The Katy Carr Series

What Katy Did

CHAPTER I: THE LITTLE CARRS

I was sitting in the meadows one day, not long ago, at a place where there was a small brook. It was a hot day. The sky was very blue, and white clouds, like great swans, went floating over it to and fro. Just opposite me was a clump of green rushes, with dark velvety spikes, and among them one single tall, red cardinal flower, which was bending over the brook as if to see its own beautiful face in the water. But the cardinal did not seem to be vain.

The picture was so pretty that I sat a long time enjoying it. Suddenly, close to me, two small voices began to talk—or to sing, for I couldn't tell exactly which it was. One voice was shrill; the other, which was a little deeper, sounded very positive and cross. They were evidently disputing about something, for they said the same words over and over again. These were the words—"Katy did." "Katy didn't." "She did." "She didn't." "She did." "She didn't." "Did." "Didn't." I think they must have repeated them at least a hundred times.

I got up from my seat to see if I could find the speakers; and sure enough, there on one of the cat-tail bulrushes, I spied two tiny pale-green creatures. Their eyes seemed to be weak, for they both wore black goggles. They had six legs apiece,—two short ones, two not so short, and two very long. These last legs had joints like the springs to buggy-tops; and as I watched, they began walking up the rush, and then I saw that they moved exactly like an old-fashioned gig. In fact, if I hadn't been too big, I *think* I should have heard them creak as they went along. They didn't say anything so long as I was there, but the moment my back was turned they began to quarrel again, and in the same old words—"Katy did." "Katy didn't." "She did." "She didn't."

As I walked home I fell to thinking about another Katy,—a Katy I once knew, who planned to do a great many wonderful things, and in the end did none of them, but something quite different,—something she didn't like at all at first, but which, on the whole, was a great deal better than any of the doings she had dreamed about. And as I thought, this little story grew in my head, and I resolved to write it down for you. I have done it; and, in memory of my two little friends on the bulrush, I give it their name. Here it is—the story of What Katy Did.

Katy's name was Katy Carr. She lived in the town of Burnet, which wasn't a very big town, but was growing as fast as it knew how. The house she lived in stood on the edge of the town. It was a large square house, white, with green blinds, and had a porch in front, over which roses and clematis made a thick bower. Four tall locust trees shaded the gravel path which led to the front gate. On one side of the house was an orchard; on the other side were wood piles and barns, and an ice-house. Behind was a kitchen garden sloping to the south; and behind that a pasture with a brook in it, and butternut trees, and four cows—two red ones, a yellow one with sharp horns tipped with tin, and a dear little white one named Daisy.

There were six of the Carr children—four girls and two boys. Katy, the oldest, was twelve years old; little Phil, the youngest, was four, and the rest fitted in between.

Dr. Carr, their Papa, was a dear, kind, busy man, who was away from home all day, and sometimes all night, too, taking care of sick people. The children hadn't any Mamma. She had died when Phil was a baby, four years before my story began. Katy could remember her pretty well; to the rest she was but a sad, sweet name, spoken on Sunday, and at prayer-times, or when Papa was especially gentle and solemn.

In place of this Mamma, whom they recollected so dimly, there was Aunt Izzie, Papa's sister, who came to take care of them when Mamma went away on that long journey, from which, for so many months, the little ones kept hoping she might return. Aunt Izzie was a small woman, sharp-faced and thin, rather old-looking, and very neat and particular about everything. She meant to be kind to the children, but they puzzled her much, because they were not a bit like herself when she was a child. Aunt Izzie had been a gentle, tidy little thing, who loved to sit as Curly Locks did, sewing long seams in the parlor, and to have her head patted by older people, and be told that she was a good girl; whereas Katy tore her dress every day, hated sewing, and didn't care a button about being called "good," while Clover and Elsie shied off like restless ponies when any one tried to pat their heads. It was very perplexing to Aunt Izzie, and she found it hard to quite forgive the children for being so "unaccountable," and so little like the good boys and girls in Sunday-school memoirs, who were the young people she liked best, and understood most about.

Then Dr. Carr was another person who worried her. He wished to have the children hardy and bold, and encouraged climbing and rough plays, in spite of the bumps and ragged clothes which resulted. In fact, there was just one half-hour of the day when Aunt Izzie was really satisfied about her charges, and that was the half-hour before breakfast, when she had made a law that they were all to sit in their little chairs and learn the Bible verse for the day. At this time she looked at them with pleased eyes, they were all so spick and span, with such nicely-brushed jackets and such neatly-combed hair. But the moment the bell rang her comfort was over. From that time on, they were what she called "not fit to be seen." The neighbors pitied her very much. They used to count the sixty stiff white pantalette legs hung out to dry every Monday morning, and say to each other what a sight of washing those children made, and what a chore it must be for poor Miss Carr to keep them so nice. But poor Miss Carr didn't think them at all nice; that was the worst of it.

"Clover, go up stairs and wash your hands! Dorry, pick your hat off the floor and hang it on the nail! Not that nail—the third nail from the corner!" These were the kind of things Aunt Izzie was saying all day long. The children minded her pretty well, but they didn't exactly love her, I fear. They called her "Aunt Izzie" always, never "Aunty." Boys and girls will know what *that* meant.

I want to show you the little Carrs, and I don't know that I could ever have a better chance than one day when five out of the six were perched on top of the ice-house, like chickens on a roost. This ice-house was one of their favorite places. It was only a low roof set over a hole in the ground, and, as it stood in the middle of the side-yard, it always seemed to the children that the shortest road to every place was up one of its slopes and down the other. They also liked to mount to the ridge-pole, and then, still keeping the sitting position, to let go, and scrape slowly down over the warm shingles to the ground. It was bad for their shoes and trousers, of course, but what of that? Shoes and trousers, and clothes generally, were Aunt Izzie's affair; theirs was to slide and enjoy themselves.

Clover, next in age to Katy, sat in the middle. She was a fair, sweet dumpling of a girl, with thick pig-tails of light brown hair, and short-sighted blue eyes, which seemed to hold tears, just ready to fall from under the blue. Really, Clover was the jolliest little thing in the world; but these eyes, and her soft cooing voice, always made people feel like petting her and taking her part. Once, when she was very small, she ran away with Katy's doll, and when Katy pursued, and tried to take it from her, Clover held fast and would not let go. Dr. Carr, who wasn't attending particularly, heard nothing but the pathetic tone of Clover's voice, as she said: "Me won't! Me want dolly!" and, without stopping to inquire, he called out sharply: "For shame, Katy! give your sister *her* doll at once!" which Katy, much surprised, did; while Clover purred in triumph, like a satisfied kitten. Clover was sunny and sweet-tempered, a little indolent, and very modest about herself, though, in fact, she was particularly clever in all sorts of games, and extremely droll and funny in a quiet way. Everybody loved her, and she loved everybody, especially Katy, whom she looked up to as one of the wisest people in the world.

Pretty little Phil sat next on the roof to Clover, and she held him tight with her arm. Then came Elsie, a thin, brown child of eight, with beautiful dark eyes, and crisp, short curls covering the whole of her small head. Poor little Elsie was the "odd one" among the Carrs. She didn't seem to belong exactly to either the older or the younger children. The great desire and ambition of her heart was to be allowed to go about with Katy and Clover and Cecy Hall, and to know their secrets, and be permitted to put notes into the little post-offices they were forever establishing in all sorts of hidden places. But they didn't want Elsie, and used to tell her to "run away and play with the children," which hurt her feelings very much. When she wouldn't run away, I am sorry to say they ran away from her, which, as their legs were longest, it was easy to do. Poor Elsie, left behind, would cry bitter tears, and, as she was too proud to play much with Dorry and John, her principal comfort was tracking the older ones about and discovering their mysteries, especially the post-offices, which were her greatest grievance. Her eyes were bright and quick as a bird's. She would peep and peer, and follow and watch, till at last, in some odd, unlikely place, the crotch of a tree, the middle of the asparagus bed, or, perhaps, on the very top step of the scuttle ladder, she spied the little paper box, with its load of notes, all ending with: "Be sure and not let Elsie know." Then she would seize the box, and, marching up to wherever the others were, she would throw it down, saying, defiantly: "There's your old post-office!" but feeling all the time just like crying. Poor little Elsie! In almost every big family, there is one of these unmated, left-out children. Katy, who had the finest plans in the world for being "heroic," and of use, never saw, as she drifted on her heedless way, that here, in this lonely little sister, was the very chance she wanted for being a comfort to somebody who needed comfort very much. She never saw it, and Elsie's heavy heart went uncheered.

    Dorry and Joanna sat on the two ends of the ridge-pole. Dorry was six years old; a pale, pudgy boy, with rather a solemn face, and smears of molasses on the sleeve of his jacket. Joanna, whom the children called "John," and "Johnnie," was a square, splendid child, a year younger than Dorry; she had big brave eyes, and a wide rosy mouth, which always looked ready to laugh. These two were great friends, though Dorry seemed like a girl who had got into boy's clothes by mistake, and Johnnie like a boy who, in a fit of fun, had borrowed his sister's frock. And now, as they all sat there chattering and giggling, the window above opened, a glad shriek was heard, and Katy's head appeared. In her hand she held a heap of stockings, which she waved triumphantly.

    "Hurray!" she cried, "all done, and Aunt Izzie says we may go. Are you tired out waiting? I couldn't help it, the holes were so big, and took so long. Hurry up, Clover, and get the things! Cecy and I will be down in a minute."

    The children jumped up gladly, and slid down the roof. Clover fetched a couple of baskets from the wood-shed. Elsie ran for her kitten. Dorry and John loaded themselves with two great fagots of green boughs. Just as they were ready, the side-door banged, and Katy and Cecy Hall came into the yard.

I must tell you about Cecy. She was a great friend of the children's, and lived in a house next door. The yards of the houses were only separated by a green hedge, with no gate, so that Cecy spent two-thirds of her time at Dr. Carr's, and was exactly like one of the family. She was a neat, dapper, pink-and-white-girl, modest and prim in manner, with light shiny hair, which always kept smooth, and slim hands, which never looked dirty. How different from my poor Katy! Katy's hair was forever in a snarl; her gowns were always catching on nails and tearing "themselves"; and, in spite of her age and size, she was as heedless and innocent as a child of six. Katy was the *longest* girl that was ever seen. What she did to make herself grow so, nobody could tell; but there she was—up above Papa's ear, and half a head taller than poor Aunt Izzie. Whenever she stopped to think about her height she became very awkward, and felt as if she were all legs and elbows, and angles and joints. Happily, her head was so full of other things, of plans and schemes, and fancies of all sorts, that she didn't often take time to remember how tall she was. She was a dear, loving child, for all her careless habits, and made bushels of good resolutions every week of her life, only unluckily she never kept any of them. She had fits of responsibility about the other children, and longed to set them a good example, but when the chance came, she generally forgot to do so. Katy's days flew like the wind; for when she wasn't studying lessons, or sewing and darning with Aunt Izzie, which she hated extremely, there were always so many delightful schemes rioting in her brains, that all she wished for was ten pairs of hands to carry them out. These same active brains got her into perpetual scrapes. She was fond of building castles in the air, and dreaming of the time when something she had done would make her famous, so that everybody would hear of her, and want to know her. I don't think she had made up her mind what this wonderful thing was to be; but while thinking about it she often forgot to learn a lesson, or to lace her boots, and then she had a bad mark, or a scolding from Aunt Izzie. At such times she consoled herself with planning how, by and by, she would be beautiful and beloved, and amiable as an angel. A great deal was to happen to Katy before that time came. Her eyes, which were black, were to turn blue; her nose was to lengthen and straighten, and her mouth, quite too large at present to suit the part of a heroine, was to be made over into a sort of rosy button. Meantime, and until these charming changes should take place, Katy forgot her features as much as she could, though still, I think, the person on earth whom she most envied was that lady on the outside of the Tricopherous bottles with the wonderful hair which sweeps the ground.

CHAPTER II: PARADISE

The place to which the children were going was a sort of marshy thicket at the bottom of a field near the house. It wasn't a big thicket, but it looked big, because the trees and bushes grew so closely that you could not see just where it ended. In winter the ground was damp and boggy, so that nobody went there, excepting cows, who don't mind getting their feet wet; but in summer the water dried away, and then it was all fresh and green, and full of delightful things—wild roses, and sassafras, and birds' nests. Narrow, winding paths ran here and there, made by the cattle as they wandered to and fro. This place the children called "Paradise," and to them it seemed as wide and endless and full of adventure as any forest of fairy land.

The way to Paradise was through some wooden bars. Katy and Cecy climbed these with a hop, skip and jump, while the smaller ones scrambled underneath. Once past the bars they were fairly in the field, and, with one consent, they all began to run till they reached the entrance of the wood. Then they halted, with a queer look of hesitation on their faces. It was always an exciting occasion to go to Paradise for the first time after the long winter. Who knew what the fairies might not have done since any of them had been there to see?

"Which path shall we go in by?" asked Clover, at last.

"Suppose we vote," said Katy. "I say by the Pilgrim's Path and the Hill of Difficulty."

"So do I!" chimed in Clover, who always agreed with Katy.

"The Path of Peace is nice," suggested Cecy.

"No, no! We want to go by Sassafras Path!" cried John and Dorry.

However, Katy, as usual, had her way. It was agreed that they should first try Pilgrim's Path, and afterward make a thorough exploration of the whole of their little kingdom, and see all that had happened since last they were there. So in they marched, Katy and Cecy heading the procession, and Dorry, with his great trailing bunch of boughs, bringing up the rear.

"Oh, there is the dear Rosary, all safe!" cried the children, as they reached the top of the Hill of Difficulty, and came upon a tall stump, out of the middle of which waved a wild rose-bush, budded over with fresh green eaves. This "Rosary" was a fascinating thing to their minds. They were always inventing stories about it, and were in constant terror lest some hungry cow should take a fancy to the rose-bush and eat it up.

"Yes," said Katy, stroking a leaf with her finger, "it was in great danger one night last winter, but it escaped."

"Oh, how? Tell us about it!" cried the others, for Katy's stories were famous in the family.

"It was Christmas Eve," continued Katy, in a mysterious tone. "The fairy of the Rosary was quite sick. She had taken a dreadful cold in her head, and the poplar-tree fairy, just over there, told her that sassafras tea is good for colds. So she made a large acorn-cup full, and then cuddled herself in where the wood looks so black and soft, and fell asleep. In the middle of the night, when she was snoring soundly, there was a noise in the forest, and a dreadful black bull with fiery eyes galloped up. He saw our poor Rosy Posy, and, opening his big mouth, he was just going to bite her in two; but at that minute a little fat man, with a wand in his hand, popped out from behind the stump. It was Santa Claus, of course. He gave the bull such a rap with his wand that he moo-ed dreadfully, and then put up his fore-paw, to see if his nose was on or not. He found it was, but it hurt him so that he 'moo-ed' again, and galloped off as fast as he could into the woods. Then Santa Claus waked up the fairy, and told her that if she didn't take better care of Rosy Posy he should put some other fairy into her place, and set her to keep guard over a prickly, scratchy, blackberry-bush."

"Is there really any fairy?" asked Dorry, who had listened to this narrative with open mouth.

"Of course," answered Katy. Then bending down toward Dorry, she added in a voice intended to be of wonderful sweetness: "I am a fairy, Dorry!"

"Pshaw!" was Dorry's reply; "you're a giraffe—Pa said so!"

The Path of Peace got its name because of its darkness and coolness. High bushes almost met over it, and trees kept it shady, even in the middle of the day. A sort of white flower grew there, which the children called Pollypods, because they didn't know the real name. They staid a long while picking bunches of these flowers, and then John and Dorry had to grub up an armful of sassafras roots; so that before they had fairly gone through Toadstool Avenue, Rabbit Hollow, and the rest, the sun was just over their heads, and it was noon.

"I'm getting hungry," said Dorry.

"Oh, no, Dorry, you mustn't be hungry till the bower is ready!" cried the little girls, alarmed, for Dorry was apt to be disconsolate if he was kept waiting for his meals. So they made haste to build the bower. It did not take long, being composed of boughs hung over skipping-ropes, which were tied to the very poplar-tree where the fairy lived who had recommended sassafras tea to the Fairy of the Rose.

When it was done they all cuddled in underneath. It was a very small bower—just big enough to hold them, and the baskets, and the kitten. I don't think there would have been room for anybody else, not even another kitten. Katy, who sat in the middle, untied and lifted the lid of the largest basket, while all the rest peeped eagerly to see what was inside.

First came a great many ginger cakes. These were carefully laid on the grass to keep till wanted: buttered biscuit came next—three apiece, with slices of cold lamb laid in between; and last of all were a dozen hard-boiled eggs, and a layer of thick bread and butter sandwiched with corn-beef. Aunt Izzie had put up lunches for Paradise before, you see, and knew pretty well what to expect in the way of appetite.

Oh, how good everything tasted in that bower, with the fresh wind rustling the poplar leaves, sunshine and sweet wood-smells about them, and birds singing overhead! No grown-up dinner party ever had half so much fun. Each mouthful was a pleasure; and when the last crumb had vanished, Katy produced the second basket, and there, oh, delightful surprise! were seven little pies—molasses pies, baked in saucers—each with a brown top and crisp candified edge, which tasted like toffy and lemon-peel, and all sorts of good things mixed up together.

There was a general shout. Even demure Cecy was pleased, and Dorry and John kicked their heels on the ground in a tumult of joy. Seven pairs of hands were held out at once toward the basket; seven sets of teeth went to work without a moment's delay. In an incredibly short time every vestige of the pie had disappeared, and a blissful stickiness pervaded the party.

"What shall we do now?" asked Clover, while little Phil tipped the baskets upside down, as if to make sure there was nothing left that could possibly be eaten.

"I don't know," replied Katy, dreamily. She had left her seat, and was half-sitting, half-lying on the low, crooked bough of a butternut tree, which hung almost over the children's heads.

"Let's play we're grown up," said Cecy, "and tell what we mean to do."

"Well," said Clover, "you begin. What do you mean to do?"

"I mean to have a black silk dress, and pink roses in my bonnet, and a white muslin long-shawl," said Cecy; "and I mean to look *exactly* like Minerva Clark! I shall be very good, too; as good as Mrs. Bedell, only a great deal prettier. All the young gentlemen will want me to go and ride, but I shan't notice them at all, because you know I shall always be teaching in Sunday-school, and visiting the poor. And some day, when I am bending over an old woman and feeding her with currant jelly, a poet will come along and see me, and he'll go home and write a poem about me," concluded Cecy, triumphantly.

"Pooh!" said Clover. "I don't think that would be nice at all. *I'm* going to be a beautiful lady—the most beautiful lady in the world! And I'm going to live in a yellow castle, with yellow pillars to the portico, and a square thing on top, like Mr. Sawyer's. My children are going to have a play-house up there. There's going to be a spy-glass in the window, to look out of. I shall wear gold dresses and silver dresses every day, and diamond rings, and have white satin aprons to tie on when I'm dusting, or doing anything dirty. In the middle of my back-yard there will be a pond-full of Lubin's Extracts, and whenever I want any I shall go just out and dip a bottle in. And I shan't teach in Sunday schools, like Cecy, because I don't want to; but every Sunday I'll go and stand by the gate, and when her scholars go by on their way home, I'll put Lubin's Extracts on their handkerchiefs."

"I mean to have just the same," cried Elsie, whose imagination was fired by this gorgeous vision, "only my pond will be the biggest. I shall be a great deal beautifuller, too," she added.

"You can't," said Katy from overhead. "Clover is going to be the most beautiful lady in the world."

"But I'll be more beautiful than the most beautiful," persisted poor little Elsie; "and I'll be big, too, and know everybody's secrets. And everybody'll be kind, then, and never run away and hide; and there won't be any post offices, or anything disagreeable."

"What'll you be, Johnnie?" asked Clover, anxious to change the subject, for Elsie's voice was growing plaintive.

But Johnnie had no clear ideas as to her future. She laughed a great deal, and squeezed Dorry's arm very tight, but that was all. Dorry was more explicit.

"I mean to have turkey every day," he declared, "and batter-puddings; not boiled ones, you know, but little baked ones, with brown shiny tops, and a great deal of pudding sauce to eat on them. And I shall be so big then that nobody will say, 'Three helps is quite enough for a little boy.'"

"Oh, Dorry, you pig!" cried Katy, while the others screamed with laughter. Dorry was much affronted.

"I shall just go and tell Aunt Izzie what you called me," he said, getting up in a great pet.

But Clover, who was a born peacemaker, caught hold of his arm, and her coaxings and entreaties consoled him so much that he finally said he would stay; especially as the others were quite grave now, and promised that they wouldn't laugh any more.

"And now, Katy, it's your turn," said Cecy; "tell us what you're going to be when you grow up."

"I'm not sure about what I'll be," replied Katy, from overhead; "beautiful, of course, and good if I can, only not so good as you, Cecy, because it would be nice to go and ride with the young gentlemen *sometimes*. And I'd like to have a large house and a splendiferous garden, and then you could all come and live with me, and we would play in the garden, and Dorry should have turkey five times a day if he liked. And we'd have a machine to darn the stockings, and another machine to put the bureau drawers in order, and we'd never sew or knit garters, or do anything we didn't want to. That's what I'd like to *be*. But now I'll tell you what I mean to *do*."

"Isn't it the same thing?" asked Cecy.

"Oh, no!" replied Katy, "quite different; for you see I mean to *do* something grand. I don't know what, yet; but when I'm grown up I shall find out." (Poor Katy always said "when I'm grown up," forgetting how very much she had grown already.) "Perhaps," she went on, "it will be rowing out in boats, and saving peoples' lives, like that girl in the book. Or perhaps I shall go and nurse in the hospital, like Miss Nightingale. Or else I'll head a crusade and ride on a white horse, with armor and a helmet on my head, and carry a sacred flag. Or if I don't do that, I'll paint pictures, or sing, or scalp—sculp,—what is it? you know—make figures in marble. Anyhow it shall be *something*. And when Aunt Izzie sees it, and reads about me in the newspapers she will say, 'The dear child! I always knew she would turn out an ornament to the family,' People very often say, afterward, that they 'always knew,'" concluded Katy sagaciously.

"Oh, Katy! how beautiful it will be!" said Clover, clasping her hands. Clover believed in Katy as she did in the Bible.

"I don't believe the newspapers would be so silly as to print things about *you*, Katy Carr," put in Elsie, vindictively.

"Yes they will!" said Clover; and gave Elsie a push.

By and by John and Dorry trotted away on mysterious errands of their own.

"Wasn't Dorry funny with his turkey?" remarked Cecy; and they all laughed again.

"If you won't tell," said Katy, "I'll let you see Dorry's journal. He kept it once for almost two weeks, and then gave it up. I found the book, this morning, in the nursery closet."

All of them promised, and Katy produced it from her pocket. It began thus:

"March 12.—Have resolved to keep a jurnal.

March 13.—Had rost befe for diner, and cabage, and potato and appel sawse, and rice puding. I do not like rice puding when it is like ours. Charley Slack's kind is rele good. Mush and sirup for tea.

March 19.—Forgit what did. John and me saved our pie to take to schule.

March 21.—Forgit what did. Gridel cakes for brekfast. Debby didn't fry enuff.

March 24.—This is Sunday. Corn befe for dinnir. Studdied my Bibel leson. Aunt Issy said I was gredy. Have resollved not to think so much about things to ete. Wish I was a beter boy. Nothing pertikeler for tea.

March 25.—Forgit what did.

March 27.—Forgit what did.

March 29.—Played.

March 31.—Forgit what did.

April 1.—Have dissided not to kepe a jurnal enny more."

Here ended the extracts; and it seemed as if only a minute had passed since they stopped laughing over them, before the long shadows began to fall, and Mary came to say that all of them must come in to get ready for tea. It was dreadful to have to pick up the empty baskets and go home, feeling that the long, delightful Saturday was over, and that there wouldn't be another for a week. But it was comforting to remember that Paradise was always there; and that at any moment when Kate and Aunt Izzie were willing, they had only to climb a pair of bars—very easy ones, and without any fear of an angel with flaming sword to stop the way—enter in, and take possession of their Eden.

CHAPTER III: THE DAY OF SCRAPES

Mrs. Knight's school, to which Katy and Clover and Cecy went, stood quite at the other end of the town from Dr. Carr's. It was a low, one-story building and had a yard behind it, in which the girls played at recess. Unfortunately, next door to it was Miss Miller's school, equally large and popular, and with a yard behind it also. Only a high board fence separated the two playgrounds.

Mrs. Knight was a stout, gentle woman, who moved slowly, and had a face which made you think of an amiable and well-disposed cow. Miss Miller, on the contrary, had black eyes, with black corkscrew curls waving about them, and was generally brisk and snappy. A constant feud raged between the two schools as to the respective merits of the teachers and the instruction. The Knight girls for some unknown reason, considered themselves genteel and the Miller girls vulgar, and took no pains to conceal this opinion; while the Miller girls, on the other hand, retaliated by being as aggravating as they knew how. They spent their recesses and intermissions mostly in making faces through the knot-holes in the fence, and over the top of it when they could get there, which wasn't an easy thing to do, as the fence was pretty high. The Knight girls could make faces too, for all their gentility. Their yard had one great advantage over the other: it possessed a wood-shed, with a climbable roof, which commanded Miss Miller's premises, and upon this the girls used to sit in rows, turning up their noses at the next yard, and irritating the foe by jeering remarks. "Knights" and "Millerites," the two schools called each other; and the feud raged so high, that sometimes it was hardly safe for a Knight to meet a Millerite in the street; all of which, as may be imagined, was exceedingly improving both to the manners and morals of the young ladies concerned.

One morning, not long after the day in Paradise, Katy was late. She could not find her things. Her algebra, as she expressed it, had "gone and lost itself," her slate was missing, and the string was off her sun-bonnet. She ran about, searching for these articles and banging doors, till Aunt Izzie was out of patience.

"As for your algebra," she said, "if it is that very dirty book with only one cover, and scribbled all over the leaves, you will find it under the kitchen-table. Philly was playing before breakfast that it was a pig: no wonder, I'm sure, for it looks good for nothing else. How you do manage to spoil your school-books in this manner, Katy, I cannot imagine. It is less than a month since your father got you a new algebra, and look at it now—not fit to be carried about. I do wish you would realize what books cost!

"About your slate," she went on, "I know nothing; but here is the bonnet-string;" taking it out of her pocket.

"Oh, thank you!" said Katy, hastily sticking it on with a pin.

"Katy Carr!" almost screamed Miss Izzie, "what are you about? Pinning on your bonnet-string! Mercy on me, what shiftless thing will you do next? Now stand still, and don't fidget. You sha'n't stir till I have sewed it on properly."

It wasn't easy to "stand still and not fidget," with Aunt Izzie fussing away and lecturing, and now and then, in a moment of forgetfulness, sticking her needle into one's chin. Katy bore it as well as she could, only shifting perpetually from one foot to the other, and now and then uttering a little snort, like an impatient horse. The minute she was released she flew into the kitchen, seized the algebra, and rushed like a whirlwind to the gate, where good little Clover stood patiently waiting, though all ready herself, and terribly afraid she should be late.

"We shall have to run," gasped Katy, quite out of breath. "Aunt Izzie kept me. She has been so horrid!"

They did run as fast as they could, but time ran faster, and before they were half-way to school the town clock struck nine, and all hope was over. This vexed Katy very much; for, though often late, she was always eager to be early.

"There," she said, stopping short, "I shall just tell Aunt Izzie that it was her fault. It is *too* bad." And she marched into school in a very cross mood.

A day begun in this manner is pretty sure to end badly, as most of us know. All the morning through, things seemed to go wrong. Katy missed twice in her grammar lesson, and lost her place in the class. Her hand shook so when she copied her composition, that the writing, not good at best, turned out almost illegible, so that Mrs. Knight said it must all be done over again. This made Katy crosser than ever; and almost before she thought, she had whispered to Clover, "How hateful!" And then, when just before recess all who had "communicated" were requested to stand up, her conscience gave such a twinge that she was forced to get up with the rest, and see a black mark put against her name on the list. The tears came into her eyes from vexation; and, for fear the other girls would notice them, she made a bolt for the yard as soon as the bell rang, and mounted up all alone to the wood-house roof, where she sat with her back to the school, fighting with her eyes, and trying to get her face in order before the rest should come.

Miss Miller's clock was about four minutes slower than Mrs. Knight's, so the next playground was empty. It was a warm, breezy day, and as Katy sat here, suddenly a gust of wind came, and seizing her sun-bonnet, which was only half tied on, whirled it across the roof. She clutched after it as it flew, but too late. Once, twice, thrice, it flapped, then it disappeared over the edge, and Katy, flying after, saw it lying a crumpled lilac heap in the very middle of the enemy's yard.

This was horrible! Not merely losing the bonnet, for Katy was comfortably indifferent as to what became of her clothes, but to lose it *so*. In another minute the Miller girls would be out. Already she seemed to see them dancing war-dances round the unfortunate bonnet, pinning it on a pole, using it as a football, waving it over the fence, and otherwise treating it as Indians treat a captive taken in war. Was it to be endured? Never! Better die first! And with very much the feeling of a person who faces destruction rather than forfeit honor, Katy set her teeth, and sliding rapidly down the roof, seized the fence, and with one bold leap vaulted into Miss Miller's yard.

Just then the recess bell tinkled; and a little Millerite who sat by the window, and who, for two seconds, had been dying to give the exciting information, squeaked out to the others: "There's Katy Carr in our back-yard!"

Out poured the Millerites, big and little. Their wrath and indignation at this daring invasion cannot be described. With a howl of fury they precipitated themselves upon Katy, but she was quick as they, and holding the rescued bonnet in her hand, was already half-way up the fence.

There are moments when it is a fine thing to be tall. On this occasion Katy's long legs and arms served her an excellent turn. Nothing but a Daddy Long Legs ever climbed so fast or so wildly as she did now. In one second she had gained the top of the fence. Just as she went over a Millerite seized her by the last foot, and almost dragged her boot off.

Almost, not quite, thanks to the stout thread with which Aunt Izzie had sewed on the buttons. With a frantic kick Katy released herself, and had the satisfaction of seeing her assailant go head over heels backward, while, with a shriek of triumph and fright, she herself plunged headlong into the midst of a group of Knights. They were listening with open mouths to the uproar, and now stood transfixed at the astonishing spectacle of one of their number absolutely returning alive from the camp of the enemy.

I cannot tell you what a commotion ensued. The Knights were beside themselves with pride and triumph. Katy was kissed and hugged, and made to tell her story over and over again, while rows of exulting girls sat on the wood-house roof to crow over the discomfited Millerites: and when, later, the foe rallied and began to retort over the fence, Clover, armed with a tack-hammer, was lifted up in the arms of one of the tall girls to rap the intruding knuckles as they appeared on the top. This she did with such good-will that the Millerites were glad to drop down again, and mutter vengeance at a safe distance. Altogether it was a great day for the school, a day to be remembered. As time went on, Katy, what with the excitement of her adventure, and of being praised and petted by the big girls, grew perfectly reckless, and hardly knew what she said or did.

A good many of the scholars lived too far from school to go home at noon, and were in the habit of bringing their lunches in baskets, and staying all day. Katy and Clover were of this number. This noon, after the dinners were eaten, it was proposed that they should play something in the school-room, and Katy's unlucky star put it into her head to invent a new game, which she called the Game of Rivers.

It was played in the following manner: Each girl took the name of a river, and laid out for herself an appointed path through the room, winding among the desks and benches, and making a low, roaring sound, to imitate the noise of water. Cecy was the Platte, Marianne Brooks, a tall girl, the Mississippi, Alice Blair, the Ohio, Clover, the Penobscot, and so on. They were instructed to run into each other once in a while, because, as Katy said, "rivers do." As for Katy herself, she was "Father Ocean," and, growling horribly, raged up and down the platform where Mrs. Knight usually sat. Every now and then, when the others were at the far end of the room, she would suddenly cry out, "Now for a meeting of the waters!" whereupon all the rivers bouncing, bounding, scrambling, screaming, would turn and run toward Father Ocean, while he roared louder than all of them put together, and made short rushes up and down, to represent the movement of waves on a beach.

Such a noise as this beautiful game made was never heard in the town of Burnet before or since. It was like the bellowing of the bulls of Bashan, the squeaking of pigs, the cackle of turkey-cocks, and the laugh of wild hyenas all at once; and, in addition, there was a great banging of furniture and scraping of many feet on an uncarpeted floor. People going by stopped and stared, children cried, an old lady asked why some one didn't run for a policeman; while the Miller girls listened to the proceedings with malicious pleasure, and told everybody that it was the noise that Mrs. Knight's scholars "usually made at recess."

Mrs. Knight coming back from dinner, was much amazed to see a crowd of people collected in front of her school. As she drew near, the sounds reached her, and then she became really frightened, for she thought somebody was being murdered on her premises. Hurrying in, she threw open the door, and there, to her dismay, was the whole room in a frightful state of confusion and uproar: chairs flung down, desks upset, ink streaming on the floor; while in the midst of the ruin the frantic rivers raced and screamed, and old Father Ocean, with a face as red as fire, capered like a lunatic on the platform.

"What *does* this mean?" gasped poor Mrs. Knight, almost unable to speak for horror.

At the sound of her voice the Rivers stood still, Father Ocean brought his prances to an abrupt close, and slunk down from the platform. All of a sudden, each girl seemed to realize what a condition the room was in, and what a horrible thing she had done. The timid ones cowered behind their desks, the bold ones tried to look unconscious, and, to make matters worse, the scholars who had gone home to dinner began to return, staring at the scene of disaster, and asking, in whispers, what had been going on?

Mrs. Knight rang the bell. When the school had come to order, she had the desks and chairs picked up, while she herself brought wet cloths to sop the ink from the floor. This was done in profound silence; and the expression of Mrs. Knight's face was so direful and solemn, that a fresh damp fell upon the spirits of the guilty Rivers, and Father Ocean wished himself thousands of miles away.

When all was in order again, and the girls had taken their seats, Mrs. Knight made a short speech. She said she never was so shocked in her life before; she had supposed that she could trust them to behave like ladies when her back was turned. The idea that they could act so disgracefully, make such an uproar and alarm people going by, had never occurred to her, and she was deeply pained. It was setting a bad example to all the neighborhood—by which Mrs. Knight meant the rival school, Miss Miller having just sent over a little girl, with her compliments, to ask if any one was hurt, and could *she* do anything? which was naturally aggravating! Mrs. Knight hoped they were sorry; she thought they must be—sorry and ashamed. The exercises could now go on as usual. Of course some punishment would be inflicted for the offense, but she should have to reflect before deciding what it ought to be. Meantime she wanted them all to think it over seriously; and if any one felt that she was more to blame than the others, now was the moment to rise and confess it.

Katy's heart gave a great thump, but she rose bravely: "I made up the game, and I was Father Ocean," she said to the astonished Mrs. Knight, who glared at her for a minute, and then replied solemnly: "Very well, Katy—sit down;" which Katy did, feeling more ashamed than ever, but somehow relieved in her mind. There is a saving grace in truth which helps truth-tellers through the worst of their troubles, and Katy found this out now.

The afternoon was long and hard. Mrs. Knight did not smile once; the lessons dragged; and Katy, after the heat and excitement of the forenoon, began to feel miserable. She had received more than one hard blow during the meetings of the waters, and had bruised herself almost without knowing it, against the desks and chairs. All these places now began to ache: her head throbbed so that she could hardly see, and a lump of something heavy seemed to be lying on her heart.

When school was over, Mrs. Knight rose and said, "The young ladies who took part in the game this afternoon are requested to remain." All the others went away, and shut the door behind them. It was a horrible moment: the girls never forgot it, or the hopeless sound of the door as the last departing scholar clapped it after her as she left.

I can't begin to tell you what it was that Mrs. Knight said to them: it was very affecting, and before long most of the girls began to cry. The penalty for their offense was announced to be the loss of recess for three weeks; but that wasn't half so bad as seeing Mrs. Knight so "religious and afflicted," as Cecy told her mother afterward. One by one the sobbing sinners departed from the schoolroom. When most of them were gone, Mrs. Knight called Katy up to the platform, and said a few words to her specially. She was not really severe, but Katy was too penitent and worn out to bear much, and before long was weeping like a water-spout, or like the ocean she had pretended to be.

At this, tender-hearted Mrs. Knight was so much affected that she let her off at once, and even kissed her in token of forgiveness, which made poor Ocean sob harder than ever. All the way home she sobbed; faithful little Clover, running along by her side in great distress, begging her to stop crying, and trying in vain to hold up the fragments of her dress, which was torn in, at least, a dozen places. Katy could not stop crying, and it was fortunate that Aunt Izzie happened to be out, and that the only person who saw her in this piteous plight was Mary, the nurse, who doted on the children, and was always ready to help them out of their troubles.

On this occasion she petted and cosseted Katy exactly as if it had been Johnnie or little Phil. She took her on her lap, bathed the hot head, brushed the hair, put arnica on the bruises, and produced a clean frock, so that by tea-time the poor child, except for her red eyes, looked like herself again, and Aunt Izzie didn't notice anything unusual.

For a wonder, Dr. Carr was at home that evening. It was always a great treat to the children when this happened, and Katy thought herself happy when, after the little ones had gone to bed, she got Papa to herself, and told him the whole story.

"Papa," she said, sitting on his knee, which, big girl as she was, she liked very much to do, "what is the reason that makes some days so lucky and other days so unlucky? Now today began all wrong, and everything that happened in it was wrong, and on other days I begin right, and all goes right, straight through. If Aunt Izzie hadn't kept me in the morning, I shouldn't have lost my mark, and then I shouldn't have been cross, and then *perhaps* I shouldn't have got in my other scrapes."

"But what made Aunt Izzie keep you, Katy?"

"To sew on the string of my bonnet, Papa."

"But how did it happen that the string was off?"

"Well," said Katy, reluctantly, "I am afraid that was *my* fault, for it came off on Tuesday, and I didn't fasten it on."

"So you see we must go back of Aunt Izzie for the beginning of this unlucky day of yours, Childie. Did you ever hear the old saying about, 'For the want of a nail the shoe was lost'?"

"No, never—tell it to me!" cried Katy, who loved stories as well as when she was three years old.

So Dr. Carr repeated—

"For the want of a nail the shoe was lost,
For the want of a shoe the horse was lost,
For the want of a horse the rider was lost,
For the want of a rider the battle was lost,
For the want of a battle the kingdom was lost,
 And all for want of a horse-shoe nail."

"Oh, Papa!" exclaimed Katy, giving him a great hug as she got off his knee, "I see what you mean! Who would have thought such a little speck of a thing as not sewing on my string could make a difference? But I don't believe I shall get in any more scrapes, for I sha'n't ever forget—

"'For the want of a nail the shoe was lost.'"

CHAPTER IV: KIKERI

But I am sorry to say that my poor, thoughtless Katy *did* forget, and did get into another scrape, and that no later than the very next Monday.

Monday was apt to be rather a stormy day at the Carrs'. There was the big wash to be done, and Aunt Izzie always seemed a little harder to please, and the servants a good deal crosser than on common days. But I think it was also, in part, the fault of the children, who, after the quiet of Sunday, were specially frisky and uproarious, and readier than usual for all sorts of mischief.

To Clover and Elsie, Sunday seemed to begin at Saturday's bed-time, when their hair was wet, and screwed up in papers, that it might curl next day. Elsie's waved naturally, so Aunt Izzie didn't think it necessary to pin her papers very tight; but Clover's thick, straight locks required to be pinched hard before they would give even the least twirl, and to her, Saturday night was one of misery. She would lie tossing, and turning, and trying first one side of her head and then the other; but whichever way she placed herself, the hard knobs and the pins stuck out and hurt her; so when at last she fell asleep, it was face down, with her small nose buried in the pillow, which was not comfortable, and gave her bad dreams. In consequence of these sufferings Clover hated curls, and when she "made up" stories for the younger children, they always commenced: "The hair of the beautiful princess was as straight as a yard-stick, and she never did it up in papers—never!"

Sunday always began with a Bible story, followed by a breakfast of baked beans, which two things were much tangled up together in Philly's mind. After breakfast the children studied their Sunday-school lessons, and then the big carryall came round, and they drove to church, which was a good mile off. It was a large, old-fashioned church, with galleries, and long pews with high red-cushioned seats.

The choir sat at the end, behind a low, green curtain, which slipped from side to side on rods. When the sermon began, they would draw the curtain aside and show themselves, all ready to listen, but the rest of the time they kept it shut. Katy always guessed that they must be having good times behind the green curtain—eating orange-peel, perhaps, or reading the Sunday-school books—and she often wished she might sit up there among them.

The seat in Dr. Carr's pew was so high that none of the children, except Katy, could touch the floor, even with the point of a toe. This made their feet go to sleep; and when they felt the queer little pin-pricks which drowsy feet use to rouse themselves with, they would slide off the seat, and sit on the benches to get over it. Once there, and well hidden from view, it was almost impossible not to whisper. Aunt

Izzie would frown and shake her head, but it did little good, especially as Phil and Dorry were sleeping with their heads on her lap, and it took both her hands to keep them from rolling off into the bottom of the pew. When good old Dr. Stone said, "Finally, my brethren," she would begin waking them up. It was hard work sometimes, but generally she succeeded, so that during the last hymn the two stood together on the seat, quite brisk and refreshed, sharing a hymn-book, and making believe to sing like the older people.

After church came Sunday-school, which the children liked very much, and then they went home to dinner, which was always the same on Sunday—cold corned-beef, baked potatoes, and rice pudding. They did not go to church in the afternoon unless they wished, but were pounced upon by Katy instead, and forced to listen to the reading of *The Sunday Visitor*, a religious paper, of which she was the editor. This paper was partly written, partly printed, on a large sheet of foolscap, and had at the top an ornamental device, in lead pencil, with "Sunday Visitor" in the middle of it. The reading part began with a dull little piece of the kind which grown people call an editorial, about "Neatness," or "Obedience," or "Punctuality." The children always fidgeted when listening to this, partly, I think, because it aggravated them to have Katy recommending on paper, as very easy, the virtues which she herself found it so hard to practise in real life. Next came anecdotes about dogs and elephants and snakes, taken from the Natural History book, and not very interesting, because the audience knew them by heart already. A hymn or two followed, or a string of original verses, and, last of all, a chapter of "Little Maria and Her Sisters," a dreadful tale, in which Katy drew so much moral, and made such personal allusions to the faults of the rest, that it was almost more than they could bear. In fact, there had just been a nursery rebellion on the subject. You must know that, for some weeks back, Katy had been too lazy to prepare any fresh *Sunday Visitors*, and so had forced the children to sit in a row and listen to the back numbers, which she read aloud from the very beginning! "Little Maria" sounded much worse when taken in these large doses, and Clover and Elsie, combining for once, made up their minds to endure it no longer. So, watching their chance, they carried off the whole edition, and poked it into the kitchen fire, where they watched it burn with a mixture of fear and delight which it was comical to witness. They dared not confess the deed, but it was impossible not to look conscious when Katy was flying about and rummaging after her lost treasure, and she suspected them, and was very irate in consequence.

The evenings of Sunday were always spent in repeating hymns to Papa and Aunt Izzie. This was fun, for they all took turns, and there was quite a scramble as to who should secure the favorites, such as, "The west hath shut its gate of gold," and "Go when the morning shineth." On the whole, Sunday was a sweet and pleasant day, and the children thought so; but, from its being so much quieter than other days, they always got up on Monday full of life and mischief, and ready to fizz over at any minute, like champagne bottles with the wires just cut.

This particular Monday was rainy, so there couldn't be any out-door play, which was the usual vent for over-high spirits. The little ones, cooped up in the nursery all the afternoon, had grown perfectly riotous. Philly was not quite well, and had been taking medicine. The medicine was called *Elixir Pro*. It was a great favorite with Aunt Izzie, who kept a bottle of it always on hand. The bottle was large and black, with a paper label tied round its neck, and the children shuddered at the sight of it.

After Phil had stopped roaring and spluttering, and play had begun again, the dolls, as was only natural, were taken ill also, and so was "Pikery," John's little yellow chair, which she always pretended was a doll too. She kept an old apron tied on his back, and generally took him to bed with her—not into bed, that would have been troublesome; but close by, tied to the bed-post. Now, as she told the others, Pikery was very sick indeed. He must have some medicine, just like Philly.

"Give him some water," suggested Dorry.

"No," said John, decidedly, "it must be black and out of a bottle, or it won't do any good."

After thinking a moment, she trotted quietly across the passage into Aunt Izzie's room. Nobody was there, but John knew where the Elixir Pro was kept—in the closet on the third shelf. She pulled one of the drawers out a little, climbed up, and reached it down. The children were enchanted when she marched back, the bottle in one hand, the cork in the other, and proceeded to pour a liberal dose on to Pikery's wooden seat, which John called his lap.

"There! there! my poor boy," she said, patting his shoulder—I mean his arm—"swallow it down—it'll do you good."

Just then Aunt Izzie came in, and to her dismay saw a long trickle of something dark and sticky running down on to the carpet. It was Pikery's medicine, which he had refused to swallow.

"What is that?" she asked sharply.

"My baby is sick," faltered John, displaying the guilty bottle.

Aunt Izzie rapped her over the head with a thimble, and told her that she was a very naughty child, whereupon Johnnie pouted, and cried a little. Aunt Izzie wiped up the slop, and taking away the Elixir, retired with it to her closet, saying that she "never knew anything like it—it was always so on Mondays."

What further pranks were played in the nursery that day, I cannot pretend to tell. But late in the afternoon a dreadful screaming was heard, and when people rushed from all parts of the house to see what was the matter, behold the nursery door was locked, and nobody could get in. Aunt Izzie called through the keyhole to have it opened, but the roars were so loud that it was long before she could get an answer. At last Elsie, sobbing violently, explained that Dorry had locked the door, and now the key wouldn't turn, and they couldn't open it. *Would* they have to stay there always, and starve?

"Of course you won't, you foolish child," exclaimed Aunt Izzie. "Dear, dear, what on earth will come next? Stop crying, Elsie—do you hear me? You shall all be got out in a few minutes."

And sure enough, the next thing came a rattling at the blinds, and there was Alexander, the hired man, standing outside on a tall ladder and nodding his head at the children. The little ones forgot their fright. They flew to open the window, and frisked and jumped about Alexander as he climbed in and unlocked the door. It struck them as being such a fine thing to be let out in this way, that Dorry began to rather plume himself for fastening them in.

But Aunt Izzie didn't take this view of the case. She scolded them well, and declared they were troublesome children, who couldn't be trusted one moment out of sight, and that she was more than half sorry she had promised to go to the Lecture that evening. "How do I know," she concluded, "that before I come home you won't have set the house on fire, or killed somebody?"

"Oh, no we won't! no we won't!" whined the children, quite moved by this frightful picture. But bless you—ten minutes afterward they had forgotten all about it.

All this time Katy had been sitting on the ledge of the bookcase in the Library, poring over a book. It was called Tasso's Jerusalem Delivered. The man who wrote it was an Italian, but somebody had done the story over into English. It was rather a queer book for a little girl to take a fancy to, but somehow Katy liked it very much. It told about knights, and ladies, and giants, and battles, and made her feel hot and cold by turns as she read, and as if she must rush at something, and shout, and strike blows. Katy was naturally fond of reading. Papa encouraged it. He kept a few books locked up, and then turned her loose in the Library. She read all sorts of things: travels, and sermons, and old magazines. Nothing was so dull that she couldn't get through with it. Anything really interesting absorbed her so that she never knew what was going on about her. The little girls to whose houses she went visiting had found this out, and always hid away their story-books when she was expected to tea. If they didn't do this, she was sure to pick one up and plunge in, and then it was no use to call her, or tug at her dress, for she neither saw nor heard anything more, till it was time to go home.

This afternoon she read the Jerusalem till It was too dark to see any more. On her way up stairs she met Aunt Izzie, with bonnet and shawl on.

"Where *have* you been?" she said. "I have been calling you for the last half-hour."

"I didn't hear you, ma'am."

"But where were you?" persisted Miss Izzie.

"In the Library, reading," replied Katy.

Her aunt gave a sort of sniff, but she knew Katy's ways, and said no more.

"I'm going out to drink tea with Mrs. Hall and attend the evening Lecture," she went on. "Be sure that Clover gets her lesson, and if Cecy comes over as usual, you must send her home early. All of you must be in bed by nine."

"Yes'm," said Katy, but I fear she was not attending much, but thinking, in her secret soul, how jolly it was to have Aunt Izzie go out for once. Miss Carr was very faithful to her duties: she seldom left the children, even for an evening, so whenever she did, they felt a certain sense of novelty and freedom, which was dangerous as well as pleasant.

Still, I am sure that on this occasion Katy meant no mischief. Like all excitable people she seldom did *mean* to do wrong, she just did it when it came into her head. Supper passed off successfully, and all might have gone well, had it not been that after the lessons were learned and Cecy had come in, they fell to talking about "Kikeri."

Kikeri was a game which had been very popular with them a year before. They had invented it themselves, and chosen for it this queer name out of an old fairy story. It was a sort of mixture of Blindman's Buff and Tag—only instead of any one's eyes being bandaged, they all played in the dark. One of the children would stay out in the hall, which was dimly lighted from the stairs, while the others hid themselves in the nursery. When they were all hidden, they would call out "Kikeri," as a signal for the one in the hall to come in and find them. Of course, coming from the light he could see nothing, while the others could see only dimly. It was very exciting to stand crouching up in a corner and watch the dark figure stumbling about and feeling to right and left, while every now and then somebody, just escaping his clutches, would slip past and gain the hall, which was "Freedom

Castle," with a joyful shout of "Kikeri, Kikeri, Kikeri, Ki!" Whoever was caught had to take the place of the catcher. For a long time this game was the delight of the Carr children; but so many scratches and black-and-blue spots came of it, and so many of the nursery things were thrown down and broken, that at last Aunt Izzie issued an order that it should not be played any more. This was almost a year since; but talking of it now put it into their heads to want to try it again.

"After all we didn't promise," said Cecy.

"No, and *Papa* never said a word about our not playing it," added Katy, to whom "Papa" was authority, and must always be minded, while Aunt Izzie might now and then be defied.

So they all went up stairs. Dorry and John, though half undressed, were allowed to join the game. Philly was fast asleep in another room.

It was certainly splendid fun. Once Clover climbed up on the mantel-piece and sat there, and when Katy, who was finder, groped about a little more wildly than usual, she caught hold of Clover's foot, and couldn't imagine where it came from. Dorry got a hard knock, and cried, and at another time Katy's dress caught on the bureau handle and was frightfully torn, but these were too much affairs of every day to interfere in the least with the pleasures of Kikeri. The fun and frolic seemed to grow greater the longer they played. In the excitement, time went on much faster than any of them dreamed. Suddenly, in the midst of the noise, came a sound—the sharp distinct slam of the carryall-door at the side entrance. Aunt Izzie had returned from her Lecture.

The dismay and confusion of that moment! Cecy slipped down stairs like an eel, and fled on the wings of fear along the path which led to her home. Mrs. Hall, as she bade Aunt Izzie good-night, and shut Dr. Carr's front door behind her with a bang, might have been struck with the singular fact that a distant bang came from her own front door like a sort of echo. But she was not a suspicious woman; and when she went up stairs there were Cecy's clothes neatly folded on a chair, and Cecy herself in bed, fast asleep, only with a little more color than usual in her cheeks.

Meantime, Aunt Izzie was on *her* way up stairs, and such a panic as prevailed in the nursery! Katie felt it, and basely scuttled off to her own room, where she went to bed with all possible speed. But the others found it much harder to go to bed; there were so many of them, all getting into each other's way, and with no lamp to see by. Dorry and John popped under the clothes half undressed, Elsie disappeared, and Clover, too late for either, and hearing Aunt Izzie's step in the hall, did this horrible thing—fell on her knees, with her face buried in a chair, and began to say her prayers very hard indeed.

Aunt Izzie, coming in with a candle in her hand, stood in the doorway, astonished at the spectacle. She sat down and waited for Clover to get through, while Clover, on her part, didn't dare to get through, but went on repeating "Now I lay me" over and over again, in a sort of despair. At last Aunt Izzie said very grimly: "That will do, Clover, you can get up!" and Clover rose, feeling like a culprit, which she was, for it was much naughtier to pretend to be praying than to disobey Aunt Izzie and be out of bed after ten o'clock, though I think Clover hardly understood this then.

Aunt Izzie at once began to undress her, and while doing so asked so many questions, that before long she had got at the truth of the whole matter. She gave Clover a sharp scolding, and leaving her to wash her tearful face, she went to the bed where John and Dorry lay, fast asleep, and snoring as conspicuously as they knew how. Something strange in the appearance of the bed made her look more closely: she lifted the clothes, and there, sure enough, they were—half dressed, and with their school-boots on.

Such a shake as Aunt Izzie gave the little scamps at this discovery, would have roused a couple of dormice. Much against their will John and Dorry were forced to wake up, and be slapped and scolded, and made ready for bed, Aunt Izzie standing over them all the while, like a dragon. She had just tucked them warmly in, when for the first time she missed Elsie.

"Where is my poor little Elsie?" she exclaimed.

"In bed," said Clover, meekly.

"In bed!" repeated Aunt Izzie, much amazed. Then stooping down, she gave a vigorous pull. The trundle-bed came into view, and sure enough, there was Elsie, in full dress, shoes and all, but so fast asleep that not all Aunt Izzie's shakes, and pinches, and calls, were able to rouse her. Her clothes were taken off, her boots unlaced, her night-gown put on; but through it all Elsie slept, and she was the only one of the children who did not get the scolding she deserved that dreadful night.

Katy did not even pretend to be asleep when Aunt Izzie went to her room. Her tardy conscience had waked up, and she was lying in bed, very miserable at having drawn the others into a scrape as well as herself, and at the failure of her last set of resolutions about "setting an example to the younger ones."

So unhappy was she, that Aunt Izzie's severe words were almost a relief; and though she cried herself to sleep, it was rather from the burden of her own thoughts than because she had been scolded.

She cried even harder the next day, for Dr. Carr talked to her more seriously than he had ever done before. He reminded her of the time when her Mamma died, and of how she said, "Katy must be a Mamma to the little ones, when she grows up." And he asked her if she didn't think the time was come for beginning to take this dear place towards the children. Poor Katy! She sobbed as if her heart would break at this, and though she made no promises, I think she was never quite so thoughtless again, after that day. As for the rest, Papa called them together and made them distinctly understand that "Kikeri" was never to be played any more. It was so seldom that Papa forbade any games, however boisterous, that this order really made an impression on the unruly brood, and they never have played Kikeri again, from that day to this.

CHAPTER V: IN THE LOFT

"I declare," said Miss Petingill, laying down her work, "if them children don't beat all! What on airth *are* they going to do now?"

Miss Petingill was sitting in the little room in the back building, which she always had when she came to the Carr's for a week's mending and making over. She was the dearest, funniest old woman who ever went out sewing by the day. Her face was round, and somehow made you think of a very nice baked apple, it was so criss-crossed, and lined by a thousand good-natured puckers. She was small and wiry, and wore caps and a false front, which was just the color of a dusty Newfoundland dog's back. Her eyes were dim, and she used spectacles; but for all that, she was an excellent worker. Every one liked Miss Petingill though Aunt Izzie *did* once say that her tongue "was hung in the middle." Aunt Izzie made this remark when she was in a temper, and was by no means prepared to have Phil walk up at once and request Miss Petingill to "stick it out," which she obligingly did; while the rest of the children crowded to look. They couldn't see that it was different from other tongues, but Philly persisted in finding something curious about it; there must be, you know—since it was hung in that queer way!

Wherever Miss Petingill went, all sorts of treasures went with her. The children liked to have her come, for it was as good as a fairy story, or the circus, to see her things unpacked. Miss Petingill was very much afraid of burglars; she lay awake half the night listening for them and nothing on earth would have persuaded her to go anywhere, leaving behind what she called her "Plate." This stately word meant six old teaspoons, very thin and bright and sharp, and a butter-knife, whose handle set forth that it was "A testimonial of gratitude, for saving the life of Ithuriel Jobson, aged seven, on the occasion of his being attacked with quinsy sore throat." Miss Petingill was very proud of her knife. It and the spoons travelled about in a little basket which hung on her arm, and was never allowed to be out of her sight, even when the family she was sewing for were the honestest people in the world.

Then, beside the plate-basket, Miss Petingill never stirred without Tom, her tortoiseshell cat. Tom was a beauty, and knew his power; he ruled Miss Petingill with a rod of iron, and always sat in the rocking-chair when there was one. It was no matter where *she* sat, Miss Petingill told people, but Tom was delicate, and must be made comfortable. A big family Bible always came too, and a special red merino pin-cushion, and some "shade pictures" of old Mr. and Mrs. Petingill and Peter Petingill, who was drowned at sea; and photographs of Mrs. Porter, who used to be Marcia Petingill, and Mrs. Porter's husband, and all the Porter children. Many little boxes and jars came also, and a long row of phials and bottles, filled with homemade physic and herb teas. Miss Petingill could not have slept without having them beside her, for, as she said, how did she know that she might not be "took sudden" with something, and die for want of a little ginger-balsam or pennyroyal?

The Carr children always made so much noise, that it required something unusual to make Miss Petingill drop her work, as she did now, and fly to the window. In fact there was a tremendous hubbub: hurrahs from Dorry, stamping of feet, and a great outcry of shrill, glad voices. Looking down, Miss Petingill saw the whole six—no, seven, for Cecy was there too—stream out of the wood-house door—which wasn't a door, but only a tall open arch—and rush noisily across the yard. Katy was at the head, bearing a large black bottle without any cork in it, while the others carried in each hand what seemed to be a cookie.

"Katherine Carr! Kather-*ine*!" screamed Miss Petingill, tapping loudly on the glass. "Don't you see that it's raining? you ought to be ashamed to let your little brothers and sisters go out and get wet in such a way!" But nobody heard her, and the children vanished into the shed, where nothing could be seen but a distant flapping of pantalettes and frilled trousers, going up what seemed to be a ladder, farther back in the shed. So, with a dissatisfied cluck, Miss Petingill drew back her head, perched the spectacles on her nose, and went to work again on Katy's plaid alpaca, which had two immense zigzag rents across the middle of the front breadth. Katy's frocks, strange to say, always tore exactly in that place!

If Miss Petingill's eyes could have reached a little farther, they would have seen that it wasn't a ladder up which the children were climbing, but a tall wooden post, with spikes driven into it about a foot apart. It required quite a stride to get from one spike to the other; in fact the littler ones couldn't have managed it at all, had it not been for Clover and Cecy "boosting" very hard from below, while Katy, making a long arm, clawed from above. At last they were all safely up, and in the delightful retreat which I am about to describe:

Imagine a low, dark loft without any windows, and with only a very little light coming in through the square hole in the floor, to which the spikey post led. There was a strong smell of corn-cobs, though the corn had been taken away, a great deal of dust and spiderweb in the corners, and some wet spots on the boards; for the roof always leaked a little in rainy weather.

This was the place, which for some reason I have never been able to find out, the Carr children preferred to any other on rainy Saturdays, when they could not play out-doors, Aunt Izzie was as much puzzled at this fancy as I am. When she was young (a vague, far-off time, which none of her nieces and nephews believed in much), she had never had any of these queer notions about getting off into holes and corners, and poke-away places. Aunt Izzie would gladly have forbidden them to go the loft, but Dr. Carr had given his permission, so all she could do was to invent stories about children who had broken their bones in various dreadful ways, by climbing posts and ladders. But these stories made no impression on any of the children except little Phil, and the self-willed brood kept on their way, and climbed their spiked post as often as they liked.

"What's in the bottle?" demanded Dorry, the minute he was fairly landed in the loft.

"Don't be greedy," replied Katy, severely; "you will know when the time comes. It is something *delicious*, I can assure you.

"Now," she went on, having thus quenched Dorry, "all of you had better give me your cookies to put away: if you don't, they'll be sure to be eaten up before the feast, and then you know there wouldn't be anything to make a feast of."

So all of them handed over their cookies. Dorry, who had begun on his as he came up the ladder, was a little unwilling, but he was too much in the habit of minding Katy to dare to disobey. The big bottle was set in a corner, and a stack of cookies built up around it.

"That's right," proceeded Katy, who, as oldest and biggest, always took the lead in their plays. "Now if we're fixed and ready to begin, the Fête (Katy pronounced it *Feet*) can commence. The opening exercise will be 'A Tragedy of the Alhambra,' by Miss Hall."

"No," cried Clover; "first 'The Blue Wizard, or Edwitha of the Hebrides,' you know, Katy."

"Didn't I tell you?" said Katy; "a dreadful accident has happened to that."

"Oh, what?" cried all the rest, for Edwitha was rather a favorite with the family. It was one of the many serial stories which Katy was forever writing, and was about a lady, a knight, a blue wizard, and a poodle named Bop. It had been going on so many months now, that everybody had forgotten the beginning, and nobody had any particular hope of living to hear the end, but still the news of its untimely fate was a shock.

"I'll tell you," said Katy. "Old Judge Kirby called this morning to see Aunt Izzie; I was studying in the little room, but I saw him come in, and pull out the big chair and sit down, and I almost screamed out 'don't!'"

"Why?" cried the children.

"Don't you see? I had stuffed 'Edwitha' down between the back and the seat. It was a *beau*tiful hiding-place, for the seat goes back ever so far; but Edwitha was such a fat bundle, and old Judge Kirby takes up so much room, that I was afraid there would be trouble. And sure enough, he had hardly dropped down before there was a great crackling of paper, and he jumped up again and called out, 'Bless me! what is that?' And then he began poking, and poking, and just as he had poked out the whole bundle, and was putting on his spectacles to see what it was, Aunt Izzie came in."

"Well, what next?" cried the children, immensely tickled.

"Oh!" continued Katy, "Aunt Izzie put on her glasses too, and screwed up her eyes—you know the way she does, and she and the judge read a little bit of it; that part at the first, you remember, where Bop steals the blue-pills, and the Wizard tries to throw him into the sea. You can't think how funny it was to hear Aunt Izzie reading 'Edwitha' out loud—" and Katy went into convulsions at the recollection "where she got to 'Oh Bop—my angel Bop—' I just rolled under the table, and stuffed the table-cover in my mouth to keep from screaming right out. By and by I heard her call Debby, and give her the papers, and say: 'Here is a mass of trash which I wish you to put at once into the kitchen fire.' And she told me afterward that she thought I would be in an insane asylum before I was twenty. It was too bad," ended Katy half laughing and half crying, "to burn up the new chapter and all. But there's one good thing—she didn't find 'The Fairy of the Dry Goods Box,' that was stuffed farther back in the seat.

"And now," continued the mistress of ceremonies, "we will begin. Miss Hall will please rise."

"Miss Hall," much flustered at her fine name, got up with very red cheeks.

"It was once upon a time," she read, "Moonlight lay on the halls of the Alhambra, and the knight, striding impatiently down the passage, thought she would never come."

"Who, the moon?" asked Clover.

"No, of course not," replied Cecy, "a lady he was in love with. The next verse is going to tell about her, only you interrupted.

"She wore a turban of silver, with a jewelled crescent. As she stole down the corregidor the beams struck it and it glittered like stars.

"'So you are come, Zuleika?'

"'Yes, my lord.'

"Just then a sound as of steel smote upon the ear, and Zuleika's mail-clad father rushed in. He drew his sword, so did the other. A moment more, and they both lay dead and stiff in the beams of the moon.

Zuleika gave a loud shriek, and threw herself upon their bodies. She was dead, too! And so ends the Tragedy of the Alhambra."

"That's lovely," said Katy, drawing a long breath, "only very sad! What beautiful stories you do write, Cecy! But I wish you wouldn't always kill the people. Why couldn't the knight have killed the father, and—no, I suppose Zuleika wouldn't have married him then. Well, the father might have—oh, bother! why must anybody be killed, anyhow? why not have them fall on each other's necks, and make up?"

"Why, Katy!" cried Cecy, "it wouldn't have been a tragedy then. You know the name was A *Tragedy* of the Alhambra."

"Oh, well," said Katy, hurriedly, for Cecy's lips were beginning to pout, and her fair, pinkish face to redden, as if she were about to cry; "perhaps it *was* prettier to have them all die; only I thought, for a change, you know!—What a lovely word that was—. 'Corregidor'—what does it mean?"

"I don't know," replied Cecy, quite consoled. "It was in the 'Conquest of Granada.' Something to walk over, I believe."

"The next," went on Katy, consulting her paper, "is 'Yap,' a Simple Poem, by Clover Carr."

All the children giggled, but Clover got up composedly, and recited the following verses:

"Did you ever know Yap?
  The best little dog
Who e'er sat on lap
  Or barked at a frog.

"His eyes were like beads,
  His tail like a mop,
And it waggled as if
  It never would stop.

"His hair was like silk
  Of the glossiest sheen,
He always ate milk,
  And once the cold-cream

"Off the nursery bureau
  (That line is too long!)
It made him quite ill,
  So endeth my song.

"For Yappy he died
  Just two months ago,
And we oughtn't to sing
  At a funeral, you know."

The "Poem" met with immense applause; all the children laughed, and shouted, and clapped, till the loft rang again. But Clover kept her face perfectly, and sat down as demure as ever, except that the little dimples came and went at the corners of her mouth; dimples, partly natural, and partly, I regret to say, the result of a pointed slate-pencil, with which Clover was in the habit of deepening them every day while she studied her lessons.

"Now," said Katy, after the noise had subsided, "now come 'Scripture Verses,' by Miss Elsie and Joanna Carr. Hold up your head, Elsie, and speak distinctly; and oh, Johnnie, you *mustn't* giggle in that way when it comes your turn!"

But Johnnie only giggled the harder at this appeal, keeping her hands very tight across her mouth, and peeping out over her fingers. Elsie, however, was solemn as a little judge, and with great dignity began:

"An angel with a fiery sword,
Came to send Adam and Eve abroad
And as they journeyed through the skies
They took one look at Paradise.
They thought of all the happy hours
Among the birds and fragrant bowers,
And Eve she wept, and Adam bawled,
And both together loudly squalled."

Dorry snickered at this, but sedate Clover hushed him.

"You mustn't," she said; "it's about the Bible, you know. Now John, it's your turn."

But Johnnie would persist in holding her hands over her mouth, while her fat little shoulders shook with laughter. At last, with a great effort, she pulled her face straight, and speaking as fast as she possibly could, repeated, in a sort of burst:

"Balaam's donkey saw the Angel,
  And stopped short in fear.
Balaam didn't see the Angel,
  Which is very queer."

After which she took refuge again behind her fingers, while Elsie went on—

"Elijah by the creek,
  He by ravens fed,
Took from their horny beak
  Pieces of meat and bread."

"Come, Johnnie," said Katy, but the incorrigible Johnnie was shaking again, and all they could make out was—

"The bears came down, and ate————and ate."

These "Verses" were part of a grand project on which Clover and Elsie had been busy for more than a year. It was a sort of rearrangement of Scripture for infant minds; and when it was finished, they meant to have it published, bound in red, with daguerreotypes of the two authoresses on the cover. "The Youth's Poetical Bible" was to be the name of it. Papa, much tickled with the scraps which he overheard, proposed, instead, "The Trundle-Bed Book," as having been composed principally in that spot, but Elsie and Clover were highly indignant, and would not listen to the idea for a moment.

After the "Scripture Verses," came Dorry's turn. He had been allowed to choose for himself, which was unlucky, as his taste was peculiar, not to say gloomy. On this occasion he had selected that cheerful hymn which begins—

"Hark, from the tombs a doleful sound."

And he now began to recite it in a lugubrious voice and with great emphasis, smacking his lips, as it were, over such lines as—

"Princes, this clay *shall* be your bed,
  In spite of all your towers."

The older children listened with a sort of fascinated horror, rather enjoying the cold chills which ran down their backs, and huddling close together, as Dorry's hollow tones echoed from the dark corners of the loft. It was too much for Philly, however. At the close of the piece he was found to be in tears.

"I don't want to st-a-a-y up here and be groaned at," he sobbed.

"There, you bad boy!" cried Katy, all the more angry because she was conscious of having enjoyed it herself, "that's what you do with your horrid hymns, frightening us to death and making Phil cry!" And she gave Dorry a little shake. He began to whimper, and as Phil was still sobbing, and Johnnie had begun to sob too, out of sympathy with the others, the *Feet* in the Loft seemed likely to come to a sad end.

"I'm goin' to tell Aunt Izzie that I don't like you," declared Dorry, putting one leg through the opening in the floor.

"No, you aren't," said Katy, seizing him, "you are going to stay, because *now* we are going to have the Feast! Do stop, Phil; and Johnnie, don't be a goose, but come and pass round the cookies."

The word "Feast" produced a speedy effect on the spirits of the party. Phil cheered at once, and Dorry changed his mind about going. The black bottle was solemnly set in the midst, and the cookies were handed about by Johnnie, who was now all smiles. The cookies had scalloped edges and caraway seeds inside, and were very nice. There were two apiece; and as the last was finished, Katy put her hand in her pocket, and amid great applause, produced the crowning addition to the repast—seven long, brown sticks of cinnamon.

"Isn't it fun?" she said. "Debby was real good-natured to-day, and let me put my own hand into the box, so I picked out the longest sticks there were. Now, Cecy, as you're company, you shall have the first drink out of the bottle."

The "something delicious" proved to be weak vinegar-and-water. It was quite warm, but somehow, drank up there in the loft, and out of a bottle, it tasted very nice. Beside, they didn't *call* it vinegar-and-water—of course not! Each child gave his or her swallow a different name, as if the bottle were like Signor Blitz's and could pour out a dozen things at once. Clover called her share "Raspberry Shrub," Dorry christened his "Ginger Pop," while Cecy, who was romantic, took her three sips under the name of "Hydomel," which she explained was something nice, made, she believed, of beeswax. The last drop gone, and the last bit of cinnamon crunched, the company came to order again, for the purpose of hearing Philly repeat his one piece,—

"Little drops of water,"

which exciting poem he had said every Saturday as far back as they could remember. After that Katy declared the literary part of the "Feet" over, and they all fell to playing "Stagecoach," which, in spite of close quarters and an occasional bump from the roof, was such good fun, that a general "Oh dear!" welcomed the ringing of the tea-bell. I suppose cookies and vinegar had taken away their appetites, for none of them were hungry, and Dorry astonished Aunt Izzie very much by eyeing the table in a disgusted way, and saying: "Pshaw! *only* plum sweatmeats and sponge cake and hot biscuit! I don't want any supper."

"What ails the child? he must be sick," said Dr. Carr; but Katy explained.

"Oh no, Papa, it isn't that—only we've been having a feast in the loft."

"Did you have a good time?" asked Papa, while Aunt Izzie gave a dissatisfied groan. And all the children answered at once: "Splendiferous!"

CHAPTER VI: INTIMATE FRIENDS

"Aunt Izzie, may I ask Imogen Clark to spend the day here on Saturday?" cried Katy, bursting in one afternoon.

"Who on earth is Imogen Clark? I never heard the name before," replied her aunt.

"Oh, the *loveliest* girl! She hasn't been going to Mrs. Knight's school but a little while, but we're the greatest friends. And she's perfectly beautiful, Aunt Izzie. Her hands are just as white as snow, and no bigger than *that*. She's got the littlest waist of any girl in school, and she's real sweet, and so self-denying and unselfish! I don't believe she has a bit good times at home, either. Do let me ask her!"

"How do you know she's so sweet and self-denying, if you've known her such a short time?" asked Aunt Izzie, in an unpromising tone.

"Oh, she tells me everything! We always walk together at recess now. I know all about her, and she's just lovely! Her father used to be real rich, but they're poor now, and Imogen had to have her boots patched twice last winter. I guess she's the flower of her family. You can't think how I love her!" concluded Katy, sentimentally.

"No, I can't," said Aunt Izzie. "I never could see into these sudden friendships of yours, Katy, and I'd rather you wouldn't invite this Imogen, or whatever her name is, till I've had a chance to ask somebody about her."

Katy clasped her hands in despair. "Oh, Aunt Izzie!" she cried, "Imogen knows that I came in to ask you, and she's standing at the gate at this moment, waiting to hear what you say. Please let me, just this once! I shall be so dreadfully ashamed not to."

"Well," said Miss Izzie, moved by the wretchedness of Katy's face, "if you've asked her already, it's no use my saying no, I suppose. But recollect, Katy, this is not to happen again. I can't have you inviting girls, and then coming for my leave. Your father won't be at all pleased. He's very particular about whom you make friends with. Remember how Mrs. Spenser turned out."

Poor Katy! Her propensity to fall violently in love with new people was always getting her into scrapes. Ever since she began to walk and talk, "Katy's intimate friends" had been one of the jokes of the household.

Papa once undertook to keep a list of them, but the number grew so great that he gave it up in despair. First on the list was a small Irish child, named Marianne O'Riley. Marianne lived in a street which Katy passed on her way to school. It was not Mrs. Knight's, but an ABC school, to which Dorry and John now went. Marianne used to be always making sand-pies in front of her mother's house, and Katy, who was about five years old, often stopped to help her. Over this mutual pastry they grew so intimate, that Katy resolved to adopt Marianne as her own little girl, and bring her up in a safe and hidden corner.

She told Clover of this plan, but nobody else. The two children, full of their delightful secret, began to save pieces of bread and cookies from their supper every evening. By degrees they collected a great heap of dry crusts, and other refreshments, which they put safely away in the garret. They also saved the apples which were given them for two weeks, and made a bed in a big empty box, with cotton quilts, and the dolls' pillows out of the baby-house. When all was ready, Katy broke the plan to her beloved Marianne, and easily persuaded her to run away and take possession of this new home.

"We won't tell Papa and Mamma till she's quite grown up," Katy said to Clover; "then we'll bring her down stairs, and *won't* they be surprised? Don't let's call her Marianne any longer, either. It isn't pretty. We'll name her Susquehanna instead—Susquehanna Carr. Recollect, Marianne, you mustn't answer if I call you Marianne—only when I say Susquehanna."

"Yes'm," replied Marianne, very meekly.

For a whole day all went on delightfully. Susquehanna lived in her wooden box, ate all the apples and the freshest cookies, and was happy. The two children took turns to steal away and play with the "Baby," as they called Marianne, though she was a great deal bigger than Clover. But when night came on, and nurse swooped on Katy and Clover, and carried them off to bed, Miss O'Riley began to think that the garret was a dreadful place. Peeping out of her box, she could see black things standing in corners, which she did not recollect seeing in the day-time. They were really trunks and brooms and warming-pans, but somehow, in the darkness, they looked different—big and awful. Poor little Marianne bore it as long as she could; but when at last a rat began to scratch in the wall close beside her, her courage gave way entirely, and she screamed at the top of her voice.

"What is that?" said Dr. Carr, who had just come in, and was on his way up stairs.

"It sounds as if it came from the attic," said Mrs. Carr (for this was before Mamma died). "Can it be that one of the children has got out of bed and wandered up stairs in her sleep?"

No, Katy and Clover were safe in the nursery; so Dr. Carr took a candle and went as fast as he could to the attic, where the yells were growing terrific. When he reached the top of the stairs, the cries ceased. He looked about. Nothing was to be seen at first, then a little head appeared over the edge of a big wooden box, and a piteous voice sobbed out:

"Ah, Miss Katy, and indeed I can't be stayin' any longer. There's rats in it!"

"Who on earth *are* you?" asked the amazed Doctor.

"Sure I'm Miss Katy's and Miss Clover's Baby. But I don't want to be a baby any longer. I want to go home and see my mother." And again the poor little midge lifted up her voice and wept.

I don't think Dr. Carr ever laughed so hard in his life, as when finally he got to the bottom of the story, and found that Katy and Clover had been "adopting" a child. But he was very kind to poor Susquehanna, and carried her down stairs in his arms, to the nursery. There, in a bed close to the other children, she soon forgot her troubles and fell asleep.

The little sisters were much surprised when they waked up in the morning, and found their Baby asleep beside them. But their joy was speedily turned to tears. After breakfast, Dr. Carr carried Marianne home to her mother, who was in a great fright over her disappearance, and explained to the children that the garret plan must be given up. Great was the mourning in the nursery; but as Marianne was allowed to come and play with them now and then, they gradually got over their grief. A few months later Mr. O'Riley moved away from Burnet, and that was the end of Katy's first friendship.

The next was even funnier. There was a queer old black woman who lived all alone by herself in a small house near the school. This old woman had a very bad temper. The neighbors told horrible stories about her, so that the children were afraid to pass the house. They used to turn always just before they reached it, and cross to the other side of the street. This they did so regularly, that their feet had worn a path in the grass. But for some reason Katy found a great fascination in the little house. She liked to dodge about the door, always holding herself ready to turn and run in case the old woman rushed out upon her with a broomstick. One day she begged a large cabbage of Alexander, and rolled it in at the door of the house. The old woman seemed to like it, and after this Katy always stopped to speak when she went by. She even got so far as to sit on the step and watch the old woman at work. There was a sort of perilous pleasure in doing this. It was like sitting at the entrance of a lion's cage, uncertain at what moment his Majesty might take it into his head to give a spring and eat you up.

After this, Katy took a fancy to a couple of twin sisters, daughters of a German jeweller. They were quite grown-up, and always wore dresses exactly alike. Hardly any one could tell them apart. They spoke very little English, and as Katy didn't know a word of German, their intercourse was confined to smiles, and to the giving of bunches of flowers, which Katy used to tie up and present to them whenever they passed the gate. She was too shy to do more than just put the flowers in their hands and run away; but the twins were evidently pleased, for one day, when Clover happened to be looking out of the window, she saw them open the gate, fasten a little parcel to a bush, and walk rapidly off. Of course she called Katy at once, and the two children flew out to see what the parcel was. It held a bonnet—a beautiful doll's bonnet of blue silk, trimmed with artificial flowers; upon it was pinned a slip of paper with these words, in an odd foreign hand:

"To the nice little girl who was so kindly to give us some flowers."

You can judge whether Katy and Clover were pleased or not.

This was when Katy was six years old. I can't begin to tell you how many different friends she had set up since then. There was an ash-man, and a steam-boat captain. There was Mrs. Sawyer's cook, a nice old woman, who gave Katy lessons in cooking, and taught her to make soft custard and sponge-cake. There was a bonnet-maker, pretty and dressy, whom, to Aunt Izzie's great indignation, Katy persisted in calling "Cousin Estelle!" There was a thief in the town-jail, under whose window Katy used to stand, saying, "I'm so sorry, poor man!" and "have you got any little girls like me?" in the most piteous way. The thief had a piece of string which he let down from the window. Katy would tie rosebuds and cherries to this string, and the thief would draw them up. It was so interesting to do this, that Katy felt dreadfully when they carried the man off to the State Prison. Then followed a short interval of Cornelia Perham, a nice, good-natured girl, whose father was a fruit-merchant. I am afraid Katy's liking for prunes and white grapes played a part in this intimacy. It was splendid fun to go with Cornelia to her father's big shop, and have whole boxes of raisins and drums of figs opened for their amusement, and be allowed to ride up and down in the elevator as much as they liked. But of all Katy's queer acquaintances, Mrs. Spenser, to whom Aunt Izzie had alluded, was the queerest.

Mrs. Spenser was a mysterious lady whom nobody ever saw. Her husband was a handsome, rather bad-looking man, who had come from parts unknown, and rented a small house in Burnet. He didn't seem to have any particular business, and was away from home a great deal. His wife was said to be an invalid, and people, when they spoke of him, shook their heads and wondered how the poor woman got on all alone in the house, while her husband was absent.

Of course Katy was too young to understand these whispers, or the reasons why people were not disposed to think well of Mr. Spenser. The romance of the closed door and the lady whom nobody saw, interested her very much. She used to stop and stare at the windows, and wonder what was going on inside, till at last it seemed as if she *must* know. So, one day she took some flowers and Victoria, her favorite doll, and boldly marched into the Spensers' yard.

She tapped at the front door, but nobody answered. Then she tapped again. Still nobody answered. She tried the door. It was locked. So shouldering Victoria, she trudged round to the back of the house. As she passed the side-door she saw that it was open a little way. She knocked for the third time, and as no one came, she went in, and passing through the little hall, began to tap at all the inside doors.

There seemed to be no people in the house, Katy peeped into the kitchen first. It was bare and forlorn. All sorts of dishes were standing about. There was no fire in the stove. The parlor was not much better. Mr. Spenser's boots lay in the middle of the floor. There were dirty glasses on the table. On the mantel-piece was a platter with bones of meat upon it. Dust lay thick over everything, and the whole house looked as if it hadn't been lived in for at least a year.

Katy tried several other doors, all of which were locked, and then she went up stairs. As she stood on the top step, grasping her flowers, and a little doubtful what to do next, a feeble voice from a bed-room called out:

"Who is there?"

This was Mrs. Spenser. She was lying on her bed, which was very tossed and tumbled, as if it hadn't been made up that morning. The room was as disorderly and dirty as all the rest of the house, and Mrs. Spenser's wrapper and night-cap were by no means clean, but her face was sweet, and she had beautiful curling hair, which fell over the pillow. She was evidently very sick, and altogether Katy felt sorrier for her than she had ever done for anybody in her life.

"Who are you, child?" asked Mrs. Spenser.

"I'm Dr. Carr's little girl," answered Katy, going straight up to the bed. "I came to bring you some flowers." And she laid the bouquet on the dirty sheet.

Mrs. Spenser seemed to like the flowers. She took them up and smelled them for a long time, without speaking.

"But how did you get in?" she said at last.

"The door was open," faltered Katy, who was beginning to feel scared at her own daring, "and they said you were sick, so I thought perhaps you would like me to come and see you."

"You are a kind little girl," said Mrs. Spenser, and gave her a kiss.

After this Katy used to go every day. Sometimes Mrs. Spenser would be up and moving feebly about; but more often she was in bed, and Katy would sit beside her. The house never looked a bit better than it did that first day, but after a while Katy used to brush Mrs. Spenser's hair, and wash her face with the corner of a towel.

I think her visits were a comfort to the poor lady, who was very ill and lonely. Sometimes, when she felt pretty well, she would tell Katy stories about the time when she was a little girl and lived at home with her father and mother. But she never spoke of Mr. Spenser, and Katy never saw him except once, when she was so frightened that for several days she dared not go near the house. At last Cecy reported that she had seen him go off in the stage with his carpet-bag, so Katy ventured in again. Mrs. Spenser cried when she saw her.

"I thought you were never coming any more," she said.

Katy was touched and flattered at having been missed, and after that she never lost a day. She always carried the prettiest flowers she could find, and if any one gave her a specially nice peach or a bunch of grapes, she saved it for Mrs. Spenser.

Aunt Izzie was much worried at all this. But Dr. Carr would not interfere. He said it was a case where grown people could do nothing, and if Katy was a comfort to the poor lady he was glad. Katy was glad too, and the visits did her as much good as they did Mrs. Spenser, for the intense pity she felt for the sick woman made her gentle and patient as she had never been before.

One day she stopped, as usual, on her way home from school. She tried the side-door—it was locked; the back-door, it was locked too. All the blinds were shut tight. This was very puzzling.

As she stood in the yard a woman put her head out of the window of the next house. "It's no use knocking," she said, "all the folks have gone away."

"Gone away where?" asked Katy.

"Nobody knows," said the woman; "the gentleman came back in the middle of the night, and this morning, before light, he had a wagon at the door, and just put in the trunks and the sick lady, and drove off. There's been more than one a-knocking besides you, since then. But Mr. Pudgett, he's got the key, and nobody can get in without goin' to him."

It was too true. Mrs. Spenser was gone, and Katy never saw her again. In a few days it came out that Mr. Spenser was a very bad man, and had been making false money—*counterfeiting*, as grown people call it. The police were searching for him to put him in jail, and that was the reason he had come back in such a hurry and carried off his poor sick wife. Aunt Izzie cried with mortification, when she heard this. She said she thought it was a disgrace that Katy should have been visiting in a counterfeiter's family. But Dr. Carr only laughed. He told Aunt Izzie that he didn't think that kind of crime was catching, and as for Mrs. Spenser, she was much to be pitied. But Aunt Izzie could not get over her vexation, and every now and then, when she was vexed, she would refer to the affair, though this all happened so long ago that most people had forgotten all about it, and Philly and John had stopped playing at "Putting Mr. Spenser in Jail," which for a long time was one of their favorite games.

Katy always felt badly when Aunt Izzie spoke unkindly of her poor sick friend. She had tears in her eyes now, as she walked to the gate, and looked so very sober, that Imogen Clark, who stood there waiting, clasped her hands and said:

"Ah, I see! Your aristocratic Aunt refuses."

Imogen's real name was Elizabeth. She was rather a pretty girl, with a screwed-up, sentimental mouth, shiny brown hair, and a little round curl on each of her cheeks. These curls must have been fastened on with glue or tin tacks, one would think, for they never moved, however much she laughed or shook her head. Imogen was a bright girl, naturally, but she had read so many novels that her brain was completely turned. It was partly this which made her so attractive to Katy, who adored stories, and thought Imogen was a real heroine of romance.

"Oh no, she doesn't," she replied, hardly able to keep from laughing, at the idea of Aunt Izzie's being called an "aristocratic relative"—"she says she shall be my hap—" But here Katy's conscience gave a prick, and the sentence ended in "um, um, um—" "So you'll come, won't you, darling? I am so glad!"

"And I!" said Imogen, turning up her eyes theatrically.

From this time on till the end of the week, the children talked of nothing but Imogen's visit, and the nice time they were going to have. Before breakfast on Saturday morning, Katy and Clover were at work building a beautiful bower of asparagus boughs under the trees. All the playthings were set out in order. Debby baked them some cinnamon cakes, the kitten had a pink ribbon tied round her neck, and the dolls, including "Pikery," were arrayed in their best clothes.

About half-past ten Imogen arrived. She was dressed in a light-blue barège, with low neck and short sleeves, and wore coral beads in her hair, white satin slippers, and a pair of yellow gloves. The gloves and slippers were quite dirty, and the barège was old and darned; but the general effect was so very gorgeous, that the children, who were dressed for play, in gingham frocks and white aprons, were quite dazzled at the appearance of their guest.

"Oh, Imogen, you look just like a young lady in a story!" said simple Katy; whereupon Imogen tossed her head and rustled her skirts about more than ever.

Somehow, with these fine clothes, Imogen seemed to have put on a fine manner, quite different from the one she used every day. You know some people always do, when they go out visiting. You would almost have supposed that this was a different Imogen, who was kept in a box most of the time, and taken out for Sundays and grand occasions. She swam about, and diddled, and lisped, and looked at herself in the glass, and was generally grown-up and airy. When Aunt Izzie spoke to her, she fluttered and behaved so queerly, that Clover almost laughed; and even Katy, who could see nothing wrong in people she loved, was glad to carry her away to the playroom.

"Come out to the bower," she said, putting her arm round the blue barège waist.

"A bower!" cried Imogen. "How sweet!" But when they reached the asparagus boughs her face fell. "Why it hasn't any roof, or pinnacles, or any fountain!" she said.

"Why no, of course not," said Clover, staring, "we made it ourselves."

"Oh!" said Imogen. She was evidently disappointed. Katy and Clover felt mortified; but as their visitor did not care for the bower, they tried to think of something else.

"Let us go to the Loft," they said.

So they all crossed the yard together. Imogen picked her way daintily in the white satin slippers, but when she saw the spiked post, she gave a scream.

"Oh, not up there, darling, not up there!". she cried; "never, never!"

"Oh, do try! It's just as easy as can be," pleaded Katy, going up and down half a dozen times in succession to show how easy it was. But Imogen wouldn't be persuaded.

"Do not ask me," she said affectedly; "my nerves would never stand such a thing! And besides—my dress!"

"What made you wear it?" said Philly, who was a plain-spoken child, and given to questions. While John whispered to Dorry, "That's a real stupid girl. Let's go off somewhere and play by ourselves."

So, one by one, the small fry crept away, leaving Katy and Clover to entertain the visitor by themselves. They tried dolls, but Imogen did not care for dolls. Then they proposed to sit down in the shade, and cap verses, a game they all liked. But Imogen said that though she adored poetry, she never could remember any. So it ended in their going to the orchard, where Imogen ate a great many plums and early apples, and really seemed to enjoy herself. But when she could eat no more, a dreadful dulness fell over the party. At last Imogen said:

"Don't you ever sit in the drawing-room?"

"The what?" asked Clover.

"The drawing-room," repeated Imogen.

"Oh, she means the parlor!" cried Katy. "No, we don't sit there except when Aunt Izzie has company to tea. It is all dark and poky, you know. Beside, it's so much pleasanter to be out-doors. Don't you think so?"

"Yes, sometimes," replied Imogen, doubtfully, "but I think it would be pleasant to go in and sit there for a while, now. My head aches dreadfully, being out here in this horrid sun."

Katy was at her wit's end to know what to do. They scarcely ever went into the parlor, which Aunt Izzie regarded as a sort of sacred place. She kept cotton petticoats over all the chairs for fear of dust, and never opened the blinds for fear of flies. The idea of children with dusty boots going in there to sit! On the other hand, Katy's natural politeness made it hard to refuse a visitor anything she asked for. And beside, it was dreadful to think that Imogen might go away and report "Katy Carr isn't allowed to sit in the best room, even when she has company!" With a quaking heart she led the way to the parlor. She dared not open the blinds, so the room looked very dark. She could just see Imogen's figure as she sat on the sofa, and Clover twirling uneasily about on the piano-stool. All the time she kept listening to hear if Aunt Izzie were not coming, and altogether the parlor was a dismal place to her; not half so pleasant as the asparagus bower, where they felt perfectly safe.

But Imogen, who, for the first time, seemed comfortable, began to talk. Her talk was about herself. Such stories she told about the things which had happened to her! All the young ladies in The Ledger put together, never had stranger adventures. Gradually, Katy and Clover got so interested that they left their seats and crouched down close to the sofa, listening with open mouths to these stories. Katy forgot to listen for Aunt Izzie. The parlor door swung open, but she did not notice it. She did not even hear the front door shut, when Papa came home to dinner.

Dr. Carr, stopping in the hall to glance over his newspaper, heard the high-pitched voice running on in the parlor. At first he hardly listened; then these words caught his ear:

"Oh, it was lovely, girls, perfectly delicious! I suppose I did look well, for I was all in white, with my hair let down, and just one rose, you know, here on top. And he leaned over me, and said in a low, deep tone, 'Lady, I am a Brigand, but I feel the enchanting power of your beauty. You are free!'"

Dr. Carr pushed the door open a little farther. Nothing was to be seen but some indistinct figures, but he heard Katy's voice in an eager tone:

"Oh, *do* go on. What happened next?"

"Who on earth have the children got in the parlor?" he asked Aunt Izzie, whom he found in the dining-room.

"The parlor!" cried Miss Izzie, wrathfully, "why, what are they there for?" Then going to the door, she called out, "Children, what are you doing in the parlor? Come out right away. I thought you were playing out-doors."

"Imogen had a head-ache," faltered Katy. The three girls came out into the hall; Clover and Katy looking scared, and even the Enchanter of the Brigand quite crest-fallen.

"Oh," said Aunt Izzie, grimly, "I am sorry to hear that. Probably you are bilious. Would you like some camphor or anything?"

"No, thank you," replied Imogen, meekly. But afterwards she whispered to Katy:

"Your aunt isn't very nice, I think. She's just like Jackima, that horrid old woman I told you about, who lived in the Brigand's Cave and did the cooking.

"I don't think you're a bit polite to tell me so," retorted Katy, very angry at this speech.

"Oh, never mind, dear, don't take it to heart!" replied Imogen, sweetly. "We can't help having relations that ain't nice, you know."

The visit was evidently not a success. Papa was very civil to Imogen at dinner, but he watched her closely, and Katy saw a comical twinkle in his eye, which she did not like. Papa had very droll eyes. They saw everything, and sometimes they seemed to talk almost as distinctly as his tongue. Katy began to feel low-spirited. She confessed afterward that she should never have got through the afternoon if she hadn't run up stairs two or three times, and comforted herself by reading a little in "Rosamond."

"Aren't you glad she's gone?" whispered Clover, as they stood at the gate together watching Imogen walk down the street.

"Oh, Clover! how can you?" said Katy But she gave Clover a great hug, and I think in her heart she *was* glad.

"Katy," said Papa, next day, "you came into the room then, exactly like your new friend Miss Clark."

"How? I don't know what you mean," answered Katy, blushing deeply.

"*So*," said Dr. Carr; and he got up, raising his shoulders and squaring his elbows, and took a few mincing steps across the room. Katy couldn't help laughing, it was so funny, and so like Imogen. Then Papa sat down again and drew her close to him.

"My dear," he said, "you're an affectionate child, and I'm glad of it. But there is such a thing as throwing away one's affection. I didn't fancy that little girl at all yesterday. What makes you like her so much?"

"I didn't like her so much, yesterday," admitted Katy, reluctantly. "She's a great deal nicer than that at school, sometimes."

"I'm glad to hear it," said her father. "For I should be sorry to think that you really admired such silly manners. And what was that nonsense I heard her telling you about Brigands?"

"It really hap—" began Katy.—Then she caught Papa's eye, and bit her lip, for he looked very quizzical. "Well," she went on, laughing, "I suppose it didn't really all happen;—but it was ever so funny, Papa, even if it was a make-up. And Imogen's just as good-natured as can be. All the girls like her."

"Make-ups are all very well," said Papa, "as long as people don't try to make you believe they are true. When they do that, it seems to me it comes too near the edge of falsehood to be very safe or pleasant. If I were you, Katy, I'd be a little shy of swearing eternal friendship for Miss Clark. She may be good-natured, as you say, but I think two or three years hence she won't seem so nice to you as she does now. Give me a kiss, Chick, and run away, for there's Alexander with the buggy."

CHAPTER VII: COUSIN HELEN'S VISIT

A little knot of the school-girls were walking home together one afternoon in July. As they neared Dr. Carr's gate, Maria Fiske exclaimed, at the sight of a pretty bunch of flowers lying in the middle of the sidewalk:

"Oh my!" she cried, "see what somebody's dropped! I'm going to have it." She stooped to pick it up. But, just as her fingers touched the stems, the nosegay, as if bewitched, began to move. Maria made a bewildered clutch. The nosegay moved faster, and at last vanished under the gate, while a giggle sounded from the other side of the hedge.

"Did you see that?" shrieked Maria; "those flowers ran away of themselves."

"Nonsense," said Katy, "it's those absurd children." Then, opening the gate, she called: "John! Dorry! come out and show yourselves." But nobody replied, and no one could be seen. The nosegay lay on the path, however, and picking it up, Katy exhibited to the girls a long end of black thread, tied to the stems.

"That's a very favorite trick of Johnnie's," she said: "she and Dorry are always tying up flowers, and putting them out on the walk to tease people. Here, Maria, take 'em if you like. Though I don't think John's taste in bouquets is very good."

"Isn't it splendid to have vacation come?" said one of the bigger girls. "What are you all going to do? We're going to the seaside."

"Pa says he'll take Susie and me to Niagara," said Maria.

"I'm going to make my aunt a visit," said Alice Blair. "She lives in a real lovely place in the country, and there's a pond there; and Tom (that's my cousin) says he'll teach me to row. What are you going to do, Katy?"

"Oh, I don't know; play round and have splendid times," replied Katy, throwing her bag of books into the air, and catching it again. But the other girls looked as if they didn't think this good fun at all, and as if they were sorry for her; and Katy felt suddenly that her vacation wasn't going to be so pleasant as that of the rest.

"I wish Papa *would* take us somewhere," she said to Clover, as they walked up the gravel path. "All the other girls' Papas do."

"He's too busy," replied Clover. "Beside, I don't think any of the rest of the girls have half such good times as we. Ellen Robbins says she'd give a million of dollars for such nice brothers and sisters as ours to play with. And, you know, Maria and Susie have *awful* times at home, though they do go to places. Mrs. Fiske is so particular. She always says 'Don't,' and they haven't got any yard to their house, or anything. I wouldn't change."

"Nor I," said Katy, cheering up at these words of wisdom. "Oh, isn't it lovely to think there won't be any school to-morrow? Vacations are just splendid!" and she gave her bag another toss. It fell to the ground with a crash.

"There, you've cracked your slate," said Clover.

"No matter, I sha'n't want it again for eight weeks," replied Katy, comfortably, as they ran up the steps.

They burst open the front door and raced up stairs, crying "Hurrah! hurrah! vacation's begun. Aunt Izzie, vacation's begun!" Then they stopped short, for lo! the upper hall was all in confusion. Sounds of beating and dusting came from the spare room. Tables and chairs were standing about; and a cot-bed, which seemed to be taking a walk all by itself, had stopped short at the head of the stairs, and barred the way.

"Why, how queer!" said Katy, trying to get by. "What *can* be going to happen? Oh, there's Aunt Izzie! Aunt Izzie, who's coming? What *are* you moving the things out of the Blue-room for?"

"Oh, gracious! is that you?" replied Aunt Izzie, who looked very hot and flurried. "Now, children, it's no use for you to stand there asking questions; I haven't got time to answer them. Let the bedstead alone, Katy, you'll push it into the wall. There, I told you so!" as Katy gave an impatient shove, "you've made a bad mark on the paper. What a troublesome child you are! Go right down stairs, both of you, and don't come up this way again till after tea. I've just as much as I can possibly attend to till then."

"Just tell us what's going to happen, and we will," cried the children.

"Your Cousin Helen is coming to visit us," said Miss Izzie, curtly, and disappeared into the Blue-room.

This was news indeed. Katy and Clover ran down stairs in great excitement, and after consulting a little, retired to the Loft to talk it over in peace and quiet. Cousin Helen coming! It seemed as strange as if Queen Victoria, gold crown and all, had invited herself to tea. Or as if some character out of a book, Robinson Crusoe, say, or "Amy Herbert," had driven up with a trunk and announced the intention of spending a week. For to the imaginations of the children, Cousin Helen was as interesting and unreal as anybody in the Fairy Tales: Cinderella, or Blue-Beard, or dear Red Riding-Hood herself. Only there was a sort of mixture of Sunday-school book in their idea of her, for Cousin Helen was very, very good.

None of them had ever seen her. Philly said he was sure she hadn't any legs, because she never went away from home, and lay on a sofa all the time. But the rest knew that this was because Cousin Helen was ill. Papa always went to visit her twice a year, and he liked to talk to the children about her, and tell how sweet and patient she was, and what a pretty room she lived in. Katy and Clover had "played Cousin Helen" so long, that now they were frightened as well as glad at the idea of seeing the real one.

"Do you suppose she will want us to say hymns to her all the time?" asked Clover.

"Not all the time," replied Katy, "because you know she'll get tired, and have to take naps in the afternoons. And then, of course, she reads the Bible a great deal. Oh dear, how quiet we shall have to be! I wonder how long she's going to stay?"

"What do you suppose she looks like?" went on Clover.

"Something like 'Lucy,' in Mrs. Sherwood, I guess, with blue eyes, and curls, and a long, straight nose. And she'll keep her hands clasped *so* all the time, and wear 'frilled wrappers,' and lie on the sofa perfectly still, and never smile, but just look patient. We'll have to take off our boots in the hall, Clover, and go up stairs in stocking feet, so as not to make a noise, all the time she stays."

"Won't it be funny!" giggled Clover, her sober little face growing bright at the idea of this variation on the hymns.

The time seemed very long till the next afternoon, when Cousin Helen was expected. Aunt Izzie, who was in a great excitement, gave the children many orders about their behavior. They were to do this and that, and not to do the other. Dorry, at last, announced that he wished Cousin Helen would just stay at home. Clover and Elsie, who had been thinking pretty much the same thing in private, were glad to hear that she was on her way to a Water Cure, and would stay only four days.

Five o'clock came. They all sat on the steps waiting for the carriage. At last it drove up. Papa was on the box. He motioned the children to stand back. Then he helped out a nice-looking young woman, who, Aunt Izzie told them, was Cousin Helen's nurse, and then, very carefully, lifted Cousin Helen in his arms and brought her in.

"Oh, there are the chicks!" were the first words the children heard, in such a gay, pleasant voice. "Do set me down somewhere, uncle. I want to see them so much!"

So Papa put Cousin Helen on the hall sofa. The nurse fetched a pillow, and when she was made comfortable, Dr. Carr called to the little ones.

"Cousin Helen wants to see you," he said.

"Indeed I do," said the bright voice. "So this is Katy? Why, what a splendid tall Katy it is! And this is Clover," kissing her; "and this dear little Elsie. You all look as natural as possible—just as if I had seen you before."

And she hugged them all round, not as if it was polite to like them because they were relations, but as if she had loved them and wanted them all her life.

There was something in Cousin Helen's face and manner, which made the children at home with her at once. Even Philly, who had backed away with his hands behind him, after staring hard for a minute or two, came up with a sort of rush to get his share of kissing.

Still, Katy's first feeling was one of disappointment. Cousin Helen was not at all like "Lucy," in Mrs. Sherwood's story. Her nose turned up the least bit in the world. She had brown hair, which didn't curl, a brown skin, and bright eyes, which danced when she laughed or spoke. Her face was thin, but except for that you wouldn't have guessed that she was sick. She didn't fold her hands, and she didn't look patient, but absolutely glad and merry. Her dress wasn't a "frilled wrapper," but a sort of loose travelling thing of pretty gray stuff, with a rose-colored bow, and bracelets, and a round hat trimmed with a gray feather. All Katy's dreams about the "saintly invalid" seemed to take wings and fly away. But the more she watched Cousin Helen the more she seemed to like her, and to feel as if she were nicer than the imaginary person which she and Clover had invented.

"She looks just like other people, don't she?" whispered Cecy, who had come over to have a peep at the new arrival.

"Y-e-s," replied Katy, doubtfully, "only a great, great deal prettier."

By and by, Papa carried Cousin Helen up stairs. All the children wanted to go too, but he told them she was tired, and must rest. So they went out doors to play till tea-time.

"Oh, do let me take up the tray," cried Katy at the tea-table, as she watched Aunt Izzie getting ready Cousin Helen's supper. Such a nice supper! Cold chicken, and raspberries and cream, and tea in a pretty pink-and-white china cup. And such a snow-white napkin as Aunt Izzie spread over the tray!

"No indeed," said Aunt Izzie; "you'll drop it the first thing." But Katy's eyes begged so hard, that Dr. Carr said, "Yes, let her, Izzie; I like to see the girls useful."

So Katy, proud of the commission, took the tray and carried it carefully across the hall. There was a bowl of flowers on the table. As she passed, she was struck with a bright idea. She set down the tray, and picking out a rose, laid it on the napkin besides the saucer of crimson raspberries. It looked very pretty, and Katy smiled to herself with pleasure.

"What are you stopping for?" called Aunt Izzie, from the dining-room. "Do be careful, Katy, I really think Bridget had better take it."

"Oh no, no!" protested Katy, "I'm most up already." And she sped up stairs as fast as she could go. Luckless speed! She had just reached the door of the Blue-room, when she tripped upon her boot-lace, which, as usual, was dangling, made a misstep, and stumbled. She caught at the door to save herself; the door flew open; and Katy, with the tray, cream, raspberries, rose and all, descended in a confused heap upon the carpet.

"I told you so!" exclaimed Aunt Izzie from the bottom of the stairs.

Katy never forgot how kind Cousin Helen was on this occasion. She was in bed, and was of course a good deal startled at the sudden crash and tumble on her floor. But after one little jump, nothing could have been sweeter than the way in which she comforted poor crest-fallen Katy, and made so merry over the accident, that even Aunt Izzie almost forgot to scold. The broken dishes were piled up and the carpet made clean again, while Aunt Izzie prepared another tray just as nice as the first.

"Please let Katy bring it up!" pleaded Cousin Helen, in her pleasant voice, "I am sure she will be careful this time. And Katy, I want just such another rose on the napkin. I guess that was your doing—wasn't it?"

Katy *was* careful.—This time all went well. The tray was placed safely on a little table beside the bed, and Katy sat watching Cousin Helen eat her supper with a warm, loving feeling at her heart. I think we are scarcely ever so grateful to people as when they help us to get back our own self-esteem.

Cousin Helen hadn't much appetite, though she declared everything was delicious. Katy could see that she was very tired.

"Now," she said, when she had finished, "if you'll shake up this pillow, *so;*—and move this other pillow a little, I think I will settle myself to sleep. Thanks—that's just right. Why, Katy dear, you are a born nurse Now kiss me. Good-night! To-morrow we will have a nice talk."

Katy went down stairs very happy.

"Cousin Helen's perfectly lovely," she told Clover. "And she's got on the most *beautiful* night-gown, all lace and ruffles. It's just like a night-gown in a book."

"Isn't it wicked to care about clothes when you're sick?" questioned Cecy.

"I don't believe Cousin Helen *could* do anything wicked," said Katy.

"I told Ma that she had on bracelets, and Ma said she feared your cousin was a worldly person," retorted Cecy, primming up her lips.

Katy and Clover were quite distressed at this opinion. They talked about it while they were undressing.

"I mean to ask Cousin Helen to-morrow," said Katy.

Next morning the children got up very early. They were so glad that it was vacation! If it hadn't been, they would have been forced to go to school without seeing Cousin Helen, for she didn't wake till late. They grew so impatient of the delay, and went up stairs so often to listen at the door, and see if she were moving, that Aunt Izzie finally had to order them off. Katy rebelled against this order a good deal, but she consoled herself by going into the garden and picking the prettiest flowers she could find, to give to Cousin Helen the moment she should see her.

When Aunt Izzie let her go up, Cousin Helen was lying on the sofa all dressed for the day in a fresh blue muslin, with blue ribbons, and cunning bronze slippers with rosettes on the toes. The sofa had been wheeled round with its back to the light. There was a cushion with a pretty fluted cover, that Katy had never seen before, and several other things were scattered about, which gave the room quite a different air. All the house was neat, but somehow Aunt Izzie's rooms never were pretty. Children's eyes are quick to perceive such things, and Katy saw at once that the Blue-room had never looked like this.

Cousin Helen was white and tired, but her eyes and smile were as bright as ever. She was delighted with the flowers, which Katy presented rather shyly.

"Oh, how lovely!" she said; "I must put them in water right away. Katy dear, don't you want to bring that little vase on the bureau and set it on this chair beside me? And please pour a little water into it first."

"What a beauty!" cried Katy, as she lifted the graceful white cup swung on a gilt stand. "Is it yours, Cousin Helen?"

"Yes, it is my pet vase. It stands on a little table beside me at home, and I fancied that the Water Cure would seem more home-like if I had it with me there, so I brought it along. But why do you look so puzzled, Katy? Does it seem queer that a vase should travel about in a trunk?"

"No," said Katy, slowly, "I was only thinking—Cousin Helen, is it worldly to have pretty things when you're sick?"

Cousin Helen laughed heartily.

"What put that idea into your head?" she asked.

"Cecy said so when I told her about your beautiful night-gown."

Cousin Helen laughed again.

"Well," she said, "I'll tell you what I think, Katy. Pretty things are no more 'worldly' than ugly ones, except when they spoil us by making us vain, or careless of the comfort of other people. And sickness is such a disagreeable thing in itself, that unless sick people take great pains, they soon grow to be eyesores to themselves and everybody about them. I don't think it is possible for an invalid to be too particular. And when one has the back-ache, and the head-ache, and the all-over ache," she added, smiling, "there isn't much danger of growing vain because of a ruffle more or less on one's night-gown, or a bit of bright ribbon."

Then she began to arrange the flowers, touching each separate one gently, and as if she loved it.

"What a queer noise!" she exclaimed, suddenly stopping.

It *was* queer—a sort of snuffing and snorting sound, as if a walrus or a sea-horse were promenading up and down in the hall. Katy opened the door. Behold! there were John and Dorry, very red in the face from flattening their noses against the key-hole, in a vain attempt to see if Cousin Helen were up and ready to receive company.

"Oh, let them come in!" cried Cousin Helen from her sofa.

So they came in, followed, before long, by Clover and Elsie. Such a merry morning as they had! Cousin Helen proved to possess a perfect genius for story-telling, and for suggesting games which could be played about her sofa, and did not make more noise than she could bear. Aunt Izzie, dropping in about eleven o'clock, found them having such a good time, that almost before she knew it, *she* was drawn into the game too. Nobody had ever heard of such a thing before! There sat Aunt Izzie on the floor, with three long lamp-lighters stuck in her hair, playing, "I'm a genteel Lady, always genteel," in the jolliest manner possible. The children were so enchanted at the spectacle, that they could hardly attend to the game, and were always forgetting how many "horns" they had. Clover privately thought that Cousin Helen must be a witch; and Papa, when he came home at noon, said almost the same thing.

"What have you been doing to them, Helen?" he inquired, as he opened the door, and saw the merry circle on the carpet. Aunt Izzie's hair was half pulled down, and Philly was rolling over and over in convulsions of laughter. But Cousin Helen said she hadn't done anything, and pretty soon Papa was on the floor too, playing away as fast as the rest.

"I must put a stop to this," he cried, when everybody was tired of laughing, and everybody's head was stuck as full of paper quills as a porcupine's back. "Cousin Helen will be worn out. Run away, all of you, and don't come near this door again till the clock strikes four. Do you hear, chicks? Run—run! Shoo! shoo!"

The children scuttled away like a brood of fowls—all but Katy. "Oh, Papa, I'll be *so* quiet!" she pleaded. "Mightn't I stay just till the dinner-bell rings?"

"Do let her!" said Cousin Helen, so Papa said "Yes."

Katy sat on the floor holding Cousin Helen's hand, and listening to her talk with Papa. It interested her, though it was about things and people she did not know.

"How is Alex?" asked Dr. Carr, at length.

"Quite well now," replied Cousin Helen, with one of her brightest looks. "He was run down and tired in the Spring, and we were a little anxious about him, but Emma persuaded him to take a fortnight's vacation, and he came back all right."

"Do you see them often?"

"Almost every day. And little Helen comes every day, you know, for her lessons."

"Is she as pretty as she used to be?"

"Oh yes—prettier, I think. She is a lovely little creature: having her so much with me is one of my greatest treats. Alex tries to think that she looks a little as I used to. But that is a compliment so great, that I dare not appropriate it."

Dr. Carr stooped and kissed Cousin Helen as if he could not help it. "My *dear* child," he said. That was all; but something in the tone made Katy curious.

"Papa," she said, after dinner, "who is Alex, that you and Cousin Helen were talking about?"

"Why, Katy? What makes you want to know?"

"I can't exactly tell—only Cousin Helen looked so;—and you kissed her;—and I thought perhaps it was something interesting."

"So it is," said Dr. Carr, drawing her on to his knee. "I've a mind to tell you about it, Katy, because you're old enough to see how beautiful it is, and wise enough (I hope) not to chatter or ask questions. Alex is the name of somebody who, long ago, when Cousin Helen was well and strong, she loved, and expected to marry."

"Oh! why didn't she?" cried Katy.

"She met with a dreadful accident," continued Dr. Carr. "For a long time they thought she would die. Then she grew slowly better, and the doctors told her that she might live a good many years, but that she would have to lie on her sofa always, and be helpless, and a cripple.

"Alex felt dreadfully when he heard this. He wanted to marry Cousin Helen just the same, and be her nurse, and take care of her always; but she would not consent. She broke the engagement, and told him that some day she hoped he would love somebody else well enough to marry her. So after a good many years, he did, and now he and his wife live next door to Cousin Helen, and are her dearest friends. Their little girl is named 'Helen.' All their plans are talked over with her, and there is nobody in the world they think so much of."

"But doesn't it make Cousin Helen feel bad, when she sees them walking about and enjoying themselves, and she can't move?" asked Katy

"No," said Dr. Carr, "it doesn't, because Cousin Helen is half an angel already, and loves other people better than herself. I'm very glad she could come here for once. She's an example to us all, Katy, and I couldn't ask anything better than to have my little girls take pattern after her."

"It must be awful to be sick," soliloquized Katy, after Papa was gone. "Why, if I had to stay in bed a whole week—I should *die*, I know I should."

Poor Katy. It seemed to her, as it does to almost all young people, that there is nothing in the world so easy as to die, the moment things go wrong!

This conversation with Papa made Cousin Helen doubly interesting in Katy's eyes. "It was just like something in a book," to be in the same house with the heroine of a love-story so sad and sweet.

The play that afternoon was much interrupted, for every few minutes somebody had to run in and see if it wasn't four o'clock. The instant the hour came, all six children galloped up stairs.

"I think we'll tell stories this time," said Cousin Helen.

So they told stories. Cousin Helen's were the best of all. There was one of them about a robber, which sent delightful chills creeping down all their backs. All but Philly. He was so excited, that he grew warlike.

"I ain't afraid of robbers," he declared, strutting up and down. "When they come, I shall just cut them in two with my sword which Papa gave me. They did come once. I did cut them in two—three, five, eleven of 'em. You'll see!"

But that evening, after the younger children were gone to bed, and Katy and Clover were sitting in the Blue-room, a lamentable howling was heard from the nursery. Clover ran to see what was the matter. Behold—there was Phil, sitting up in bed, and crying for help.

"There's robbers under the bed," he sobbed; "ever so many robbers."

"Why no, Philly!" said Clover, peeping under the valance to satisfy him; "there isn't anybody there."

"Yes, there is, I tell you," declared Phil, holding her tight. "I heard one. They were *chewing my india-rubbers.*"

"Poor little fellow!" said Cousin Helen, when Clover, having pacified Phil, came back to report. "It's a warning against robber stories. But this one ended so well, that I didn't think of anybody's being frightened."

It was no use, after this, for Aunt Izzie to make rules about going into the Blue-room. She might as well have ordered flies to keep away from a sugar-bowl. By hook or by crook, the children *would* get up stairs. Whenever Aunt Izzie went in, she was sure to find them there, just as close to Cousin Helen as they could get. And Cousin Helen begged her not to interfere.

"We have only three or four days to be together," she said. "Let them come as much as they like. It won't hurt me a bit."

Little Elsie clung with a passionate love to this new friend. Cousin Helen had sharp eyes. She saw the wistful look in Elsie's face at once, and took special pains to be sweet and tender to her. This preference made Katy jealous. She couldn't bear to share her cousin with anybody.

When the last evening came, and they went up after tea to the Blue-room, Cousin Helen was opening a box which had just come by Express.

"It is a Good-by Box," she said. "All of you must sit down in a row, and when I hide my hands behind me, *so*, you must choose in turn which you will take."

So they all chose in turn, "Which hand will you have, the right or the left?" and Cousin Helen, with the air of a wise fairy, brought out from behind her pillow something pretty for each one. First came a vase exactly like her own, which Katy had admired so much. Katy screamed with delight as it was placed in her hands:

"Oh, how lovely! how lovely!" she cried. "I'll keep it as long as I live and breathe."

"If you do, it'll be the first time you ever kept anything for a week without breaking it," remarked Aunt Izzie.

Next came a pretty purple pocket-book for Clover. It was just what she wanted, for she had lost her porte-monnaie. Then a cunning little locket on a bit of velvet ribbon, which Cousin Helen tied round Elsie's neck.

"There's a piece of my hair in it," she said. "Why, Elsie, darling, what's the matter? Don't cry so!"

"Oh, you're s-o beautiful, and s-o sweet!" sobbed Elsie; "and you're go-o-ing away."

Dorry had a box of dominoes, and John a solitaire board. For Phil there appeared a book—"The History of the Robber Cat."

"That will remind you of the night when the thieves came and chewed your india-rubbers," said Cousin Helen, with a mischievous smile. They all laughed, Phil loudest of all.

Nobody was forgotten. There was a notebook for Papa, and a set of ivory tablets for Aunt Izzie. Even Cecy was remembered. Her present was "The Book of Golden Deeds," with all sorts of stories about boys and girls who had done brave and good things. She was almost too pleased to speak.

"Oh, thank you, Cousin Helen!" she said at last. Cecy wasn't a cousin, but she and the Carr children were in the habit of sharing their aunts and uncles, and relations generally, as they did their other good things.

Next day came the sad parting. All the little ones stood at the gate, to wave their pocket-handkerchiefs as the carriage drove away. When it was quite out of sight, Katy rushed off to "weep a little weep," all by herself.

"Papa said he wished we were all like Cousin Helen," she thought, as she wiped her eyes, "and I mean to try, though I don't suppose if I tried a thousand years I should ever get to be half so good. I'll study, and keep my things in order, and be ever so kind to the little ones. Dear me—if only Aunt Izzie was Cousin Helen, how easy it would be! Never mind—I'll think about her all the time, and I'll begin to-morrow."

CHAPTER VIII: TO-MORROW

"To-morrow I will begin," thought Katy, as she dropped asleep that night. How often we all do so! And what a pity it is that when morning comes and to-morrow is to-day, we so frequently wake up feeling quite differently; careless or impatient, and not a bit inclined to do the fine things we planned overnight.

Sometimes it seems as if there must be wicked little imps in the world, who are kept tied up so long as the sun shines, but who creep into our bed-rooms when we are asleep, to tease us and ruffle our tempers. Else, why, when we go to rest good-natured and pleasant, should we wake up so cross? Now there was Katy. Her last sleepy thought was an intention to be an angel from that time on, and as much like Cousin Helen as she could; and when she opened her eyes she was all out of sorts, and as fractious as a bear! Old Mary said that she got out of bed on the wrong side. I wonder, by the way, if anybody will ever be wise enough to tell us which side that is, so that we may always choose the other? How comfortable it would be if they could!

You know how, if we begin the day in a cross mood, all sorts of unfortunate accidents seem to occur to add to our vexations. The very first thing Katy did this morning was to break her precious vase—the one Cousin Helen had given her.

It was standing on the bureau with a little cluster of blush-roses in it. The bureau had a swing-glass. While Katy was brushing her hair, the glass tipped a little so that she could not see. At a good-humored moment, this accident wouldn't have troubled her much. But being out of temper to begin with, it made her angry. She gave the glass a violent push. The lower part swung forward, there was a smash, and the first thing Katy knew, the blush-roses lay scattered all over the floor, and Cousin Helen's pretty present was ruined.

Katy just sat down on the carpet and cried as hard as if she had been Phil himself. Aunt Izzie heard her lamenting, and came in.

"I'm very sorry," she said, picking up the broken glass, "but it's no more than I expected, you're so careless, Katy. Now don't sit there in that foolish way! Get up and dress yourself. You'll be late to breakfast."

"What's the matter?" asked Papa, noticing Katy's red eyes as she took her seat at the table.

"I've broken my vase," said Katy, dolefully.

"It was extremely careless of you to put it in such a dangerous place," said her aunt. "You might have known that the glass would swing and knock it off." Then, seeing a big tear fall in the middle of Katy's plate, she added: "Really, Katy, you're too big to behave like a baby. Why Dorry would be ashamed to do so. Pray control yourself!"

This snub did not improve Katy's temper. She went on with her breakfast in sulky silence.

"What are you all going to do to-day?" asked Dr. Carr, hoping to give things a more cheerful turn.

"Swing!" cried John and Dorry both together. "Alexander's put us up a splendid one in the wood-shed."

"No you're not," said Aunt Izzie in a positive tone, "the swing is not to be used till to-morrow. Remember that, children. Not till to-morrow. And not then, unless I give you leave."

This was unwise of Aunt Izzie. She would better have explained farther. The truth was, that Alexander, in putting up the swing, had cracked one of the staples which fastened it to the roof. He meant to get a new one in the course of the day, and, meantime, he had cautioned Miss Carr to let no one use the swing, because it really was not safe. If she had told this to the children, all would have been right; but Aunt Izzie's theory was, that young people must obey their elders without explanation.

John, and Elsie, and Dorry, all pouted when they heard this order. Elsie recovered her good-humor first.

"I don't care," she said, "'cause I'm going to be very busy; I've got to write a letter to Cousin Helen about somefing." (Elsie never could quite pronounce the *th*.)

"What?" asked Clover.

"Oh, somefing," answered Elsie, wagging her head mysteriously. "None of the rest of you must know, Cousin Helen said so, it's a secret she and me has got."

"I don't believe Cousin Helen said so at all," said Katy, crossly. "She wouldn't tell secrets to a silly little girl like you."

"Yes she would too," retorted Elsie angrily. "She said I was just as good to trust as if I was ever so big. And she said I was her pet. So there! Katy Carr!"

"Stop disputing," said Aunt Izzie. "Katy your top-drawer is all out of order. I never saw anything look so badly. Go up stairs at once and straighten it, before you do anything else. Children, you must keep in the shade this morning. It's too hot for you to be running about in the sun. Elsie, go into the kitchen and tell Debby I want to speak to her."

"Yes," said Elsie, in an important tone, "And afterwards I'm coming back to write my letter to Cousin Helen."

Katy went slowly up stairs, dragging one foot after the other. It was a warm, languid day. Her head ached a little, and her eyes smarted and felt heavy from crying so much. Everything seemed dull and hateful. She said to herself, that Aunt Izzie was very unkind to make her work in vacation, and she pulled the top-drawer open with a disgusted groan.

It must be confessed that Miss Izzie was right. A bureau-drawer could hardly look worse than this one did. It reminded one of the White Knight's recipe for a pudding, which began with blotting-paper, and ended with sealing-wax and gunpowder. All sorts of things were mixed together, as if somebody had put in a long stick and stirred them well up. There were books and paint-boxes and bits of scribbled paper, and lead-pencils and brushes. Stocking-legs had come unrolled, and twisted themselves about pocket-handkerchiefs, and ends of ribbon, and linen collars.

Ruffles, all crushed out of shape, stuck up from under the heavier things, and sundry little paper boxes lay empty on top, the treasures they once held having sifted down to the bottom of the drawer, and disappeared beneath the general mass.

It took much time and patience to bring order out of this confusion. But Katy knew that Aunt Izzie would be up by and by, and she dared not stop till all was done. By the time it was finished, she was very tired. Going down stairs, she met Elsie coming up with a slate in her hand, which, as soon as she saw Katy, she put behind her.

"You mustn't look," she said, "it's my letter to Cousin Helen. Nobody but me knows the secret. It's all written, and I'm going to send it to the office. See—there's a stamp on it;" and she exhibited a corner of the slate. Sure enough, there was a stamp stuck on the frame.

"You little goose!" said Katy, impatiently, "you can't send *that* to the post-office. Here, give me the slate. I'll copy what you've written on paper, and Papa'll give you an envelope."

"No, no," cried Elsie, struggling, "you mustn't! You'll see what I've said and Cousin Helen said I wasn't to tell. It's a secret. Let go of my slate, I say! I'll tell Cousin Helen what a mean girl you are, and then she won't love you a bit."

"There, then, take your old slate!" said Katy, giving her a vindictive push. Elsie slipped, screamed, caught at the banisters, missed them, and rolling over and over, fell with a thump on the hall floor.

It wasn't much of a fall, only half-a-dozen steps, but the bump was a hard one, and Elsie roared as if she had been half killed. Aunt Izzie and Mary came rushing to the spot.

"Katy—pushed—me," sobbed Elsie. "She wanted me to tell her my secret, and I wouldn't. She's a bad, naughty girl!"

"Well, Katy Carr, I *should* think you'd be ashamed of yourself," said Aunt Izzie, "wreaking your temper on your poor little sister! I think your Cousin Helen will be surprised when she hears this. There, there, Elsie! Don't cry any more, dear. Come up stairs with me. I'll put on some arnica, and Katy sha'n't hurt you again."

So they went up stairs. Katy, left below, felt very miserable: repentant, defiant, discontented, and sulky all at once. She knew in her heart that she had not meant to hurt Elsie, but was thoroughly ashamed of that push; but Aunt Izzie's hint about telling Cousin Helen, had made her too angry to allow of her confessing this to herself or anybody else.

"I don't care!" she murmured, choking back her tears. "Elsie is a real cry-baby, anyway. And Aunt Izzie always takes her part. Just because I told the little silly not to go and send a great heavy slate to the post-office!"

She went out by the side-door into the yard. As she passed the shed, the new swing caught her eye.

"How exactly like Aunt Izzie," she thought, "ordering the children not to swing till she gives them leave. I suppose she thinks it's too hot, or something. *I* sha'n't mind her, anyhow."

She seated herself in the swing. It was a first-rate one, with a broad, comfortable seat, and thick new ropes. The seat hung just the right distance from the floor. Alexander was a capital hand at putting up swings, and the wood-shed the nicest possible spot in which to have one.

It was a big place, with a very high roof. There was not much wood left in it just now, and the little there was, was piled neatly about the sides of the shed, so as to leave plenty of room. The place felt cool and dark, and the motion of the swing seemed to set the breeze blowing. It waved Katy's hair like a great fan, and made her dreamy and quiet. All sorts of sleepy ideas began to flit through her brain. Swinging to and fro like the pendulum of a great clock, she gradually rose higher and higher, driving herself along by the motion of her body, and striking the floor smartly with her foot, at every sweep. Now she was at the top of the high arched door. Then she could almost touch the cross-beam above it, and through the small square window could see pigeons sitting and pluming themselves on the eaves of the barn, and white clouds blowing over the blue sky. She had never swung so high before. It was like flying, she thought, and she bent and curved more strongly in the seat, trying to send herself yet higher, and graze the roof with her toes.

Suddenly, at the very highest point of the sweep, there was a sharp noise of cracking. The swing gave a violent twist, spun half round, and tossed Katy into the air. She clutched the rope,—felt it dragged from her grasp,—then, down,—down—down—she fell. All grew dark, and she knew no more.

When she opened her eyes she was lying on the sofa in the dining-room. Clover was kneeling beside her with a pale, scared face, and Aunt Izzie was dropping something cold and wet on her forehead.

"What's the matter?" said Katy, faintly.

"Oh, she's alive—she's alive!" and Clover put her arms round Katy's neck and sobbed.

"Hush, dear!" Aunt Izzie's voice sounded unusually gentle. "You've had a bad tumble, Katy. Don't you recollect?"

"A tumble? Oh, yes—out of the swing," said Katy, as it all came slowly back to her. "Did the rope break, Aunt Izzie? I can't remember about it."

"No, Katy, not the rope. The staple drew out of the roof. It was a cracked one, and not safe. Don't you recollect my telling you not to swing to-day? Did you forget?"

"No, Aunt Izzie—I didn't forget. I—" but here Katy broke down. She closed her eyes, and big tears rolled from under the lids.

"Don't cry," whispered Clover, crying herself, "please don't. Aunt Izzie isn't going to scold you." But Katy was too weak and shaken not to cry.

"I think I'd like to go up stairs and lie on the bed," she said. But when she tried to get off the sofa, everything swam before her, and she fell back again on the pillow.

"Why, I can't stand up!" she gasped, looking very much frightened.

"I'm afraid you've given yourself a sprain somewhere," said Aunt Izzie, who looked rather frightened herself. "You'd better lie still a while, dear, before you try to move. Ah, here's the doctor! well, I am glad." And she went forward to meet him. It wasn't Papa, but Dr. Alsop, who lived quite near them.

"I am so relieved that you could come," Aunt Izzie said. "My brother is gone out of town not to return till to-morrow, and one of the little girls has had a bad fall."

Dr. Alsop sat down beside the sofa and counted Katy's pulse. Then he began feeling all over her.

"Can you move this leg?" he asked.

Katy gave a feeble kick.

"And this?"

The kick was a good deal more feeble.

"Did that hurt you?" asked Dr. Alsop, seeing a look of pain on her face.

"Yes, a little," replied Katy, trying hard not to cry.

"In your back, eh? Was the pain high up or low down?" And the doctor punched Katy's spine for some minutes, making her squirm uneasily.

"I'm afraid she's done some mischief," he said at last, "but it's impossible to tell yet exactly what. It may be only a twist, or a slight sprain," he added, seeing the look of terror on Katy's face. "You'd better get her up stairs and undress her as soon as you can, Miss Carr. I'll leave a prescription to rub her with." And Dr. Alsop took out a bit of paper and began to write.

"Oh, must I go to bed?" said Katy. "How long will I have to stay there, doctor?"

"That depends on how fast you get well," replied the doctor; "not long, I hope. Perhaps only a few days.

"A few days!" repeated Katy, in a despairing tone.

After the doctor was gone, Aunt Izzie and Debby lifted Katy, and carried her slowly up stairs. It was not easy, for every motion hurt her, and the sense of being helpless hurt most of all. She couldn't help crying after she was undressed and put into bed. It all seemed so dreadful and strange. If only Papa was here, she thought. But Dr. Carr had gone into the country to see somebody who was very sick, and couldn't possibly be back till to-morrow.

Such a long, long afternoon as that was! Aunt Izzie sent up some dinner, but Katy couldn't eat. Her lips were parched and her head ached violently. The sun began to pour in, the room grew warm. Flies buzzed in the window, and tormented her by lighting on her face. Little prickles of pain ran up and down her back. She lay with her eyes shut, because it hurt to keep them open, and all sorts of uneasy thoughts went rushing through her mind.

"Perhaps, if my back is really sprained, I shall have to lie here as much as a week," she said to herself. "Oh dear, dear! I *can't*. The vacation is only eight weeks, and I was going to do such lovely things! How can people be as patient as Cousin Helen when they have to lie still? Won't she be sorry when she hears! Was it really yesterday that she went away? It seems a year. If only I hadn't got into that nasty old swing!" And then Katy began to imagine how it would have been if she *hadn't*, and how she and Clover had meant to go to Paradise that afternoon. They might have been there under the cool trees now. As these thoughts ran through her mind, her head grew hotter and her position in the bed more uncomfortable.

Suddenly she became conscious that the glaring light from the window was shaded, and that the wind seemed to be blowing freshly over her. She opened her heavy eyes. The blinds were shut, and there beside the bed sat little Elsie, fanning her with a palm-leaf fan.

"Did I wake you up, Katy?" she asked in a timid voice.

Katy looked at her with startled, amazed eyes.

"Don't be frightened," said Elsie, "I won't disturb you. Johnnie and me are so sorry you're sick," and her little lips trembled. "But we mean to keep real quiet, and never bang the nursery door, or make noises on the stairs, till you're well again. And I've brought you somefing real nice. Some of it's from John, and some from me. It's because you got tumbled out of the swing. See—" and Elsie pointed triumphantly to a chair, which she had pulled up close to the bed, and on which were solemnly set forth: 1st. A pewter tea-set; 2d. A box with a glass lid, on which flowers were painted; 3d. A jointed doll; 4th. A transparent slate; and lastly, two new lead pencils!

"They're all yours—yours to keep," said generous little Elsie. "You can have Pikery, too, if you want. Only he's pretty big, and I'm afraid he'd be lonely without me. Don't you like the fings, Katy? They're real pretty!"

It seemed to Katy as if the hottest sort of a coal of fire was burning into the top of her head as she looked at the treasures on the chair, and then at Elsie's face all lighted up with affectionate self-sacrifice. She tried to speak, but began to cry instead, which frightened Elsie very much.

"Does it hurt you so bad?" she asked, crying, too, from sympathy.

"Oh, no! it isn't that," sobbed Katy, "but I was so cross to you this morning, Elsie, and pushed you. Oh, please forgive me, please do!"

"Why, it's got well!" said Elsie, surprised. "Aunt Izzie put a fing out of a bottle on it, and the bump all went away. Shall I go and ask her to put some on you too—I will." And she ran toward the door.

"Oh, no!" cried Katy, "don't go away, Elsie. Come here and kiss me, instead."

Elsie turned as if doubtful whether this invitation could be meant for her. Katy held out her arms. Elsie ran right into them, and the big sister and the little, exchanged an embrace which seemed to bring their hearts closer together than they had ever been before.

"You're the most *precious* little darling," murmured Katy, clasping Elsie tight. "I've been real horrid to you, Elsie. But I'll never be again. You shall play with me and Clover, and Cecy, just as much as you like, and write notes in all the post-offices, and everything else."

"Oh, goody! goody!" cried Elsie, executing little skips of transport. "How sweet you are, Katy! I mean to love you next best to Cousin Helen and Papa! And"—racking her brains for some way of repaying this wonderful kindness—"I'll tell you the secret, if you want me to *very* much. I guess Cousin Helen would let me."

"No!" said Katy; "never mind about the secret. I don't want you to tell it to me. Sit down by the bed, and fan me some more instead."

"No!" persisted Elsie, who, now that she had made up her mind to part with the treasured secret, could not bear to be stopped. "Cousin Helen gave me a half-dollar, and told me to give it to Debby, and tell her she was much obliged to her for making her such nice things to eat. And I did. And Debby was real pleased. And I wrote Cousin Helen a letter, and told her that Debby liked the half-dollar. That's the secret! Isn't it a nice one? Only you mustn't tell anybody about it, ever—just as long as you live."

"No!" said Katy, smiling faintly, "I won't."

All the rest of the afternoon Elsie sat beside the bed with her palm-leaf fan, keeping off the flies, and "shue"-ing away the other children when they peeped in at the door. "Do you really like to have me here?" she asked, more than once, and smiled, oh, *so* triumphantly! when Katy said "Yes!" But though Katy said yes, I am afraid it was only half the truth, for the sight of the dear little forgiving girl, whom she had treated unkindly, gave her more pain than pleasure.

"I'll be *so* good to her when I get well," she thought to herself, tossing uneasily to and fro.

Aunt Izzie slept in her room that night. Katy was feverish. When morning came, and Dr. Carr returned, he found her in a good deal of pain, hot and restless, with wide-open, anxious eyes.

"Papa!" she cried the first thing, "must I lie here as much as a week?"

"My darling, I'm afraid you must," replied her father, who looked worried, and very grave.

"Dear, dear!" sobbed Katy, "how can I bear it?"

CHAPTER IX: DISMAL DAYS

If anybody had told Katy, that first afternoon, that at the end of a week she would still be in bed, and in pain, and with no time fixed for getting up, I think it would have almost killed her. She was so restless and eager, that to lie still seemed one of the hardest things in the world. But to lie still and have her back ache all the time, was worse yet. Day after day she asked Papa with quivering lip: "Mayn't I get up and go down stairs this morning?" And when he shook his head, the lip would quiver more, and tears would come. But if she tried to get up, it hurt her so much, that in spite of herself she was glad to sink back again on the soft pillows and mattress, which felt so comfortable to her poor bones.

Then there came a time when Katy didn't even ask to be allowed to get up. A time when sharp, dreadful pain, such as she never imagined before, took hold of her. When days and nights got all confused and tangled up together, and Aunt Izzie never seemed to go to bed. A time when Papa was constantly in her room. When other doctors came and stood over her, and punched and felt her back, and talked to each other in low whispers. It was all like a long, bad dream, from which she couldn't wake up, though she tried ever so hard. Now and then she would rouse a little, and catch the sound of voices, or be aware that Clover or Elsie stood at the door, crying softly; or that Aunt Izzie, in creaking slippers, was going about the room on tiptoe. Then all these things would slip away again, and she would drop off into a dark place, where there was nothing but pain, and sleep, which made her forget pain, and so seemed the best thing in the world.

We will hurry over this time, for it is hard to think of our bright Katy in such a sad plight. By and by the pain grew less, and the sleep quieter. Then, as the pain became easier still, Katy woke up as it were—began to take notice of what was going on about her; to put questions.

"How long have I been sick?" she asked one morning.

"It is four weeks yesterday," said Papa.

"Four weeks!" said Katy. "Why, I didn't know it was so long as that. Was I very sick, Papa?"

"Very, dear. But you are a great deal better now."

"How did I hurt me when I tumbled out of the swing?" asked Katy, who was in an unusually wakeful mood.

"I don't believe I could make you understand, dear."

"But try, Papa!"

"Well—did you know that you had a long bone down your back, called a spine?"

"I thought that was a disease," said Katy. "Clover said that Cousin Helen had the spine!"

"No—the spine is a bone. It is made up of a row of smaller bones—or knobs—and in the middle of it is a sort of rope of nerves called the spinal cord. Nerves, you know, are the things we feel with. Well, this spinal cord is rolled up for safe keeping in a soft wrapping, called membrane. When you fell out of the swing, you struck against one of these knobs, and bruised the membrane inside, and the nerve inflamed, and gave you a fever in the back. Do you see?"

"A little," said Katy, not quite understanding, but too tired to question farther. After she had rested a while, she said: "Is the fever well now, Papa? Can I get up again and go down stairs right away?"

"Not right away, I'm afraid," said Dr. Carr, trying to speak cheerfully.

Katy didn't ask any more questions then. Another week passed, and another. The pain was almost gone. It only came back now and then for a few minutes. She could sleep now, and eat, and be raised in bed without feeling giddy. But still the once active limbs hung heavy and lifeless, and she was not able to walk, or even stand alone.

"My legs feel so queer," she said one morning, "they are just like the Prince's legs which were turned to black marble in the Arabian Nights. What do you suppose is the reason, Papa? Won't they feel natural soon?"

"Not soon," answered Dr. Carr. Then he said to himself: "Poor child! she had better know the truth." So he went on, aloud, "I am afraid, my darling, that you must make up your mind to stay in bed a long time."

"How long?" said Katy, looking frightened: "a month more?"

"I can't tell exactly how long," answered her father. "The doctors think, as I do, that the injury to your spine is one which you will outgrow by and by, because you are so young and strong. But it may take a good while to do it. It may be that you will have to lie here for months, or it may be more. The only cure for such a hurt is time and patience. It is hard, darling"—for Katy began to sob wildly—"but you have Hope to help you along. Think of poor Cousin Helen, bearing all these years without hope!"

"Oh, Papa!" gasped Katy, between her sobs, "doesn't it seem dreadful, that just getting into the swing for a few minutes should do so much harm? Such a little thing as that!"

"Yes, such a little thing!" repeated Dr. Carr, sadly. "And it was only a little thing, too, forgetting Aunt Izzie's order about the swing. Just for the want of the small 'horseshoe nail' of Obedience, Katy."

Years afterwards, Katy told somebody that the longest six weeks of her life were those which followed this conversation with Papa. Now that she knew there was no chance of getting well at once, the days dragged dreadfully. Each seemed duller and dismaller than the day before. She lost heart about herself, and took no interest in anything. Aunt Izzie brought her books, but she didn't want to read, or to sew. Nothing amused her. Clover and Cecy would come and sit with her, but hearing them tell about their plays, and the things they had been doing, made her cry so miserably, that Aunt Izzie wouldn't let them come often. They were very sorry for Katy, but the room was so gloomy, and Katy so cross, that they didn't mind much not being allowed to see her. In those days Katy made Aunt Izzie keep the blinds shut tight, and she lay in the dark, thinking how miserable she was, and how wretched all the rest of her life was going to be. Everybody was very kind and patient with her, but she was too selfishly miserable to notice it. Aunt Izzie ran up and down stairs, and was on her feet all day, trying to get something which would please her, but Katy hardly said "Thank you," and never saw how tired Aunt Izzie looked. So long as she was forced to stay in bed, Katy could not be grateful for anything that was done for her.

But doleful as the days were, they were not so bad as the nights, when, after Aunt Izzie was asleep, Katy would lie wide awake, and have long, hopeless fits of crying. At these times she would think of all the plans she had made for doing beautiful things when she was grown up. "And now I shall never do any of them," she would say to herself, "only just lie here. Papa says I may get well by and by, but I sha'n't, I know I sha'n't. And even if I do, I shall have wasted all these years, and the others will grow up and get ahead of me, and I sha'n't be a comfort to them or to anybody else. Oh dear! oh dear! how dreadful it is!"

The first thing which broke in upon this sad state of affairs, was a letter from Cousin Helen, which Papa brought one morning and handed to Aunt Izzie.

"Helen tells me she's going home this week," said Aunt Izzie, from the window, where she had gone to read the letter. "Well, I'm sorry, but I think she's quite right not to stop. It's just as she says: one invalid at a time is enough in a house. I'm sure I have my hands full with Katy."

"Oh, Aunt Izzie!" cried Katy, "is Cousin Helen coming this way when she goes home? Oh! do make her stop. If it's just for one day, do ask her! I want to see her so much! I can't tell you how much! Won't you? Please! Please, dear Papa!"

She was almost crying with eagerness.

"Why, yes, darling, if you wish it so much," said Dr. Carr. "It will cost Aunt Izzie some trouble, but she's so kind that I'm sure she'll manage it if it is to give you so much pleasure. Can't you, Izzie?" And he looked eagerly at his sister.

"Of course I will!" said Miss Izzie, heartily. Katy was so glad, that, for the first time in her life, she threw her arms of her own accord round Aunt Izzie's neck, and kissed her.

"Thank you, dear Aunty!" she said.

Aunt Izzie looked as pleased as could be. She had a warm heart hidden under her fidgety ways—only Katy had never been sick before, to find it out.

For the next week Katy was feverish with expectation. At last Cousin Helen came. This time Katy was not on the steps to welcome her, but after a little while Papa brought Cousin Helen in his arms, and sat her in a big chair beside the bed.

"How dark it is!" she said, after they had kissed each other and talked for a minute or two; "I can't see your face at all. Would it hurt your eyes to have a little more light?"

"Oh no!" answered Katy. "It don't hurt my eyes, only I hate to have the sun come in. It makes me feel worse, somehow."

"Push the blind open a little bit then Clover;" and Clover did so.

"Now I can see," said Cousin Helen.

It was a forlorn-looking child enough which she saw lying before her. Katy's face had grown thin, and her eyes had red circles about them from continual crying. Her hair had been brushed twice that morning by Aunt Izzie, but Katy had run her fingers impatiently through it, till it stood out above her head like a frowsy bush. She wore a calico dressing-gown, which, though clean, was particularly ugly in pattern; and the room, for all its tidiness, had a dismal look, with the chairs set up against the wall, and a row of medicine-bottles on the chimney-piece.

"Isn't it horrid?" sighed Katy, as Cousin Helen looked around. "Everything's horrid. But I don't mind so much now that you've come. Oh, Cousin Helen, I've had such a dreadful, *dreadful* time!"

"I know," said her cousin, pityingly. "I've heard all about it, Katy, and I'm so very sorry for you! It is a hard trial, my poor darling."

"But how do *you* do it?" cried Katy.

"How do you manage to be so sweet and beautiful and patient, when you're feeling badly all the time, and can't do anything, or walk, or stand?"—her voice was lost in sobs.

Cousin Helen didn't say anything for a little while. She just sat and stroked Katy's hand.

"Katy," she said at last, "has Papa told you that he thinks you are going to get well by and by?"

"Yes," replied Katy, "he did say so. But perhaps it won't be for a long, long time. And I wanted to do so many things. And now I can't do anything at all!"

"What sort of things?"

"Study, and help people, and become famous. And I wanted to teach the children. Mamma said I must take care of them, and I meant to. And now I can't go to school or learn anything myself. And if I ever do get well, the children will be almost grown up, and they won't need me."

"But why must you wait till you get well?" asked Cousin Helen, smiling.

"Why, Cousin Helen, what can I do lying here in bed?"

"A good deal. Shall I tell you, Katy, what it seems to me that I should say to myself if I were in your place?"

"Yes, please!" replied Katy wonderingly.

"I should say this: 'Now, Katy Carr, you wanted to go to school and learn to be wise and useful, and here's a chance for you. God is going to let you go to *His* school—where He teaches all sorts of beautiful things to people. Perhaps He will only keep you for one term, or perhaps it may be for three or four; but whichever it is, you must make the very most of the chance, because He gives it to you Himself.'"

"But what is the school?" asked Katy. "I don't know what you mean."

"It is called The School of Pain," replied Cousin Helen, with her sweetest smile. "And the place where the lessons are to be learned is this room of yours. The rules of the school are pretty hard, but the good scholars, who keep them best, find out after a while how right and kind they are. And the lessons aren't easy, either, but the more you study the more interesting they become."

"What are the lessons?" asked Katy, getting interested, and beginning to feel as if Cousin Helen were telling her a story.

"Well, there's the lesson of Patience. That's one of the hardest studies. You can't learn much of it at a time, but every bit you get by heart, makes the next bit easier. And there's the lesson of Cheerfulness. And the lesson of Making the Best of Things."

"Sometimes there isn't anything to make the best of," remarked Katy, dolefully.

"Yes there is, always! Everything in the world has two handles. Didn't you know that? One is a smooth handle. If you take hold of it, the thing comes up lightly and easily, but if you seize the rough handle, it hurts your hand and the thing is hard to lift. Some people always manage to get hold of the wrong handle."

"Is Aunt Izzie a 'thing?'" asked Katy. Cousin Helen was glad to hear her laugh.

"Yes—Aunt Izzie is a *thing*—and she has a nice pleasant handle too, if you just try to find it. And the children are 'things,' also, in one sense. All their handles are different. You know human beings aren't made just alike, like red flower-pots. We have to feel and guess before we can make out just how other people go, and how we ought to take hold of them. It is very interesting, I advise you to try it. And while you are trying, you will learn all sorts of things which will help you to help others."

"If I only could!" sighed Katy. "Are there any other studies in the School, Cousin Helen?"

"Yes, there's the lesson of Hopefulness. That class has ever so many teachers. The Sun is one. He sits outside the window all day waiting a chance to slip in and get at his pupil. He's a first-rate teacher, too. I wouldn't shut him out, if I were you.

"Every morning, the first thing when I woke up, I would say to myself: 'I am going to get well, so Papa thinks. Perhaps it may be to-morrow. So, in case this *should* be the last day of my sickness, let me spend it *beauti*-fully, and make my sick-room so pleasant that everybody will like to remember it.'

"Then, there is one more lesson, Katy—the lesson of Neatness. School-rooms must be kept in order, you know. A sick person ought to be as fresh and dainty as a rose."

"But it is such a fuss," pleaded Katy. "I don't believe you've any idea what a bother it is to always be nice and in order. You never were careless like me, Cousin Helen; you were born neat."

"Oh, was I?" said her Cousin. "Well, Katy, we won't dispute that point, but I'll tell you a story, if you like, about a girl I once knew, who *wasn't* born neat."

"Oh, do!" cried Katy, enchanted. Cousin Helen had done her good, already. She looked brighter and less listless than for days.

"This girl was quite young," continued Cousin Helen; "she was strong and active, and liked to run, and climb, and ride, and do all sorts of jolly things. One day something happened—an accident—and they told her that all the rest of her life she had got to lie on her back and suffer pain, and never walk any more, or do any of the things she enjoyed most."

"Just like you and me!" whispered Katy, squeezing Cousin Helen's hand.

"Something like me; but not so much like you, because, you know, we hope *you* are going to get well one of these days. The girl didn't mind it so much when they first told her, for she was so ill that she felt sure she should die. But when she got better, and began to think of the long life which lay before her, that was worse than ever the pain had been. She was so wretched, that she didn't care what became of anything, or how anything looked. She had no Aunt Izzie to look after things, so her room soon got into a dreadful state. It was full of dust and confusion, and dirty spoons and phials of physic. She kept the blinds shut, and let her hair tangle every which way, and altogether was a dismal spectacle.

"This girl had a dear old father," went on Cousin Helen, "who used to come every day and sit beside her bed. One morning he said to her:

"'My daughter, I'm afraid you've got to live in this room for a long time. Now there's one thing I want you to do for my sake.'

"'What's that?' she asked, surprised to hear there was anything left which she could *do* for anybody.

"'I want you to turn out all these physic bottles, and make your room pleasant and pretty for *me* to come and sit in. You see, I shall spend a good deal of my time here! Now I don't like dust and darkness. I like to see flowers on the table, and sunshine in at the window. Will you do this to please me?'

"'Yes,' said the girl, but she gave a sigh, and I am afraid she felt as if it was going to be a dreadful trouble.

"'Then, another thing,' continued her father, 'I want *you* to look pretty. Can't nightgowns and wrappers be trimmed and made becoming just as much as dresses? A sick woman who isn't neat is a disagreeable object. Do, to please me, send for something pretty, and let me see you looking nice again. I can't bear to have my Helen turn into a slattern.'"

"Helen!" exclaimed Katy, with wide-open eyes, "was it *you*?"

"Yes," said her cousin, smiling. "It was I though I didn't mean to let the name slip out so soon. So, after my father was gone away, I sent for a looking-glass. Such a sight, Katy! My hair was a perfect mouse's nest, and I had frowned so much that my forehead was all criss-crossed with lines of pain, till it looked like an old woman's."

Katy stared at Cousin Helen's smooth brow and glossy hair. "I can't believe it," she said; "your hair never could be rough."

"Yes it was—worse, a great deal, than yours looks now. But that peep in the glass did me good. I began to think how selfishly I was behaving, and to desire to do better. And after that, when the pain came on, I used to lie and keep my forehead smooth with my fingers, and try not to let my face show what I was enduring. So by and by the wrinkles wore away, and though I am a good deal older now, they have never come back.

"It was a great deal of trouble at first to have to think and plan to keep my room and myself looking nice. But after a while it grew to be a habit, and then it became easy. And the pleasure it gave my dear father repaid for all. He had been proud of his active, healthy girl, but I think she was never such a comfort to him as his sick one, lying there in her bed. My room was his favorite sitting-place, and he spent so much time there, that now the room, and everything in it, makes me think of him."

There were tears in Cousin Helen's eyes as she ceased speaking. But Katy looked bright and eager. It seemed somehow to be a help, as well as a great surprise, that ever there should have been a time when Cousin Helen was less perfect than she was now.

"Do you really think I could do so too?" she asked.

"Do what? Comb your hair?" Cousin Helen was smiling now.

"Oh no! Be nice and sweet and patient, and a comfort to people. You know what I mean."

"I am sure you can, if you try."

"But what would you do first?" asked Katy; who, now that her mind had grasped a new idea, was eager to begin.

"Well—first I would open the blinds, and make the room look a little less dismal. Are you taking all those medicines in the bottles now?"

"No—only that big one with the blue label."

"Then you might ask Aunt Izzy to take away the others. And I'd get Clover to pick a bunch of fresh flowers every day for your table. By the way, I don't see the little white vase."

"No—it got broken the very day after you went away; the day I fell out of the swing," said Katy, sorrowfully.

"Never mind, pet, don't look so doleful. I know the tree those vases grow upon, and you shall have another. Then, after the room is made pleasant, I would have all my lesson-books fetched up, if I were you, and I would study a couple of hours every morning."

"Oh!" cried Katy, making a wry face at the idea.

Cousin Helen smiled. "I know," said she, "it sounds like dull work, learning geography and doing sums up here all by yourself. But I think if you make the effort you'll be glad by and by. You won't lose so much ground, you see—won't slip back quite so far in your education. And then, studying will be like working at a garden, where things don't grow easily. Every flower you raise will be a sort of triumph, and you will value it twice as much as a common flower which has cost no trouble."

"Well," said Katy, rather forlornly, "I'll try. But it won't be a bit nice studying without anybody to study with me. Is there anything else, Cousin Helen?"

Just then the door creaked, and Elsie timidly put her head into the room.

"Oh, Elsie, run away!" cried Katy. "Cousin Helen and I are talking. Don't come just now."

Katy didn't speak unkindly, but Elsie's face fell, and she looked disappointed. She said nothing, however, but shut the door and stole away.

Cousin Helen watched this little scene without speaking. For a few minutes after Elsie was gone she seemed to be thinking.

"Katy," she said at last, "you were saying just now, that one of the things you were sorry about was that while you were ill you could be of no use to the children. Do you know, I don't think you have that reason for being sorry."

"Why not?" said Katy, astonished.

"Because you can be of use. It seems to me that you have more of a chance with the children now, than you ever could have had when you were well, and flying about as you used. You might do almost anything you liked with them."

"I can't think what you mean," said Katy, sadly. "Why, Cousin Helen, half the time I don't even know where they are, or what they are doing. And I can't get up and go after them, you know."

"But you can make your room such a delightful place, that they will want to come to you! Don't you see, a sick person has one splendid chance—she is always on hand. Everybody who wants her knows just where to go. If people love her, she gets naturally to be the heart of the house.

"Once make the little ones feel that your room is the place of all others to come to when they are tired, or happy, or grieved, or sorry about anything, and that the Katy who lives there is sure to give them a loving reception—and the battle is won. For you know we never do people good by lecturing; only by living their lives with them, and helping a little here, and a little there, to make them better. And when one's own life is laid aside for a while, as yours is now, that is the very time to take up other people's lives, as we can't do when we are scurrying and bustling over our own affairs. But I didn't mean to preach a sermon. I'm afraid you're tired."

"No, I'm not a bit," said Katy, holding Cousin Helen's hand tight in hers; "you can't think how much better I feel. Oh, Cousin Helen, I will try!"

"It won't be easy," replied her cousin. "There will be days when your head aches, and you feel cross and fretted, and don't want to think of any one but yourself. And there'll be other days when Clover and the rest will come in, as Elsie did just now, and you will be doing something else, and will feel as if their coming was a bother. But you must recollect that every time you forget, and are impatient or selfish, you chill them and drive them farther away. They are loving little things, and are so sorry for you now, that nothing you do makes them angry. But by and by they will get used to having you sick, and if you haven't won them as friends, they will grow away from you as they get older."

Just then Dr. Carr came in.

"Oh, Papa! you haven't come to take Cousin Helen, have you?" cried Katy.

"Indeed I have," said her father. "I think the big invalid and the little invalid have talked quite long enough. Cousin Helen looks tired."

For a minute, Katy felt just like crying. But she choked back the tears. "My first lesson in Patience," she said to herself, and managed to give a faint, watery smile as Papa looked at her.

"That's right, dear," whispered Cousin Helen, as she bent forward to kiss her. "And one last word, Katy. In this school, to which you and I belong, there is one great comfort, and that is that the Teacher is always at hand. He never goes away. If things puzzle us, there He is, close by, ready to explain and make all easy. Try to think of this, darling, and don't be afraid to ask Him for help if the lesson seems too hard."

Katy had a strange dream that night. She thought she was trying to study a lesson out of a book which wouldn't come quite open. She could just see a little bit of what was inside, but it was in a language which she did not understand. She tried in vain; not a word could she read; and yet, for all that, it looked so interesting that she longed to go on.

"Oh, if somebody would only help me!" she cried impatiently.

Suddenly a hand came over her shoulder and took hold of the book. It opened at once, and showed the whole page. And then the forefinger of the hand began to point to line after line, and as it moved the words became plain, and Katy could read them easily. She looked up. There, stooping over her, was a great beautiful Face. The eyes met hers. The lips smiled.

"Why didn't you ask me before, Little Scholar?" said a voice.

"Why, it is You, just as Cousin Helen told me!" cried Katy.

She must have spoken in her sleep, for Aunt Izzie half woke up, and said:

"What is it? Do you want anything?"

The dream broke, and Katy roused, to find herself in bed, with the first sunbeams struggling in at the window, and Aunt Izzie raised on her elbow, looking at her with a sort of sleepy wonder.

CHAPTER X: ST. NICHOLAS AND ST. VALENTINE

"What are the children all doing to-day?" said Katy laying down "Norway and the Norwegians," which she was reading for the fourth time; "I haven't seen them since breakfast."

Aunt Izzie, who was sewing on the other side of the room, looked up from her work.

"I don't know," she said, "they're over at Cecy's, or somewhere. They'll be back before long, I guess."

Her voice sounded a little odd and mysterious, but Katy didn't notice it.

"I thought of such a nice plan yesterday," she went on. "That was that all of them should hang their stockings up here to-morrow night instead of in the nursery. Then I could see them open their presents, you know. Mayn't they, Aunt Izzie? It would be real fun."

"I don't believe there will be any objection," replied her aunt. She looked as if she were trying not to laugh. Katy wondered what was the matter with her.

It was more than two months now since Cousin Helen went away, and Winter had fairly come. Snow was falling out-doors. Katy could see the thick flakes go whirling past the window, but the sight did not chill her. It only made the room look warmer and more cosy. It was a pleasant room now. There was a bright fire in the grate. Everything was neat and orderly, the air was sweet with mignonette, from a little glass of flowers which stood on the table, and the Katy who lay in bed, was a very different-looking Katy from the forlorn girl of the last chapter.

Cousin Helen's visit, though it lasted only one day, did great good. Not that Katy grew perfect all at once. None of us do that, even in books. But it is everything to be started in the right path. Katy's feet were on it now; and though she often stumbled and slipped, and often sat down discouraged, she kept on pretty steadily, in spite of bad days, which made her say to herself that she was not getting forward at all.

These bad days, when everything seemed hard, and she herself was cross and fretful, and drove the children out of her room, cost Katy many bitter tears. But after them she would pick herself up, and try again, and harder. And I think that in spite of drawbacks, the little scholar, on the whole, was learning her lesson pretty well.

Cousin Helen was a great comfort all this time. She never forgot Katy. Nearly every week some little thing came from her. Sometimes it was a pencil note, written from her sofa. Sometimes it was an interesting book, or a new magazine, or some pretty little thing for the room. The crimson wrapper which Katy wore was one of her presents, so were the bright chromos of Autumn leaves which hung on the wall, the little stand for the books—all sorts of things. Katy loved to look about her as she lay. All the room seemed full of Cousin Helen and her kindness.

"I wish I had something pretty to put into everybody's stocking," she went on, wistfully; "but I've only got the muffetees for Papa, and these reins for Phil." She took them from under her pillow as she spoke—gay worsted affairs, with bells sewed on here and there. She had knit them herself, a very little bit at a time.

"There's my pink sash," she said suddenly, "I might give that to Clover. I only wore it once, you know, and I don't think I got any spots on it. Would you please fetch it and let me see, Aunt Izzie? It's in the top drawer."

Aunt Izzie brought the sash. It proved to be quite fresh, and they both decided that it would do nicely for Clover.

"You know I sha'n't want sashes for ever so long," said Katy, in rather a sad tone, "And this is a beauty."

When she spoke next, her voice was bright again.

"I wish I had something real nice for Elsie. Do you know, Aunt Izzie—I think Elsie is the dearest little girl that ever was."

"I'm glad you've found it out," said Aunt Izzie, who had always been specially fond of Elsie.

"What she wants most of all is a writing-desk," continued Katy. "And Johnnie wants a sled. But, oh dear! these are such big things. And I've only got two dollars and a quarter."

Aunt Izzie marched out of the room without saying anything. When she came back she had something folded up in her hand.

"I didn't know what to give you for Christmas, Katy," she said, "because Helen sends you such a lot of things that there don't seem to be anything you haven't already. So I thought I'd give you this, and let you choose for yourself. But if you've set your heart on getting presents for the children, perhaps you'd rather have it now." So saying, Aunt Izzie laid on the bed a crisp, new five-dollar bill!

"How good you are!" cried Katy, flushed with pleasure. And indeed Aunt Izzie *did* seem to have grown wonderfully good of late. Perhaps Katy had got hold of her smooth handle!

Being now in possession of seven dollars and a quarter, Katy could afford to be gorgeously generous. She gave Aunt Izzie an exact description of the desk she wanted.

"It's no matter about its being very big," said Katy, "but it must have a blue velvet lining, and an inkstand, with a silver top. And please buy some little sheets of paper and envelopes, and a pen-handle; the prettiest you can find. Oh! and there must be a lock and key. Don't forget that, Aunt Izzie."

"No, I won't. What else?"

"I'd like the sled to be green," went on Katy, "and to have a nice name. Sky-Scraper would be nice, if there was one. Johnnie saw a sled once called Sky-Scraper, and she said it was splendid. And if there's money enough left, Aunty, won't you buy me a real nice book for Dorry, and another for Cecy, and a silver thimble for Mary? Her old one is full of holes. Oh! and some candy. And something for Debby and Bridget—some little thing, you know. I think that's all!"

Was ever seven dollars and a quarter expected to do so much? Aunt Izzie must have been a witch, indeed, to make it hold out. But she did, and next day all the precious bundles came home. How Katy enjoyed untying the strings!

Everything was exactly right.

"There wasn't any Sky-Scraper," said Aunt Izzie, "so I got 'Snow-Skimmer' instead."

"It's beautiful, and I like it just as well," said Katy contentedly.

"Oh, hide them, hide them!" she cried with sudden terror, "somebody's coming." But the somebody was only Papa, who put his head into the room as Aunt Izzie, laden with bundles, scuttled across the hall.

Katy was glad to catch him alone. She had a little private secret to talk over with him. It was about Aunt Izzie, for whom she, as yet, had no present.

"I thought perhaps you'd get me a book like that one of Cousin Helen's, which Aunt Izzie liked so much," she said. "I don't recollect the name exactly. It was something about a Shadow. But I've spent all my money."

"Never mind about that," said Dr. Carr. "We'll make that right. 'The Shadow of the Cross'—was that it? I'll buy it this afternoon."

"Oh, thank you, Papa! And please get a brown cover, if you can, because Cousin Helen's was brown. And you won't let Aunt Izzie know, will you? Be careful, Papa!"

"I'll swallow the book first, brown cover and all," said Papa, making a funny face. He was pleased to see Katy so interested about anything again.

These delightful secrets took up so much of her thoughts, that Katy scarcely found time to wonder at the absence of the children, who generally haunted her room, but who for three days back had hardly been seen. However, after supper they all came up in a body, looking very merry, and as if they had been having a good time somewhere.

"You don't know what we've been doing," began Philly.

"Hush, Phil!" said Clover, in a warning voice. Then she divided the stockings which she held in her hand. And everybody proceeded to hang them up.

Dorry hung his on one side of the fireplace, and John hers exactly opposite. Clover and Phil suspended theirs side by side, on two handles of the bureau.

"I'm going to put mine here, close to Katy, so that she can see it the first fing in the mornin'," said Elsie, pinning hers to the bed-post.

Then they all sat down round the fire to write their wishes on bits of paper, and see whether they would burn, or fly up the chimney. If they did the latter, it was a sign that Santa Claus had them safe, and would bring the things wished for.

John wished for a sled and a doll's tea-set, and the continuation of the Swiss Family Robinson. Dorry's list ran thus:

"A plum-cake,

A new Bibel,

Harry and Lucy,

A Kellidescope,

Everything else Santa Claus likes."

When they had written these lists they threw them into the fire. The fire gave a flicker just then, and the papers vanished. Nobody saw exactly how. John thought they flew up chimney, but Dorry said they didn't. Phil dropped his piece in very solemnly. It flamed for a minute, then sank into ashes.

"There, you won't get it, whatever it was!" said Dorry. "What did you write, Phil?"

"Nofing," said Phil, "only just Philly Carr."

The children shouted.

"I wrote 'a writing-desk' on mine," remarked Elsie, sorrowfully, "but it all burned up."

Katy chuckled when she heard this.

And now Clover produced her list. She read aloud:

"'Strive and Thrive,'

A pair of kid gloves,

A muff,

A good temper!"

Then she dropped it into the fire. Behold, it flew straight up chimney.

"How queer!" said Katy; "none of the rest of them did that."

The truth was, that Clover, who was a canny little mortal, had slipped across the room and opened the door just before putting her wishes in. This, of course, made a draft, and sent the paper right upward.

Pretty soon Aunt Izzie came in and swept them all off to bed.

"I know how it will be in the morning," she said, "you'll all be up and racing about as soon as it is light. So you must get your sleep now, if ever."

After they had gone, Katy recollected that nobody had offered to hang a stocking up for her. She felt a little hurt when she thought of it. "But I suppose they forgot," she said to herself.

A little later Papa and Aunt Izzie came in, and they filled the stockings. It was great fun. Each was brought to Katy, as she lay in bed, that she might arrange it as she liked.

The toes were stuffed with candy and oranges. Then came the parcels, all shapes and sizes, tied in white paper, with ribbons, and labelled.

"What's that?" asked Dr. Carr, as Aunt Izzie rammed a long, narrow package into Clover's stocking.

"A nail-brush," answered Aunt Izzie. "Clover needed a new one."

How Papa and Katy laughed! "I don't believe Santa Claus ever had such a thing before," said Dr. Carr.

"He's a very dirty old gentleman, then," observed Aunt Izzie, grimly.

The desk and sled were too big to go into any stocking, so they were wrapped in paper and hung beneath the other things. It was ten o'clock before all was done, and Papa and Aunt Izzie went away. Katy lay a long time watching the queer shapes of the stocking-legs as they dangled in the firelight. Then she fell asleep.

It seemed only a minute, before something touched her and woke her up. Behold, it was day-time, and there was Philly in his nightgown, climbing up on the bed to kiss her! The rest of the children, half dressed, were dancing about with their stockings in their hands.

"Merry Christmas! Merry Christmas!" they cried. "Oh, Katy, such beautiful, beautiful things!"

"Oh!" shrieked Elsie, who at that moment spied her desk, "Santa Claus *did* bring it, after all! Why, it's got 'from Katy' written on it! Oh, Katy, it's so sweet, and I'm *so* happy!" and Elsie hugged Katy, and sobbed for pleasure.

But what was that strange thing beside the bed! Katy stared, and rubbed her eyes. It certainly had not been there when she went to sleep. How had it come?

It was a little evergreen tree planted in a red flower-pot. The pot had stripes of gilt paper stuck on it, and gilt stars and crosses, which made it look very gay. The boughs of the tree were hung with oranges, and nuts, and shiny red apples, and pop-corn balls, and strings of bright berries. There were also a number of little packages tied with blue and crimson ribbon, and altogether the tree looked so pretty, that Katy gave a cry of delighted surprise.

"It's a Christmas-tree for you, because you're sick, you know!" said the children, all trying to hug her at once.

"We made it ourselves," said Dorry, hopping about on one foot; "I pasted the black stars on the pot."

"And I popped the corn!" cried Philly.

"Do you like it?" asked Elsie, cuddling close to Katy. "That's my present—that one tied with a green ribbon. I wish it was nicer! Don't you want to open 'em right away?"

Of course Katy wanted to. All sorts of things came out of the little bundles. The children had arranged every parcel themselves. No grown person had been allowed to help in the least.

Elsie's present was a pen-wiper, with a gray flannel kitten on it. Johnnie's, a doll's tea-tray of scarlet tin.

"Isn't it beau-ti-ful?" she said, admiringly.

Dorry's gift, I regret to say, was a huge red-and-yellow spider, which whirred wildly when waved at the end of its string.

"They didn't want me to buy it," said he, "but I did! I thought it would amoose you. Does it amoose you, Katy?"

"Yes, indeed," said Katy, laughing and blinking as Dorry waved the spider to and fro before her eyes.

"You can play with it when we ain't here and you're all alone, you know," remarked Dorry, highly gratified.

"But you don't notice what the tree's standing upon," said Clover.

It was a chair, a very large and curious one, with a long-cushioned back, which ended in a footstool.

"That's Papa's present," said Clover; "see, it tips back so as to be just like a bed. And Papa says he thinks pretty soon you can lie on it, in the window, where you can see us play."

"Does he really?" said Katy, doubtfully. It still hurt her very much to be touched or moved.

"And see what's tied to the arm of the chair," said Elsie.

It was a little silver bell, with "Katy" engraved on the handle.

"Cousin Helen sent it. It's for you to ring when you want anybody to come," explained Elsie.

More surprises. To the other arm of the chair was fastened a beautiful book. It was "The Wide Wide World"—and there Was Katy's name written on it, 'from her affectionate Cecy.' On it stood a great parcel of dried cherries from Mrs. Hall. Mrs. Hall had the most *delicious* dried cherries, the children thought.

"How perfectly lovely everybody is!" said Katy, with grateful tears in her eyes.

That was a pleasant Christmas. The children declared it to be the nicest they had ever had. And though Katy couldn't quite say that, she enjoyed it too, and was very happy.

It was several weeks before she was able to use the chair, but when once she became accustomed to it, it proved very comfortable. Aunt Izzie would dress her in the morning, tip the chair back till it was on a level with the bed, and then, very gently and gradually, draw her over on to it. Wheeling across the room was always painful, but sitting in the window and looking out at the clouds, the people going by, and the children playing in the snow, was delightful. How delightful nobody knows, excepting those who, like Katy, have lain for six months in bed, without a peep at the outside world. Every day she grew brighter and more cheerful.

"How jolly Santa Claus was this year!" She happened to say one day, when she was talking with Cecy. "I wish another Saint would come and pay us a visit. But I don't know any more, except Cousin Helen, and she can't."

"There's St. Valentine," suggested Cecy.

"Sure enough. What a bright thought!" cried Katy, clapping her hands. "Oh, Cecy, let's do something funny on Valentine's-Day! Such a good idea has just popped into my mind."

So the two girls put their heads together and held a long, mysterious confabulation. What it was about, we shall see farther on.

Valentine's-Day was the next Friday. When the children came home from school on Thursday afternoon, Aunt Izzie met them, and, to their great surprise, told them that Cecy was come to drink tea, and they must all go up stairs and be made nice.

"But Cecy comes most every day," remarked Dorry, who didn't see the connection between this fact and having his face washed.

"Yes—but to-night you are to take tea in Katy's room," said Aunt Izzie; "here are the invitations: one for each of you."

Sure enough, there was a neat little note for each, requesting the pleasure of their company at "Queen Katharine's Palace," that afternoon, at six o'clock.

This put quite a different aspect on the affair. The children scampered up stairs, and pretty soon, all nicely brushed and washed, they were knocking formally at the door of the "Palace." How fine it sounded!

The room looked bright and inviting. Katy, in her chair, sat close to the fire, Cecy was beside her, and there was a round table all set out with a white cloth and mugs of milk and biscuit, and strawberry-Jam and doughnuts. In the middle was a loaf of frosted cake. There was something on the icing which looked like pink letters, and Clover, leaning forward, read aloud, "St. Valentine."

"What's that for?" asked Dorry.

"Why, you know this is St. Valentine's-Eve," replied Katy. "Debbie remembered it, I guess, so she put that on."

Nothing more was said about St. Valentine just then. But when the last pink letter of his name had been eaten, and the supper had been cleared away, suddenly, as the children sat by the fire, there was a loud rap at the door.

"Who can that be?" said Katy; "please see, Clover!"

So Clover opened the door. There stood Bridget, trying very hard not to laugh, and holding a letter in her hand.

"It's a note as has come for you, Miss Clover," she said.

"For *me*!" cried Clover, much amazed. Then she shut the door, and brought the note to the table.

"How very funny!" she exclaimed, as she looked at the envelope, which was a green and white one. There was something hard inside. Clover broke the seal. Out tumbled a small green velvet pincushion made in the shape of a clover-leaf, with a tiny stem of wire wound with green silk. Pinned to the cushion was a paper, with these verses:

"Some people love roses well,
　Tulips, gayly dressed,
Some love violets blue and sweet,—
　I love Clover best.

"Though she has a modest air,
　Though no grace she boast,
Though no gardener call her fair,
　I love Clover most.

"Butterfly may pass her by,
　He is but a rover,
I'm a faithful, loving Bee—
　And I stick to Clover."

This was the first valentine Clover had ever had. She was perfectly enchanted.

"Oh, who *do* you suppose sent it?" she cried.

But before anybody could answer, there came another loud knock at the door, which made them all jump. Behold, Bridget again, with a second letter!

"It's for you, Miss Elsie, this time," she said with a grin.

There was an instant rush from all the children, and the envelope was torn open in the twinkling of an eye. Inside was a little ivory seal with "Elsie" on it in old English letters, and these rhymes:

"I know a little girl,
She is very dear to me,
She is just as sweet as honey
When she chooses so to be,
And her name begins with E, and ends with E.

"She has brown hair which curls,
And black eyes for to see
With, teeth like tiny pearls,
And dimples, one, two—three,
And her name begins with E, and ends with E.
  "Her little feet run faster
Than other feet can flee,
As she brushes quickly past, her
Voice hums like a bee,
And her name begins with E, and ends with E.
  "Do you ask me why I love her?
Then I shall answer thee,
Because I can't help loving,
She is so sweet to me,
This little girl whose name begins and ends with 'E.'"

  "It's just like a fairy story," said Elsie, whose eyes had grown as big as saucers from surprise, while these verses were being read aloud by Cecy.

  Another knock. This time there was a perfect handful of letters. Everybody had one. Katy, to her great surprise, had *two*.

  "Why, what *can* this be?" she said. But when she peeped into the second one, she saw Cousin Helen's handwriting, and she put it into her pocket, till the valentines should be read.

  Dorry's was opened first. It had the picture of a pie at the top—I ought to explain that Dorry had lately been having a siege with the dentist.

  "Little Jack Horner
Sat in his corner,
    Eating his Christmas pie,
When a sudden grimace
Spread over his face,
    And he began loudly to cry.
  "His tender Mamma
Heard the sound from afar,
    And hastened to comfort her child;
'What aileth my John?'
She inquired in a tone
    Which belied her question mild.
  "'Oh, Mother,' he said,
'Every tooth in my head
    Jumps and aches and is loose, O my!
And it hurts me to eat

Anything that is sweet—
 So what *will* become of my pie?'
"It were vain to describe
How he roared and he cried,
 And howled like a miniature tempest;
Suffice it to say,
That the very next day
 He had all his teeth pulled by a dentist!"

This valentine made the children laugh for a long time. Johnnie's envelope held a paper doll named "Red Riding-Hood." These were the verses:

"I send you my picture, dear Johnnie, to show
 That I'm just as alive as you,
And that you needn't cry over my fate
 Any more, as you used to do.
"The wolf didn't hurt me at all that day,
 For I kicked and fought and cried,
Till he dropped me out of his mouth, and ran
 Away in the woods to hide.
"And Grandma and I have lived ever since
 In the little brown house so small,
And churned fresh butter and made cream cheeses,
 Nor seen the wolf at all.
"So cry no more for fear I am eaten,
 The naughty wolf is shot,
And if you will come to tea some evening
 You shall see for yourself I'm not."

Johnnie was immensely pleased at this, for Red Riding-Hood was a great favorite of hers.

Philly had a bit of india-rubber in his letter, which was written with very black ink on a big sheet of foolscap:

"I was once a naughty man,
 And I hid beneath the bed,
To steal your india-rubbers,
 But I chewed them up instead.
"Then you called out, 'Who is there?'
 I was thrown most in a fit,
And I let the india-rubbers fall—
 All but this little bit.
"I'm sorry for my naughty ways,
 And now, to make amends,
I send the chewed piece back again,
 And beg we may be friends.

"ROBBER."

"Just listen to mine," said Cecy, who had all along pretended to be as much surprised as anybody, and now behaved as if she could hardly wait till Philly's was finished. Then she read aloud:

"TO CECY.

"If I were a bird
And you were a bird,
What would we do?
Why you should be little and I would be big,
And, side by side on a cherry-tree twig,
We'd kiss with our yellow bills, and coo—
That's what we'd do!

"If I were a fish
And you were a fish,
What would we do?
We'd frolic, and whisk our little tails,
And play all sorts of tricks with the whales,
And call on the oysters, and order a 'stew,'
That's what we'd do!

"If I were a bee
And you were a bee,
What would we do?
We'd find a home in a breezy wood,
And store it with honey sweet and good.
You should feed me and I would feed you,
That's what we'd do!

"VALENTINE."

"I think that's the prettiest of all," said Clover.

"I don't," said Elsie. "I think mine is the prettiest. Cecy didn't have any seal in hers, either." And she fondled the little seal, which all this time she had held in her hand.

"Katy, you ought to have read yours first because you are the oldest," said Clover.

"Mine isn't much," replied Katy, and she read:
"The rose is red the violet blue,
  Sugar is sweet, and so are you."

"What a mean valentine!" cried Elsie, with flashing eyes. "It's a real shame, Katy! You ought to have had the best of all."

Katy could hardly keep from laughing. The fact was that the verses for the others had taken so long, that no time had been left for writing a valentine to herself. So, thinking it would excite suspicion to have none, she had scribbled this old rhyme at the last moment.

"It isn't very nice," she said, trying to look as pensive as she could, "but never mind."

"It's a shame!" repeated Elsie, petting her very hard to make up for the injustice.

"Hasn't it been a funny evening?" said John; and Dorry replied, "Yes; we never had such good times before Katy was sick, did we?"

Katy heard this with a mingled feeling of pleasure and pain. "I think the children do love me a little more of late," she said to herself. "But, oh, why couldn't I be good to them when I was well and strong!"

She didn't open Cousin Helen's letter until the rest were all gone to bed. I think somebody must have written and told about the valentine party, for instead of a note there were these verses in Cousin Helen's own clear, pretty hand. It wasn't a valentine, because it was too solemn, as Katy explained to Clover, next day. "But," she added, "it is a great deal beautifuller than any valentine that ever was written." And Clover thought so too.

These were the verses:
"IN SCHOOL.

"I used to go to a bright school
Where Youth and Frolic taught in turn;
But idle scholar that I was,
I liked to play, I would not learn;
So the Great Teacher did ordain
That I should try the School of Pain.

"One of the infant class I am
With little, easy lessons, set
In a great book; the higher class
Have harder ones than I, and yet
I find mine hard, and can't restrain
My tears while studying thus with Pain.

"There are two Teachers in the school,
One has a gentle voice and low,
And smiles upon her scholars, as
She softly passes to and fro.
Her name is Love; 'tis very plain
She shuns the sharper teacher, Pain.

"Or so I sometimes think; and then,
At other times, they meet and kiss,
And look so strangely like, that I
Am puzzled to tell how it is,
Or whence the change which makes it vain
To guess if it be—Love or Pain.

"They tell me if I study well,
And learn my lessons, I shall be
Moved upward to that higher class
Where dear Love teaches constantly;
And I work hard, in hopes to gain
Reward, and get away from Pain.
  "Yet Pain is sometimes kind, and helps
Me on when I am very dull;
I thank him often in my heart;
But Love is far more beautiful;
Under her tender, gentle reign
I must learn faster than of Pain.
  "So I will do my very best,
Nor chide the clock, nor call it slow;
That when the Teacher calls me up
To see if I am fit to go,
I may to Love's high class attain,
And bid a sweet good-by to Pain."

CHAPTER XI: A NEW LESSON TO LEARN

It was a long time before the children ceased to talk and laugh over that jolly evening. Dorry declared he wished there could be a Valentine's-Day every week.

"Don't you think St. Valentine would be tired of writing verses?" asked Katy. But she, too, had enjoyed the frolic, and the bright recollection helped her along through the rest of the long, cold winter.

Spring opened late that year, but the Summer, when it came, was a warm one. Katy felt the heat very much. She could not change her seat and follow the breeze about from window to window as other people could. The long burning days left her weak and parched. She hung her head, and seemed to wilt like the flowers in the garden-beds. Indeed she was worse off than they, for every evening Alexander gave them a watering with the hose, while nobody was able to bring a watering-pot and pour out what she needed—a shower of cold, fresh air.

It wasn't easy to be good-humored under these circumstances, and one could hardly have blamed Katy if she had sometimes forgotten her resolutions and been cross and fretful. But she didn't—not very often. Now and then bad days came, when she was discouraged and forlorn. But Katy's long year of schooling had taught her self-control, and, as a general thing, her discomforts were borne patiently. She could not help growing pale and thin however, and Papa saw with concern that, as the summer went on, she became too languid to read, or study, or sew, and just sat hour after hour, with folded hands, gazing wistfully out of the window.

He tried the experiment of taking her to drive. But the motion of the carriage, and the being lifted in and out, brought on so much pain, that Katy begged that he would not ask her to go again. So there was nothing to be done but wait for cooler weather. The summer dragged on, and all who loved Katy rejoiced when it was over.

When September came, with cool mornings and nights, and fresh breezes, smelling of pine woods, and hill-tops, all things seemed to revive, and Katy with them. She began to crochet and to read. After a while she collected her books again, and tried to study as Cousin Helen had advised. But so many idle weeks made it seem harder work than ever. One day she asked Papa to let her take French lessons.

"You see I'm forgetting all I knew," she said, "and Clover is going to begin this term, and I don't like that she should get so far ahead of me. Don't you think Mr. Bergèr would be willing to come here, Papa? He does go to houses sometimes."

"I think he would if we asked him," said Dr. Carr, pleased to see Katy waking up with something like life again.

So the arrangement was made. Mr. Bergèr came twice every week, and sat beside the big chair, correcting Katy's exercises and practising her in the verbs and pronunciation. He was a lively little old Frenchman, and knew how to make lesson-time pleasant.

"You take more pain than you used, Mademoiselle," he said one day; "if you go on so, you shall be my best scholar. And if to hurt the back make you study, it would be well that some other of my young ladies shall do the same."

Katy laughed. But in spite of Mr. Bergèr and his lessons, and in spite of her endeavors to keep cheerful and busy, this second winter was harder than the first. It is often so with sick people. There is a sort of excitement in being ill which helps along just at the beginning. But as months go on, and everything grows an old story, and one day follows another day, all just alike and all tiresome, courage is apt to flag and spirits to grow dull. Spring seemed a long, long way off whenever Katy thought about it.

"I wish something would happen," she often said to herself. And something was about to happen. But she little guessed what it was going to be.

"Katy!" said Clover, coming in one day in November, "do you know where the camphor is? Aunt Izzie has got *such* a headache."

"No," replied Katy, "I don't. Or—wait—Clover, it seems to me that Debby came for it the other day. Perhaps if you look in her room you'll find it."

"How very queer!" she soliloquized, when Clover was gone; "I never knew Aunt Izzie to have a headache before."

"How is Aunt Izzie?" she asked, when Papa came in at noon.

"Well, I don't know. She has some fever and a bad pain in her head. I have told her that she had better lie still, and not try to get up this evening. Old Mary will come in to undress you, Katy. You won't mind, will you, dear?"

"N-o!" said Katy, reluctantly. But she did mind. Aunt Izzie had grown used to her and her ways. Nobody else suited her so well.

"It seems so strange to have to explain just how every little thing is to be done," she remarked to Clover, rather petulantly.

It seemed stranger yet, when the next day, and the next, and the next after that passed, and still no Aunt Izzie came near her. Blessings brighten as they take their flight. Katy began to appreciate for the first time how much she had learned to rely on her aunt. She missed her dreadfully.

"When *is* Aunt Izzie going to get well?" she asked her father; "I want her so much."

"We all want her," said Dr. Carr, who looked disturbed and anxious.

"Is she very sick?" asked Katy, struck by the expression of his face.

"Pretty sick, I'm afraid," he replied. "I'm going to get a regular nurse to take care of her."

Aunt Izzie's attack proved to be typhoid fever. The doctors said that the house must be kept quiet, so John, and Dorry, and Phil were sent over to Mrs. Hall's to stay. Elsie and Clover were to have gone too, but they begged so hard, and made so many promises of good behavior, that finally Papa permitted them to remain. The dear little things stole about the house on tiptoe, as quietly as mice, whispering to each other, and waiting on Katy, who would have been lonely enough without them, for everybody else was absorbed in Aunt Izzie.

It was a confused, melancholy time. The three girls didn't know much about sickness, but Papa's grave face, and the hushed house, weighed upon their spirits, and they missed the children very much.

"Oh dear!" sighed Elsie. "How I wish Aunt Izzie would hurry and get well."

"We'll be real good to her when she does, won't we?" said Clover. "I never mean to leave my rubbers in the hat-stand any more, because she don't like to have me. And I shall pick up the croquet-balls and put them in the box every night."

"Yes," added Elsie, "so will I, when she gets well."

It never occurred to either of them that perhaps Aunt Izzie might not get well. Little people are apt to feel as if grown folks are so strong and so big, that nothing can possibly happen to them.

Katy was more anxious. Still she did not fairly realize the danger. So it came like a sudden and violent shock to her, when, one morning on waking up, she found old Mary crying quietly beside the bed, with her apron at her eyes. Aunt Izzie had died in the night!

All their kind, penitent thoughts of her; their resolutions to please—their plans for obeying her wishes and saving her trouble, were too late! For the first time, the three girls, sobbing in each other's arms, realized what a good friend Aunt Izzie had been to them. Her worrying ways were all forgotten now. They could only remember the many kind things she had done for them since they were little children. How they wished that they had never teased her, never said sharp words about her to each other! But it was no use to wish.

"What shall we do without Aunt Izzie?" thought Katy, as she cried herself to sleep that night. And the question came into her mind again and again, after the funeral was over and the little ones had come back from Mrs. Hall's, and things began to go on in their usual manner.

For several days she saw almost nothing of her father. Clover reported that he looked very tired and scarcely said a word.

"Did Papa eat any dinner?" asked Katy, one afternoon.

"Not much. He said he wasn't hungry. And Mrs. Jackson's boy came for him before we were through."

"Oh dear!" sighed Katy, "I do hope *he* isn't going to be sick. How it rains! Clovy, I wish you'd run down and get out his slippers and put them by the fire to warm. Oh, and ask Debby to make some cream-toast for tea! Papa likes cream-toast."

After tea, Dr. Carr came up stairs to sit a while in Katy's room. He often did so, but this was the first time since Aunt Izzie's death.

Katy studied his face anxiously. It seemed to her that it had grown older of late, and there was a sad look upon it, which made her heart ache. She longed to do something for him, but all she could do was to poke the fire bright, and then to possess herself of his hand, and stroke it gently with both hers. It wasn't much, to be sure, but I think Papa liked it.

"What have you been about all day?" he asked.

"Oh, nothing, much," said Katy. "I studied my French lesson this morning. And after school, Elsie and John brought in their patchwork, and we had a 'Bee.' That's all."

"I've been thinking how we are to manage about the housekeeping," said Dr. Carr. "Of course we shall have to get somebody to come and take charge. But it isn't easy to find just the right person. Mrs. Hall knows of a woman who might do, but she is out West, just now, and it will be a week or two before we can hear from her. Do you think you can get on as you are for a few days?"

"Oh, Papa!" cried Katy, in dismay, "must we have anybody?"

"Why, how did you suppose we were going to arrange it? Clover is much too young for a housekeeper. And beside, she is at school all day."

"I don't know—I hadn't thought about it," said Katy, in a perplexed tone.

But she did think about it—all that evening, and the first thing when she woke in the morning.

"Papa," she said, the next time she got him to herself, "I've been thinking over what you were saying last night, about getting somebody to keep the house, you know. And I wish you wouldn't. I wish you would let *me* try. Really and truly, I think I could manage."

"But how?" asked Dr. Carr, much surprised. "I really don't see. If you were well and strong, perhaps—but even then you would be pretty young for such a charge, Katy."

"I shall be fourteen in two weeks," said Katy, drawing herself up in her chair as straight as she could. "And if I *were* well, Papa, I should be going to school, you know, and then of course I couldn't. No, I'll tell you my plan. I've been thinking about it all day. Debby and Bridget have been with us so long, that they know all Aunt Izzie's ways, and they're such good women, that all they want is just to be told a little now and then. Now, why couldn't they come up to me when anything is wanted—just as well as to have me go down to them? Clover and old Mary will keep watch, you know, and see if anything is wrong. And you wouldn't mind if things were a little crooked just at first, would you? because, you know, I should be learning all the time. Do let me try! It will be real nice to have something to think about as I sit up here alone, so much better than having a stranger in the house who doesn't know the children or anything. I am sure it will make me happier. Please say 'Yes,' Papa, please do!"

"It's too much for you, a great deal too much," replied Dr. Carr. But it was not easy to resist Katy's "Please! Please!" and after a while it ended with—

"Well, darling, you may try, though I am doubtful as to the result of the experiment. I will tell Mrs. Hall to put off writing to Wisconsin for a month, and we will see.

"Poor child, anything to take her thoughts off herself!" he muttered, as he walked down stairs. "She'll be glad enough to give the thing up by the end of the month."

But Papa was mistaken. At the end of a month Katy was eager to go on. So he said,

"Very well—she might try it till Spring."

It was not such hard work as it sounds. Katy had plenty of quiet thinking-time for one thing. The children were at school all day, and few visitors came to interrupt her, so she could plan out her hours and keep to the plans. That is a great help to a housekeeper.

Then Aunt Izzie's regular, punctual ways were so well understood by the servants, that the house seemed almost to keep itself. As Katy had said, all Debby and Bridget needed was a little "telling" now and then.

As soon as breakfast was over, and the dishes were washed and put away, Debby would tie on a clean apron, and come up stairs for orders. At first Katy thought this great fun. But after ordering dinner a good many times, it began to grow tiresome. She never saw the dishes after they were cooked; and, being inexperienced, it seemed impossible to think of things enough to make a variety.

"Let me see—there is roast beef—leg of mutton—boiled chicken," she would say, counting on her fingers, "roast beef—leg of mutton—boiled chicken. Debby, you might roast the chickens. Dear!—I wish somebody would invent a new animal! Where all the things to eat are gone to, I can't imagine!"

Then Katy would send for every recipe-book in the house, and pore over them by the hour, till her appetite was as completely gone as if she had swallowed twenty dinners. Poor Debby learned to dread these books. She would stand by the door with her pleasant red face drawn up into a pucker, while Katy read aloud some impossible-sounding rule.

"This looks as if it were delicious, Debby, I wish you'd try it: Take a gallon of oysters, a pint of beef stock, sixteen soda crackers, the juice of two lemons, four cloves, a glass of white wine, a sprig of marjoram, a sprig of thyme, a sprig of bay, a sliced shalott—"

"Please, Miss Katy, what's them?"

"Oh, don't you know, Debby? It must be something quite common, for it's in almost all the recipes."

"No, Miss Katy, I never heard tell of it before. Miss Carr never gave me no shell-outs at all at all!"

"Dear me, how provoking!" Katy would cry, flapping over the leaves of her book; "then we must try something else."

Poor Debby! If she hadn't loved Katy so dearly, I think her patience must have given way. But she bore her trials meekly, except for an occasional grumble when alone with Bridget. Dr. Carr had to eat a great many queer things in those days. But he didn't mind, and as for the children, they enjoyed it. Dinner-time became quite exciting, when nobody could tell exactly what any dish on the table was made of. Dorry, who was a sort of Dr. Livingstone where strange articles of food were concerned, usually made the first experiment, and if he said that it was good, the rest followed suit.

After a while Katy grew wiser. She ceased teasing Debby to try new things, and the Carr family went back to plain roast and boiled, much to the advantage of all concerned. But then another series of experiments began. Katy got hold of a book upon "The Stomach," and was seized with a rage for wholesome food. She entreated Clover and the other children to give up sugar, and butter, and gravy, and pudding-sauce, and buckwheat cakes, and pies, and almost everything else that they particularly liked. Boiled rice seemed to her the most sensible dessert, and she kept the family on it until finally John and Dorry started a rebellion, and Dr. Carr was forced to interfere.

"My dear, you are overdoing it sadly," he said, as Katy opened her book and prepared to explain her views; "I am glad to have the children eat simple food—but really, boiled rice five times in a week is too much."

Katy sighed, but submitted. Later, as the Spring came on, she had a fit of over-anxiousness, and was always sending Clover down to ask Debby if her bread was not burning, or if she was sure that the pickles were not fermenting in their jars? She also fidgeted the children about wearing india-rubbers, and keeping on their coats, and behaved altogether as if the cares of the world were on her shoulders.

But all these were but the natural mistakes of a beginner. Katy was too much in earnest not to improve. Month by month she learned how to manage a little better, and a little better still. Matters went on more smoothly. Her cares ceased to fret her. Dr. Carr watching the increasing brightness of her face and manner, felt that the experiment was a success. Nothing more was said about "somebody else," and Katy, sitting up stairs in her big chair, held the threads of the house firmly in her hands.

CHAPTER XII: TWO YEARS AFTERWARD

It was a pleasant morning in early June. A warm wind was rustling the trees, which were covered thickly with half-opened leaves, and looked like fountains of green spray thrown high into the air. Dr. Carr's front door stood wide open. Through the parlor window came the sound of piano practice, and on the steps, under the budding roses, sat a small figure, busily sewing.

This was Clover, little Clover still, though more than two years had passed since we saw her last, and she was now over fourteen. Clover was never intended to be tall. Her eyes were as blue and sweet as ever, and her apple-blossom cheeks as pink. But the brown pig-tails were pinned up into a round knot, and the childish face had gained almost a womanly look. Old Mary declared that Miss Clover was getting quite young-ladyfied, and "Miss Clover" was quite aware of the fact, and mightily pleased with it. It delighted her to turn up her hair; and she was very particular about having her dresses made to come below the tops of her boots. She had also left off ruffles, and wore narrow collars instead, and little cuffs with sleeve-buttons to fasten them. These sleeve-buttons, which were a present from Cousin Helen, Clover liked best of all her things. Papa said that he was sure she took them to bed with her, but of course that was only a joke, though she certainly was never seen without them in the daytime. She glanced frequently at these beloved buttons as she sat sewing, and every now and then laid down her work to twist them into a better position, or give them an affectionate pat with her forefinger.

Pretty soon the side-gate swung open, and Philly came round the corner of the house. He had grown into a big boy. All his pretty baby curls were cut off, and his frocks had given place to jacket and trousers. In his hand he held something. What, Clover could not see.

"What's that?" she said, as he reached the steps.

"I'm going up stairs to ask Katy if these are ripe," replied Phil, exhibiting some currants faintly streaked with red.

"Why, of course they're not ripe!" said Clover, putting one into her mouth. "Can't you tell by the taste? They're as green as can be."

"I don't care, if Katy says they're ripe I shall eat 'em," answered Phil, defiantly, marching into the house.

"What did Philly want?" asked Elsie, opening the parlor door as Phil went up stairs.

"Only to know if the currants are ripe enough to eat."

"How particular he always is about asking now!" said Elsie; "he's afraid of another dose of salts."

"I should think he would be," replied Clover, laughing. "Johnnie says she never was so scared in her life as when Papa called them, and they looked up, and saw him standing there with the bottle in one hand and a spoon in the other!"

"Yes," went on Elsie, "and you know Dorry held his in his mouth for ever so long, and then went round the corner of the house and spat it out! Papa said he had a good mind to make him take another spoonful, but he remembered that after all Dorry had the bad taste a great deal longer than the others, so he didn't. I think it was an *awful* punishment, don't you?"

"Yes, but it was a good one, for none of them have ever touched the green gooseberries since. Have you got through practising? It doesn't seem like an hour yet."

"Oh, it isn't—it's only twenty-five minutes. But Katy told me not to sit more than half an hour at a time without getting up and running round to rest. I'm going to walk twice down to the gate, and twice back. I promised her I would." And Elsie set off, clapping her hands briskly before and behind her as she walked.

"Why—what is Bridget doing in Papa's room?" she asked, as she came back the second time. "She's flapping things out of the window. Are the girls up there? I thought they were cleaning the dining-room."

"They're doing both. Katy said it was such a good chance, having Papa away, that she would have both the carpets taken up at once. There isn't going to be any dinner today, only just bread and butter, and milk, and cold ham, up in Katy's room, because Debby is helping too, so as to get through and save Papa all the fuss. And see," exhibiting her sewing, "Katy's making a new cover for Papa's pincushion, and I'm hemming the ruffle to go round it."

"How nicely you hem!" said Elsie. "I wish I had something for Papa's room too. There's my washstand mats—but the one for the soap-dish isn't finished. Do you suppose, if Katy would excuse me from the rest of my practising, I could get it done? I've a great mind to go and ask her."

"There's her bell!" said Clover, as a little tinkle sounded up stairs; "I'll ask her, if you like."

"No, let me go. I'll see what she wants." But Clover was already half-way across the hall, and the two girls ran up side by side. There was often a little strife between them as to which should answer Katy's bell. Both liked to wait on her so much.

Katy came to meet them as they entered. Not on her feet: that, alas! was still only a far-off possibility; but in a chair with large wheels, with which she was rolling herself across the room. This chair was a great comfort to her. Sitting in it, she could get to her closet and her bureau-drawers, and help herself to what she wanted without troubling anybody. It was only lately that she had been able to use it. Dr. Carr considered her doing so as a hopeful sign, but he had never told Katy this. She had grown accustomed to her invalid life at last, and was cheerful in it, and he thought it unwise to make her restless, by exciting hopes which might after all end in fresh disappointment.

She met the girls with a bright smile as they came in, and said:

"Oh, Clovy, it was you I rang for! I am troubled for fear Bridget will meddle with the things on Papa's table. You know he likes them to be left just so. Will you please go and remind her that she is not to touch them at all? After the carpet is put down, I want you to dust the table, so as to be sure that everything is put back in the same place. Will you?"

"Of course I will!" said Clover, who was a born housewife, and dearly loved to act as Katy's prime minister.

"Sha'n't I fetch you the pincushion too, while I'm there?"

"Oh yes, please do! I want to measure."

"Katy," said Elsie, "those mats of mine are most done, and I would like to finish them and put them on Papa's washstand before he comes back. Mayn't I stop practising now, and bring my crochet up here instead?"

"Will there be plenty of time to learn the new exercise before Miss Phillips comes, if you do?"

"I think so, plenty. She doesn't come till Friday, you know."

"Well, then it seems to me that you might just as well as not. And Elsie, dear, run into papa's room first, and bring me the drawer out of his table. I want to put that in order myself."

Elsie went cheerfully. She laid the drawer across Katy's lap, and Katy began to dust and arrange the contents. Pretty soon Clover joined them.

"Here's the cushion," she said. "Now we'll have a nice quiet time all by ourselves, won't we? I like this sort of day, when nobody comes in to interrupt us."

Somebody tapped at the door, as she spoke. Katy called out, "Come!" And in marched a tall, broad-shouldered lad, with a solemn, sensible face, and a little clock carried carefully in both his hands. This was Dorry. He has grown and improved very much since we saw him last, and is turning out clever in several ways. Among the rest, he has developed a strong turn for mechanics.

"Here's your clock, Katy," he said. "I've got it fixed so that it strikes all right. Only you must be careful not to hit the striker when you start the pendulum."

"Have you, really?" said Katy. "Why, Dorry, you're a genius! I'm ever so much obliged."

"It's four minutes to eleven now," went on Dorry. "So it'll strike pretty soon. I guess I'd better stay and hear it, so as to be sure that it is right. That is," he added politely, "unless you're busy, and would rather not."

"I'm never too busy to want you, old fellow," said Katy, stroking his arm. "Here, this drawer is arranged now. Don't you want to carry it into Papa's room and put it back into the table? Your hands are stronger than Elsie's."

Dorry looked gratified. When he came back the clock was just beginning to strike.

"There!" he exclaimed; "that's splendid, isn't it?"

But alas! the clock did not stop at eleven. It went on—Twelve, Thirteen, Fourteen, Fifteen, Sixteen!

"Dear me!" said Clover, "what does all this mean? It must be day after to-morrow, at least."

Dorry stared with open mouth at the clock, which was still striking as though it would split its sides. Elsie, screaming with laughter, kept count.

"Thirty, Thirty-one—Oh, Dorry! Thirty-two! Thirty-three! Thirty-four!"

"You've bewitched it, Dorry!" said Katy, as much entertained as the rest.

Then they all began counting. Dorry seized the clock—shook it, slapped it, turned it upside-down. But still the sharp, vibrating sounds continued, as if the clock, having got its own way for once, meant to go on till it was tired out. At last, at the one-hundred-and-thirtieth stroke, it suddenly ceased; and Dorry, with a red, amazed countenance, faced the laughing company.

"It's very queer," he said, "but I'm sure it's not because of anything I did. I can fix it, though, if you'll let me try again. May I, Katy? I'll promise not to hurt it."

For a moment Katy hesitated. Clover pulled her sleeve, and whispered, "Don't!" Then seeing the mortification on Dorry's face, she made up her mind.

"Yes! take it, Dorry. I'm sure you'll be careful. But if I were you, I'd carry it down to Wetherell's first of all, and talk it over with them. Together you could hit on just the right thing. Don't you think so?"

"Perhaps," said Dorry; "yes, I think I will." Then he departed with the clock under his arm, while Clover called after him teasingly, "Lunch at 132 o'clock; don't forget!"

"No, I won't!" said Dorry. Two years before he would not have borne to be laughed at so good-naturedly.

"How could you let him take your clock again?" said Clover, as soon as the door was shut. "He'll spoil it. And you think so much of it."

"I thought he would feel mortified if I didn't let him try," replied Katy, quietly, "I don't believe he'll hurt it. Wetherell's man likes Dorry, and he'll show him what to do."

"You were real good to do it," responded Clover; "but if it had been mine I don't think I could."

Just then the door flew open, and Johnnie rushed in, two years taller, but otherwise looking exactly as she used to do.

"Oh, Katy!" she gasped, "won't you please tell Philly not to wash the chickens in the rain-water tub? He's put in every one of Speckle's, and is just beginning on Dame Durden's. I'm afraid one little yellow one is dead already—"

"Why, he mustn't—of course he mustn't!" said Katy; "what made him think of such a thing?"

"He says they're dirty, because they've just come out of egg-shells! And he insists that the yellow on them is yolk-of-egg. I told him it wasn't, but he wouldn't listen to me." And Johnnie wrung her hands.

"Clover!" cried Katy, "won't you run down and ask Philly to come up to me? Speak pleasantly, you know!"

"I spoke pleasantly—real pleasantly, but it wasn't any use," said Johnnie, on whom the wrongs of the chicks had evidently made a deep impression.

"What a mischief Phil is getting to be!" said Elsie. "Papa says his name ought to be Pickle."

"Pickles turn out very nice sometimes, you know," replied Katy, laughing.

Pretty soon Philly came up, escorted by Clover. He looked a little defiant, but Katy understood how to manage him. She lifted him into her lap, which, big boy as he was, he liked extremely; and talked to him so affectionately about the poor little shivering chicks, that his heart was quite melted.

"I didn't mean to hurt 'em, really and truly," he said, "but they were all dirty and yellow—with egg, you know, and I thought you'd like me to clean 'em up."

"But that wasn't egg, Philly—it was dear little clean feathers, like a canary-bird's wings."

"Was it?"

"Yes. And now the chickies are as cold and forlorn as you would feel if you tumbled into a pond and nobody gave you any dry clothes. Don't you think you ought to go and warm them?"

"How?"

"Well—in your hands, very gently. And then I would let them run round in the sun."

"I will!" said Philly, getting down from her lap. "Only kiss me first, because I didn't mean to, you know!"—Philly was very fond of Katy. Miss Petingill said it was wonderful to see how that child let himself be managed. But I think the secret was that Katy didn't "manage," but tried to be always kind and loving, and considerate of Phil's feelings.

Before the echo of Phil's boots had fairly died away on the stairs, old Mary put her head into the door. There was a distressed expression on her face.

"Miss Katy," she said, "I wish *you'd* speak to Alexander about putting the woodshed in order. I don't think you know how bad it looks."

"I don't suppose I do," said Katy, smiling, and then sighing. She had never seen the wood-shed since the day of her fall from the swing. "Never mind, Mary, I'll talk to Alexander about it, and he shall make it all nice."

Mary trotted down stairs satisfied. But in the course of a few minutes she was up again.

"There's a man come with a box of soap, Miss Katy, and here's the bill. He says it's resated."

It took Katy a little time to find her purse, and then she wanted her pencil and account book, and Elsie had to move from her seat at the table.

"Oh dear!" she said, "I wish people wouldn't keep coming and interrupting us. Who'll be the next, I wonder?"

She was not left to wonder long. Almost as she spoke, there was another knock at the door.

"Come in!" said Katy, rather wearily. The door opened.

"Shall I?" said a voice. There was a rustle of skirts, a clatter of boot-heels, and Imogen Clark swept into the room. Katy could not think who it was, at first. She had not seen Imogen for almost two years.

"I found the front door open," explained Imogen, in her high-pitched voice, "and as nobody seemed to hear when I rang the bell, I ventured to come right up stairs. I hope I'm not interrupting anything private?"

"Not at all," said Katy, politely. "Elsie, dear, move up that low chair, please. Do sit down, Imogen! I'm sorry nobody answered your ring, but the servants are cleaning house to-day, and I suppose they didn't hear."

So Imogen sat down and began to rattle on in her usual manner, while Elsie, from behind Katy's chair, took a wide-awake survey of her dress. It was of cheap material, but very gorgeously made and trimmed, with flounces and puffs, and Imogen wore a jet necklace and long black ear-rings, which jingled and clicked when she waved her head about. She still had the little round curls stuck on to her cheeks, and Elsie wondered anew what kept them in their places.

By and by the object of Imogen's visit came out. She had called to say good-by. The Clark family were all going back to Jacksonville to live.

"Did you ever see the Brigand again?" asked Clover, who had never forgotten that eventful tale told in the parlor.

"Yes," replied Imogen, "several times. And I get letters from him quite often. He writes *beau*tiful letters. I wish I had one with me, so that I could read you a little bit. You would enjoy it, I know. Let me see—perhaps I have." And she put her hand into her pocket. Sure enough there *was* a letter. Clover couldn't help suspecting that Imogen knew it all the time.

The Brigand seemed to write a bold, black hand, and his note-paper and envelope was just like anybody else's. But perhaps his band had surprised a pedlar with a box of stationery.

"Let me see," said Imogen, running her eye down the page. "'Adored Imogen'—that wouldn't interest you—hm, hm, hm—ah, here's something! 'I took dinner at the Rock House on Christmas. It was lonesome without you. I had roast turkey, roast goose, roast beef, mince pie, plum pudding, and nuts and raisins. A pretty good dinner, was it not? But nothing tastes first-rate when friends are away.'"

Katy and Clover stared, as well they might. Such language from a Brigand!

"John Billings has bought a new horse," continued Imogen; "hm, hm, hm—him. I don't think there is anything else you'd care about. Oh, yes! just here, at the end, is some poetry:

"'Come, little dove, with azure wing,
And brood upon my breast,'

"That's sweet, ain't it?"

"Hasn't he reformed?" said Clover; "he writes as if he had."

"Reformed!" cried Imogen, with a toss of the jingling ear-rings. "He was always just as good as he could be!"

There was nothing to be said in reply to this. Katy felt her lips twitch, and for fear she should be rude, and laugh out, she began to talk as fast as she could about something else. All the time she found herself taking measure of Imogen, and thinking—"Did I ever really like her? How queer! Oh, what a wise man Papa is!"

Imogen stayed half an hour. Then she took her leave.

"She never asked how you were!" cried Elsie, indignantly; "I noticed, and she didn't—not once."

"Oh well—I suppose she forgot. We were talking about her, not about me," replied Katy.

The little group settled down again to their work. This time half an hour went by without any more interruptions. Then the door bell rang, and Bridget, with a disturbed face, came up stairs.

"Miss Katy," she said, "it's old Mrs. Worrett, and I reckon's she's come to spend the day, for she's brought her bag. What ever shall I tell her?"

Katy looked dismayed. "Oh dear!" she said, "how unlucky. What can we do?"

Mrs. Worrett was an old friend of Aunt Izzie's, who lived in the country, about six miles from Burnet, and was in the habit of coming to Dr. Carr's for lunch, on days when shopping or other business brought her into town. This did not occur often; and, as it happened, Katy had never had to entertain her before.

"Tell her ye're busy, and can't see her," suggested Bridget; "there's no dinner nor nothing, you know."

The Katy of two years ago would probably have jumped at this idea. But the Katy of to-day was more considerate.

"N-o," she said; "I don't like to do that. We must just make the best of it, Bridget. Run down, Clover, dear, that's a good girl! and tell Mrs. Worrett that the dining-room is all in confusion, but that we're going to have lunch here, and, after she's rested, I should be glad to have her come up. And, oh, Clovy! give her a fan the first thing. She'll be *so* hot. Bridget, you can bring up the luncheon just the same, only take out some canned peaches, by way of a dessert, and make Mrs. Worrett a cup of tea. She drinks tea always, I believe.

"I can't bear to send the poor old lady away when she has come so far," she explained to Elsie, after the others were gone. "Pull the rocking-chair a little this way, Elsie. And oh! push all those little chairs back against the wall. Mrs. Worrett broke down in one the last time she was here—don't you recollect?"

It took some time to cool Mrs. Worrett off, so nearly twenty minutes passed before a heavy, creaking step on the stairs announced that the guest was on her way up. Elsie began to giggle. Mrs. Worrett always made her giggle. Katy had just time to give her a warning glance before the door opened.

Mrs. Worrett was the most enormously fat person ever seen. Nobody dared to guess how much she weighed, but she looked as if it might be a thousand pounds. Her face was extremely red. In the coldest weather she appeared hot, and on a mild day she seemed absolutely ready to melt. Her bonnet-strings were flying loose as she came in, and she fanned herself all the way across the room, which shook as she walked.

"Well, my dear," she said, as she plumped herself into the rocking-chair, "and how do you do?"

"Very well, thank you," replied Katy, thinking that she never saw Mrs. Worrett look half so fat before, and wondering how she *was* to entertain her.

"And how's your Pa?" inquired Mrs. Worrett. Katy answered politely, and then asked after Mrs. Worrett's own health.

"Well, I'm so's to be round," was the reply, which had the effect of sending Elsie off into a fit of convulsive laughter behind Katy's chair.

"I had business at the bank," continued the visitor, "and I thought while I was about it I'd step up to Miss Petingill's and see if I couldn't get her to come and let out my black silk. It was made quite a piece back, and I seem to have fleshed up since then, for I can't make the hooks and eyes meet at all. But when I got there, she was out, so I'd my walk for nothing. Do you know where she's sewing now?"

"No," said Katy, feeling her chair shake, and keeping her own countenance with difficulty, "she was here for three days last week to make Johnnie a school-dress. But I haven't heard anything about her since. Elsie, don't you want to run down stairs and ask Bridget to bring a—a—a glass of iced water for Mrs. Worrett? She looks warm after her walk."

Elsie, dreadfully ashamed, made a bolt from the room, and hid herself in the hall closet to have her laugh out. She came back after a while, with a perfectly straight face. Luncheon was brought up. Mrs. Worrett made a good meal, and seemed to enjoy everything. She was so comfortable that she never stirred till four o'clock! Oh, how long that afternoon did seem to the poor girls, sitting there and trying to think of something to say to their vast visitor!

At last Mrs. Worrett got out of her chair, and prepared to depart.

"Well," she said, tying her bonnet-strings, "I've had a good rest, and feel all the better for it. Ain't some of you young folks coming out to see me one of these days? I'd like to have you, first-rate, if you will. 'Tain't every girl would know how to take care of a fat old woman, and make her feel to home, as you have me, Katy. I wish your aunt could see you all as you are now. She'd be right pleased; I know that."

Somehow, this sentence rang pleasantly in Katy's ears.

"Ah! don't laugh at her," she said later in the evening, when the children, after their tea in the clean, fresh-smelling dining-room, were come up to sit with her, and Cecy, in her pretty pink lawn and white shawl, had dropped in to spend an hour or two; "she's a real kind old woman, and I don't like to have you. It isn't her fault that she's fat. And Aunt Izzie was fond of her, you know. It is doing something for her when we can show a little attention to one of her friends. I was sorry when she came, but now it's over, I'm glad."

"It feels so nice when it stops aching," quoted Elsie, mischievously, while Cecy whispered to Clover.

"Isn't Katy sweet?"

"Isn't she!" replied Clover. "I wish I was half so good. Sometimes I think I shall really be sorry if she ever gets well. She's such a dear old darling to us all, sitting there in her chair, that it wouldn't seem so nice to have her anywhere else. But then, I know it's horrid in me. And I don't believe she'd be different, or grow slam-bang and horrid, like some of the girls, even if she were well."

"Of course she wouldn't!" replied Cecy.

CHAPTER XIII: AT LAST

It was about six weeks after this, that one day, Clover and Elsie were busy down stairs, they were startled by the sound of Katy's bell ringing in a sudden and agitated manner. Both ran up two steps at a time, to see what was wanted.

Katy sat in her chair, looking very much flushed and excited.
"Oh, girls!" she exclaimed, "what do you think? I stood up!"
"What?" cried Clover and Elsie.
"I really did! I stood up on my feet! by myself!"

The others were too much astonished to speak, so Katy went on explaining.

"It was all at once, you see. Suddenly, I had the feeling that if I tried I could, and almost before I thought, I *did* try, and there I was, up and out of the chair. Only I kept hold of the arm all the time! I don't know how I got back, I was so frightened. Oh, girls!"—and Katy buried her face in her hands.

"Do you think I shall ever be able to do it again?" she asked, looking up with wet eyes.

"Why, of course you will!" said Clover; while Elsie danced about, crying out anxiously: "Be careful! Do be careful!"

Katy tried, but the spring was gone. She could not move out of the chair at all. She began to wonder if she had dreamed the whole thing.

But next day, when Clover happened to be in the room, she heard a sudden exclamation, and turning, there stood Katy, absolutely on her feet.

"Papa! papa!" shrieked Clover, rushing down stairs. "Dorry, John, Elsie—come! Come and see!"

Papa was out, but all the rest crowded up at once. This time Katy found no trouble in "doing it again." It seemed as if her will had been asleep; and now that it had waked up, the limbs recognized its orders and obeyed them.

When Papa came in, he was as much excited as any of the children. He walked round and round the chair, questioning Katy and making her stand up and sit down.

"Am I really going to get well?" she asked, almost in a whisper.

"Yes, my love, I think you are," replied Dr. Carr, seizing Phil and giving him a toss into the air. None of the children had ever before seen Papa behave so like a boy. But pretty soon, noticing Katy's burning cheeks and excited eyes, he calmed himself, sent the others all away, and sat down to soothe and quiet her with gentle words.

"I think it is coming, my darling," he said, "but it will take time, and you must have a great deal of patience. After being such a good child all the years, I am sure you won't fail now. Remember, any imprudence will put you back. You must be content to gain a very little at a time. There is no royal road to walking any more than there is to learning. Every baby finds that out."

"Oh, Papa!" said Katy, "it's no matter if it takes a year—if only I get well at last."

How happy she was that night—too happy to sleep. Papa noticed the dark circles under her eyes in the morning, and shook his head.

"You must be careful," he told her, "or you'll be laid up again. A course of fever would put you back for years."

Katy knew Papa was right, and she was careful, though it was by no means easy to be so with that new life tingling in every limb. Her progress was slow, as Dr. Carr had predicted. At first she only stood on her feet a few seconds, then a minute, then five minutes, holding tightly all the while by the chair. Next she ventured to let go the chair, and stand alone. After that she began to walk a step at a time, pushing a chair before her, as children do when they are learning the use of their feet. Clover and Elsie hovered about her as she moved, like anxious mammas. It was droll, and a little pitiful, to see tall Katy with her feeble, unsteady progress, and the active figures of the little sisters following her protectingly. But Katy did not consider it either droll or pitiful; to her it was simply delightful—the most delightful thing possible. No baby of a year old was ever prouder of his first steps than she.

Gradually she grew adventurous, and ventured on a bolder flight. Clover, running up stairs one day to her own room, stood transfixed at the sight of Katy sitting there, flushed, panting, but enjoying the surprise she caused.

"You see," she explained, in an apologizing tone, "I was seized with a desire to explore. It is such a time since I saw any room but my own! But oh dear, how long that hall is! I had forgotten it could be so long. I shall have to take a good rest before I go back."

Katy did take a good rest, but she was very tired next day. The experiment, however, did no harm. In the course of two or three weeks, she was able to walk all over the second story.

This was a great enjoyment. It was like reading an interesting book to see all the new things, and the little changes. She was forever wondering over something.

"Why, Dorry," she would say, "what a pretty book-shelf! When did you get it?"

"That old thing! Why, I've had it two years. Didn't I ever tell you about it?"

"Perhaps you did," Katy would reply, "but you see I never saw it before, so it made no impression."

By the end of August she was grown so strong, that she began to talk about going down stairs. But Papa said, "Wait."

"It will tire you much more than walking about on a level," he explained, "you had better put it off a little while—till you are quite sure of your feet."

"I think so too," said Clover; "and beside, I want to have the house all put in order and made nice, before your sharp eyes see it, Mrs. Housekeeper. Oh, I'll tell you! Such a beautiful idea has come into my head! You shall fix a day to come down, Katy, and we'll be all ready for you, and have a 'celebration' among ourselves. That would be just lovely! How soon may she, Papa?"

"Well—in ten days, I should say, it might be safe."

"Ten days! that will bring it to the seventh of September, won't it?" said Katy. "Then Papa, if I may, I'll come down stairs the first time on the eighth. It was Mamma's birthday, you know," she added in a lower voice.

So it was settled. "How delicious!" cried Clover, skipping about and clapping her hands: "I never, never, never *did* hear of anything so perfectly lovely. Papa, when are you coming down stairs? I want to speak to you *dreadfully*."

"Right away—rather than have my coat-tails pulled off," answered Dr. Carr, laughing, and they went away together. Katy sat looking out of the window in a peaceful, happy mood.

"Oh!" she thought, "can it really be? Is School going to 'let out,' just as Cousin Helen's hymn said? Am I going to 'Bid a sweet good-bye to Pain?' But there was Love in the Pain. I see it now. How good the dear Teacher has been to me!"

Clover seemed to be very busy all the rest of that week. She was "having windows washed," she said, but this explanation hardly accounted for her long absences, and the mysterious exultation on her face, not to mention certain sounds of hammering and sawing which came from down stairs. The other children had evidently been warned to say nothing; for once or twice Philly broke out with, "Oh, Katy!" and then hushed himself up, saying, "I 'most forgot!" Katy grew very curious. But she saw that the secret, whatever it was, gave immense satisfaction to everybody except herself; so, though she longed to know, she concluded not to spoil the fun by asking any questions.

At last it wanted but one day of the important occasion.

"See," said Katy, as Clover came into the room a little before tea-time. "Miss Petingill has brought home my new dress. I'm going to wear it for the first time to go down stairs in."

"How pretty!" said Clover, examining the dress, which was a soft, dove-colored cashmere, trimmed with ribbon of the same shade. "But

Katy, I came up to shut your door. Bridget's going to sweep the hall, and I don't want the dust to fly in, because your room was brushed this morning, you know."

"What a queer time to sweep a hall!" said Katy, wonderingly. "Why don't you make her wait till morning?"

"Oh, she can't! There are—she has—I mean there will be other things for her to do to-morrow. It's a great deal more convenient that she should do it now. Don't worry, Katy, darling, but just keep your door shut. You will, won't you? Promise me!"

"Very well," said Katy, more and more amazed, but yielding to Clover's eagerness, "I'll keep it shut." Her curiosity was excited. She took a book and tried to read, but the letters danced up and down before her eyes, and she couldn't help listening. Bridget was making a most ostentatious noise with her broom, but through it all, Katy seemed to hear other sounds—feet on the stairs, doors opening and shutting—once, a stifled giggle. How queer it all was!

"Never mind," she said, resolutely stopping her ears, "I shall know all about it to-morrow."

To-morrow dawned fresh and fair—the very ideal of a September day.

"Katy!" said Clover, as she came in from the garden with her hands full of flowers, "that dress of yours is sweet. You never looked so nice before in your life!" And she stuck a beautiful carnation pink under Katy's breast-pin and fastened another in her hair.

"There!" she said, "now you're adorned. Papa is coming up in a few minutes to take you down."

Just then Elsie and Johnnie came in. They had on their best frocks. So had Clover. It was evidently a festival-day to all the house. Cecy followed, invited over for the special purpose of seeing Katy walk down stairs. She, too, had on a new frock.

"How fine we are!" said Clover, as she remarked this magnificence. "Turn round, Cecy—a panier, I do declare— and a sash! You are getting awfully grown up, Miss Hall."

"None of us will ever be so 'grown up' as Katy," said Cecy, laughing.

And now Papa appeared. Very slowly they all went down stairs, Katy leaning on Papa, with Dorry on her other side, and the girls behind, while Philly clattered ahead. And there were Debby and Bridget and Alexander, peeping out of the kitchen door to watch her, and dear old Mary with her apron at her eyes crying for joy.

"Oh, the front door is open!" said Katy, in a delighted tone. "How nice! And what a pretty oil-cloth. That's new since I was here."

"Don't stop to look at *that*!" cried Philly, who seemed in a great hurry about something. "It isn't new. It's been there ever and ever so long! Come into the parlor instead."

"Yes!" said Papa, "dinner isn't quite ready yet, you'll have time to rest a little after your walk down stairs. You have borne it admirably, Katy. Are you very tired?"

"Not a bit!" replied Katy, cheerfully. "I could do it alone, I think. Oh! the bookcase door has been mended! How nice it looks."

"Don't wait, oh, don't wait!" repeated Phil, in an agony of impatience.

So they moved on. Papa opened the parlor door. Katy took one step into the room—then stopped. The color flashed over her face, and she held by the door-knob to support herself. What was it that she saw?

Not merely the room itself, with its fresh muslin curtains and vases of flowers. Nor even the wide, beautiful window which had been cut toward the sun, or the inviting little couch and table which stood there, evidently for her. No, there was something else! The sofa was pulled out and there upon it, supported by pillows, her bright eyes turned to the door, lay—Cousin Helen! When she saw Katy, she held out her arms.

Clover and Cecy agreed afterward that they never were so frightened in their lives as at this moment; for Katy, forgetting her weakness, let go of Papa's arm, and absolutely *ran* toward the sofa. "Oh, Cousin Helen! dear, dear Cousin Helen!" she cried. Then she tumbled down by the sofa somehow, the two pairs of arms and the two faces met, and for a moment or two not a word more was heard from anybody.

"Isn't a nice 'prise?" shouted Philly, turning a somerset by way of relieving his feelings, while John and Dorry executed a sort of war-dance round the sofa.

Phil's voice seemed to break the spell of silence, and a perfect hubbub of questions and exclamations began.

It appeared that this happy thought of getting Cousin Helen to the "Celebration," was Clover's. She it was who had proposed it to Papa, and made all the arrangements. And, artful puss! she had set Bridget to sweep the hall, on purpose that Katy might not hear the noise of the arrival.

"Cousin Helen's going to stay three weeks this time—isn't that nice?" asked Elsie, while Clover anxiously questioned: "Are you sure that you didn't suspect? Not one bit? Not the least tiny, weeny mite?"

"No, indeed—not the least. How could I suspect anything so perfectly delightful?" And Katy gave Cousin Helen another rapturous kiss.

Such a short day as that seemed! There was so much to see, to ask about, to talk over, that the hours flew, and evening dropped upon them all like another great surprise.

Cousin Helen was perhaps the happiest of the party. Beside the pleasure of knowing Katy to be almost well again, she had the additional enjoyment of seeing for herself how many changes for the better had taken place, during the four years, among the little cousins she loved so much.

It was very interesting to watch them all. Elsie and Dorry seemed to her the most improved of the family. Elsie had quite lost her plaintive look and little injured tone, and was as bright and beaming a maiden of twelve as any one could wish to see. Dorry's moody face had grown open and sensible, and his manners were good-humored and obliging. He was still a sober boy, and not specially quick in catching an idea, but he promised to turn out a valuable man. And to him, as to all the other children, Katy was evidently the centre and the sun. They all revolved about her, and trusted her for everything. Cousin Helen looked on as Phil came in crying, after a hard tumble, and was consoled; as Johnnie whispered an important secret, and Elsie begged for help in her work. She saw Katy meet them all pleasantly and sweetly, without a bit of the dictatorial elder-sister in her manner, and with none of her old, impetuous tone. And best of all, she saw the change in Katy's own face: the gentle expression of her eyes, the womanly look, the pleasant voice, the politeness, the tact in advising the others, without seeming to advise.

"Dear Katy," she said a day or two after her arrival, "this visit is a great pleasure to me—you can't think how great. It is such a contrast to the last I made, when you were so sick, and everybody so sad. Do you remember?"

"Indeed I do! And how good you were, and how you helped me! I shall never forget that."

"I'm glad! But what I could do was very little. You have been learning by yourself all this time. And Katy, darling, I want to tell you how pleased I am to see how bravely you have worked your way up. I can perceive it in everything—in Papa, in the children, in yourself. You have won the place, which, you recollect, I once told you an invalid should try to gain, of being to everybody 'The Heart of the House.'"

"Oh, Cousin Helen, don't!" said Katy, her eyes filling with sudden tears. "I haven't been brave. You can't think how badly I sometimes have behaved—how cross and ungrateful I am, and how stupid and slow. Every day I see things which ought to be done, and I don't do them. It's too delightful to have you praise me—but you mustn't. I don't deserve it."

But although she said she didn't deserve it I think that Katy did!

What Katy Did at School

CHAPTER I. CONIC SECTION.

It was just after that happy visit of which I told at the end of "What Katy Did," that Elsie and John made their famous excursion to Conic Section; an excursion which neither of them ever forgot, and about which the family teased them for a long time afterward.

The summer had been cool; but, as often happens after cool summers, the autumn proved unusually hot. It seemed as if the months had been playing a game, and had "changed places" all round; and as if September were determined to show that he knew how to make himself just as disagreeable as August, if only he chose to do so. All the last half of Cousin Helen's stay, the weather was excessively sultry. She felt it very much, though the children did all they could to make her comfortable, with shaded rooms, and iced water, and fans. Every evening the boys would wheel her sofa out on the porch, in hopes of coolness; but it was of no use: the evenings were as warm as the days, and the yellow dust hanging in the air made the sunshine look thick and hot. A few bright leaves appeared on the trees, but they were wrinkled, and of an ugly color. Clover said she thought they had been *boiled* red like lobsters. Altogether, the month was a trying one, and the coming of October made little difference: still the dust continued, and the heat; and the wind, when it blew, had no refreshment in it, but seemed to have passed over some great furnace which had burned out of it all life and flavor.

In spite of this, however it was wonderful to see how Katy gained and improved. Every day added to her powers. First she came down to dinner, then to breakfast. She sat on the porch in the afternoons; she poured the tea. It was like a miracle to the others, in the beginning, to watch her going about the house; but they got used to it surprisingly soon,—one does to pleasant things. One person, however, never got used to it, never took it as a matter of course; and that was Katy herself. She could not run downstairs, or out into the garden; she could not open the kitchen door to give an order, without a sense of gladness and exultation which was beyond words. The wider and more active life stimulated her in every way. Her cheeks grew round and pink, her eyes bright. Cousin Helen and papa watched this change with indescribable pleasure; and Mrs. Worrett, who dropped in to lunch one day, fairly screamed with surprise at the sight of it.

"To think of it!" she cried, "why, the last time I was here you looked as if you had took root in that chair of yours for the rest of your days, and here you are stepping around as lively as I be. Well, well! wonders will never cease. It does my eyes good to see you, Katherine. I wish your poor aunt were here to-day; that I do. How pleased she'd be?"

It is doubtful whether Aunt Izzie would have been so pleased, for the lived-in look of the best parlor would have horrified her extremely; but Katy did not recollect that just then. She was touched at the genuine kindness of Mrs. Worrett's voice, and took very willingly her offered kiss. Clover brought lemonade and grapes, and they all devoted themselves to making the poor lady comfortable. Just before she went away she said,

"How is it that I can't never get any of you to come out to the Conic Section? I'm sure I've asked you often enough. There's Elsie, now, and John, they're just the age to enjoy being in the country. Why won't you send 'em out for a week? Johnnie can feed chickens, and chase 'em, too, if she likes," she added, as Johnnie dashed just then into view, pursuing one of Phil's bantams round the house. "Tell her so, won't you, Katherine? There is lots of chickens on the farm. She can chase 'em from morning to night, if she's a mind to."

Katy thanked her, but she didn't think the children would care to go. She gave Johnnie the message, and then the whole matter passed out of her mind. The family were in low spirits that morning because of Cousin Helen's having just gone away; and Elsie was lying on the sofa fanning herself with a great palm-leaf fan.

"Oh, dear!" she sighed. "Do you suppose it's every going to be cool again? It does seem as if I couldn't bear it any longer."

"Aren't you well, darling?" inquired Katy, anxiously.

"Oh, yes! well enough," replied Elsie. "It's only this horrid heat, and never going away to where it's cooler. I keep thinking about the country, and wishing I were there feeling the wind blow. I wonder if papa wouldn't let John and me go to Conic Section, and see Mrs. Worrett. Do you think he would, if you asked him?"

"But," said Katy, amazed, "Conic Section isn't exactly country, you know. It is just out of the city,—only six miles from here. And Mrs. Worrett's house is close to the road, papa said. Do you think you'd like it, dear? It *can't* be very much cooler than this."

"Oh, yes! it can," rejoined Elsie, in a tone which was a little fretful. "It's *always* cooler on a farm. There's more room for the wind, and—oh, every thing's pleasanter! You can't think how tired I am of this hot house. Last night I hardly slept at all; and, when I did, I dreamed that I was a loaf of brown bread, and Debby was putting me into the oven to bake. It was a horrid dream. I was so glad to wake up. Won't you ask papa if we may go, Katy?"

"Why, of course I will, if you wish it so much. Only"—Katy stopped and did not finish her sentence. A vision of fat Mrs. Worrett had risen before her, and she could not help doubting if Elsie would find the farm as pleasant as she expected. But sometimes the truest kindness is in giving people their own unwise way, and Elsie's eyes looked so wistful that Katy had no heart to argue or refuse.

Dr. Carr looked doubtful when the plan was proposed to him.

"It's too hot," he said. "I don't believe the girls will like it."

"Oh, yes! we will, papa; indeed we will," pleaded Elsie and John, who had lingered near the door to learn the fate of their request.

Dr. Carr smiled at the imploring faces, but he looked a little quizzical. "Very well," he said, "you may go. Mr. Worrett is coming into town to-morrow, on some bank business. I'll send word by him; and in the afternoon, when it is cooler, Alexander can drive you out."

"Goody! Goody!" cried John, jumping up and down, while Elsie put her arms round papa's neck and gave him a hug.

"And Thursday I'll send for you," he continued.

"But, papa," expostulated Elsie, "That's only two days. Mrs. Worrett said a week."

"Yes, she said a week," chimed in John; "and she's got ever so many chickens, and I'm to feed 'em, and chase 'em as much as I like. Only it's too hot to run much," she added reflectively.

"You won't really send for us on Thursday, will you, papa?" urged Elsie, anxiously. "I'd like to stay ever and ever so long; but Mrs. Worrett said a week."

"I shall send on Thursday," repeated Dr. Carr, in a decided tone. Then, seeing that Elsie's lip was trembling, and her eyes were full of tears, he continued: "Don't look so woeful, Pussy. Alexander shall drive out for you; but if you want to stay longer, you may send him back with a note to say what day you would like to have him come again. Will that do?"

"Oh, yes!" said Elsie, wiping her eyes; "that will do beautifully, papa. Only, it seems such a pity that Alexander should have to go twice when it's so hot; for we're perfectly sure to want to stay a week."

Papa only laughed, as he kissed her. All being settled the children began to get ready. It was quite an excitement packing the bags, and deciding what to take and what not to take. Elsie grew bright and gay with the bustle. Just to think of being in the country,—the cool green country,—made her perfectly happy, she declared. The truth was, she was a little feverish and not quite well, and didn't know exactly how she felt or what she wanted.

The drive out was pleasant, except that Alexander upset John's gravity, and hurt Elsie's dignity very much, by inquiring, as they left the gate, "Do the little misses know where it is that they want to go?" Part of the way the road ran through woods. They were rather boggy woods; but the dense shade kept off the sun, and there was a spicy smell of evergreens and sweet fern. Elsie felt that the good time had fairly begun and her spirits rose with every turn of the wheels.

By and by they left the woods, and came out again into the sunshine. The road was dusty, and so were the fields, and the ragged sheaves of corn-stalks, which dotted them here and there, looked dusty too. Piles of dusty red apples lay on the grass, under the orchard trees. Some cows going down a lane toward their milking shed, mooed in a dispirited and thirsty way, which made the children feel thirsty also.

"I want a drink of water awfully," said John. "Do you suppose it's much farther? How long will it be before we get to Mrs. Worrett's, Alexander?"

"'Most there, miss," replied Alexander, laconically.

Elsie put her head out of the carriage, and looked eagerly round. Where was the delightful farm? She saw a big, pumpkin-colored house by the roadside, a little farther on; but surely that couldn't be it. Yes: Alexander drew up at the gate, and jumped down to lift. them out. It really was! The surprise quite took away her breath.

She looked about. There were the woods, to be sure, but half a mile away across the fields. Near the house, there were no trees at all; only some lilac bushes at one side; there was no green grass either. A gravel path took up the whole of the narrow front yard; and, what with the blazing color of the paint and the wide-awake look of the blindless windows, the house had somehow the air of standing on tip-toe and staring hard at something,—the dust in the road, perhaps; for there seemed to be nothing to stare at.

Elsie's heart sank indescribably, as she and John got very slowly out of the carryall, and Alexander, putting his arm over the fence, rapped loudly at the front door. It was some minutes before the rap was answered. Then a heavy step was heard creaking through the hall, and somebody began fumbling at an obstinate bolt, which would not move. Next, a voice which they recognized as Mrs. Worrett's called: "Isaphiny, Isaphiny, come and see if you can open this door."

"How funny!" whispered Johnnie, beginning to giggle.

"Isaphiny" seemed to be upstairs; for presently they heard her running down, after which a fresh rattle began at the obstinate bolt. But still the door did not open, and at length Mrs. Worrett put her lips to the keyhole, and asked,—

"Who is it?"

The voice sounded so hollow and ghostly, that Elsie jumped, as she answered: "It's I, Mrs. Worrett,—Elsie Carr. And Johnnie's here, too."

"Ts, ts, ts!" sounded from within, and then came a whispering; after which Mrs. Worrett put her mouth again to the keyhole, and called out:

"Go round to the back, children. I can't make this door open anyway. It's swelled up with the damp."

"Damp!" whispered Johnnie; "why, it hasn't rained since the third week in August; papa said so yesterday."

"That's nothing, Miss Johnnie," put in Alexander, overhearing her. "Folks hereaway don't open their front doors much,—only for weddings and funerals and such like. Very likely this has stood shut these five years. I know the last time I drove Miss Carr out, before she died, it was just so; and she had to go round to the back, as you're a-doing now."

John's eyes grew wide with wonder; but there was no time to say any thing, for they had turned the corner of the house, and there was Mrs. Worrett waiting at the kitchen door to receive them. She looked fatter than ever, Elsie thought; but she kissed them both, and said she was real glad to see a Carr in her house at last.

"It was too bad," she went on, "to keep you waiting so. But the fact is I got asleep and when you knocked, I waked up all in a daze, and for a minute it didn't come to me who it must be. Take the bags right upstairs, Isaphiny; and put them in the keeping-room chamber. How's your pa, Elsie,—and Katy? Not laid up again, I hope."

"Oh, no; she seems to get better all the time."

"That's right," responded Mrs. Worrett, heartily. "I didn't know but what, with hot weather, and company in the house, and all,—there's a chicken, Johnnie," she exclaimed, suddenly interrupting herself, as a long-legged hen ran past the door. "Want to chase it right away? You can, if you like. Or would you rather go upstairs first?"

"Upstairs, please," replied John, while Elsie went to the door, and watched Alexander driving away down the dusty road. She felt as if their last friend had deserted them. Then she and Johnnie followed Isaphiny upstairs. Mrs. Worrett never "mounted" in hot weather she told them.

The spare chamber was just under the roof. It was very hot, and smelt as if the windows had never been opened since the house was built. As soon as they were alone, Elsie ran across the room, and threw up the sash; but the moment she let go, it fell again with a crash which shook the floor and made the pitcher dance and rattle in the wash-bowl. The children were dreadfully frightened, especially when they heard Mrs. Worrett at the foot of the stairs calling to ask what was the matter.

"It's only the window," explained Elsie, going into the hall. "I'm so sorry; but it won't stay open. Something's the matter with it."

"Did you stick the nail in?" inquired Mrs. Worrett.

"The nail? No, ma'am."

"Why, how on earth did you expect it do stay up then? You young folks never see what's before your eyes. Look on the window-sill, and you'll find it. It's put there a purpose."

Elsie returned, much discomfited. She looked, and, sure enough, there was a big nail, and there was a hole in the side of the window-frame in which to stick it. This time she got the window open without accident; but a long blue paper shade caused her much embarrassment. It hung down, and kept the air from coming in. She saw no way of fastening it.

"Roll it up, and put in a pin," suggested John.

"I'm afraid of tearing the paper. Dear, what a horrid thing it is!" Replied Elsie in a disgusted tone.

However, she stuck in a couple of pins and fastened the shade out of the way. After that, they looked about the room. It was plainly furnished, but very nice and neat. The bureau was covered with a white towel, on which stood a pincushion, with "Remember Ruth" stuck upon it in pins. John admired this very much, and felt that she could never make up her mind to spoil the pattern by taking out a pin, however great her need of one might be.

"What a high bed!" she exclaimed. "Elsie, you'll have to climb on a chair to get into it; and so shall I."

Elsie felt of it. "Feathers!" she cried a tone of horror. "O John! why did we come? What shall we do?"

"I guess we shan't mind it much," replied John, who was perfectly well, and considered these little variations on home habits rather as fun than otherwise. But Elsie gave a groan. Two nights on a feather-bed! How should she bear it!

Tea was ready in the kitchen when they went downstairs. A small fire had been lighted to boil the water. It was almost out, but the room felt stiflingly warm, and the butter was so nearly melted that Mrs. Worrett had to help it with a tea-spoon. Buzzing flies hovered above the table, and gathered thick on the plate of cake. The bread was excellent, and so were the cottage cheeses and the stewed quinces; but Elsie could eat nothing. She was in a fever of heat. Mrs. Worrett was distressed at this want of appetite; and so was Mr. Worrett, to whom the children had just been introduced. He was a kindly-looking old man, with a bald head, who came to supper in his shirt-sleeves, and was a thin as his wife was fat.

"I'm afraid the little girl don't like her supper, Lucinda," he said. "You must see about getting her something different for to-morrow."

"Oh! it isn't that. Every thing is very nice, only, I'm not hungry," pleaded Elsie, feeling as if she should like to cry. She did cry a little after tea, as they sat in the dusk; Mr. Worrett smoking his pipe and slapping mosquitoes outside the door, and Mrs. Worrett sleeping rather noisily in a big rocking-chair. But not even Johnnie found out that she was crying; for Elsie felt that she was the naughtiest child in the world to behave so badly when everybody was so kind to her. She repeated this to herself many times, but it didn't do much good. As often as the thought of home and Katy and papa came, a wild longing to get back to them would rush over her, and her eyes would fill again with sudden tears.

The night was very uncomfortable. Not a breath of wind was stirring, or none found its way to the stifling bed where the little sisters lay. John slept pretty well, in spite of heat and mosquitoes, but Elsie hardly closed her eyes. Once she got up and went to the window, but the blue paper shade had become unfastened, and rattled down upon her head with a sudden bump, which startled her very much. She could find no pins in the dark, so she left it hanging; whereupon it rustled and flapped through the rest of the night, and did its share toward keeping her awake. About three o'clock she fell into a doze; and it seemed only a minute after that before she waked up to find bright sunshine in the room, and half a dozen roosters crowing and calling under the windows. Her head ached violently. She longed to stay in bed, but was afraid it would be thought impolite, so she dressed and went down with Johnnie; but she looked so pale and ate so little breakfast that Mrs. Worrett was quite troubled, and said she had better not try to go out, but just lie on the lounge in the best room, and amuse herself with a book.

The lounge in the best room was covered with slippery purple chintz. It was a high lounge and very narrow. There was nothing at the end to hold the pillow in its place; so the pillow constantly tumbled off and jerked Elsie's head suddenly backward, which was not at all comfortable. Worse,—Elsie having dropped into a doze, she herself tumbled to the floor, rolling from the glassy, smooth chintz as if it had been a slope of ice. This adventure made her so nervous that she dared not go to sleep again, though Johnnie fetched two chairs, and placed them beside the sofa to hold her on. So she followed Mrs. Worretts advice, and "amused herself with a book." There were not many books in the best room. The one Elsie chose was a fat black volume called "The Complete Works of Mrs. Hannah More." Part of it was prose, and part was poetry. Elsie began with a chapter called "Hints on the Formation of the Character of a Youthful Princess." But there were a great many long words in it; so she turned to a story named "Coelebs in Search of a Wife." It was about a young gentleman who wanted to get married, but who didn't feel sure that there were any young ladies nice enough for him; so he went about making visits, first to one and then to another; and, when he had stayed a few days at a house, he would always say, "No, she won't do," and then he would go away. At last, he found a young lady who seemed the very person, who visited the poor, and got up early in the morning, and always wore white, and never forgot to wind up her watch or do her duty; and Elsie almost thought that now the difficult young gentleman must be satisfied, and say, "This is the very thing." When, lo! her attention wandered a little, and the next thing she knew she was rolling off the lounge for the second time, in company with Mrs. Hannah More. They landed in the chairs, and Johnnie ran and picked them both up. Altogether, lying on the best parlor sofa was not very restful; and as the day went on, and the sun beating on the blindless windows made the room hotter, Elsie grew continually more and more feverish and homesick and disconsolate.

Meanwhile Johnnie was kept in occupation by Mrs. Worrett, who had got the idea firmly fixed in her mind, that the chief joy of a child's life was to chase chickens. Whenever a hen fluttered past the kitchen door, which was about once in three minutes, she would cry: "Here, Johnnie, here's another chicken for you to chase;" and poor Johnnie would feel obliged to dash out into the sun. Being a very polite little girl, she did not like to say to Mrs. Worrett that running in the heat was disagreeable: so by dinner-time she was thoroughly tired out, and would have been cross if she had known how; but she didn't— Johnnie was never cross. After dinner it was even worse; for the sun was hotter, and the chickens, who didn't mind sun, seemed to be walking all the time. "Hurry, Johnnie, here's another," came so constantly, that at last Elsie grew desperate, got up, and went to the kitchen with a languid appeal: "Please, Mrs. Worrett, won't you let Johnnie stay by me, because my head aches so hard?" After that, Johnnie had a rest; for Mrs. Worrett was the kindest of women, and had no idea that she was not amusing her little guest in the most delightful manner.

A little before six, Elsie's head felt better; and she and Johnnie put on their hats, and went for a walk in the garden. There was not much to see: beds of vegetables,—a few currant bushes,—that was all. Elsie was leaning against a paling, and trying to make out why the Worrett house had that queer tiptoe expression, when a sudden loud grunt startled her, and something touched the top of her head. She turned, and there was an enormous pig, standing on his hind legs, on the other side of the paling. He was taller than Elsie, as he stood thus, and it was his cold nose which had touched her head. Somehow, appearing in this unexpected way, he seemed to the children like some dreadful wild beast. They screamed with fright, and fled to the house, from which Elsie never ventured to stir again during their visit. John chased chickens at intervals, but it was a doubtful pleasure; and all the time she kept a wary eye on the distant pig.

That evening, while Mrs. Worrett slept and Mr. Worrett smoked outside the door, Elsie felt so very miserable that she broke down altogether. She put her head in Johnnie's lap, as they sat together in the darkest corner of the room, and sobbed and cried, making as little noise as she possibly could. Johnnie comforted her with soft pats and strokings; but did not dare to say a word, for fear Mrs. Worrett should wake up and find them out.

When the morning came, Elsie's one thought was, would Alexander come for them in the afternoon? All day she watched the clock and the road with feverish anxiety. Oh! if papa had changed his mind,—had decided to let them stay for a week at Conic Section,—what should she do? It was just possible to worry through and keep alive till afternoon, she thought; but if they were forced to spend another night in that feather-bed, with those mosquitoes, hearing the blue shad rattle and quiver hour after hour,—she should die, she was sure she should die!

But Elsie was not called upon to die, or even to discover how easy it is to survive a little discomfort. About five, her anxious watch was rewarded by the appearance of a cloud of dust, out of which presently emerged old Whitey's ears and the top of the well-known carryall. They stopped at the gate. There was Alexander, brisk and smiling, very glad to see his "little misses" again, and to find them so glad to go home. Mrs. Worrett, however, did not discover that they were glad; no indeed! Elsie and John were much too polite for that. They thanked the old lady, and said good-by so prettily that, after they were gone, she told Mr. Worrett that it hadn't been a bit of trouble having them there, and she hoped they would come again; they enjoyed every thing so much; only it was a pity that Elsie looked so peaked. And at that very moment Elsie was sitting on the floor of the carryall, with her head in John's lap, crying and sobbing for joy that the visit was over and that she was on the way home. "If only I live to get there," she said, "I'll never, no, never, go into the country again!" which was silly enough; but we must forgive her because she was half sick.

Ah, how charming home did look, with the family grouped in the shady porch, Katy in her white wrapper, Clover with rose-buds in her belt, and everybody ready to welcome and pet the little absentees! There was much hugging and kissing, and much to tell of what had happened in the two days: how a letter had come from Cousin Helen; how Daisy White had four kittens as white as herself; how Dorry had finished his water-wheel,—a wheel which turned in the bath-tub, and was "really ingenious," papa said; and Phil had "swapped" one of his bantam chicks for on of Eugene Slack's Bramapootras. It was not till they were all seated round the tea-table that anybody demanded an account of the visit. Elsie felt this a relief, and was just thinking how delicious every thing was, from the sliced peaches to the clinking ice in the milk-pitcher, when papa put the dreaded question,—

"Well, Elsie, so you decided to come, after all. How was it? Why didn't you stay your week out? You look pale, it seems to me. Have you been enjoying yourself too much? Tell us all about it."

Elsie looked at papa, and papa looked at Elsie. Dr. Carr's eyes twinkled just a little, but otherwise he was perfectly grave. Elsie began to speak, then to laugh, then to cry, and the explanation, when it came, was given in a mingled burst of all three.

"O papa, it was horrid! That is, Mrs. Worrett was just as kind as could be, but so fat; and oh, such a pig! I never imagined such a pig! And the calico on that horrid sofa was so slippery that I rolled off five times, and once I hurt myself real badly. And we had a feather-bed; and I was so homesick that I cried all the evening."

"That must have been gratifying to Mrs. Worrett," put in Dr. Carr.

"Oh! she didn't know it, papa. She was asleep, and snoring so that nobody could hear. And the flies!—such flies, Katy!—and the mosquitoes, and our window wouldn't open till I put in a nail. I am so glad to get home! I never want to go into the country again, never, never! Oh, if Alexander hadn't come!—why, Clover, what are you laughing for? And Dorry,—I think it's very unkind," and Elsie ran to Katy, hid her face, and began to cry.

"Never mind, darling, they didn't mean to be unkind. Papa, her hands are quite hot; you must give her something." Katy's voice shook a little; but she would not hurt Elsie's feeling by showing that she was amused. Papa gave Elsie "something" before she went to bed,— a very mild dose I fancy; for doctors' little girls, as a general rule, do not take medicine, and next day she was much better. As the adventures of the Conic Section visit leaked out bit by bit, the family laughed till it seemed as if they would never stop. Phil was forever enacting the pig, standing on his triumphant hind legs, and patting Elsie's head with his nose; and many and many a time, "It will end like your visit to Mrs. Worrett," proved a useful check when Elsie was in a self-willed mood and bent on some scheme which for the moment struck her as delightful. For one of the good things about our childish mistakes is, that each one teaches us something; and so, blundering on, we grow wiser, till, when the time comes, we are ready to take our places among the wonderful grown-up people who never make mistakes.

CHAPTER II. A NEW YEAR AND A NEW PLAN.

When summer lingers on into October, it often seems as if winter, anxious to catch a glimpse of her, hurries a little; and so people are cheated out of their autumn. It was so that year. Almost as soon as it ceased to be hot it began to be cold. The leaves, instead of drifting away in soft, dying colors, like sunset clouds, turned yellow all at once; and were whirled off the trees in a single gusty night, leaving every thing bare and desolate. Thanksgiving came; and before the smell of the turkey was fairly out of the house, it was time to hang up stockings and dress the Christmas tree. They had a tree that year in honor of Katy's being downstairs. Cecy, who had gone away to boarding-school, came home; and it was all delightful, except that the days flew too fast. Clover said it seemed to her very queer that there was so much less time than usual in the world. She couldn't imagine what had become of it: there used to be plenty. And she was certain that Dorry must have been tinkering all the clocks,—they struck so often.

It was just after New Year that Dr. Carr walked in one day with a letter in his hand, and remarked: "Mr. and Mrs. Page are coming to stay with us."

"Mr. and Mrs. Page," repeated Katy; "who are they, papa? Did I ever see them?"

"Once, when you were four years old, and Elsie a baby. Of chouse you don't remember it."

"But who are they, papa?"

"Mrs. Page was your dear mother's second cousin; and at one time she lived in your grandfather's family, and was like a sister to mamma and Uncle Charles. It is a good many years since I have seen her. Mr. Page is a railroad engineer. He is coming this way on business, and they will stop for a few days with us. Your Cousin Olivia writes that she is anxious to see all you children. Have every thing as nice as you can, Katy."

"Of course, I will. What day are the coming?"

"Thursday,—no, Friday," replied Dr. Carr, consulting the letter, "Friday evening, at half-past six. Order something substantial for tea that night, Katy. They'll be hungry after traveling."

Katy worked with a will for the next two days. Twenty times, at least, she went into the blue room to make sure that nothing was forgotten; repeating, as if it had been a lesson in geography: "Bath towels, face towels, matches, soap, candles, cologne, extra blanket, ink." A nice little fire was lighted in the bedroom on Friday afternoon, and a big, beautiful one in the parlor, which looked very pleasant with the lamp lit and Clover's geraniums and china roses in the window. The tea- table was set with the best linen and the pink-and-white china. Debby's muffins were very light. The crab-apple jelly came out of its mould clear and whole, and the cold chicken looked appetizing, with its green wreath of parsley. There was stewed potato, too, and, of course, oysters. Everybody in Burnet had oysters for tea when company was expected. They were counted a special treat; because they were rather dear, and could not always be procured. Burnet was a thousand miles from the sea, so the oysters were of the tin- can variety. The cans gave the oysters a curious taste,—tinny, or was it more like solder? At all events, Burnet people liked it, and always insisted that it was a striking improvement on the flavor which oysters have on their native shores. Every thing was as nice as could be, when Katy stood in the dining-room to take a last look at her arrangements; and she hoped papa would be pleased, and that mamma's cousin would think her a good housekeeper.

"I don't want to have on my other jacket," observed Phil, putting his head in at the door. "Need I? This is nice."

"Let me see," said Katy, gently turning him round. "Well, it does pretty well; but I think I'd rather you should put on the other, if you don't mind much. We want every thing as nice as possible, you know; because this is papa's company, and he hardly ever has any."

"Just one little sticky place isn't much," said Phil, rather gloomily, wetting his finger a rubbing at a shiny place on his sleeve. "Do you really thing I'd better? Well, then I will."

"That's a dear,"—kissing him. "Be quick, Philly, for it's almost time they were here. And please tell Dorry to make haste. It's ever so long since he went upstairs."

"Dorry's an awful prink," remarked Phil, confidentially. "He looks in the glass, and makes faces if he can't get his parting straight. I wouldn't care so much about my clothes for a good deal. It's like a girl. Jim Slack says a boy who shines his hair up like that, never'll get to be president, not if he lives a thousand years."

"Well," said Katy, laughing: "it's something to be clean, even if you can't be president." She was not at all alarmed by Dorry's recent reaction in favor of personal adornment. He came down pretty soon, very spick and span in his best suit, and asked her to fasten the blue ribbon under his collar, which she did most obligingly; though he was very particular as to the size of the bows and length of the ends, and made her tie and retie more than once. She had just arranged it to suit him when a carriage stopped.

"There they are," she cried. "Run and open the door, Dorry."

Dorry did so; and Katy, following, found papa ushering in a tall gentleman, and a lady who was not tall, but whose Roman nose and long neck, and general air of style and fashion, made her look so. Katy bent quite over to be kissed; but for all that she felt small and young and unformed, as the eyes of mamma's cousin looked her over and over, and through and through, and Mrs. Page said,—

"Why, Philip! is it possible that this tall girl is one of yours? Dear me! how time flies! I was thinking of the little creatures I saw when I was here last. And this other great creature can't be Elsie? That mite of a baby! Impossible! I cannot realize it. I really cannot realize it in the least."

"Won't you come to the fire, Mrs. Page?" said Katy, rather timidly.

"Don't call me Mrs. Page, my dear. Call me Cousin Olivia." Then the new-comer rustled into the parlor, where Johnnie and Phil were waiting to be introduced; and again she remarked that she "couldn't realize it." I don't know why Mrs. Page's not realizing it should have made Katy uncomfortable; but it did.

Supper went off well. The guests ate and praised; and Dr. Carr looked pleased, and said: "We think Katy an excellent housekeeper for her age;" at which Katy blushed and was delighted, till she caught Mrs. Page's eyes fixed upon her, with a look of scrutiny and amusement, whereupon she felt awkward and ill at ease. It was so all the evening. Mamma's cousin was entertaining and bright, and told lively stories; but the children felt that she was watching them, and passing judgment on their ways. Children are very quick to suspect when older people hold within themselves these little private courts of inquiry, and they always resent it.

Next morning Mrs. Page sat by while Katy washed the breakfast things, fed the birds, and did various odd jobs about the room and house. "My dear," she said at last, "what a solemn girl you are! I should think from your face that you were at least five and thirty. Don't you ever laugh or frolic, like other girls your age? Why, my Lilly, who is four months older than you, is a perfect child still; impulsive as a baby, bubbling over with fun from morning till night."

"I've been shut up a good deal," said Katy, trying to defend herself; "but I didn't know I was solemn."

"My dear, that's the very thing I complain of: you don't know it! You are altogether ahead of your age. It's very bad for you, in my opinion. All this housekeeping and care, for young girls like you and Clover, is wrong and unnatural. I don't like it; indeed I don't."

"Oh! housekeeping doesn't hurt me a bit," protested Katy, trying to smile. "We have lovely times; indeed we do, Cousin Olivia."

Cousin Olivia only pursed up her mouth, and repeated: "It's wrong, my dear. It's unnatural. It's not the thing for you. Depend upon it, it's not the thing."

This was unpleasant; but what was worse had Katy known it, Mrs. Page attacked Dr. Carr upon the subject. He was quite troubled to learn that she considered Katy grave and careworn, and unlike what girls of her age should be. Katy caught him looking at her with a puzzled expression.

"What is it, dear papa? Do you want anything?"

"No, child, nothing. What are you doing there? Mending the parlor curtain, eh? Can't old Mary attend to that, and give you a chance to frisk about with the other girls?"

"Papa! As if I wanted to frisk! I declare you're as bad as Cousin Olivia. She's always telling me that I ought to bubble over with mirth. I don't wish to bubble. I don't know how."

"I'm afraid you don't," said Dr. Carr, with an odd sigh, which set Katy to wondering. What should papa sigh for? Had she done any thing wrong? She began to rack her brains and memory as to whether it could be this or that; or, if not, what could it be? Such needless self-examination does no good. Katy looked more "solemn" than ever after it.

Altogether, Mrs. Page was not a favorite in the family. She had every intention of being kind to her cousin's children, "so dreadfully in want of a mother, poor things!" but she could not hide the fact that their ways puzzled and did not please her; and the children detected this, as children always will. She and Mr. Page were very polite. They praised the housekeeping, and the excellent order or every thing, and said there never were better children in the world than John and Dorry and Phil. But, through all, Katy perceived the hidden disapproval; and she couldn't help feeling glad when the visit ended, and they went away.

With their departure, matters went back to their old train, and Katy forgot her disagreeable feelings. Papa seemed a little grave and preoccupied; but the doctors often are when they have bad cases to think of, and nobody noticed it particularly, or remarked that several letters came from Mrs. Page, and nothing was heard of their contents, except that "Cousin Olivia sent her love." So it was a shock, when one day papa called Katy into the study to tell of a new plan. She knew at once that it was something important when she heard his voice: it sounded so grave. Beside, he said "My daughter," he began, "I want to talk to you about something which I have been thinking of. How would you and Clover like going away to school together?"

"To school? To Mrs. Knight's?"

"No, not to Mrs. Knight's. To a boarding-school at the East, where Lilly Page has been for two years. Didn't you hear Cousin Olivia speak of it when she was here?"

"I believe I did. But, papa, you won't really?"

"Yes, I think so," said Dr. Carr, gently. "Listen, Katy, and don't feel so badly, my dear child. I've thought the plan over carefully; and it seems to me a good one, though I hate to part from you. It is pretty much as your cousin says: these home-cares, which I can't take from you while you are at home, are making you old before your time. Heaven knows I don't want to turn you into a silly giggling miss; but I should like you to enjoy your youth while you have it, and not grow middle-aged before you are twenty."

"What is the name of the school?" asked Katy. Her voice sound a good deal like a sob.

"The girls call it 'The Nunnery.' It is at Hillsover, on the Connecticut River, pretty cold, I fancy; but the air is sure to be good and bracing. That is one thing which has inclined me to the plan. The climate is just what you need."

"Hillsover? Isn't there a college there too?"

"Yes: Arrowmouth College. I believe there is always a college where there is a boarding-school; though why, I can't for the life of me imagine. That's neither here nor there, however. I'm not afraid of your getting into silly scrapes, as girls sometimes do."

"College scrapes? Why, how could I. We don't have any thing to do with the college, do we?" said Katy, opening her candid eyes with such a wondering stare that Dr. Carr laughed and replied: "No, my dear, not a thing."

"The term opens the third week in April," he went on. "You must begin to get ready at once. Mrs. Hall has just fitted out Cecy: so she can tell you what you will need. You'd better consult her, to-morrow."

"But, papa," cried Katy, beginning to realize it, "what are *you* going to do? Elsie's a darling, but she's so very little. I don't see how you can possibly manage. I'm sure you'll miss us, and so will the children."

"I rather think we shall," said Dr. Carr, with a smile, which ended in a sigh; "but we shall do very well, Katy; never fear. Miss Finch will see to us."

"Miss Finch? Do you mean Mrs. Knight's sister-in-law?"

"Yes. Her mother died in the summer; so she has no particular home now, and is glad to come for a year and keep house for us. Mrs. Knight says she is a good manager; and I dare say she'll fill your place sufficiently well, as far as that goes. We can't expect her to be *you*, you know: that would be unreasonable." And Dr. Carr put his arm round Katy, and kissed her so fondly that she was quite overcome and clung to him, crying,—

"O papa! don't make us go. I'll frisk, and be as young as I can, and not grow middle-aged or any thing disagreeable, if only you'll let us stay. Never mind what Cousin Olivia says; she doesn't know. Cousin Helen wouldn't say so, I'm sure."

"On the contrary, Helen thinks well of the plan; only she wishes the school were nearer," said Dr. Carr. "No, Katy, don't coax. My mind is made up. It will do you and Clover both good, and once you are settled at Hillsover, you'll be very happy, I hope."

When papa spoke in this decided tone, it was never any use to urge him. Katy knew this, and ceased her pleadings. She went to find Clover and tell her the news, and the two girls had a hearty cry together. A sort of "clearing-up shower" it turned out to be; for when once they had wiped their eyes, every thing looked brighter, and they began to see a pleasant side to the plan.

"The travelling part of it will be very nice," pronounced Clover. "We never went so far away from home before."

Elsie, who was still looking very woeful, burst into tears afresh at this remark.

"Oh, don't darling!" said Katy. "Think how pleasant it will be to send letters, and to get them from us. I shall write to you every Saturday. Run for the big atlas,—there's a dear, and let us see where we are going."

Elsie brought the atlas; and the three heads bent eagerly over it, as Clover traced the route of the journey with her forefinger. How exciting it looked! There was the railroad, twisting and curving over half-a-dozen States. The black dots which followed it were towns and villages, all of which they should see. By and by the road made a bend, and swept northward by the side of the Connecticut River and toward the hills. They had heard how beautiful the Connecticut valley is.

"Only think! we shall be close to it," remarked Clover; "and we shall see the hills. I suppose they are very high, a great deal higher than the hill at Bolton."

"I hope so," laughed Dr. Carr, who came into the room just then. The hill at Bolton was one of his favorite jokes. When mamma first came to Burnet, she had paid a visit to some friends at Bolton, and one day, when they were all out walking, they asked her if she felt strong enough to go to the top of the hill. Mamma was used to hills, so she said yes, and walked on, very glad to find that there was a hill in that flat country, but wondering a little why they did not see it. At last she asked where it was, and, behold, they had just reached the top! The slope had been so gradual that she had never found out that they were going uphill at all. Dr. Carr had told this story to the children, but had never been able to make them see the joke very clearly. In fact, when Clover went to Bolton, she was quite struck with the hill: it was so much higher than the sand-bank which bordered the lake at Burnet.

There was a great deal to do to make the girls ready for school by the third week in April. Mrs. Hall was very kind, and her advice was sensible; though, except for Dr. Carr, the girls would hardly have had furs and flannels enough for so cold a place as Hillsover. Every thing for winter as well as for summer had to be thought of; for it had been arranged that the girls should not come home for the autumn vacation, but should spend it with Mrs. Page. This was the hardest thing about the plan. Katy begged very hard for Christmas; but when she learned that it would take three days to come and three days to go, and that the holidays lasted less than a week, she saw it was of no use, and gave up the idea, while Elsie tried to comfort herself by planning a Christmas-box. The preparations kept them so busy that there was no time for any thing else. Mrs. Hall was always wanting them to go with her to shops, or Miss Petingill demanding that they should try on linings, and so the days flew by. At last all was ready. The nice half-dozens of pretty underclothes came home from the sewing-machine woman's, and were done up by Bridget, who dropped many a tear into the bluing water, at the thought of the young ladies going away. Mrs. Hall, who was a good packer, put the things into the new trunks. Everybody gave the girls presents, as if they had been brides starting on a wedding journey.

Papa's was a watch for each. They were not new, but the girls thought them beautiful. Katy's had belonged to her mother. It was large and old-fashioned, with a finely wrought case. Clover's, which had been her grandmother's, was larger still. It had a quaint ornament on the back,— a sort of true-love knot, done in gold of different tints. The girls were excessively pleased with these watches. They wore them with guard-chains of black watered ribbon, and every other minute they looked to see what the time was.

Elsie had been in papa's confidence, so her presents were watch cases, embroidered on perforated paper. Johnnie gave Katy a case of pencils, and Clover a pen-knife with a pearl handle. Dorry and Phil clubbed to buy a box of note-paper and envelopes, which the girls were requested to divide between them. Miss Petingill contributed a bottle of ginger balsam, and a box of opodeldoc salve, to be used in case of possible chilblains. Old Mary's offering was a couple of needle-books, full of bright sharp needles.

"I wouldn't give you scissors," she said; "but you can't cut love—or, for the matter of that, any thing else—with a needle."

Miss Finch, the new housekeeper, arrived a few days before they started: so Katy had time to take her over the house and explain all the different things she wanted done and not done, to secure papa's comfort and the children's. Miss Finch was meek and gentle. She seemed glad of a comfortable home. And Katy felt that she would be kind to the boys, and not fret Debby, and drive her into marrying Alexander and going away,—an event which Aunt Izzie had been used to predict. Now that all was settled, she and Clover found themselves looking forward to the change with pleasure. There was something new and interesting about it which excited their imaginations.

The last evening was a melancholy one. Elsie had been too much absorbed in the preparations to realize her loss; but, when it came to locking the trunks, her courage gave way altogether. She was in such a state of affliction that everybody else became afflicted too; and there is no knowing what would have happened, had not a parcel arrived by express and distracted their attention. The parcel was from Cousin Helen, whose things, like herself, had a knack of coming at the moment when most wanted. It contained two pretty silk umbrellas—one brown, and one dark-green, with Katy's initials on one handle and Clover's on the other. Opening these treasures, and exclaiming over them, helped the family through the evening wonderfully; and next morning there was such a bustle of getting off that nobody had time to cry.

After the last kisses had been given, and Philly, who had climbed on the horse-block, was clamoring for "one more,—just one more," Dr. Carr, looking at the sober faces, was struck by a bright idea, and, calling Alexander, told him to hurry old Whitey into the carryall, and drive the children down to Willett's Point, that they might wave there handkerchiefs to the boat as she went by. This suggestion worked like a charm on the spirits of the party. Phil began to caper, and Elsie and John ran in to get their hats. Half an hour later, when the boat rounded the point, there stood the little crew, radiant with smiles, fluttering the handkerchiefs and kissing their hands as cheerfully as possible. It was a pleasant last look to the two who stood beside papa on the deck; and, as they waved back their greetings to the little ones, and then looked forward across the blue water to the unknown places they were going to see, Katy and Clover felt that the new life opened well, and promised to be very interesting indeed.

CHAPTER III. ON THE WAY.

The journey from Burnet to Hillsover was a very long one. It took the greater part of three days, and as Dr. Carr was in a hurry to get back to his patients, they travelled without stopping; spending the first night on the boat, and the second on a railroad train. Papa found this tiresome; but the girls, to whom every thing was new, thought it delightful. They enjoyed their state-room, with its narrow shelves of beds, as much as if it had been a baby house, and they two children playing in it. To tuck themselves away for the night in a car-section seemed the greatest fun in the world. When older people fretted, they laughed. Every thing was interesting, from the telegraph poles by the wayside to the faces of their fellow-passengers. It amused them to watch people, and make up stories about them,—where they were going, and what relation they could be to each other. The strange people, in their turn, cast curious glances toward the bright, happy-faced sisters; but Katy and Clover did not mind that, or, in fact, notice it. They were too much absorbed to think of themselves, or the impression they were making on others.

It was early on the third morning that the train, puffing and shrieking, ran into the Springfield depot. Other trains stood waiting; and there was such a chorus of snorts and whistles, and such clouds of smoke, that Katy was half frightened. Papa, who was half asleep, jumped up, and told the girls to collect their bags and books; for they were to breakfast here, and to meet Lilly Page, who was going on to Hillsover with them.

"Do you suppose she is here already?" asked Katy, tucking the railway guide into the shawl-strap, and closing her bag with a snap.

"Yes: we shall meet her at the Massasoit. She and her father were to pass the night there."

The Massasoit was close at hand, and in less then five minutes the girls and papa were seated at a table in its pleasant dining-room. They were ordering their breakfast, when Mr. Page came in, accompanied by his daughter,—a pretty girl, with light hair, delicate, rather sharp features, and her mother's stylish ease of manner. Her travelling dress was simple, but had the finish which a French dressmaker knows how to give to a simple thing; and all its appointments—boots, hat, gloves, collar, neck ribbon—were so perfect, each in its way, that Clover, glancing down at her own gray alpaca, and then at Katy's, felt suddenly countrified and shabby.

"Well, Lilly, here they are: here are your cousins," said Mr. Page, giving the girls a cordial greeting. Lilly only said, "How do you do?" Clover saw her glancing at the gray alpacas, and was conscious of a sudden flush. But perhaps Lilly looked at something inside the alpaca; for after a minute her manner changed, and became more friendly.

"Did you order waffles?" she asked.

"Waffles? no, I think not," replied Katy.

"Oh! why not? Don't you know how celebrated they are for waffles at this hotel? I thought everybody knew *that*." Then she tinkled her fork against her glass, and, when the waiter came, said, "Waffles, please," with an air which impressed Clover extremely. Lilly seemed to her like a young lady in a story,—so elegant and self-possessed. She wondered if all the girls at Hillsover were going to be like her?

The waffles came, crisp and hot, with delicious maple syrup to eat on them; and the party made a satisfactory breakfast. Lilly, in spite of all her elegance, displayed a wonderful appetite. "You see," she explained to Clover, "I don't expect to have another decent thing to eat till next September,—not a thing; so I'm making the most of this." Accordingly she disposed of nine waffles, in quick succession, before she found time to utter any thing farther, except "Butter, please," or, "May I trouble you for the molasses?" As she swallowed the last morsel, Dr. Carr, looking at his watch, said that it was time to start for the train; and they set off. As they crossed the street, Katy was surprised to see that Lilly, who had seemed quite happy only a minute before, had begun to cry. After they reached the car, her tears increased to sobs: she grew almost hysterical.

"Oh! don't make me go, papa," she implored, clinging to her father's arm. "I shall be so homesick! It will kill me; I know it will. Please let me stay. Please let me go home with you."

"Now, my darling," protested Mr. Page, "this is foolish; you know it is."

"I can't help it," blubbered Lilly. "I ca—n't help it. Oh! don't make me go. Don't, papa dear. I ca—n't bear it."

Katy and Clover felt embarrassed during this scene. They had always been used to considering tears as things to be rather ashamed of,— to be kept back, if possible; or, if not, shed in private corners, in dark closets, or behind the bed in the nursery. To see the stylish Lilly crying like a baby in the midst of a railway carriage, with strangers looking on, quite shocked them. It did not last long, however. The whistle sounded; the conductor shouted, "All aboard!" and Mr. Page, giving Lilly a last kiss, disengaged her clinging arms, put her into the seat beside Clover, and hurried out of the car. Lilly sobbed loudly for a few seconds; then she dried her eyes, lifted her head, adjusted her veil and the wrists of her three- buttoned gloves, and remarked,—

"I always go on in this way. Ma says I am a real cry-baby; and I suppose I am. I don't see how people can be calm and composed when they're leaving home, do you? You'll be just as bad to-morrow, when you come to say good-by to your papa."

"Oh! I hope not," said Katy. "Because papa would feel so badly."

Lilly stared. "I shall think you real cold-hearted if you don't," she said, in an offended tone.

Katy took no notice of the tone; and before long Lilly recovered from her pettishness, and began to talk about the school. Katy and Clover asked eager questions. They were eager to hear all that Lily could tell.

"You'll adore Mrs. Florence," she said. "All the girls do. She's the most fascinating woman! She does just what she likes with everybody. Why, even the students think her perfectly splendid, and yet she's just as strict as she can be."

"Strict with the students?" asked Clover, looking puzzled.

"No; strict with us girls. She never lets any one call, unless it's a brother or a first cousin; and then you have to have a letter from you parents, asking permission. I wanted ma to write and say that George Hickman might call on me. He isn't a first cousin exactly, but his father married pa's sister-in-law's sister. So it's just as good. But ma was real mean about it. She says I'm too young to have gentlemen coming to see me! I can't think why. Ever so many girls have them, who are younger than I."

"Which Row are you going to room in?" she went on.

"I don't know. Nobody told us that there were any rows."

"Oh, yes! Shaker Row and Quaker Row and Attic Row. Attic Row is the

nicest, because it's highest up, and furthest away from Mrs. Florence. My room is in Attic Row. Annie Silsbie and I engaged it last term. You'll be in Quaker Row, I guess. Most of the new girls are."

"Is that a nice row?" asked Clover, greatly interested.

"Pretty nice. It isn't so good as Attic, but it's ever so much better than Shaker; Because there you're close to Mrs. Florence, and can't have a bit of fun without her hearing you. I'd try to get the end room, if I were you. Mary Andrews and I had it once. There is a splendid view of Berry Searles's window."

"Berry Searles?"

"Yes; President Searles, you know; his youngest son. He's an elegant fellow. All the girls are cracked about him,—perfectly cracked! The president's house is next door to the Nunnery, you know; and Berry rooms at the very end of the back building, just opposite Quaker Row. It used to be such fun! He'd sit at his window, and we'd sit at ours, in silent study hour, you know; and he'd pretend to read, and all the time keep looking over the top of his book at us, and trying to make us laugh. Once Mary did laugh right out; and Miss Jane heard her, and came in. But Berry is just as quick as a flash, and he ducked down under the window-sill; so she didn't see him. It was such fun!"

"Who's Miss Jane?" asked Katy.

"The horridest old thing. She's Mrs. Florence's niece, and engaged to a missionary. Mrs. Florence keeps her on purpose to spy us girls, and report when we break the rules. Oh, those rules! Just wait till you come to read 'em over. They're nailed up on all the doors,— thirty-two of them, and you can't help breaking 'em if you try ever so much."

"What are they? what sort of rules?" cried Katy and Clover in a breath.

"Oh! about being punctual to prayers, and turning you mattress, and smoothing over the under-sheet before you leave your room, and never speaking a word in the hall, or in private study hour, and hanging your towel on your own nail in the wash-room, and all that."

"Wash-room? what *do* you mean?" said Katy, aghast.

"At the head of Quaker Row, you know. All the girls wash there, except on Saturdays when they go to the bath-house. You have your own bowl and soap-dish, and a hook for you towel. Why, what's the matter? How big your eyes are!"

"I never heard any thing so horrid!" cried Katy, when she had recovered her breath. "Do you really mean that girls don't have wash-stands in their own rooms?"

"You'll get used to it. All the girls do," responded Lilly.

"I don't want to get used to it," said Katy, resolving to appeal to papa; but papa had gone into the smoking-car, and she had to wait. Meantime Lilly went on talking.

"If you have that end room in Quaker Row, you'll see all the fun that goes on at commencement time. Mrs. Searles always has a big party, and you can look right in, and watch the people and the supper-table, just as if you were there. Last summer, Berry and Alpheus Seccomb got a lot of cakes and mottoes from the table and came out into the yard, and threw them up one by one to Rose Red and her room-mate. They didn't have the end room, though; but the one next to it."

"What a funny name!—Rose Red," said Clover.

"Oh! her real name is Rosamond Redding; but the girls call her Rose Red. She's the greatest witch in the school; not exactly pretty, you know, but sort of killing and fascinating. She's always getting into the most awful scrapes. Mrs. Florence would had expelled her long ago, if she hadn't been such a favorite; and Mr. Redding's daughter, beside. He's a member of Congress, you know, and all that; and Mrs. Florence is quite proud of having Rose in her school.

"Berry Searles is so funny!" she continued. "His mother is a horrid old thing, and always interfering with him. Sometimes when he has a party of fellows in his room, and they're playing cards, we can see her coming with her candle through the house; and when she gets to his door, she tries it, and then she knocks, and calls out, 'Abernathy, my son!' And the fellows whip the cards into their pockets, and stick the bottles under the table, and get out their books and dictionaries like a flash; and when Berry unlocks the door, there they sit, studying away; and Mrs. Searles looks so disappointed! I thought I should die one night, Mary Andrews and I laughed so."

I verily believe that if Dr. Carr had been present at this conversation, he would have stopped at the next station, and taken the girls back to Burnet. But he did not return from the smoking-car till the anecdotes about Berry were finished, and Lilly had begun again on Mrs. Florence.

"She's a sort of queen, you know. Everybody minds her. She's tall, and always dresses beautifully. Her eyes are lovely; but, when she gets angry, they're perfectly awful. Rose Red says she'd rather face a mad bull any day than Mrs. Florence in a fury; and Rose ought to know, for she's had more reprimands than any girl in school."

"How many girls are there?" inquired Dr. Carr.

"There were forty-eight last term. I don't know how many there'll be this, for they say Mrs. Florence is going to give up. It's she who makes the school so popular."

All this time the train was moving northward. With every mile the country grew prettier. Spring had not fairly opened; but the grass was green, and the buds on the tress gave a tender mist-like color to the woods. The road followed the river, which here and there turned upon itself in long links and windings. Ranges of blue hills closed the distance. Now and then a nearer mountain rose, single and alone, from the plain. The air was cool, and full of brilliant zest, which the Western girls had never before tasted. Katy felt as if she were drinking champagne. She and Clover flew from window to window, exclaiming with such delight that Lilly was surprised.

"I can't see what there is to make such a fuss about," she remarked. "That's only Deerfield. It's quite a small place."

"But how pretty it looks, nestled in among the hills! Hills are lovely, Clover, aren't they?"

"These hills are nothing. You should see the White Mountains," said the experienced Lilly. "Ma and I spent three weeks at the Profile House last vacation. It was perfectly elegant."

In the course of the afternoon, Katy drew papa away to a distant seat, and confided her distress about the wash-stands.

"Don't you think it is horrid, papa? Aunt Izzie always said that it isn't lady-like not to take a sponge-bath every morning; but how can we, with forty-eight girls in the room? I don't see what we are going to do."

"I fancy we can arrange it; don't be distressed, my dear," replied Dr. Carr. And Katy was satisfied; for when papa undertook to arrange things, they were very apt to be done.

It was almost evening when they reached their final stopping place.

"Now, two miles in the stage, and then we're at the horrid old Nunnery," said Lilly. "Ugh! look at that snow. It never melts here till long after it's all gone at home. How I do hate this station! I'm going to be awfully homesick: I know I am."

But just then she caught sight of the stagecoach, which stood waiting; and her mood changed, for the stage was full of girls who had come by the other train.

"Hurrah! there's Mary Edwards and Mary Silver," she exclaimed; "and I declare, Rose Red! O you precious darling! how do you do?" Scrambling up the steps, who plunged at a girl with waving hair, and a rosy, mischievous face; and began kissing her with effusion.

Rose Red did not seem equally enchanted.

"Well, Lilly, how are you?" she said, and then went on talking to a girl who sat by her side, and whose hand she held; while Lilly rushed up and down the line, embracing and being embraced. She did not introduce Katy and Clover; and, as papa was outside, on the driver's box, they felt a little lonely, and strange. All the rest were chattering merrily, and were evidently well acquainted: they were the only ones left out.

Clover watched Rose Red, to whose face she had taken a fancy. It made her think of a pink carnation, or of a twinkling wild rose, with saucy whiskers of brown calyx. Whatever she said or did seemed full of a flavor especially her own. Here eyes, which were blue, and not very large, sparkled with fun and mischief. Her cheeks were round and soft, like a baby's; when she laughed, two dimples broke their pink, and, and made you want to laugh too. A cunning white throat supported this pretty head, as a stem supports a flower; and, altogether, she was like a flower, except that flowers don't talk, and she talked all the time. What she said seemed droll, for the girls about here were in fits of laughter; but Clover only caught a word now and then, the stage made such a noise.

Suddenly Rose Red leaned forward, and touched Clover's hand.

"What's your name?" she said. "You've got eyes like my sister's. Are you coming to the Nunnery?"

"Yes," replied Clover, smiling back. "My name is Clover,—Clover Carr."

"What a dear little name! It sounds just as you look!"

"So does your name,—Rose Red," said Clover, shyly.

"It's a ridiculous name," protested Rose Red, trying to pout. Just then the stage stopped.

"Why? Who's going to the hotel?" cried the school-girls, in a chorus.

"I am," said Dr. Carr, putting his head in at the door, with a smile which captivated every girl there. "Come, Katy; come, Clover. I've decided that you sha'n't begin school till to-morrow."

"Oh, my! Don't I wish he was my pa!" cried Rose Red. Then the stage moved on.

"Who are they? What's their name?" asked the girls. "They look nice."

"They're sort of cousins of mine, and they come from the West," replied Lilly, not unwilling to own the relationship, now that she perceived that Dr. Carr had made a favorable impression.

"Why on earth didn't you introduce them, then? I declare that was just like you, Lilly Page," put in Rose Red, indignantly. "They looked so lonesome that I wanted to pat and stroke both of 'em. That little one has the sweetest eyes!"

Meantime Katy and Clover entered the hotel, very glad of the reprieve, and of one more quiet evening alone with papa. They needed to get their ideas straightened out and put to rights, after the confusions of the day and Lilly's extraordinary talk. It was very evident that the Nunnery was to be quite different from their expectations; but another thing was equally evident,—it would not be dull! Rose Red by herself, and without any one to help her, would be enough to prevent that!

CHAPTER IV. THE NUNNERY.

The night seemed short; for the girls, tired by their journey, slept like dormice. About seven o'clock, Katy was roused by the click of a blind, and, opening her eyes, saw Clover standing in the window, and peeping out through the half-opened shutters. When she heard Katy move, she cried out,—

"Oh, do come! It's so interesting! I can see the colleges and the church, and, I guess, the Nunnery; only I am not quite sure, because the houses are all so much alike."

Katy jumped up and hurried to the window. The hotel stood on one side of a green common, planted with trees. The common had a lead-colored fence, and gravel paths, which ran across it from corner to corner. Opposite the hotel was a long row of red buildings, broken by one or two brown ones, with cupolas. These were evidently the colleges, and a large gray building with a spire was as evidently the church; but which one of the many white, green-blinded house which filled the other sides of the common, was the Nunnery, the girls could not tell. Clover thought it was one with a garden at the side; but Katy thought not, because Lilly had said nothing of a garden. They discussed the point so long that the breakfast bell took them by surprise, and they were forced to rush through their dressing as fast as possible, so as not to keep papa waiting.

When breakfast was over, Dr. Carr told them to put on their hats, and get ready to walk with him to the school. Clover took one arm, and Katy the other, and the three passed between some lead-colored posts, and took one of the diagonal paths which led across the common.

"That's the house," said Dr. Carr, pointing.

"It isn't the one you picked out, Clover," said Katy.

"No," replied Clover, a little disappointed. The house papa indicated was by no means so pleasant as the one she had chosen.

It was a tall, narrow building, with dormer windows in the roof, and a square porch supported by whitewashed pillars. A pile of trunks stood in the porch. From above came sounds of voices. Girls' heads were popped out of upper widows at the swinging of the gate, and, as the door opened, more heads appeared looking over the balusters from the hall above.

The parlor into which they were taken was full of heavy, old-fashioned furniture, stiffly arranged. The sofa and chairs were covered with black haircloth, and stood closely against the wall. Some books lay upon the table, arranged two by two; each upper book being exactly at a right angle with each lower book. A bunch of dried grasses stood in the fire-place. There were no pictures, except one portrait in oils, of a forbidding old gentleman in a wig and glasses, sitting with his finger majestically inserted in a half-open Bible. Altogether, it was not a cheerful room, nor one calculated to raise the spirits of new-comers; and Katy, whose long seclusion had made her sensitive on the subject of rooms, shrank instinctively nearer papa as they went in.

Two ladies rose to receive them. One, a tall dignified person, was Mrs. Florence. The other she introduced as "my assistant principal, Mrs. Nipson." Mrs. Nipson was not tall. She had a round face, pinched lips, and half-shut gray eyes.

"This lady is fully associated with me in the management of the school," explained Mrs. Florence. "When I go, she will assume entire control."

"Is that likely to be soon?" inquired Dr. Carr, surprised, and not well pleased that the teacher of whom he had heard, and with whom he had proposed to leave his children, was planning to yield her place to a stranger.

"The time is not yet determined," replied Mrs. Florence. Then she changed the subject, gracefully, but so decidedly that Dr. Carr had no chance for further question. She spoke of classes, and discussed what Katy and Clover were to study. Finally, she proposed to take them upstairs to see their room. Papa might come too, she said.

"I dare say that Lilly Page, who tells me that she is a cousin of yours, has described the arrangements of the house," she remarked to Katy. "The room I have assigned to you is in the back building. 'Quaker Row,' the girls call it." She smiled as she spoke; and Katy, meeting her eyes for the fist time, felt that there was something in what Lilly had said. Mrs. Florence *was* a sort of queen.

They went upstairs. Some girls who were peeping over the baluster hurried away at their approach. Mrs. Florence shook her head at them.

"The first day is always one of license," she said, leading the way along an uncarpeted entry to a door at the end, from which, by a couple of steps, they went down into a square room; round three sides of which, ran a shelf, on which stood rows of wash-bowls and pitchers. Above were hooks for towels. Katy perceived that this was the much-dreaded wash-room.

"Our lavatory," remarked Mrs. Florence blandly.

Opening from the wash-room was a very long hall, lighted at each end by a window. The doors on either side were numbered "one, two, three," and so on. Some of them were half open; as they went by, Katy and Clover caught glimpses of girls and trunks, and beds strewed with things. At No. 6 Mrs. Florence paused.

"Here is the room which I propose to give you," she said.

Katy and Clover looked eagerly about. It was a small room, but the sun shone in cheerfully at the window. There was a maple bedstead and table, a couple of chairs, and a row of hooks; that was all, except that in the wall was set a case of black-handled drawers, with cupboard-doors above them.

"These take the place of a bureau, and hold your clothes," explained Mrs. Florence, pulling out one of the drawers. "I hope, when once you are settled, you will find yourselves comfortable. The rooms are small; but young people do not require so much space as older ones. Though, indeed, your elder daughter, Dr. Carr, looks more advanced and grown-up that I was prepared to find her. What did you say was her age?"

"She is past sixteen; but she has been so long confined to her room by the illness of which I wrote, that you may probably find her behind in some respects, which reminds me" (this was very adroit of papa!) "I am anxious that she should keep up the system to which she has been accustomed at home,—among other things, sponge-baths of cold water every morning; and, as I see that the bedrooms are not furnished with wash-stands, I will ask your permission to provide one for the use of my little girls. Perhaps you will kindly tell me where I would look for it?"

Mrs. Florence was not pleased, but she could not object; so she mentioned a shop. Katy's heart gave a bound of relief. She thought No. 6, with a wash-stand, might be very comfortable. Its bareness and simplicity had the charm of novelty. Then there was something very interesting to her in the idea of a whole house full of girls.

They did not stay long, after seeing the room, but went off on a shopping excursion. Shops were few and far between at Hillsover; but they found a neat little maple wash-stand and rocking-chair, and papa also bought a comfortable low chair, with a slatted back and a cushion. This was for Katy.

"Never study till your back aches," he told her: "when you are tired, lie flat on the bed for half an hour, and tell Mrs. Florence that it was by my direction."

"Or Mrs. Nipson," said Katy, laughing rather ruefully. She had taken no fancy to Mrs. Nipson, and did not enjoy the idea of a divided authority.

A hurried lunch at the hotel followed, and then it was time for Dr. Carr to go away. They all walked to the school together, and said good-by upon the steps. The girls would not cry, but they clung very tightly to papa, and put as much feeling into their last kisses as would have furnished forth half a dozen fits of tears. Lilly might have thought them cold-hearted, but papa did not; he knew better.

"That's my brave girls!" he said. Then he kissed them once more, and hurried away. Perhaps he did not wish them to see that his eyes too were a little misty.

As the door closed behind them, Katy and Clover realized that they were alone among strangers. The sensation was not pleasant; and they felt forlorn, as they went upstairs, and down Quaker Row, toward No. 6.

"Aha! so you're going to be next door," said a gay voice, as they passed No. 5, and Rose Red popped her head into the hall. "Well, I'm glad," she went on, shaking hands cordially; "I sort of thought you would, and yet I didn't know; and there are some awful stiffies among the new girls. How do you both do?"

"Oh! are we next door to you?" cried Clover, brightening.

"Yes. It's rather good of me not to hate you; for I wanted the end room myself, and Mrs. Florence wouldn't give it to me. Come in, and let me introduce you to my room-mate. It's against the rules, but that's no matter: nobody pretends to keep rules the first day."

They went in. No.5 was precisely like No. 6, in shape, size and furniture; but Rose had unpacked her trunk, and decorated the room with odds and ends of all sorts. The table was covered with books and boxes; colored lithographs were pinned on the walls; a huge blue rosette ornamented the head-board of the bed; the blinds were tied together with pink ribbon; over the top of the window was a festoon of hemlock boughs, fresh and spicy. The effect was fantastic, but cheery; and Katy and Clover exclaimed, with one voice, "How pretty!"

The room-mate was a pale, shy girl, with a half-scared look in her eyes, and small hands which twisted uneasily together when she moved and spoke. Her name was Mary Silver. She and Rose were so utterly unlike, that Katy thought it odd they should have chosen to be together. Afterward she understood it better. Rose liked to protect, and Mary to be protected; Rose to talk, and Mary to listen. Mary evidently considered Rose the most entertaining creature in the world; she giggled violently at all her jokes, and then stopped short and covered her mouth with her fingers, in a frightened way, as if giggling were wrong.

"Only think, Mary," began Rose, after introducing Katy and Clover, "these young ladies have got the end room. What do you suppose was the reason that Mrs. Florence did not give it to us? It's very peculiar."

Mary laughed her uneasy laugh. She looked as if she could tell the reason, but did not dare.

"Never mind," continued Rose. "Trials are good for one, they say. It's something to have nice people in the room, if we can't be there ourselves. You are nice, aren't you?" turning to Clover.

"Very," replied Clover, laughing.

"I thought so. I can almost always tell without asking; still, it is something to have it on the best authority. We'll be good neighbors, won't we? Look here!" and she pulled one of the black-handled drawers completely out and laid it on the bed. "Do you see? your drawers are exactly behind ours. At any time in silent study hour, if I have something I want to say, I'll rap and pop a note into your drawer, and you can do the same to me. Isn't it fun?"

Clover said, "Yes;" but Katy, though she laughed, shook her head. "Don't entice us into mischief," she said.

"Oh, gracious!" exclaimed Rose. "Now, are you going to be good,—you two? If you are, just break the news at once, and have it over. I can bear it." She fanned herself in such a comical way that no one could help laughing. Mary Silver joined, but stopped pretty soon in her sudden manner.

"There's Mary, now," went on Rose: "she's a Paragon. But, if any more are coming into the entry, just give me fair notice, and I pack and move up among the sinners in Attic Row. Somehow, you don't look like Paragons either,—you especially," nodding to Clover. "Your eyes are like violets; but so are Sylvia's—that's my sister,—and she's the greatest witch in Massachusetts. Eyes are dreadfully deceitful things. As for you,"—to Katy,—"you're so tall that I can't take you in all at once; but the piece I see doesn't look dreadful a bit."

Rose was sitting in the window as she made these remarks; and, leaning forward suddenly, she gave a pretty, blushing nod to some one below. Katy glanced down, and saw a handsome young man replacing the cap he had lifted from his head.

"That's Berry Searles," said Rose. "He's the president's son, you know. He always comes through the side yard to get to his room. That's it,—the one with the red curtain. It's exactly opposite your window: don't you see?"

"So it is!" exclaimed Katy, remembering what Lilly had said. "Oh! was that the reason?"—she stopped, afraid of being rude.

"The reason we wanted the room?" inquired Rose, coolly. "Well, I don't know. It hadn't occurred to me to look at it in that light. Mary!" with sudden severity, "is it possible that you had Berry Searles in your mind when you were so pertinacious about that room?"

"Rose! How can you? You know I never thought of such a thing," protested poor Mary.

"I hope not; otherwise I should feel it my duty to consult with Mrs. Florence on the subject," went on Rose, with an air of dignified admonition. "I consider myself responsible for you and your morals, Mary. Let us change this painful subject." She looked gravely at the three girls for a moment; then her lips began to twitch, the irresistible dimples appeared in her cheeks, and, throwing herself back in her chair, she burst into a fit of laughter.

"O Mary, you blessed goose! Some day or other you'll be the death of me! Dear, dear! how I am behaving! It's perfectly horrid of me. And I didn't mean it. I'm going to be real good this term; I promised mother. Please forget it, and don't take a dislike to me, and never come again," she added, coaxingly, as Katy and Clover rose to go.

"Indeed we won't," replied Katy. As for sensible Clover, she was already desperately in love with Rose, on that very first day!

After a couple of hours of hard work, No. 6 was in order, and looked like a different place. Fringed towels were laid over the wash-stand and the table. Dr. Carr's photograph and some pretty chromos ornamented the walls; the rocking-chair and the study-chair stood by the window; the trunks were hidden by chintz covers, made for the purpose by old Mary. On the window-sill stood Cousin Helen's vase, which Katy had brought carefully packed among her clothes.

"Now," she said, tying the blinds together with a knot of ribbon in imitation of Rose Red's, "when we get a bunch of wild flowers for my vase, we shall be all right."

A tap at the door. Rose entered.

"Are you done?" she asked; "may I come in and see?"

"Oh, this is pretty!" she exclaimed, looking about: "how you can tell in one minute what sort of a girl one is, just by looking at her room! I should know you had been neat and dainty and housekeepery all your days. And you would see in a minute that I'm a Madge Wildfire, and that Ellen Gray is a saint, and Sally Satterlee a scatterbrain, and Lilly Page an affected little hum— oh, I forgot, she is your cousin, isn't she? How dreadfully rude of me!" dimpling at Clover, who couldn't help dimpling back again.

"Oh, my!" she went on, "a wash-stand, I declare! Where did you get it?"

"Papa bought it," explained Katy: "he asked Mrs. Florence's permission."

"How bright of him! I shall just write to my father to ask for permission too." Which she did; and the result was that it set the fashion of wash-stands, and so many papas wrote to "ask permission," that Mrs. Florence found it necessary to give up the lavatory system, and provide wash-stands for the whole house. Katy's request had been the opening wedge. I do not think this fact made her more popular with the principals.

"By the way, where is Lilly?" asked Katy; "I haven't seen her to-day."

"Do you want to know? I can tell you. She's sitting on the edge of one chair, with her feet on the rung of another chair, and her head on the shoulder of her room-mate (who is dying to get away and arrange her drawers); and she's crying"—

"How do you know? Have you been up to see her?"

"Oh! I haven't seen her. It isn't necessary. I saw her last term, and the term before. She always spends the first day at school in that way. I'll take you up, if you'd like to examine for yourselves."

Katy and Clover, much amused, followed as she led the way upstairs. Sure enough, Lilly was sitting exactly as Rose had predicted. Her face was swollen from crying. When she saw the girls, her sobs redoubled.

"Oh! isn't it dreadful?" she demanded. "I shall die, I know I shall. Oh! why did pa make me come?"

"Now, Lilly, don't be an idiot," said the unsympathizing Rose. Then she sat down and proceeded to make a series of the most grotesque faces, winking her eyes and twinkling her fingers round the head of "Niobe," as she called Lilly, till the other girls were in fits of laughter, and Niobe, though she shrugged her shoulders pettishly and said, "Don't be so ridiculous, Rose Red," was forced to give way. First she smiled, then a laugh was heard; afterward she announced that she felt better.

"That's right, Niobe," said Rose. "Wash your face now, and get ready for tea, for the bell is just going to ring. As for you, Annie, you might as well put your drawers in order," with a wicked wink. Annie hurried away with a laugh, which she tried in vain to hide.

"You heartless creature!" cried the exasperated Lilly. "I believe you're made of marble; you haven't one bit of feeling. Nor you either, Katy. You haven't cried a drop."

"Given this problem," said the provoking Rose: "when the nose without is as red as a lobster, what must be the temperature of the heart within, and *vice versa?*"

The tea-bell rang just in time to avert a fresh flood of tears from Lilly. She brushed her hair in angry haste, and they all hurried down by a side staircase which, as Rose explained, the school-girls were expected to use. The dining-room was not large; only part of the girls could be seated at a time; so they took turns at dining at the first table, half one week and half the next.

Mrs. Nipson sat at the tea-tray, with Mrs. Florence beside her. At the other end of the long board sat a severe-looking person, whom Lilly announced in a whisper as "that horrid Miss Jane." The meal was very simple,—tea, bread and butter, and dried beef:—it was eaten in silence; the girls were not allowed to speak, except to ask for what they wanted. Rose Red indeed, who sat next to Mrs. Florence, talked to her, and even ventured once or twice on daring little jokes, which caused Clover to regard her with admiring astonishment. No one else said any thing, except "Butter, please," or "Pass the bread." As they filed upstairs after this cheerless meal, they were met by rows of hungry girls, who were waiting to go down, and who whispered, "How long you have been! What's for tea?"

The evening passed in making up classes and arranging for recitation-rooms and study-hours. Katy was glad when bed-time came. The day, with all its new impressions and strange faces, seemed to her like a confused dream. She and Clover undressed very quietly. Among the printed rules, which hung on the bedroom door, they read: "All communication between room-mates, after the retiring bell has rung, is strictly prohibited." Just then it did not seem difficult to keep this rule. It was only after the candle was blown out, that Clover ventured to whisper,—very low indeed, for who knew but Miss Jane was listening outside the door?—"Do you think you're going to like it?" and Katy, in the same cautious whisper, responded, "I'm not quite sure." And so ended the first day at the nunnery.

CHAPTER V. ROSES AND THORNS.

"Oh! what is it? What has happened?" cried Clover, starting up in bed, the next morning, as a clanging sound roused her suddenly from sleep. It was only the rising-bell, ringing at the end of Quaker Row.

Katy held her watch up to the dim light. She could just see the hands. Yes: they pointed to six. It was actually morning! She and Clover jumped up, and began to dress as fast as possible.

"We've only got half an hour," said Clover, unhooking the rules, and carrying them to the window,—"Half an hour; and this says that we must turn the mattress, smooth the under-sheet over the bolster, and spend five minutes in silent devotion! We'll have to be quick to do all that besides dressing ourselves!"

It is never easy to be quick, when one is in a hurry. Every thing sets itself against you. Fingers turn into thumbs; dresses won't button, nor pins keep their place. With all their haste, Katy and Clover were barely ready when the second bell sounded. As they hastened downstairs, Katy fastening her breast-pin, and Clover her cuffs, they met other girls, some looking half asleep, some half dressed; all yawning, rubbing their eyes, and complaining of the early hour.

"Isn't it horrid?" said Lilly Page, hurrying by with no collar on, and her hair hastily tucked into a net. "I never get up till nine o'clock when I'm at home. Ma saves my breakfast for me. She says I shall have my sleep out while I have the chance."

"You don't look quite awake now," remarked Clover.

"No, because I haven't washed my face. Half the time I don't, before breakfast. There's that old mattress has to be turned; and, when I sleep over, I just do that first, and then scramble my clothes on the best way I can. Any thing not to be marked!"

After prayers and breakfast were done, the girls had half an hour for putting their bedrooms to rights, during which interval it is to be hoped that Lilly found time to wash her face. After that, lessons began, and lasted till one o'clock. Dinner followed, with an hour's "recreation;" then the bell rang for "silent study hour," when the girls sat with their books in their bedrooms, but were not allowed to speak to each other. Next came a walk.

"Who are you going to walk with?" asked Rose Red, meeting Clover in
Quaker Row.

"I don't know. Katy, I guess."

"Are you really? You and she like each other, don't you? Do you know you're the first sisters I ever knew at school who did! Generally, they quarrel awfully. The Stearns girls, who were here last term, scarcely spoke to each other. They didn't even room together; and

Sarah Stearns was always telling tales against Sue, and Sue against Sara."

"How disgusting! I never heard of any thing so mean," cried Clover, indignantly. "Why, I wouldn't tell tales about Katy if we quarrelled ever so much. We never do, though, Katy is so sweet."

"I suppose she is," said Rose, rather doubtfully; "but, do you know, I'm sort of afraid of her. It's because she's so tall. Tall people always scare me. And then she looks so grave and grown up! Don't tell her I said so, though; for I want her to like me."

"Oh, she isn't a bit grave or grown up. She's the funniest girl in the world. Wait till you know her," replied loyal Clover.

"I'd give any thing if I could walk with you part of this term," went on Rose, putting her arm round Clover's waist. "But you see, unluckily, I'm engaged straight through. All of us old girls are. I walk with May Mather this week and next, then Esther Dearborn for a month, then Lilly Page for two weeks, and all the rest of the time with Mary. I can't think why I promised Lilly. I'm sure I don't want to go with her. I'd ask Mary to let me off, only I'm afraid she'd feel bad. I say, suppose we engage now to walk with each other for the first half of next term!"

"Why, that's not till October!" said Clover

"I know it; but it's nice to be beforehand. Will you?"

"Of course I will; provided that Katy has somebody pleasant to go with," replied Clover, immensely flattered at being asked by the popular Rose. Then they ran downstairs, and took their places in the long procession of girls, who were ranged two and two, ready to start. Miss Jane walked at the head; and Miss Marsh, another teacher, brought up the rear. Rose Red whispered that it was like a funeral and a caravan mixed,—"as cheerful as hearses at both ends, and wild beasts in the middle."

The walk was along a wooded road; a mile out and a mile back. The procession was not permitted to stop or straggle, or take any of the liberties which make walking pleasant. Still, Katy and Clover enjoyed it. There was a spring smell in the air, and the woods were beginning to be pretty. They even found a little trailing aributis blossoming in a sunny hollow. Lilly was just in front of them, and amused them with histories of different girls, whom she pointed out in the long line. That was Esther Dearborn,—Rose Red's friend. Handsome, wasn't she? but awfully sarcastic. The two next were Amy Alsop and Ellen Gray. They always walked together, because they were so intimate. Yes; they were nice enough, only so distressingly good. Amy did not get one single mark last term! That child with pig-tails was Bella Arkwright. Why on earth did Katy want to know her? She was a nasty little thing.

"She's just about Elsie's height," replied Katy. "Who's that pretty girl with pink velvet on her hat?"

"Dear me! Do you think she's pretty? I don't. Her name is Louisa Agnew. She lives at Ashburn,—quite near us; but we don't know them. Her family are not at all in good society."

"What a pity! She looks sweet and lady-like."

Lilly tossed her head. "They're quite common people," she said. "They live in a little mite of a house, and her father paints portraits."

"But I should think that would be nice. Doesn't she ever take you to see his pictures?"

"Take me!" cried Lilly, indignantly. "I should think not. I tell you we don't visit. I just speak when we're here, but I never see her when I'm at home."

"Move on, young ladies. What are you stopping for?" cried Miss Jane.

"Yes; move on," muttered Rose Red, from behind. "Don't you hear Policeman X?"

From walking-hour till tea-time was "recreation" again. Lilly improved this opportunity to call at No. 6. She had waited to see how the girls were likely to take in the school before committing herself to intimacy; but, now that Rose Red had declared in their favor, she was ready to begin to be friendly.

"How lovely!" she said, looking about. "You got the end room, after all, didn't you? What splendid times you'll have! Oh, how plainly you can see Berry Searles's window! Has he spoken to you yet?"

"Spoken to us,—of course not! Why should he?" replied Katy: "he doesn't know us, and we don't know him."

"That's nothing: half the girls in the school bow, and speak, and carry on with young men they don't know. You won't have a bit of fun if you're so particular."

"I don't want that kind of fun," replied Katy, with energy in her voice; "neither does Clover. And I can't imagine how the girls can behave so. It isn't lady-like at all."

Katy was very fond of this word, lady-like. She always laid great stress upon it. It seemed in some way to be connected with Cousin Helen, and to mean every thing that was good, and graceful, and sweet.

"Dear me! I'd no idea you were so dreadfully proper," said Lilly, pouting. "Mother said you were as prim and precise as your grandmother; but I didn't suppose"—

"How unkind!" broke in Clover, taking fire, as usual, at any affront to Katy. "Katy prim and precise! She isn't a bit! She's twice as much fun as the rest of you girls; but it's nice fun,—not this horrid stuff about students. I wish your mother wouldn't say such things!"

"I didn't—she didn't—I don't mean exactly that," stammered Lilly, frightened by Clover's indignant eyes. "All I meant was, that Katy is dreadfully dignified for her age, and we bad girls will have to look out. You needn't be so mad, Clover; I'm sure it's very nice to be proper and good, and set an example."

"I don't want to preach to anybody," said Katy, coloring, "and I wasn't thinking about examples. But really and truly, Lilly, wouldn't your mother, and all the girls' mothers, be shocked if they knew about these performances here?"

"Gracious! I should think so; ma would kill me. I wouldn't have her know of my goings on for all the world."

Just then Rose pulled out a drawer, and called through to ask if Clover would please come in and help her a minute. Lilly took advantage of her absence to say,—

"I came on purpose to ask you to walk with me for four weeks. Will you?"

"Thank you; but I'm engaged to Clover."

"To Clover! But she's your sister; you can get off."

"I don't want to get off. Clover and I like dearly to go together."

Lilly stared. "Well, I never heard of such a thing," she said, "you're really romantic. The girls will call you 'The Inseparables.'"

"I wouldn't mind being inseparable from Clover," said Katy, laughing.

Next day was Saturday. It was nominally a holiday; but so many tasks were set for it, that it hardly seemed like one. The girls had to practise in the gymnasium, to do their mending, and have all drawers in apple-pie order, before afternoon, when Miss Jane went through the rooms on a tour of inspection. Saturday, also, was the day for writing home letters; so, altogether, it was about the busiest of the week.

Early in the morning Miss Jane appeared in Quaker Row with some slips of paper in her hand, one of which she left at each door. They told the hours at which the girls were to go to the bath-house.

"You will carry, each, a crash towel, a sponge, and soap," she announced to Katy, "and will be in the entry, at the foot of the stairs, at twenty-five minutes after nine precisely. Failures in punctuality will be punished by a mark." Miss Jane always delivered her words like a machine, and closed her mouth with a snap at the end of the sentence.

"Horrid thing! Don't I wish her missionary would come and carry her off. Not that I blame him for staying away," remarked Rose Red, from her door; making a face at Miss Jane, as she walked down the entry.

"I don't understand about the bath-house," said Katy. "Does it belong to us? And where is it?"

"No, it doesn't belong to us. It belongs to Mr. Perrit, and anybody can use it; only on Saturday it is reserved for us nuns. Haven't you every noticed it when we have been out walking? It's in that street by the bakery, which we pass to take the Lebanon road. We go across the green, and down by Professor Seccomb's, and we are in plain sight from the college all the way; and, of course, those abominable boys sit there with spy-glasses, and stare as hard as ever they can. It's perfectly horrid. 'A crash towel, a sponge, and soap,' indeed! I wish I could make Miss Jane eat the pieces of soap which she has forced me to carry across this village."

"O Rose!" remonstrated Mary Silver.

"Well, I do. And the crash towels afterward, by way of a dessert," replied the incorrigible Rose. "Never mind! Just wait! A bright idea strikes me!"

"Oh! what?" cried the other three; but Rose only pursed up her mouth, arched he eye-brows, and vanished into her own room, locking the door behind her. Mary Silver, finding herself shut out, sat down meekly in the hall till such time as it should please Rose to open the door. This was not till the bath hour. As Katy and Clover went by, Rose put her head out, and called that she would be down in a minute.

The bathing party consisted of eight girls, with Miss Jane for escort. They were half way across the common before Miss Jane noticed that everybody was shaking with stifled laughter, except Rose, who walked along demurely, apparently unconscious that there was any thing to laugh at. Miss Jane looked sharply from one to another for a moment, then stopped short and exclaimed, "Rosamond Redding! how dare you?"

"What is it ma'am?" asked Rose, with the face of a lamb.

"Your bath towel! your sponge!" gasped Miss Jane.

"Yes, ma'am, I have them all," replied the audacious Rose, putting her hand to her hat. There, to be sure, was the long crash towel, hanging down behind like a veil, while the sponge was fastened on one side like a great cockade; and in front appeared a cake of pink soap, neatly pinned into the middle of a black velvet bow.

Miss Jane seized Rose, and removed these ornaments in a twinkling. "We shall see what Mrs. Florence thinks of this conduct," she grimly remarked. Then, dropping the soap and sponge in her own pocket, she made Rose walk beside her, as if she were a criminal in custody.

The bath-house was a neat place, with eight small rooms, well supplied with hot and cold water. Katy would have found her bath very nice, had it not been for the thought of the walk home. They must look so absurd, she reflected, with their sponges and damp towels.

Miss Jane was as good as her word. After dinner, Rose was sent for by Mrs. Florence, and had an interview of two hours with her: she came out with red eyes, and shut herself into her room with a disconsolate bang. Before long, however, she revived sufficiently to tap on the drawers and push through a note with the following words:—
"My heart is broken!
"R.R."

Clover hastened in to comfort her. Rose was sitting on the floor, with a very clean pocket-handkerchief in her hand. She wept, and put her head against Clover's knee.

"I suppose I'm the nastiest girl in the world," she said. "Mrs. Florence thinks so. She said I was an evil influence in the school. Wasn't that un—kind?" with a little sob.

"I meant to be so good this term," she went on; "but what's the use? A codfish might as well try to play the piano! It was always so, even when I was a baby. Sylvia says I have got a little fiend inside of me. Do you believe I have? Is it that makes me so horrid?"

Clover purred over her. She could not bear to have Rose feel badly. "Wasn't Miss Jane funny?" went on Rose, with a sudden twinkle; "and did you see Berry, and Alfred Seccomb?"

"No: where were they?"

"Close to us, standing by the fence. All the time Miss Jane was unpinning the towel, they were splitting their sides, and Berry made such a face at me that I nearly laughed out. That boy has a perfect genius for faces. He used to frighten Sylvia and me into fits, when we were little tots, up here on visits."

"Then you knew him before you came to school?"

"Oh dear, yes! I know all the Hillsover boys. We used to make mud pies together. They're grown up now, most of 'em, and in college; and when we meet, we're very dignified, and say, 'Miss Redding,' and 'Mr. Seccomb,' and 'Mr. Searles;' but we're just as good friends as ever. When I go to take tea with Mrs. Seccomb, Alfred always invites Berry to drop in, and we have the greatest fun. Mrs. Florence won't let me go this term, though, I guess, she's so mad about the towel."

Katy was quite relieved when Clover reported this conversation. Rose, for all her wickedness, seemed to be a little lady. Katy did not like to class her among the girls who flirted with students whom they did not know.

It was wonderful how soon they all settled down, and became accustomed to their new life. Before six weeks were over, Katy and Clover felt as if they had lived at Hillsover for years. This was partly because there was so much to do. Nothing makes time fly like having every moment filled, and every hour set apart for a distinct employment.

They made several friends, chief among whom were Ellen Gray and Louisa Agnew. This last intimacy Lilly resented highly, and seemed to consider as an affront to herself. With no one, however, was Katy so intimate as Clover was with Rose Red. This cost Katy some jealous pangs at first. She was so used to considering Clover her own exclusive property that it was not easy to share her with another; and she had occasional fits of feeling resentful, and injured, and left out. These were but momentary, however. Katy was too healthy of mind to let unkind feelings grow, and by and by she grew fond of Rose and Rose of her, so that in the end the sisters share their friend as they did other nice things, and neither of them was jealous of the other.

But, charming as she was, a certain price had to be paid for the pleasure of intimacy with Rose. Her overflowing spirits, and "the little fiend inside her," were always provoking scrapes, in which her friends were apt to be more or less involved. She was very pen intent and afflicted after these scrapes; but it didn't make a bit of difference: the next time she was just as naughty as ever.

"What are you?" said Katy, one day, meeting her in the hall with a heap of black shawls and aprons on her arm.

"Hush!" whispered Rose, mysteriously, "don't say a word. Senator Brown is dead—our senator, you know. I'm going to put my window into mourning for him, that's all. It's a proper token of respect."

Two hours later, Mrs. Nipson, walking sedately across the common, noticed quite a group of students, in the president's yard, looking up at the Nunnery. She drew nearer. They were admiring Rose's window, hung with black, and decorated with a photograph of the deceased senator, suspended in the middle of a wreath of weeping- willow. Of course she hurried upstairs, and tore down the shawls and aprons; and, equally of course, Rose had a lecture and a mark; but, dear me! what good did it do? The next day but one, as Katy and Clover sat together in silent study hour, their lower drawer was pushed open very noiselessly and gently, till it came out entirely, and lay on the floor, and in the aperture thus formed appeared Roses's saucy face flushed with mischief. She was crawling through from her own room!

"Such fun!" she whispered; "I never thought of this before! We can have parties in study hours, and all sorts of things."

"Oh, go back, Rosy!" whispered Clover in agonized entreaty, though laughing all the time.

"Go back? Not at all! I'm coming in," answered Rose, pulling herself through a little farther. But at that moment the door opened: there stood

Miss Jane! She had caught the buzz of voices, as she passed in the hall, and had entered to see what was going on.

Rose, dreadfully frightened, made a rapid movement to withdraw. But the space was narrow, and she had wedged herself, and could move neither backward nor forward. She had to submit to being helped through by Miss Jane, in a series of pulls, while Katy and Clover sat by, not daring to laugh or to offer assistance. When Rose was on her feet, Miss Jane released her with a final shake, which she seemed unable to refrain from giving.

"Go to your room," she said; "I shall report all of you young ladies for this flagrant act of disobedience."

Rose went, and in two minutes the drawer, which Miss Jane had replaced, opened again, and there was this note:—

"If I'm never heard of more, give my love to my family, and mention how I died. I forgive my enemies; and leave Clover my band bracelet.

"My blessings on you both.

"With the deepest regard,

"Your afflicted friend, R. R."

Mrs. Florence was very angry on this occasion, and would listen to no explanations, but gave Katy and Clover a "disobedience mark" also. This was very unfair, and Rose felt dreadfully about it. She begged and entreated; but Mrs. Florence only replied: "There is blame on both sides, I have no doubt."

"She's entirely changed from what she used to be," declared Rose. "I don't know what's the matter; I don't like her half so much as I did."

The truth was, that Mrs. Florence had secretly determined to give up her connection with the school at midsummer; and, regarding it now rather as Mrs. Nipson's school than her own, she took no pains to study character or mete out justice carefully among scholars with whom she was not likely to have much to do.

CHAPTER VI. THE S. S. U. C.

It was Saturday afternoon; and Clover, having finished her practising, dusting, and mending, had settle herself in No. 6 for a couple of hours of quiet enjoyment. Every thing was in beautiful order to meet Miss Jane's inspecting eye; and Clover, as she sat in the rocking chair, writing-case in lap, looked extremely cosy and comfortable.

A half-finished letter to Elsie lay in the writing-case; but Clover felt lazy, and instead of writing was looking out of window in a dreamy way, to where Berry Searles and some other young men were playing ball in the yard below. She was not thinking of them or of any thing else in particular. A vague sense of pleasant idleness possessed her, and it was like the breaking of a dream when the door opened and Katy came in, not quietly after her wont, but with a certain haste and indignant rustle as if vexed by something. When she saw Clover at the window, she cried out hastily, "O Clover, don't'!"

"Don't what?" asked Clover, without turning her head.

"Don't sit there looking at those boys."

"Why? why not? They can't see me. The blinds are shut."

"No matter for that. It's just as bad as if they could see you. Don't do it. I can't bear to have you."

"Well, I won't then," said Clover good-humoredly, facing round with her back to the window. "I wasn't looking at them either,—not exactly. I was thinking about Elsie and John, and wondering—But what's the matter, Katy? What makes you fire up so about it? You've watched the ball-playing yourself plenty of times."

"I know I have, and I didn't mean to be cross, Clovy. The truth is I am all put out. These girls with incessant talk about the students make me absolutely sick. It is so unladylike, and so bad, especially for the little ones. Fancy that mite of a Carrie Steele informing me that she is "in love" with Harry Crosby. In love! A baby like that! She has no business to know that there is such a thing."

"Yes," said Clover laughing: "she wrote his name on a wintergreen lozenge, and bored a hole and hung it round her neck on a blue ribbon. But it melted and stuck to her frock, and she had to take it off."

"Whereupon she ate it," added Rose, who came in at that moment.

The girls shouted, but Katy soon grew grave. "One can't help laughing," she said, "but isn't it a shame to have such things going on? Just fancy our Elsie behaving so, Clover! Why, papa would have a fit. I declare, I've a great mind to get up a society to put down flirting."

"Do!" said Rose. "What fun it would be! Call it 'The Society for the Suppression of Young Men.' I'll join."

"You, indeed!" replied Katy, shaking her head. "Didn't I see Berry Searles throw a bunch of syringa into your window only this morning?"

"Dear me! did he? I shall have to speak to Mary again. It's quite shocking to have her go on so. But really and truly do let us have a Society. It would be so jolly. We could meet on Saturday afternoons, and write pieces and have signals and a secret, as Sylvia's Society did when she was at school. Get one up, Katy,— that's a dear."

"But," said Katy, taken aback by having her random idea so suddenly adopted, "if I did get one up, it would be in real earnest, and it would be a society against flirting. And you know you can't help it, Rosy."

"Yes, I can. You are doing me great injustice. I don't behave like those girls in Attic Row. I never did. I just bow to Berry and the rest whom I really know,—never to anybody else. And you must see, Katherine darling, that it would be the height of ingratitude if I didn't bow to the boys who made mud pies for me when I was little, and lent me their marbles, and did all sorts of kind things. Now wouldn't it?"— coaxingly.

"Per—haps," admitted Katy, with a smile. "But you're such a witch!"

"I'm not,—indeed I'm not. I'll be a pillar of society if only you'll provide a Society for me to be a pillar of. Now, Katy, do—ah, do, do!"

When Rose was in a coaxing mood, few people could resist her. Katy yielded, and between jest and earnest the matter was settled. Katy was to head the plan and invite the members.

"Only a few at first," suggested Rose. "When it is proved to be a success, and everybody wants to join, we can let in two or three more as a great favor. What shall the name be? We'll keep it a secret, whatever it is. There's no fun in a society without a secret."

What should the name be? Rose invented half a dozen, each more absurd than the last. "The Anti-Jane Society" would sound well, she insisted. Or, no!—the "Put-him-down-Club" was better yet! Finally they settled upon "The Society for the Suppression of Unladylike Conduct."

"Only we'll never use the whole name," said Rose: "We'll say, 'The S. S .U. C.' That sounds brisk and snappy, and will drive the whole school wild with curiosity. What larks! How I long to begin!"

The next Saturday was fixed upon for the first meeting. During the week Katy proposed the plan to the elect few, all of whom accepted enthusiastically. Lilly Page was the only person who declined. She said it would be stupid; that for her part she didn't set up to be "proper" or better than she was, and that in any case she shouldn't wish to be mixed up in a Society of which "Miss Agnew" was a member. The girls did not break their hearts over this refusal. They had felt obliged to ask her for relationship's sake, but everybody was a little relieved that she did not wish to join.

No. 6 looked very full indeed that Saturday afternoon when the S. S. U. C. came together for the first time. Ten members were present. Mary Silver and Louisa were two; and Rose's crony, Esther Dearborn, another. The remaining four were Sally Alsop and Amy Erskine; Alice Gibbons, one of the new scholars, whom they all liked, but did not know very well; and Ellen Gray, a pale, quiet girl, with droll blue eyes, a comical twist to her mouth, and a trick of saying funny things in such a demure way that half the people who listened never found out that they were funny. All Rose's chairs had been borrowed for the occasion. Three girls sat on the bed, and three on the floor. With a little squeezing, there was plenty of room for everybody.

Katy was chosen President, and requested to take the rocking-chair as a sign of office. This she did with much dignity, and proceeded to read the Constitution and By-Laws of the Society, which had been drawn up by Rose Red, and copied on an immense sheet of blue paper.

They ran thus:—

CONSTITUTION FOR THE SOCIETY FOR THE SUPPRESSION OF UNLADYLIKE CONDUCT, KNOWN TO THE UNINITIATED AS THE S. S. U. C.

ARTICLE I.

>The object of this Society is twofold: it combines having a good time with the Pursuit of VIRTUE.

ARTICLE II.

>The good time is to take place once a week in No. 6 Quaker Row, between the hours of four and six P. M.

ARTICLE III.

>The nature of the good time is to be decided upon by a Committee to be appointed each Saturday by the members of the Society.

ARTICLE IV.

>VIRTUE is to be pursued at all times and in all seasons, by the members of the Society setting their faces against the practice of bowing and speaking to young gentlemen who are not acquaintances; waving of pocket handkerchiefs, signals from windows, and any species of conduct which would be thought unladylike by nice people anywhere, and especially by the mammas of the Society.

ARTICLE V.

>The members of the Society pledge themselves to use their influence against these practices, both by precept and example.

In witness whereof we sign.

Katherine Carr, President.
Rosamond Redding, Secretary.
Clover E. Carr.
Mary L. Silver.
Esther Dearborn.
Sally P. Alsop.
Amy W. Erskine.
Alice Gibbons.
Ellen Whitworth Gray.

Next followed the By-Laws. Katy had not been able to see the necessity of having any By-Laws, but Rose had insisted. She had never heard of a Society without them, she said, and she didn't think it would be "legal" to leave them out. It had cost her some trouble to invent them, but at last they stood thus:—

BY-LAW NO. 1.

The members of the S. S. U. C. will observe the following signals:—

1st. The Grip.—This is given by inserting the first and middle finger of the right hand between the thumb and fourth finger of the respondent's left, and describing a rotatory motion in the air with the little finger. N. B. Much practice is necessary to enable members to exchange this signal in such a manner as not to attract attention.

2nd. The Signal of Danger.—This signal is for use when Miss Jane, or any other foe-woman, heaves into sight. It consists in rubbing the nose violently, and at the same time giving three stamps on the floor with the left foot. It must be done with an air of unconsciousness.

3rd. The Signal for Consultation.—This signal is for use when immediate communication is requisite between members of the Society. It consists of a pinch on the back of the right hand, accompanied by the word "Holofernes" pronounced in a low voice.

BY-LAW NO. 2.

The members of the S. S. U. C. pledge themselves to inviolable secrecy about all Society proceedings.

BY-LAW NO. 3

The members of the S. S. U. C. will bring their Saturday corn-balls to swell the common entertainment.

BY-LAW NO. 4.

Members having boxes from home are at liberty to contribute such part of the contents as they please to the aforementioned common entertainment.

Here the By-Laws ended. There was much laughter over them, especially over the last.

"Why did you put that in, Rosy?" asked Ellen Gray: "it strikes me as hardly necessary."

"Oh," replied Rose, "I put that in to encourage Silvery Mary there. She's expecting a box soon, and I knew that she would pine to give the Society a share, but would be too timid to propose it; so I thought I would just pave the way."

"How truly kind!" laughed Clover.

"Now," said the President, "the entertainment of the meeting will begin by the reading of 'Trailing Arbutus,' a poem by C. E. C."

Clover had been very unwilling to read the first piece, and had only yielded after much coaxing from Rose, who had bestowed upon her in consequence the name of Quintia Curtia. She felt very shy as she stood up with her paper in hand, and her voice trembled perceptibly; but after a minute she grew used to the sound of it, and read steadily.

TRAILING ARBUTUS.

> I always think, when looking
> At its mingled rose and white,
> Of the pink lips of children
> Put up to say good-night.
> Cuddled its green leaves under,
> Like babies in their beds,
> Its blossoms shy and sunny
> Conceal their pretty heads.
> And when I lift the blanket up,
> And peep inside of it,
> They seem to give me smile for smile,
> Nor be afraid a bit.
> Dear little flower, the earliest
> Of all the flowers that are;
> Twinkling upon the bare, brown earth,
> As on the clouds a star.
> How can we fail to love it well,
> Or prize it more and more!
> It is the first small signal
> That winter time is o'er;
> That spring has not forgotten us,
> Though late and slow she be,
> But is upon her flying way,
> And we her face shall see.

This production caused quite a sensation among the girls. They had never heard any of Clover's verses before, and thought these wonderful.

"Why!" cried Sally Alsop, "it is almost as good as Tupper!" Sally meant this for a great compliment, for she was devoted to the "Proverbial Philosophy."

"A Poem by E.D." was the next thing on the list. Esther Dearborn rose with great pomp and dignity, cleared her throat, put on a pair of eye-glasses, and began.

MISS JANE.

> Who ran to catch me on the spot,
> If I the slightest rule forgot,
> Believing and excusing not?
> > Miss Jane.
>
> Who lurked outside my door all day
> In hopes that I would disobey,
> And some low whispered word would say?
> > Miss Jane.
>
> Who caught our Rose-bud half way through
> The wall which parted her from two
> Friends, and that small prank made her rue?
> > Miss Jane.
>
> Who is our bane, our foe, our fear?
> Who's always certain to appear
> Just when we do not think her near?
> > Miss Jane.

—"Who down the hall is creeping now
With stealthy step, but knowing not how
Exactly to discover"—

broke in Rose, improvising rapidly. Next moment came a knock at the door. It was Miss Jane.

"Your drawers, Miss Carr,—your cupboard,"—she said, going across the room and examining each in turn. There was no fault to be found with either, so she withdrew, giving the laughing girls a suspicious glance, and remarking that it was a bad habit to sit on beds,—it always injured them.

"Do you suppose she heard?" whispered Mary Silver.

"No, I don't think she did," replied Rose. "Of course she suspected us of being in some mischief or other,—she always does that. Now, Mary, it's you turn to give us an intellectual treat. Begin."

Poor Mary shrank back, blushing and protesting.

"You know I can't," she said, "I'm too stupid."

"Rubbish!" cried Rose, "You're the dearest girl that ever was." She gave Mary's shoulder a reassuring pat.

"Mary is excused this time," put in Katy. "It is the first meeting, so I shall be indulgent. But, after this, every member will be expected to contribute something for each meeting. I mean to be very strict."

"Oh, I never, never can!" cried Mary. Rose was down on her at once. "Nonsense! hush!" she said. "Of course you can. You shall, if I have to write it for you myself!"

"Order!" said the President, rapping on the table with a pencil. "Rose has something to read us."

Rose stood up with great gravity. "I would ask for a moment's delay, that the Society may get out its pocket-handkerchiefs," she said. "My piece is an affecting one. I didn't mean it, but it came so. We cannot always be cheerful." Here she heaved a sigh, which set the S. S. U. C. to laughing, and began.

A SCOTCH POEM.

    Wee, crimson-tippet Willie Wink,
      Wae's me, drear, dree, and dra,
    A waeful thocht, a fearsome flea,
      A wuther wind, and a'.
    Sair, sair thy mither sabs her lane,
      Her een, her mou, are wat;
    Her cauld kail hae the corbies ta'en,
      And grievously she grat.
    Ah, me, the suthering of the wind!
    Ah, me, the waesom mither!
    Ah, me the bairnies left ahind,
      The shither, hither, blither!

"What *does* it mean?" cried the girls, as Rose folded up the paper and sat down.

"Mean?" said Rose, "I'm sure I don't know. It's Scotch, I tell you! It's the kind of thing that people read, and then they say, 'One of the loveliest gems that Burns ever wrote!' I thought I'd see if I couldn't do one too. Anybody can, I find: it's not at all difficult."

All the poems having been read, Katy now proposed that they should play "Word and Question." She and Clover were accustomed to the game at home, but to some of the others it was quite new.

Each girl was furnished with a slip of paper and a pencil, and was told to write a word at the top of the paper, fold it over, and pass it to her next left-hand neighbor.

"Dear me! I don't know what to write," said Mary Silver.

"Oh, write any thing," said Clover. So Mary obediently wrote "Any thing," and folded it over.

"What next?" asked Alice Gibbons.

"Now a question," said Katy. "Write it under the word, and fold over again. No, Amy, not *on* the fold. Don't you see, if you do, the writing will be on the wrong side of the paper when we come to read?"

The questions were more troublesome than the words, and the girls sat frowning and biting their pencil-tops for some minutes before all were done. As the slips were handed in, Katy dropped them into the lid of her work-basket, and thoroughly mixed and stirred them up.

"Now," she said, passing it about, "each draw one, read, and write a rhyme in which the word is introduced and the question answered. It needn't be more than two lines, unless you like. Here, Rose, it's your turn first."

"Oh, what a hard game!" cried some of the girls; but pretty soon they grew interested, and began to work over their verses.

"I should uncommonly like to know who wrote this abominable word," said Rose, in a tone of despair. "Clover, you rascal, I believe it was you."

Clover peeped over her shoulder, nodded, and laughed.

"Very well then!" snatching up Clover's slip, and putting her own in its place, "you can just write on it yourself,—I shan't! I never heard of such a word in my life! You made it up for the occasion, you know you did!"

"I didn't! it's in the Bible," replied Clover, setting to work composedly on the fresh paper. But when Rose opened Clover's slip she groaned again.

"It's just as bad as the other!" she cried. "Do change back again, Clovy,—that's a dear."

"No, indeed!" said Clover, guarding her paper: "you've changed once, and now you must keep what you have."

Rose made a face, chewed her pencil awhile, and then began to write rapidly. For some minutes not a word was spoken.

"I've done!" said Esther Dearborn at last, flinging her paper into the basket-lid.

"So have I!" said Katy.

One by one the papers were collected and jumbled into a heap. Then Katy, giving all a final shake, drew out one, opened it, and read.

WORD.—Radishes.

QUESTION.—How do you like your clergymen done?

    How do I like them done? Well, that depends.

  I like them *done* on sleepy, drowsy Sundays;

  I like them under-done on other days;

    Perhaps a little *over*-done on Mondays.

  But always I prefer them old as pa,

  And not like radishes, all red and raw.

"Oh, *what* a rhyme! cried Clover.

"Well,—what is one to do?" said Ellen Gray. Then she stopped and bit her lip, remembering that no one was supposed to know who wrote the separate papers.

"Aha! it's your, is it, Ellen?" said Rose. "You're an awfully clever girl, and an ornament to the S. S. U. C. Go on, Katy."

Katy opened the second slip.

WORD.—Anything.

QUESTION.—Would you rather be a greater fool than you seem, or seem

> a greater fool than you are?
> I wouldn't seem a fool for anything, my dear,
> If I could help it; but I can't, I fear.

"Not bad," said Rose, nodding her head at Sally Alsop, who blushed crimson.

The third paper ran,—

WORD.—Mahershahalhashbaz.

QUESTION.—Does your mother know you're out?

Rose and Clover exchanged looks.

> Why, of course my mother knows it,
> For she sent me out herself.
> She told me to run quickly, for
> It wasn't but a mile;
> But I found it was much farther,
> And my feet grew tired and weary,
> And I couldn't hurry greatly,
> So I took a long, long while.
> Beside, I stopped to read your word,
> A stranger one I never heard!
> I've met with *Pa*-pistical,
> That's pat;
> But _Ma-hershahalhashbaz,
> What's that?

"Oh, Clovy, you bright little thing!" cried Rose, in fits of laughter. But Mary Silver looked quite pale.

"I never heard of any thing so awful!" she said. "If that word had come to me, I should have fainted away on the spot,—I know I should!"

Next came—

WORD.—Buttons.

QUESTION.—What is the best way to make home happy?

> To me 'tis quite clear I can answer this right:
> Sew on the buttons, and sew them on tight.

"I suspect that is Amy's," said Esther: "she's such a model for mending and keeping things in order."

"It's not fair, guessing aloud in this way," said Sally Alsop. Sally always spoke for Amy, and Amy for Sally. "Voice and Echo" Rose called them: only, as she remarked, nobody could tell which was Echo and which Voice.

The next word was "Mrs. Nipson," and the question, "Do you like flowers?"

> Do I like flowers? I will not write a sonnet,
> Singing their beauty as a poet might do:
> I just detest those on Aunt Nipson's bonnet,
> Because they are like her,—all gray and blue,
> Dusty and pinched, and fastened on askew!
> And as for heaven's own buttercups and daisies,
> I am not good enough to sing their praises.

Nobody knew who wrote this verse. Katy suspected Louisa, and Rose suspected Katy.

The sixth slip was a very brief one.

WORD.—When?
QUESTION.—Are you willing?

> If I wasn't willing, I would tell you;
> But when— Oh, dear, I *can't!*

"What an extraordinary rhyme!" began Clover, but Rose spied poor Mary blushing and looking distressed, and hastily interposed,—

"It's very good, I'm sure. I wish I'd written it. Go on, Katy."

So Katy went on.

WORD.—Unfeeling.
QUESTION.—Which would you rather do, or go fishing?

> I don't feel up to fishing or such;
> And so, if you please, I'd rather do—which?

"I don't seem to see the word in that poem," said Rose. "The distinguished author will please write another."

"The distinguished author" made no reply to this suggestion; but, after a minute or two, Esther Dearborn, "quite disinterestedly," as she stated, remarked that, after all, to "don't feel" was pretty much the same as unfeeling. There was a little chorus of groans at this, and Katy said she should certainly impose a fine if such dodges and evasions were practised again. This was the first meeting, however, and she would be merciful. After this speech she unfolded another paper. It ran,—

WORD.—Flea.
QUESTION.—What would you do, love?

> What would I do, love? Well, I do not know.
> How can I tell till you are more explicit?

>   If 'twere a rose you held me, I would smell it;
>   If 'twere a mouth you held me, I would kiss it;
>   If 'twere a frog, I'd scream than furies louder'
>   If 'twere a flea, I'd fetch the Lyons Powder.

Only two slips remained. One was Katy's own. She knew it by the way in which it was folded, and had almost instinctively avoided and left it for the last. Now, however, she took courage and opened it. The word was "Measles," and the question, "Who was the grandmother of Invention?" These were the lines:—

>   The night was horribly dark,
>   The measles broke out in the Ark:
>   Little Japher, and Shem, and all the young Hams,
>   Were screaming at once for potatoes and clams.
>   And "What shall I do," said poor Mrs. Noah,
>   "All alone by myself in this terrible shower:
>   I know what I'll do: I'll step down in the hold,
>   And wake up a lioness grim and old,
>   And tie her close to the children's door,
>   And giver her a ginger-cake to roar
>   At the top of her voice for an hour or more;
>   And I'll tell the children to cease their din,
>   Or I'll let that grim old party in,
>   To stop their squeazles and likewise their measles."—
>   She practised this with the greatest success.
>   She was every one's grandmother, I guess.

"That's much the best of all!" pronounced Alice Gibbons. "I wonder who wrote it?"

"Dear me! did you like it so much?" said Rose, simpering, and doing her best to blush.

"Did you really write it?" said Mary; but Louisa laughed, and exclaimed, "No use, Rosy! you can't take us in,—we know better!"

"Now for the last," said Katy. "The word is 'Buckwheat,' and the question, 'What is the origin of dreams?'"

>   When the nuns are sweetly sleeping,
>   Mrs. Nipson comes a-creeping,
>   Creeping like a kitty-cat from door to door;
>   And she listens to their slumbers,
>   And most carefully she numbers,
>   Counting for every nun a nunlet snore!
>   And the nuns in sweet forgetfulness who lie,
>   Dreaming of buckwheat cakes, parental love, and—pie;
>   Moan softly, twist and turn, and see
>   Black cats and fiends, who frolic in their glee;

And nightmares prancing wildly do abound
　　While Mrs. Nipson makes her nightly round.

"Who did write that?" exclaimed Rose. Nobody answered. The girls looked at each other, and Rose scrutinized them all with sharp glances.

"Well! I never saw such creatures for keeping their countenances," she said. "Somebody is as bold as brass. Didn't you see how I blushed when my piece was read?"

"You monkey!" whispered Clover, who at that moment caught sight of the handwriting on the paper. Rose gave her a warning pinch, and the both subsided into an unseen giggle.

"What! The tea-bell!" cried everybody. "We wanted to play another game."

"It's a complete success!" whispered Rose, ecstatically, as they went down the hall. "The girls all say they never had such a good time in their lives. I'm so glad I didn't die with the measles when I was little!"

"Well," demanded Lilly, "so the high and mighty Society has had a meeting! How did it go off?"

"_De_licious!" replied Rose, smacking her lips as at the recollection of something very nice. "But you mustn't ask any questions, Lilly. Outsiders have nothing to do with the S. S. U. C. Our proceedings are strictly private." She ran downstairs with Katy.

"I think you're real mean!" called Lilly after them. Then she said to herself, "They're just trying to tease. I know it was stupid."

CHAPTER VII. INJUSTICE.

Summer was always slow in getting to Hillsover, but at last she arrived, and woods and hills suddenly put on new colors and became beautiful. The sober village shared in the glorifying process. Vines budded on piazzas. Wistaria purpled white-washed walls. The brown elm boughs which hung above the Common turned into trailing garlands of fresh green. Each walk revealed some change, or ended in some delightful discovery, trilliums, dog-tooth violets, apple- trees in blossom, or wild strawberries turning red. The wood flowers and mosses, even the birds and bird-songs, were new to our Western girls. Hillsover, in summer, was a great deal prettier than Burnet, and Katy and Clover began to enjoy school very much indeed.

Toward the end of June, however, something took place which gave them quite a different feeling,—something so disagreeable that I hate to tell about it: but, as it really happened, I must.

It was on a Saturday morning. They had just come upstairs, laughing, and feeling very merry; for Clover had written a droll piece for the S. S. U. C. meeting, and was telling Katy about it, when, just at the head of the stairs, they met Rose Red. She was evidently in trouble, for she looked flushed and excited, and was under escort of Miss Barnes, who marched before her with the air of a policeman. As she passed the girls, Rose opened her eyes very wide, and made a face expressive of dismay.

"What's the matter?" whispered Clover. Rose only made another grimace, clawed with her fingers at Miss Barnes's back, and vanished down the entry which led to Mrs. Florence's room. They stood looking after her.

"Oh, dear!" sighed Clover, "I'm so afraid Rose is in a scrape."

They walked on toward Quaker Row. In the wash-room was a knot of girls, with their heads close together, whispering. When they saw Katy and Clover, they became silent, and gazed at them curiously.

"What has Rose Red gone to Mrs. Florence about?" asked Clover, too anxious to notice the strange manner of the girls. But at that moment she caught sight of something which so amazed her that she forgot her question. It was nothing less than her own trunk, with "C. E. C." at the end, being carried along the entry by two men. Miss Jane followed close behind, with her arms full of clothes and books. Katy's well-know scarlet pin-cushion topped the pile; in Miss Jane's hand were Clover's comb and brush.

"Why, what does this mean?" gasped Clover, as she and Katy darted after Miss Jane, who had turned into one of the rooms. It was No. 1, at the head of the row,—a room which no one had wanted, on account of its smallness and lack of light. The window looked out on a brick wall not ten feet away; there was never a ray of sun to make it cheerful; and Mrs. Nipson had converted it into a store-room for empty trunks. The trunks were taken away now, and the bed was strewn with Katy's and Clovers possessions.

"Miss Jane, what is the matter? What are you moving our things for?" exclaimed the girls in great excitement.

Miss Jane laid down her load of dress, and looked them sternly.

"You know the reason as well as I do," she said icily.

"No, I don't. I haven't the least idea what you mean!" cried Katy. "Oh, please be careful!" as Miss Jane flung a pair of boots on top of Cousin Helen's vase, "you'll break it! Dear, dear! Clover, there's your Cologne bottle tipped over, and all the Cologne spilt! What does it mean? Is our room going to be painted, or what?"

"Your room," responded Miss Jane, "is for the future to be this,—No. 1. Miss Benson and Miss James will take No. 6; and, it is to be hoped, will conduct themselves more properly than you have done."

"Than we have done!" cried Katy, hardly believing her ears.

"Do not repeat my words in that rude way!" said Miss Jane, tartly. "Yes, than you have done!"

"But what have we done? There is some dreadful mistake! Do tell us what you mean, Miss Jane! We have done nothing wrong, so far as I know!"

"Indeed!" replied Miss Jane, sarcastically. "Your ideas of right and wrong must be peculiar! I advise you to say no more on the subject, but be thankful that Mrs. Florence keeps you in the school at all, instead of dismissing you. Nothing but the fact that your home is at such a distance prevents her from doing so."

Katy felt as if all the blood in her body were turned to fire as she heard these words, and met Miss Jane's eyes. Her old, hasty temper, which had seemed to die out during years of pain and patience, flashed into sudden life, as a smouldering coal flashes, when you least expect it, into flame. She drew herself up to her full height, gave Miss Jane a look of scorching indignation, and, with a rapid impulse, darted out of the room and along the hall towards Mrs. Florence's door. The girls she met scattered from her path right and left. She looked so tall and moved so impetuously that she absolutely frightened them.

"Come in," said Mrs. Florence, in answer to her sharp, quivering knock. Katy entered. Rose was not there, and Mrs. Florence and Mrs. Nipson sat together, side by side, in close consultation.

"Mrs. Florence," said Katy, too much excited to feel in the least afraid, "will you please tell me why our things are being changed to No. 1?"

Mrs. Florence flushed with anger. She looked Katy all over for a minute before she answered, then she said, in a sever voice, "It is done by my orders, and for good and sufficient reasons. What those reasons are, you know as well as I."

"No, I don't!" replied Katy, as angry as Mrs. Florence. "I haven't the least idea what they are, and I insist on knowing!"

"I cannot answer questions put in such an improper manner," said Mrs. Florence, with a wave of the hand which meant that Katy was to go. But Katy did not stir.

"I am sorry if my manner was improper," she said, trying to speak quietly, "but I think I have a right to ask what this means. If we are accused of doing wrong, it is only fair to tell us what it is."

Mrs. Florence only waved her hand again; but Mrs. Nipson, who had been twisting uneasily in her chair, said, "Excuse me, Mrs. Florence, but perhaps it would better—would satisfy Miss Carr better—if you were to be explicit."

"It does not seem to me that Miss Carr can be in need of any explanation," replied Mrs. Florence. "When a young lady writes underhand notes to young gentlemen, and throws them from her window, and they are discovered, she must naturally expect that persons of correct ideas will be shocked and disgusted. Your note to Mr. Abernathy Searles, Miss Carr, was found by his mother while mending his pocket, and was handed by her to me. After this statement you will hardly be surprised that I do not consider it best to permit you to room longer on that side of the house. I did not suppose I had a girl in my school capable of such conduct."

For a moment Katy was too much stunned to speak. She took hold of a chair to steady herself, and her color changed so quickly from red to pale and back again to red, that Mrs. Florence and Mrs. Nipson, who sat watching her, might be pardoned for thinking that she looked guilty. As soon as she recovered her voice, she stammered out, "But I didn't! I never did! I haven't written any note! I wouldn't for the world! Oh, Mrs. Florence, please believe me!"

"I prefer to believe the evidence of my eyes," replied Mrs. Florence, as she drew a paper from her pocket. "Here is the note! I suppose you will hardly deny your own signature."

Katy seized the note. It was written in a round, unformed hand, and ran thus:—

"Dear Berry,—I saw you last night on the green. I think you are splendid. All the nuns think so. I look at you very often out of my window. If I let down a string, would you tie a cake to it, like that kind which you threw to Mary Andrews last term? Tie two cakes, please;

one for me and one for my room-mate. The string will be at the end of the Row. "Miss Carr."

In spite of her agitation, Katy could hardly keep back a smile as she read this absurd production. Mrs. Florence saw the smile, and her tone was more severe than ever, as she said,—

"Give that back to me, if you please, It will be my justification with your father if he objects to your change of room."

"But, Mrs. Florence," cried Katy, "I never wrote that note. It isn't my handwriting; it isn't my— Oh, surely you can't think so! It's too ridiculous."

"Go to your room at once," said Mrs. Florence, "and be thankful that your punishment is such a mild one. If your home were not so distant, I should write to ask your father to remove you from the school; instead of which, I merely put you on the other side of the entry, out of reach of farther correspondence of this sort."

"But *I* shall write him, and he will take us away immediately," cried Katy, stung to the quick by this obstinate injustice. "I will not stay, neither shall Clover, where our word is disbelieved, and we are treated like this. Papa knows! Papa will never doubt us a moment when we tell him that this isn't true."

With these passionate words she left the room. I do not think that either Mrs. Florence or Mrs. Nipson felt very comfortable after she was gone.

That was a dreadful afternoon. The girls had no heart to arrange No. 1, or do any thing toward making it comfortable, but lay on the bed in the midst of their belongings, crying, and receiving visits of condolence from their friends. The S. S. U. C. meeting was put off. Katy was in no humor to act as president, or Clover to read her funny poem. Rose and Mary Silver sat by, kissing them at intervals, and declaring that it was a shame, while the other members dropped in one by one to re-echo the same sentiments.

"If it had been anybody else!" said Alice Gibbons; "but Katy of all persons! It is too much!"

"So I told Mrs. Florence," sobbed Rose Red. "Oh, why was I born so bad? If I'd always been good, and a model to the rest of you, perhaps she'd have believed me instead of scolding harder than ever."

The idea of Rose as a "model" made Clover smile in the midst of her dolefulness.

"It's an outrageous thing," said Ellen Gray, "if Mrs. Florence only knew it, you two have done more to keep the rest of us steady than any girls in school."

"So they have," blubbered Rose, whose pretty face was quite swollen with crying. "I've been getting better and better every day since they came." She put her arms round Clover as she spoke, and sobbed harder than ever.

It was in the midst of this excitement that Miss Jane saw fit to come in and "inspect the room." When she saw the crying girls and the general confusion of every thing, she was very angry.

"I shall mark you both for disorder," she said. "Get off the bed, Miss Carr. Hang your dresses up at once, Clover, and put your shoes in the shoe-bag. I never saw any thing so disgraceful. All these things must be in order when I return, fifteen minutes from now, or I shall report you to Mrs. Florence."

"It's of no consequence what you do. We are not going to stay," muttered Katy. But soon she was ashamed of having said this. Her anger was melting, and grief taking its place. "Oh, papa! papa! Elsie! Elsie!" she whispered to herself, as she slowly hung up the dresses; and, unseen by the girls, she hid her face in the folds of Clover's gray alpaca, and shed some hot tears. Till then she had been too angry to cry.

This softer mood followed her all through the evening. Clover and Rose sat by, talking over the affair and keeping their wrath warm with discussion. Katy said hardly a word. She felt too weary and depressed to speak.

"Who could have written the note?" asked Clover again and again. It was impossible to guess. It seemed absurd to suspect any of the older girls; but then, as Rose suggested, the absurdity as well as the signature might have been imitated to avoid detection.

"I know one thing" remarked Rose, "and that is that I should like to kill Mrs. Searles. Horrid old thing!—peeping and prying into pockets. She has no business to be alive at all."

Rose's ferocious speeches always sounded specially comical when taken in connection with her pink cheeks and her dimples.

"Shall you write to papa to-night, Katy?" asked Clover.

Katy shook her head. She was too heavy-hearted to talk. Big tears rolled down unseen and fell upon the pillow. After Rose was gone, and the candle out, she cried herself to sleep.

Waking early in the dim dawn, she lay and thought it over, Clover slumbering soundly beside her meanwhile. "Morning brings counsel," says the old proverb. In this case it seemed true. Katy, to her surprise, found a train of fresh thoughts filling her mind, which were not there when she fell asleep. She recalled her passionate words and feelings of the day before. Now that the mood had passed, they seemed to her worse than the injury which provoked them. Quick- tempered and generous people often experience this. It was easier for Katy to forgive

Mrs. Florence, because it was needful also that she should forgive herself.

"I said I would write to papa to take us away," she thought "Why did I say that? What good would it do? It wouldn't make anybody disbelieve this hateful story. They'd only think I wanted to get away because I was found out. And papa would be so worried and disappointed. It has cost him a great deal to get us ready and send us here, and he wants us to stay a year. If we went home now, all the money would be wasted. And yet how horrid it is going to be after this! I don't feel as if I could ever bear to see Mrs. Florence again. I must write.

"But then," her thoughts flowed on, "home wouldn't seem like home if we went away from school in disgrace, and knew that everybody here was believing such things. Suppose, instead, I were to write to papa to come on and make things straight. He'd find out the truth, and force Mrs. Florence to see it. It would be very expensive, though; and I know he oughtn't to leave home again so soon. Oh, dear! How hard it is to know what to do!"

"What would Cousin Helen say?" she continued, going in imagination to the sofa-side of the dear friend who was to her like a second conscience. She shut her eyes and invented a long talk,—her questions, Cousin Helen's replies. But, as everybody knows, it is impossible to play croquet by yourself and be strictly impartial to all the four balls. Katy found that she was making Cousin Helen play (that is, answer) as she herself wished, and not, as something whispered, she would answer were she really there.

"It is just the 'Little Scholar' over again," she said, half aloud, "I can't see. I don't know how to act." She remembered the dream she once had, of a great beautiful Face and a helping hand. "And it was real," she murmured, "and just as real, and just as near, now as then."

The result of this long meditation was that, when Clover woke up, she found Katy leaning over, ready to kiss her for good morning, and looking bright and determined.

"Clovy," she said, "I've been thinking; and I'm not going to write to papa about this affair at all!"

"Aren't you? Why not?" asked Clover, puzzled.

"Because it would worry him, and be of no use. He would come on and take us right away, I'm sure; but Mrs. Florence and all the teachers, and a great many of the girls, would always believe that this horrid, ridiculous story is true. I can't bear to have them. Let's stay, instead, and convince them that it isn't. I think we can."

"I would a great deal rather go home," said Clover. "It won't ever be nice here again. We shall have this dark room, and Miss Jane will be more unkind than ever, and the girls will think you wrote that note, and Lilly Page will say hateful things!" She buttoned her boots with a vindictive air.

"Never mind," said Katy, trying to feel brave. "I don't suppose it will be pleasant, but I'm pretty sure it's right. And Rosy and all the girls we really care for know how it is."

"I can't bear it," sighed Clover, with tears in her eyes. "It is so cruel that they should say such things about you."

"I mean that they shall say something quite different before we go away," replied Katy, stroking her hair. "Cousin Helen would tell us to stay, I'm pretty sure. I was thinking about her just now, and I seemed to hear her voice in the air, saying over and over, 'Live it down! Live it down! Live it down!'" She half sang this, and took two or three dancing steps across the room.

"What a girl you are!" said Clover, consoled by seeing Katy look so bright.

Mrs. Florence was surprised that morning, as she sat in her room, by the appearance of Katy. She looked pale, but perfectly quiet and gentle.

"Mrs. Florence," she said, "I've come to say that I shall not write to my father to take us away, as I told you I should."

Mrs. Florence bowed stiffly, by way of answer.

"Not," went on Katy, with a little flash in her eyes, "that he would hesitate, or doubt my word one moment, if I did. But he wished us to stay here a year, and I don't want to disappoint him. I'd rather stay. And, Mrs. Florence, I'm sorry I was angry, and felt that you were unjust."

"And to-day you own that I was not?"

"Oh, no!" replied Katy, "I can't do that. You *were* unjust, because neither Clover nor I wrote that note. We wouldn't do such a horrid thing for the world, and I hope some day you will believe us. But I oughtn't to have spoken so."

Katy's face and voice were so truthful as she said this, that Mrs. Florence was almost shaken in her opinion.

"We will say no more about the matter," she remarked, in a kinder tone. "If your conduct is perfectly correct in future, it will go far to make this forgotten."

Few things are more aggravating than to be forgiven when one has done no wrong. Katy felt this as she walked away from Mrs. Florence's room. But she would not let herself grow angry again. "Live it down!" she whispered, as she went into the school-room.

She and Clover had a good deal to endure for the next two or three weeks. They missed their old room with its sunny window and pleasant outlook. They missed Rose, who, down at the far end of Quaker Row, could not drop in half so often as had been her custom. Miss Jane was specially grim and sharp; and some of the upstairs girls, who resented Katy's plain speaking, and the formation of a society against flirting, improved the chance to be provoking. Lilly Page was one of these. She didn't really believe Katy guilty, but she liked to tease her by pretending to believe it.

"Only to think of the President of the Saintly Stuck-Up Society being caught like this!" she remarked, maliciously. "What are our great reformers coming to? Now if it had been a sinner like me, no one would be surprised!"

All this naturally was vexatious. Even sunny Clover shed many tears in private over her mortifications. But the girls bore their trouble bravely, and never said one syllable about the matter in the letters home. There were consolations, too, mixed with the annoyances. Rose Red clung to her two friends closely, and loyally fought their battles. The S. S. U. C. to a girl rallied round its chief. After that sad Saturday the meetings were resumed with as much spirit as ever. Katy's steadiness and uniform politeness and sweet temper impressed even those who would have been glad to believe a tale against her, and in short time the affair ceased to be a subject for discussion,— was almost forgotten, in fact, except for a sore spot in Katy's heart, and one page in Rose Red's album, upon which, under the date of that fatal day, were written these words, headed by an appalling skull and cross-bones in pen-and-ink:—

"N. B.—Pay Miss Jane off."

CHAPTER VIII. CHANGES.

"Clover, where's Clover?" cried Rose Red, popping her head into the schoolroom, where Katy sat writing her composition. "Oh, Katy! there you are. I want you too. Come down to my room right away. I've such a thing to tell you!"

"What is it?" Tell me too!" said Bella Arkwright. Bella was a veritable "little pitcher," of the kind mentioned in the Proverb, and had an insatiable curiosity to know every thing that other people knew.

"Tell you, Miss? I should really like to know why!" replied Rose, who was not at all fond of Bella.

"You're real mean, and real unkind," whined Bella. "You think you're a great grown-up lady, and can have secrets. But you ain't! You're a little girl too,—most as little as me. So there!"

Rose made a face at her, and a sort of growling rush, which had the effect of sending Bella screaming down the hall. Then, returning to the school-room,—

"Do come, Katy," she said: "find Clover, and hurry! Really and truly I want you. I feel as if I should burst if I don't tell somebody right away what I've found out."

Katy began to be curious. She went in pursuit of Clover, who was practising in one of the recitation-rooms, and the three girls ran together down Quaker Row.

"Now," said Rose, locking the door, and pushing forward a chair for Katy and another for Clover, "swear that you won't tell, for this is a real secret,—the greatest secret that ever was, and Mrs. Florence would flay me alive if she knew that I knew!" She paused to enjoy the effect of her words, and suddenly began to snuff the air in a peculiar manner.

"Girls," she said, solemnly, "that little wretch of a Bella is in this room. I am sure of it."

"What makes you think so?" cried the others supervised.

"I smell that dreadful pomatum that she puts on her hair! Don't you notice it? She's hidden somewhere." Rose looked sharply about for a minute, then made a pounce, and from under the bed dragged a small kicking heap. It was the guilty Bella.

"What were you doing there, you bad child?" demanded Rose, seizing the kicking feet and holding them fast.

"I don't care," blubbered Bella, "you wouldn't tell me your secret. You're a real horrid girl, Rose Red. I don't love you a bit."

"Your affection is not a thing which I particularly pine for," retorted Rose, seating herself, and holding the culprit before her by the ends of her short pig-tails. "I don't want little girls who peep and hide to love me. I'd rather they wouldn't. Now listen. Do you know what I shall do if you ever come again into my room without leave. First, I shall cut off your hair, pomatum and all, with my penknife,"—Bella screamed,—"and then I'll turn myself into a bear—a great brown bear —and eat you up." Rose pronounced this threat with tremendous energy, and accompanied it with a snarl which showed all her teeth. Bella roared with fright, twitched away her pig-tails, unlocked the door and fled, Rose not pursuing, but sitting comfortably in her chair and growling at intervals, till her victim was out of hearing. Then she rose and bolted the door again.

"How lucky that the imp is so fond of that smelly pomatum!" she remarked: "one always knows where to look for her. It's as good as a bell round her neck! Now, for the secret. You promise not to tell? Well, then, Mrs. Florence is going away week after next, and, what's more,—she's going to be married!"

"Not really!" cried the others.

"Really and truly. She's going to be married to a clergyman."

"How did you find out?"

"Why, it's the most curious thing. You know my blue lawn, which Miss James is making. This morning I went to try it on, Miss Barnes with me of course, and while Miss James was fitting the waist Mrs. Seccomb came in and sat down on the sofa by Miss Barnes. They began to talk, and pretty soon Mrs. Seccomb said, 'What day does Mrs. Florence go?'

"'Thursday week,' said Miss Barnes. She sort of mumbled it, and looked to see if I were listening. I wasn't; but of course after that I did,—as hard as I could.

"'And where does the important event take place?' asked Mrs. Seccomb.
She's so funny with her little bit of a mouth and her long words. She always looks as if each of them was a big pill, and she wanted to swallow it and couldn't.

"'In Lewisberg, at her sister's house,' said Miss Barnes. She mumbled more than ever, but I heard.

"'What a deplorable loss she will be to our limited circle!' said Mrs. Seccomb. I couldn't imagine what they meant. But don't you think, when I got home there was this letter from Sylvia, and she says, 'Your adored Mrs. Florence is going to be married. I'm afraid you'll all break your hearts about it. Mother met the gentleman at a party the other night. She says he looks clever, but isn't at all handsome, which is a pity, for Mrs. Florence is a raving beauty in my opinion. He's an excellent preacher, we hear; and won't she manage the parish to perfection? How shall you like being left to the tender mercies of Mrs. Nipson?' Now did you ever hear any thing so droll in your life?" went on Rose, folding up her letter. "Just think of those two things coming together the same day! It's like a sum in arithmetic, with an answer which 'proves' the sum, isn't it?"

Rose had counted on producing an effect, and she certainly was not disappointed. The girls could think and talk of nothing else for the remainder of that afternoon.

It was a singular fact that before two days were over every scholar in the school knew that Mrs. Florence was going to be married! How the secret got out, nobody could guess. Rose protested that it wasn't her fault,—she had been a miracle of discretion, a perfect sphinx; but there was a guilty laugh in her eyes, and Katy suspected that the sphinx had unbent a little. Nothing so exciting had ever happened at the Nunnery before. Some of the older scholars were quite inconsolable. They bemoaned themselves, and got together in corners to enjoy the luxury of woe. Nothing comforted them but the project of getting up a "testimonial" for Mrs. Florence.

What this testimonial should be caused great discussion in the school. Everybody had a different idea, and everybody was sure that her idea was better than anybody's else. All the school contributed. The money collected amounted to nearly forty dollars, and the question was, What should be bought?

Every sort of thing was proposed. Lilly Page insisted that nothing could possibly be so appropriate as a bouquet of wax flowers and a glass shade to put over it. There was a strong party in favor of spoons. Annie Silsbie suggested "a statue;" somebody else a clock. Rose Red was for a cabinet piano, and Katy had some trouble in convincing her that forty dollars would not buy one. Bella demanded that they should get "an organ."

"You can go along with it as monkey," said Rose, which remark made
Bella caper with indignation.

At last, after long discussion and some quarelling, a cake-basket was fixed upon. Sylvia Redding happened to be making a visit in Boston, and Rose was commissioned to write and ask her to select the gift and send it up by express. The girls could hardly wait till it came.

"I do hope it will be pretty, don't you?" they said over and over again. When the box arrived, they all gathered to see it opened. Esther Dearborn took out the nails, half a dozen hands lifted the lid, and Rose unwrapped the tissue paper and displayed the basket up to general view.

"Oh, what a beauty!" cried everybody. It was woven of twisted silver wire. Two figures of children with wings and garlands supported the handle on either side. In the middle of the handle were a pair of silver doves, billing and cooing in the most affectionate way, over a tiny shield, on which were engraved Mrs. Florence's initials.

"I never saw one like it!" "Doesn't it look heavy?" cried a chorus of voices, as Rose, highly gratified, held up the basket.

"Who shall present it?" asked Louisa Agnew.

"Rose Red," said some of the girls.

"No, indeed, I'm not tall enough," protested Rose, "it must be somebody who'd kind of sweep into the room and be impressive. I vote for Katy."

"Oh, no!" said Katy, shrinking back, "I shouldn't do it well at all. Suppose we put it to a vote."

Ellen Gray cut some slips of paper, and each girl wrote a name and dropped it into the box. When the votes were counted, Katy's name appeared on all but three.

"I propose that we make this vote unanimous," said Rose, highly delighted. The girls agreed; and Rose, jumping on a chair, exclaimed, "Three cheers for Katy Carr! keep time, girls,—one, two, hip, hip, hurrah!"

The hurrahs were given with enthusiasm, for Katy, almost without knowing it, had become popular. She was too much touched and pleased to speak at first. When she did, it was to protest against her election.

"Esther would do it beautifully," she said, "and I think Mrs. Florence would like the basket better if she gave it. You know ever since"— she stopped. Even now she could not refer with composure to the affair of the note.

"Oh!" cried Louisa, "she's thinking of that ridiculous note Mrs. Florence made such a fuss about. As if anybody supposed you wrote it, Katy! I don't believe even Miss Jane is such a goose as that. Any way, if she is, that's one reason more why you should present the basket, to show that we don't think so." She gave Katy a kiss by way of period.

"Yes, indeed, you're chosen, and you must give it," cried the others.

"Very well," said Katy, extremely gratified, "what am I to say?"

"We'll compose a speech for you," replied Rose, "sugar your voice, Katy, and, whatever you do, stand up straight. Don't crook over, as if you thought you were tall. It's a bad trick you have, child, and I'm always sorry to see it," concluded Rose, with the air of a wise mamma giving a lecture.

It is droll how much can go on in a school unseen and unsuspected by its teachers. Mrs. Florence never dreamed that the girls had guessed her secret. Her plan was to go away as if for a visit, and leave Mrs. Nipson to explain at her leisure. She was therefore quite unprepared for the appearance of Katy, holding the beautiful basket, which was full of fresh roses, crimson, white, and pink. I am afraid the rules of the S. S. U. C. had been slightly relaxed to allow of Rose Red's getting these flowers; certainly they grew nowhere in Hillsover except in Professor Seccomb's garden!

"The girls wanted me to give you this, with a great deal of love from us all," said Katy, feeling strangely embarrassed, and hardly venturing to raise her eyes. She set the basket on the table. "We hope that you will be happy," she added in a low voice, and moved toward the door. Mrs. Florence had been to much surprised to speak, but now she called, "Wait! Come back a moment."

Katy came back. Mrs. Florence's cheeks were flushed. She looked very handsome. Katy almost thought there were tears in her eyes.

"Tell the girls that I thank them very much. Their present is beautiful. I shall always value it." She blushed as she spoke, and Katy blushed too. It made her shy to see the usually composed Mrs. Florence so confused.

"What did she say? What did she say?" demanded the others, who were collected in groups round the school-room door to hear a report of the interview.

Katy repeated her message. Some of the girls were disappointed.

"Is that all?" they said. "We thought she would stand up and make a speech."

"Or a short poem," put in Rose Red,—"a few stanzas thrown off on the spur of the moment; like this, for instance:—

> "Thank you, kindly, for your basket,
> Which I didn't mean to ask it;
> But I'll very gladly take it,
> And when 'tis full of cake, it
> Will frequently remind me
> Of the girls I left behind me!

There was a universal giggle, which brought Miss Jane out of the school-room.

"Order!" she said, ringing the bell. "Young ladies, what are you about? Study hour has begun."

"We're so sorry Mrs. Florence is going away," said some of the girls.

"How did you know that she is going?" demanded Miss Jane, sharply.

Nobody answered.

Next day Mrs. Florence left. Katy saw her go with a secret regret.

"If only she would have said that she didn't believe I wrote that note!" she told Clover.

"I don't care what she believes! She's a stupid, unjust woman!" replied independent little Clover.

Mrs. Nipson was now in sole charge of the establishment. She had never tried school-keeping before, and had various pet plans and theories of her own, which she had only been waiting for Mrs. Florence's departure to put into practice.

One of these was that the school was to dine three times a week on pudding and bread and butter. Mrs. Nipson had a theory,—very convenient and economical for herself, but highly distasteful to her scholars,—that it was injurious for young people to eat meat every day in hot weather.

The puddings were made of batter, with a sprinkling of blackberries or raisins. Now, rising at six, and studying four hours and a half on a light breakfast, has wonderful effect on the appetite, as all who have tried it will testify. The poor girls would go down to dinner as hungry as wolves, and eye the large, pale slices on their plates with a wrath and dismay which I cannot describe. Very thick the slices were, and there was plenty of thin, sugared sauce to eat with them, and plenty of bread and butter; but, somehow, the whole was unsatisfying, and the hungry girls would go upstairs almost as ravenous as when they came down. The second-table-ites were always hanging over the balusters to receive them, and when to the demand, "What did you have for dinner?" "Pudding!" was answered, a low groan would run from one to another, and a general gloom seemed to drop down and envelop the party.

It may have been in consequence of this experience of starvation that the orders for fourth of July were that year so unusually large. It was an old custom in the school that the girls should celebrate the National Independence by buying as many goodies as they liked. There was no candy-shop in Hillsover, so Mrs. Nipson took the orders, and sent to Boston for the things, which were charged on the bills with other extras. Under these blissful circumstances, the girls felt that they could afford to be extravagant, and made out their lists regardless of expense. Rose Red's, for this Fourth, ran thus:—

"Two pounds of Chocolate Caramels.
Two pounds of Sugar almonds.
Two pounds of Lemon Drops.
Two pounds of Mixed Candy.
Two pounds of Maccaroons.
A dozen Oranges.
A dozen Lemons.
A drum of Figs.
A box of French Plums.
A loaf of Almond Cake."

The result of this liberal order was that, after the great wash-basket of parcels had been distributed, and the school had rioted for twenty- four hours upon these unaccustomed luxuries, Rose was found lying on her bed, ghastly and pallid.

"Never speak to me of any thing sweet again so long as I live!" she gasped. "Talk of vinegar, or pickles, or sour apples, but don't allude to sugar in any form, if you love me! Oh, why, why did I send for those fatal things?"

In time all the candy was eaten up, and the school went back to its normal condition. Three weeks later came College commencement.

"Are you and Clover Craters or Symposiums?" demanded Lilly Page, meeting Katy in the hall, a few days before this important event.

"What do you mean?"

"Why, has nobody told you about them? They are the two great College Societies. All the girls belong to one or the other, and make the wreaths to dress their halls. We work up in the Gymnasium; the Crater girls take the east side, and the Symposium girls the west, and when the wreaths grow too long we hang them out of the windows. It's the greatest fun in the world! Be a Symposium, do! I'm one!"

"I shall have to think about it before deciding," said Katy, privately resolving to join Rose Red's Society, whichever it was. The Crater it proved to be, so Katy and Clover enrolled themselves with the Craters. Three days before Commencement wreath-making began. The afternoons were wholly given up to the work, and, instead of walking or piano practice, the girls sat plaiting oak-leaves into garlands many yards long. Baskets of fresh leaves were constantly brought in, and there was a strife between the rival Societies as to which should accomplish most.

It was great fun, as Lilly had said, to sit there amid the green boughs, and pleasant leafy smells, a buzz of gay voices in the air, and a general sense of holiday. The Gymnasium would have furnished many a pretty picture for an artist during those three afternoons, only, unfortunately, no artist was let in to see it.

One day, Rose Red, emptying a basket, lighted upon a white parcel, hidden beneath the leaves.

"Lemon drops!" she exclaimed, applying finger and thumb with all the dexterity of Jack Horner. "Here, Crater girls, here's something for you! Don't you pity the Symposiums?"

But next day a big package of peppermints appeared in the Symposium basket, so neither Society could boast advantage over the other. They were pretty nearly equal, too, in the quantity of wreath made,—the Craters measuring nine hundred yards, and the Symposiums nine hundred and two. As for the Halls, which they were taken over to see the evening before Commencement, it was impossible to say which was most beautifully trimmed. Each faction preferred its own, and President Searles said that both did the young ladies credit.

They all sat in the gallery of the church on Commencement Day, and heard the speeches. It was very hot, and the speeches were not exactly interesting, being on such subjects as "The Influence of a Republic on Men of Letters," and "The Abstract Law of Justice, as applied to Human Affairs;" but the music, and the crowd, and the spectacle of six hundred ladies all fanning themselves at once, were entertaining, and the girls would not have missed them for the world. Later in the day another diversion was afforded them by the throngs of pink and blue ladies and white-gloved gentlemen who passed the house, on their way to the President's Levee; but they were not allowed to enjoy this amusement long, for Miss Jane, suspecting what was going on, went from room to room, and ordered everybody summarily off to bed.

With the close of Commencement Day, a deep sleep seemed to settle over Hillsover. Most of the Professors' families went off to enjoy themselves at the mountains or the sea-side, leaving their houses shut up. This gave the village a drowsy and deserted air. There were no boys playing balls on the Common, or swinging on the College fence; no look of life in the streets. The weather continued warm, the routine of study and excercise grew dull, and teachers and scholars alike were glad when the middle of September arrived, and with it the opening of the autumn vacation.

CHAPTER IX. THE AUTUMN VACATION.

The last day of the term was one of confusion. Every part of the house was given over to trunks and packing. Mrs. Nipson sat at her desk making out bills, and listening to requests about rooms and room-mates. Miss Jane counted books and atlases, taking note of each ink-spot and dog-eared page. The girls ran about, searching for missing articles, deciding what to take home and what to leave, engaging each other for the winter walks. All rules were laid aside. The sober Nunnery seemed turned into a hive of buzzing bees. Bella slid twice down the baluster of the front stairs without being reproved, and Rose Red threw her arm round Katy's waist and waltzed the whole length of Quaker Row.

"I'm so happy that I should like to scream!" she announced, as their last whirl brought them up against the wall. "Isn't vacation just lovely? Katy, you don't look half glad."

"We're not going home, you know," replied Katy, in rather a doleful tone. She and Clover were not so enraptured at the coming of vacation as the rest of the girls. Spending a month with Mrs. Page and Lilly was by no means the same thing as spending it with papa and the children.

Next morning, however, when the big stage drove up, and the girls crowded in; when Mrs. Nipson stood in the door-way, blandly waving farewell, and the maids flourished their dusters out of the upper windows, they found themselves sharing the general excitement, and joining heartily in the cheer which arose as the stage moved away. The girls felt so happy and good-natured that some of them even kissed their hands to Miss Jane.

Such a wild company is not often met with on a railroad train. They all went together as far as the Junction: and Mr. Gray, Ellen's father, who had been put in charge of the party by Mrs. Nipson, had his hands full to keep them in any sort of order. He was a timid old gentleman, and, as Rose suggested, his expression resembled that of a sedate hen who suddenly finds herself responsible for the conduct of a brood of ducklings.

"My dear, my dear!" he feebly remonstrated, "would you buy any more candy? Do you not think so many pea-nuts may be bad for you?"

"Oh, no, sir!" replied Rose, "they never hurt me a bit. I can eat thousands!" Then, as a stout lady entered the car, and made a motion toward the vacant seat beside her, she rolled her eyes wildly, and said, "Excuse me, but perhaps I had better take the end seat so as to get out easily in case I have a fit."

"Fits!" cried the stout lady, and walked away with the utmost dispatch. Rose gave a wicked chuckle, the girls tittered, and Mr. Gray visibly trembled.

"Is she really afflicted in this way?" he whispered.

"Oh, no, papa! it's only Rose's nonsense!" apologized Ellen, who was laughing as hard as the rest. But Mr. Gray did not feel comfortable, and he was very glad when they reached the Junction, and half of his troublesome charge departed on the branch road.

At six o'clock they arrived in Springfield. Half a dozen papas were waiting for their daughters, trains stood ready, there was a clamor of good-bys. Mr. Page was absorbed by Lilly, who kissed him incessantly, and chattered so fast that he had no eyes for any one else. Louisa was borne away by an uncle, with whom she was to pass the night, and Katy and Clover found themselves left alone. They did not like to interrupt Lilly, so they retreated to a bench, and sat down feeling rather left-out and home-sick; and, though they did not say so, I am sure that each was thinking about papa.

It was only for a moment. Mr. Page spied them, and came up with such a kind greeting that the forlorn feeling fled at once. They were to pass the night at the Massasoit, it seemed; and he collected their bags, and led the way across the street to the hotel, where rooms were already engaged for them.

"Now for waffles," whispered Lilly, as they went upstairs; and when, after a few minutes of washing and brushing, they came down again into the dining-room, she called for so many things, and announced herself "starved" in such a tragical tone, that two amused waiters at once flew to the rescue, and devoted themselves to supplying her wants. Waffle after waffle—each hotter and crisper than the last—did those long-suffering men produce, till even Lilly's appetite gave out, and she was forced to own that she could not swallow another morsel. This climax reached, they went into the parlor, and the girls sat down in the window to watch the people in the street, which, after quiet Hillsover, looked as brilliant and crowded as Broadway.

There were not many persons in the parlor. A grave-looking couple sat at a table at some distance, and a pretty little boy in a velvet jacket was playing around the room. He seemed about five years old; and Katy, who was fond of children, put out her hand as he went by, caught him, and lifted him into her lap. He did not seem shy, but looked her in the face composedly, like a grown person.

"What is your name, dear?" she asked.

"Daniel D'Aubigny Sparks," answered the little boy, His voice was prim and distinct.

"Do you live at this hotel?"

"Yes, ma'am. I reside here with my father and mother."

"And what do you do all day? Are there some other little boys for you to play with?"

"I do not wish to play with any little boys," replied Daniel D'Aubigny, in a dignified tone: "I prefer to be with my parents. To-day we have taken a walk. We went to see a beautiful conservatory outside the city. There is a Victoria Regia there. I had often heard of this wonderful lily, and in the last number of the London 'Musee' there is a picture of it, represented with a small negro child standing upon one of its leaves. My father said that he did not think this possible, but when we saw the plant we perceived that the print was not an exaggeration. Such is the size of the leaf, that a small negro child might very easily supported upon it."

"Oh, my!" cried Katy, feeling as if she had accidentally picked up an elderly gentleman or a college professor. "Pray, how old are you?"

"Nearly nine, ma'am," replied the little fellow with a bow.

Katy, too much appalled for farther speech, let him slide off her lap. But Mr. Page, who was much diverted, continued the conversation; and Daniel, mounting a chair, crossed his short legs, and discoursed with all the gravity of an old man. The talk was principally about himself, —his tastes, his adventures, his ideas about art and science. Now and then he alluded to his papa and mamma, and once to his grandfather.

"My maternal grandfather," he said, "was a remarkable man. In his youth he spent a great deal of time in France. He was there at the time of the French Revolution, and, as it happened, was present at the execution of the unfortunate Queen Marie Antoinette. This of course was not intentional. It chanced thus. My grandfather was in a barber's shop, having his hair cut. He saw a great crowd going by, and went out to ask what was the cause. The crowd was so immense that he could not extricate himself; he was carried along against his will, and not only so, but was forced to the front and compelled to witness every part of the dreadful scene. He has often told my mother that, after the execution, the executioner held up the queen's head to the people: the eyes were open, and there was in them an expression, not of pain, not of fear, but of great astonishment and surprise."

This anecdote carried "great astonishment and surprise" into the company who listened to it. Mr. Page gave a sort of chuckle, and saying, "By George!" got up and left the room. The girls put their heads out of the window that they might laugh unseen. Daniel gazed at their shaking shoulders with an air of wonder, while the grave couple at the end of the room, who for some moments had been looking disturbed, drew near and informed the youthful prodigy that it was time for him to go to bed.

"Good-night, young ladies," said the small condescending voice. Katy alone had "presence of countenance" enough to return this salutation. It was a relief to find that Daniel went to bed at all.

Next morning at breakfast they saw him seated between his parents, eating bread and milk. He bowed to them over the edge of the bowl.

"Dreadful little prig! They should bottle him in spirits of wine as a specimen. It's the only thing he'll ever be fit for," remarked Mr. Page, who rarely said so sharp a thing about anybody.

Louisa joined them at the station. She was to travel under Mr. Page's care, and Katy was much annoyed at Lilly's manner with her. It grew colder and less polite with every mile. By the time they reached Ashburn it was absolutely rude.

"Come and see me very soon, girls," said Louisa, as they parted in the station. "I long to have you know mother and little Daisy. Oh, there's papa!" and she rushed up to a tall, pleasant-looking man, who kissed her fondly, shook hands with Mr. Page, and touched his hat to Lilly, who scarcely bowed in return.

"Boarding-school is so horrid," she remarked, "you get all mixed up with people you don't want to know,—people not in society at all."

"How can you talk such nonsense?" said her father: "the Agnews are thoroughly respectable, and Mr. Agnew is one of the cleverest men I know."

Katy was pleased when Mr. Page said this, but Lilly shrugged her shoulders and looked cross.

"Papa is so democratic," she whispered to Clover, "he don't care a bit who people are, so long as they are respectable and clever."

"Well, why should he?" replied Clover. Lilly was more disgusted than ever.

Ashburn was a large and prosperous town. It was built on the slopes of a picturesque hill, and shaded with fine elms. As they drove through the streets, Katy and Clover caught glimpses of conservatories and shrubberies and beautiful houses with bay-windows and piazzas.

"That's ours," said Lilly, as the carriage turned in at a gate. It stopped, and Mr. Page jumped out.

"Here we are," he said. "Gently, Lilly, you'll hurt yourself. Well, my dears, we're very glad to see you in our home at last."

This was kind and comfortable, and the girls were glad of it, for the size and splendor of the house quite dazzled and made them shy. They had never seen any thing like it before. The hall had a marble floor, and busts and statues. Large rooms opened on either side; and Mrs. Page, who came forward to receive them, wore a heavy silk with a train and laces, and looked altogether as if she were dressed for a party.

"This is the drawing-room," said Lilly, delighted to see the girls looking so impressed. "Isn't it splendid?" And she led the way into a stiff, chilly, magnificent apartment, where all the blinds were closed, and all the shades pulled down, and all the furniture shrouded in linen covers. Even the picture frames and mirrors were sewed up in muslin to keep off flies; and the bronzes and alabaster ornaments on the chimney-piece and *etagere* gleamed through the dim light in a ghostly way. Katy thought it very dismal. She couldn't imagine anybody sitting down there to read or sew, or do any thing pleasant, and probably it was not intended that any one should do so; for Mrs. Page soon showed them out, and led the way into a smaller room at the back of the hall.

"Well, Katy," she said, "how do you like Hillsover?"

"Very well, ma'am," replied Katy; but she did not speak enthusiastically.

"Ah!" said Mrs. Page shaking her head, "it takes time to shake off home habits, and to learn to get along with young people after living with older ones and catching their ways. You'll like it better as you go on."

Katy privately doubted whether this was true, but she did not say so. Pretty soon Lilly offered to show them upstairs to their room. She took them first into three large and elegant chambers, which she explained were kept for grand company, and then into a much smaller one in a wing.

"Mother always puts my friends in here," she remarked: "she says it's plenty good enough for school-girls to thrash about in!"

"What does she mean?" cried Clover, indignantly, as Lilly closed the door. "We don't thrash!"

"I can't imagine," answered Katy, who was vexed too. But pretty soon she began to laugh.

"People are so funny!" she said. "Never mind, Clovy, this room is good enough, I'm sure."

"Must we unpack, or will it do to go down in our alpacas?" asked Clover.

"I don't know," replied Katy, in a doubtful tone. "Perhaps we had better change our gowns. Cousin Olivia always dresses so much! Here's your blue muslin right on top of the trunk. You might put on that, and I'll wear my purple."

The girls were glad that they had done this, for it was evidently expected, and Lilly had dressed her hair and donned a fresh white pique. Mrs. Page examined their dresses, and said that Clover's was a lovely blue, but that ruffles were quite gone out, and every thing must be made with basques. She supposed they needed quantities of things, and she had already engaged a dressmaker to work for them.

"Thank you," said Katy, "but I don't think we need any thing. We had our winter dresses made before we left home."

"Winter dresses! last spring! My dear, what were you thinking of? They must be completely out of fashion."

"You can't think how little Hillsover people know about fashions," replied Katy, laughing.

"But, my dear, for your own sake!" exclaimed Mrs. Page, distressed by these lax remarks. "I'll look over your things to-morrow and see what you need."

Katy did not dare to say "No," but she felt rebellious. When they were half through tea, the door opened, and a boy came in.

"You are late, Clarence," said Mr. Page, while Mrs. Page groaned and observed, "Clarence makes a point of being late. He really deserves to be made to go without his supper. Shut the door, Clarence. O mercy! don't bang it in that way. I wish you would learn to shut a door properly. Here are your cousins, Katy and Clover Carr. Now let me see if you can shake hands with them like a gentleman, and not like a ploughboy."

Clarence, a square, freckled boy of thirteen, with reddish hair, and a sort of red sparkle in his eyes, looked very angry at this address. He did not offer to shake hands at all, but elevating his shoulders said, "How d'you do?" in a sulky voice, and sitting down at the table buried his nose without delay in a glass of milk. His mother gave a disgusted sigh.

"What a boy you are!" she said. "Your cousins will think that you have never been taught any thing, which is not the case; for I'm sure I've taken twice the pains with you that I have with Lilly. Pray excuse him, Katy. It's no use trying to make boys polite!"

"Isn't it?" said Katy, thinking of Phil and Dorry, and wondering what Mrs. Page could mean.

"Hullo, Lilly!" broke in Clarence, spying his sister as it seemed for the first time.

"How d'you do?" said Lilly, carelessly. "I was wondering how long it would be before you would condescend to notice my existence."

"I didn't see you."

"I know you didn't. I never knew such a boy! You might as well have no eyes at all."

Clarence scowled, and went on with his supper. His mother seemed unable to let him alone. "Clarence, don't take such large mouthfuls! Clarence, pray use your napkin! Clarence, your elbows are on the table, sir! Now, Clarence, don't try to speak until you have swallowed all that bread,"—came every other moment. Katy felt very sorry for Clarence. His manners were certainly bad, but it seemed quite dreadful that public attention should be thus constantly called to them.

The evening was rather dull. There was a sort of put-in-order-for-company air about the parlor, which made everybody stiff. Mrs. Page did not sew or read, but sat in a low chair looking like a lady in a fashion plate, and asked questions about Hillsover, some of which were not easy to answer, as, for example, "Have you any other intimate friends among the school-girls beside Lilly?" About eight o'clock a couple of young, very young, gentlemen came in, at the sight of whom Lilly, who was half asleep, brightened and became lively and talkative. One of them was the Mr. Hickman, whose father married Mr. Page's sister-in-law's sister, thus making him in some mysterious way a "first cousin" of Lilly's. He was an Arrowmouth student, and seemed to have so many jokes to laugh over with Lilly that before long they conversed in whispers. The other youth, introduced as Mr. Eels, was left to entertain the other three ladies, which duty he performed by sucking the head of his cane in silence while they talked to him. He too was an Arrowmouth Sophomore.

In the midst of the conversation, the door, which stood ajar, opened a little wider, and a dog's head appeared, followed by a tail, which waggled so beseechingly for leave to come farther that Clover, who liked dogs, put out her hand at once. He was not pretty, being of a pepper-and-salt color, with a blunt nose and no particular sort of a tail, but looked good-natured; and Clover fondled him cordially, while Mr. Eels took his cane out of his mouth to ask, "What kind of a dog is that, Mrs. Page?"

"I'm sure I don't know," she replied; while Lilly, from the distance, added affectedly, "Oh, he's the most dreadful dog, Mr. Eels. My brother picked him up in the street, and none of us know the least thing about him, except that he's the commonest kind of dog,—a sort of cur, I believe."

"That's not true!" broke in a stern voice from the hall, which made everybody jump; and Katy, looking that way, was aware of a vengeful eye glaring at Lilly through the crack of the door. "He's a very valuable dog, indeed,—half mastiff and half terrier, with a touch of the bull-dog,—so there, Miss!"

The effect of this remark was startling. Lilly gave a scream; Mrs. Page rose, and hurried to the door; while the dog, hearing his master's voice, rushed that way also, got before her, and almost threw her down. Katy and Clover could not help laughing, and Mr. Eels, meeting their amused eyes, removed the cane from his mouth, and grew conversible.

"That Clarence is a droll chap!" he remarked confidentially. "Bright, too! He'd be a nice fellow if he wasn't picked at so much. It never does a fellow any good to be picked at,—now does it, Miss Carr?"

"No: I don't think it does."

"I say," continued Mr. Eels, "I've seen you young ladies up at Hillsover, haven't I? Aren't you both at the Nunnery?"

"Yes. It's vacation now, you know."

"I was sure I'd seen you. You had a room on the side next the President's, didn't you? I thought so. We fellows didn't know your names, so we called you 'The Real Nuns.'"

"Real Nuns?"

"Yes, because you never looked out of the window at us. Real nuns and sham nuns,—don't you see?" Almost all the young ladies are sham nuns, except you, and two pretty little ones in the story above, fifth window from the end."

"Oh, I know!" said Clover, much amused. "Sally Alsop, you know, Katy, and Amy Erskine. They are such nice girls!"

"Are they?" replied Mr. Eels, with the air of one who notes down names for future reference. "Well, I thought so. Not so much fun in them as some of the others, I guess; but a fellow likes other things as well as fun. I know if my sister was there, I'd rather have her take the dull line than the other."

Katy treasured up this remark for the benefit of the S. S. U. C. Mrs. Page came back just then, and Mr. Eels resumed his cane. Nothing more was heard of Clarence that night.

Next morning Cousin Olivia fulfilled her threat of inspecting the girls' wardrobe. She shook her head over the simple, untrimmed merinos and thick cloth coats.

"There's no help for it," she said, "but it's a great pity. You would much better have waited, and had things fresh. Perhaps it may be possible to match the merino, and have some sort of basque arrangement added on. I will talk to Madame Chonfleur about it. Meantime, I shall get one handsome thick dress for each of you, and have it stylishly made. That, at least, you really need."

Katy was too glad to be so easily let off to raise objections. So that afternoon she and Clover were taken out to "choose their material," Mrs. Page said, but really to sit by while she chose it for them. At the dressmaker's it was the same: they stood passive while the orders were given, and every thing decided upon.

"Isn't it funny!" whispered Clover; "but I don't like it a bit, do you? It's just like Elsie saying how she'll have her doll's things made."

"Oh, this dress isn't mine! it's Cousin Olivia's!" replied Katy. "She's welcome to have it trimmed just as she likes!"

But when the suits came home she was forced to be pleased. There was no over-trimming, no look of finery: every thing fitted perfectly, and had the air of finish which they had noticed and admired in Lilly's clothes. Katy almost forgot that she had objected to the dresses as unnecessary.

"After all, it is nice to look nice," she confessed to Clover.

Excepting going to the dressmaker's there was not much to amuse the girls during the first half of vacation. Mrs. Page took them to drive now and then, and Katy found some pleasant books in the library, and read a good deal. Clover meantime made friends with Clarence. I think his heart was won that first evening by her attentions to Guest the dog, that mysterious composite, "half mastiff and half terrier, with a touch of the bull-dog." Clarence loved Guest dearly, and was gratified that Clover liked him; for the poor animal had few friends in the household. In a little while Clarence became quite sociable with her, and tolerably so with Katy. They found him, as Mr. Eels said, "a bright fellow," and pleasant and good-humored enough when taken in the right way. Lilly always seemed to take him wrong, and his treatment of her was most disagreeable, snappish, and quarrelsome to the last degree.

"Much you don't like oranges!" he said one day at dinner, in answer to an innocent remark of hers. "Much! I've seen you eat two at a time, without stopping. Pa, Lilly says she don't like oranges! I've seen her eat two at a time, without stopping! Much she doesn't! I've seen her eat two at a time, without stopping!" He kept this up for five minutes, looking from one person to another, and repeating, "Much she don't! Much!" till Lilly was almost crying from vexation, and even Clover longed to box his ears. Nobody was sorry when Mr. Page ordered him to leave the room, which he did with a last vindictive "Much!" addressed to Lilly.

"How can Clarence behave so?" said Katy, when she and Clover were alone.

"I don't know," replied Clover. "He's such a nice boy, sometimes; but when he isn't nice, he's the horridest boy I ever saw. I wish you'd talk to him, Katy, and tell him how dreadfully it sounds when he says such things."

"No, indeed! He'd take it much better from you. You're nearer his age, and could do it nicely and pleasantly, and not make him feel as if he were being scolded. Poor fellow, he gets plenty of that!"

Clover said no more about the subject, but she meditated. She had a good deal of tact for so young a girl, and took care to get Clarence into a specially amicable mood before she began her lecture. "Look here, you bad boy, how could you tease poor Lilly so yesterday? Guest, speak up, sir, and tell your massa how naughty it was!"

"Oh, dear! now you're going to nag!" growled Clarence, in an injured voice.

"No, I'm not,—not the least in the world. I'll promise not to. But just tell me,"—and Clover put her hand on the rough, red-brown hair, and stroked it,—"just tell me why you 'go for to do' such things? They're not a bit nice."

"Lilly's so hateful!" grumbled Clarence.

"Well,—she is sometimes, I know," admitted Clover, candidly. "But because she is hateful is no reason why you should be unmanly."

"Unmanly!" cried Clarence, flushing.

"Yes. I call it unmanly to tease and quarrel, and contradict like that. It's like girls. They do it sometimes, but I didn't think a boy would. I thought he'd be ashamed!"

"Doesn't Dorry ever quarrel or tease?" asked Clarence, who liked to hear about Clover's brothers and sisters.

"Not now, and never in that way. He used to sometimes when he was little, but now he's real nice. He wouldn't speak to a girl as you speak to Lilly for any thing in the world. He'd think it wasn't being a gentleman."

"Stuff about gentleman, and all that!" retorted Clarence. "Mother dings the word in my ears till I hate it!"

"Well, it is rather teasing to be reminded all the time, I admit; but you can't wonder that your mother wants you to be a gentleman, Clarence. It's the best thing in the world, I think. I hope Phil and Dorry will grow up just like papa, for everybody says he's the most perfect gentleman, and it makes me so proud to hear them."

"But what does it mean any way! Mother says it's how you hold your fork, and how you chew, and how you put on your hat. If that's all, I don't think it amounts to much."

"Oh, that isn't all. It's being gentle, don't you see? Gentle and nice to everybody, and just as polite to poor people as to rich ones," said Clover, talking fast, in her eagerness to explain her meaning,— "and never being selfish, or noisy, or pushing people out of their place. Forks, and hats, and all that are only little ways of making one's self more agreeable to other people. A gentleman is a gentleman inside,— all through! Oh, I wish I could make you see what I mean!"

"Oh, that's it, is it?" said Clarence. Whether he understood or not, Clover could not tell; or whether she had done any good or not; but she had the discretion to say no more; and certainly Clarence was not offended, for after that day he grew fonder of her than ever. Lilly became absolutely jealous. She had never cared particularly for Clarence's affection, but she did not like to have any one preferred above herself.

"It's pretty hard, I think," she told Clover. "Clare does every thing you tell him, and he treats me awfully. It isn't a bit fair! I'm his sister, and you're only a second cousin."

All this time the girls had seen almost nothing of Louisa Agnew. She called once, but Lilly received the call with them, and so cool and stiff that Louisa grew stiff also, and made but a short stay; and when the girls returned the visit she was out. A few days before the close of vacation, however, a note came from her.

>"Dear Katy,—I am so sorry not to have seen more of you and Clover. Won't you come and spend Wednesday with us? Mamma sends her love, and hopes you will come early, so as to have a long day, for she wants to know you. I long to show you the baby and every thing. Do come. Papa will see you home in the evening. Remember me to Lilly. She has so many friends to see during vacation that I am sure she will forgive me for stealing you for one day. "Yours affectionately, "Louisa."

Katy thought this message very politely expressed, but Lilly, when she heard it, tossed her head, and said she "really thought Miss Agnew might let her name alone when she wrote notes." Mrs. Page seemed to pity the girls for having to go. They must, she supposed, as it was a schoolmate; but she feared it would be stupid for them. The Agnews were queer sort of people, not in society at all. Mr. Agnew was clever, people said; but, really, she knew very little about the family. Perhaps it would not do to decline.

Katy and Clover had no idea of declining. They sent a warm little note of acceptance, and on the appointed day set off bright and early with a good deal of pleasant anticipation. The vacation had been rather dull at Cousin Olivia's. Lilly was a good deal with her own friends, and Mrs. Page with hers; and there never seemed any special place where they might sit, or any thing in particular for then to do.

Louisa's home was at some distance from Mr. Page's, and in a less fashionable street. It looked pleasant and cosy as the girls opened the gate. There was a small garden in front with gay flower-beds; and on the piazza, which was shaded with vines, sat Mrs. Agnew with a little work-table by her side. She was a pretty and youthful- looking woman, and her voice and smile made them feel at home immediately.

"There is no need of anybody to introduce you," she said. "Lulu has described you so often that I know perfectly well which is Katy and which is Clover. I am so glad you could come. Won't you go right in my bed-room by that long window and take off your things? Lulu has explained to you that I am lame and never walk, so you won't think it strange that I do not show you the way. She will be here in a moment. She ran upstairs to fetch the baby."

The girls went into the bed-room. It was a pretty and unusual-looking apartment. The furniture was simple as could be, but bed and toilet and windows were curtained and frilled with white, and the walls were covered thick with pictures, photographs, and pen-and-ink sketches, and water-color drawings, unframed most of them, and just pinned up without regularity, so as to give each the best possible light. It was an odd way of arranging pictures; but Katy liked it, and would gladly have lingered to look at each one, only that she feared Mrs. Agnew would expect them and would think it strange that they did not come back.

Just as they went out again to the piazza, Louisa came running downstairs with her little sister in her arms.

"I was curling her hair," she explained, "and did not hear you come in. Daisy, give Katy a kiss. Now another for Clover. Isn't she a darling?" embracing the child rapturously herself, "now isn't she a little beauty?"

"Perfectly lovely?" cried the others, and soon all three were seated on the floor of the piazza, with Daisy in the midst, passing her from hand to hand as if she had been something good to eat. She was used to it, and submitted with perfect good nature to being kissed, trotted, carried up and down, and generally made love to. Mrs. Agnew sat by and laughed at the spectacle. When Baby was taken off for her noonday nap, Louisa took the girls into the parlor, another odd and pretty room, full of prints and sketches, and pictures of all sorts, some with frames, others with a knot of autumn leaves or a twist of ivy around them by way of a finish. There was a bowl of beautiful autumn roses on the table; and, though the price of one of Mrs. Page's damask curtains would probably have bought the whole furniture of the room, every thing was so bright and homelike and pleasant-looking that Katy's heart warmed at the sight. They were examining a portrait of Louisa with Daisy in her lap, painted by her father, when Mr. Agnew came in. The girls liked his face at once. It was fine and frank; and nothing could be prettier than to see him pick up his sweet invalid wife as if she had been a child, and carry her into the dining-room to her place at the head of the table.

Katy and Clover agreed afterward that it was the merriest dinner they had had since they left home. Mr. Agnew told stories about painters and painting, and was delightful. No less so was the nice gossip upstairs in Louisa's room which followed dinner, or the afternoon frolic with Daisy, or the long evening spent in looking over books and photographs. Altogether the day seemed only too short. As they went out of the gate at ten o'clock, Mr. Agnew following, lo! a dark figure emerged from behind a tree and joined Clover. It was Clarence!

"I thought I'd just walk this way," he explained, "the house has been dreadfully dull all day without you."

Clover was immensely flattered, but Mrs. Page's astonishment next day knew no bounds.

"Really," she said, "I have hopes of Clarence at last. I never knew him volunteer to escort anybody anywhere before in his life."

"I say," remarked Clarence, the evening before the girls went back to school,—"I say, suppose you write to a fellow sometimes, Clover."

"Do you mean yourself by 'a fellow'?" laughed Clover.

"You don't suppose I meant George Hickman or that donkey of an Eels, did you?" retorted Clarence.

"No, I didn't. Well, I've no objection to writing to a fellow, if that fellow is you, provided the fellow answers my letters. Will you?"

"Yes," gruffly, "but you mustn't show 'em to any girls or laugh at my writing, or I'll stop. Lilly says my writing is like beetle tracks. Little she knows about it though! I don't write to her! Promise, Clover!"

"Yes, I promise," said Clover, pleased at the notion of Clare's proposing a correspondence of his own accord. Next morning they all left for Hillsover. Clarence's friendship and the remembrance of their day with the Agnews were the pleasantest things that the girls carried away with them from their autumn vacation.

CHAPTER X. A BUDGET OF LETTERS.

"Hillsover, October 21st.

Dearest Elsie,—I didn't write you last Saturday, because that was the day we came back to school, and there hasn't been one minute since when I could. We thought perhaps Miss Jane would let us off from the abstracts on Sunday, because it was the first day, and school was hardly begun; and, if she had, I was going to write to you instead, but she didn't. She said the only way to keep girls out of mischief was to keep them busy. Rose Red is sure that something has gone wrong with Miss Jane's missionary during the vacation,—she's so dreadfully cross. Oh, dear, how I do hate to come back and be scolded by her again!

"I forget if I told you about the abstracts. They are of the sermons on Sunday, you know, and we have to give the texts, and the heads, and as much as we can remember of the rest. Sometimes Dr. Prince begins: 'I shall divide my subject into three parts,' and tells what they are going to be. When he does that, most of the girls take out their pencils and put them down, and then they don't listen any more. Katy and I don't, for she says it isn't right not to listen some. Miss Jane pretends that she reads all the abstracts through, but she doesn't; for once Rose Red, just to try her, wrote in the middle of hers, 'I am sitting by my window at this moment, and a red cow is going down the street. I wonder if she is any relation to Mrs. Seccomb's cow?' and Miss Jane never noticed it, but marked her 'perfect' all the same. Wasn't it funny?

"But I must tell you about our journey back. Mr. Page came all the way with us, and was ever so nice. Clarence rode down in the carriage to the depot. He gave me a real pretty india-rubber and gold pencil for a good-by present. I think you and Dorry would like Clarence, only just at first you might say he was rather rude and cross. I did; but now I like him ever so much. Cousin Olivia gave Katy a worked collar and sleeves, and me an embroidered pocket-handkerchief with clover leaves in the corner. Wasn't it kind? I'm sorry I said in my last letter that we didn't enjoy our vacation. We didn't much; but it wasn't exactly Cousin Olivia's fault. She meant we should, but she didn't know how. Some people don't, you know. And don't tell any one I said so, will you?

"Rose Red got here in the train before we did. She was so glad when we came that she cried. It was because she was home-sick waiting four hours at the Nunnery without us, she said. Rose is such a darling! She had a splendid vacation, and went to three parties and a picnic. Isn't it queer? her winter bonnet is black velvet trimmed with pink, and so is mine. I wanted blue at first, but Cousin Olivia said pink was more stylish; and now I am glad, because I like to be like Rose.

"Katy and I have got No. 2 this term. It's a good deal pleasanter than our old room, and the entry-stove is just outside the door, so we shall keep warm. There is sun, too, only Mrs. Nipson has nailed thick cotton over all the window except a little place at top. Every window in the house is just so. You can't think how mad the girls are about it. The first night we had an indignation meeting, and passed resolutions, and some of the girls said they wouldn't stay,— they should write to their fathers to come and take them home. None of them did, though. It's perfectly forlorn, not being able to look out. Oh, dear, how I wish it were spring!

"We've got a new dining-room. It's a great deal bigger than the old one, so now we all eat together, and don't have any first and second tables. It's ever so much nicer, for I used to get so dreadfully hungry waiting that I didn't know what to do. One thing is horrid, though, and that is, that every girl has to make a remark in French every day at dinner. The remarks are about a subject. Mrs. Nipson gives out the subjects. To-day the subject was 'Les oiseaux,' and Rose Red said, 'J'aime beaucoup les oiseaux, et surtout ceux qui sont rotis,' which made us all laugh. That ridiculous little Bella Arkwright said, 'J'aime beaucoup les oiseaux qui sing.' She thought sing was French! Every girl in school began, 'J'aime beaucoup les oiseaux'! To-morrow the subject is 'Jules Cesar.' I'm sure I don't know what to say. There isn't a word in Ollendorf about him.

"There aren't so many new scholars this term as there were last. The girls think it is because Mrs. Nipson isn't so popular as Mrs. Florence used to be. Two or three of the new ones look pleasant, but I don't know them yet. Louisa Agnew is the nicest girl here next to Rose. Lilly Page says she is vulgar, because her father paints portraits and they don't know the same people that Cousin Olivia know, but she isn't a bit. We went to spend the day there just before we left Ashburn, and her father and mother are splendid. Their house is just full of all sorts of queer, interesting things, and pictures; and Mr. Agnew told us ever so many stories about painters, and what they did. One was about a boy who used to make figures of lions in butter, and afterward he became famous. I forget his name. We had a lovely time. I wish you could see Lou's little sister Daisy. She's only two, and a perfect little beauty. She has got ten teeth, and hardly ever cries.

"Please ask papa"—

Just as Clover had got to this point she was interrupted by Katy, who walked in with her hat on, and a whole handful of letters.

"See here!" she cried. "Isn't this delightful? Miss Marsh took me with her to the Post-Office, and we found these. Three for you and two for me, and one for rose. Wait a minute till I give Rose hers, and we'll read them together."

In another moment the two were cosily seated with their heads close together, opening their budget. First came one from papa.

"My dear Daughters,"—

"It's for you too, you see," said Katy.

"Last week came your letter of the 31st, and we were glad to hear that you were well and ready to go back to school. By the time this reaches you, you will be in Hillsover, and your winter term begun. Make the most of it, for we all feel as if we could never let you go from home again. Johnnie says she shall rub Spalding's Prepared Glue all over your dresses when you come back, so that you cannot stir. I am a little of the same way of thinking myself. Cecy has returned from boarding-school, and set up as a young lady. Elsie is much excited over the party dresses which Mrs. Hall is having made for her, and goes over every day to see if any thing new has come. I am glad on this account that you are away just now, for it would not be easy to keep steady heads and continue you studies, with so much going on next door. I have sent Cousin Olivia a check to pay for the things she bought for you, and am much obliged to her for seeing that you were properly fitted out. Katy was very right to consider expense, but I wish you to have all things needful. I enclose two ten-dollar bills, one for each of you, for pocket-money; and, with much love from the children, am, "Yours affectionately, P. Carr."

"P. S.—Cousin Helen has had a sharp attack, but is better."

"I wish papa would write longer letters," said Katy. "He always sends us money, but he don't send half enough words with it." She folded the letter, and fondled it affectionately.

"He's always so busy," replied Clover. "Don't you remember how he used to sit down at his desk and scrabble off his letters, and how somebody always was sure to ring the bell before he got through? I'm very glad to have some money, for now I can pay the sixty-two cents I owe you. It's my turn to read. This is from Elsie, and a real long one. Put away the bills first, Katy, or they'll be lost. That's right; now we'll begin together."

"Dear Clover,—You don't know how glad I am when my turn comes to get a letter all to myself. Of course I read papa's, and all the rest you write to the family, but it never seems as if you were talking to me unless you begin 'Dear Elsie.' I wish some time you'd put in a little note marked 'private,' just for me, which nobody else need see. It would be such fun! Please do. I should think you would have hated staying at Cousin Olivia's. When I read what she said about your travelling dresses looking as if they had come out of the Ark, I was too mad for any thing. But I shouldn't think you'd want much to go back to school either, though sometimes it must be splendid. John has named her old stockinet doll, which she used to call 'Scratch-face,' 'Nippy,' after Mrs. Nipson; and I made her a muslin cap, and Dorry drew a pair of black spectacles round her eyes. She is a perfect fright, and John plays all the time that dreadful things happen to her. She pricks her with pins, and pretends she has the ear-ache, and lets her tumble down and hurt herself, till sometimes I nearly feel sorry, though it's all make-believe. When you wrote us about only having pudding for dinner, I didn't a bit. John put her into the rag-closet that very day, and has been starving her to death ever since, and Phil says it serves her right. You can't think how awfully lonely I sometimes get without you. If it wasn't for Helen Gibbs, that new girl I told you about, I shouldn't know what to do. She is the prettiest girl in Miss McCrane's school. Her hair curls just like mine, only it is four times as long and a million times as thick, and her waist is really and truly not much bigger round than a bed-post. We're the greatest friends. She says she loves me just exactly as much as if I was her sister, but she never had any real sisters. She was quite mad the other day because I said I couldn't love her quite so well as you and Katy; and all recess-time she wouldn't speak to me, but now we've made up. Dorry is so awfully in love with her that I never can get him to come into the room when she is here, and he blushes when we tease him about her. But this is a great secret. Dorry and I play chess every evening. He almost always beats unless papa comes behind and helps me. Phil has learned too, because he always wants to do every thing that we do. Dorry gives him a castle, and a bishop, and a knight, and four pawns, and then beats him in six moves. Phil gets so mad that we can't help laughing. Last night he buttoned his king up inside his jacket, and said, 'There! you can't checkmate me now, any way!'

"Cecy has come home. She is a young lady now. She does her hair up quite different, and wears long dresses. This winter she is going to parties, and Mrs. Hall is going to have a party for her on Thursday, with real, grown-up young ladies and gentlemen at it. Cecy has got some beautiful new dresses,—a white muslin, a blue tarlatan, and a pink silk. The pink silk is the prettiest, I think. Cecy is real kind, and lets me see all her things. She has got a lovely breast-pin too, and a new fan with ivory sticks, and all sorts of things. I wish I was grown up. It must be so nice. I was to tell you something, only you mustn't tell any body except Katy. Don't you remember how Cecy used to say that she never was going out to drive with young gentlemen, but was going to stay at home and read the Bible to poor people? Well, she didn't tell the truth, for she has been out three times already with Sylvester Slack in his buggy. When I told her she oughtn't to do so, because it was breaking a promise, she only laughed, and said I was a silly little girl. Isn't it queer?

"I want to tell you what an awful thing I did the other night. Maria Avery invited me to tea, and papa said I might go. I didn't want to much, but I didn't know what to tell Maria, so I went. You know how poor they are, and how aunt Izzie used to say that they were 'touchy,' so I thought I would take great care not to hurry home right after tea, for fear they would think I wasn't having a good time. So I waited, and waited, and waited, and got so sleepy that I had to pinch my fingers to keep awake. At last I was sure that it must be almost nine, so I asked Mr. Avery if he'd please take me home; and don't you believe, when we got there, it was a quarter past ten, and papa was coming for me! Dorry said he guessed I must be enjoying myself to stay so late. I didn't tell anybody about it for three days, because I knew they'd laugh at me, and they did. Wasn't it funny? And old Mrs. Avery looked as sleepy as I felt, and kept yawning behind her hand. I told papa if I had a watch of my own I shouldn't make such mistakes, and he laughed, and said, 'We'll see.' Oh, do you suppose that means he's going to give me one?

"We are so proud of Dorry's having taken two prizes at the examination yesterday. He took the second Latin prize, and the first Mathematics. Dr. Pullman says he thinks Dorry is one of the most thorough boys he ever saw. Isn't that nice? The prizes were books: one was the life of Benjamin Franklin, and the other the Life of General Butler. Papa says he doesn't think much of the Life of Butler; but Dorry has begun it, and says it is splendid. Phil says when he takes a prize he wants candy and a new knife; but he'll have to wait a good while unless he studies harder than he does now. He has just come in to tease me to go up into the garret and help him to get down his sled, because he thinks it is going to snow; but there isn't a sign of it, and the weather is quite warm. I asked him what I should say for him to you, and he said, 'Oh, tell her to come home, and any thing you please.' I said, 'Shall I give her your love, and say that you are very well?' and he says, 'Oh, yes, Miss Elsie, I guess you'd think yourself mighty well if your head ached as much as mine does every day.' Don't be frightened, however, for he's just as fat and rosey as can be; but almost every day he says he feels sick about school-time. When papa was at Moorfield, Miss Finch believed him, and let him stay at home two mornings. I don't wonder at it, for you can think what a face he makes up; but he got well so fast that she pays no attention to him now. The other day, about eleven o'clock, papa met him coming along the road, shying stones at the birds, and making lots of noise. He told papa he felt so sick that his teacher had let him go home; but papa noticed that his mouth looked sticky, so he opened his dinner-basket, and found that the little scamp had eaten up all his dinner on the road, corned beef, bread and butter, a great piece of mince pie, and six pears. Papa couldn't help laughing, but he made him turn around and go right back to school again.

"I told you in my last about Johnnie's going to school with me now. She is very proud of it, and is always talking about 'Elsie's and my school.' She is twice as smart as the other girls of her age. Miss McCrane has put her into the composition class, where they write compositions on their slates. The first subject was, 'A Kitten;' and John's began, 'She's a dear, little, soft scratching thing, only you'd better not pull her by the tail, but she's real cunning.' All the girls laughed, and Johnnie called out, 'Well, it's true, anyhow.'

"I can't write any more, for I must study my Latin. Beside, this is the longest letter that ever was. I have been four days writing it. Please send me one just as long. Old Mary and the children send lots of love, and papa says, 'Tell Katy if a pudding diet sets her to growing again she must come home at once, for he couldn't afford it.' Oh, dear, how I wish I could see you! Please give my love to Rose Red. She must be perfectly splendid. "Your affectionate Elsie."

"Oh, the dear little duck! Isn't that just like her?" said Clover. "I think Elsie has a real genius for writing, don't you? She tells all the little things, and is so droll and cunning. Nobody writes such nice letters. Who's that from, Katy?"

"Cousin Helen, and it's been such a long time coming. Just look at this date! September 22, a whole month ago!" Then she began to read.

"Dear Katy,—It seems a long time since we have had a talk, but I have been less well lately, so that it has been difficult to write. Yesterday I sat up for the first time in several weeks, and to-day I am dressed and beginning to feel like myself. I wish you could see my room this morning,—I often wish this,—but it is so particularly pretty, for little Helen has been in with a great basket full of leaves and flowers, and together we have dressed it to perfection. There are four vases of roses, a bowl full of chrysanthemums, and red leaves round all my pictures. The leaves are Virginia creeper. It doesn't last long, but is lovely while it lasts. Helen also brought a bird's nest which the gardener found in a hawthorn-tree on the lawn. It hangs on a branch, and she has tied it to one side of my bookshelves. On the opposite side is another nest quite different,—a great, gray hornets' nest, as big as a band-box, which came from the mountains a year ago. I wonder if any such grow in the woods about Hillsover. In spite of the red leaves, the day is warm as summer, and the windows stand wide open. I suppose it is cooler with you, but I know it is delicious cold. Now that I think of it, you must be in Ashburn by this time. I hope you will enjoy every moment of your vacation.

"Oct. 19th. I did not finish my letter the day it as begun, dear Katy, and the next morning it proved that I was not so strong as I fancied, and I had to go to bed again. I am still there, and, as you see, writing with a pencil; but do not be worried about me, for the doctor says I am mending, and soon I hope to be up and in my chair. The red leaves are gone, but the roses are lovely as ever, for little Helen keeps bringing me fresh ones. She has just been in to read me her composition. The subject was 'Stars,' and you can't think how much she found to say about them, She is a bright little creature, and it is a great pleasure to teach her. I am hardly ever so sick that she cannot come for her lessons, and she gets on fast. We have made an arrangement that when she knows more than I do she is to give me lessons, and I am not sure that the time is so very far off.

"I must tell you about my Ben. He is a new canary which was given me in the summer, and lately he has grown so delightfully tame that I feel as if it were not a bird at all, but a fairy prince come to live with me and amuse me. The cage door is left open always now, and he flies in and out as he likes. He is a restless, inquisitive fellow, and visits any part of the room, trying each fresh thing with his bill to see if it is good to eat, and then perching on it to see if it good to sit upon. He mistakes his own reflection in the looking- glass for another canary, and sits on the pin-cushion twittering and making love to himself for half an hour at a time. To watch him is one of my greatest amusements, especially just now when I am in bed so much. Sometimes he hides and keeps so still that I have not the least idea where he is. but the moment I call, 'Ben, Ben,' and hold out my finger, wings begin to rustle, and out he flies and perches on my finger. He isn't the least bit in the world afraid, but sits on my head or shoulder, eats out of my mouth, and kisses me with his beak. He is on the pillow at this moment making runs at my pencil, of which he is mortally jealous. It is just so with my combs and brushes if I attempt to do my hair; he cannot bear to have me do any thing but play with him. I do wish I could show him to you and Clover.

"Little Helen, my other pet, has just come in with a sponge cake which she frosted herself. She sends her love, and says when you come to me next summer she will frost you each one just like it. Good-by, my Katy. I had nothing to write about and have written it, but I never like to keep silent too long, or let you feel as if you were forgotten by your loving cousin, Helen."

"P.S. Be sure to wear plenty of warm wraps for your winter walks. And, Katy, dear, you must eat meat every day. Mrs. Nipson will probably give up her favorite pudding now that the cold weather has begun; but, if not, write to papa."

"Isn't that letter Cousin Helen all over?" said Katy, "So little about her illness, and so bright and merry, and yet she has really been sick. Papa says 'a sharp attack.' Isn't she the dearest person in the world, next to papa I mean?"

"Yes, indeed. There's nobody like her. I do hope we can go to see her next summer. Now it's my turn. I can't think who this letter is from. Oh, Clarence! Katy, I can't let you see this. I promised I wouldn't show his letters to anybody, not even you!"

"Oh, very well. But you've got another. Dorry, isn't it? Read that first, and I'll go away and leave you in peace."

So Clover read:—

"Dear Clover,—Elsie says she is going to write you to-day; but I won't stop because next Saturday I'm going out fishing with the Slacks. There are a great many trout now in Blue Brook. Eugene caught six the other day,—no, five, one was a minnow. Papa has given me a splendid rod, it lets out as tall as a house. I hope I shall catch with it. Alexander says the trout will admire it so much that they can't help biting; but he was only funning. Elsie and I play chess most every night. She plays a real good game for a girl. Sometimes pa helps, and then she beats. Miss Finch is well. She don't keep house quite like Katy did, and I don't like her so well as I do you, but she's pretty nice. The other day we had a nutting picnic, and she gave me and Phil a loaf of Election cake and six quince turnovers to carry. The boys gave three cheers for her when they saw them. Did Elsie tell you that I have invented a new machine? It is called 'The Intellectual Peach Parer.' There is a place to hold a book while you pare the peaches. It is very convenient. I don't think of any thing else to tell you. Cecy has got home, and is going to have a party next week. She's grown up now, she says, and she wears her hair quite different. It's a great deal thicker than it used to be. Elsie says it's because there are rats in it; but I don't believe her. Elsie has got a new friend. Her name is Helen Gibbs. She's quite pretty. "Your affectionate brother, Dorry."

P.S.—John wants to put in a note."

John's note was written in a round hand, as easy to read as print.

"Dear Clover,—I am well, and hope you are the same. I wish you would write me a letter of my own. I go to school with Elsie now. We write compossizions. They are hard to write. We don't go up into the loft half so much as we used to when you ware at home. Mrs. Worrett came to dinner last week. She says she ways two hundred and atey pounds. I should think it would be dredful to way that. I only way 76. My head comes up to the mark on the door where you ware mesured when you ware twelve. Isn't that tal? Good-bye. I send a kiss to Katy. Your loving "John."

After they had finished this note, Katy went away, leaving Clover to open Clarence's letter by herself. It was not so well written or spelt as Dorry's by any means.

"Dear Clover,—Don't forget what you promised. I mene about not showing this. And don't tell Lilly I rote. If you do, she'll be as mad as hops. I haven't been doing much since you went away. School begun yesterday, and I am glad; for it's awfully dull now that you girls have gone. Mother says Guest has got flees on him, so she won't let him come into the house any more. I stay out in the barn with him insted. He is well, and sends you a wag of his tail. Jim and me are making him a colar. It is black, with G.P. on it, for Guest Page, you know. A lot of the boys had a camping out last week. I went. It was real jolly; but ma wouldn't let me stay all night, so I lost the best part. They roasted scullpins for supper, and had a bon-fire. The camp was on Harstnet Hill. Next time you come I'll take you out there. Pa has gone to Mane on bizness. He said I must take care of the house, so I've borrowed Jim's gun, and if any robers come I mean to shoot them. I always go to sleep with a broom agenst the door, so as to wake up when they open it. This morning I thought they had come, for the broom was gone, and the gun too; but it was only Briget. She opened the door, and it fell down; but I didn't wake up, so she took it away, and put the gun in the closset. I was mad, I can tell you.

"This is only a short letter, but I hope you will answer it soon. Give my love to Katy, and tell Dorry that if he likes I'll send him my compas for his machenery, because I've got two.
    "Your affectionate Cousin,
     "Clarence Page."

This was the last of the budget. As Clover folded it up, she was dismayed by the tinkle of the tea-bell.

"Oh, dear!" she cried, "there's tea, and I have not finished my letter to Elsie. Where has the afternoon gone! How splendid it has been! I wish I could have four letters every day as long as I live."

CHAPTER XI. CHRISTMAS BOXES.

October was a delightful month, clear and sparkling; but early in November the weather changed, and became very cold. Thick frosts fell, every leaf vanished from the woods, in the gardens only blackened stalks remained to show where once the summer flowers had been. In spite of the stove outside the door, No. 2 began to be chilly; more than once Katy found her tooth-brush stiff with ice in the morning. It was a fore-taste of the what the winter was to be, and the girls shivered at the prospect.

Toward the end of November Miss Jane caught a heavy cold. Unsparing of herself as of others, she went on hearing her classes as usual; and nobody paid much attention to her hoarseness and flushed cheeks, until she grew so much worse that she was forced to go to bed. There she stayed for nearly four weeks. It made a great change in the school; and the girls found it such a relief to have her sharp voice and eyes taken away that I am afraid they were rather glad of her illness than otherwise.

Katy shared in this feeling of relief. She did not like Miss Jane; it was pleasant not to have to see her or hear of her. But as day after day passed, and still she continued ill, Katy's conscience began to prick. One night she lay awake a long time, and heard Miss Jane coughing violently. Katy feared she was very sick, and wondered who took care of her all night and all day. None of the girls went near her. The servants were always busy. And Mrs. Nipson, who did not love Miss Jane, was busy too.

In the morning, while studying and practising, Katy caught herself thinking over this question. At last she asked Miss Marsh,—

"How is Miss Jane to-day?"

"About the same. She is not dangerously ill, the doctor says; but she coughs a great deal, and has some fever."

"Is anybody sitting with her?"

"Oh, no! there's no need of any one. Susan answers the bell, and she has her medicine on the table within reach."

It sounded forlorn enough. Katy had lived in a sick-room so long herself that she knew just how dreary it is for an invalid to be left alone with "medicine within reach," and some one to answer a bell. She began to feel sorry for Miss Jane, and almost without intending it went down the entry, and tapped at her door. The "Come in!" sounded very faint; and Miss Jane as she lay in bed looked weak and dismal, and quite unlike the sharp, terrible person whom the girls feared so much. She was amazed at the sight of Katy, and made a feeble attempt to hold up her head and speak as usual.

"What is it, Miss Carr?"

"I only came to see how you are," said Katy, abashed at her own daring, "You coughed so much last night that I was afraid you were worse. Isn't there something I could do for you?"

"Thank you," said Miss Jane, "you are very kind." Think of Miss Jane's thanking anybody, and calling anybody kind!

"I should be very glad. Isn't there any thing?" repeated Katy, encouraged.

"Well, I don't know: you might put another stick of wood on the fire," said Miss Jane, in an ungracious tone. Katy did so; and seeing that the iron cup on top of the stove was empty, she poured some water into it. Then she took a look about the room. Books and papers were scattered over the table; clean clothes from the wash lay on the chairs; nothing was in its place; and Katy, who knew how particular Miss Jane was on the subject of order, guessed at the discomfort which this untidy state of affairs must have caused her.

"Wouldn't you like to have me put these away?" she asked, touching the pile of clothes.

Miss Jane sighed impatiently, but she did not say no; so Katy, taking silence for consent, opened the drawers, and laid the clothes inside, guessing at the right places with a sort of instinct, and making as little noise and bustle as possible. Next she moved quietly to the table, where she sorted and arranged the papers, piled up the books, and put the pens and pencils in a small tray which stood there for the purpose. Lastly she began to dust the table with her pocket handkerchief, which proceeding roused Miss Jane at once.

"Don't," she said, "there is a duster in the cupboard."

Katy could not help smiling, but she found the duster, and proceeded to put the rest of the room into nice order, laying a fresh towel over the bedside table, and arranging watch, medicine, and spoon within reach. Miss Jane lay and watched her. I think she was as much surprised at herself for permitting all this, as Katy was at being permitted to do it. Sick people often consent because they feel too weak to object. After all, it *was* comfortable to have some one come in and straighten the things which for ten days past had vexed her neat eyes with their untidiness.

Lastly, smoothing the quilt, Katy asked if Miss Jane wouldn't like to have her pillow shaken up?

"I don't care," was the answer. It sounded discouraging; but Katy boldly seized the pillow, beat, smoothed, and put it again in place. Then she went out of the room as noiselessly as she could, Miss Jane never saying, "Thank you," or seeming to observe whether she went or stayed.

Rose Red and Clover could hardly believe their ears when told where she had been. They stared at her as people stare at Van Amburgh when he comes safely out of the lion's den.

"My stars!" exclaimed Rose, drawing a long breath. "You didn't really?
And she hasn't bitten your head off!"

"Not a bit," said Katy, laughing. "What's more, I'm going again."

She was as good as her word. After that she went to see Miss Jane very often. Almost always there was some little thing which she could do, the fire needed mending, or the pitcher to be filled with ice-water, or Miss Jane wanted the blinds opened or shut. Gradually she grew used to seeing Katy about the room. One morning she actually allowed her to brush her hair; and Katy's touch was so light and pleasant that afterwards Miss Jane begged her to do it every day.

"What makes you such a good nurse?" she asked one afternoon, rather abruptly.

"Being sick myself," replied Katy, gently. Then in answer to farther questioning, she told of her four years' illness, and her life upstairs, keeping house and studying lessons all alone by herself. Miss Jane did not say any thing when she got through; but Katy fancied she looked at her in a new and kinder way.

So time went on till Christmas. It fell on a Friday that year, which shortened the holidays by a day, and disappointed many of the girls. Only a few went home, the rest were left to pass the time as best they might till Monday, when lessons were to begin again.

"It isn't much like merry Christmas," sighed Clover to herself, as she looked up at the uncottoned space at the top of the window, and saw great snow-flakes wildly whirling by. No. 2 felt cold and dreary, and she was glad to exchange it for the school-room, round whose warm stove a cluster of girls was huddling. Everybody was in bad spirits; there was a tendency to talk about home, and the nice time which people were having there, and the very bad time they themselves were having at the Nunnery.

"Isn't it mis-e-ra-ble? I shall cry all night, I know I shall, I am so homesick," gulped Lilly, who had taken possession of her room-mate's shoulder and was weeping ostentatiously.

"I declare, you're just Mrs. Gummidge in 'David Copperfield' over again," said Rose. "You recollect her, girls, don't you? When the porridge was burnt, you know,—'All of us felt the disappointment, but Mrs. Gummidge felt it the most.' Isn't Lilly a real Mrs. Gummidge, girls?"

The observation changed Lilly's tears into anger. "You're as hateful and as horrid as you can be, Rose Red," she exclaimed angrily. Then she flew out of the room, and shut the door behind her with a bang.

"There! she's gone upstairs to be mad," said Louisa Agnew.

"I don't care if she has," replied Rose, who was in a perverse mood.

"I wish you hadn't said that, Rosy," whispered Clover. "Lilly really felt badly."

"Well, what if she did? So do I feel badly, and you, and the rest of us. Lilly hasn't taken out a patent for bad feelings, which nobody must infringe. What business has she to make us feel badder, by setting up to be so much worse than the rest of the world?"

Clover said nothing, but went on with a book she was reading. In less than ten minutes, Rose, whose sun seldom stayed long behind a cloud, was at her elbow, dimpling and coaxing.

"I forgive you," she whispered, giving Clover's arm a little pinch.

"What for?"

"For being in the right. About Lilly, I mean. I was rather hateful to her, I confess. Never mind. When she comes downstairs, I'll make up. She's a crocodile, if ever there was one; but, as she's your cousin, I'll be good to her. Kiss me quick to prove that you're not vexed."

"Vexed indeed!" said Clover, kissing the middle of the pink cheek. "I wonder if anybody ever stayed vexed with you for ten minutes together, You Rosy-Posy you?"

"Bless you, yes! Miss Jane, for example. She hates me like poison, and all the time. Well, what of it? I know she's sick, but I 'can't tell a lie, pa,' on that account. Where's Katy?"

"Gone in to see her, I believe."

"One of these days," prophesied Rose, solemnly, "she'll go into that room, and she'll never come out again! Miss Jane is getting back into biting condition. I advise Katy to be careful. What's that noise? Sleigh-bells, I declare! Girls,"—mounting a desk, and peeping out of the window,—"somebody's got a big box,—a big one! Here's old Joyce at the door, with his sledge. Now who do you suppose it is?"

"It's for me. I'm sure it's for me," cried half a dozen voices.

"Bella, my love, peep over the balusters, and see if you can't see the name," cried Louisa; and Bella, nothing loath, departed at once on this congenial errand.

"No, I can't," she reported, coming back from the hall. "The name's tipped up against the wall. There's two boxes! One is big, and one is little!"

"Oh, who can they be for?" clamored the girls. Half the school expected boxes, and had been watching the storm all day, with a dreadful fear that it would block the roads, and delay the expected treasures.

At this moment Mrs. Nipson came in.

"There will be the usual study-hour this evening," she announced. "All of you will prepare lessons for Monday morning. Miss Carr, come her for a moment, if you please."

Clover, wondering, followed her into the entry.

"A parcel has arrived for you, and a box," said Mrs. Nipson. "I presume that they contain articles for Christmas. I will have the nails removed, and both of them placed in you room this evening, but I expect you to refrain from examining them until to-morrow. The vacation does not open until after study-hour to-night, and it will then be too late for you to begin."

"Very well, ma'am," said Clover, demurely. But the minute Mrs. Nipson's back was turned, she gave a jump, and rushed into the school-room.

"O girls," she cried, "what do you think? Both the boxes are for Katy and me!"

"Both!" cried a disappointed chorus.

"Yes, both. Nipson said so. I'm so sorry for you. But isn't it nice for us? We've never had a box from home before, you know; and I didn't think we should, it's so far off. It's too lovely! But I do hope yours will come to-night."

Clover's voice was so sympathizing, for all its glee, that nobody could help being glad with her.

"You little darling!" said Louisa, giving her a hug. "I'm rejoiced that the box is yours. The rest of us are always getting them, and you and Katy never had a thing before. I hope it's a nice one!"

Study-hour seemed unusually long that night. The minute it was over, the sisters ran to No. 2. There stood the boxes, a big wooden one, with all the nails taken out of the lid, and a small paper one, carefully tied up and sealed. It was almost more than the girls could do to obey orders and not peep.

"I feel something hard," announced Clover, inserting a finger-top under the lid.

"Oh, do you?" cried Katy. Then, making an heroic effort, she jumped into the bed.

"It's the only way," she said, "you'd better come too, Clovy. Blow the candle out and let's get to sleep as fast as we can, so as to make morning come quicker."

Katy dreamed of home that night. Perhaps it was that which made her wake so early. It was not five o'clock, and the room was perfectly dark. She did not like to disturb Clover, so she lay perfectly still, for hours as it seemed, till a faint gray dawn crept in, and revealed the outlines of the big box standing by the window. Then she could wait no longer, but crept out of bed, crossed the floor on tip-toe, and raising the lid a little put in her hand. Something crumby and sugary met it, and when she drew it out, there, fitting on her finger like a ring, was a round cake with a hole in the middle of it.

"Oh! it's one of Debby's jumbles!" she exclaimed.

"Where? What are you doing? Give me one too!" cried Clover, starting up. Katy rummaged till she found another, then, half frozen, she ran back to bed; and the two lay nibbling the jumbles, and talking about home, till dawn deepened into daylight, and morning was fairly come.

Breakfast was half an hour later than usual, which was comfortable. As soon as it was over, the girls proceeded to unpack their box. The day was so cold that they wrapped themselves in shawls, and Clover put on a hood and thick gloves. Rose Red, passing the door, burst out laughing, and recommended that she should add india rubbers and an umbrella.

"Come in," cried the sisters,—"come in, and help us open our box."

"Oh, by the way, you have a box, haven't you?" said Rose, who was perfectly aware of the important fact, and had presented herself with the hope of being asked to look on. "Thank you, but perhaps I would better come some other time. I shall be in your way."

"You humbug!" said Clover, while Katy seized Rose and pulled her into the room. "There, sit on the bed, you ridiculous goose, and put on my gray cloak. How can you be so absurd as to say you won't? You know we want you, and you know you came on purpose!"

"Did I? Well, perhaps I did," laughed Rose. Then Katy lifted off the lid and set it against the door. It was an exciting moment.

"Just look here!" cried Katy.

The top of the box was mostly taken up with four square paper boxes, round which parcels of all shapes and sized were wedged and fitted. The whole was a miracle of packing. It had taken Miss Finch three mornings, with assistance from old Mary, and much advice from Elsie, to do it so beautifully.

Each box held a different kind of cake. One was of jumbles, another of ginger-snaps, a third of crullers, and the fourth contained a big square loaf of frosted plum-cake, with a circle of sugar almonds set in the frosting. How the trio exclaimed at this!

"I never imagined any thing so nice," declared Rose, with her mouth full of jumble. "As for those snaps, they're simply perfect. What can be in all those fascinating bundles? Do hurry and open one, Katy."

Dear little Elsie! The first two bundles opened were hers, a white hood for Katy, and a blue one for Clover, both of her own knitting, and so nicely done. The girls were enchanted.

"How she has improved!" said Katy. "She knits better than either of us, Clover."

"There never was such a clever little darling!" responded Clover, and they patted the hoods, tried them on before the glass, and spent so much time in admiring them that Rose grew impatient.

"I declare," she cried, "it isn't any of my funeral, I know; but if you don't open another parcel soon, I shall certainly fall to myself. It seems as if, what with cold and curiosity, I couldn't wait."

"Very well," said Katy, laying aside her hood, with one final glance. "Take out a bundle, Clover. It's your turn."

Clover's bundle was for herself, "Evangeline," in blue and gold; and pretty soon "Golden Legend," in the same binding, appeared for Katy. Both these were from Dorry. Next came a couple of round packages of exactly the same size. These proved to be ink-stands, covered with Russia leather: one marked, "Katy from Johnnie," and the other, "Clover from Phil." It was evident that the children had done their shopping together, for presently two long narrow parcels revealed the carved pen-handles, precisely alike; and these were labelled, "Katy from Phil," and "Clover from Johnnie."

What fun it was opening those bundles! The girls made a long business of it, taking out but one at a time, exclaiming, admiring, and exhibiting to Rose, before they began upon another. They laughed, they joked, but I do not think it would have taken much to make either of them cry. It was almost too tender a pleasure, these proofs of loving remembrance from the little one; and each separate article seemed full of the very look and feel of home.

"What can this be?" said Katy, as she unrolled a paper and disclosed a pretty round box. She opened. Nothing was visible but pink cotton wool. Katy peeped beneath, and gave a cry.

"O Clovy! Such a lovely thing! It's from papa,—of course it's from papa. How could he? It's a great deal too pretty."

The "lovely thing" was a long slender chain for Katy's watch, worked in fine yellow gold. Clover admired it extremely; and her joy knew no bounds when farther search revealed another box with a precisely similar chain for herself. It was too much. The girls fairly cried with pleasure.

"There never was such a papa in the world!" they said.

"Yes, there is. Mine is just as good," declared Rose, twinkling away a little tear-drop from her own eyes. "Now don't cry, honeys. Your papa's an angel, there's no doubt about it. I never saw such pretty chains in my life,—never. As for the children, they're little ducks. You certainly are a wonderful family. Katy, I'm dying to know what is in the blue parcel."

The blue parcel was from Cecy, and contained a pretty blue ribbon for Clover. There was a pink one also, with a pink ribbon for Katy. Everybody had thought of the girls. Old Mary sent them each a yard measure; Miss Finch, a thread-case, stocked with differently colored cottons. Alexander had cracked a bag full of hickory nuts.

"Did you ever?" said, Rose, when this last was produced. "What a thing it is to be popular! Mrs. Hall? Who's Mrs. Hall?" as Clover unwrapped a tiny carved easel.

"She's Cecy's mother," explained Clover. "Wasn't she kind to send me this, Katy? And here's Cecy's photograph in a little frame for you."

Never was such a wonderful box. It appeared to have no bottom whatever. Under the presents were parcels of figs, prunes, almonds, raisins, candy; under those, apples and pears. There seemed no end to the surprises.

At last all were out.

"Now," said Katy, "let's throw back the apples and pears, and then I want you to help divide the other things, and make some packages for the girls. They are all disappointed not to have their boxes. I should like to have them share ours. Wouldn't you, Clover?"

"Yes, indeed. I was just going to propose it."

So Clover cut twenty-nine squares of white paper, Rose and Katy sorted and divided, and pretty soon ginger-snaps and almonds and sugar-plums were walking down all the entries, and a gladsome crunching showed that the girls had found pleasant employment. None of the snowed-up boxes got through till Monday, so except for Katy and Clover the school would have had no Christmas treat at all.

They carried Mrs. Nipson a large slice of cake, and a basket full of the beautiful red apples. All the teachers were remembered, and the servants. The S. S. U. C. was convened and feasted; and as for Rose, Louisa, and other special cronies, dainties were heaped upon them with such unsparing hand that they finally remonstrated.

"You're giving everything away. You'll have none left for yourselves."

"Yes, we shall,—plenty," said Clover. "O Rosy! here's such a splendid pear! You must have this."

"No! no!" protested Rose; but Clover forced it into her pocket. "The Carrs' Box" was always quoted in the Nunnery afterward, as an example of what papas and mammas could accomplish, when they were of the right sort, and really wanted to make school-girls happy. Distributing their treasures kept Katy and Clover so busy that it was not until after dinner that they found time to open the smaller box. When they did so, they were sorry for the delay. The box was full of flowers, roses, geranium-leaves, heliotrope, beautiful red and white carnations, all so bedded in cotton that the frost had not touched them. But they looked chilled, and Katy hastened to put them in warm water, which she had been told was the best way to revive drooping flowers.

Cousin Helen had sent them; and underneath, sewed to the box, that they might not shake about and do mischief, were two flat parcels wrapped in tissue paper, and tied with white ribbon, in Cousin Helen's, dainty way. They were glove-cases, of quilted silk, delicately scented, one white, and one lilac; and to each was pinned a loving note, wishing the girls a Merry Christmas.

"How awfully good people are!" said Clover. "I do think we ought to be the best girls in the world."

Last of all, Katy made a choice little selection from her stores, a splendid apple, a couple of fine pears, and handful of raisins and figs, and, with a few of the freshest flowers in a wine-glass, she went down the Row and tapped at Miss Jane's door.

Miss Jane was sitting up for the first time, wrapped in a shawl, and looking very thin and pale. Katy, who had almost ceased to be afraid of her, went in cheerily.

"We've had a delicious box from home, Miss Jane, full of all sorts of things. It has been such fun unpacking it! I've brought you an apple, some pears, and this little bunch of flowers. Wasn't it a nice Christmas for us?"

"Yes," said Miss Jane, "very nice indeed. I heard some one saying in the entry that you had a box. Thank you," as Katy set the basket and glass on the table. "Those flowers are very sweet. I wish you a Merry Christmas, I'm sure."

This was much from Miss Jane, who couldn't help speaking shortly, even when she was pleased. Katy withdrew in high glee.

But that night, just before bed-time, something happened so surprising that Katy, telling Clover of it afterward, said she half fancied that she must have dreamed it all. It was about eight o'clock in the evening: she was passing down Quaker Row, and Miss Jane called and asked her to come in. Miss Jane's cheeks were flushed, and she spoke fast, as if she had resolved to say something, and thought the sooner it was over the better.

"Miss Carr," she began, "I wish to tell you that I made up my mind some time since that we did you an injustice last term. It is not your attentions to me during my illness which have changed my opinion,— that was done before I fell ill. It is your general conduct, and the good influence which I have seen you exert over other girls, which convinced me that we must have been wrong about you. That is all. I thought you might like to hear me say this, and I shall say the same to Mrs. Nipson."

"Thank you," said Katy, "you don't know how glad I am!" She half thought she would kiss Miss Jane, but somehow it didn't seem possible; so she shook hands very heartily instead, and flew to her room, feeling as if her feet were wings.

"It seems too good to be true. I want to cry, I am so happy," she told Clover. "What a lovely day this has been!"

And of all that she had received, I think Katy considered this explanation with Miss Jane as her very best Christmas box.

CHAPTER XII. WAITING FOR SPRING.

School was a much happier place after this. Mrs. Nipson never alluded to the matter, but her manner altered. Katy felt that she was no longer watched or distrusted, and her heart grew light.

In another week Miss Jane was so much better as to be hearing her classes again. Illness had not changed her materially. It is only in novels that rheumatic fever sweetens tempers, and makes disagreeable people over into agreeable ones. Most of the girls disliked her as much as ever. Her tongue was just as sharp, and her manner as grim. But for Katy, from that time forward, there was a difference. Miss Jane was not affectionate to her,—it was not in her nature to be that,—but she was civil and considerate, and in a dry way, friendly, and gradually Katy grew to have an odd sort of liking for her.

Do any of you know how incredibly long winter seems in climates where for weeks together the thermometer stands at zero? There is something hopeless in such cold. You think of summer as of a thing read about somewhere in a book, but which has no actual existence. Winter seems the only reality in the world.

Katy and Clover felt this hopelessness growing upon them as the days went on, and the weather became more and more severe. Ten, twenty, even thirty degrees below zero, was no unusual register for the Hillsover thermometers. Such cold half frightened them, but nobody else was frightened or surprised. It was dry, brilliant cold. The December snows lay unmelted on the ground in March, and the paths cut then were crisp and hard still, only the white walls on either side had risen higher and higher, till only a moving line of hoods and tippets was visible above them, when the school went out for its daily walk. Morning after morning the girls woke to find thick crusts of frost on their window-panes, and every drop of water in the wash-bowl or pitcher turned to solid ice. Night after night, Clover, who was a chilly little creature, lay shivering and unable to sleep, notwithstanding the hot bricks at her feet, and the many wraps which Katy piled upon her. To Katy herself the cold was more bracing than depressing. There was something in her blood which responded to the sharp tingle of frost, and she gained in strength in a remarkable way during this winter. But the long storms told upon her spirits. She pined for spring and home more than she liked to tell, and felt the need of variety in their monotonous life, where the creeping days appeared like weeks, and the weeks stretched themselves out, and seemed as long as months do in other places.

The girls resorted to all sorts of devices to keep themselves alive during this dreary season. They had little epidemics of occupation. At one time it was "spattering," when all faces and fingers had a tendency to smudges of India ink; and there was hardly a fine comb or toothbrush fit for use in the establishment. Then a rage for tatting set in, followed by a fever of fancy-work, every one falling in love with the same pattern at the same time, and copying and recopying, till nobody could bear the sight of it. At one time Clover counted eighteen girls all at work on the same bead and canvas pin-cushion. Later there was a short period of *decalcomanie;* and then came the grand album craze, when thirty-three girls out of the thirty-nine sent for blank books bound in red morocco, and began to collect signatures and sentiments. Here, also, there was a tendency toward repetition.

Sally Austin added to her autograph these lines of her own composition:—

> When on this page your beauteous eyes you bend,
> Let it remind you of your absent friend.
> Sally J. Austin,
> Galveston, Texas.

The girls found this sentiment charming, at least a dozen borrowed it, and in half the albums in the school you might read,—

"When on this page your beauteous eyes," &c.

Esther Dearborn wrote in Clover's book: "The better part of Valor is Discretion." Why she wrote it, nobody knew, or why it was more applicable to Clover than to any one else; but the sentiment proved popular, and was repeated over and over again, above various neatly written signatures. There was a strife as to who should display the largest collection. Some of the girls sent home for autographs of distinguished persons, which they pasted in their books. Rose Red, however, out-did them all.

"Did I ever show you mine?" she asked one day, when most of the girls were together in the school-room.

"No, never!" cried a number of voices. "Have you got one? Oh, do let us see it."

"Certainly, I'll get it right away, if you like," said Rose, obligingly.

She went to her room, and returned with a shabby old blank book in her hand. Some of the girls looked disappointed.

"The cover of mine isn't very nice," explained Rose. "I'm going to have it rebound one of these days. You see it's not a new album at all, nor a school album; but it's very valuable to me." Here she heaved a sentimental sigh. "All my friends have written in it," she said.

The girls were quite impressed by the manner in which Rose said this. But, when they turned over the pages of the album, they were even more impressed. Rose had evidently been on intimate terms with a circle of most distinguished persons. Half the autographs in the book were from gentlemen, and they were dated all over the world.

"Just listen to this!" cried Louisa, and she read,—
"Thou may'st forget me, but never, never shall I forget thee!"
Alphonso of Castile.
The Escurial, April 1st.

'Who's he?" asked a circle of awe-struck girls.

"Didn't you ever hear of him? Youngest brother of the King of Spain," replied Rose carelessly.

"Oh, my! and just hear this," exclaimed Annie Silsbie.

If you ever deign to cast a thought in my direction, Miss Rose, remember me always as
Thy devoted servitor,
Potemkin Montmorency.
St. Petersburg, July 10th.

"And this," shrieked Alice White.

"They say love is a thorn, I say it is a dart,
And yet I cannot tear thee from my heart."
Antonio, Count of Vallambrosa.

"Do you really and truly know a Count?" asked Bella, backing away from Rose with eyes as big as saucers.

"Know Antonio de Vallambrosa! I should think I did," replied Rose. "Nobody in this country knows him so well, I fancy."

"And he wrote that for you?"

"How else could it get into my book, goosey?"

This was unanswerable; and Rose was installed from that time forward in the minds of Bella and the rest as a heroine of the first water. Katy, however, knew better; and the first time she caught Rose alone she attacked her on the subject.

"Now, Rosy-Posy, confess. Who wrote all those absurd autographs in your book?"

"Absurd autographs! What can you mean?"

"All those Counts and things. No, it's no use. You shan't wriggle away till you tell me."

"Oh, Antonio and dear Potemkin, do you mean them?"

"Yes, of course I do."

"And you really want to know?"

"Yes."

"And will swear not to tell?"

"Yes."

"Well, then," bursting into a laugh, "I wrote every one of them myself."

"Did you really? When?"

"Day before yesterday. I thought Lilly needed taking down, she was so set up with her autographs of Wendell Phillips and Mr. Seward, so

I just sat down and wrote a book full. It only took me half an hour. I meant to write some more: in fact, I had one all ready,—

'I am dead, or pretty near:
David's done for me I fear'
Goliath of Gath.

but I was afraid even Bella wouldn't swallow that, so I tore out the page. I'm sorry I did now, for I really think the geese would have believed it. Written in his last moments, you know, to oblige an ancestor of my own," added Rose, in a tone of explanation.

"You monkey!" cried Katy, highly diverted. But she kept Rose's counsel, and I daresay some of the Hillsover girls believe in that wonderful album to this day.

It was not long after that a sad piece of news came for Bella. Her father was dead. Their home was in Iowa, too far to allow of her returning for the funeral; so the poor little girl stayed at school, to bear her trouble as best she might. Katy, who was always kind to children, and had somewhat affected Bella from the first on account of her resemblance to Elsie in height and figure, was especially tender to her now, which Bella repaid with the gift of her whole queer little heart. Her affectionate demonstrations were rather of the monkey order, and not un frequently troublesome; but Katy was never otherwise than patient and gentle with her, though Rose, and even Clover, remonstrated on what they called this "singular intimacy."

"Poor little soul! It's so hard for her, and she's only eleven years old," she told them.

"She has such a funny way of looking at you sometimes," said Rose, who was very observant. "It is just the air of a squirrel who has hidden a nut, and doesn't want you to find out where, and yet can hardly help indicating it with his paw. She's got something on her mind, I'm sure."

"Half a dozen things, very likely," added Clover: "she's such a mischief."

But none of them guessed what this "something" was.

Early in January Mrs. Nipson announced that in four weeks she proposed to give a "Soiree," to which all young ladies whose records were entirely free from marks during the intervening period would be allowed to come. This announcement created great excitement, and the school set itself to be good; but marks were easy to get, and gradually one girl after another lost her chance, till by the appointed day only a limited party descended to join the festivities, and nearly half the school was left upstairs to sigh over past sins. Katy and Rose were among the unlucky ones. Rose had incurred a mark by writing a note in study-hour, and Katy by being five minutes late to dinner. They consoled themselves by dressing Clover's hair, and making her look as pretty as possible, and then stationed themselves in the upper hall at the head of the stairs to watch her career, and get as much fun out of the occasion as they could.

Pretty soon they saw Clover below on Professor Seccomb's arm. He was a kingly, pleasant man, with a bald head, and it was a fashion among the girls to admire him.

"Doesn't she look pretty?" said Rose. "Just notice Mrs. Searles, Katy. She's grinning at Clover like the Cheshire cat. What a wonderful cap that is of hers! She had it when Sylvia was here at school, eight years ago."

"Hush! she'll hear you."

"No, she won't. There's Ellen beginning her piece. I know she's frightened by the way she plays. Hark! how she hurries the time!"

"There, they are going to have refreshments, after all!" cried Esther Dearborn, as trays of lemonade and cake-baskets appeared below on their way to the parlor. "Isn't it a shame to have to stay up here?"

"Professor Seccomb! Professor!" called Rose, in a daring whisper. "Take pity upon us. We are starving for a piece of cake."

The Professor gave a jump; then retreated, and looked upward. When he saw the circle of hungry faces peering down, he doubled up with laughter. "Wait a moment," he whispered back, and vanished into the parlor. Pretty soon the girls saw him making his way through the crowd with an immense slice of pound-cake in each hand.

"Here, Miss Rose," he said,—"catch it." But Rose ran half-way downstairs, received the cake, dimpled her thanks, and retreated to the darkness above, whence sounds proceeded which sent the amused Professor into the parlor convulsed with suppressed laughter. Pretty soon Clover stole up the back stairs to report.

"Are you having a nice time? Is the lemon-ade good? Who have you been talking with?" inquired a chorus of voices.

"Pretty nice. Everybody is very old. I haven't been talking to anybody in particular, and the lemonade is only cream-of-tartar water. I guess it's jollier up here with you," replied Clover. "I must go now: my turn to play comes next." Down she ran.

"Except for the glory of the thing, I think we're having more fun than she," answered Rose.

Next week came St. Valentine's Day. Several of the girls received valentines from home, and they wrote them to each other. Katy and Clover both had one from Phil, exactly alike, with the same purple bird in the middle of the page, and "I love you" printed underneath; and they joined in fabricating a gorgeous one for Rose, which was supposed to come from Potemkin de Montmorencey, the hero of the album. But the most surprising valentine was received by Miss Jane. It came with the others, while all the household were at dinner. The girls saw her redden and look angry, but she put the letter in her pocket, and said nothing.

In the afternoon, it came out through Bella that "Miss Jane's letter was in poetry, and that she was just mad as fire about it." Just before tea, Louisa came running down the Row, to No. 5, where Katy was sitting with Rose.

"Girls, what do you think? That letter which Miss Jane got this morning was a valentine, the most dreadful thing, but so funny!" she stopped to laugh.

"How do you know?" cried the other two.

"Miss Marsh told Alice Gibbons. She's a sort of cousin, you know; and Miss Marsh often tells her things. She says Miss Jane and Mrs. Nipson are furious, and are determined to find out who sent it. It was from Mr. Hardhack, Miss Jane's missionary,—or no, not from Mr. Hardhack, but from a cannibal who had just eaten Mr. Hardhack up; and he sent Miss Jane a lock of his hair, and the recipe the tribe cooked him by. They found him 'very nice,' he said, and 'He turned out quite tender.' That was one of the lines in the poem. Did you ever hear of any thing like it? Who do you suppose could have sent it?"

"Who could it have been?" cried the others. Katy had one moment's awful misgiving; but a glance at Rose's face, calm and innocent as a baby's, reassured her. It was impossible that she could have done this mischievous thing. Katy, you see, was not privy to that entry in Rose's journal, "Pay Miss Jane off," nor aware that Rose had just written underneath, "Did it. Feb. 14, 1869."

Nobody ever found out the author of this audacious valentine. Rose kept her own counsel, and Miss Jane probably concluded that "the better part of valor was discretion," for the threatened inquiries were never made.

And now it lacked but six weeks to the end of the term. The girls counted the days, and practised various devices to make them pass more quickly. Esther Dearborn, who had a turn for arithmetic, set herself to a careful calculation of how many hours, minutes, and seconds must pass before the happy time should come. Annie Silsbie strung forty-two tiny squares of card-board on a thread and each night slipped one off and burned it up in the candle. Others made diagrams of the time, with a division for each day, and every night blotted one out with a sense of triumph. None of these devices made the time hasten. It never moved more slowly than now, when life seemed to consist of a universal waiting.

But though Katy's heart bounded at the thought of home till she could hardly bear the gladness, she owned to Clover,—"Do you know, much as I long to get away, I am half sorry to go! It is parting with something which we shall never have any more. Home is lovely, and I would rather be there than anywhere else; but, if you and I live to be a hundred, we shall never be girls at boarding-school again."

CHAPTER XIII. PARADISE REGAINED.

"Only seven days more to cross off," said Clover, drawing her pencil through one of the squares on the diagram pinned beside her looking-glass, "seven more, and then—oh, joy!—papa will be here, and we shall start for home."

She was interrupted by the entrance of Katy, holding a letter and looking pale and aggrieved.

"Oh, Clover," she cried, "just listen to this! Papa can't come for us. Isn't it too bad?" And she read:—

"Burnet, March 20.

"My dear Girls,—I find that it will not be possible for me to come for you next week, as I intended. Several people are severely ill, and old Mrs. Barlow struck down suddenly with paralysis, so I cannot leave. I am sorry, and so will you be; but there is no help for it. Fortunately, Mrs. Hall has just heard that some friends of hers are coming westward with their family, and she has written to ask them to take charge of you. The drawback to this plan is, that you will have to travel alone as far as Albany, where Mr. Peters (Mrs. Hall's friend) will meet you. I have written to ask Mr. Page to put you on the train, and under the care of the conductor, on Tuesday morning. I hope you will get through without embarrassment. Mr. Peters will be at the station in Albany to receive you; or, if any thing should hinder him, you are to drive at once to the Delavan House where they are staying. I enclose a check for your journey. If Dorry were five years older, I should send him after you.

"The children are most impatient to have you back. Miss Finch has been suddenly called away by the illness of her sister-in-law, so Elsie is keeping house till you return.

"God bless you, my dear daughters, and send you safe.
                "Yours affectionately,
                        P. Carr."

"Oh, dear!" said Clover, with her lip trembling, "now papa won't see Rosy."

"No," said Katy, "and Rosy and Louisa and the rest won't see him. That is the worst of all. I wanted them to so much. And just think how dismal it will be to travel with people we don't know. It's too, too bad, I declare."

"I do think old Mrs. Barlow might have put off being ill just one week longer," grumbled Clover. "It takes away half the pleasure of going home."

The girls might be excused for being cross, for this was a great disappointment. There was no help for it, however, as papa said. They could only sigh and submit. But the journey, to which they had looked forward so much, was no longer thought of as a pleasure, only a disagreeable necessity, something which must be endured in order that they might reach home.

Five, four, three days,—the last little square was crossed off, the last dinner was eaten, the last breakfast. There was much mourning over Katy and Clover among the girls who were to return for another year. Louisa and Ellen Gray were inconsolable; and Bella, with a very small pocket handkerchief held tightly in her hand, clung to Katy every moment, crying, and declaring that she would not let her go. The last evening she followed her into No. 2 (where she was dreadfully in the way of the packing), and after various odd contortions and mysterious, half-spoken sentences, said:—

"Say, won't you tell if I tell you something?"

"What is it?" asked Katy, absently, as she folded and smoothed her best gown.

"Something," repeated Bella, wagging her head mysteriously, and looking more like a thievish squirrel than ever.

"Well, what is it? Tell me."

To Katy's surprise, Bella burst into a violent fit of crying.

"I'm real sorry I did it," she sobbed,—"real sorry! And now you'll never love me any more."

"Yes, I will. What is it? Do stop crying, Bella dear, and tell me," said Katy, alarmed at the violence of the sobs.

"It was for fun, really and truly it was. But I wanted some cake too," —protested Bella, sniffing very hard.

"What!"

"And I didn't think anybody would know. Berry Searles doesn't care a bit for us little girls, only for big ones. And I knew if I said "Bella," he'd never give me the cake. So I said 'Miss Carr' instead."

"Bella, did you write that note?" inquired Katy, almost to much surprised to speak.

"Yes. And I tied a string to your blind, because I knew I could go in and draw it up when you were practising. But I didn't mean to do any harm; and when Mrs. Florence was so mad, and changed your room, I was real sorry," moaned Bella, digging her knuckles into her eyes.

"Won't you ever love me any more?" she demanded. Katy lifted her into her lap, and talked so tenderly and seriously that her contrition, which was only half genuine, became real; and she cried in good earnest when Katy kissed her in token of forgiveness.

"Of course you'll go at once to Mrs. Nipson," said Clover and Rose, when Katy imparted this surprising discovery.

"No, I think not. Why should I? It would only get poor little Bella into a dreadful scrape, and she's coming back again, you know. Mrs.

Nipson does not believe that story now,—nobody does. We had 'lived it down,' just as I hope we should. That is much better than having it contradicted."

"I don't think so; and I should enjoy seeing that little wretch of a Bella well whipped," persisted Rose. But Katy was not to be shaken.

"To please me, promise that not a word shall be said about it," she urged; and, to please her, the girls consented.

I think Katy was right in saying that Mrs. Nipson no longer believed her guilty in the affair of the note. She had been very friendly to both the sisters of late; and when Clover carried in her album and asked for an autograph, she waxed quite sentimental and wrote, "I would not exchange the modest Clover for the most beautiful parterre, so bring it back, I pray thee, to your affectionate teacher, Marianne Nipson;" which effusion quite overwhelmed "the modest Clover," and called out the remark from Rose,—"Don't she wish she may get you!" Miss Jane said twice, "I shall miss you, Katy," a speech which, to quote Rose again, made Katy look as "surprised as Balaam." Rose herself was not coming back to school. She and the girls were half broken-hearted at parting. They lavished tears, kisses, promises of letters, and vows of eternal friendship. Neither of them, it was agreed, was ever to love anybody else so well. The final moment would have been almost too tragical, had it not been for a last bit of mischief on the part of Rose. It was after the stage was actually at the door, and she had her foot upon the step, that, struck by a happy thought, she rushed upstairs again, collected the girls, and, each taking a window, they tore down the cotton, flung open sashes, and startled Mrs. Nipson, who stood below, by the simultaneous waving therefrom of many white flags. Katy, who was already in the stage, had the full benefit of this performance. Always after that, when she thought of the Nunnery, her memory recalled this scene,—Mrs. Nipson in the door-way, Bella blubbering behind, and overhead the windows crowded with saucy girls, laughing and triumphantly flapping the long cotton strips which had for so many months obscured the daylight for them all.

At Springfield next morning she and Clover said good-by to Mr. Page and Lilly. The ride to Albany was easy and safe. With every mile their spirits rose. At last they were actually on the way home.

At Albany they looked anxiously about the crowded depot for "Mr. Peters." Nobody appeared at first, and they had time to grow nervous before they saw a gentle, careworn little man coming toward them in company with the conductor.

"I believe you are the young ladies I have come to meet," he said. "You must excuse my being late, I was detained by business. There is a great deal to do to move a family out West," he wiped his forehead in a dispirited way. Then he put the girls into a carriage, and gave the driver a direction.

"We'd better leave your baggage at the office as we pass," he said, "because we have to get off so early in the morning."

"How early?"

"The boat goes at six, but we ought to be on board by half-past five, so as to be well settled before she starts."

"The boat?" said Katy, opening her eyes.

"Yes. Erie Canal, you know. Our furniture goes that way, so we judged it best to do the same, and keep an eye on it ourselves. Never be separated from your property, if you can help it, that's my maxim. It's the Prairie Belle,—one of the finest boats on the Canal."

"When do we get to Buffalo?" asked Katy, with an uneasy recollection of having heard that canal boats travel slowly.

"Buffalo? Let me see. This is Tuesday,—Wednesday, Thursday,—well, if we're lucky we ought to be there Friday evening; so, if we're not too late to catch the night boat on the lake, you'll reach home Saturday afternoon."

Four days! The girls looked at each other with dismay too deep for words. Elsie was expecting them by Thursday at latest. What should they do?

"Telegraph," was the only answer that suggested itself. So Katy scribbled a despatch, "Coming by canal. Don't expect us till Saturday," which she begged Mr. Peters to send; and she and Clover agreed in whispers that it was dreadful, but they must bear it as patiently as they could.

Oh, the patience which is needed on a canal! The motion which is not so much motion as standing still! The crazy impulse to jump out and help the crawling boat along by pushing it from behind! How one grows to hate the slow, monotonous glide, the dull banks, and to envy every swift-moving thing in sight, each man on horseback, each bird flying through the air.

Mrs. Peters was a thin, anxious woman, who spent her life anticipating disasters of all sorts. She had her children with her, three little boys, and a teething baby; and such a load of bundles, and baskets, and brown paper parcels, that Katy and Clover privately wondered how she could possibly have got through the journey without their help. Willy, the eldest boy, was always begging leave to go ashore and ride the towing horses; Sammy, the second could only be kept quiet by means of crooked pins and fish-lines of blue yarn; while Paul, the youngest, was possessed with a curiosity as to the under side of the boat, which resulted in his dropping his new hat overboard five times in three days, Mr. Peters and the cabin-boy rowing back in a small boat each time to recover it. Mrs. Peters sat on deck with her baby in her lap, and was in a perpetual agony lest the locks should work wrongly, or the boys be drowned, or some one fail to notice the warning cry, "Bridge!" and have their heads carried off from their shoulders. Nobody did; but the poor lady suffered the anguish of ten accidents in dreading the one which never took place. The berths at night were small and cramped, restless children woke and cried, the cabins were close, the decks cold and windy. There was nothing to see, and nothing to do. Katy and Clover agreed that they never wanted to see a canal boat again.

They were very helpful to Mrs. Peters, amused the boys, and kept them out of mischief; and she told her husband that she really thought she shouldn't have lived through the journey if it hadn't been for the Miss Carrs, they were such kind girls, and so fond of children. But the three days were terribly long. At last they ended. Buffalo was reached in time for the lake boat; and once established on board, feeling the rapid motion, and knowing that each stroke of the paddles took them nearer home, the girls were rewarded for their long trial of patience.

At four o'clock the next afternoon Burnet was in sight. Long before they touched the wharf Clover discovered old Whitey and the carryall, and Alexander, waiting for them among the crowd of carriages. Standing on the edge of the dock appeared a well-known figure.

"Papa! papa!" she shrieked. It seemed as if the girls could not wait for the boat to stop, and the plank to be lowered. How delightful it was to feel papa again! Such a sense of home and comfort and shelter as came with his touch!

"I'll never go away from you again, never, never!" repeated Clover, keeping tight hold of his hand as they drove up the hill. Dr. Carr, as he gazed at his girls, was equally happy,—they were so bright, affectionate and loving. No, he could never spare them again, for the boarding-school or any thing else, he thought.

"You must be very tired," he said.

"Not a bit. I'm hardly ever tired now," replied Katy.

"Oh, dear! I forgot to thank Mr. Peters for taking care of us," said Clover.

"Never mind. I did it for you," answered her father.

"Oh, that baby!" she continued: "how glad I am that it has gone to Toledo, and I needn't hear it cry any more! Katy! Katy! there's home! We are at the gate!"

The girls looked eagerly out, but no children were visible. They hurried up the gravel path, under the locust boughs just beginning to bud. There, over the front door, was an arch of evergreens, with "Katy" and "Clover" upon it in scarlet letters; and as they reached the porch, the door flew open, and out poured the children in a tumultuous little crowd. They had been on the roof, looking through a spy-glass after the boat.

"We never knew you had come till we heard the gate," explained John and Dorry; while Elsie hugged Clover, and Phil, locking his arms round Katy's neck, took his feet off the floor, and swung them in and ecstasy of affection, until she begged for mercy.

"How you are grown! Dorry, you're as tall as I am! Elsie, darling, how well you look! Oh, isn't it delicious, delicious, delicious, to be at home again!" There was such a hubbub of endearments and explanations that Dr. Carr could hardly make himself heard.

"Clover, your waist has grown as small as a pin. You look just like the beautiful princess in Elsie's story," said Johnnie.

"Take the girls into the parlor," repeated Dr. Carr: "it is cold out here, with the door open."

"Take 'em upstairs! You don't know what is upstairs!" shouted Phil, whereupon Elsie frowned and shook her head at him.

The parlor was gay with daffodils and hyacinths, and vases of blue violets, which smelt delightfully. Cecy had helped to arrange them, Elsie said. And just at that moment Cecy herself came in. Her hair was arranged in a sort of pin-cushion of puffs, with a row of curls on top, where no curls used to grow, and her appearance generally was very fine and fashionable; but she was the same affectionate Cecy as ever, and hugged the girls, and danced round them as she used to do at twelve. She had waited until they had had time to kiss once all round, she said, and then she really couldn't wait any longer.

"Now come upstairs," suggested Elsie, when Clover had warmed her feet, and the flowers had been admired, and everybody had said ten times over how nice it was to have the girls back, and the girls had replied that it was just as nice to come back.

So they all went upstairs, Elsie leading the way.

"Where are you going?" cried Katy: "that's the Blue Room." But Elsie did not pause.

"You see," she explained, with the door-knob in her hand, "papa and I thought you ought to have a bigger room now, because you are grown-up young ladies! So we have fixed this for you, and your old one is going to be the spare room instead." Then she threw the door open, and led the girls in.

"See, Katy," she said, "this is your bureau, and this is Clover's. And look what nice drawers papa has had put in the closet,—two for you, and two for her. Aren't they convenient? Don't you like it? And isn't it a great deal pleasanter than the old room?"

"Oh, a great deal," cried the girls. "It is delightful, every thing about it." All Katy's old treasures had been transferred from her old quarters to this. There was her cushioned chair, her table, her book-shelf, the pictures from the walls. There were some new things too, —a blue carpet, blue paper on the walls, window curtains of fresh chintz; and Elsie had made a tasteful pin-cushion for each bureau, and Johnnie crocheted mats for the wash-stand. Altogether, it was as pretty a bower as two sisters just grown into ladies could desire.

"What are those lovely things hanging on either side of the bed?" asked Clover.

They were two illuminated texts, sent as a "welcome home," by Cousin Helen. One was a morning text, and other an evening text, Elsie explained. The evening text, which bore the words, "I will lay me down to sleep, and take my rest, for it is thou, Lord, only who makest me dwell in safety," was painted in soft purples and grays, and among the poppies and silver lilies which wreathed it appeared a cunning little downy bird, fast asleep, with his head under his wing. The morning text, "When I awake, I am still with Thee," was in bright colors, scarlet and blue and gold, and had a frame of rose garlands and wide-awake-looking butterflies and humming-birds. The girls thought they had never seen any thing so pretty.

Such a gay supper as they had that night! Katy would not take her old place at the tea-tray. She wanted to know how Elsie looked as housekeeper, she said. So she sat on one side of papa, and Clover on the other, and Elsie poured the tea, with a mixture of delight and dignity which was worth seeing.

"I'll begin to-morrow," said Katy.

And with that morrow, when she came out of her pretty room and took her place once more as manager of the household, her grown-up life may be said to have begun. So it is time that I should cease to write about her. Grown-up lives may be very interesting, but they have no rightful place in a child's book. If little girls will forget to be little, and take it upon them to become young ladies, they must bear the consequences, one of which is, that we can follow their fortunes no longer.

. . . .

I wrote these last words sitting in the same green meadow where the first words of "What Katy Did" were written. A year had passed, but a cardinal-flower which seemed the same stood looking at itself in the brook, and from the bulrush-bed sounded tiny voices. My little goggle-eyed friends were discussing Katy and her conduct, as they did then, but with less spirit; for one voice came seldom and faintly, while the other, bold and defiant as ever, repeated over and over again, "Katy didn't! Katy didn't! She didn't, didn't, didn't"

"Katy did!" sounded faintly from the farther rush.

"She didn't, she didn't," chirped the undaunted partisan. Silence followed. His opponent was either convinced or tired of the discussion.

"Katy didn't." The words repeated themselves in my mind as I walked homeward. How much room for "Didn'ts" there is in the world, I thought What an important part they play! And how glad I am that, with all her own and other people's doings, so many of these "Didn'ts" were included among the things which my Katy did at School!

What Katy Did Next

CHAPTER I. AN UNEXPECTED GUEST.

The September sun was glinting cheerfully into a pretty bedroom furnished with blue. It danced on the glossy hair and bright eyes of two girls, who sat together hemming ruffles for a white muslin dress. The half-finished skirt of the dress lay on the bed; and as each crisp ruffle was completed, the girls added it to the snowy heap, which looked like a drift of transparent clouds or a pile of foamy white-of-egg beaten stiff enough to stand alone.

These girls were Clover and Elsie Carr, and it was Clover's first evening dress for which they were hemming ruffles. It was nearly two years since a certain visit made by Johnnie to Inches Mills, of which some of you have read in "Nine Little Goslings;" and more than three since Clover and Katy had returned home from the boarding-school at Hillsover.

Clover was now eighteen. She was a very small Clover still, but it would have been hard to find anywhere a prettier little maiden than she had grown to be. Her skin was so exquisitely fair that her arms and wrists and shoulders, which were round and dimpled like a baby's, seemed cut out of daisies or white rose leaves. Her thick, brown hair waved and coiled gracefully about her head. Her smile was peculiarly sweet; and the eyes, always Clover's chief beauty, had still that pathetic look which made them irresistible to tender-hearted people.

Elsie, who adored Clover, considered her as beautiful as girls in books, and was proud to be permitted to hem ruffles for the dress in which she was to burst upon the world. Though, as for that, not much "bursting" was possible in Burnet, where tea-parties of a middle-aged description, and now and then a mild little dance, represented "gayety" and "society." Girls "came out" very much, as the sun comes out in the morning,—by slow degrees and gradual approaches, with no particular one moment which could be fixed upon as having been the crisis of the joyful event.

"There," said Elsie, adding another ruffle to the pile on the bed,— "there's the fifth done. It's going to be ever so pretty, I think. I'm glad you had it all white; it's a great deal nicer."

"Cecy wanted me to have a blue bodice and sash," said Clover, "but I wouldn't. Then she tried to persuade me to get a long spray of pink roses for the skirt."

"I'm so glad you didn't! Cecy was always crazy about pink roses. I only wonder she didn't wear them when she was married!"

Yes; the excellent Cecy, who at thirteen had announced her intention to devote her whole life to teaching Sunday School, visiting the poor, and setting a good example to her more worldly contemporaries, had actually forgotten these fine resolutions, and before she was twenty had become the wife of Sylvester Slack, a young lawyer in a neighboring town! Cecy's wedding and wedding-clothes, and Cecy's house-furnishing had been the great excitement of the preceding year in Burnet; and a fresh excitement had come since in the shape of Cecy's baby, now about two months old, and named "Katherine Clover," after her two friends. This made it natural that Cecy and her affairs should still be of interest in the Carr household; and Johnnie, at the time we write of, was making her a week's visit.

"She *was* rather wedded to them," went on Clover, pursuing the subject of the pink roses. "She was almost vexed when I wouldn't buy the spray. But it cost lots, and I didn't want it in the least, so I stood firm. Besides, I always said that my first party dress should be plain white. Girls in novels always wear white to their first balls; and fresh flowers are a great deal prettier, any way, than artificial. Katy says she'll give me some violets to wear."

"Oh, will she? That will be lovely!" cried the adoring Elsie. "Violets look just like you, somehow. Oh, Clover, what sort of a dress do you think I shall have when I grow up and go to parties and things? Won't it be awfully interesting when you and I go out to choose it?"

Just then the noise of some one running upstairs quickly made the sisters look up from their work. Footsteps are very significant at times, and these footsteps suggested haste and excitement.

Another moment, the door opened, and Katy dashed in, calling out, "Papa!—Elsie, Clover, where's papa?"

"He went over the river to see that son of Mr. White's who broke his leg. Why, what's the matter?" asked Clover.

"Is somebody hurt?" inquired Elsie, startled at Katy's agitated looks.

"No, not hurt, but poor Mrs. Ashe is in such trouble."

Mrs. Ashe, it should be explained, was a widow who had come to Burnet some months previously, and had taken a pleasant house not far from the Carrs'. She was a pretty, lady-like woman, with a particularly graceful, appealing manner, and very fond of her one child, a little girl. Katy and papa both took a fancy to her at once; and the families had grown neighborly and intimate in a short time, as people occasionally do when circumstances are favorable.

"I'll tell you all about it in a minute," went on Katy. "But first I must find Alexander, and send him off to meet papa and beg him to hurry home." She went to the head of the stairs as she spoke, and called "Debby! Debby!" Debby answered. Katy gave her direction, and then came back again to the room where the other two were sitting.

"Now," she said, speaking more collectedly, "I must explain as fast as I can, for I have got to go back. You know that Mrs. Ashe's little nephew is here for a visit, don't you?"

"Yes, he came on Saturday."

"Well, he was ailing all day yesterday, and to-day he is worse, and she is afraid it is scarlet-fever. Luckily, Amy was spending the day with the Uphams yesterday, so she scarcely saw the boy at all; and as soon as her mother became alarmed, she sent her out into the garden to play, and hasn't let her come indoors since, so she can't have been exposed to any particular danger yet. I went by the house on my way down street, and there sat the poor little thing all alone in the arbor, with her dolly in her lap, looking so disconsolate. I spoke to her over the fence, and Mrs. Ashe heard my voice, and opened the upstairs window and called to me. She said Amy had never had the fever, and that the very idea of her having it frightened her to death. She is such a delicate child, you know."

"Oh, poor Mrs. Ashe!" cried Clover; "I am so sorry for her! Well, Katy, what did you do?"

"I hope I didn't do wrong, but I offered to bring Amy here. Papa won't object, I am almost sure."

"Why, of course he won't. Well?"

"I am going back now to fetch Amy. Mrs. Ashe is to let Ellen, who hasn't been in the room with the little boy, pack a bagful of clothes and put it out on the steps, and I shall send Alexander for it by and by. You can't think how troubled poor Mrs. Ashe was. She couldn't help crying when she said that Amy was all she had left in the world. And I nearly cried too, I was so sorry for her. She was so relieved when I said that we would take Amy. You know she has a great deal of confidence in papa."

"Yes, and in you too. Where will you put Amy to sleep, Katy?"

"What do you think would be best? In Dorry's room?"

"I think she'd better come in here with you, and I'll go into Dorry's room. She is used to sleeping with her mother, you know, and she would be lonely if she were left to herself."

"Perhaps that will be better, only it is a great bother for you, Clovy dear."

"I don't mind," responded Clover, cheerfully. "I rather like to change about and try a new room once in a while. It's as good as going on a journey—almost."

She pushed aside the half-finished dress as she spoke, opened a drawer, took out its contents, and began to carry them across the entry to Dorry's room, doing everything with the orderly deliberation that was characteristic of whatever Clover did. Her preparations were almost complete before Katy returned, bringing with her little Amy Ashe.

Amy was a tall child of eight, with a frank, happy face, and long light hair hanging down her back. She looked like the pictures of "Alice in Wonderland;" but just at that moment it was a very woful little Alice indeed that she resembled, for her cheeks were stained with tears and her eyes swollen with recent crying.

"Why, what is the matter?" cried kind little Clover, taking Amy in her arms, and giving her a great hug. "Aren't you glad that you are coming to make us a visit? We are."

"Mamma didn't kiss me for good-by," sobbed the little girl. "She didn't come downstairs at all. She just put her head out of the window and said, 'Good-by; Amy, be very good, and don't make Miss Carr any trouble,' and then she went away. I never went anywhere before without kissing mamma for good-by."

"Mamma was afraid to kiss you for fear she might give you the fever," explained Katy, taking her turn as a comforter. "It wasn't because she forgot. She felt worse about it than you did, I imagine. You know the thing she cares most for is that you shall not be ill as your cousin Walter is. She would rather do anything than have that happen. As soon as he gets well she will kiss you dozens of times, see if she doesn't. Meanwhile, she says in this note that you must write her a little letter every day, and she will hang a basket by a string out of the window, and you and I will go and drop the letters into the basket, and stand by the gate and see her pull it up. That will be funny, won't it? We will play that you are my little girl, and that you have a real mamma and a make-believe mamma."

"Shall I sleep with you?" demanded Amy,

"Yes, in that bed over there."

"It's a pretty bed," pronounced Amy after examining it gravely for a moment. "Will you tell me a story every morning?"

"If you don't wake me up too early. My stories are always sleepy till seven o'clock. Let us see what Ellen has packed in that bag, and then I'll give you some drawers of your own, and we will put the things away."

The bag was full of neat little frocks and underclothes stuffed hastily in all together. Katy took them out, smoothing the folds, and crimping the tumbled ruffles with her fingers. As she lifted the last skirt, Amy, with a cry of joy, pounced on something that lay beneath it.

"It is Maria Matilda," she said, "I'm glad of that. I thought Ellen would forget her, and the poor child wouldn't know what to do with me and her little sister not coming to see her for so long. She was having the measles on the back shelf of the closet, you know, and nobody would have heard her if she had cried ever so loud."

"What a pretty face she has!" said Katy, taking the doll out of Amy's hands.

"Yes, but not so pretty as Mabel. Miss Upham says that Mabel is the prettiest child she ever saw. Look, Miss Clover," lifting the other doll from the table where she had laid it; "hasn't she got *sweet* eyes? She's older than Maria Matilda, and she knows a great deal more. She's begun on French verbs!"

"Not really! Which ones?"

"Oh, only 'J'aime, tu aimes, il aime,' you know,—the same that our class is learning at school. She hasn't tried any but that. Sometimes she says it quite nicely, but sometimes she's very stupid, and I have to scold her." Amy had quite recovered her spirits by this time.

"Are these the only dolls you have?"

"Oh, please don't call them *that!*" urged Amy. "It hurts their feelings dreadfully. I never let them know that they are dolls. They think that they are real children, only sometimes when they are very bad I use the word for a punishment. I've got several other children. There's old Ragazza. My uncle named her, and she's made of rag, but she has such bad rheumatism that I don't play with her any longer; I just give her medicine. Then there's Effie Deans, she's only got one leg; and Mopsa the Fairy, she's a tiny one made out of china; and Peg of Linkinvaddy,—but she don't count, for she's all come to pieces."

"What very queer names your children have!" said Elsie, who had come in during the enumeration.

"Yes; Uncle Ned named them. He's a very funny uncle, but he's nice. He's always so much interested in my children."

"There's papa now!" cried Katy; and she ran downstairs to meet him.

"Did I do right?" she asked anxiously after she had told her story.

"Yes, my dear, perfectly right," replied Dr. Carr. "I only hope Amy was taken away in time. I will go round at once to see Mrs. Ashe and the boy; and, Katy, keep away from me when I come back, and keep the others away, till I have changed my coat."

It is odd how soon and how easily human beings accustom themselves to a new condition of things. When sudden illness comes, or sudden sorrow, or a house is burned up, or blown down by a tornado, there are a few hours or days of confusion and bewilderment, and then people gather up their wits and their courage and set to work to repair damages. They clear away ruins, plant, rebuild, very much as ants whose hill has been trodden upon, after running wildly about for a little while, begin all together to reconstruct the tiny cone of sand which is so important in their eyes. In a very short time the changes which at first seem so sad and strange become accustomed and matter-of-course things which no longer surprise us.

It seemed to the Carrs after a few days as if they had always had Amy in the house with them. Papa's daily visit to the sick-room, their avoidance of him till after he had "changed his coat," Amy's lessons and games of play, her dressing and undressing, the walks with the make-believe mamma, the dropping of notes into the little basket, seemed part of a system of things which had been going on for a long, long time, and which everybody would miss should they suddenly stop.

But they by no means suddenly stopped. Little Walter Ashe's case proved to be rather a severe one; and after he had begun to mend, he caught cold somehow and was taken worse again. There were some serious symptoms, and for a few days Dr. Carr did not feel sure how things would turn. He did not speak of his anxiety at home, but kept silence and a cheerful face, as doctors know how to do. Only Katy, who was more intimate with her father than the rest, guessed that things were going gravely at the other house, and she was too well trained to ask questions. The threatening symptoms passed off, however, and little Walter slowly got better; but it was a long convalescence, and Mrs. Ashe grew thin and pale before he began to look rosy. There was no one on whom she could devolve the charge of the child. His mother was dead; his father, an overworked business man, had barely time to run up once a week to see about him; there was no one at his home but a housekeeper, in whom Mrs. Ashe had not full confidence. So the good aunt denied herself the sight of her own child, and devoted her strength and time to Walter; and nearly two months passed, and still little Amy remained at Dr. Carr's.

She was entirely happy there. She had grown very fond of Katy, and was perfectly at home with the others. Phil and Johnnie, who had returned from her visit to Cecy, were by no means too old or too proud to be play-fellows to a child of eight; and with all the older members of the family Amy was a chosen pet. Debby baked turnovers, and twisted cinnamon cakes into all sorts of fantastic shapes to please her; Alexander would let her drive if she happened to sit on the front seat of the carryall; Dr. Carr was seldom so tired that he could not tell her a story,—and nobody told such nice stories as Dr. Carr, Amy thought; Elsie invented all manner of charming games for the hour before bedtime; Clover made wonderful capes and bonnets for Mabel and Maria Matilda; and Katy—Katy did all sorts of things.

Katy had a peculiar gift with children which is not easy to define. Some people possess it, and some do not; it cannot be learned, it comes by nature. She was bright and firm and equable all at once. She both amused and influenced them. There was something about her which excited the childish imagination, and always they felt her sympathy. Amy was a tractable child, and intelligent beyond her age, but she was never quite so good with any one as with Katy. She followed her about like a little lover; she lavished upon her certain special words and caresses which she gave to no one else; and would kneel on her lap, patting Katy's shoulders with her soft hand, and cooing up into her face like a happy dove, for a half-hour together. Katy laughed at these demonstrations, but they pleased her very much. She loved to be loved, as all affectionate people do, but most of all to be loved by a child.

At last, the long convalescence ended, Walter was carried away to his father, with every possible precaution against fatigue and exposure, and an army of workpeople was turned into Mrs. Ashe's house. Plaster was scraped and painted, wall-papers torn down, mattresses made over, and clothing burned. At last Dr. Carr pronounced the premises in a sanitary condition, and Mrs. Ashe sent for her little girl to come home again.

Amy was overjoyed at the prospect of seeing her mother; but at the last moment she clung to Katy and cried as if her heart would break.

"I want you too," she said. "Oh, if Dr. Carr would only let you come and live with me and mamma, I should be so happy! I shall be so lone-ly!"

"Nonsense!" cried Clover. "Lonely with mamma, and those poor children of yours who have been wondering all these weeks what has become of you! They'll want a great deal of attention at first, I am sure; medicine and new clothes and whippings,—all manner of things. You remember I promised to make a dress for Effie Deans out of that blue and brown plaid like Johnnie's balmoral. I mean to begin it to-morrow."

"Oh, will you?"—forgetting her grief—"that will be lovely. The skirt needn't be *very* full, you know. Effie doesn't walk much, because of only having one leg. She will be *so* pleased, for she hasn't had a new dress I don't know when."

Consoled by the prospect of Effie's satisfaction, Amy departed quite cheerfully, and Mrs. Ashe was spared the pain of seeing her only child in tears on the first evening of their reunion. But Amy talked so constantly of Katy, and seemed to love her so much, that it put a plan into her mother's head which led to important results, as the next chapter will show.

CHAPTER II. AN INVITATION.

It is a curious fact, and makes life very interesting, that, generally speaking, none of us have any expectation that things are going to happen till the very moment when they do happen. We wake up some morning with no idea that a great happiness is at hand, and before night it has come, and all the world is changed for us; or we wake bright and cheerful, with never a guess that clouds of sorrow are lowering in our sky, to put all the sunshine out for a while, and before noon all is dark. Nothing whispers of either the joy or the grief. No instinct bids us to delay or to hasten the opening of the letter or telegram, or the lifting of the latch of the door at which stands the messenger of good or ill. And because it may be, and often is, happy tidings that come, and joyful things which happen, each fresh day as it dawns upon us is like an unread story, full of possible interest and adventure, to be made ours as soon as we have cut the pages and begun to read.

Nothing whispered to Katy Carr, as she sat at the window mending a long rent in Johnnie's school coat, and saw Mrs. Ashe come in at the side gate and ring the office bell, that the visit had any special significance for her. Mrs. Ashe often did come to the office to consult Dr. Carr. Amy might not be quite well, Katy thought, or there might be a letter with something about Walter in it, or perhaps matters had gone wrong at the house, where paperers and painters were still at work. So she went calmly on with her darning, drawing the "ravelling," with which her needle was threaded, carefully in and out, and taking nice even stitches without one prophetic thrill or tremor; while, if only she could have looked through the two walls and two doors which separated the room in which she sat from the office, and have heard what Mrs. Ashe was saying, the school coat would have been thrown to the winds, and for all her tall stature and propriety, she would have been skipping with delight and astonishment. For Mrs. Ashe was asking papa to let her do the very thing of all others that she most longed to do; she was asking him to let Katy go with her to Europe!

"I am not very well," she told the Doctor. "I got tired and run down while Walter was ill, and I don't seem to throw it off as I hoped I should. I feel as if a change would do me good. Don't you think so yourself?"

"Yes, I do," Dr. Carr admitted.

"This idea of Europe is not altogether a new one," continued Mrs. Ashe. "I have always meant to go some time, and have put it off, partly because I dreaded going alone, and didn't know anybody whom I exactly wanted to take with me. But if you will let me have Katy, Dr. Carr, it will settle all my difficulties. Amy loves her dearly, and so do I;

she is just the companion I need; if I have her with me, I sha'n't be afraid of anything. I do hope you will consent."

"How long do you mean to be away?" asked Dr. Carr, divided between pleasure at these compliments to Katy and dismay at the idea of losing her.

"About a year, I think. My plans are rather vague as yet; but my idea was to spend a few weeks in Scotland and England first,—I have some cousins in London who will be good to us; and an old friend of mine married a gentleman who lives on the Isle of Wight; perhaps we might go there. Then we could cross over to France and visit Paris and a few other places; and before it gets cold go down to Nice, and from there to Italy. Katy would like to see Italy. Don't you think so?"

"I dare say she would," said Dr. Carr, with a smile. "She would be a queer girl if she didn't."

"There is one reason why I thought Italy would be particularly pleasant this winter for me and for her too," went on Mrs. Ashe; "and that is, because my brother will be there. He is a lieutenant in the navy, you know, and his ship, the 'Natchitoches,' is one of the Mediterranean squadron. They will be in Naples by and by, and if we were there at the same time we should have Ned to go about with; and he would take us to the receptions on the frigate, and all that, which would be a nice chance for Katy. Then toward spring I should like to go to Florence and Venice, and visit the Italian lakes and Switzerland in the early summer. But all this depends on your letting Katy go. If you decide against it, I shall give the whole thing up. But you won't decide against it,"—coaxingly,—"you will be kinder than that. I will take the best possible care of her, and do all I can to make her happy, if only you will consent to lend her to me; and I shall consider it *such* a favor. And it is to cost you nothing. You understand, Doctor, she is to be my guest all through. That is a point I want to make clear in the outset; for she goes for my sake, and I cannot take her on any other conditions. Now, Dr. Carr, please, please! I am sure you won't deny me, when I have so set my heart upon having her."

Mrs. Ashe was very pretty and persuasive, but still Dr. Carr hesitated. To send Katy for a year's pleasuring in Europe was a thing that had never occurred to his mind as possible. The cost alone would have prevented; for country doctors with six children are not apt to be rich men, even in the limited and old-fashioned construction of the word "wealth." It seemed equally impossible to let her go at Mrs. Ashe's expense; at the same time, the chance was such a good one, and Mrs. Ashe so much in earnest and so urgent, that it was difficult to refuse point blank. He finally consented to take time for consideration before making his decision.

"I will talk it over with Katy," he said. "The child ought to have a say in the matter; and whatever we decide, you must let me thank you in her name as well as my own for your great kindness in proposing it."

"Doctor, I'm not kind at all, and I don't want to be thanked. My desire to take Katy with me to Europe is purely selfish. I am a lonely person," she went on; "I have no mother or sister, and no cousins of my own age. My brother's profession keeps him at sea; I scarcely ever see him. I have no one but a couple of old aunts, too feeble in health to travel with me or to be counted on in case of any emergency. You see, I am a real case for pity."

Mrs. Ashe spoke gayly, but her brown eyes were dim with tears as she ended her little appeal. Dr. Carr, who was soft-hearted where women were concerned, was touched. Perhaps his face showed it, for Mrs. Ashe added in a more hopeful tone,—

"But I won't tease any more. I know you will not refuse me unless you think it right and necessary; and," she continued mischievously, "I have great faith in Katy as an ally. I am pretty sure that she will say that she wants to go."

And indeed Katy's cry of delight when the plan was proposed to her said that sufficiently, without need of further explanation. To go to Europe for a year with Mrs. Ashe and Amy seemed simply too delightful to be true. All the things she had heard about and read about—cathedrals, pictures, Alpine peaks, famous places, famous people—came rushing into her mind in a sort of bewildering tide as dazzling as it was overwhelming. Dr. Carr's objections, his reluctance to part with her, melted before the radiance of her satisfaction. He had no idea that Katy would care so much about it. After all, it was a great chance,—perhaps the only one of the sort that she would ever have. Mrs. Ashe could well afford to give Katy this treat, he knew; and it was quite true what she said, that it was a favor to her as well as to Katy. This train of reasoning led to its natural results. Dr. Carr began to waver in his mind.

But, the first excitement over, Katy's second thoughts were more sober ones. How could papa manage without her for a whole year, she asked herself. He would miss her, she well knew, and might not the charge of the house be too much for Clover? The preserves were almost all made, that was one comfort; but there were the winter clothes to be seen to; Dorry needed new flannels, Elsie's dresses must be altered over for Johnnie,—there were cucumbers to pickle, the coal to order! A host of housewifely cares began to troop through Katy's mind, and a little pucker came into her forehead, and a worried look across the face which had been so bright a few minutes before. Strange to say, it was that little pucker and the look of worry which decided Dr. Carr.

"She is only twenty-one," he reflected; "hardly out of childhood. I don't want her to settle into an anxious, drudging state and lose her youth with caring for us all. She shall go; though how we are to manage without her I don't see. Little Clover will have to come to the fore, and show what sort of stuff there is in her."

"Little Clover" came gallantly "to the fore" when the first shock of surprise was over, and she had relieved her mind with one long private cry over having to do without Katy for a year. Then she wiped her eyes, and began to revel unselfishly in the idea of her sister's having so great a treat. Anything and everything seemed possible to secure it for her; and she made light of all Katy's many anxieties and apprehensions.

"My dear child, I know a flannel undershirt when I see one, just as well as you do," she declared. "Tucks in Johnnie's dress, forsooth! why, of course. Ripping out a tuck doesn't require any superhuman ingenuity! Give me your scissors, and I'll show you at once. Quince marmalade? Debby can make that. Hers is about as good as yours; and if it wasn't, what should we care, as long as you are ascending Mont Blanc, and hob-nobbing with Michael Angelo and the crowned heads of Europe? I'll make the spiced peaches! I'll order the kindling! And if there ever comes a time when I feel lost and can't manage without advice, I'll go across to Mrs. Hall. Don't worry about us. We shall get on happily and easily; in fact, I shouldn't be surprised if I developed such a turn for housekeeping, that when you come back the family refused to change, and you had just to sit for the rest of your life and twirl your thumbs and watch me do it! Wouldn't that be fine?" and Clover laughed merrily. "So, Katy darling, cast that shadow from your brow, and look as a girl ought to look who's going to Europe. Why, if it were I who were going, I should simply stand on my head every moment of the time!"

"Not a very convenient position for packing," said Katy, smiling.

"Yes, it is, if you just turn your trunk upside down! When I think of all the delightful things you are going to do, I can hardly sit still. I *love* Mrs. Ashe for inviting you."

"So do I," said Katy, soberly. "It was the kindest thing! I can't think why she did it."

"Well, I can," replied Clover, always ready to defend Katy even against herself. "She did it because she wanted you, and she wanted you because you are the dearest old thing in the world, and the nicest to have about. You needn't say you're not, for you are! Now, Katy, don't waste another thought on such miserable things as pickles and undershirts. We shall get along perfectly well, I do assure you. Just fix your mind instead on the dome of St. Peter's, or try to fancy how you'll feel the first time you step into a gondola or see the Mediterranean. There will be a moment! I feel a forty-horse power of housekeeping developing within me; and what fun it will be to get your letters! We shall fetch out the Encyclopaedia and the big Atlas and the 'History of Modern Europe,' and read all about everything you see and all the places you go to; and it will be as good as a lesson in geography and history and political economy all combined, only a great deal more interesting! We shall stick out all over with knowledge before you come back; and this makes it a plain duty to go, if it were only for our sakes." With these zealous promises, Katy was forced to be content. Indeed, contentment was not difficult with such a prospect of delight before her. When once her little anxieties had been laid aside, the idea of the coming journey grew in pleasantness every moment. Night after night she and papa and the children pored over maps and made out schemes for travel and sight-seeing, every one of which was likely to be discarded as soon as the real journey began. But they didn't know that, and it made no real difference. Such schemes are the preliminary joys of travel, and it doesn't signify that they come to nothing after they have served their purpose.

Katy learned a great deal while thus talking over what she was to see and do. She read every scrap she could lay her hand on which related to Rome or Florence or Venice or London. The driest details had a charm for her now that she was likely to see the real places. She went about with scraps of paper in her pocket, on which were written such things as these: "Forum. When built? By whom built? More than one?" "What does *Cenacola* mean?" "Cecilia Metella. Who was she?" "Find out about Saint Catherine of Siena." "Who was Beatrice Cenci?" How she wished that she had studied harder and more carefully before this wonderful chance came to her. People always wish this when they are starting for Europe; and they wish it more and more after they get there, and realize of what value exact ideas and information and a fuller knowledge of the foreign languages are to all travellers; how they add to the charm of everything seen, and enhance the ease of everything done.

All Burnet took an interest in Katy's plans, and almost everybody had some sort of advice or help, or some little gift to offer. Old Mrs. Worrett, who, though fatter than ever, still retained the power of locomotion, drove in from Conic Section in her roomy carryall with the present of a rather obsolete copy of "Murray's Guide," in faded red covers, which her father had used in his youth, and which she was sure Katy would find convenient; also a bottle of Brown's Jamaica Ginger, in case of sea-sickness. Debby's sister-in-law brought a bundle of dried chamomile for the same purpose. Some one had told her it was the "handiest thing in the world to take along with you on them steamboats." Cecy sent a wonderful old-gold and scarlet contrivance to hang on the wall of the stateroom. There were pockets for watches, and pockets for medicines, and pockets for handkerchief and hairpins,—in short, there were pockets for everything; besides a pincushion with "Bon Voyage" in rows of shining pins, a bottle of eau-de-cologne, a cake of soap, and a hammer and tacks to nail the whole up with. Mrs. Hall's gift was a warm and very pretty woollen wrapper of dark blue flannel, with a pair of soft knitted slippers to match. Old Mr. Worrett sent a note of advice, recommending Katy to take a quinine pill every day that she was away, never to stay out late, because the dews "over there" were said to be unwholesome, and on no account to drink a drop of water which had not been boiled.

From Cousin Helen came a delightful travelling-bag, light and strong at once, and fitted up with all manner of nice little conveniences. Miss Inches sent a "History of Europe" in five fat volumes, which was so heavy that it had to be left at home. In fact, a good many of Katy's presents had to be left at home, including a bronze paper-weight in the shape of a griffin, a large pair of brass screw candlesticks, and an ormolu inkstand with a pen-rest attached, which weighed at least a pound and a half. These Katy laid aside to enjoy after her return. Mrs. Ashe and Cousin Helen had both warned her of the inconvenient consequences of weight in baggage; and by their advice she had limited herself to a single trunk of moderate size, besides a little flat valise for use in her stateroom.

Clover's gift was a set of blank books for notes, journals, etc. In one of these, Katy made out a list of "Things I must see," "Things I must do," "Things I would like to see," "Things I would like to do." Another she devoted to various good shopping addresses which had been given her; for though she did not expect to do any shopping herself, she thought Mrs. Ashe might find them useful. Katy's ideas were still so simple and unworldly, and her experience of life so small, that it had not occurred to her how very tantalizing it might be to stand in front of shop windows full of delightful things and not be able to buy any of them. She was accordingly overpowered with surprise, gratitude, and the sense of sudden wealth, when about a week before the start her father gave her three little thin strips of paper, which he told her were circular notes, and worth a hundred dollars apiece. He also gave her five English sovereigns.

"Those are for immediate use," he said. "Put the notes away carefully, and don't lose them. You had better have them cashed one at a time as you require them. Mrs. Ashe will explain how. You will need a gown or so before you come back, and you'll want to buy some photographs and so on, and there will be fees—"

"But, papa," protested Katy, opening wide her candid eyes, "I didn't expect you to give me any money, and I'm afraid you are giving me too much. Do you think you can afford it? Really and truly, I don't want to buy things. I shall see everything, you know, and that's enough."

Her father only laughed.

"You'll be wiser and greedier before the year is out, my dear," he replied. "Three hundred dollars won't go far, as you'll find. But it's all I can spare, and I trust you to keep within it, and not come home with any long bills for me to pay."

"Papa! I should think not!" cried Katy, with unsophisticated horror.

One very interesting thing was to happen before they sailed, the thought of which helped both Katy and Clover through the last hard days, when the preparations were nearly complete, and the family had leisure to feel dull and out of spirits. Katy was to make Rose Red a visit.

Rose had by no means been idle during the three years and a half which had elapsed since they all parted at Hillsover, and during which the girls had not seen her. In fact, she had made more out of the time than any of the rest of them, for she had been engaged for eighteen months, had been married, and was now keeping house near Boston with a little Rose of her own, who, she wrote to Clover, was a perfect angel, and more delicious than words could say! Mrs. Ashe had taken passage in the "Spartacus," sailing from Boston; and it was arranged that Katy should spend the last two days before sailing, with Rose, while Mrs. Ashe and Amy visited an old aunt in Hingham. To see Rose in her own home, and Rose's husband, and Rose's baby, was only next in interest to seeing Europe. None of the changes in her lot seemed to have changed her particularly, to judge by the letter she sent in reply to Katy's announcing her plans, which letter ran as follows:—

"LONGWOOD, September 20.

"My dearest child,—Your note made me dance with delight. I stood on my head waving my heels wildly to the breeze till Deniston thought I must be taken suddenly mad; but when I explained he did the same. It is too enchanting, the whole of it. I put it at the head of all the nice things that ever happened, except my baby. Write the moment you get this by what train you expect to reach Boston, and when you roll into the station you will behold two forms, one tall and stalwart, the other short and fatsome, waiting for you. They will be those of Deniston and myself. Deniston is not beautiful, but he is good, and he is prepared to *adore* you. The baby is both good and beautiful, and you will adore her. I am neither; but you know all about me, and I always did adore you and always shall. I am going out this moment to the butcher's to order a calf fatted for your special behoof; and he shall be slain and made into cutlets the moment I hear from you. My funny little house, which is quite a dear little house too, assumes a new interest in my eyes from the fact that you so soon are to see it. It is somewhat queer, as you might know my house would be; but I think you will like it.

"I saw Silvery Mary the other day and told her you were coming. She is the same mouse as ever. I shall ask her and some of the other girls to come out to lunch on one of your days. Good-by, with a hundred and fifty kisses to Clovy and the rest.

"Your loving

"ROSE RED."

"She never signs herself Browne, I observe," said Clover, as she finished the letter.

"Oh, Rose Red Browne would sound too funny. Rose Red she must stay till the end of the chapter; no other name could suit her half so well, and I can't imagine her being called anything else. What fun it will be to see her and little Rose!"

"And Deniston Browne," put in Clover.

"Somehow I find it rather hard to take in the fact that there is a Deniston Browne," observed Katy.

"It will be easier after you have seen him, perhaps."

The last day came, as last days will. Katy's trunk, most carefully and exactly packed by the united efforts of the family, stood in the hall, locked and strapped, not to be opened again till the party reached London. This fact gave it a certain awful interest in the eyes of Phil and Johnnie, and even Elsie gazed upon it with respect. The little valise was also ready; and Dorry, the neat-handed, had painted a red star on both ends of both it and the trunk, that they might be easily picked from among a heap of luggage. He now proceeded to prepare and paste on two square cards, labelled respectively, "Hold" and "State-room." Mrs. Hall had told them that this was the correct thing to do.

Mrs. Ashe had been full of business likewise in putting her house to rights for a family who had rented it for the time of her absence, and Katy and Clover had taken a good many hours from their own preparations to help her. All was done at last; and one bright morning in October, Katy stood on the wharf with her family about her, and a lump in her throat which made it difficult to speak to any of them. She stood so very still and said so very little, that a bystander not acquainted with the circumstances might have dubbed her "unfeeling;" while the fact was that she was feeling too much!

The first bell rang. Katy kissed everybody quietly and went on board with her father. Her parting from him, hardest of all, took place in the midst of a crowd of people; then he had to leave her, and as the wheels began to revolve she went out on the side deck to have a last glimpse of the home faces. There they were: Elsie crying tumultuously, with her head on papa's coat-sleeve; John laughing, or trying to laugh, with big tears running down her cheeks the while; and brave little Clover waving her handkerchief encouragingly, but with a very sober look on her face. Katy's heart went out to the little group with a sudden passion of regret and yearning. Why had she said she would go? What was all Europe in comparison with what she was leaving? Life was so short, how could she take a whole year out of it to spend away from the people she loved best? If it had been left to her to choose, I think she would have flown back to the shore then and there, and given up the journey, I also think she would have been heartily sorry a little later, had she done so.

But it was not left for her to choose. Already the throb of the engines was growing more regular and the distance widening between the great boat and the wharf. Gradually the dear faces faded into distance; and after watching till the flutter of Clover's handkerchief became an undistinguishable speck, Katy went to the cabin with a heavy heart. But there were Mrs. Ashe and Amy, inclined to be homesick also, and in need of cheering; and Katy, as she tried to brighten them, gradually grew bright herself, and recovered her hopeful spirits. Burnet pulled less strongly as it got farther away, and Europe beckoned more brilliantly now that they were fairly embarked on their journey. The sun shone, the lake was a beautiful, dazzling blue, and Katy said to herself, "After all, a year is not very long, and how happy I am going to be!"

CHAPTER III. ROSE AND ROSEBUD.

Thirty-six hours later the Albany train, running smoothly across the green levels beyond the Mill Dam, brought the travellers to Boston.

Katy looked eagerly from the window for her first glimpse of the city of which she had heard so much. "Dear little Boston! How nice it is to see it again!" she heard a lady behind her say; but why it should be called "little Boston" she could not imagine. Seen from the train, it looked large, imposing, and very picturesque, after flat Burnet with its one bank down to the edge of the lake. She studied the towers, steeples, and red roofs crowding each other up the slopes of the Tri-Mountain, and the big State House dome crowning all, and made up her mind that she liked the looks of it better than any other city she had ever seen.

The train slackened its speed, ran for a few moments between rows of tall, shabby brick walls, and with a long, final screech of its whistle came to halt in the station-house. Every one made a simultaneous rush for the door; and Katy and Mrs. Ashe, waiting to collect their books and bags, found themselves wedged into their seats and unable to get out. It was a confusing moment, and not comfortable; such moments never are.

But the discomfort brightened into a sense of relief as, looking out of the window, Katy caught sight of a face exactly opposite, which had evidently caught sight of her,—a fresh, pretty face, with light, waving hair, pink cheeks all a-dimple, and eyes which shone with laughter and welcome. It was Rose herself, not a bit changed during the years since they parted. A tall young man stood beside her, who must, of course, be her husband, Deniston Browne.

"There is Rose Red," cried Katy to Mrs. Ashe. "Oh, doesn't she look dear and natural? Do wait and let me introduce you. I want you to know her."

But the train had come in a little behind time, and Mrs. Ashe was afraid of missing the Hingham boat; so she only took a hasty peep from the window at Rose, pronounced her to be charming-looking, kissed Katy hurriedly, reminded her that they must be on the steamer punctually at twelve o'clock the following Saturday, and was gone, with Amy beside her; so that Katy, following last of all the slow-moving line of passengers, stepped all alone down from the platform into the arms of Rose Red.

"You darling!" was Rose's first greeting. "I began to think you meant to spend the night in the car, you were so long in getting out. Well, how perfectly lovely this is! Deniston, here is Katy; Katy, this is my husband."

Rose looked about fifteen as she spoke, and so absurdly young to have a "husband," that Katy could not help laughing as she shook hands with "Deniston;" and his own eyes twinkled with fun and evident recognition of the same joke. He was a tall young man, with a pleasant, "steady" face, and seemed to be infinitely amused, in a quiet way, with everything which his wife said and did.

"Let us make haste and get out of this hole," went on Rose. "I can scarcely see for the smoke. Deniston, dear, please find the cab, and have Katy's luggage put on it. I am wild to get her home, and exhibit baby before she chews up her new sash or does something else that is dreadful, to spoil her looks. I left her sitting in state, Katy, with all her best clothes on, waiting to be made known to you."

"My large trunk is to go straight to the steamer," explained Katy, as she gave her checks to Mr. Browne. "I only want the little one taken out to Longwood, please."

"Now, this is cosey," remarked Rose, when they were seated in the cab with Katy's bag at their feet. "Deniston, my love, I wish you were going out with us. There's a nice little bench here all ready and vacant, which is just suited to a man of your inches. You won't? Well, come in the early train, then. Don't forget.—Now, isn't he just as nice as I told you he was?" she demanded, the moment the cab began to move.

"He looks very nice indeed, as far as I can judge in three minutes and a quarter."

"My dear, it ought not to take anybody of ordinary discernment a minute and a quarter to perceive that he is simply the dearest fellow that ever lived," said Rose. "I discovered it three seconds after I first beheld him, and was desperately in love with him before he had fairly finished his first bow after introduction."

"And was he equally prompt?" asked Katy.

"He says so," replied Rose, with a pretty blush. "But then, you know, he could hardly say less after such a frank confession on my part. It is no more than decent of him to make believe, even if it is not true. Now, Katy, look at Boston, and see if you don't *love* it!"

The cab had now turned into Boylston Street; and on the right hand lay the Common, green as summer after the autumn rains, with the elm arches leafy still. Long, slant beams of afternoon sun were filtering through the boughs and falling across the turf and the paths, where people were walking and sitting, and children and babies playing together. It was a delightful scene; and Katy received an impression of space and cheer and air and freshness, which ever after was associated with her recollection of Boston.

Rose was quite satisfied with her raptures as they drove through Charles Street, between the Common and the Public Garden, all ablaze with autumn flowers, and down the length of Beacon Street with the blue bay shining between the handsome houses on the water side. Every vestibule and bay-window was gay with potted plants and flower-boxes; and a concourse of happy-looking people, on foot, on horseback, and in carriages, was surging to and fro like an equal, prosperous tide, while the sunlight glorified all.

"'Boston shows a soft Venetian side,'" quoted Katy, after a while. "I know now what Mr. Lowell meant when he wrote that. I don't believe there is a more beautiful place in the world."

"Why, of course there isn't," retorted Rose, who was a most devoted little Bostonian, in spite of the fact that she had lived in Washington nearly all her life. "I've not seen much beside, to be sure, but that is no matter; I know it is true. It is the dream of my life to come into the city to live. I don't care what part I live in,—West End, South End, North End; it's all one to me, so long as it is Boston!"

"But don't you like Longwood?" asked Katy, looking out admiringly at the pretty places set amid vines and shrubberies, which they were now passing. "It looks so very pretty and pleasant."

"Yes, it's well enough for any one who has a taste for natural beauties," replied Rose. "I haven't; I never had. There is nothing I hate so much as Nature! I'm a born cockney. I'd rather live in one room over Jordan and Marsh's, and see the world wag past, than be the owner of the most romantic villa that ever was built, I don't care where it may be situated."

The cab now turned in at a gate and followed a curving drive bordered with trees to a pretty stone house with a porch embowered with Virginia creepers, before which it stopped.

"Here we are!" cried Rose, springing out. "Now, Katy, you mustn't even take time to sit down before I show you the dearest baby that ever was sent to this sinful earth. Here, let me take your bag; come straight upstairs, and I will exhibit her to you."

They ran up accordingly, and Rose took Katy into a large sunny nursery, where, tied with pink ribbon into a little basket-chair and watched over by a pretty young nurse, sat a dear, fat, fair baby, so exactly like Rose in miniature that no one could possibly have mistaken the relationship. The baby began to laugh and coo as soon as it caught sight of its gay little mother, and exhibited just such another dimple as hers, in the middle of a pink cheek. Katy was enchanted.

"Oh, you darling!" she said. "Would she come to me, do you think, Rose?"

"Why, of course she shall," replied Rose, picking up the baby as if she had been a pillow, and stuffing her into Katy's arms head first. "Now, just look at her, and tell me if ever you saw anything so enchanting in the whole course of your life before? Isn't she big? Isn't she beautiful? Isn't she good? Just see her little hands and her hair! She never cries except when it is clearly her duty to cry. See her turn her head to look at me! Oh, you angel!" And seizing the long-suffering baby, she smothered it with kisses. "I never, never, never did see anything so sweet. Smell her, Katy! Doesn't she smell like heaven?"

Little Rose was indeed a delicious baby, all dimples and good-humor and violet-powder, with a skin as soft as a lily's leaf, and a happy capacity for allowing herself to be petted and cuddled without remonstrance. Katy wanted to hold her all the time; but this Rose would by no means permit; in fact, I may as well say at once that the two girls spent a great part of their time during the visit in fighting for the possession of the baby, who looked on at the struggle, and smiled on the victor, whichever it happened to be, with all the philosophic composure of Helen of Troy. She was so soft and sunny and equable, that it was no more trouble to care for and amuse her than if she had been a bird or a kitten; and, as Rose remarked, it was "ten times better fun."

"I was never allowed as much doll as I wanted in my infancy," she said. "I suppose I tore them to pieces too soon; and they couldn't give me tin ones to play with, as they did wash-bowls when I broke the china ones."

"Were you such a very bad child?" asked Katy.

"Oh, utterly depraved, I believe. You wouldn't think so now, would you? I recollect some dreadful occasions at school. Once I had my head pinned up in my apron because I *would* make faces at the other scholars, and they laughed; but I promptly bit a bay-window through the apron, and ran my tongue out of it till they laughed worse than ever. The teacher used to send me home with notes fastened to my pinafore with things like this written in them: 'Little Frisk has been more troublesome than usual to-day. She has pinched all the younger children, and bent the bonnets of all the older ones. We hope to see an amendment soon, or we do not know what we shall do.'"

"Why did they call you Little Frisk?" inquired Katy, after she had recovered from the laugh which Rose's reminiscences called forth.

"It was a term of endearment, I suppose; but somehow my family never seemed to enjoy it as they ought. I cannot understand," she went on reflectively, "why I had not sense enough to suppress those awful little notes. It would have been so easy to lose them on the way home, but somehow it never occurred to me. Little Rose will be wiser than that; won't you, my angel? She will tear up the horrid notes—mammy will show her how!"

All the time that Katy was washing her face and brushing the dust of the railway from her dress, Rose sat by with the little Rose in her lap, entertaining her thus. When she was ready, the droll little mamma tucked her baby under her arm and led the way downstairs to a large square parlor with a bay-window, through which the westering sun was shining. It was a pretty room, and had a flavor about it "just like Rose," Katy declared. No one else would have hung the pictures or looped back the curtains in exactly that way, or have hit upon the happy device of filling the grate with a great bunch of marigolds, pale brown, golden, and orange, to simulate the fire, which would have been quite too warm on so mild an evening. Morris papers and chintzes and "artistic" shades of color were in their infancy at that date; but Rose's taste was in advance of her time, and with a foreshadowing of the coming "reaction," she had chosen a "greenery, yallery" paper for her walls, against which hung various articles which looked a great deal queerer then than they would to-day. There was a mandolin, picked up at some Eastern sale, a warming-pan in shining brass from her mother's attic, two old samplers worked in faded silks, and a quantity of gayly tinted Japanese fans and embroideries. She had also begged from an old aunt at Beverly Farms a couple of droll little armchairs in white painted wood, with covers of antique needle-work. One had "Chit" embroidered on the middle of its cushion; the other, "Chat." These stood suggestively at the corners of the hearth.

"Now, Katy," said Rose, seating herself in "Chit," "pull up 'Chat' and let us begin."

So they did begin, and went on, interrupted only by Baby Rose's coos and splutters, till the dusk fell, till appetizing smells floated through from the rear of the house, and the click of a latch-key announced Mr. Browne, come home just in time for dinner.

The two days' visit went only too quickly. There is nothing more fascinating to a girl than the menage of a young couple of her own age. It is a sort of playing at real life without the cares and the sense of responsibility that real life is sure to bring. Rose was an adventurous housekeeper. She was still new to the position, she found it very entertaining, and she delighted in experiments of all sorts. If they turned out well, it was good fun; if not, that was funnier still! Her husband, for all his serious manner, had a real boy's love of a lark, and he aided and abetted her in all sorts of whimsical devices. They owned a dog who was only less dear than the baby, a cat only less dear than the dog, a parrot whose education required constant supervision, and a hutch of ring-doves whose melancholy little "whuddering" coos were the delight of Rose the less. The house seemed astir with young life all over. The only elderly thing in it was the cook, who had the reputation of a dreadful temper; only, unfortunately, Rose made her laugh so much that she never found time to be cross.

Katy felt quite an old, experienced person amid all this movement and liveliness and cheer. It seemed to her that nobody in the world could possibly be having such a good time as Rose; but Rose did not take the same view of the situation.

"It's all very well now," she said, "while the warm weather lasts; but in winter Longwood is simply grewsome. The wind never stops blowing day nor night. It howls and it roars and it screams, till I feel as if every nerve in my body were on the point of snapping in two. And the snow, ugh! And the wind, ugh! And burglars! Every night of our lives they come,—or I think they come,—and I lie awake and hear them sharpening their tools and forcing the locks and murdering the cook and kidnapping Baby, till I long to die, and have done with them forever! Oh, Nature is the most unpleasant thing!"

"Burglars are not Nature," objected Katy.

"What are they, then? Art? High Art? Well, whatever they are, I do not like them. Oh, if ever the happy day comes when Deniston consents to move into town, I never wish to set my eyes on the country again as long as I live, unless—well, yes, I should like to come out just once more in the horse-cars and *kick* that elm-tree by the fence! The number of times that I have lain awake at night listening to its creaking!"

"You might kick it without waiting to have a house in town."

"Oh, I shouldn't dare as long as we are living here! You never know what Nature may do. She has ways of her own of getting even with people," remarked her friend, solemnly.

No time must be lost in showing Boston to Katy, Rose said. So the morning after her arrival she was taken in bright and early to see the sights. There were not quite so many sights to be seen then as there are today. The Art Museum had not got much above its foundations; the new Trinity Church was still in the future; but the big organ and the bronze statue of Beethoven were in their glory, and every day at high noon a small straggling audience wandered into Music Hall to hear the instrument played. To this extempore concert Katy was taken, and to Faneuil Hall and the Athenaeum, to Doll and Richards's, where was an exhibition of pictures, to the Granary Graveyard, and the Old South. Then the girls did a little shopping; and by that time they were quite tired enough to make the idea of luncheon agreeable, so they took the path across the Common to the Joy Street Mall.

Katy was charmed by all she had seen. The delightful nearness of so many interesting things surprised her. She perceived what is one of Boston's chief charms,—that the Common and its surrounding streets make a natural centre and rallying-point for the whole city; as the heart is the centre of the body and keeps up a quick correspondence and regulates the life of all its extremities. The stately old houses on Beacon Street, with their rounded fronts, deep window-casements, and here and there a mauve or a lilac pane set in the sashes, took her fancy greatly; and so did the State House, whose situation made it sufficiently imposing, even before the gilding of the dome.

Up the steep steps of the Joy Street Mall they went, to the house on Mt. Vernon Street which the Reddings had taken on their return from Washington nearly three years before. Rose had previously shown Katy the site of the old family house on Summer Street, where she was born, now given over wholly to warehouses and shops. Their present residence was one of those wide old-fashioned brick houses on the crest of the hill, whose upper windows command the view across to the Boston Highlands; in the rear was a spacious yard, almost large enough to be called a garden, walled in with ivies and grapevines, under which were long beds full of roses and chrysanthemums and marigolds and mignonette.

Rose carried a latch-key in her pocket, which she said had been one of her wedding-gifts; with this she unlocked the front door and let Katy into a roomy white-painted hall.

"We will go straight through to the back steps," she said. "Mamma is sure to be sitting there; she always sits there till the first frost; she says it makes her think of the country. How different people are! I don't want to think of the country, but I'm never allowed to forget it for a moment. Mamma is so fond of those steps and the garden."

There, to be sure, Mrs. Redding was found sitting in a wicker-work chair under the shade of the grapevines, with a big basket of mending at her side. It looked so homely and country-like to find a person thus occupied in the middle of a busy city, that Katy's heart warmed to her at once.

Mrs. Redding was a fair little woman, scarcely taller than Rose and very much like her. She gave Katy a kind welcome.

"You do not seem like a stranger," she said, "Rose has told us so much about you and your sister. Sylvia will be very disappointed not to see you. She went off to make some visits when we broke up in the country, and is not to be home for three weeks yet."

Katy was disappointed, too, for she had heard a great deal about Sylvia and had wished very much to meet her. She was shown her picture, from which she gathered that she did not look in the least like

Rose; for though equally fair, her fairness was of the tall aquiline type, quite different from Rose's dimpled prettiness. In fact, Rose resembled her mother, and Sylvia her father; they were only alike in little peculiarities of voice and manner, of which a portrait did not enable Katy to judge.

The two girls had a cosey little luncheon with Mrs. Redding, after which Rose carried Katy off to see the house and everything in it which was in any way connected with her own personal history,—the room where she used to sleep, the high-chair in which she sat as a baby and which was presently to be made over to little Rose, the sofa where Deniston offered himself, and the exact spot on the carpet on which she had stood while they were being married! Last of all,—

"Now you shall see the best and dearest thing in the whole house," she said, opening the door of a room in the second story.— "Grandmamma, here is my friend Katy Carr, whom you have so often heard me tell about."

It was a large pleasant room, with a little wood-fire blazing in a grate, by which, in an arm-chair full of cushions, with a Solitaire-board on a little table beside her, sat a sweet old lady. This was Rose's father's mother. She was nearly eighty; but she was beautiful still, and her manner had a gracious old-fashioned courtesy which was full of charm. She had been thrown from a carriage the year before, and had never since been able to come downstairs or to mingle in the family life.

"They come to me instead," she told Katy. "There is no lack of pleasant company," she added; "every one is very good to me. I have a reader for two hours a day, and I read to myself a little, and play Patience and Solitaire, and never lack entertainment."

There was something restful in the sight of such a lovely specimen of old age. Katy realized, as she looked at her, what a loss it had been to her own life that she had never known either of her grandparents. She sat and gazed at old Mrs. Redding with a mixture of regret and fascination. She longed to hold her hand, and kiss her, and play with her beautiful silvery hair, as Rose did. Rose was evidently the old lady's peculiar darling. They were on the most intimate terms; and Rose dimpled and twinkled, and made saucy speeches, and told all her little adventures and the baby's achievements, and made jests, and talked nonsense as freely as to a person of her own age. It was a delightful relation.

"Grandmamma has taken a fancy to you, I can see," she told Katy, as they drove back to Longwood. "She always wants to know my friends; and she has her own opinions about them, I can tell you."

"Do you really think she liked me?" said Katy, warmly. "I am so glad if she did, for I *loved* her. I never saw a really beautiful old person before."

"Oh, there's nobody like her," rejoined Rose. "I can't imagine what it would be not to have her." Her merry little face was quite sad and serious as she spoke. "I wish she were not so old," she added with a sigh. "If we could only put her back twenty years! Then, perhaps, she would live as long as I do."

But, alas! there is no putting back the hands on the dial of time, no matter how much we may desire it.

The second day of Katy's visit was devoted to the luncheon-party of which Rose had written in her letter, and which was meant to be a reunion or "side chapter" of the S.S.U.C. Rose had asked every old Hillsover girl who was within reach. There was Mary Silver, of course, and Esther Dearborn, both of whom lived in Boston; and by good luck Alice Gibbons happened to be making Esther a visit, and Ellen Gray came in from Waltham, where her father had recently been settled over a parish, so that all together they made six of the original nine of the society; and Quaker Row itself never heard a merrier confusion of tongues than resounded through Rose's pretty parlor for the first hour after the arrival of the guests.

There was everybody to ask after, and everything to tell. The girls all seemed wonderfully unchanged to Katy, but they professed to find her very grown up and dignified.

"I wonder if I am," she said. "Clover never told me so. But perhaps she has grown dignified too."

"Nonsense!" cried Rose; "Clover could no more be dignified than my baby could. Mary Silver, give me that child this moment! I never saw such a greedy thing as you are; you have kept her to yourself at least a quarter of an hour, and it isn't fair."

"Oh, I beg your pardon," said Mary, laughing and covering her mouth with her hand exactly in her old, shy, half-frightened way.

"We only need Mrs. Nipson to make our little party complete," went on Rose, "or dear Miss Jane! What has become of Miss Jane, by the way? Do any of you know?"

"Oh, she is still teaching at Hillsover and waiting for her missionary. He has never come back. Berry Searles says that when he goes out to walk he always walks away from the United States, for fear of diminishing the distance between them."

"What a shame!" said Katy, though she could not help laughing. "Miss Jane was really quite nice,—no, not nice exactly, but she had good things about her."

"Had she!" remarked Rose, satirically. "I never observed them. It required eyes like yours, real 'double million magnifying-glasses of h'extra power,' to find them out. She was all teeth and talons as far as I was concerned; but I think she really did have a softish spot in her old heart for you, Katy, and it's the only good thing I ever knew about her."

"What has become of Lilly Page?" asked Ellen.

"She's in Europe with her mother. I dare say you'll meet, Katy, and what a pleasure that will be! And have you heard about Bella? she's teaching school in the Indian Territory. Just fancy that scrap teaching school!"

"Isn't it dangerous?" asked Mary Silver.

"Dangerous? How? To her scholars, do you mean? Oh, the Indians! Well, her scalp will be easy to identify if she has adhered to her favorite pomatum; that's one comfort," put in naughty Rose.

It was a merry luncheon indeed, as little Rose seemed to think, for she laughed and cooed incessantly. The girls were enchanted with her, and voted her by acclamation an honorary member of the S.S.U.C. Her health was drunk in Apollinaris water with all the honors, and Rose returned thanks in a droll speech. The friends told each other their histories for the past three years; but it was curious how little, on the whole, most of them had to tell. Though, perhaps, that was because they did not tell all; for Alice Gibbons confided to Katy in a whisper that she strongly suspected Esther of being engaged, and at the same moment Ellen Gray was convulsing Rose by the intelligence that a theological student from Andover was "very attentive" to Mary Silver.

"My dear, I don't believe it," Rose said, "not even a theological student would dare! and if he did, I am quite sure Mary would consider it most improper. You must be mistaken, Ellen."

"No, I'm not mistaken; for the theological student is my second cousin, and his sister told me all about it. They are not engaged exactly, but she hasn't said no; so he hopes she will say yes."

"Oh, she'll never say no; but then she will never say yes, either. He would better take silence as consent! Well, I never did think I should live to see Silvery Mary married. I should as soon have expected to find the Thirty-nine Articles engaged in a flirtation. She's a dear old thing, though, and as good as gold; and I shall consider your second cousin a lucky man if he persuades her."

"I wonder where we shall all be when you come back, Katy," said Esther Dearborn as they parted at the gate. "A year is a long time; all sorts of things may happen in a year."

These words rang in Katy's ears as she fell asleep that night. "All sorts of things may happen in a year," she thought, "and they may not be all happy things, either." Almost she wished that the journey to Europe had never been thought of!

But when she waked the next morning to the brightest of October suns shining out of a clear blue sky, her misgivings fled. There could not have been a more beautiful day for their start.

She and Rose went early into town, for old Mrs. Bedding had made Katy promise to come for a few minutes to say good-by. They found her sitting by the fire as usual, though her windows were open to admit the sun-warmed air. A little basket of grapes stood on the table beside her, with a nosegay of tea-roses on top. These were from Rose's mother, for Katy to take on board the steamer; and there was something else, a small parcel twisted up in thin white paper.

"It is my good-by gift," said the dear old lady. "Don't open it now. Keep it till you are well out at sea, and get some little thing with it as a keepsake from me."

Grateful and wondering, Katy put the little parcel in her pocket. With kisses and good wishes she parted from these new made friends, and she and Rose drove to the steamer, stopping for Mr. Browne by the way. They were a little late, so there was not much time for farewells after they arrived; but Rose snatched a moment for a private interview with the stewardess, unnoticed by Katy, who was busy with Mrs. Ashe and Amy.

The bell rang, and the great steam-vessel slowly backed into the stream. Then her head was turned to sea, and down the bay she went, leaving Rose and her husband still waving their handkerchiefs on the pier. Katy watched them to the last, and when she could no longer distinguish them, felt that her final link with home was broken.

It was not till she had settled her things in the little cabin which was to be her home for the next ten days, had put her bonnet and dress for safe keeping in the upper berth, nailed up her red and yellow bag, and donned the woollen gown, ulster, and soft felt hat which were to do service during the voyage, that she found time to examine the mysterious parcel.

Behold, it was a large, beautiful gold-piece, twenty dollars!

"What a darling old lady!" said Katy; and she gave the gold-piece a kiss. "How did she come to think of such a thing? I wonder if there is anything in Europe good enough to buy with it?"

CHAPTER IV. ON THE "SPARTACUS."

The ulster and the felt hat soon came off again, for a head wind lay waiting in the offing, and the "Spartacus" began to pitch and toss in a manner which made all her unseasoned passengers glad to betake themselves to their berths. Mrs. Ashe and Amy were among the earliest victims of sea-sickness; and Katy, after helping them to settle in their staterooms, found herself too dizzy and ill to sit up a moment longer, and thankfully resorted to her own.

As the night came on, the wind grew stronger and the motion worse. The "Spartacus" had the reputation of being a dreadful "roller," and seemed bound to justify it on this particular voyage. Down, down, down the great hull would slide till Katy would hold her breath with fear lest it might never right itself again; then slowly, slowly the turn would be made, and up, up, up it would go, till the cant on the other side was equally alarming. On the whole, Katy preferred to have her own side of the ship, the downward one; for it was less difficult to keep herself in the berth, from which she was in continual danger of being thrown. The night seemed endless, for she was too frightened to sleep except in broken snatches; and when day dawned, and she looked through the little round pane of glass in the port-hole, only gray sky and gray weltering waves and flying spray and rain met her view.

"Oh, dear, why do people ever go to sea, unless they must?" she thought feebly to herself. She wanted to get up and see how Mrs. Ashe had lived through the night, but the attempt to move made her so miserably ill that she was glad to sink again on her pillows.

The stewardess looked in with offers of tea and toast, the very idea of which was simply dreadful, and pronounced the other lady "'orridly ill, worse than you are, Miss," and the little girl "takin' on dreadful in the h'upper berth." Of this fact Katy soon had audible proof; for as her dizzy senses rallied a little, she could hear Amy in the opposite stateroom crying and sobbing pitifully. She seemed to be angry as well as sick, for she was scolding her poor mother in the most vehement fashion.

"I hate being at sea," Katy heard her say. "I won't stay in this nasty old ship. Mamma! Mamma! do you hear me? I won't stay in this ship! It wasn't a bit kind of you to bring me to such a horrid place. It was very unkind; it was cru-el. I want to go back, mamma. Tell the captain to take me back to the land. Mamma, why don't you speak to me? Oh, I am so sick and so very un-happy. Don't you wish you were dead? I do!"

And then came another storm of sobs, but never a sound from Mrs. Ashe, who, Katy suspected, was too ill to speak. She felt very sorry for poor little Amy, raging there in her high berth like some imprisoned creature, but she was powerless to help her. She could only resign herself to her own discomforts, and try to believe that somehow, sometime, this state of things must mend,—either they should all get to land or all go to the bottom and be drowned, and at that moment she didn't care very much which it turned out to be.

The gale increased as the day wore on, and the vessel pitched dreadfully. Twice Katy was thrown out of her berth on the floor; then the stewardess came and fixed a sort of movable side to the berth, which held her in, but made her feel like a child fastened into a railed crib. At intervals she could still hear Amy crying and scolding her mother, and conjectured that they were having a dreadful time of it in the other stateroom. It was all like a bad dream. "And they call this travelling for pleasure!" thought poor Katy.

One droll thing happened in the course of the second night,—at least it seemed droll afterward; at the time Katy was too uncomfortable to enjoy it. Amid the rush of the wind, the creaking of the ship's timbers, and the shrill buzz of the screw, she heard a sound of queer little footsteps in the entry outside of her open door, hopping and leaping together in an odd irregular way, like a regiment of mice or toy soldiers. Nearer and nearer they came; and Katy opening her eyes saw a procession of boots and shoes of all sizes and shapes, which had evidently been left on the floors or at the doors of various staterooms, and which in obedience to the lurchings of the vessel had collected in the cabin. They now seemed to be acting in concert with one another, and really looked alive as they bumped and trotted side by side, and two by two, in at the door and up close to her bedside. There they remained for several moments executing what looked like a dance; then the leading shoe turned on its heel as if giving a signal to the others, and they all hopped slowly again into the passage-way and disappeared. It was exactly like one of Hans Christian Andersen's fairy-tales, Katy wrote to Clover afterward. She heard them going down the cabin; but how it ended, or whether the owners of the boots and shoes ever got their own particular pairs again, she never knew.

Toward morning the gale abated, the sea became smoother, and she dropped asleep. When she woke the sun was struggling through the clouds, and she felt better.

The stewardess opened the port-hole to freshen the air, and helped her to wash her face and smooth her tangled hair; then she produced a little basin of gruel and a triangular bit of toast, and Katy found that her appetite was come again and she could eat.

"And 'ere's a letter, ma'am, which has come for you by post this morning," said the nice old stewardess, producing an envelope from her pocket, and eying her patient with great satisfaction.

"By post!" cried Katy, in amazement; "why, how can that be?" Then catching sight of Rose's handwriting on the envelope, she understood, and smiled at her own simplicity.

The stewardess beamed at her as she opened it, then saying again, "Yes, 'm, by post, m'm," withdrew, and left Katy to enjoy the little surprise.

The letter was not long, but it was very like its writer. Rose drew a picture of what Katy would probably be doing at the time it reached her,—a picture so near the truth that Katy felt as if Rose must have the spirit of prophecy, especially as she kindly illustrated the situation with a series of pen-and-ink drawings, in which Katy was depicted as prone in her berth, refusing with horror to go to dinner, looking longingly backward toward the quarter where the United States was supposed to be, and fishing out of her port-hole with a crooked pin in hopes of grappling the submarine cable and sending a message to her family to come out at once and take her home. It ended with this short "poem," over which Katy laughed till Mrs. Ashe called feebly across the entry to ask what *was* the matter?

"Break, break, break   And mis-behave, O sea,   And I wish that my tongue could utter   The hatred I feel for thee!   "Oh, well for the fisherman's child   On the sandy beach at his play;   Oh, well for all sensible folk   Who are safe at home to-day!   "But this horrible ship keeps on,   And is never a moment still,   And I yearn for the touch of the nice dry land,   Where I needn't feel so ill!   "Break! break! break!
There is no good left in me;   For the dinner I ate on the shore so late
Has vanished into the sea!"

Laughter is very restorative after the forlornity of sea-sickness; and Katy was so stimulated by her letter that she managed to struggle into her dressing-gown and slippers and across the entry to Mrs. Ashe's stateroom. Amy had fallen asleep at last and must not be waked up, so their interview was conducted in whispers. Mrs. Ashe had by no means got to the tea-and-toast stage yet, and was feeling miserable enough.

"I have had the most dreadful time with Amy," she said. "All day yesterday, when she wasn't sick she was raging at me from the upper berth, and I too ill to say a word in reply. I never knew her so naughty! And it seemed very neglectful not to come to see after you, poor dear child! but really I couldn't raise my head."

"Neither could I, and I felt just as guilty not to be taking care of you," said Katy. "Well, the worst is over with all of us, I hope. The vessel doesn't pitch half so much now, and the stewardess says we shall feel a great deal better as soon as we get on deck. She is coming presently to help me up; and when Amy wakes, won't you let her be dressed, and I will take care of her while Mrs. Barrett attends to you."

"I don't think I can be dressed," sighed poor Mrs. Ashe. "I feel as if I should just lie here till we get to Liverpool."

"Oh no, h'indeed, mum,—no, you won't," put in Mrs. Barrett, who at that moment appeared, gruel-cup in hand. "I don't never let my ladies lie in their berths a moment longer than there is need of. I h'always gets them on deck as soon as possible to get the h'air. It's the best medicine you can 'ave, ma'am, the fresh h'air; h'indeed it h'is."

Stewardesses are all-powerful on board ship, and Mrs. Barrett was so persuasive as well as positive that it was not possible to resist her. She got Katy into her dress and wraps, and seated her on deck in a chair with a great rug wrapped about her feet, with very little effort on Katy's part. Then she dived down the companion-way again, and in the course of an hour appeared escorting a big burly steward, who carried poor little pale Amy in his arms as easily as though she had been a kitten. Amy gave a scream of joy at the sight of Katy, and cuddled down in her lap under the warm rug with a sigh of relief and satisfaction.

"I thought I was never going to see you again," she said, with a little squeeze. "Oh, Miss Katy, it has been so horrid! I never thought that going to Europe meant such dreadful things as this!"

"This is only the beginning; we shall get across the sea in a few days, and then we shall find out what going to Europe really means. But what made you behave so, Amy, and cry and scold poor mamma when she was sick? I could hear you all the way across the entry."

"Could you? Then why didn't you come to me?"

"I wanted to; but I was sick too, so sick that I couldn't move. But why were you so naughty?—you didn't tell me."

"I didn't mean to be naughty, but I couldn't help crying. You would have cried too, and so would Johnnie, if you had been cooped up in a dreadful old berth at the top of the wall that you couldn't get out of, and hadn't had anything to eat, and nobody to bring you any water when you wanted some. And mamma wouldn't answer when I called to her."

"She couldn't answer; she was too ill," explained Katy. "Well, my pet, it *was* pretty hard for you. I hope we sha'n't have any more such days. The sea is a great deal smoother now."

"Mabel looks quite pale; she was sick, too," said Amy, regarding the doll in her arms with an anxious air. "I hope the fresh h'air will do her good."

"Is she going to have any fresh hair?" asked Katy, wilfully misunderstanding.

"That was what that woman called it,—the fat one who made me come up here. But I'm glad she did, for I feel heaps better already; only I keep thinking of poor little Maria Matilda shut up in the trunk in that dark place, and wondering if she's sick. There's nobody to explain to her down there."

"They say that you don't feel the motion half so much in the bottom of the ship," said Katy. "Perhaps she hasn't noticed it at all. Dear me, how good something smells! I wish they would bring us something to eat."

A good many passengers had come up by this time; and Robert, the deck steward, was going about, tray in hand, taking orders for lunch. Amy and Katy both felt suddenly ravenous; and when Mrs. Ashe awhile later was helped up the stairs, she was amazed to find them eating cold beef and roasted potatoes, with the finest appetites in the world. "They had served out their apprenticeships," the kindly old captain told them, "and were made free of the nautical guild from that time on." So it proved; for after these two bad days none of the party were sick again during the voyage.

Amy had a clamorous appetite for stories as well as for cold beef; and to appease this craving, Katy started a sort of ocean serial, called "The History of Violet and Emma," which she meant to make last till they got to Liverpool, but which in reality lasted much longer. It might with equal propriety have been called "The Adventures of two little Girls who didn't have any Adventures," for nothing in particular happened to either Violet or Emma during the whole course of their long-drawn-out history. Amy, however, found them perfectly enchanting, and was never weary of hearing how they went to school and came home again, how they got into scrapes and got out of them, how they made good resolutions and broke them, about their Christmas presents and birthday treats, and what they said and how they felt. The first instalment of this un-exciting romance was given that first afternoon on deck; and after that, Amy claimed a new chapter daily, and it was a chief ingredient of her pleasure during the voyage.

On the third morning Katy woke and dressed so early, that she gained the deck before the sailors had finished their scrubbing and holystoning. She took refuge within the companion-way, and sat down on the top step of the ladder, to wait till the deck was dry enough to venture upon it. There the Captain found her and drew near for a talk.

Captain Bryce was exactly the kind of sea-captain that is found in story-books, but not always in real life. He was stout and grizzled and brown and kind. He had a bluff weather-beaten face, lit up with a pair of shrewd blue eyes which twinkled when he was pleased; and his manner, though it was full of the habit of command, was quiet and pleasant. He was a Martinet on board his ship. Not a sailor under him would have dared dispute his orders for a moment; but he was very popular with them, notwithstanding; they liked him as much as they feared him, for they knew him to be their best friend if it came to sickness or trouble with any of them.

Katy and he grew quite intimate during their long morning talk. The Captain liked girls. He had one of his own, about Katy's age, and was fond of talking about her. Lucy was his mainstay at home, he told Katy. Her mother had been "weakly" now this long time back, and Bess and Nanny were but children yet, so Lucy had to take command and keep things ship-shape when he was away.

"She'll be on the lookout when the steamer comes in," said the Captain. "There's a signal we've arranged which means 'All's well,' and when we get up the river a little way I always look to see if it's flying. It's a bit of a towel hung from a particular window; and when I see it I say to myself, 'Thank God! another voyage safely done and no harm come of it.' It's a sad kind of work for a man to go off for a twenty-four days' cruise leaving a sick wife on shore behind him. If it wasn't that I have Lucy to look after things, I should have thrown up my command long ago."

"Indeed, I am glad you have Lucy; she must be a great comfort to you," said Katy, sympathetically; for the Captain's hearty voice trembled a little as he spoke. She made him tell her the color of Lucy's hair and eyes, and exactly how tall she was, and what she had studied, and what sort of books she liked. She seemed such a very nice girl, and Katy thought she should like to know her.

The deck had dried fast in the fresh sea-wind, and the Captain had just arranged Katy in her chair, and was wrapping the rug about her feet in a fatherly way, when Mrs. Barrett, all smiles, appeared from below.

"Oh, 'ere you h'are, Miss. I couldn't think what 'ad come to you so early; and you're looking ever so well again, I'm pleased to see; and 'ere's a bundle just arrived, Miss, by the Parcels Delivery."

"What!" cried simple Katy. Then she laughed at her own foolishness, and took the "bundle," which was directed in Rose's unmistakable hand.

It contained a pretty little green-bound copy of Emerson's Poems, with Katy's name and "To be read at sea," written on the flyleaf. Somehow the little gift seemed to bridge the long misty distance which stretched between the vessel's stern and Boston Bay, and to bring home and friends a great deal nearer. With a half-happy, half-tearful pleasure Katy recognized the fact that distance counts for little if people love one another, and that hearts have a telegraph of their own whose messages are as sure and swift as any of those sent over the material lines which link continent to continent and shore with shore.

Later in the morning, Katy, going down to her stateroom for something, came across a pallid, exhausted-looking lady, who lay stretched on one of the long sofas in the cabin, with a baby in her arms and a little girl sitting at her feet, quite still, with a pair of small hands folded in her lap. The little girl did not seem to be more than four years old. She had two pig-tails of thick flaxen hair hanging over her shoulders, and at Katy's approach raised a pair of solemn blue eyes, which had so much appeal in them, though she said nothing, that Katy stopped at once.

"Can I do anything for you?" she asked. "I am afraid you have been very ill."

At the sound of her voice the lady on the sofa opened her eyes. She tried to speak, but to Katy's dismay began to cry instead; and when the words came they were strangled with sobs.

"You are so kin-d to ask," she said. "If you would give my little girl something to eat! She has had nothing since yesterday, and I have been so ill; and no-nobody has c-ome near us!"

"Oh!" cried Katy, with horror, "nothing to eat since yesterday! How did it happen?"

"Everybody has been sick on our side the ship," explained the poor lady, "and I suppose the stewardess thought, as I had a maid with me, that I needed her less than the others. But my maid has been sick, too; and oh, so selfish! She wouldn't even take the baby into the berth with her; and I have had all I could do to manage with him, when I couldn't lift up my head. Little Gretchen has had to go without anything; and she has been so good and patient!"

Katy lost no time, but ran for Mrs. Barrett, whose indignation knew no bounds when she heard how the helpless party had been neglected.

"It's a new person that stewardess h'is, ma'am," she explained, "and most h'inefficient! I told the Captain when she come aboard that I didn't 'ave much opinion of her, and now he'll see how it h'is. I'm h'ashamed that such a thing should 'appen on the 'Spartacus,' ma'am,—I h'am, h'indeed. H'it never would 'ave ben so h'under h'Eliza, ma'am,—she's the one that went h'off and got herself married the trip before last, when this person came to take her place."

All the time that she talked Mrs. Barrett was busy in making Mrs. Ware—for that, it seemed, was the sick lady's name—more comfortable; and Katy was feeding Gretchen out of a big bowl full of bread and milk which one of the stewards had brought. The little uncomplaining thing was evidently half starved, but with the mouthfuls the pink began to steal back into her cheeks and lips, and the dark circles lessened under the blue eyes. By the time the bottom of the bowl was reached she could smile, but still she said not a word except a whispered *Danke schon*. Her mother explained that she had been born in Germany, and always till now had been cared for by a German nurse, so that she knew that language better than English.

Gretchen was a great amusement to Katy and Amy during the rest of the voyage. They kept her on deck with them a great deal, and she was perfectly content with them and very good, though always solemn and quiet. Pleasant people turned up among the passengers, as always happens on an ocean steamship, and others not so pleasant, perhaps, who were rather curious and interesting to watch.

Katy grew to feel as if she knew a great deal about her fellow travellers as time went on. There was the young girl going out to join her parents under the care of a severe governess, whom everybody on board rather pitied. There was the other girl on her way to study art, who was travelling quite alone, and seemed to have nobody to meet her or to go to except a fellow student of her own age, already in Paris, but who seemed quite unconscious of her lonely position and competent to grapple with anything or anybody. There was the queer old gentleman who had "crossed" eleven times before, and had advice and experience to spare for any one who would listen to them; and the other gentleman, not so old but even more queer, who had "frozen his stomach," eight years before, by indulging, on a hot summer's day, in sixteen successive ice-creams, alternated with ten glasses of equally cold soda-water, and who related this exciting experience in turn to everybody on board. There was the bad little boy, whose parents were powerless to oppose him, and who carried terror to the hearts of all beholders whenever he appeared; and the pretty widow who filled the role of reigning belle; and the other widow, not quite so pretty or so much a belle, who had a good deal to say, in a voice made discreetly low, about what a pity it was that dear Mrs. So-and-so should do this or that, and "Doesn't it strike you as very unfortunate that she should not consider" the other thing? A great sea-going steamer is a little world in itself, and gives one a glimpse of all sorts and conditions of people and characters.

On the whole, there was no one on the "Spartacus" whom Katy liked so well as sedate little Gretchen except the dear old Captain, with whom she was a prime favorite. He gave Mrs. Ashe and herself the seats next to him at table, looked after their comfort in every possible way, and each night at dinner sent Katy one of the apple-dumplings made specially for him by the cook, who had gone many voyages with the Captain and knew his fancies. Katy did not care particularly for the dumpling, but she valued it as a mark of regard, and always ate it when she could.

Meanwhile, every morning brought a fresh surprise from that dear, painstaking Rose, who had evidently worked hard and thought harder in contriving pleasures for Katy's first voyage at sea. Mrs. Barrett was enlisted in the plot, there could be no doubt of that, and enjoyed the joke as much as any one, as she presented herself each day with the invariable formula, "A letter for you, ma'am," or "A bundle, Miss, come by the Parcels Delivery." On the fourth morning it was a photograph of Baby Rose, in a little flat morocco case. The fifth brought a wonderful epistle, full of startling pieces of news, none of them true. On the sixth appeared a long narrow box containing a fountain pen. Then came Mr. Howells's "A Foregone Conclusion," which Katy had never seen; then a box of quinine pills; then a sachet for her trunk; then another burlesque poem; last of all, a cake of delicious violet soap, "to wash the sea-smell from her hands," the label said. It grew to be one of the little excitements of ship life to watch for the arrival of these daily gifts; and "What did the mail bring for you this time, Miss Carr?" was a question frequently asked. Each arrival Katy thought must be the final one; but Rose's forethought had gone so far even as to provide an extra parcel in case the voyage was a day longer than usual, and "Miss Carr's mail" continued to come in till the very last morning.

Katy never forgot the thrill that went through her when, after so many days of sea, her eyes first caught sight of the dim line of the Irish coast. An exciting and interesting day followed as, after stopping at Queenstown to leave the mails, they sped northeastward between shores which grew more distinct and beautiful with every hour,—on one side Ireland, on the other the bold mountain lines of the Welsh coast. It was late afternoon when they entered the Mersey, and dusk had fallen before the Captain got out his glass to look for the white fluttering speck in his own window which meant so much to him. Long he studied before he made quite sure that it was there. At last he shut the glass with a satisfied air.

"It's all right," he said to Katy, who stood near, almost as much interested as he. "Lucy never forgets, bless her! Well, there's another voyage over and done with, thank God, and my Mary is where she was. It's a load taken from my mind."

The moon had risen and was shining softly on the river as the crowded tender landed the passengers from the "Spartacus" at the Liverpool docks.

"We shall meet again in London or in Paris," said one to another, and cards and addresses were exchanged. Then after a brief delay at the Custom House they separated, each to his own particular destination; and, as a general thing, none of them ever saw any of the others again.

It is often thus with those who have been fellow voyagers at sea; and it is always a surprise and perplexity to inexperienced travellers that it can be so, and that those who have been so much to each other for ten days can melt away into space and disappear as though the brief intimacy had never existed.

"Four-wheeler or hansom, ma'am?" said a porter to Mrs. Ashe.

"Which, Katy?"

"Oh, let us have a hansom! I never saw one, and they look so nice in 'Punch.'"

So a hansom cab was called, the two ladies got in, Amy cuddled down between them, the folding-doors were shut over their knees like a lap-robe, and away they drove up the solidly paved streets to the hotel where they were to pass the night. It was too late to see or do anything but enjoy the sense of being on firm land once more.

"How lovely it will be to sleep in a bed that doesn't tip or roll from side to side!" said Mrs. Ashe.

"Yes, and that is wide enough and long enough and soft enough to be comfortable!" replied Katy. "I feel as if I could sleep for a fortnight to make up for the bad nights at sea."

Everything seemed delightful to her,—the space for undressing, the great tub of fresh water which stood beside the English-looking washstand with its ample basin and ewer, the chintz-curtained bed, the coolness, the silence,—and she closed her eyes with the pleasant thought in her mind, "It is really England and we are really here!"

CHAPTER V. STORYBOOK ENGLAND.

"Oh, is it raining?" was Katy's first question next morning, when the maid came to call her. The pretty room, with its gayly flowered chintz, and china, and its brass bedstead, did not look half so bright as when lit with gas the night before; and a dim gray light struggled in at the window, which in America would certainly have meant bad weather coming or already come.

"Oh no, h'indeed, ma'am, it's a very fine day,—not bright, ma'am, but very dry," was the answer.

Katy couldn't imagine what the maid meant, when she peeped between the curtains and saw a thick dull mist lying over everything, and the pavements opposite her window shining with wet. Afterwards, when she understood better the peculiarities of the English climate, she too learned to call days not absolutely rainy "fine," and to be grateful for them; but on that first morning her sensations were of bewildered surprise, almost vexation.

Mrs. Ashe and Amy were waiting in the coffee-room when she went in search of them.

"What shall we have for breakfast," asked Mrs. Ashe,—"our first meal in England? Katy, you order it."

"Let's have all the things we have read about in books and don't have at home," said Katy, eagerly. But when she came to look over the bill of fare there didn't seem to be many such things. Soles and muffins she finally decided upon, and, as an after-thought, gooseberry jam.

"Muffins sound so very good in Dickens, you know," she explained to Mrs. Ashe; "and I never saw a sole."

The soles when they came proved to be nice little pan-fish, not unlike what in New England are called "scup." All the party took kindly to them; but the muffins were a great disappointment, tough and tasteless, with a flavor about them as of scorched flannel.

"How queer and disagreeable they are!" said Katy. "I feel as if I were eating rounds cut from an old ironing-blanket and buttered! Dear me! what did Dickens mean by making such a fuss about them, I wonder? And I don't care for gooseberry jam, either; it isn't half as good as the jams we have at home. Books are very deceptive."

"I am afraid they are. We must make up our minds to find a great many things not quite so nice as they sound when we read about them," replied Mrs. Ashe.

Mabel was breakfasting with them, of course, and was heard to remark at this juncture that she didn't like muffins, either, and would a great deal rather have waffles; whereupon Amy reproved her, and explained that nobody in England knew what waffles were, they were such a stupid nation, and that Mabel must learn to eat whatever was given her and not find fault with it!

After this moral lesson it was found to be dangerously near train-time; and they all hurried to the railroad station, which, fortunately, was close by. There was rather a scramble and confusion for a few moments; for Katy, who had undertaken to buy the tickets, was puzzled by the unaccustomed coinage; and Mrs. Ashe, whose part was to see after the luggage, found herself perplexed and worried by the absence of checks, and by no means disposed to accept the porter's statement, that if she'd only bear in mind that the trunks were in the second van from the engine, and get out to see that they were safe once or twice during the journey, and call for them as soon as they reached London, she'd have no trouble,—"please remember the porter, ma'am!" However all was happily settled at last; and without any serious inconveniences they found themselves established in a first-class carriage, and presently after running smoothly at full speed across the rich English midlands toward London and the eastern coast.

The extreme greenness of the October landscape was what struck them first, and the wonderfully orderly and trim aspect of the country, with no ragged, stump-dotted fields or reaches of wild untended woods. Late in October as it was, the hedgerows and meadows were still almost summer-like in color, though the trees were leafless. The delightful-looking old manor-houses and farm-houses, of which they had glimpses now and again, were a constant pleasure to Katy, with their mullioned windows, twisted chimney-stacks, porches of quaint build, and thick-growing ivy. She contrasted them with the uncompromising ugliness of farm-houses which she remembered at home, and wondered whether it could be that at the end of another thousand years or so, America would have picturesque buildings like these to show in addition to her picturesque scenery.

Suddenly into the midst of these reflections there glanced a picture so vivid that it almost took away her breath, as the train steamed past a pack of hounds in full cry, followed by a galloping throng of scarlet-coated huntsmen. One horse and rider were in the air, going over a wall. Another was just rising to the leap. A string of others, headed by a lady, were tearing across a meadow bounded by a little brook, and beyond that streamed the hounds following the invisible fox. It was like one of Muybridge's instantaneous photographs of "The Horse in Motion," for the moment that it lasted; and Katy put it away in her memory, distinct and brilliant, as she might a real picture.

Their destination in London was Batt's Hotel in Dover Street. The old gentleman on the "Spartacus," who had "crossed" so many times, had furnished Mrs. Ashe with a number of addresses of hotels and lodging-houses, from among which Katy had chosen Batt's for the reason that it was mentioned in Miss Edgeworth's "Patronage." "It was the place," she explained, "where Godfrey Percy didn't stay when Lord Oldborough sent him the letter." It seemed an odd enough reason for going anywhere that a person in a novel didn't stay there. But Mrs. Ashe knew nothing of London, and had no preference of her own; so she was perfectly willing to give Katy hers, and Batt's was decided upon.

"It is just like a dream or a story," said Katy, as they drove away from the London station in a four-wheeler. "It is really ourselves, and this is really London! Can you imagine it?"

She looked out. Nothing met her eyes but dingy weather, muddy streets, long rows of ordinary brick or stone houses. It might very well have been New York or Boston on a foggy day, yet to her eyes all things had a subtle difference which made them unlike similar objects at home.

"Wimpole Street!" she cried suddenly, as she caught sight of the name on the corner; "that is the street where Maria Crawford in Mansfield Park, you know, 'opened one of the best houses' after she married Mr. Rushworth. Think of seeing Wimpole Street! What fun!" She looked eagerly out after the "best houses," but the whole street looked uninteresting and old-fashioned; the best house to be seen was not of a kind, Katy thought, to reconcile an ambitious young woman to a dull husband. Katy had to remind herself that Miss Austen wrote her novels nearly a century ago, that London was a "growing" place, and that things were probably much changed since that day.

More "fun" awaited them when they arrived at Batt's, and exactly such a landlady sailed forth to welcome them as they had often met with in books,—an old landlady, smiling and rubicund, with a towering lace cap on her head, a flowered silk gown, a gold chain, and a pair of fat mittened hands demurely crossed over a black brocade apron. She alone would have been worth crossing the ocean to see, they all declared. Their telegram had been received, and rooms were ready, with a bright, smoky fire of soft coals; the dinner-table was set, and a nice, formal, white-cravated old waiter, who seemed to have stepped out of the same book with the landlady, was waiting to serve it. Everything was dingy and old-fashioned, but very clean and comfortable; and Katy concluded that on the whole Godfrey Percy would have done wisely to go to Batt's, and could have fared no better at the other hotel where he did stay.

The first of Katy's "London sights" came to her next morning before she was out of her bedroom. She heard a bell ring and a queer squeaking little voice utter a speech of which she could not make out a single word. Then came a laugh and a shout, as if several boys were amused at something or other; and altogether her curiosity was roused, so that she finished dressing as fast as she could, and ran to the drawing-room window which commanded a view of the street. Quite a little crowd was collected under the window, and in their midst was a queer box raised high on poles, with little red curtains tied back on either side to form a miniature stage, on which puppets were moving and vociferating. Katy knew in a moment that she was seeing her first Punch and Judy!

The box and the crowd began to move away. Katy in despair ran to Wilkins, the old waiter who was setting the breakfast-table.

"Oh, please stop that man!" she said. "I want to see him."

"What man is it, Miss?" said Wilkins.

When he reached the window and realized what Katy meant, his sense of propriety seemed to receive a severe shock. He even ventured on remonstrance.

"H'I wouldn't, Miss, h'if h'I was you. Them Punches are a low lot, Miss; they h'ought to be put down, really they h'ought. Gentlefolks, h'as a general thing, pays no h'attention to them."

But Katy didn't care what "gentlefolks" did or did not do, and insisted upon having Punch called back. So Wilkins was forced to swallow his remonstrances and his dignity, and go in pursuit of the objectionable object. Amy came rushing out, with her hair flying and Mabel in her arms; and she and Katy had a real treat of Punch and Judy, with all the well-known scenes, and perhaps a few new ones thrown in for their especial behoof; for the showman seemed to be inspired by the rapturous enjoyment of his little audience of three at the first-floor windows. Punch beat Judy and stole the baby, and Judy banged Punch in return, and the constable came in and Punch outwitted him, and the hangman and the devil made their appearance duly; and it was all perfectly satisfactory, and "just exactly what she hoped it would be, and it quite made up for the muffins," Katy declared.

Then, when Punch had gone away, the question arose as to what they should choose, out of the many delightful things in London, for their first morning.

Like ninety-nine Americans out of a hundred, they decided on Westminster Abbey; and indeed there is nothing in England better worth seeing, or more impressive, in its dim, rich antiquity, to eyes fresh from the world which still calls itself "new." So to the Abbey they went, and lingered there till Mrs. Ashe declared herself to be absolutely dropping with fatigue.

"If you don't take me home and give me something to eat," she said, "I shall drop down on one of these pedestals and stay there and be exhibited forever after as an 'h'effigy' of somebody belonging to ancient English history."

So Katy tore herself away from Henry the Seventh and the Poets' Corner, and tore Amy away from a quaint little tomb shaped like a cradle, with the marble image of a baby in it, which had greatly taken her fancy. She could only be consoled by the promise that she should soon come again and stay as long as she liked. She reminded Katy of this promise the very next morning.

"Mamma has waked up with rather a bad headache, and she thinks she will lie still and not come to breakfast," she reported. "And she sends her love, and says will you please have a cab and go where you like; and if I won't be a trouble, she would be glad if you would take me with you. And I won't be a trouble, Miss Katy, and I know where I wish you would go."

"Where is that!"

"To see that cunning little baby again that we saw yesterday. I want to show her to Mabel,—she didn't go with us, you know, and I don't like to have her mind not improved; and, darling Miss Katy, mayn't I buy some flowers and put them on the Baby? She's so dusty and so old that I don't believe anybody has put any flowers for her for ever so long."

Katy found this idea rather pretty, and willingly stopped at Covent Garden, where they bought a bunch of late roses for eighteen pence, which entirely satisfied Amy. With them in her hand, and Mabel in her arms, she led the way through the dim aisles of the Abbey, through grates and doors and up and down steps; the guide following, but not at all needed, for Amy seemed to have a perfectly clear recollection of every turn and winding. When the chapel was reached, she laid the roses on the tomb with gentle fingers, and a pitiful, reverent look in her gray eyes. Then she lifted Mabel up to kiss the odd little baby effigy above the marble quilt; whereupon the guide seemed altogether surprised out of his composure, and remarked to Katy,—

"Little Miss is an h'American, as is plain to see; no h'English child would be likely to think of doing such a thing."

"Do not English children take any interest in the tombs of the Abbey?" asked Katy.

"Oh yes, m'm,—h'interest; but they don't take no special notice of one tomb above h'another."

Katy could scarcely keep from laughing, especially as she heard Amy, who had been listening to the conversation, give an audible sniff, and inform Mabel that she was glad *she* was not an English child, who didn't notice things and liked grown-up graves as much as she did dear little cunning ones like this!

Later in the day, when Mrs. Ashe was better, they all drove together to the quaint old keep which has been the scene of so many tragedies, and is known as the Tower of London. Here they were shown various rooms and chapels and prisons; and among the rest the apartments where Queen Elizabeth, when a friendless young Princess, was shut up for many months by her sister, Queen Mary. Katy had read somewhere, and now told Amy, the pretty legend of the four little children who lived with their parents in the Tower, and used to play with the royal captive; and how one little boy brought her a key which he had picked up on the ground, and said, "Now you can go out when you will, lady;" and how the Lords of the Council, getting wind of it, sent for the children to question them, and frightened them and their friends almost to death, and forbade them to go near the Princess again.

A story about children always brings the past much nearer to a child, and Amy's imagination was so excited by this tale, that when they got to the darksome closet which is said to have been the prison of Sir Walter Raleigh, she marched out of it with a pale and wrathful face.

"If this is English history, I never mean to learn any more of it, and neither shall Mabel," she declared.

But it is not possible for Amy or any one else not to learn a great deal of history simply by going about London. So many places are associated with people or events, and seeing the places makes one care so much more for the people or the events, that one insensibly questions and wonders. Katy, who had "browsed" all through her childhood in a good old-fashioned library, had her memory stuffed with all manner of little scraps of information and literary allusions, which now came into use. It was like owning the disjointed bits of a puzzle, and suddenly discovering that properly put together they make a pattern. Mrs. Ashe, who had never been much of a reader, considered her young friend a prodigy of intelligence; but Katy herself realized how inadequate and inexact her knowledge was, and how many bits were missing from the pattern of her puzzle. She wished with all her heart, as every one wishes under such circumstances, that she had studied harder and more wisely while the chance was in her power. On a journey you cannot read to advantage. Remember that, dear girls, who are looking forward to travelling some day, and be industrious in time.

October is not a favorable month in which to see England. Water, water is everywhere; you breathe it, you absorb it; it wets your clothes and it dampens your spirits. Mrs. Ashe's friends advised her not to think of Scotland at that time of the year. One by one their little intended excursions were given up. A single day and night in Oxford and Stratford-on-Avon; a short visit to the Isle of Wight, where, in a country-place which seemed provokingly pretty as far as they could see it for the rain, lived that friend of Mrs. Ashe who had married an Englishman and in so doing had, as Katy privately thought, "renounced the sun;" a peep at Stonehenge from under the shelter of an umbrella, and an hour or two in Salisbury Cathedral,—was all that they accomplished, except a brief halt at Winchester, that Katy might have the privilege of seeing the grave of her beloved Miss Austen. Katy had come abroad with a terribly long list of graves to visit, Mrs. Ashe declared. They laid a few rain-washed flowers upon the tomb, and listened with edification to the verger, who inquired,—

"Whatever was it, ma'am, that lady did which brings so many h'Americans to h'ask about her? Our h'English people don't seem to take the same h'interest."

"She wrote such delightful stories," explained Katy; but the old verger shook his head.

"I think h'it must be some other party, Miss, you've confused with this here. It stands to reason, Miss, that we'd have heard of 'em h'over 'ere in England sooner than you would h'over there in h'America, if the books 'ad been h'anything so h'extraordinary."

The night after their return to London they were dining for the second time with the cousins of whom Mrs. Ashe had spoken to Dr. Carr; and as it happened Katy sat next to a quaint elderly American, who had lived for twenty years in London and knew it much better than most Londoners do. This gentleman, Mr. Allen Beach, had a hobby for antiquities, old books especially, and passed half his time at the British Museum, and the other half in sales rooms and the old shops in Wardour Street.

Katy was lamenting over the bad weather which stood in the way of their plans.

"It is so vexatious," she said. "Mrs. Ashe meant to go to York and Lincoln and all the cathedral towns and to Scotland; and we have had to give it all up because of the rains. We shall go away having seen hardly anything."

"You can see London."

"We have,—that is, we have seen the things that everybody sees."

"But there are so many things that people in general do not see. How much longer are you to stay, Miss Carr?"

"A week, I believe."

"Why don't you make out a list of old buildings which are connected with famous people in history, and visit them in turn? I did that the second year after I came. I gave up three months to it, and it was most interesting. I unearthed all manner of curious stories and traditions."

"Or," cried Katy, struck with a sudden bright thought, "why mightn't I put into the list some of the places I know about in books,—novels as well as history,—and the places where the people who wrote the books lived?"

"You might do that, and it wouldn't be a bad idea, either," said Mr. Beach, pleased with her enthusiasm. "I will get a pencil after dinner and help you with your list if you will allow me."

Mr. Beach was better than his word. He not only suggested places and traced a plan of sight-seeing, but on two different mornings he went with them himself; and his intelligent knowledge of London added very much to the interest of the excursions. Under his guidance the little party of four—for Mabel was never left out; it was *such* a chance for her to improve her mind, Amy declared—visited the Charter-House, where Thackeray went to school, and the Home of the Poor Brothers connected with it, in which Colonel Newcome answered "Adsum" to the roll-call of the angels. They took a look at the small house in Curzon Street, which is supposed to have been in Thackeray's mind when he described the residence of Becky Sharpe; and the other house in Russell Square which is unmistakably that where George Osborne courted Amelia Sedley. They went to service in the delightful old church of St. Mary in the Temple, and thought of Ivanhoe and Brian de Bois-Guilbert and Rebecca the Jewess. From there Mr. Beach took them to Lamb's Court, where Pendennis and George Warrington dwelt in chambers together; and to Brick Court, where Oliver Goldsmith passed so much of his life, and the little rooms in which Charles and Mary Lamb spent so many sadly happy years. On another day they drove to Whitefriars, for the sake of Lord Glenvarloch and the old privilege of Sanctuary in the "Fortunes of Nigel;" and took a peep at Bethnal Green, where the Blind Beggar and his "Pretty Bessee" lived, and at the old Prison of the Marshalsea, made interesting by its associations with "Little Dorrit." They also went to see Milton's house and St. Giles Church, in which he is buried; and stood a long time before St. James Palace, trying to make out which could have been Miss Burney's windows when she was dresser to Queen Charlotte of bitter memory. And they saw Paternoster Row and No. 5 Cheyne Walk, sacred forevermore to the memory of Thomas Carlyle, and Whitehall, where Queen Elizabeth lay in state and King Charles was beheaded, and the state rooms of Holland House; and by great good luck had a glimpse of George Eliot getting out of a cab. She stood for a moment while she gave her fare to the cabman, and Katy looked as one who might not look again, and carried away a distinct picture of the unbeautiful, interesting, remarkable face.

With all this to see and to do, the last week sped all too swiftly, and the last day came before they were at all ready to leave what Katy called "Story-book England." Mrs. Ashe had decided to cross by Newhaven and Dieppe, because some one had told her of the beautiful old town of Rouen, and it seemed easy and convenient to take it on the way to Paris. Just landed from the long voyage across the Atlantic, the little passage of the Channel seemed nothing to our travellers, and they made ready for their night on the Dieppe steamer with the philosophy which is born of ignorance. They were speedily undeceived!

The English Channel has a character of its own, which distinguishes it from other seas and straits. It seems made fractious and difficult by Nature, and set as on purpose to be barrier between two nations who are too unlike to easily understand each other, and are the safer neighbors for this wholesome difficulty of communication between them. The "chop" was worse than usual on the night when our travellers crossed; the steamer had to fight her way inch by inch. And oh, such a little steamer! and oh, such a long night!

CHAPTER VI. ACROSS THE CHANNEL.

Dawn had given place to day, and day was well advanced toward noon, before the stout little steamer gained her port. It was hours after the usual time for arrival; the train for Paris must long since have started, and Katy felt dejected and forlorn as, making her way out of the terrible ladies'-cabin, she crept on deck for her first glimpse of France.

The sun was struggling through the fog with a watery smile, and his faint beams shone on a confusion of stone piers, higher than the vessel's deck, intersected with canal-like waterways, through whose intricate windings the steamer was slowly threading her course to the landing-place. Looking up, Katy could see crowds of people assembled to watch the boat come in,—workmen, peasants, women, children, soldiers, custom-house officers, moving to and fro,—and all this crowd were talking all at once and all were talking French!

I don't know why this should have startled her as it did. She knew, of course, that people of different countries were liable to be found speaking their own languages; but somehow the spectacle of the chattering multitude, all seeming so perfectly at ease with their preterits and subjunctives and never once having to refer to Ollendorf or a dictionary, filled her with a sense of dismayed surprise.

"Good gracious!" she said to herself, "even the babies understand it!" She racked her brains to recall what she had once known of French, but very little seemed to have survived the horrors of the night!

"Oh dear! what is the word for trunk-key?" she asked herself. "They will all begin to ask questions, and I shall not have a word to say; and Mrs. Ashe will be even worse off, I know." She saw the red-trousered custom-house officers pounce upon the passengers as they landed one by one, and she felt her heart sink within her.

But after all, when the time came it did not prove so very bad. Katy's pleasant looks and courteous manner stood her in good stead. She did not trust herself to say much; but the officials seemed to understand without saying. They bowed and gestured, whisked the keys in and out, and in a surprisingly short time all was pronounced right, the baggage had "passed," and it and its owners were free to proceed to the railway-station, which fortunately was close at hand.

Inquiry revealed the fact that no train for Paris left till four in the afternoon.

"I am rather glad," declared poor Mrs. Ashe, "for I feel too used up to move. I will lie here on this sofa; and, Katy dear, please see if there is an eating-place, and get some breakfast for yourself and Amy, and send me a cup of tea."

"I don't like to leave you alone," Katy was beginning; but at that moment a nice old woman who seemed to be in charge of the waiting-room appeared, and with a flood of French which none of them could follow, but which was evidently sympathetic in its nature, flew at Mrs. Ashe and began to make her comfortable. From a cupboard in the wall she produced a pillow, from another cupboard a blanket; in a trice she had one under Mrs. Ashe's head and the other wrapped round her feet.

"Pauvre madame," she said, "si pâle! si souffrante! Il faut avoir quelque chose à boire et à manger tout de suite." She trotted across the room and into the restaurant which opened out of it, while Mrs. Ashe smiled at Katy and said, "You see you can leave me quite safely; I am to be taken care of." And Katy and Amy passed through the same door into the *buffet*, and sat down at a little table.

It was a particularly pleasant-looking place to breakfast in. There were many windows with bright polished panes and very clean short muslin curtains, and on the window-sills stood rows of thrifty potted plants in full bloom,—marigolds, balsams, nasturtiums, and many colored geraniums. Two birds in cages were singing loudly; the floor was waxed to a glass-like polish; nothing could have been whiter than the marble of the tables except the napkins laid over them. And such a good breakfast as was presently brought to them,—delicious coffee in bowl-like cups, crisp rolls and rusks, an omelette with a delicate flavor of fine herbs, stewed chicken, little pats of freshly churned butter without salt, shaped like shells and tasting like solidified cream, and a pot of some sort of nice preserve. Amy made great delighted eyes at Katy, and remarking, "I think France is heaps nicer than that old England," began to eat with a will; and Katy herself felt that if this railroad meal was a specimen of what they had to expect in the future, they had indeed come to a land of plenty.

Fortified with the satisfactory breakfast, she felt equal to a walk; and after they had made sure that Mrs. Ashe had all she needed, she and Amy (and Mabel) set off by themselves to see the sights of Dieppe. I don't know that travellers generally have considered Dieppe an interesting place, but Katy found it so. There was a really old church and some quaint buildings of the style of two centuries back, and even the more modern streets had a novel look to her unaccustomed eyes. At first they only ventured a timid turn or two, marking each corner, and going back now and then to reassure themselves by a look at the station; but after a while, growing bolder, Katy ventured to ask a question or two in French, and was surprised and charmed to find herself understood. After that she grew adventurous, and, no longer fearful of being lost, led Amy straight down a long street lined with shops, almost all of which were for the sale of articles in ivory.

Ivory wares are one of the chief industries of Dieppe. There were cases full, windows full, counters full, of the most exquisite combs and brushes, some with elaborate monograms in silver and colors, others plain; there were boxes and caskets of every size and shape, ornaments, fans, parasol handles, looking-glasses, frames for pictures large and small, napkin-rings.

Katy was particularly smitten with a paper-knife in the form of an angel with long slender wings raised over its head and meeting to form a point. Its price was twenty francs, and she was strongly tempted to buy it for Clover or Rose Red. But she said to herself sensibly, "This is the first shop I have been into and the first thing I have really wanted to buy, and very likely as we go on I shall see things I like better and want more, so it would be foolish to do it. No, I won't." And she resolutely turned her back on the ivory angel, and walked away.

The next turn brought them to a gay-looking little market-place, where old women in white caps were sitting on the ground beside baskets and panniers full of apples, pears, and various queer and curly vegetables, none of which Katy recognized as familiar; fish of all shapes and colors were flapping in shallow tubs of sea-water; there were piles of stockings, muffetees, and comforters in vivid blue and red worsted, and coarse pottery glazed in bright patterns. The faces of the women were brown and wrinkled; there were no pretty ones among them, but their black eyes were full of life and quickness, and their fingers one and all clicked with knitting-needles, as their tongues flew equally fast in the chatter and the chaffer, which went on without stop or stay, though customers did not seem to be many and sales were few.

Returning to the station they found that Mrs. Ashe had been asleep during their absence, and seemed so much better that it was with greatly amended spirits that they took their places in the late afternoon train which was to set them down at Rouen. Katy said they were like the Wise Men of the East, "following a star," in their choice of a hotel; for, having no better advice, they had decided upon one of those thus distinguished in Baedeker's Guide-book.

The star did not betray their confidence; for the Hôtel de la Cloche, to which it led them, proved to be quaint and old, and very pleasant of aspect. The lofty chambers, with their dimly frescoed ceilings, and beds curtained with faded patch, might to all appearances have been furnished about the time when "Columbus crossed the ocean blue;" but everything was clean, and had an air of old-time respectability. The dining-room, which was evidently of more modern build, opened into a square courtyard where oleanders and lemon trees in boxes stood round the basin of a little fountain, whose tinkle and plash blended agreeably with the rattle of the knives and forks. In one corner of the room was a raised and railed platform, where behind a desk sat the mistress of the house, busy with her account-books, but keeping an eye the while on all that went forward.

Mrs. Ashe walked past this personage without taking any notice of her, as Americans are wont to do under such circumstances; but presently the observant Katy noticed that every one else, as they went in or out of the room, addressed a bow or a civil remark to this lady. She quite blushed at the recollection afterward, as she made ready for bed.

"How rude we must have seemed!" she thought. "I am afraid the people here think that Americans have *awful* manners, everybody is so polite. They said 'Bon soir' and 'Merci' and 'Voulez-vous avoir la bonté,' to the waiters even! Well, there is one thing,—I am going to reform. To-morrow I will be as polite as anybody. They will think that I am miraculously improved by one night on French soil; but, never mind! I am going to do it."

She kept her resolution, and astonished Mrs. Ashe next morning, by bowing to the dame on the platform in the most winning manner, and saying, "Bon jour, madame," as they went by.

"But, Katy, who is that person? Why do you speak to her?"

"Don't you see that they all do? She is the landlady, I think; at all events, everybody bows to her. And just notice how prettily these ladies at the next table speak to the waiter. They do not order him to do things as we do at home. I noticed it last night, and I liked it so much that I made a resolution to get up and be as polite as the French themselves this morning."

So all the time that they went about the sumptuous old city, rich in carvings and sculptures and traditions, while they were looking at the Cathedral and the wonderful church of St. Ouen, and the Palace of Justice, and the "Place of the Maid," where poor Jeanne d'Arc was burned and her ashes scattered to the winds, Katy remembered her manners, and smiled and bowed, and used courteous prefixes in a soft pleasant voice; and as Mrs. Ashe and Amy fell in with her example more or less, I think the guides and coachmen and the old women who showed them over the buildings felt that the air of France was very civilizing indeed, and that these strangers from savage countries over the sea were in a fair way to be as well bred as if they had been born in a more favored part of the world!

Paris looked very modern after the peculiar quaint richness and air of the Middle Ages which distinguish Rouen. Rooms had been engaged for Mrs. Ashe's party in a *pension* near the Arc d'Étoile, and there they drove immediately on arriving. The rooms were not in the *pension* itself, but in a house close by,—a sitting-room with six mirrors, three clocks, and a pinched little grate about a foot wide, a dining-room just large enough for a table and four chairs, and two bedrooms. A maid called Amandine had been detailed to take charge of these rooms and serve their meals.

Dampness, as Katy afterward wrote to Clover, was the first impression they received of "gay Paris." The tiny fire in the tiny grate had only just been lighted, and the walls and the sheets and even the blankets felt chilly and moist to the touch. They spent their first evening in hanging the bedclothes round the grate and piling on fuel; they even set the mattresses up on edge to warm and dry! It was not very enlivening, it must be confessed. Amy had taken a cold, Mrs. Ashe looked worried, and Katy thought of Burnet and the safety and comfort of home with a throb of longing.

The days that ensued were not brilliant enough to remove this impression. The November fogs seemed to have followed them across the Channel, and Paris remained enveloped in a wet blanket which dimmed and hid its usually brilliant features. Going about in cabs with the windows drawn up, and now and then making a rush through the drip into shops, was not exactly delightful, but it seemed pretty much all that they could do. It was worse for Amy, whose cold kept her indoors and denied her even the relaxation of the cab. Mrs. Ashe had engaged a well-recommended elderly English maid to come every morning and take care of Amy while they were out; and with this respectable functionary, whose ideas were of a rigidly British type and who did not speak a word of any language but her own, poor Amy was compelled to spend most of her time. Her only consolation was in persuading this serene attendant to take a part in the French lessons which she made a daily point of giving to Mabel out of her own little phrase-book.

"Wilkins is getting on, I think," she told Katy one night. "She says 'Biscuit glacé' quite nicely now. But I never will let her look at the book, though she always wants to; for if once she saw how the words are spelled, she would never in the world pronounce them right again. They look so very different, you know."

Katy looked at Amy's pale little face and eager eyes with a real heartache. Her rapture when at the end of the long dull afternoons her mother returned to her was touching. Paris was very *triste* to poor Amy, with all her happy facility for amusing herself; and Katy felt that the sooner they got away from it the better it would be. So, in spite of the delight which her brief glimpses at the Louvre gave her, and the fun it was to go about with Mrs. Ashe and see her buy pretty things, and the real satisfaction she took in the one perfectly made walking-suit to which she had treated herself, she was glad when the final day came, when the belated dressmakers and artistes in jackets and wraps had sent home their last wares, and the trunks were packed. It had been rather the fault of circumstances than of Paris; but Katy had not learned to love the beautiful capital as most Americans do, and did not feel at all as if she wanted that her "reward of virtue" should be to go there when she died! There must be more interesting places for live people, and ghosts too, to be found on the map of Europe, she was sure.

Next morning as they drove slowly down the Champs Élysées, and looked back for a last glimpse of the famous Arch, a bright object met their eyes, moving vaguely against the mist. It was the gay red wagon of the Bon Marché, carrying bundles home to the dwellers of some up-town street.

Katy burst out laughing. "It is an emblem of Paris," she said,—"of our Paris, I mean. It has been all Bon Marché and fog!"

"Miss Katy," interrupted Amy, "*do* you like Europe? For my part, I was never so disgusted with any place in my life!"

"Poor little bird, her views of 'Europe' are rather dark just now, and no wonder," said her mother. "Never mind, darling, you shall have something pleasanter by and by if I can find it for you."

"Burnet is a great deal pleasanter than Paris," pronounced Amy, decidedly. "It doesn't keep always raining there, and I can take walks, and I understand everything that people say."

All that day they sped southward, and with every hour came a change in the aspect of their surroundings. Now they made brief stops in large busy towns which seemed humming with industry. Now they whirled through grape countries with miles of vineyards, where the brown leaves still hung on the vines. Then again came glimpses of old Roman ruins, amphitheatres, viaducts, fragments of wall or arch; or a sudden chill betokened their approach to mountains, where snowy peaks could be seen on the far horizon. And when the long night ended and day roused them from broken slumbers, behold, the world was made over! Autumn had vanished, and the summer, which they thought fled for good, had taken his place. Green woods waved about them, fresh leaves were blowing in the wind, roses and hollyhocks beckoned from white-walled gardens; and before they had done with exclaiming and rejoicing, the Mediterranean shot into view, intensely blue, with white fringes of foam, white sails blowing across, white gulls flying above it, and over all a sky of the same exquisite blue, whose clouds were white as the drifting sails on the water below, and they were at Marseilles.

It was like a glimpse of Paradise to eyes fresh from autumnal grays and glooms, as they sped along the lovely coast, every curve and turn showing new combinations of sea and shore, olive-crowned cliff and shining mountain-peak. With every mile the blue became bluer, the wind softer, the feathery verdure more dense and summer-like. Hyères and Cannes and Antibes were passed, and then, as they rounded a long point, came the view of a sunshiny city lying on a sunlit shore; the train slackened its speed, and they knew that their journey's end was come and they were in Nice.

The place seemed to laugh with gayety as they drove down the Promenade des Anglais and past the English garden, where the band was playing beneath the acacias and palm-trees. On one side was a line of bright-windowed hotels and *pensions*, with balconies and striped awnings; on the other, the long reach of yellow sand-beach, where ladies were grouped on shawls and rugs, and children ran up and down in the sun, while beyond stretched the waveless sea. The December sun felt as warm as on a late June day at home, and had the same soft caressing touch. The pavements were thronged with groups of leisurely-looking people, all wearing an unmistakable holiday aspect; pretty girls in correct Parisian costumes walked demurely beside their mothers, with cavaliers in attendance; and among these young men appeared now and again the well-known uniform of the United States Navy.

"I wonder," said Mrs. Ashe, struck by a sudden thought, "if by any chance our squadron is here." She asked the question the moment they entered the hotel; and the porter, who prided himself on understanding "zose Eenglesh," replied,—

"Mais oui, Madame, ze Americaine fleet it is here; zat is, not here, but at Villefranche, just a leetle four mile away,—it is ze same zing exactly."

"Katy, do you hear that?" cried Mrs. Ashe. "The frigates *are* here, and the 'Natchitoches' among them of course; and we shall have Ned to go about with us everywhere. It is a real piece of good luck for us. Ladies are at such a loss in a place like this with nobody to escort them. I am perfectly delighted."

"So am I," said Katy. "I never saw a frigate, and I always wanted to see one. Do you suppose they will let us go on board of them?"

"Why, of course they will." Then to the porter, "Give me a sheet of paper and an envelope, please.—I must let Ned know that I am here at once."

Mrs. Ashe wrote her note and despatched it before they went upstairs to take off their bonnets. She seemed to have a half-hope that some bird of the air might carry the news of her arrival to her brother, for she kept running to the window as if in expectation of seeing him. She was too restless to lie down or sleep, and after she and Katy had lunched, proposed that they should go out on the beach for a while.

"Perhaps we may come across Ned," she remarked.

They did not come across Ned, but there was no lack of other delightful objects to engage their attention. The sands were smooth and hard as a floor. Soft pink lights were beginning to tinge the western sky. To the north shone the peaks of the maritime Alps, and the same rosy glow caught them here and there, and warmed their grays and whites into color.

"I wonder what that can be?" said Katy, indicating the rocky point which bounded the beach to the east, where stood a picturesque building of stone, with massive towers and steep pitches of roof. "It looks half like a house and half like a castle, but it is quite fascinating, I think. Do you suppose that people live there?"

"We might ask," suggested Mrs. Ashe.

Just then they came to a shallow river spanned by a bridge, beside whose pebbly bed stood a number of women who seemed to be washing clothes by the simple and primitive process of laying them in the water on top of the stones, and pounding them with a flat wooden paddle till they were white. Katy privately thought that the clothes stood a poor chance of lasting through these cleansing operations; but she did not say so, and made the inquiry which Mrs. Ashe had suggested, in her best French.

"Celle-là?" answered the old woman whom she had addressed. "Mais c'est la Pension Suisse."

"A *pension*; why, that means a boarding-house," cried Katy. "What fun it must be to board there!"

"Well, why shouldn't we board there!" said her friend. "You know we meant to look for rooms as soon as we were rested and had found out a little about the place. Let us walk on and see what the Pension Suisse is like. If the inside is as pleasant as the outside, we could not do better, I should think."

"Oh, I do hope all the rooms are not already taken," said Katy, who had fallen in love at first sight with the Pension Suisse. She felt quite oppressed with anxiety as they rang the bell.

The Pension Suisse proved to be quite as charming inside as out. The thick stone walls made deep sills and embrasures for the casement windows, which were furnished with red cushions to serve as seats and lounging-places. Every window seemed to command a view, for those which did not look toward the sea looked toward the mountains. The house was by no means full, either. Several sets of rooms were to be had; and Katy felt as if she had walked straight into the pages of a romance When Mrs. Ashe engaged for a month a delightful suite of three, a sitting-room and two sleeping-chambers, in a round tower, with a balcony overhanging the water, and a side window, from which a flight of steps led down into a little walled garden, nestled in among the masonry, where tall laurestinus and lemon trees grew, and orange and brown wallflowers made the air sweet. Her contentment knew no bounds.

"I am so glad that I came," she told Mrs. Ashe. "I never confessed it to you before; but sometimes.—when we were sick at sea, you know, and when it would rain all the time, and after Amy caught that cold in Paris—I have almost wished, just for a minute or two at a time, that we hadn't. But now I wouldn't not have come for the world! This is perfectly delicious. I am glad, glad, glad we are here, and we are going to have a lovely time, I know."

They were passing out of the rooms into the hall as she said these words, and two ladies who were walking up a cross passage turned their heads at the sound of her voice. To her great surprise Katy recognized Mrs. Page and Lilly.

"Why, Cousin Olivia, is it you?" she cried, springing forward with the cordiality one naturally feels in seeing a familiar face in a foreign land.

Mrs. Page seemed rather puzzled than cordial. She put up her eyeglass and did not seem to quite make out who Katy was.

"It is Katy Carr, mamma," explained Lilly. "Well, Katy, this *is* a surprise! Who would have thought of meeting you in Nice!"

There was a decided absence of rapture in Lilly's manner. She was prettier than ever, as Katy saw in a moment, and beautifully dressed in soft brown velvet, which exactly suited her complexion and her pale-colored wavy hair.

"Katy Carr! why, so it is," admitted Mrs. Page. "It is a surprise indeed. We had no idea that you were abroad. What has brought you so far from Tunket,—Burnet, I mean? Who are you with?"

"With my friend Mrs. Ashe," explained Katy, rather chilled by this cool reception.

"Let me introduce you. Mrs. Ashe, these are my cousins Mrs. Page and Miss Page. Amy,—why where is Amy?"

Amy had walked back to the door of the garden staircase, and was standing there looking down upon the flowers.

Cousin Olivia bowed rather distantly. Her quick eye took in the details of Mrs. Ashe's travelling-dress and Katy's dark blue ulster.

"Some countrified friend from that dreadful Western town where they live," she said to herself. "How foolish of Philip Carr to try to send his girls to Europe! He can't afford it, I know." Her voice was rather rigid as she inquired,—

"And what brings you here?—to this house, I mean?"

"Oh, we are coming to-morrow to stay; we have taken rooms for a month," explained Katy. "What a delicious-looking old place it is."

"Have you?" said Lilly, in a voice which did not express any particular pleasure. "Why, we are staying here too."

CHAPTER VII. THE PENSION SUISSE.

"What do you suppose can have brought Katy Carr to Europe?" inquired Lilly, as she stood in the window watching the three figures walk slowly down the sands. "She is the last person I expected to turn up here. I supposed she was stuck in that horrid place—what is the name of it?—where they live, for the rest of her life."

"I confess I am surprised at meeting her myself," rejoined Mrs. Page. "I had no idea that her father could afford so expensive a journey."

"And who is this woman that she has got along with her?"

"I have no idea, I'm sure. Some Western friend, I suppose."

"Dear me, I wish they were going to some other house than this," said Lilly, discontentedly. "If they were at the Rivoir, for instance, or one of those places at the far end of the beach, we shouldn't need to see anything of them, or even know that they were in town! It's a real nuisance to have people spring upon you this way, people you don't want to meet; and when they happen to be relations it is all the worse. Katy will be hanging on us all the time, I'm afraid."

"Oh, my dear, there is no fear of that. A little repression on our part will prevent her from being any trouble, I'm quite certain. But we *must* treat her politely, you know, Lilly; her father is my cousin."

"That's the saddest part of it! Well, there's one thing, I shall *not* take her with me every time we go to the frigates," said Lilly, decisively. "I am not going to inflict a country cousin on Lieutenant Worthington, and spoil all my own fun beside. So I give you fair warning, mamma, and you must manage it somehow."

"Certainly, dear, I will. It would be a great pity to have your visit to Nice spoiled in any way, with the squadron here too, and that pleasant Mr. Worthington so very attentive."

Unconscious of these plans for her suppression, Katy walked back to the hotel in a mood of pensive pleasure. Europe at last promised to be as delightful as it had seemed when she only knew it from maps and books, and Nice so far appeared to her the most charming place in the world.

Somebody was waiting for them at the Hotel des Anglais,—a tall, bronzed, good-looking somebody in uniform, with pleasant brown eyes beaming from beneath a gold-banded cap; at the sight of whom Amy rushed forward with her long locks flying, and Mrs. Ashe uttered an exclamation of pleasure. It was Ned Worthington, Mrs. Ashe's only brother, whom she had not met for two years and a half; and you can easily imagine how glad she was to see him.

"You got my note then?" she said after the first eager greetings were over and she had introduced him to Katy.

"Note? No. Did you write me a note?"

"Yes; to Villefranche."

"To the ship? I shan't get that till tomorrow. No; finding out that you were here is just a bit of good fortune. I came over to call on some friends who are staying down the beach a little way, and dropping in to look over the list of arrivals, as I generally do, I saw your names; and the porter not being able to say which way you had gone, I waited for you to come in."

"We have been looking at such a delightful old place, the Pension Suisse, and have taken rooms."

"The Pension Suisse, eh? Why, that was where I was going to call. I know some people who are staying there. It seems a pleasant house; I'm glad you are going there, Polly. It's first-rate luck that the ships happen to be here just now. I can see you every day."

"But, Ned, surely you are not leaving me so soon? Surely you will stay and dine with us?" urged his sister, as he took up his cap.

"I wish I could, but I can't to-night, Polly. You see I had engaged to take some ladies out to drive, and they will expect me. I had no idea that you would be here, or I should have kept myself free," apologetically. "Tomorrow I will come over early, and be at your service for whatever you like to do."

"That's right, dear boy. We shall expect you." Then, the moment he was gone, "Now, Katy, isn't he nice?"

"Very nice, I should think," said Katy, who had watched the brief interview with interest. "I like his face so much, and how fond he is of you!"

"Dear fellow! so he is. I am seven years older than he, but we have always been intimate. Brothers and sisters are not always intimate, you know,—or perhaps you don't know, for all of yours are."

"Yes, indeed," said Katy, with a happy smile. "There is nobody like Clover and Elsie, except perhaps Johnnie and Dorry and Phil," she added with a laugh.

The remove to the Pension Suisse was made early the next morning. Mrs. Page and Lilly did not appear to welcome them. Katy rather rejoiced in their absence, for she wanted the chance to get into order without interruptions.

There was something comfortable in the thought that they were to stay a whole month in these new quarters; for so long a time, it seemed worth while to make them pretty and homelike. So, while Mrs. Ashe unpacked her own belongings and Amy's, Katy, who had a natural turn for arranging rooms, took possession of the little parlor, pulled the furniture into new positions, laid out portfolios and work-cases and their few books, pinned various photographs which they had bought in Oxford and London on the walls, and tied back the curtains to admit the sunshine. Then she paid a visit to the little garden, and came back with a long branch of laurestinus, which she trained across the mantelpiece, and a bunch of wallflowers for their one little vase. The maid, by her orders, laid a fire of wood and pine cones ready for lighting; and when all was done she called Mrs. Ashe to pronounce upon the effect.

"It is lovely," she said, sinking into a great velvet arm-chair which Katy had drawn close to the seaward window. "I haven't seen anything so pleasant since we left home. You are a witch, Katy, and the comfort of my life. I am so glad I brought you! Now, pray go and unpack your own things, and make yourself look nice for the second breakfast. We have been a shabby set enough since we arrived. I saw those cousins of yours looking askance at our old travelling-dresses yesterday. Let us try to make a more respectable impression to-day."

So they went down to breakfast, Mrs. Ashe in one of her new Paris gowns, Katy in a pretty dress of olive serge, and Amy all smiles and ruffled pinafore, walking hand in hand with her uncle Ned, who had just arrived and whose great ally she was; and Mrs. Page and Lilly, who were already seated at table, had much ado to conceal their somewhat unflattering surprise at the conjunction. For one moment Lilly's eyes opened into a wide stare of incredulous astonishment; then she remembered herself, nodded as pleasantly as she could to Mrs. Ashe and Katy, and favored Lieutenant Worthington with a pretty blushing smile as he went by, while she murmured,—

"Mamma, do you see that? What does it mean?"

"Why, Ned, do you know those people?" asked Mrs. Ashe at the same moment.

"Do *you* know them!"

"Yes; we met yesterday. They are connections of my friend Miss Carr."

"Really? There is not the least family likeness between them." And Mr. Worthington's eyes travelled deliberately from Lilly's delicate, golden prettiness to Katy, who, truth to say, did not shine by the contrast.

"She has a nice, sensible sort of face," he thought, "and she looks like a lady, but for beauty there is no comparison between the two." Then he turned to listen to his sister as she replied,—

"No, indeed, not the least; no two girls could be less like." Mrs. Ashe had made the same comparison, but with quite a different result.

Katy's face was grown dear to her, and she had not taken the smallest fancy to Lilly Page.

Her relationship to the young naval officer, however, made a wonderful difference in the attitude of Mrs. Page and Lilly toward the party. Katy became a person to be cultivated rather than repressed, and thenceforward there was no lack of cordiality on their part.

"I want to come in and have a good talk," said Lilly, slipping her arm through Katy's as they left the dining-room. "Mayn't I come now while mamma is calling on Mrs. Ashe?" This arrangement brought her to the side of Lieutenant Worthington, and she walked between him and Katy down the hall and into the little drawing-room.

"Oh, how perfectly charming! You have been fixing up ever since you came, haven't you? It looks like home. I wish we had a *salon*, but mamma thought it wasn't worth while, as we were only to be here such a little time. What a delicious balcony over the water, too! May I go out on it? Oh, Mr. Worthington, do see this!"

She pushed open the half-closed window and stepped out as she spoke. Mr. Worthington, after hesitating a moment, followed. Katy paused uncertain. There was hardly room for three in the balcony, yet she did not quite like to leave them. But Lilly had turned her back, and was talking in a low tone; it was nothing more in reality than the lightest chit-chat, but it had the air of being something confidential; so Katy, after waiting a little while, retreated to the sofa, and took up her work, joining now and then in the conversation which Mrs. Ashe was keeping up with Cousin Olivia. She did not mind Lilly's ill-breeding, nor was she surprised at it. Mrs. Ashe was less tolerant.

"Isn't it rather damp out there, Ned?" she called to her brother; "you had better throw my shawl round Miss Page's shoulders."

"Oh, it isn't a bit damp," said Lilly, recalled to herself by this broad hint. "Thank you so much for thinking of it, Mrs. Ashe, but I am just coming in." She seated herself beside Katy, and began to question her rather languidly.

"When did you leave home, and how were they all when you came away?"

"All well, thank you. We sailed from Boston on the 14th of October; and before that I spent two days with Rose Red,—you remember her? She is married now, and has the dearest little home and such a darling baby."

"Yes, I heard of her marriage. It didn't seem much of a match for Mr. Redding's daughter to make, did it? I never supposed she would be satisfied with anything less than a member of Congress or a Secretary of Legation."

"Rose isn't particularly ambitious, I think, and she seems perfectly happy," replied Katy, flushing.

"Oh, you needn't fire up in her defence; you and Clover always did adore Rose Red, I know, but I never could see what there was about her that was so wonderfully fascinating. She never had the least style, and she was always just as rude to me as she could be."

"You were not intimate at school, but I am sure Rose was never rude," said Katy, with spirit.

"Well, we won't fight about her at this late day. Tell me where you have been, and where you are going, and how long you are to stay in Europe."

Katy, glad to change the subject, complied, and the conversation diverged into comparison of plans and experiences. Lilly had been in Europe nearly a year, and had seen "almost everything," as she phrased it. She and her mother had spent the previous winter in Italy, had taken a run into Russia, "done" Switzerland and the Tyrol thoroughly, and France and Germany, and were soon going into Spain, and from there to Paris, to shop in preparation for their return home in the spring.

"Of course we shall want quantities of things," she said. "No one will believe that we have been abroad unless we bring home a lot of clothes. The *lingerie* and all that is ordered already; but the dresses must be made at the last moment, and we shall have a horrid time of it, I suppose. Worth has promised to make me two walking-suits and two ball-dresses, but he's very bad about keeping his word. Did you do much when you were in Paris, Katy?"

"We went to the Louvre three times, and to Versailles and St. Cloud," said Katy, wilfully misunderstanding her.

"Oh, I didn't mean that kind of stupid thing; I meant gowns. What did you buy?"

"One tailor-made suit of dark blue cloth."

"My! what moderation!"

Shopping played a large part in Lilly's reminiscences. She recollected places, not from their situation or beauty or historical associations, or because of the works of art which they contained, but as the places where she bought this or that.

"Oh, that dear Piazza di Spagna!" she would say; "that was where I found my rococo necklace, the loveliest thing you ever saw, Katy." Or, "Prague—oh yes, mother got the most enchanting old silver chatelaine there, with all kinds of things hanging to it,—needlecases and watches and scent-bottles, all solid, and so beautifully chased." Or again, "Berlin was horrid, we thought; but the amber is better and cheaper than anywhere else,—great strings of beads, of the largest size and that beautiful pale yellow, for a hundred francs. You must get yourself one, Katy."

Poor Lilly! Europe to her was all "things." She had collected trunks full of objects to carry home, but of the other collections which do not go into trunks, she had little or none. Her mind was as empty, her heart as untouched as ever; the beauty and the glory and the pathos of art and history and Nature had been poured out in vain before her closed and indifferent eyes.

Life soon dropped into a peaceful routine at the Pension Suisse, which was at the same time restful and stimulating. Katy's first act in the morning, as soon as she opened her eyes, was to hurry to the window in hopes of getting a glimpse of Corsica. She had discovered that this elusive island could almost always be seen from Nice at the dawning, but that as soon as the sun was fairly up, it vanished to appear no more for the rest of the day. There was something fascinating to her imagination in the hovering mountain outline between sea and sky. She felt as if she were under an engagement to be there to meet it, and she rarely missed the appointment. Then, after Corsica had pulled the bright mists over its face and melted from view, she would hurry with her dressing, and as soon as was practicable set to work to make the *salon* look bright before the coffee and rolls should appear, a little after eight o'clock. Mrs. Ashe always found the fire lit, the little meal cosily set out beside it, and Katy's happy untroubled face to welcome her when she emerged from her room; and the cheer of these morning repasts made a good beginning for the day.

Then came walking and a French lesson, and a long sitting on the beach, while Katy worked at her home letters and Amy raced up and down in the sun; and then toward noon Lieutenant Ned generally appeared, and some scheme of pleasure was set on foot. Mrs. Ashe ignored his evident *penchant* for Lilly Page, and claimed his time and attentions as hers by right. Young Worthington was a good deal "taken" with the pretty Lilly; still, he had an old-time devotion for his sister and the habit of doing what she desired, and he yielded to her behests with no audible objections. He made a fourth in the carriage while they drove over the lovely hills which encircle Nice toward the north, to Cimiers and the Val de St. André, or down the coast toward Ventimiglia. He went with them to Monte-Carlo and Mentone, and was their escort again and again when they visited the great war-ships as they lay at anchor in a bay which in its translucent blue was like an enormous sapphire.

Mrs. Page and her daughter were included in these parties more than once; but there was something in Mrs. Ashe's cool appropriation of her brother which was infinitely vexatious to Lilly, who before her arrival had rather looked upon Lieutenant Worthington as her own especial property.

"I wish *that* Mrs. Ashe had stayed at home," she told her mother. "She quite spoils everything. Mr. Worthington isn't half so nice as he was before she came. I do believe she has a plan for making him fall in love with Katy; but there she makes a miss of it, for he doesn't seem to care anything about her."

"Katy is a nice girl enough," pronounced her mother, "but not of the sort to attract a gay young man, I should fancy. I don't believe *she* is thinking of any such thing. You needn't be afraid, Lilly."

"I'm not afraid," said Lilly, with a pout; "only it's so provoking."

Mrs. Page was quite right. Katy was not thinking of any such thing. She liked Ned Worthington's frank manners; she owned, quite honestly, that she thought him handsome, and she particularly admired the sort of deferential affection which he showed to Mrs. Ashe, and his nice ways with Amy. For herself, she was aware that he scarcely noticed her except as politeness demanded that he should be civil to his sister's friend; but the knowledge did not trouble her particularly. Her head was full of interesting things, plans, ideas. She was not accustomed to being made the object of admiration, and experienced none of the vexations of a neglected belle. If Lieutenant Worthington happened to talk to her, she responded frankly and freely; if he did not, she occupied herself with something else; in either case she was quite unembarrassed both in feeling and manner, and had none of the awkwardness which comes from disappointed vanity and baffled expectations, and the need for concealing them.

Toward the close of December the officers of the flag-ship gave a ball, which was the great event of the season to the gay world of Nice. Americans were naturally in the ascendant on an American frigate; and of all the American girls present, Lilly Page was unquestionably the prettiest. Exquisitely dressed in white lace, with bands of turquoises on her neck and arms and in her hair, she had more partners than she knew what to do with, more bouquets than she could well carry, and compliments enough to turn any girl's head. Thrown off her guard by her triumphs, she indulged a little vindictive feeling which had been growing in her mind of late on account of what she chose to consider certain derelictions of duty on the part of Lieutenant Worthington, and treated him to a taste of neglect. She was engaged three deep when he asked her to dance; she did not hear when he invited her to walk; she turned a cold shoulder when he tried to talk, and seemed absorbed by the other cavaliers, naval and otherwise, who crowded about her.

Piqued and surprised, Ned Worthington turned to Katy. She did not dance, saying frankly that she did not know how and was too tall;

and she was rather simply dressed in a pearl-gray silk, which had been her best gown the winter before in Burnet, with a bunch of red roses in the white lace of the tucker, and another in her hand, both the gifts of little Amy; but she looked pleasant and serene, and there was something about her which somehow soothed his disturbed mind, as he offered her his arm for a walk on the decks.

For a while they said little, and Katy was quite content to pace up and down in silence, enjoying the really beautiful scene,—the moonlight on the Bay, the deep wavering reflections of the dark hulls and slender spars, the fairy effect of the colored lamps and lanterns, and the brilliant moving maze of the dancers.

"Do you care for this sort of thing?" he suddenly asked.

"What sort of thing do you mean?"

"Oh, all this jigging and waltzing and amusement."

"I don't know how to 'jig,' but it's delightful to look on," she answered merrily. "I never saw anything so pretty in my life."

The happy tone of her voice and the unruffled face which she turned upon him quieted his irritation.

"I really believe you mean it," he said; "and yet, if you won't think me rude to say so, most girls would consider the thing dull enough if they were only getting out of it what you are,—if they were not dancing, I mean, and nobody in particular was trying to entertain them."

"But everything *is* being done to entertain me," cried Katy. "I can't imagine what makes you think that it could seem dull. I am in it all, don't you see,—I have my share—. Oh, I am stupid, I can't make you understand."

"Yes, you do. I understand perfectly, I think; only it is such a different point of view from what girls in general would take." (By girls he meant Lilly!) "Please do not think me uncivil."

"You are not uncivil at all; but don't let us talk any more about me. Look at the lights between the shadows of the masts on the water. How they quiver! I never saw anything so beautiful, I think. And how warm it is! I can't believe that we are in December and that it is nearly Christmas."

"How is Polly going to celebrate her Christmas? Have you decided?"

"Amy is to have a Christmas-tree for her dolls, and two other dolls are coming. We went out this morning to buy things for it,—tiny little toys and candles fit for Lilliput. And that reminds me, do you suppose one can get any Christmas greens here?"

"Why not? The place seems full of green."

"That's just it; the summer look makes it unnatural. But I should like some to dress the parlor with if they could be had."

"I'll see what I can find, and send you a load."

I don't know why this very simple little talk should have made an impression on Lieutenant Worthington's mind, but somehow he did not forget it.

"'Don't let us talk any more about me,'" he said to himself that night when alone in his cabin. "I wonder how long it would be before the other one did anything to divert the talk from herself. Some time, I fancy." He smiled rather grimly as he unbuckled his sword-belt. It is unlucky for a girl when she starts a train of reflection like this. Lilly's little attempt to pique her admirer had somehow missed its mark.

The next afternoon Katy in her favorite place on the beach was at work on the long weekly letter which she never failed to send home to Burnet. She held her portfolio in her lap, and her pen ran rapidly over the paper, as rapidly almost as her tongue would have run could her correspondents have been brought nearer.

"Nice, December 22.

"Dear Papa and everybody,—Amy and I are sitting on my old purple cloak, which is spread over the sand just where it was spread the last time I wrote you. We are playing the following game: I am a fairy and she is a little girl. Another fairy—not sitting on the cloak at present—has enchanted the little girl, and I am telling her various ways by which she can work out her deliverance. At present the task is to find twenty-four dull red pebbles of the same color, failing to do which she is to be changed into an owl. When we began to play, I was the wicked fairy; but Amy objected to that because I am 'so nice,' so we changed the characters. I wish you could see the glee in her pretty gray eyes over this infantile game, into which she has thrown herself so thoroughly that she half believes in it. 'But I needn't really be changed into an owl!' she says, with a good deal of anxiety in her voice.

"To think that you are shivering in the first snow-storm, or sending the children out with their sleds and india-rubbers to slide! How I wish instead that you were sharing the purple cloak with Amy and me, and could sit all this warm balmy afternoon close to the surf-line which fringes this bluest of blue seas! There is plenty of room for you all. Not many people come down to this end of the beach, and if you were very good we would let you play.

"Our life here goes on as delightfully as ever. Nice is very full of people, and there seem to be some pleasant ones among them. Here at the Pension Suisse we do not see a great many Americans. The fellow-boarders are principally Germans and Austrians with a sprinkling of French. (Amy has found her twenty-four red pebbles, so she is let off from being an owl. She is now engaged in throwing them one by one into the sea. Each must hit the water under penalty of her being turned into a Muscovy duck. She doesn't know exactly what a Muscovy duck is, which makes her all the more particular about her shots.) But, as I was saying, our little *suite* in the round tower is so on one side of the rest of the Pension that it is as good as having a house of our own. The *salon* is very bright and sunny; we have two sofas and a square table and a round table and a sort of what-not and two easy-chairs and two uneasy chairs and a lamp of our own and a clock. There is also a sofa-pillow. There's richness for you! We have pinned up all our photographs on the walls, including Papa's and Clovy's and that bad one of Phil and Johnnie making faces at each other, and three lovely red and yellow Japanese pictures on muslin which Rose Red put in my trunk the last thing, for a spot of color. There are some autumn leaves too; and we always have flowers and in the mornings and evenings a fire.

"Amy is now finding fifty snow-white pebbles, which when found are to be interred in one common grave among the shingle. If she fails to do this, she is to be changed to an electrical eel. The chief difficulty is that she loses her heart to particular pebbles. 'I can't bury you,' I hear her saying.

"To return,—we have jolly little breakfasts together in the *salon*. They consist of coffee and rolls, and are served by a droll, snappish little *garçon* with no teeth, and an Italian-French patois which is very hard to understand when he sputters. He told me the other day that he had been a *garçon* for forty-six years, which seemed rather a long boyhood.

"The company, as we meet them at table, are rather entertaining. Cousin Olivia and Lilly are on their best behavior to me because I am travelling with Mrs. Ashe, and Mrs. Ashe is Lieutenant Worthington's sister, and Lieutenant Worthington is Lilly's admirer, and they like him very much. In fact, Lilly has intimated confidentially that she is all but engaged to him; but I am not sure about it, or if that was what she meant; and I fear, if it proves true, that dear Polly will not like it at all. She is quite unmanageable, and snubs Lilly continually in a polite way, which makes me fidgety for fear Lilly will be offended, but she never seems to notice it. Cousin Olivia looks very handsome and gorgeous. She quite takes the color out of the little Russian Countess who sits next to her, and who is as dowdy and meek as if she came from Akron or Binghampton, or any other place where countesses are unknown. Then there are two charming, well-bred young Austrians. The one who sits nearest to me is a 'Candidat' for a Doctorate of Laws, and speaks eight languages well. He has only studied English for the past six weeks, but has made wonderful progress. I wish my French were half as good as his English is already.

"There is a very gossiping young woman on the story beneath ours, whom I meet sometimes in the garden, and from her I hear all manner of romantic tales about people in the house. One little French girl is dying of consumption and a broken heart, because of a quarrel with her lover, who is a courier; and the *padrona*, who is young and pretty, and has only been married a few months to our elderly landlord, has a story also. I forget some of the details; but there was a stern parent and an admirer, and a cup of cold poison, and now she says she wishes she were dying of consumption like poor Alphonsine. For all that, she looks quite fat and rosy, and I often see her in her best gown with a great deal of Roman scarf and mosaic jewelry, stationed in the doorway, 'making the Pension look attractive to the passers-by.' So she has a sense of duty, though she is unhappy.

"Amy has buried all her pebbles, and says she is tired of playing fairy. She is now sitting with her head on my shoulder, and professedly studying her French verb for to-morrow, but in reality, I am sorry to say, she is conversing with me about be-headings,—a subject which, since her visit to the Tower, has exercised a horrible fascination over her mind. 'Do people die right away?' she asks. 'Don't they feel one minute, and doesn't it feel awfully?' There is a good deal of blood, she supposes, because there was so much straw laid about the block in the picture of Lady Jane Gray's execution, which enlivened our walls in Paris. On the whole, I am rather glad that a fat little white dog has come waddling down the beach and taken off her attention.

"Speaking of Paris seems to renew the sense of fog which we had there. Oh, how enchanting sunshine is after weeks of gloom! I shall never forget how the Mediterranean looked when we saw it first,—all blue, and such a lovely color. There ought, according to Morse's Atlas, to have been a big red letter T on the water about where we were, but I didn't see any. Perhaps they letter it so far out from shore that only people in boats notice it.

"Now the dusk is fading, and the odd chill which hides under these warm afternoons begins to be felt. Amy has received a message written on a mysterious white pebble to the effect—"

Katy was interrupted at this point by a crunching step on the gravel behind her.

"Good afternoon," said a voice. "Polly has sent me to fetch you and Amy in. She says it is growing cool."

"We were just coming," said Katy, beginning to put away her papers.

Ned Worthington sat down on the cloak beside her. The distance was now steel gray against the sky; then came a stripe of violet, and then a broad sheet of the vivid iridescent blue which one sees on the necks of peacocks, which again melted into the long line of flashing surf.

"See that gull," he said, "how it drops plumb into the sea, as if bound to go through to China!"

"Mrs. Hawthorne calls skylarks 'little raptures,'" replied Katy. "Sea-gulls seem to me like grown-up raptures."

"Are you going?" said Lieutenant Worthington in a tone of surprise, as she rose.

"Didn't you say that Polly wanted us to come in?"

"Why, yes; but it seems too good to leave, doesn't it? Oh, by the way, Miss Carr, I came across a man to-day and ordered your greens. They will be sent on Christmas Eve. Is that right?"

"Quite right, and we are ever so much obliged to you." She turned for a last look at the sea, and, unseen by Ned Worthington, formed her lips into a "good-night." Katy had made great friends with the Mediterranean.

The promised "greens" appeared on the afternoon before Christmas Day, in the shape of an enormous fagot of laurel and laurestinus and holly and box; orange and lemon boughs with ripe fruit hanging from them, thick ivy tendrils whole yards long, arbutus, pepper tree, and great branches of acacia, covered with feathery yellow bloom. The man apologized for bringing so little. The gentleman had ordered two francs worth, he said, but this was all he could carry; he would fetch some more if the young lady wished! But Katy, exclaiming with delight over her wealth, wished no more; so the man departed, and the three friends proceeded to turn the little *salon* into a fairy bower. Every photograph and picture was wreathed in ivy, long garlands hung on either side the windows, and the chimney-piece and door-frames became clustering banks of leaf and blossom. A great box of flowers had come with the greens, and bowls of fresh roses and heliotrope and carnations were set everywhere; violets and primroses, gold-hearted brown auriculas, spikes of veronica, all the zones and all the seasons, combining to make the Christmas-tide sweet, and to turn winter topsy-turvy in the little parlor.

Mabel and Mary Matilda, with their two doll visitors, sat gravely round the table, in the laps of their little mistresses; and Katy, putting on an apron and an improvised cap, and speaking Irish very fast, served them with a repast of rolls and cocoa, raspberry jam, and delicious little almond cakes. The fun waxed fast and furious; and Lieutenant Worthington, coming in with his hands full of parcels for the Christmas-tree, was just in time to hear Katy remark in a strong County Kerry brogue,—

"Och, thin indade, Miss Amy, and it's no more cake you'll be getting out of me the night. That's four pieces you've ate, and it's little slape your poor mother'll git with you a tossin' and tumblin' forenenst her all night long because of your big appetite."

"Oh, Miss Katy, talk Irish some more!" cried the delighted children.

"Is it Irish you'd be afther having me talk, when it's me own langwidge, and sorrow a bit of another do I know?" demanded Katy. Then she caught sight of the new arrival and stopped short with a blush and a laugh.

"Come in, Mr. Worthington," she said; "we're at supper, as you see, and I am acting as waitress."

"Oh, Uncle Ned, please go away," pleaded Amy, "or Katy will be polite, and not talk Irish any more."

"Indade, and the less ye say about politeness the betther, when ye're afther ordering the jantleman out of the room in that fashion!" said the waitress. Then she pulled off her cap and untied her apron.

"Now for the Christmas-tree," she said.

It was a very little tree, but it bore some remarkable fruits; for in addition to the "tiny toys and candles fit for Lilliput," various parcels were found to have been hastily added at the last moment for various people. The "Natchitoches" had lately come from the Levant, and delightful Oriental confections now appeared for Amy and Mrs. Ashe; Turkish slippers, all gold embroidery; towels, with richly decorated ends in silks and tinsel;—all the pretty superfluities which the East holds out to charm gold from the pockets of her Western visitors. A pretty little dagger in agate and silver fell to Katy's share out of what Lieutenant Worthington called his "loot;" and beside, a most beautiful specimen of the inlaid work for which Nice is famous,—a looking-glass, with a stand and little doors to close it in,—which was a present from Mrs. Ashe. It was quite unlike a Christmas Eve at home, but altogether delightful; and as Katy sat next morning on the sand, after the service in the English church, to finish her home letter, and felt the sun warm on her cheek, and the perfumed air blow past as softly as in June, she had to remind herself that Christmas is not necessarily synonymous with snow and winter, but means the great central heat and warmth, the advent of Him who came to lighten the whole earth.

A few days after this pleasant Christmas they left Nice. All of them felt a reluctance to move, and Amy loudly bewailed the necessity.

"If I could stay here till it is time to go home, I shouldn't be homesick at all," she declared.

"But what a pity it would be not to see Italy!" said her mother. "Think of Naples and Rome and Venice."

"I don't want to think about them. It makes me feel as if I was studying a great long geography lesson, and it tires me so to learn it."

"Amy, dear, you're not well."

"Yes, I am,—quite well; only I don't want to go away from Nice."

"You only have to learn a little bit at a time of your geography lesson, you know," suggested Katy; "and it's a great deal nicer way to study it than out of a book." But though she spoke cheerfully she was conscious that she shared Amy's reluctance.

"It's all laziness," she told herself. "Nice has been so pleasant that it has spoiled me."

It was a consolation and made going easier that they were to drive over the famous Cornice Road as far as San Remo, instead of going to Genoa by rail as most travellers now-a-days do. They departed from the Pension Suisse early on an exquisite morning, fair and balmy as June, but with a little zest and sparkle of coolness in the air which made it additionally delightful. The Mediterranean was of the deepest violet-blue; a sort of bloom of color seemed to lie upon it. The sky was like an arch of turquoise; every cape and headland shone jewel-like in the golden sunshine. The carriage, as it followed the windings of the road cut shelf-like on the cliffs, seemed poised between earth and heaven; the sea below, the mountain summits above, with a fairy world of verdure between. The journey was like a dream of enchantment and rapidly changing surprises; and when it ended in a quaint hostelry at San Remo, with palm-trees feathering the Bordighera Point and Corsica, for once seen by day, lying in bold, clear outlines against the sunset, Katy had to admit to herself that Nice, much as she loved it, was not the only, not even the most beautiful place in Europe. Already she felt her horizon growing, her convictions changing; and who should say what lay beyond?

The next day brought them to Genoa, to a hotel once the stately palace of an archbishop, where they were lodged, all three together, in an enormous room, so high and broad and long that their three little curtained beds set behind a screen of carved wood made no impression on the space. There were not less than four sofas and double that number of arm-chairs in the room, besides a couple of monumental wardrobes; but, as Katy remarked, several grand pianos could still have been moved in without anybody's feeling crowded. On one side of them lay the port of Genoa, filled with craft from all parts of the world, and flying the flags of a dozen different nations. From the other they caught glimpses of the magnificent old city, rising in tier over tier of churches and palaces and gardens; while nearer still were narrow streets, which glittered with gold filigree and the shops of jewel-workers. And while they went in and out and gazed and wondered, Lilly Page, at the Pension Suisse, was saying,—

"I am so glad that Katy and *that* Mrs. Ashe are gone. Nothing has been so pleasant since they came. Lieutenant Worthington is dreadfully stiff and stupid, and seems quite different from what he used to be. But now that we have got rid of them it will all come right again."

"I really don't think that Katy was to blame," said Mrs. Page. "She never seemed to me to be making any effort to attract him."

"Oh, Katy is sly," responded Lilly, vindictively. "She never *seems* to do anything, but somehow she always gets her own way. I suppose she thought I didn't see her keeping him down there on the beach the other day when he was coming in to call on us, but I did. It was just out of spite, and because she wanted to vex me; I know it was."

"Well, dear, she's gone now, and you won't be worried with her again," said her mother, soothingly. "Don't pout so, Lilly, and wrinkle up your forehead. It's very unbecoming."

"Yes, she's gone," snapped Lilly; "and as she's bound for the East, and we for the West, we are not likely to meet again, for which I am devoutly thankful."

CHAPTER VIII. ON THE TRACK OF ULYSSES.

"We are going to follow the track of Ulysses," said Katy, with her eyes fixed on the little travelling-map in her guide-book. "Do you realize that, Polly dear? He and his companions sailed these very seas before us, and we shall see the sights they saw,—Circe's Cape and the Isles of the Sirens, and Polyphemus himself, perhaps, who knows?"

The "Marco Polo" had just cast off her moorings, and was slowly steaming out of the crowded port of Genoa into the heart of a still rosy sunset. The water was perfectly smooth; no motion could be felt but the engine's throb. The trembling foam of the long wake showed glancing points of phosphorescence here and there, while low on the eastern sky a great silver planet burned like a signal lamp.

"Polyphemus was a horrible giant. I read about him once, and I don't want to see him," observed Amy, from her safe protected perch in her mother's lap.

"He may not be so bad now as he was in those old times. Some missionary may have come across him and converted him. If he were good, you wouldn't mind his being big, would you?" suggested Katy.

"N-o," replied Amy, doubtfully; "but it would take a great lot of missionaries to make *him* good, I should think. One all alone would be afraid to speak to him. We shan't really see him, shall we?"

"I don't believe we shall; and if we stuff cotton in our ears and look the other way, we need not hear the sirens sing," said Katy, who was in the highest spirits.—"And oh, Polly dear, there is one delightful thing I forgot to tell you about. The captain says he shall stay in Leghorn all day to-morrow taking on freight, and we shall have plenty of time to run up to Pisa and see the Cathedral and the Leaning Tower and everything else. Now, that is something Ulysses didn't do! I am so glad I didn't die of measles when I was little, as Rose Red used to say." She gave her book a toss into the air as she spoke, and caught it again as it fell, very much as the Katy Carr of twelve years ago might have done.

"What a child you are!" said Mrs. Ashe, approvingly; "you never seem out of sorts or tired of things."

"Out of sorts? I should think not! And pray why should I be, Polly dear?"

Katy had taken to calling her friend "Polly dear" of late,—a trick picked up half unconsciously from Lieutenant Ned. Mrs. Ashe liked it; it was sisterly and intimate, she said, and made her feel nearer Katy's age.

"Does the tower really lean?" questioned Amy,—"far over, I mean, so that we can see it?"

"We shall know to-morrow," replied Katy. "If it doesn't, I shall lose all my confidence in human nature."

Katy's confidence in human nature was not doomed to be impaired. There stood the famous tower, when they reached the Place del Duomo in Pisa, next morning, looking all aslant, exactly as it does in the pictures and the alabaster models, and seeming as if in another moment it must topple over, from its own weight, upon their heads. Mrs. Ashe declared that it was so unnatural that it made her flesh creep; and when she was coaxed up the winding staircase to the top, she turned so giddy that they were all thankful to get her safely down to firm ground again. She turned her back upon the tower, as they crossed the grassy space to the majestic old Cathedral, saying that if she thought about it any more, she should become a disbeliever in the attraction of gravitation, which she had always been told all respectable people *must* believe in.

The guide showed them the lamp swinging by a long slender chain, before which Galileo is said to have sat and pondered while he worked out his theory of the pendulum. This lamp seemed a sort of own cousin to the attraction of gravitation, and they gazed upon it with respect. Then they went to the Baptistery to see Niccolo Pisano's magnificent pulpit of creamy marble, a mass of sculpture supported on the backs of lions, and the equally lovely font, and to admire the extraordinary sound which their guide evoked from a mysterious echo, with which he seemed to be on intimate terms, for he made it say whatever he would and almost "answer back."

It was in coming out of the Baptistery that they met with an adventure which Amy could never quite forget. Pisa is the mendicant city of Italy, and her streets are infested with a band of religious beggars who call themselves the Brethren of the Order of Mercy. They wear loose black gowns, sandals laced over their bare feet, and black cambric masks with holes, through which their eyes glare awfully; and they carry tin cups for the reception of offerings, which they thrust into the faces of all strangers visiting the city, whom they look upon as their lawful prey.

As our party emerged from the Baptistery, two of these Brethren espied them, and like great human bats came swooping down upon them with long strides, their black garments flying in the wind, their eyes rolling strangely behind their masks, and brandishing their alms-cups, which had "Pour les Pauvres" lettered upon them, and gave forth a clapping sound like a watchman's rattle. There was something terrible in their appearance and the rushing speed of their movements. Amy screamed and ran behind her mother, who visibly shrank. Katy stood her ground; but the bat-winged fiends in Doré's illustrations to Dante occurred to her, and her fingers trembled as she dropped some money in the cups.

Even mendicant friars are human. Katy ceased to tremble as she observed that one of them, as he retreated, walked backward for some distance in order to gaze longer at Mrs. Ashe, whose cheeks were flushed with bright pink and who was looking particularly handsome. She began to laugh instead, and Mrs. Ashe laughed too; but Amy could not get over the impression of having been attacked by demons, and often afterward recurred with a shudder to the time when those awful black *things* flew at her and she hid behind mamma. The ghastly pictures of the Triumph of Death, which were presently exhibited to them on the walls of the Campo Santo, did not tend to reassure her, and it was with quite a pale, scared little face that she walked toward the hotel where they were to lunch, and she held fast to Katy's hand.

Their way led them through a narrow street inhabited by the poorer classes,—a dusty street with high shabby buildings on either side and wide doorways giving glimpses of interior courtyards, where empty hogsheads and barrels and rusty caldrons lay, and great wooden trays of macaroni were spread out in the sun to dry. Some of the macaroni was gray, some white, some yellow; none of it looked at all desirable to eat, as it lay exposed to the dust, with long lines of ill-washed clothes flapping above on wires stretched from one house to another. As is usual in poor streets, there were swarms of children; and the appearance of little Amy with her long bright hair falling over her shoulders and Mabel clasped in her arms created a great sensation. The children in the street shouted and exclaimed, and other children within the houses heard the sounds and came trooping out, while mothers and older sisters peeped from the doorways. The very air seemed full of eager faces and little brown and curly heads bobbing up and down with excitement, and black eyes all fixed upon big beautiful Mabel, who with her thick wig of flaxen hair, her blue velvet dress and jacket, feathered hat, and little muff, seemed to them like some strange small marvel from another world. They could not decide whether she was a living child or a make-believe one, and they dared not come near enough to find out; so they clustered at a little distance, pointed with their fingers, and whispered and giggled, while Amy, much pleased with the admiration shown for her darling, lifted Mabel up to view.

At last one droll little girl with a white cap on her round head seemed to make up *her* mind, and darting indoors returned with her doll,—a poor little image of wood, its only garment a coarse shirt of red cotton. This she held out for Amy to see. Amy smiled for the first time since her encounter with the bat-like friars; and Katy, taking Mabel from her, made signs that the two dolls should kiss each other.

But though the little Italian screamed with laughter at the idea of a *bacio* between two dolls, she would by no means allow it, and hid her treasure behind her back, blushing and giggling, and saying something very fast which none of them understood, while she waved two fingers at them with a curious gesture.

"I do believe she is afraid Mabel will cast the evil eye on her doll," said Katy at last, with a sudden understanding as to what this pantomime meant.

"Why, you silly thing!" cried the outraged Amy; "do you suppose for one moment that my child could hurt your dirty old dolly? You ought to be glad to have her noticed at all by anybody that's clean."

The sound of the foreign tongue completed the discomfiture of the little Italian. With a shriek she fled, and all the other children after her; pausing at a distance to look back at the alarming creatures who didn't speak the familiar language. Katy, wishing to leave a pleasant impression, made Mabel kiss her waxen fingers toward them. This sent the children off into another fit of laughter and chatter, and they followed our friends for quite a distance as they proceeded on their way to the hotel.

All that night, over a sea as smooth as glass, the "Marco Polo" slipped along the coasts past which the ships of Ulysses sailed in those old legendary days which wear so charmed a light to our modern eyes. Katy roused at three in the morning, and looking from her cabin window had a glimpse of an island, which her map showed her must be Elba, where that war-eagle Napoleon was chained for a while. Then she fell asleep again, and when she roused in full daylight the steamer was off the coast of Ostia and nearing the mouth of the Tiber. Dreamy mountain-shapes rose beyond the far-away Campagna, and every curve and indentation of the coast bore a name which recalled some interesting thing.

About eleven a dim-drawn bubble appeared on the horizon, which the captain assured them was the dome of St. Peter's, nearly thirty miles distant. This was one of the "moments" which Clover had been fond of speculating about; and Katy, contrasting the real with the imaginary moment, could not help smiling. Neither she nor Clover had ever supposed that her first glimpse of the great dome was to be so little impressive.

On and on they went till the air-hung bubble disappeared; and Amy, grown very tired of scenery with which she had no associations, and grown-up raptures which she did not comprehend, squeezed herself into the end of the long wooden settee on which Katy sat, and began to beg for another story concerning Violet and Emma.

"Just a little tiny chapter, you know, Miss Katy, about what they did on

New Year's Day or something. It's so dull to keep sailing and sailing all day and have nothing to do, and it's ever so long since you told me anything about them, really and truly it is!"

Now, Violet and Emma, if the truth is to be told, had grown to be the bane of Katy's existence. She had rung the changes on their uneventful adventures, and racked her brains to invent more and more details, till her imagination felt like a dry sponge from which every possible drop of moisture had been squeezed. Amy was insatiable. Her interest in the tale never flagged; and when her exhausted friend explained that she really could not think of another word to say on the subject, she would turn the tables by asking, "Then, Miss Katy, mayn't I tell *you* a chapter?" whereupon she would proceed somewhat in this fashion:—

"It was the day before Christmas—no, we won't have it the day before Christmas; it shall be three days before Thanksgiving. Violet and Emma got up in the morning, and—well, they didn't do anything in particular that day. They just had their breakfasts and dinners, and played and studied a little, and went to bed early, you know, and the next morning —well, there didn't much happen that day, either; they just had their breakfasts and dinners, and played."

Listening to Amy's stories was so much worse than telling them to her, that Katy in self-defence was driven to recommence her narrations, but she had grown to hate Violet and Emma with a deadly hatred. So when Amy made this appeal on the steamer's deck, a sudden resolution took possession of her, and she decided to put an end to these dreadful children once for all.

"Yes, Amy," she said, "I will tell you one more story about Violet and Emma; but this is positively the last."

So Amy cuddled close to her friend, and listened with rapt attention as Katy told how on a certain day just before the New Year, Violet and Emma started by themselves in a little sleigh drawn by a pony, to carry to a poor woman who lived in a lonely house high up on a mountain slope a basket containing a turkey, a mould of cranberry jelly, a bunch of celery, and a mince-pie.

"They were so pleased at having all these nice things to take to poor widow Simpson and in thinking how glad she would be to see them," proceeded the naughty Katy, "that they never noticed how black the sky was getting to be, or how the wind howled through the bare boughs of the trees. They had to go slowly, for the road was up hill all the way, and it was hard work for the poor pony. But he was a stout little fellow, and tugged away up the slippery track, and Violet and Emma talked and laughed, and never thought what was going to happen. Just half-way up the mountain there was a rocky cliff which overhung the road, and on this cliff grew an enormous hemlock tree.

The branches were loaded with snow, which made them much heavier than usual. Just as the sleigh passed slowly underneath the cliff, a violent blast of wind blew up from the ravine, struck the hemlock and tore it out of the ground, roots and all. It fell directly across the sleigh, and Violet and Emma and the pony and the basket with the turkey and the other things in it were all crushed as flat as pancakes!"

"Well," said Amy, as Katy stopped, "go on! what happened then?"

"Nothing happened then," replied Katy, in a tone of awful solemnity; "nothing could happen! Violet and Emma were dead, the pony was dead, the things in the basket were broken all to little bits, and a great snowstorm began and covered them up, and no one knew where they were or what had become of them till the snow melted in the spring."

With a loud shriek Amy jumped up from the bench.

"No! no! no!" she cried; "they aren't dead! I won't let them be dead!" Then she burst into tears, ran down the stairs, locked herself into her mother's stateroom, and did not appear again for several hours.

Katy laughed heartily at first over this outburst, but presently she began to repent and to think that she had treated her pet unkindly. She went down and knocked at the stateroom door; but Amy would not answer. She called her softly through the key-hole, and coaxed and pleaded, but it was all in vain. Amy remained invisible till late in the afternoon; and when she finally crept up again to the deck, her eyes were red with crying, and her little face as pale and miserable as if she had been attending the funeral of her dearest friend.

Katy's heart smote her.

"Come here, my darling," she said, holding out her hand; "come and sit in my lap and forgive me. Violet and Emma shall not be dead. They shall go on living, since you care so much for them, and I will tell stories about them to the end of the chapter."

"No," said Amy, shaking her head mournfully; "you can't. They're dead, and they won't come to life again ever. It's all over, and I'm so so-o-rry."

All Katy's apologies and efforts to resuscitate the story were useless. Violet and Emma were dead to Amy's imagination, and she could not make herself believe in them any more.

She was too woe-begone to care for the fables of Circe and her swine which Katy told as they rounded the magnificent Cape Circello, and the isles where the sirens used to sing appealed to her in vain. The sun set, the stars came out; and under the beams of their countless lamps and the beckonings of a slender new moon, the "Marco Polo" sailed into the Bay of Naples, past Vesuvius, whose dusky curl of smoke could be seen outlined against the luminous sky, and brought her passengers to their landing-place.

They woke next morning to a summer atmosphere full of yellow sunshine and true July warmth. Flower-vendors stood on every corner, and pursued each newcomer with their fragrant wares. Katy could not stop exclaiming over the cheapness of the flowers, which were thrust in at the carriage windows as they drove slowly up and down the streets. They were tied into flat nosegays, whose centre was a white camellia, encircled with concentric rows of pink tea rosebuds, ring after ring, till the whole was the size of an ordinary milk-pan; all to be had for the sum of ten cents! But after they had bought two or three of these enormous bouquets, and had discovered that not a single rose boasted an inch of stem, and that all were pierced with long wires through their very hearts, she ceased to care for them.

"I would rather have one Souvenir or General Jacqueminot, with a long stem and plenty of leaves, than a dozen of these stiff platters of bouquets," Katy told Mrs. Ashe. But when they drove beyond the city gates, and the coachman came to anchor beneath walls overhung with the same roses, and she found that she might stand on the seat and pull down as many branches of the lovely flowers as she desired, and gather wallflowers for herself out of the clefts in the masonry, she was entirely satisfied.

"This is the Italy of my dreams," she said.

With all its beauty there was an underlying sense of danger about Naples, which interfered with their enjoyment of it. Evil smells came in at the windows, or confronted them as they went about the city. There seemed something deadly in the air. Whispered reports met their ears of cases of fever, which the landlords of the hotels were doing their best to hush up. An American gentleman was said to be lying very ill at one house. A lady had died the week before at another. Mrs. Ashe grew nervous.

"We will just take a rapid look at a few of the principal things," she told Katy, "and then get away as fast as we can. Amy is so on my mind that I have no peace of my life. I keep feeling her pulse and imagining that she does not look right; and though I know it is all my fancy, I am impatient to be off. You won't mind, will you, Katy?"

After that everything they did was done in a hurry. Katy felt as if she were being driven about by a cyclone, as they rushed from one sight to another, filling up all the chinks between with shopping, which was irresistible where everything was so pretty and so wonderfully cheap. She herself purchased a tortoise-shell fan and chain for Rose Red, and had her monogram carved upon it; a coral locket for Elsie;

some studs for Dorry; and for her father a small, beautiful vase of bronze, copied from one of the Pompeian antiques.

"How charming it is to have money to spend in such a place as this!" she said to herself with a sigh of satisfaction as she surveyed these delightful buyings. "I only wish I could get ten times as many things and take them to ten times as many people. Papa was so wise about it. I can't think how it is that he always knows beforehand exactly how people are going to feel, and what they will want!"

Mrs. Ashe also bought a great many things for herself and Amy, and to take home as presents; and it was all very pleasant and satisfactory except for that subtle sense of danger from which they could not escape and which made them glad to go. "See Naples and die," says the old adage; and the saying has proved sadly true in the case of many an American traveller.

Beside the talk of fever there was also a good deal of gossip about brigands going about, as is generally the case in Naples and its vicinity. Something was said to have happened to a party on one of the heights above Sorrento; and though nobody knew exactly what the something was, or was willing to vouch for the story, Mrs. Ashe and Katy felt a good deal of trepidation as they entered the carriage which was to take them to the neighborhood where the mysterious "something" had occurred.

The drive between Castellamare and Sorrento is in reality as safe as that between Boston and Brookline; but as our party did not know this fact till afterward, it did them no good. It is also one of the most beautiful drives in the world, following the windings of the exquisite coast mile after mile, in long links of perfectly made road, carved on the face of sharp cliffs, with groves of oranges and lemons and olive orchards above, and the Bay of Naples beneath, stretching away like a solid sheet of lapis-lazuli, and gemmed with islands of the most picturesque form.

It is a pity that so much beauty should have been wasted on Mrs. Ashe and Katy, but they were too frightened to half enjoy it. Their carriage was driven by a shaggy young savage, who looked quite wild enough to be a bandit himself. He cracked his whip loudly as they rolled along, and every now and then gave a long shrill whistle. Mrs. Ashe was sure that these were signals to his band, who were lurking somewhere on the olive-hung hillsides. She thought she detected him once or twice making signs to certain questionable-looking characters as they passed; and she fancied that the people they met gazed at them with an air of commiseration, as upon victims who were being carried to execution. Her fears affected Katy; so, though they talked and laughed, and made jokes to amuse Amy, who must not be scared or led to suppose that anything was amiss, and to the outward view seemed a very merry party, they were privately quaking in their shoes all the way, and enjoying a deal of highly superfluous misery. And after all they reached Sorrento in perfect safety; and the driver, who looked so dangerous, turned out to be a respectable young man enough, with a wife and family to support, who considered a plateful of macaroni and a glass of sour red wine as the height of luxury, and was grateful for a small gratuity of thirty cents or so, which would enable him to purchase these dainties. Mrs. Ashe had a very bad headache next day, to pay for her fright; but she and Katy agreed that they had been very foolish, and resolved to pay no more attention to unaccredited rumors or allow them to spoil their enjoyment, which was a sensible resolution to make.

Their hotel was perched directly over the sea. From the balcony of their sitting-room they looked down a sheer cliff some sixty feet high, into the water; their bedrooms opened on a garden of roses, with an orange grove beyond. Not far from them was the great gorge which cuts the little town of Sorrento almost in two, and whose seaward end makes the harbor of the place. Katy was never tired of peering down into this strange and beautiful cleft, whose sides, two hundred feet in depth, are hung with vines and trailing growths of all sorts, and seem all a-tremble with the fairy fronds of maiden-hair ferns growing out of every chink and crevice. She and Amy took walks along the coast toward Massa, to look off at the lovely island shapes in the bay, and admire the great clumps of cactus and Spanish bayonet which grew by the roadside; and they always came back loaded with orange-flowers, which could be picked as freely as apple-blossoms from New England orchards in the spring. The oranges themselves at that time of the year were very sour, but they answered as well for a romantic date, "From an orange grove," as if they had been the sweetest in the world.

They made two different excursions to Pompeii, which is within easy distance of Sorrento. They scrambled on donkeys over the hills, and had glimpses of the far-away Calabrian shore, of the natural arch, and the temples of Pæstum shining in the sun many miles distant. On Katy's birthday, which fell toward the end of January, Mrs. Ashe let her have her choice of a treat; and she elected to go to the Island of Capri, which none of them had seen. It turned out a perfect day, with sea and wind exactly right for the sail, and to allow of getting into the famous "Blue Grotto," which can only be entered under particular conditions of tide and weather. And they climbed the great cliff-rise at the island's end, and saw the ruins of the villa built by the wicked emperor Tiberius, and the awful place known as his "Leap," down which, it is said, he made his victims throw themselves; and they lunched at a hotel which bore his name, and just at sunset pushed off again for the row home over the charmed sea. This return voyage was almost the pleasantest thing of all the day. The water was smooth, the moon at its full. It was larger and more brilliant than American moons are, and seemed to possess an actual warmth and color. The boatmen timed their oar-strokes to the cadence of Neapolitan *barcaroles* and folk-songs, full of rhythmic movement, which seemed caught from the pulsing tides. And when at last the bow grated on the sands of the Sorrento landing-place, Katy drew a long, regretful breath, and declared that this was her best birthday-gift of all, better than Amy's flowers, or the pretty tortoise-shell locket that Mrs. Ashe had given her, better even than the letter from home, which, timed by happy accident, had arrived by the morning's post to make a bright opening for the day.

All pleasant things must come to an ending.

"Katy," said Mrs. Ashe, one afternoon in early February, "I heard some ladies talking just now in the *salon*, and they said that Rome is filling up very fast. The Carnival begins in less than two weeks, and everybody wants to be there then. If we don't make haste, we shall not be able to get any rooms."

"Oh dear!" said Katy, "it is very trying not to be able to be in two places at once. I want to see Rome dreadfully, and yet I cannot bear to leave Sorrento. We have been very happy here, haven't we?"

So they took up their wandering staves again, and departed for Rome, like the Apostle, "not knowing what should befall them there."

CHAPTER IX. A ROMAN HOLIDAY.

"Oh dear!" said Mrs. Ashe, as she folded her letters and laid them aside, "I wish those Pages would go away from Nice, or else that the frigates were not there."

"Why! what's the matter?" asked Katy, looking up from the many-leaved journal from Clover over which she was poring.

"Nothing is the matter except that those everlasting people haven't gone to Spain yet, as they said they would, and Ned seems to keep on seeing them," replied Mrs. Ashe, petulantly.

"But, dear Polly, what difference does it make? And they never did promise you to go on any particular time, did they?"

"N-o, they didn't; but I wish they would, all the same. Not that Ned is such a goose as really to care anything for that foolish Lilly!" Then she gave a little laugh at her own inconsistency, and added, "But I oughtn't to abuse her when she is your cousin."

"Don't mention it," said Katy, cheerfully. "But, really, I don't see why poor Lilly need worry you so, Polly dear."

The room in which this conversation took place was on the very topmost floor of the Hotel del Hondo in Rome. It was large and many-windowed; and though there was a little bed in one corner half hidden behind a calico screen, with a bureau and washing-stand, and a sort of stout mahogany hat-tree on which Katy's dresses and jackets were hanging, the remaining space, with a sofa and easy-chairs grouped round a fire, and a round table furnished with books and a lamp, was ample enough to make a good substitute for the private sitting-room which Mrs. Ashe had not been able to procure on account of the near approach of the Carnival and the consequent crowding of strangers to Rome. In fact, she was assured that under the circumstances she was lucky in finding rooms as good as these; and she made the most of the assurance as a consolation for the somewhat unsatisfactory food and service of the hotel, and the four long flights of stairs which must be passed every time they needed to reach the dining-room or the street door.

The party had been in Rome only four days, but already they had seen a host of interesting things. They had stood in the strange sunken space with its marble floor and broken columns, which is all that is left of the great Roman Forum. They had visited the Coliseum, at that period still overhung with ivy garlands and trailing greeneries, and not, as now, scraped clean and bare and "tidied" out of much of its picturesqueness. They had seen the Baths of Caracalla and the Temple of Janus and St. Peter's and the Vatican marbles, and had driven out on the Campagna and to the Pamphili-Doria Villa to gather purple and red anemones, and to the English cemetery to see the grave of Keats. They had also peeped into certain shops, and attended a reception at the American Minister's,—in short, like most unwarned travellers, they had done about twice as much as prudence and experience would have permitted, had those worthies been consulted.

All the romance of Katy's nature responded to the fascination of the ancient city,—the capital of the world, as it may truly be called. The shortest drive or walk brought them face to face with innumerable and unexpected delights. Now it was a wonderful fountain, with plunging horses and colossal nymphs and Tritons, holding cups and horns from which showers of white foam rose high in air to fall like rushing rain into an immense marble basin. Now it was an arched doorway with traceries as fine as lace,—sole-remaining fragment of a heathen temple, flung and stranded as it were by the waves of time on the squalid shore of the present. Now it was a shrine at the meeting of three streets, where a dim lamp burned beneath the effigy of the Madonna, with always a fresh rose beside it in a vase, and at its foot a peasant woman kneeling in red bodice and blue petticoat, with a lace-trimmed towel folded over her hair. Or again it would be a sunlit terrace lifted high on a hillside, and crowded with carriages full of beautifully dressed people, while below all Rome seemed spread out like a panorama, dim, mighty, majestic, and bounded by the blue wavy line of the Campagna and the Alban hills. Or perhaps it might be a wonderful double flight of steps with massive balustrades and pillars with urns, on which sat a crowd of figures in strange costumes and attitudes, who all looked as though they had stepped out of pictures, but who were in reality models waiting for artists to come by and engage them. No matter what it was,—a bit of oddly tinted masonry with a tuft of brown and orange wallflowers hanging upon it, or a vegetable stall where endive and chiccory and curly lettuces were arranged in wreaths with tiny orange gourds and scarlet peppers for points of color,—it was all Rome, and, by virtue of that word, different from any other place,—more suggestive, more interesting, ten times more mysterious than any other could possibly be, so Katy thought.

This fact consoled her for everything and anything,—for the fleas, the dirt, for the queer things they had to eat and the still queerer odors they were forced to smell! Nothing seemed of any particular consequence except the deep sense of enjoyment, and the newly discovered world of thought and sensation of which she had become suddenly conscious.

The only drawback to her happiness, as the days went on, was that little Amy did not seem quite well or like herself. She had taken a cold on the journey from Naples, and though it did not seem serious, that, or something, made her look pale and thin. Her mother said she was growing fast, but the explanation did not quite account for the wistful look in the child's eyes and the tired feeling of which she continually complained. Mrs. Ashe, with vague uneasiness, began to talk of cutting short their Roman stay and getting Amy off to the more bracing air of Florence. But meanwhile there was the Carnival close at hand, which they must by no means lose; and the feeling that their opportunity might be a brief one made her and Katy all the more anxious to make the very most of their time. So they filled the days full with sights to see and things to do, and came and went; sometimes taking Amy with them, but more often leaving her at the hotel under the care of a kind German chambermaid, who spoke pretty good English and to whom Amy had taken a fancy.

"The marble things are so cold, and the old broken things make me so sorry," she explained; "and I hate beggars because they are dirty, and the stairs make my back ache; and I'd a great deal rather stay with Maria and go up on the roof, if you don't mind, mamma."

This roof, which Amy had chosen as a playplace, covered the whole of the great hotel, and had been turned into a sort of upper-air garden by the simple process of gravelling it all over, placing trellises of ivy here and there, and setting tubs of oranges and oleanders and boxes of gay geraniums and stock-gillyflowers on the balustrades. A tame fawn was tethered there. Amy adopted him as a playmate; and what with his company and that of the flowers, the times when her mother and Katy were absent from her passed not unhappily.

Katy always repaired to the roof as soon as they came in from their long mornings and afternoons of sight-seeing. Years afterward, she would remember with contrition how pathetically glad Amy always was to see her. She would put her little head on Katy's breast and hold her tight for many minutes without saying a word. When she did speak it was always about the house and the garden that she talked. She never asked any questions as to where Katy had been, or what she had done; it seemed to tire her to think about it.

"I should be very lonely sometimes if it were not for my dear little fawn," she told Katy once. "He is so sweet that I don't miss you and mamma very much while I have him to play with. I call him Florio,—don't you think that is a pretty name? I like to stay with him a great deal better than to go about with you to those nasty-smelling old churches, with fleas hopping all over them!"

So Amy was left in peace with her fawn, and the others made haste to see all they could before the time came to go to Florence.

Katy realized one of the "moments" for which she had come to Europe when she stood for the first time on the balcony overhanging the Corso, which Mrs. Ashe had hired in company with some acquaintances made at the hotel, and looked down at the ebb and surge of the just-begun Carnival. The narrow street seemed humming with people of all sorts and conditions. Some were masked; some were not. There were ladies and gentlemen in fashionable clothes, peasants in the gayest costumes, surprised-looking tourists in tall hats and linen dusters, harlequins, clowns, devils, nuns, dominoes of every color,—red, white, blue, black; while above, the balconies bloomed like a rose-garden with pretty faces framed in lace veils or picturesque hats. Flowers were everywhere, wreathed along the house-fronts, tied to the horses' ears, in ladies' hands and gentlemen's button-holes, while venders went up and down the street bearing great trays of violets and carnations and camellias for sale. The air was full of cries and laughter, and the shrill calls of merchants advertising their wares,—candy, fruit, birds, lanterns, and *confetti*, the latter being merely lumps of lime, large or small, with a pea or a bean embedded in each lump to give it weight. Boxes full of this unpleasant confection were suspended in front of each balcony, with tin scoops to use in ladling it out and flinging it about. Everybody wore or carried a wire mask as protection against this white, incessant shower; and before long the air became full of a fine dust which hung above the Corso like a mist, and filled the eyes and noses and clothes of all present with irritating particles.

Pasquino's Car was passing underneath just as Katy and Mrs. Ashe arrived,—a gorgeous affair, hung with silken draperies, and bearing as symbol an enormous egg, in which the Carnival was supposed to be in act of incubation. A huge wagon followed in its wake, on which was a house some sixteen feet square, whose sole occupant was a gentleman attended by five servants, who kept him supplied with *confetti*, which he showered liberally on the heads of the crowd. Then came a car in the shape of a steamboat, with a smoke-pipe and sails, over which flew the Union Jack, and which was manned with a party wearing the dress of British tars. The next wagon bore a company of jolly maskers equipped with many-colored bladders, which they banged and rattled as they went along. Following this was a troupe of beautiful circus horses, cream-colored with scarlet trappings, or sorrel with blue, ridden by ladies in pale green velvet laced with silver, or blue velvet and gold. Another car bore a bird-cage which was an exact imitation of St. Peter's, within which perched a lonely old parrot. This device evidently had a political signification, for it was alternately hissed and applauded as it went along. The whole scene was like a brilliant, rapidly shifting dream; and Katy, as she stood with lips apart and eyes wide open with wonderment and pleasure, forgot whether she was in the body or not,—forgot everything except what was passing before her gaze.

She was roused by a stinging shower of lime-dust. An Englishman in the next balcony had take courteous advantage of her preoccupation, and had flung a scoopful of *confetti* in her undefended face! It is generally Anglo-Saxons of the less refined class, English or Americans, who do these things at Carnival times. The national love of a rough joke comes to the surface, encouraged by the license of the moment, and all the grace and prettiness of the festival vanish. Katy laughed, and dusted herself as well as she could, and took refuge behind her mask; while a nimble American boy of the party changed places with her, and thenceforward made that particular Englishman his special target, plying such a lively and adroit shovel as to make Katy's assailant rue the hour when he evoked this national reprisal. His powdered head and rather clumsy efforts to retaliate excited shouts of laughter from the adjoining balconies. The young American, fresh from tennis and college athletics, darted about and dodged with an agility impossible to his heavily built foe; and each effective shot and parry on his side was greeted with little cries of applause and the clapping of hands on the part of those who were watching the contest.

Exactly opposite them was a balcony hung with white silk, in which sat a lady who seemed to be of some distinction; for every now and then an officer in brilliant uniform, or some official covered with orders and stars, would be shown in by her servants, bow before her with the utmost deference, and after a little conversation retire, kissing her gloved hand as he went. The lady was a beautiful person, with lustrous black eyes and dark hair, over which a lace mantilla was fastened with diamond stars. She wore pale blue with white flowers, and altogether, as Katy afterward wrote to Clover, reminded her exactly of one of those beautiful princesses whom they used to play about in their childhood and quarrel over, because every one of them wanted to be the Princess and nobody else.

"I wonder who she is," said Mrs. Ashe in a low tone. "She might be almost anybody from her looks. She keeps glancing across to us, Katy. Do you know, I think she has taken a fancy to you."

Perhaps the lady had; for just then she turned her head and said a word to one of her footmen, who immediately placed something in her hand. It was a little shining bonbonniere, and rising she threw it straight at Katy. Alas! it struck the edge of the balcony and fell into the street below, where it was picked up by a ragged little peasant girl in a red jacket, who raised a pair of astonished eyes to the heavens, as if sure that the gift must have fallen straight from thence. Katy bent forward to watch its fate, and went through a little pantomime of regret and despair for the benefit of the opposite lady, who only laughed, and taking another from her servant flung with better aim, so that it fell exactly at Katy's feet. This was a gilded box in the shape of a mandolin, with sugar-plums tucked cunningly away inside. Katy kissed both her hands in acknowledgment for the pretty toy, and tossed back a bunch of roses which she happened to be wearing in her dress. After that it seemed the chief amusement of the fair unknown to throw bonbons at Katy. Some went straight and some did not; but before the afternoon ended, Katy had quite a lapful of confections and trifles,—roses, sugared almonds, a satin casket, a silvered box in the shape of a horseshoe, a tiny cage with orange blossoms for birds on the perches, a minute gondola with a *marron glacée* by way of passenger, and, prettiest of all, a little ivory harp strung with enamelled violets instead of wires. For all these favors she had nothing better to offer, in return, than a few long-tailed bonbons with gay streamers of ribbon. These the lady opposite caught very cleverly, rarely missing one, and kissing her hand in thanks each time.

"Isn't she exquisite?" demanded Katy, her eyes shining with excitement. "Did you ever see any one so lovely in your life, Polly dear? I never did. There, now! she is buying those birds to set them free, I do believe."

It was indeed so. A vender of larks had, by the aid of a long staff, thrust a cage full of wretched little prisoners up into the balcony; and "Katy's lady," as Mrs. Ashe called her, was paying for the whole. As they watched she opened the cage door, and with the sweetest look on her face encouraged the birds to fly away. The poor little creatures cowered and hesitated, not knowing at first what use to make of their new liberty; but at last one, the boldest of the company, hopped to the door and with a glad, exultant chirp flew straight upward. Then the others, taking courage from his example, followed, and all were lost to view in the twinkling of an eye.

"Oh, you angel!" cried Katy, leaning over the edge of the balcony and kissing both hands impulsively, "I never saw any one so sweet as you are in my life. Polly dear, I think carnivals are the most perfectly bewitching things in the world. How glad I am that this lasts a week, and that we can come every day. Won't Amy be delighted with these bonbons! I do hope my lady will be here tomorrow."

How little she dreamed that she was never to enter that balcony again! How little can any of us see what lies before us till it comes so near that we cannot help seeing it, or shut our eyes, or turn away!

The next morning, almost as soon as it was light, Mrs. Ashe tapped at Katy's door. She was in her dressing-gown, and her eyes looked large and frightened.

"Amy is ill," she cried. "She has been hot and feverish all night, and she says that her head aches dreadfully. What shall I do, Katy? We ought to have a doctor at once, and I don't know the name even of any doctor here."

Katy sat up in bed, and for one bewildered moment did not speak. Her brain felt in a whirl of confusion; but presently it cleared, and she saw what to do.

"I will write a note to Mrs. Sands," she said. Mrs. Sands was the wife of the American Minister, and one of the few acquaintances they had made since they came to Rome. "You remember how nice she was the other day, and how we liked her; and she has lived here so long that of course she must know all about the doctors. Don't you think that is the best thing to do!"

"The very best," said Mrs. Ashe, looking relieved. "I wonder I did not think of it myself, but I am so confused that I can't think. Write the note at once, please, dear Katy. I will ring your bell for you, and then I must hurry back to Amy."

Katy made haste with the note. The answer came promptly in half an hour, and by ten o'clock the physician recommended appeared. Dr.

Hilary was a dark little Italian to all appearance; but his mother had been a Scotch-woman, and he spoke English very well,—a great comfort to poor Mrs. Ashe, who knew not a word of Italian and not a great deal of French. He felt Amy's pulse for a long time, and tested her temperature; but he gave no positive opinion, only left a prescription, and said that he would call later in the day and should then be able to judge more clearly what the attack was likely to prove.

Katy augured ill from this reserve. There was no talk of going to the Carnival that afternoon; no one had any heart for it. Instead, Katy spent the time in trying to recollect all she had ever heard about the care of sick people,—what was to be done first and what next,—and in searching the shops for a feather pillow, which luxury Amy was imperiously demanding. The pillows of Roman hotels are, as a general thing, stuffed with wool, and very hard.

"I won't have this horrid pillow any longer," poor Amy was screaming. "It's got bricks in it. It hurts the back of my neck. Take it away, mamma, and give me a nice soft American pillow. I won't have this a minute longer. Don't you hear me, mamma! Take it away!"

So, while Mrs. Ashe pacified Amy to the best of her ability, Katy hurried out in quest of the desired pillow. It proved almost an unattainable luxury; but at last, after a long search, she secured an air-cushion, a down cushion about twelve inches square, and one old feather pillow which had come from some auction, and had apparently lain for years in the corner of the shop. When this was encased in a fresh cover of Canton flannel, it did very well, and stilled Amy's complaints a little; but all night she grew worse, and when Dr. Hilary came next day, he was forced to utter plainly the dreaded words "Roman fever." Amy was in for an attack,—a light one he hoped it might be,—but they had better know the truth and make ready for it.

Mrs. Ashe was utterly overwhelmed by this verdict, and for the first bewildered moments did not know which way to turn. Katy, happily, kept a steadier head. She had the advantage of a little preparation of thought, and had decided beforehand what it would be necessary to do "in case." Oh, that fateful "in case"! The doctor and she consulted together, and the result was that Katy sought out the padrona of the establishment, and without hinting at the nature of Amy's attack, secured some rooms just vacated, which were at the end of a corridor, and a little removed from the rooms of other people. There was a large room with corner windows, a smaller one opening from it, and another, still smaller, close by, which would serve as a storeroom or might do for the use of a nurse.

These rooms, without much consultation with Mrs. Ashe,—who seemed stunned and sat with her eyes fixed on Amy, just answering,

"Certainly, dear, anything you say," when applied to,—Katy had arranged according to her own ideas of comfort and hygienic necessity, as learned from Miss Nightingale's excellent little book on nursing. From the larger room she had the carpet, curtains, and nearly all the furniture taken away, the floor scrubbed with hot soapsuds, and the bed pulled out from the wall to allow of a free circulation of air all round it. The smaller one she made as comfortable as possible for the use of Mrs. Ashe, choosing for it the softest sofa and the best mattresses that were obtainable; for she knew that her friend's strength was likely to be severely tried if Amy's illness proved serious. When all was ready, Amy, well wrapped in her coverings, was carried down the entry and laid in the fresh bed with the soft pillows about her; and Katy, as she went to and fro, conveying clothes and books and filling drawers, felt that they were perhaps making arrangements for a long, hard trial of faith and spirits.

By the next day the necessity of a nurse became apparent, and in the afternoon Katy started out in a little hired carriage in search of one. She had a list of names, and went first to the English nurses; but finding them all engaged, she ordered the coachman to drive to a convent where there was hope that a nursing sister might be procured.

Their route lay across the Corso. So utterly had the Carnival with all its gay follies vanished from her mind, that she was for a moment astonished at finding herself entangled in a motley crowd, so dense that the coachman was obliged to rein in his horses and stand still for some time.

There were the same masks and dominos, the same picturesque peasant costumes which had struck her as so gay and pretty only three days before. The same jests and merry laughter filled the air, but somehow it all seemed out of tune. The sense of cold, lonely fear that had taken possession of her killed all capacity for merriment; the apprehension and solicitude of which her heart was full made the gay chattering and squeaking of the crowd sound harsh and unfeeling. The bright colors affronted her dejection; she did not want to see them. She lay back in the carriage, trying to be patient under the detention, and half shut her eyes.

A shower of lime dust aroused her. It came from a party of burly figures in white cotton dominos, whose carriage had been stayed by the crowd close to her own. She signified by gestures that she had no *confetti* and no protection, that she "was not playing," in fact; but her appeal made no difference. The maskers kept on shovelling lime all over her hair and person and the carriage, and never tired of the sport till an opportune break in the procession enabled their vehicle to move on.

Katy was shaking their largesse from her dress and parasol as well as she could, when an odd gibbering sound close to her ear, and the laughter of the crowd attracted her attention to the back of the carriage. A masker attired as a scarlet devil had climbed into the hood, and was now perched close behind her. She shook her head at him; but he only shook his in return, and chattered and grimaced, and bent over till his fiery mask almost grazed her shoulder. There was no hope but in good humor, as she speedily realized; and recollecting that in her shopping-bag one or two of the Carnival bonbons still remained, she took these out and offered them in the hope of propitiating him. The fiend bit one to insure that it was made of sugar and not lime, while the crowd laughed more than ever; then, seeming satisfied, he made Katy a little speech in rapid Italian, of which she did not comprehend a word, kissed her hand, jumped down from the carriage and disappeared in the crowd to her great relief.

Presently after that the driver spied an opening, of which he took advantage. They were across the Corso now, the roar and rush of the Carnival dying into silence as they drove rapidly on; and Katy, as she finished wiping away the last of the lime dust, wiped some tears from her cheeks as well.

"How hateful it all was!" she said to herself. Then she remembered a sentence read somewhere, "How heavily roll the wheels of other people's joys when your heart is sorrowful!" and she realized that it is true.

The convent was propitious, and promised to send a sister next morning, with the proviso that every second day she was to come back to sleep and rest. Katy was too thankful for any aid to make objections, and drove home with visions of saintly nuns with pure pale faces full of peace and resignation, such as she had read of in books, floating before her eyes.

Sister Ambrogia, when she appeared next day, did not exactly realize these imaginations. She was a plump little person, with rosy cheeks, a pair of demure black eyes, and a very obstinate mouth and chin. It soon appeared that natural inclination combined with the rules of her convent made her theory of a nurse's duties a very limited one.

If Mrs. Ashe wished her to go down to the office with an order, she was told: "We sisters care for the sick; we are not allowed to converse with porters and hotel people."

If Katy suggested that on the way home she should leave a prescription at the chemist's, it was: "We sisters are for nursing only; we do not visit shops." And when she was asked if she could make beef tea, she replied calmly but decisively, "We sisters are not cooks."

In fact, all that Sister Ambrogia seemed able or willing to do, beyond the bathing of Amy's face and brushing her hair, which she accomplished handily, was to sit by the bedside telling her rosary, or plying a little ebony shuttle in the manufacture of a long strip of tatting. Even this amount of usefulness was interfered with by the fact that Amy, who by this time was in a semi-delirious condition, had taken an aversion to her at the first glance, and was not willing to be left with her for a single moment.

"I won't stay here alone with Sister Embroidery," she would cry, if her mother and Katy went into the next room for a moment's rest or a private consultation; "I hate Sister Embroidery! Come back, mamma, come back this moment! She's making faces at me, and chattering just like an old parrot, and I don't understand a word she says. Take Sister Embroidery away, mamma, I tell you! Don't you hear me? Come back, I say!"

The little voice would be raised to a shrill scream; and Mrs. Ashe and Katy, hurrying back, would find Amy sitting up on her pillow with wet, scarlet-flushed cheeks and eyes bright with fever, ready to throw herself out of bed; while, calm as Mabel, whose curly head lay on the pillow beside her little mistress, Sister Ambrogia, unaware of the intricacies of the English language, was placidly telling her beads and muttering prayers to herself. Some of these prayers, I do not doubt, related to Amy's recovery if not to her conversion, and were well meant; but they were rather irritating under the circumstances!

CHAPTER X. CLEAR SHINING AFTER RAIN.

When the first shock is over and the inevitable realized and accepted, those who tend a long illness are apt to fall into a routine of life which helps to make the days seem short. The apparatus of nursing is got together. Every day the same things need to be done at the same hours and in the same way. Each little appliance is kept at hand; and sad and tired as the watchers may be, the very monotony and regularity of their proceedings give a certain stay for their thoughts to rest upon.

But there was little of this monotony to help Mrs. Ashe and Katy through with Amy's illness. Small chance was there for regularity or exact system; for something unexpected was always turning up, and needful things were often lacking. The most ordinary comforts of the sick-room, or what are considered so in America, were hard to come by, and much of Katy's time was spent in devising substitutes to take their places.

Was ice needed? A pailful of dirty snow would be brought in, full of straws, sticks, and other refuse, which had apparently been scraped from the surface of the street after a frosty night. Not a particle of it could be put into milk or water; all that could be done was to make the pail serve the purpose of a refrigerator, and set bowls and tumblers in it to chill.

Was a feeding-cup wanted? It came of a cumbrous and antiquated pattern, which the infant Hercules may have enjoyed, but which the modern Amy abominated and rejected. Such a thing as a glass tube could not be found in all Rome. Bed-rests were unknown. Katy searched in vain for an India-rubber hot-water bag.

But the greatest trial of all was the beef tea. It was Amy's sole food, and almost her only medicine; for Dr. Hilary believed in leaving Nature pretty much to herself in cases of fever. The kitchen of the hotel sent up, under that name, a mixture of grease and hot water, which could not be given to Amy at all. In vain Katy remonstrated and explained the process. In vain did she go to the kitchen herself to translate a carefully written recipe to the cook, and to slip a shining five-franc piece in his hand, which it was hoped would quicken his energies and soften his heart. In vain did she order private supplies of the best of beef from a separate market. The cooks stole the beef and ignored the recipe; and day after day the same bottle-full of greasy liquid came upstairs, which Amy would not touch, and which would have done her no good had she swallowed it all. At last, driven to desperation, Katy procured a couple of stout bottles, and every morning slowly and carefully cut up two pounds of meat into small pieces, sealed the bottle with her own seal ring, and sent it down to be boiled for a specified time. This answered better, for the thieving cook dared not tamper with her seal; but it was a long and toilsome process, and consumed more time than she well knew how to spare,—for there were continual errands to be done which no one could attend to but herself, and the interminable flights of stairs taxed her strength painfully, and seemed to grow longer and harder every day.

At last a good Samaritan turned up in the shape of an American lady with a house of her own, who, hearing of their plight from Mrs. Sands, undertook to send each day a supply of strong, perfectly made beef tea, from her own kitchen, for Amy's use. It was an inexpressible relief, and the lightening of this one particular care made all the rest seem easier of endurance.

Another great relief came, when, after some delay, Dr. Hilary succeeded in getting an English nurse to take the places of the unsatisfactory Sister Ambrogia and her substitute, Sister Agatha, whom Amy in her half-comprehending condition persisted in calling "Sister Nutmeg Grater." Mrs. Swift was a tall, wiry, angular person, who seemed made of equal parts of iron and whalebone. She was never tired; she could lift anybody, do anything; and for sleep she seemed to have a sort of antipathy, preferring to sit in an easy-chair and drop off into little dozes, whenever it was convenient, to going regularly to bed for a night's rest.

Amy took to her from the first, and the new nurse managed her beautifully. No one else could soothe her half so well during the delirious period, when the little shrill voice seemed never to be still, and went on all day and all night in alternate raving or screaming or, what was saddest of all to hear, low pitiful moans. There was no shutting in these sounds. People moved out of the rooms below and on either side, because they could get no sleep; and till the arrival of Nurse Swift, there was no rest for poor Mrs. Ashe, who could not keep away from her darling for a moment while that mournful wailing sounded in her ears.

Somehow the long, dry Englishwoman seemed to have a mesmeric effect on Amy, who was never quite so violent after she arrived. Katy was more thankful for this than can well be told; for her great underlying dread—a dread she dared not whisper plainly even to herself—was that "Polly dear" might break down before Amy was better, and then what *should* they do?

She took every care that was possible of her friend. She made her eat; she made her lie down. She forced daily doses of quinine and port-wine down her throat, and saved her every possible step. But no one, however affectionate and willing, could do much to lift the crushing burden of care, which was changing Mrs. Ashe's rosy fairness to wan pallor and laying such dark shadows under the pretty gray eyes. She had taken small thought of looks since Amy's illness. All the little touches which had made her toilette becoming, all the crimps and fluffs, had disappeared; yet somehow never had she seemed to Katy half so lovely as now in the plain black gown which she wore all day long, with her hair tucked into a knot behind her ears. Her real beauty of feature and outline seemed only enhanced by the rigid plainness of her attire, and the charm of true expression grew in her face. Never had Katy admired and loved her friend so well as during those days of fatigue and wearing suspense, or realized so strongly the worth of her sweetness of temper, her unselfishness and power of devoting herself to other people.

"Polly bears it wonderfully," she wrote her father; "she was all broken down for the first day or two, but now her courage and patience are surprising. When I think how precious Amy is to her and how lonely her life would be if she were to die, I can hardly keep the tears out of my eyes. But Polly does not cry. She is quiet and brave and almost cheerful all the time, keeping herself busy with what needs to be done; she never complains, and she looks—oh, so pretty! I think I never knew how much she had in her before."

All this time no word had come from Lieutenant Worthington. His sister had written him as soon as Amy was taken ill, and had twice telegraphed since, but no answer had been received, and this strange silence added to the sense of lonely isolation and distance from home and help which those who encounter illness in a foreign land have to bear.

So first one week and then another wore themselves away somehow. The fever did not break on the fourteenth day, as had been hoped, and must run for another period, the doctor said; but its force was lessened, and he considered that a favorable sign. Amy was quieter now and did not rave so constantly, but she was very weak. All her pretty hair had been shorn away, which made her little face look tiny and sharp. Mabel's golden wig was sacrificed at the same time. Amy had insisted upon it, and they dared not cross her.

"She has got a fever, too, and it's a great deal badder than mine is," she protested. "Her cheeks are as hot as fire. She ought to have ice on her head, and how can she when her bang is so thick? Cut it all off, every bit, and then I will let you cut mine."

"You had better give ze child her way," said Dr. Hilary. "She's in no state to be fretted with triffles [trifles, the doctor meant], and in ze end it will be well; for ze fever infection might harbor in zat doll's head as well as elsewhere, and I should have to disinfect it, which would be bad for ze skin of her."

"She isn't a doll," cried Amy, overhearing him; "she's my child, and you sha'n't call her names." She hugged Mabel tight in her arms, and glared at Dr. Hilary defiantly.

So Katy with pitiful fingers slashed away at Mabel's blond wig till her head was as bare as a billiard-ball; and Amy, quite content, patted her child while her own locks were being cut, and murmured, "Perhaps your hair will all come out in little round curls, darling, as Johnnie Carr's did;" then she fell into one of the quietest sleeps she had yet had.

It was the day after this that Katy, coming in from a round of errands, found Mrs. Ashe standing erect and pale, with a frightened look in her eyes, and her back against Amy's door, as if defending it from somebody. Confronting her was Madame Frulini, the *padrona* of the hotel. Madame's cheeks were red, and her eyes bright and fierce; she was evidently in a rage about something, and was pouring out a torrent of excited Italian, with now and then a French or English word slipped in by way of punctuation, and all so rapidly that only a trained ear could have followed or grasped her meaning.

"What is the matter?" asked Katy, in amazement.

"Oh, Katy, I am so glad you have come," cried poor Mrs. Ashe. "I can hardly understand a word that this horrible woman says, but I think she wants to turn us out of the hotel, and that we shall take Amy to some other place. It would be the death of her,—I know it would. I never, never will go, unless the doctor says it is safe. I oughtn't to,—I couldn't; she can't make me, can she, Katy?"

"Madame," said Katy,—and there was a flash in her eyes before which the landlady rather shrank,—"what is all this? Why do you come to trouble madame while her child is so ill?"

Then came another torrent of explanation which didn't explain; but Katy gathered enough of the meaning to make out that Mrs. Ashe was quite correct in her guess, and that Madame Frulini was requesting, nay, insisting, that they should remove Amy from the hotel at once. There were plenty of apartments to be had now that the Carnival was over, she said,—her own cousin had rooms close by,—it could easily be arranged, and people were going away from the Del Mondo every day because there was fever in the house. Such a thing could not be, it should not be,—the landlady's voice rose to a shriek, "the child must go!"

"You are a cruel woman," said Katy, indignantly, when she had grasped the meaning of the outburst. "It is wicked, it is cowardly, to come thus and attack a poor lady under your roof who has so much already to bear. It is her only child who is lying in there,—her only one, do you understand, madame?—and she is a widow. What you ask might kill the child. I shall not permit you or any of your people to enter that door till the doctor comes, and then I shall tell him how you have behaved, and we shall see what he will say." As she spoke she turned the key of Amy's door, took it out and put it in her pocket, then faced the *padrona* steadily, looking her straight in the eyes.

"Mademoiselle," stormed the landlady, "I give you my word, four people have left this house already because of the noises made by little miss. More will go. I shall lose my winter's profit,—all of it,—all; it will be said there is fever at the Del Mondo,—no one will hereafter come to me. There are lodgings plenty, comfortable,—oh, so comfortable! I will not have my season ruined by a sickness; no, I will not!"

Madame Frulini's voice was again rising to a scream.

"Be silent!" said Katy, sternly; "you will frighten the child. I am sorry that you should lose any customers, madame, but the fever is here and we are here, and here we must stay till it is safe to go. The child shall not be moved till the doctor gives permission. Money is not the only thing in the world! Mrs. Ashe will pay anything that is fair to make up your losses to you, but you must leave this room now, and not return till Dr. Hilary is here."

Where Katy found French for all these long coherent speeches, she could never afterward imagine. She tried to explain it by saying that excitement inspired her for the moment, but that as soon as the moment was over the inspiration died away and left her as speechless and confused as ever. Clover said it made her think of the miracle of Balaam; and Katy merrily rejoined that it might be so, and that no donkey in any age of the world could possibly have been more grateful than was she for the sudden gift of speech.

"But it is not the money,—it is my prestige," declared the landlady.

"Thank Heaven! here is the doctor now," cried Mrs. Ashe.

The doctor had in fact been standing in the doorway for several moments before they noticed him, and had overheard part of the colloquy with Madame Frulini. With him was some one else, at the sight of whom Mrs. Ashe gave a great sob of relief. It was her brother, at last.

When Italian meets Italian, then comes the tug of expletive. It did not seem to take one second for Dr. Hilary to whirl the *padrona* out into the entry, where they could be heard going at each other like two furious cats. Hiss, roll, sputter, recrimination, objurgation! In five minutes Madame Frulini was, metaphorically speaking, on her knees, and the doctor standing over her with drawn sword, making her take back every word she had said and every threat she had uttered.

"Prestige of thy miserable hotel!" he thundered; "where will that be when I go and tell the English and Americans—all of whom I know, every one!—how thou hast served a countrywoman of theirs in thy house? Dost thou think thy prestige will help thee much when Dr. Hilary has fixed a black mark on thy door! I tell thee no; not a stranger shalt thou have next year to eat so much as a plate of macaroni under thy base roof! I will advertise thy behavior in all the foreign papers,—in Figaro, in Galignani, in the Swiss Times, and the English one which is read by all the nobility, and the Heraldo of New York, which all Americans peruse—"

"Oh, doctor—pardon me—I regret what I said—I am afflicted—"

"I will post thee in the railroad stations," continued the doctor, implacably; "I will bid my patients to write letters to all their friends, warning them against thy flea-ridden Del Mondo; I will apprise the steamboat companies at Genoa and Naples. Thou shalt see what comes of it,—truly, thou shalt see."

Having thus reduced Madame Frulini to powder, the doctor now condescended to take breath and listen to her appeals for mercy; and presently he brought her in with her mouth full of protestations and apologies, and assurances that the ladies had mistaken her meaning, she had only spoken for the good of all; nothing was further from her intention than that they should be disturbed or offended in any way, and she and all her household were at the service of "the little sick angel of God." After which the doctor dismissed her with an air of contemptuous tolerance, and laid his hand on the door of Amy's room. Behold, it was locked!

"Oh, I forgot," cried Katy, laughing; and she pulled the key out of her pocket.

"You are a hee-roine, mademoiselle," said Dr. Hilary. "I watched you as you faced that tigress, and your eyes were like a swordsman's as he regards his enemy's rapier."

"Oh, she was so brave, and such a help!" said Mrs. Ashe, kissing her impulsively. "You can't think how she has stood by me all through, Ned, or what a comfort she has been."

"Yes, I can," said Ned Worthington, with a warm, grateful look at Katy. "I can believe anything good of Miss Carr."

"But where have *you* been all this time?" said Katy, who felt this flood of compliment to be embarrassing; "we have so wondered at not hearing from you."

"I have been off on a ten-days' leave to Corsica for moufflon-shooting," replied Mr. Worthington. "I only got Polly's telegrams and letters day before yesterday, and I came away as soon as I could get my leave extended. It was a most unlucky absence. I shall always regret it."

"Oh, it is all right now that you have come," his sister said, leaning her head on his arm with a look of relief and rest which was good to see. "Everything will go better now, I am sure."

"Katy Carr has behaved like a perfect angel," she told her brother when they were alone.

"She is a trump of a girl. I came in time for part of that scene with the landlady, and upon my word she was glorious! I didn't suppose she could look so handsome."

"Have the Pages left Nice yet?" asked his sister, rather irrelevantly.

"No,—at least they were there on Thursday, but I think that they were to start to-day."

Mr. Worthington answered carelessly, but his face darkened as he spoke. There had been a little scene in Nice which he could not forget. He was sitting in the English garden with Lilly and her mother when his sister's telegrams were brought to him; and he had read them aloud, partly as an explanation for the immediate departure which they made necessary and which broke up an excursion just arranged with the ladies for the afternoon. It is not pleasant to have plans interfered with; and as neither Mrs. Page nor her daughter cared personally for little Amy, it is not strange that disappointment at the interruption of their pleasure should have been the first impulse with them. Still, this did not excuse Lilly's unstudied exclamation of "Oh, bother!" and though she speedily repented it as an indiscretion, and was properly sympathetic, and "hoped the poor little thing would soon be better," Amy's uncle could not forget the jarring impression. It completed a process of disenchantment which had long been going on; and as hearts are sometimes caught at the rebound, Mrs. Ashe was not so far astray when she built certain little dim sisterly hopes on his evident admiration for Katy's courage and this sudden awakening to a sense of her good looks.

But no space was left for sentiment or match-making while still Amy's fate hung in the balance, and all three of them found plenty to do during the next fortnight. The fever did not turn on the twenty-first day, and another weary week of suspense set in, each day bringing a decrease of the dangerous symptoms, but each day as well marking a lessening in the childish strength which had been so long and severely tested. Amy was quite conscious now, and lay quietly, sleeping a great deal and speaking seldom. There was not much to do but to wait and hope; but the flame of hope burned low at times, as the little life flickered in its socket, and seemed likely to go out like a wind-blown torch.

Now and then Lieutenant Worthington would persuade his sister to go with him for a few minutes' drive or walk in the fresh air, from which she had so long been debarred, and once or twice he prevailed on Katy to do the same; but neither of them could bear to be away long from Amy's bedside.

Intimacy grows fast when people are thus united by a common anxiety, sharing the same hopes and fears day after day, speaking and thinking of the same thing. The gay young officer at Nice, who had counted so little in Katy's world, seemed to have disappeared, and the gentle, considerate, tender-hearted fellow who now filled his place was quite a different person in her eyes. Katy began to count on Ned Worthington as a friend who could be trusted for help and sympathy and comprehension, and appealed to and relied upon in all emergencies. She was quite at ease with him now, and asked him to do this and that, to come and help her, or to absent himself, as freely as if he had been Dorry or Phil.

He, on his part, found this easy intimacy charming. In the reaction of his temporary glamour for the pretty Lilly, Katy's very difference from her was an added attraction. This difference consisted, as much as anything else, in the fact that she was so truly in earnest in what she said and did. Had Lilly been in Katy's place, she would probably have been helpful to Mrs. Ashe and kind to Amy so far as in her lay; but the thought of self would have tinctured all that she did and said, and the need of keeping to what was tasteful and becoming would have influenced her in every emergency, and never have been absent from her mind.

Katy, on the contrary, absorbed in the needs of the moment, gave little heed to how she looked or what any one was thinking about her. Her habit of neatness made her take time for the one thorough daily dressing,—the brushing of hair and freshening of clothes, which were customary with her; but, this tax paid to personal comfort, she gave little further heed to appearances. She wore an old gray gown, day in and day out, which Lilly would not have put on for half an hour without a large bribe, so unbecoming was it; but somehow Lieutenant Worthington grew to like the gray gown as a part of Katy herself. And if by chance he brought a rose in to cheer the dim stillness of the sick-room, and she tucked it into her buttonhole, immediately it was as though she were decked for conquest. Pretty dresses are very pretty on pretty people,—they certainly play an important part in this queer little world of ours; but depend upon it, dear girls, no woman ever has established so distinct and clear a claim on the regard of her lover as when he has ceased to notice or analyze what she wears, and just accepts it unquestioningly, whatever it is, as a bit of the dear human life which has grown or is growing to be the best and most delightful thing in the world to him.

The gray gown played its part during the long anxious night when they all sat watching breathlessly to see which way the tide would turn with dear little Amy. The doctor came at midnight, and went away to come again at dawn. Mrs. Swift sat grim and watchful beside the pillow of her charge, rising now and then to feel pulse and skin, or to put a spoonful of something between Amy's lips. The doors and windows stood open to admit the air. In the outer room all was hushed. A dim Roman lamp, fed with olive oil, burned in one corner behind a screen. Mrs. Ashe lay on the sofa with her eyes closed, bearing the strain of suspense in absolute silence. Her brother sat beside her, holding in his one of the hot hands whose nervous twitches alone told of the surgings of hope and fear within. Katy was resting in a big chair near by, her wistful eyes fixed on Amy's little figure seen in the dim distance, her ears alert for every sound from the sick-room.

So they watched and waited. Now and then Ned Worthington or Katy would rise softly, steal on tiptoe to the bedside, and come back to whisper to Mrs. Ashe that Amy had stirred or that she seemed to be asleep. It was one of the nights which do not come often in a lifetime, and which people never forget. The darkness seems full of meaning; the hush, of sound. God is beyond, holding the sunrise in his right hand, holding the sun of our earthly hopes as well,—will it dawn in sorrow or in joy? We dare not ask, we can only wait.

A faint stir of wind and a little broadening of the light roused Katy from a trance of half-understood thoughts. She crept once more into Amy's room. Mrs. Swift laid a warning finger on her lips; Amy was sleeping, she said with a gesture. Katy whispered the news to the still figure on the sofa, then she went noiselessly out of the room. The great hotel was fast asleep; not a sound stirred the profound silence of the dark halls. A longing for fresh air led her to the roof.

There was the dawn just tingeing the east. The sky, even thus early, wore the deep mysterious blue of Italy. A fresh *tramontana* was blowing, and made Katy glad to draw her shawl about her.

Far away in the distance rose the Alban Hills above the dim Campagna, with the more lofty Sabines beyond, and Soracte, clear cut against the sky like a wave frozen in the moment of breaking. Below lay the ancient city, with its strange mingling of the old and the new, of past things embedded in the present; or is it the present thinly veiling the rich and mighty past,—who shall say?

Faint rumblings of wheels and here and there a curl of smoke showed that Rome was waking up. The light insensibly grew upon the darkness. A pink flush lit up the horizon. Florio stirred in his lair, stretched his dappled limbs, and as the first sun-ray glinted on the roof, raised himself, crossed the gravelled tiles with soundless feet, and ran his soft nose into Katy's hand. She fondled him for Amy's sake as she stood bent over the flower-boxes, inhaling the scent of the mignonette and gilly-flowers, with her eyes fixed on the distance; but her heart was at home with the sleepers there, and a rush of strong desire stirred her. Would this dreary time come to an end presently, and should they be set at liberty to go their ways with no heavy sorrow to press them down, to be care-free and happy again in their own land?

A footstep startled her. Ned Worthington was coming over the roof on tiptoe as if fearful of disturbing somebody. His face looked resolute and excited.

"I wanted to tell you," he said in a hushed voice, "that the doctor is here, and he says Amy has no fever, and with care may be considered out of danger."

"Thank God!" cried Katy, bursting into tears. The long fatigue, the fears kept in check so resolutely, the sleepless night just passed, had their revenge now, and she cried and cried as if she could never stop, but with all the time such joy and gratitude in her heart! She was conscious that Ned had his arm round her and was holding both her hands tight; but they were so one in the emotion of the moment that it did not seem strange.

"How sweet the sun looks!" she said presently, releasing herself, with a happy smile flashing through her tears; "it hasn't seemed really bright for ever so long. How silly I was to cry! Where is dear Polly? I must go down to her at once. Oh, what does she say?"

CHAPTER XI. NEXT.

Lieut. Worthington's leave had nearly expired. He must rejoin his ship; but he waited till the last possible moment in order to help his sister through the move to Albano, where it had been decided that Amy should go for a few days of hill air before undertaking the longer journey to Florence.

It was a perfect morning in late March when the pale little invalid was carried in her uncle's strong arms, and placed in the carriage which was to take them to the old town on the mountain slopes which they had seen shining from far away for so many weeks past. Spring had come in her fairest shape to Italy. The Campagna had lost its brown and tawny hues and taken on a tinge of fresher color. The olive orchards were budding thickly. Almond boughs extended their dazzling shapes across the blue sky. Arums and acanthus and ivy filled every hollow, roses nodded from over every gate, while a carpet of violets and cyclamen and primroses stretched over the fields and freighted every wandering wind with fragrance.

When once the Campagna with its long line of aqueducts, arches, and hoary tombs was left behind, and the carriage slowly began to mount the gradual rises of the hill, Amy revived. With every breath of the fresher air her eyes seemed to brighten and her voice to grow stronger. She held Mabel up to look at the view; and the sound of her laugh, faint and feeble as it was, was like music to her mother's ears.

Amy wore a droll little silk-lined cap on her head, over which a downy growth of pale-brown fuzz was gradually thickening. Already it showed a tendency to form into tiny rings, which to Amy, who had always hankered for curls, was an extreme satisfaction. Strange to say, the same thing exactly had happened to Mabel; her hair had grown out into soft little round curls also! Uncle Ned and Katy had ransacked Rome for this baby-wig, which filled and realized all Amy's hopes for her child. On the same excursion they had bought the materials for the pretty spring suit which Mabel wore, for it had been deemed necessary to sacrifice most of her wardrobe as a concession to possible fever-germs. Amy admired the pearl-colored dress and hat, the fringed jacket and little lace-trimmed parasol so much, that she was quite consoled for the loss of the blue velvet costume and ermine muff which had been the pride of her heart ever since they left Paris, and whose destruction they had scarcely dared to confess to her.

So up, up, up, they climbed till the gateway of the old town was passed, and the carriage stopped before a quaint building once the residence of the Bishop of Albano, but now known as the Hôtel de la Poste. Here they alighted, and were shown up a wide and lofty staircase to their rooms, which were on the sunny side of the house, and looked across a walled garden, where roses and lemon trees grew beside old fountains guarded by sculptured lions and heathen divinities with broken noses and a scant supply of fingers and toes, to the Campagna, purple with distance and stretching miles and miles away to where Rome sat on her seven hills, lifting high the Dome of St. Peter's into the illumined air.

Nurse Swift said that Amy must go to bed at once, and have a long rest. But Amy nearly wept at the proposal, and declared that she was not a bit tired and couldn't sleep if she went to bed ever so much. The change of air had done her good already, and she looked more like herself than for many weeks past. They compromised their dispute on a sofa, where Amy, well wrapped up, was laid, and where, in spite of her protestations, she presently fell asleep, leaving the others free to examine and arrange their new quarters.

Such enormous rooms as they were! It was quite a journey to go from one side of them to another. The floors were of stone, with squares of carpet laid down over them, which looked absurdly small for the great spaces they were supposed to cover. The beds and tables were of the usual size, but they seemed almost like doll furniture because the chambers were so big. A quaint old paper, with an enormous pattern of banyan trees and pagodas, covered the walls, and every now and then betrayed by an oblong of regular cracks the existence of a hidden door, papered to look exactly like the rest of the wall.

These mysterious doors made Katy nervous, and she never rested till she had opened every one of them and explored the places they led to. One gave access to a queer little bathroom. Another led, through a narrow dark passage, to a sort of balcony or loggia overhanging the garden. A third ended in a dusty closet with an artful chink in it from which you could peep into what had been the Bishop's drawing-room but which was now turned into the dining-room of the hotel. It seemed made for purposes of espial; and Katy had visions of a long line of reverend prelates with their ears glued to the chink, overhearing what was being said about them in the apartment beyond.

The most surprising of all she did not discover till she was going to bed on the second night after their arrival, when she thought she knew all about the mysterious doors and what they led to. A little unexplained draught of wind made her candle flicker, and betrayed the existence of still another door so cunningly hid in the wall pattern that she had failed to notice it. She had quite a creepy feeling as she drew her dressing-gown about her, took a light, and entered the narrow passage into which it opened. It was not a long passage, and ended presently in a tiny oratory. There was a little marble altar, with a kneeling-step and candlesticks and a great crucifix above. Ends of wax candles still remained in the candlesticks, and bunches of dusty paper flowers filled the vases which stood on either side of them. A faded silk cushion lay on the step. Doubtless the Bishop had often knelt there. Katy felt as if she were the first person to enter the place since he went away. Her common-sense told her that in a hotel bedroom constantly occupied by strangers for years past, some one *must* have discovered the door and found the little oratory before her; but common-sense is sometimes less satisfactory than romance. Katy liked to think that she was the first, and to "make believe" that no one else knew about it; so she did so, and invented legends about the place which Amy considered better than any fairy story.

Before he left them Lieutenant Worthington had a talk with his sister in the garden. She rather forced this talk upon him, for various things were lying at her heart about which she longed for explanation; but he yielded so easily to her wiles that it was evident he was not averse to the idea.

"Come, Polly, don't beat about the bush any longer," he said at last, amused and a little irritated at her half-hints and little feminine *finesses*. "I know what you want to ask; and as there's no use making a secret of it, I will take my turn in asking. Have I any chance, do you think?"

"Any chance?—about Katy, do you mean? Oh, Ned, you make me so happy."

"Yes; about her, of course."

"I don't see why you should say 'of course,'" remarked his sister, with the perversity of her sex, "when it's only five or six weeks ago that I was lying awake at night for fear you were being gobbled up by that Lilly Page."

"There was a little risk of it," replied her brother, seriously. "She's awfully pretty and she dances beautifully, and the other fellows were all wild about her, and—well, you know yourself how such things go. I can't see now what it was that I fancied so much about her, I don't suppose I could have told exactly at the time; but I can tell without the smallest trouble what it is in—the other."

"In Katy? I should think so," cried Mrs. Ashe, emphatically; "the two are no more to be compared than—than—well, bread and syllabub! You can live on one, and you can't live on the other."

"Come, now, Miss Page isn't so bad as that. She is a nice girl enough, and a pretty girl too,—prettier than Katy; I'm not so far gone that I can't see that. But we won't talk about her, she's not in the present question at all; very likely she'd have had nothing to say to me in any case. I was only one out of a dozen, and she never gave me reason to suppose that she cared more for me than the rest. Let us talk about this friend of yours; have I any chance at all, do you think, Polly?"

"Ned, you are the dearest boy! I would rather have Katy for a sister than any one else I know. She's so nice all through,—so true and sweet and satisfactory."

"She is all that and more; she's a woman to tie to for life, to be perfectly sure of always. She would make a splendid wife for any man. I'm not half good enough for her; but the question is,—and you haven't answered it yet, Polly,—what's my chance?"

"I don't know," said his sister, slowly.

"Then I must ask herself, and I shall do so to-day."

"I don't know," repeated Mrs. Ashe. "'She is a woman, therefore to be won:' and I don't think there is any one ahead of you; that is the best hope I have to offer, Ned. Katy never talks of such things; and though she's so frank, I can't guess whether or not she ever thinks about them. She likes you, however, I am sure of that. But, Ned, it will not be wise to say anything to her yet."

"Not say anything? Why not?"

"No. Recollect that it is only a little while since she looked upon you as the admirer of another girl, and a girl she doesn't like very much, though they are cousins. You must give her time to get over that impression. Wait awhile; that's my advice, Ned."

"I'll wait any time if only she will say yes in the end. But it's hard to go away without a word of hope, and it's more like a man to speak out, it seems to me."

"It's too soon," persisted his sister. "You don't want her to think you a fickle fellow, falling in love with a fresh girl every time you go into port, and falling out again when the ship sails. Sailors have a bad reputation for that sort of thing. No woman cares to win a man like that."

"Great Scott! I should think not! Do you mean to say that is the way my conduct appears to her, Polly?"

"No, I don't mean just that; but wait, dear Ned, I am sure it is better."

Fortified by this sage counsel, Lieutenant Worthington went away next morning, without saying anything to Katy in words, though perhaps eyes and tones may have been less discreet. He made them promise that some one should send a letter every day about Amy; and as Mrs. Ashe frequently devolved the writing of these bulletins upon Katy, and the replies came in the shape of long letters, she found herself conducting a pretty regular correspondence without quite intending it. Ned Worthington wrote particularly nice letters. He had the knack, more often found in women than men, of giving a picture with a few graphic touches, and indicating what was droll or what was characteristic with a single happy phrase. His letters grew to be one of Katy's pleasures; and sometimes, as Mrs. Ashe watched the color deepen in her cheeks while she read, her heart would bound hopefully within her. But she was a wise woman in her way, and she wanted Katy for a sister very much; so she never said a word or looked a look to startle or surprise her, but left the thing to work itself out, which is the best course always in love affairs.

Little Amy's improvement at Albano was something remarkable. Mrs. Swift watched over her like a lynx. Her vigilance never relaxed. Amy was made to eat and sleep and walk and rest with the regularity of a machine; and this exact system, combined with the good air, worked like a charm. The little one gained hour by hour. They could absolutely see her growing fat, her mother declared. Fevers, when they do not kill, operate sometimes as spring bonfires do in gardens, burning up all the refuse and leaving the soil free for the growth of fairer things; and Amy promised in time to be only the better and stronger for her hard experience.

She had gained so much before the time came to start for Florence, that they scarcely dreaded the journey; but it proved worse than their expectations. They had not been able to secure a carriage to themselves, and were obliged to share their compartment with two English ladies, and three Roman Catholic priests, one old, the others young. The older priest seemed to be a person of some consequence; for quite a number of people came to see him off, and knelt for his blessing devoutly as the train moved away. The younger ones Katy guessed to be seminary students under his charge. Her chief amusement through the long dusty journey was in watching the terrible time that one of these young men was having with his own hat. It was a large three-cornered black affair, with sharp angles and excessively stiff; and a perpetual struggle seemed to be going on between it and its owner, who was evidently unhappy when it was on his head and still more unhappy when it was anywhere else. If he perched it on his knees it was sure to slide away from him and fall with a thump on the floor, whereupon he would pick it up, blushing furiously as he did so. Then he would lay it on the seat when the train stopped at a station, and jump out with an air of relief; but he invariably forgot, and sat down upon it when he returned, and sprang up with a look of horror at the loud crackle it made; after which he would tuck it into the baggage-rack overhead, from which it would presently descend, generally into the lap of one of the staid English ladies, who would hand it back to him with an air of deep offence, remarking to her companion,—

"I never knew anything like it. Fancy! that makes four times that hat has fallen on me. The young man is a feedgit! He's the most feegitty creature I ever saw in my life."

The young *seminariat* did not understand a word she said; but the tone needed no interpreter, and set him to blushing more painfully than ever. Altogether, the hat was never off his mind for a moment. Katy could see that he was thinking about it, even when he was thumbing his Breviary and making believe to read.

At last the train, steaming down the valley of the Arno, revealed fair Florence sitting among olive-clad hills, with Giotto's beautiful Bell-tower, and the great, many-colored, soft-hued Cathedral, and the square tower of the old Palace, and the quaint bridges over the river, looking exactly as they do in the photographs; and Katy would have felt delighted, in spite of dust and fatigue, had not Amy looked so worn out and exhausted. They were seriously troubled about her, and for the moment could think of nothing else. Happily the fatigue did no permanent harm, and a day or two of rest made her all right again. By good fortune, a nice little apartment in the modern quarter of the city had been vacated by its winter occupants the very day of their arrival, and Mrs. Ashe secured it for a month, with all its conveniences and advantages, including a maid named Maria, who had been servant to the just departed tenants.

Maria was a very tall woman, at least six feet two, and had a splendid contralto voice, which she occasionally exercised while busy over her pots and pans. It was so remarkable to hear these grand arias and recitatives proceeding from a kitchen some eight feet square, that Katy was at great pains to satisfy her curiosity about it. By aid of the dictionary and much persistent questioning, she made out that Maria in her youth had received a partial training for the opera; but in the end it was decided that she was too big and heavy for the stage, and the poor "giantess," as Amy named her, had been forced to abandon her career, and gradually had sunk to the position of a maid-of-all-work. Katy suspected that heaviness of mind as well as of body must have stood in her way; for Maria, though a good-natured giantess, was by no means quick of intelligence.

"I do think that the manner in which people over here can make homes for themselves at five minutes' notice is perfectly delightful," cried Katy, at the end of their first day's housekeeping. "I wish we could do the same in America. How cosy it looks here already!"

It was indeed cosy. Their new domain consisted of a parlor in a corner, furnished in bright yellow brocade, with windows to south and west; a nice little dining-room; three bedrooms, with dimity-curtained beds; a square entrance hall, lighted at night by a tall slender brass lamp whose double wicks were fed with olive oil; and the aforesaid tiny kitchen, behind which was a sleeping cubby, quite too small to be a good fit for the giantess. The rooms were full of conveniences,— easy-chairs, sofas, plenty of bureaus and dressing-tables, and corner fireplaces like Franklin stoves, in which odd little fires burned on cool days, made of pine cones, cakes of pressed sawdust exactly like Boston brown bread cut into slices, and a few sticks of wood thriftily adjusted, for fuel is worth its weight in gold in Florence. Katy's was the smallest of the bedrooms, but she liked it best of all for the reason that its one big window opened on an iron balcony over which grew a Banksia rose-vine with a stem as thick as her wrist. It was covered just now with masses of tiny white blossoms, whose fragrance was inexpressibly delicious and made every breath drawn in their neighborhood a delight. The sun streamed in on all sides of the little apartment, which filled a narrowing angle at the union of three streets; and from one window and another, glimpses could be caught of the distant heights about the city,—San Miniato in one direction, Bellosguardo in another, and for the third the long olive-hung ascent of Fiesole, crowned by its gray cathedral towers.

It was astonishing how easily everything fell into train about the little establishment. Every morning at six the English baker left two small sweet brown loaves and a dozen rolls at the door. Then followed the dairyman with a supply of tiny leaf-shaped pats of freshly churned butter, a big flask of milk, and two small bottles of thick cream, with a twist of vine leaf in each by way of a cork. Next came a *contadino* with a flask of red Chianti wine, a film of oil floating on top to keep it sweet. People in Florence must drink wine, whether they like it or not, because the lime-impregnated water is unsafe for use without some admixture.

Dinner came from a *trattoria*, in a tin box, with a pan of coals inside to keep it warm, which box was carried on a man's head. It was furnished at a fixed price per day,—a soup, two dishes of meat, two vegetables, and a sweet dish; and the supply was so generous as always to leave something toward next day's luncheon. Salad, fruit, and fresh eggs Maria bought for them in the old market. From the confectioners came loaves of *pane santo*, a sort of light cake made with arrowroot instead of flour; and sometimes, by way of treat, a square of *pan forte da Siena*, compounded of honey, almonds, and chocolate,—a mixture as pernicious as it is delicious, and which might take a medal anywhere for the sure production of nightmares.

Amy soon learned to know the shops from which these delicacies came. She had her favorites, too, among the strolling merchants who sold oranges and those little sweet native figs, dried in the sun without sugar, which are among the specialties of Florence. They, in their turn, learned to know her and to watch for the appearance of her little capped head and Mabel's blond wig at the window, lingering about till she came, and advertising their wares with musical modulations, so appealing that Amy was always running to Katy, who acted as housekeeper, to beg her to please buy this or that, "because it is my old man, and he wants me to so much."

"But, chicken, we have plenty of figs for to-day."

"No matter; get some more, please do. I'll eat them all; really, I will."

And Amy was as good as her word. Her convalescent appetite was something prodigious.

There was another branch of shopping in which they all took equal delight. The beauty and the cheapness of the Florence flowers are a continual surprise to a stranger. Every morning after breakfast an old man came creaking up the two long flights of stairs which led to Mrs. Ashe's apartment, tapped at the door, and as soon as it opened, inserted a shabby elbow and a large flat basket full of flowers. Such flowers! Great masses of scarlet and cream-colored tulips, and white and gold narcissus, knots of roses of all shades, carnations, heavy-headed trails of wistaria, wild hyacinths, violets, deep crimson and orange ranunculus, *giglios*, or wild irises,—the Florence emblem, so deeply purple as to be almost black,—anemones, spring-beauties, faintly tinted wood-blooms tied in large loose nosegays, ivy, fruit blossoms,— everything that can be thought of that is fair and sweet. These enticing wares the old man would tip out on the table. Mrs. Ashe and Katy would select what they wanted, and then the process of bargaining would begin, without which no sale is complete in Italy. The old man would name an enormous price, five times as much as he hoped to get. Katy would offer a very small one, considerably less than she expected to give. The old man would dance with dismay, wring his hands, assure them that he should die of hunger and all his family with him if he took less than the price named; he would then come down half a franc in his demand. So it would go on for five minutes, ten, sometimes for a quarter of an hour, the old man's price gradually descending, and Katy's terms very slowly going up, a cent or two at a time. Next the giantess would mingle with the fray. She would bounce out of her kitchen, berate the flower-vender, snatch up his flowers, declare that they smelt badly, fling them down again, pouring out all the while a voluble tirade of reproaches and revilings, and looking so enormous in her excitement that Katy wondered that the old man dared to answer her at all. Finally, there would be a sudden lull. The old man would shrug his shoulders, and remarking that he and his wife and his aged grandmother must go without bread that day since it was the Signora's will, take the money offered and depart, leaving such a mass of flowers behind him that Katy would begin to think that they had paid an unfair price for them and to feel a little rueful, till she observed that the old man was absolutely dancing downstairs with rapture over the good bargain he had made, and that Maria was black with indignation over the extravagance of her ladies!

"The Americani are a nation of spend-thrifts," she would mutter to herself, as she quickened the charcoal in her droll little range by fanning it with a palm-leaf fan; "they squander money like water. Well, all the better for us Italians!" with a shrug of her shoulders.

"But, Maria, it was only sixteen cents that we paid, and look at those flowers! There are at least half a bushel of them."

"Sixteen cents for garbage like that! The Signorina would better let me make her bargains for her. *Già! Già!* No Italian lady would have paid more than eleven sous for such useless *roba*. It is evident that the Signorina's countrymen eat gold when at home, they think so little of casting it away!"

Altogether, what with the comfort and quiet of this little home, the numberless delightful things that there were to do and to see, and Viessieux's great library, from which they could draw books at will to make the doing and seeing more intelligible, the month at Florence passed only too quickly, and was one of the times to which they afterward looked back with most pleasure. Amy grew steadily stronger, and the freedom from anxiety about her after their long strain of apprehension was restful and healing beyond expression to both mind and body.

Their very last excursion of all, and one of the pleasantest, was to the old amphitheatre at Fiesole; and it was while they sat there in the soft glow of the late afternoon, tying into bunches the violets which they had gathered from under walls whose foundations antedate Rome itself, that a cheery call sounded from above, and an unexpected surprise descended upon them in the shape of Lieutenant Worthington, who having secured another fifteen days' furlough, had come to take his sister on to Venice.

"I didn't write you that I had applied for leave," he explained, "because there seemed so little chance of my getting off again so soon; but as luck had it, Carruthers, whose turn it was, sprained his ankle and was laid up, and the Commodore let us exchange. I made all the capital I could out of Amy's fever; but upon my word, I felt like a humbug when I came upon her and Mrs. Swift in the Cascine just now, as I was hunting for you. How she has picked up! I should never have known her for the same child."

"Yes, she seems perfectly well again, and as strong as before she had the fever, though that dear old Goody Swift is just as careful of her as ever. She would not let us bring her here this afternoon, for fear we should stay out till the dew fell. Ned, it is perfectly delightful that you were able to come. It makes going to Venice seem quite a different thing, doesn't it, Katy?"

"I don't want it to seem quite different, because going to Venice was always one of my dreams," replied Katy, with a little laugh.

"I hope at least it doesn't make it seem less pleasant," said Mr. Worthington, as his sister stopped to pick a violet.

"No, indeed, I am glad," said Katy; "we shall all be seeing it for the first time, too, shall we not? I think you said you had never been there." She spoke simply and frankly, but she was conscious of an odd shyness.

"I simply couldn't stand it any longer," Ned Worthington confided to his sister when they were alone. "My head is so full of her that I can't attend to my work, and it came to me all of a sudden that this might be my last chance. You'll be getting north before long, you know, to Switzerland and so on, where I cannot follow you. So I made a clean breast of it to the Commodore; and the good old fellow, who has a soft spot in his heart for a love-story, behaved like a brick, and made it all straight for me to come away."

Mrs. Ashe did not join in these commendations of the Commodore; her attention was fixed on another part of her brother's discourse.

"Then you won't be able to come to me again? I sha'n't see you again after this!" she exclaimed. "Dear me! I never realized that before. What shall I do without you?"

"You will have Miss Carr. She is a host in herself," suggested Ned Worthington. His sister shook her head.

"Katy is a jewel," she remarked presently; "but somehow one wants a man to call upon. I shall feel lost without you, Ned."

The month's housekeeping wound up that night with a "thick tea" in honor of Lieutenant Worthington's arrival, which taxed all the resources of the little establishment. Maria was sent out hastily to buy *pan forte da Siena* and *vino d'Asti*, and fresh eggs for an omelette, and chickens' breasts smothered in cream from the restaurant, and artichokes for a salad, and flowers to garnish all; and the guest ate and praised and admired; and Amy and Mabel sat on his knee and explained everything to him, and they were all very happy together. Their merriment was so infectious that it extended to the poor giantess, who had been very pensive all day at the prospect of losing her good place, and who now raised her voice in the grand aria from "Orfeo," and made the kitchen ring with the passionate demand "Che farò senza Eurydice?" The splendid notes, full of fire and lamentation, rang out across the saucepans as effectively as if they had been footlights; and Katy, rising softly, opened the kitchen door a little way that they might not lose a sound.

The next day brought them to Venice. It was a "moment," indeed, as Katy seated herself for the first time in a gondola, and looked from beneath its black hood at the palace walls on the Grand Canal, past which they were gliding. Some were creamy white and black, some orange-tawny, others of a dull delicious ruddy color, half pink, half red; but all, in build and ornament, were unlike palaces elsewhere. High on the prow before her stood the gondolier, his form defined in dark outline against the sky, as he swayed and bent to his long oar, raising his head now and again to give a wild musical cry, as warning to other approaching gondolas. It was all like a dream. Ned Worthington sat beside her, looking more at the changes in her expressive face than at the palaces. Venice was as new to him as to Katy; but she was a new feature in his life also, and even more interesting than Venice. They seemed to float on pleasures for the next ten days. Their arrival had been happily timed to coincide with a great popular festival which for nearly a week kept Venice in a state of continual brilliant gala. All the days were spent on the water, only landing now and then to look at some famous building or picture, or to eat ices in the Piazza with the lovely façade of St. Mark's before them. Dining or sleeping seemed a sheer waste of time! The evenings were spent on the water too; for every night, immediately after sunset, a beautiful drifting pageant started from the front of the Doge's Palace to make the tour of the Grand Canal, and our friends always took a part in it. In its centre went a barge hung with embroideries and filled with orange trees and musicians. This was surrounded by a great convoy of skiffs and gondolas bearing colored lanterns and pennons and gay awnings, and managed by gondoliers in picturesque uniforms. All these floated and shifted and swept on together with a sort of rhythmic undulation as if keeping time to the music, while across their path dazzling showers and arches of colored fire poured from the palace fronts and the hotels. Every movement of the fairy flotilla was repeated in the illuminated water, every torch-tip and scarlet lantern and flake of green or rosy fire; above all the bright full moon looked down as if surprised. It was magically beautiful in effect. Katy felt as if her previous sober ideas about life and things had melted away. For the moment the world was turned topsy-turvy. There was nothing hard or real or sordid left in it; it was just a fairy tale, and she was in the middle of it as she had longed to be in her childhood. She was the Princess, encircled by delights, as when she and Clover and Elsie played in "Paradise,"—only, this was better; and, dear me! who was this Prince who seemed to belong to the story and to grow more important to it every day?

Fairy tales must come to ending. Katy's last chapter closed with a sudden turn-over of the leaf when, toward the end of this happy fortnight, Mrs. Ashe came into her room with the face of one who has unpleasant news to communicate.

"Katy," she began, "should you be *awfully* disappointed, should you consider me a perfect wretch, if I went home now instead of in the autumn?"

Katy was too much astonished to reply.

"I am grown such a coward, I am so knocked up and weakened by what I suffered in Rome, that I find I cannot face the idea of going on to Germany and Switzerland alone, without Ned to take care of me. You are a perfect angel, dear, and I know that you would do all you could to make it easy for me, but I am such a fool that I do not dare. I think my nerves must have given way," she continued half tearfully; "but the very idea of shifting for myself for five months longer makes me so miserably homesick that I cannot endure it. I dare say I shall repent afterward, and I tell myself now how silly it is; but it's no use,— I shall never know another easy moment till I have Amy safe again in America and under your father's care."

"I find," she continued after another little pause, "that we can go down with Ned to Genoa and take a steamer there which will carry us straight to New York without any stops. I hate to disappoint you dreadfully, Katy, but I have almost decided to do it. Shall you mind very much? Can you ever forgive me?" She was fairly crying now.

Katy had to swallow hard before she could answer, the sense of disappointment was so sharp; and with all her efforts there was almost a sob in her voice as she said,—

"Why yes, indeed, dear Polly, there is nothing to forgive. You are perfectly right to go home if you feel so." Then with another swallow she added: "You have given me the loveliest six months' treat that ever was, and I should be a greedy girl indeed if I found fault because it is cut off a little sooner than we expected."

"You are so dear and good not to be vexed," said her friend, embracing her. "It makes me feel doubly sorry about disappointing you. Indeed I wouldn't if I could help it, but I simply can't. I *must* go home. Perhaps we'll come back some day when Amy is grown up, or safely married to somebody who will take good care of her!"

This distant prospect was but a poor consolation for the immediate disappointment. The more Katy thought about it the sorrier did she feel. It was not only losing the chance—very likely the only one she would ever have—of seeing Switzerland and Germany; it was all sorts of other little things besides. They must go home in a strange ship with a captain they did not know, instead of in the "Spartacus," as they had planned; and they should land in New York, where no one would be waiting for them, and not have the fun of sailing into Boston Bay and seeing Rose on the wharf, where she had promised to be. Furthermore, they must pass the hot summer in Burnet instead of in the cool Alpine valleys; and Polly's house was let till October. She and Amy would have to shift for themselves elsewhere. Perhaps they would not be in Burnet at all. Oh dear, what a pity it was! what a dreadful pity!

Then, the first shock of surprise and discomfiture over, other ideas asserted themselves; and as she realized that in three weeks more, or four at the longest, she was to see papa and Clover and all her dear people at home, she began to feel so very glad that she could hardly wait for the time to come. After all, there was nothing in Europe quite so good as that.

"No, I'm not sorry," she told herself; "I am glad. Poor Polly! it's no wonder she feels nervous after all she has gone through. I hope I wasn't cross to her! And it will be *very* nice to have Lieutenant Worthington to take care of us as far as Genoa."

The next three days were full of work. There was no more floating in gondolas, except in the way of business. All the shopping which they had put off must be done, and the trunks packed for the voyage. Every one recollected last errands and commissions; there was continual coming and going and confusion, and Amy, wild with excitement, popping up every other moment in the midst of it all, to demand of everybody if they were not glad that they were going back to America.

Katy had never yet bought her gift from old Mrs. Redding. She had waited, thinking continually that she should see something more tempting still in the next place they went to; but now, with the sense that there were to be no more "next places," she resolved to wait no longer, and with a hundred francs in her pocket, set forth to choose something from among the many tempting things for sale in the Piazza. A bracelet of old Roman coins had caught her fancy one day in a bric-à-brac shop, and she walked straight toward it, only pausing by the way to buy a pale blue iridescent pitcher at Salviate's for Cecy Slack, and see it carefully rolled in seaweed and soft paper.

The price of the bracelet was a little more than she expected, and quite a long process of bargaining was necessary to reduce it to the sum she had to spend. She had just succeeded and was counting out the money when Mrs. Ashe and her brother appeared, having spied her from the opposite side of the Piazza, where they were choosing last photographs at Naga's. Katy showed her purchase and explained that it was a present; "for of course I should never walk out in cold blood and buy a bracelet for myself," she said with a laugh.

"This is a fascinating little shop," said Mrs. Ashe. "I wonder what is the price of that queer old chatelaine with the bottles hanging from it."

The price was high; but Mrs. Ashe was now tolerably conversant with shopping Italian, which consists chiefly of a few words repeated many times over, and it lowered rapidly under the influence of her *troppo's* and *è molto caro's*, accompanied with telling little shrugs and looks of surprise. In the end she bought it for less than two thirds of what had been originally asked for it. As she put the parcel in her pocket, her brother said,—

"If you have done your shopping now, Polly, can't you come out for a last row?"

"Katy may, but I can't," replied Mrs. Ashe. "The man promised to bring me gloves at six o'clock, and I must be there to pay for them. Take her down to the Lido, Ned. It's an exquisite evening for the water, and the sunset promises to be delicious. You can take the time, can't you, Katy?"

Katy could.

Mrs. Ashe turned to leave them, but suddenly stopped short.

"Katy, look! Isn't that a picture!"

The "picture" was Amy, who had come to the Piazza with Mrs. Swift, to feed the doves of St. Mark's, which was one of her favorite amusements. These pretty birds are the pets of all Venice, and so accustomed to being fondled and made much of by strangers, that they are perfectly tame. Amy, when her mother caught sight of her, was sitting on the marble pavement, with one on her shoulder, two perched on the edge of her lap, which was full of crumbs, and a flight of others circling round her head. She was looking up and calling them in soft tones. The sunlight caught the little downy curls on her head and made them glitter. The flying doves lit on the pavement, and crowded round her, their pearl and gray and rose-tinted and white feathers, their scarlet feet and gold-ringed eyes, making a shifting confusion of colors, as they hopped and fluttered and cooed about the little maid, unstartled even by her clear laughter. Close by stood Nurse Swift, observant and grimly pleased.

The mother looked on with happy tears in her eyes. "Oh, Katy, think what she was a few weeks ago and look at her now! Can I ever be thankful enough?"

She squeezed Katy's hand convulsively and walked away, turning her head now and then for another glance at Amy and the doves; while Ned and Katy silently crossed to the landing and got into a gondola. It was the perfection of a Venice evening, with silver waves lapsing and lulling under a rose and opal sky; and the sense that it was their last row on those enchanted waters made every moment seem doubly precious.

I cannot tell you exactly what it was that Ned Worthington said to Katy during that row, or why it took so long to say it that they did not get in till after the sun was set, and the stars had come out to peep at their bright, glinting faces, reflected in the Grand Canal. In fact, no one can tell; for no one overheard, except Giacomo, the brown yellow-jacketed gondolier, and as he did not understand a word of English he could not repeat the conversation. Venetian boatmen, however, know pretty well what it means when a gentleman and lady, both young, find so much to say in low tones to each other under the gondola hood, and are so long about giving the order to return; and Giacomo, deeply sympathetic, rowed as softly and made himself as imperceptible as he could,—a display of tact which merited the big silver piece with which Lieutenant Worthington "crossed his palm" on landing.

Mrs. Ashe had begun to look for them long before they appeared, but I think she was neither surprised nor sorry that they were so late. Katy kissed her hastily and went away at once,—"to pack," she said,—and Ned was equally undemonstrative; but they looked so happy, both of them, that "Polly dear" was quite satisfied and asked no questions.

Five days later the parting came, when the "Florio" steamer put into the port of Genoa for passengers. It was not an easy good-by to say. Mrs. Ashe and Amy both cried, and Mabel was said to be in deep affliction also. But there were alleviations. The squadron was coming home in the autumn, and the officers would have leave to see their friends, and of course Lieutenant Worthington must come to Burnet—to visit his sister. Five months would soon go, he declared; but for all the cheerful assurance, his face was rueful enough as he held Katy's hand in a long tight clasp while the little boat waited to take him ashore.

After that it was just a waiting to be got through with till they sighted Sandy Hook and the Neversinks,—a waiting varied with peeps at Marseilles and Gibraltar and the sight of a whale or two and one distant iceberg. The weather was fair all the way, and the ocean smooth. Amy was never weary of lamenting her own stupidity in not having taken Maria Matilda out of confinement before they left Venice.

"That child has hardly been out of the trunk since we started," she said. "She hasn't seen anything except a little bit of Nice. I shall really be ashamed when the other children ask her about it. I think I shall play that she was left at boarding-school and didn't come to Europe at all! Don't you think that would be the best way, mamma?"

"You might play that she was left in the States-prison for having done something naughty," suggested Katy; but Amy scouted this idea.

"She never does naughty things," she said, "because she never does anything at all. She's just stupid, poor child! It's not her fault."

The thirty-six hours between New York and Burnet seemed longer than all the rest of the journey put together, Katy thought. But they ended at last, as the "Lake Queen" swung to her moorings at the familiar wharf, where Dr. Carr stood surrounded with all his boys and girls just as they had stood the previous October, only that now there were no clouds on anybody's face, and Johnnie was skipping up and down for joy instead of grief. It was a long moment while the plank was being lowered from the gangway; but the moment it was in place, Katy darted across, first ashore of all the passengers, and was in her father's arms.

Mrs. Ashe and Amy spent two or three days with them, while looking up temporary quarters elsewhere; and so long as they stayed all seemed a happy confusion of talking and embracing and exclaiming, and distributing of gifts. After they went away things fell into their customary train, and a certain flatness became apparent. Everything had happened that could happen. The long-talked-of European journey was over. Here was Katy at home again, months sooner than they expected; yet she looked remarkably cheerful and content! Clover could not understand it; she was likewise puzzled to account for one or two private conversations between Katy and papa in which she had not been invited to take part, and the occasional arrival of a letter from "foreign parts" about whose contents nothing was said.

"It seems a dreadful pity that you had to come so soon," she said one day when they were alone in their bedroom. "It's delightful to have you, of course; but we had braced ourselves to do without you till October, and there are such lots of delightful things that you could have been doing and seeing at this moment."

"Oh, yes, indeed," replied Katy, but not at all as if she were particularly disappointed.

"Katy Carr, I don't understand you," persisted Clover. "Why don't you feel worse about it? Here you have lost five months of the most splendid time you ever had, and you don't seem to mind it a bit! Why, if I were in your place my heart would be perfectly broken. And you needn't have come, either; that's the worst of it. It was just a whim of Polly's. Papa says Amy might have stayed as well as not. Why aren't you sorrier, Katy?"

"Oh, I don't know. Perhaps because I had so much as it was,— enough to last all my life, I think, though I *should* like to go again. You can't imagine what beautiful pictures are put away in my memory."

"I don't see that you had so awfully much," said the aggravated Clover; "you were there only a little more than six months,—for I don't count the sea,—and ever so much of that time was taken up with nursing Amy. You can't have any pleasant pictures of *that* part of it."

"Yes, I have, some."

"Well, I should really like to know what. There you were in a dark room, frightened to death and tired to death, with only Mrs. Ashe and the old nurse to keep you company—Oh, yes, that brother was there part of the time; I forgot him—"

Clover stopped short in sudden amazement. Katy was standing with her back toward her, smoothing her hair, but her face was reflected in the glass. At Clover's words a sudden deep flush had mounted in Katy's cheeks. Deeper and deeper it burned as she became conscious of Clover's astonished gaze, till even the back of her neck was pink. Then, as if she could not bear it any longer, she put the brush down, turned, and fled out of the room; while Clover, looking after her, exclaimed in a tone of sudden comical dismay,—

"What does it mean? Oh, dear me! is that what Katy is going to do next?"

Clover

CHAPTER I. A TALK ON THE DOORSTEPS.

It was one of those afternoons in late April which are as mild and balmy as any June day. The air was full of the chirps and twitters of nest-building birds, and of sweet indefinable odors from half-developed leaf-buds and cherry and pear blossoms. The wisterias overhead were thickly starred with pointed pearl-colored sacs, growing purpler with each hour, which would be flowers before long; the hedges were quickening into life, the long pensile willow-boughs and the honey-locusts hung in a mist of fine green against the sky, and delicious smells came with every puff of wind from the bed of white violets under the parlor windows.

Katy and Clover Carr, sitting with their sewing on the door-steps, drew in with every breath the sense of spring. Who does not know the delightfulness of that first sitting out of doors after a long winter's confinement? It seems like flinging the gauntlet down to the powers of cold. Hope and renovation are in the air. Life has conquered Death, and to the happy hearts in love with life there is joy in the victory. The two sisters talked busily as they sewed, but all the time an only half-conscious rapture informed their senses,—the sympathy of that which is immortal in human souls with the resurrection of natural things, which is the sure pledge of immortality.

It was nearly a year since Katy had come back from that too brief journey to Europe with Mrs. Ashe and Amy, about which some of you have read, and many things of interest to the Carr family had happened during the interval. The "Natchitoches" had duly arrived in New York in October, and presently afterward Burnet was convulsed by the appearance of a tall young fellow in naval uniform, and the announcement of Katy's engagement to Lieutenant Worthington.

It was a piece of news which interested everybody in the little town, for Dr. Carr was a universal friend and favorite. For a time he had been the only physician in the place; and though with the gradual growth of population two or three younger men had appeared to dispute the ground with him, they were forced for the most part to content themselves with doctoring the new arrivals, and with such fragments and leavings of practice as Dr. Carr chose to intrust to them. None of the old established families would consent to call in any one else if they could possibly get the "old" doctor.

A skilful practitioner, who is at the same time a wise adviser, a helpful friend, and an agreeable man, must necessarily command a wide influence. Dr. Carr was "by all odds and far away," as our English cousins would express it, the most popular person in Burnet, wanted for all pleasant occasions, and doubly wanted for all painful ones.

So the news of Katy's engagement was made a matter of personal concern by a great many people, and caused a general stir, partly because she was her father's daughter, and partly because she was herself; for Katy had won many friends by her own merit. So long as Ned Worthington stayed, a sort of tide of congratulation and sympathy seemed to sweep through the house all day long. Tea-roses and chrysanthemums, and baskets of pears and the beautiful Burnet grapes flooded the premises, and the door-bell rang so often that Clover threatened to leave the door open, with a card attached,—"Walk straight in. *He* is in the parlor!"

Everybody wanted to see and know Katy's lover, and to have him as a guest. Ten tea-drinkings a week would scarcely have contented Katy's well-wishers, had the limitations of mortal weeks permitted such a thing; and not a can of oysters would have been left in the place if Lieutenant Worthington's leave had lasted three days longer. Clover and Elsie loudly complained that they themselves never had a chance to see him; for whenever he was not driving or walking with Katy, or having long *tête-à-têtes* in the library, he was eating muffins somewhere, or making calls on old ladies whose feelings would be dreadfully hurt if he went away without their seeing him.

"Sisters seem to come off worst of all," protested Johnnie. But in spite of their lamentations they all saw enough of their future brother-in-law to grow fond of him; and notwithstanding some natural pangs of jealousy at having to share Katy with an outsider, it was a happy visit, and every one was sorry when the leave of absence ended, and Ned had to go away.

A month later the "Natchitoches" sailed for the Bahamas. It was to be a six months' cruise only; and on her return she was for a while to make part of the home squadron. This furnished a good opportunity for her first lieutenant to marry; so it was agreed that the wedding should take place in June, and Katy set about her preparations in the leisurely and simple fashion which was characteristic of her. She had no ambition for a great *trousseau*, and desired to save her father expense; so her outfit, as compared with that of most modern brides, was a very moderate one, but being planned and mostly made at home, it necessarily involved thought, time, and a good deal of personal exertion.

Dear little Clover flung herself into the affair with even more interest than if it had been her own. Many happy mornings that winter did the sisters spend together over their dainty stitches and "white seam." Elsie and Johnnie were good needle-women now, and could help in many ways. Mrs. Ashe often joined them; even Amy could contribute aid in the plainer sewing, and thread everybody's needles. But the most daring and indefatigable of all was Clover, who never swerved in her determination that Katy's "things" should be as nice and as pretty as love and industry combined could make them. Her ideas as to decoration soared far beyond Katy's. She hem-stitched, she cat-stitched, she feather-stitched, she lace-stitched, she tucked and frilled and embroidered, and generally worked her fingers off; while the bride vainly protested that all this finery was quite unnecessary, and that simple hems and a little Hamburg edging would answer just as well. Clover merely repeated the words, "Hamburg edging!" with an accent of scorn, and went straight on in her elected way.

As each article received its last touch, and came from the laundry white and immaculate, it was folded to perfection, tied with a narrow blue or pale rose-colored ribbon, and laid aside in a sacred receptacle known as "The Wedding Bureau." The handkerchiefs, grouped in dozens, were strewn with dried violets and rose-leaves to make them sweet. Lavender-bags and sachets of orris lay among the linen; and perfumes as of Araby were discernible whenever a drawer in the bureau was pulled out.

So the winter passed, and now spring was come; and the two girls on the doorsteps were talking about the wedding, which seemed very near now.

"Tell me just what sort of an affair you want it to be," said Clover.

"It seems more your wedding than mine, you have worked so hard for it," replied Katy. "You might give your ideas first."

"My ideas are not very distinct. It's only lately that I have begun to think about it at all, there has been so much to do. I'd like to have you have a beautiful dress and a great many wedding-presents and everything as pretty as can be, but not so many bridesmaids as Cecy, because there is always such a fuss in getting them nicely up the aisle in church and out again,—that is as far as I've got. But so long as you are pleased, and it goes off well, I don't care exactly how it is managed."

"Then, since you are in such an accommodating frame of mind, it seems a good time to break my views to you. Don't be shocked, Clovy; but, do you know, I don't want to be married in church at all, or to have any bridesmaids, or anything arranged for beforehand particularly. I should like things to be simple, and to just *happen*."

"But, Katy, you can't do it like that. It will all get into a snarl if there is no planning beforehand or rehearsals; it would be confused and horrid."

"I don't see why it would be confused if there were nothing to confuse. Please not be vexed; but I always have hated the ordinary kind of wedding, with its fuss and worry and so much of everything, and just like all the other weddings, and the bride looking tired to death, and nobody enjoying it a bit. I'd like mine to be different, and more—more—real. I don't want any show or processing about, but just to have things nice and pretty, and all the people I love and who love me to come to it, and nothing cut and dried, and nobody tired, and to make it a sort of dear, loving occasion, with leisure to realize how dear it is and what it all means. Don't you think it would really be nicer in that way?"

"Well, yes, as you put it, and 'viewed from the higher standard,' as Miss Inches would say, perhaps it would. Still, bridesmaids and all that are very pretty to look at; and folks will be surprised if you don't have them."

"Never mind folks," remarked the irreverent Katy. "I don't care a button for that argument. Yes; bridesmaids and going up the aisle in a long procession and all the rest *are* pretty to look at,—or were before they got to be so hackneyed. I can imagine the first bridal procession up the aisle of some early cathedral as having been perfectly beautiful. But nowadays, when the butcher and baker and candlestick-maker and everybody else do it just alike, the custom seems to me to have lost its charm. I never did enjoy having things exactly as every one else has them,—all going in the same direction like a flock of sheep. I would like my little wedding to be something especially my own. There was a poetical meaning in those old customs; but now that the custom has swallowed up so much of the meaning, it would please me better to retain the meaning and drop the custom."

"I see what you mean," said Clover, not quite convinced, but inclined as usual to admire Katy and think that whatever she meant must be right. "But tell me a little more. You mean to have a wedding-dress, don't you?" doubtfully.

"Yes, indeed!"

"Have you thought what it shall be?"

"Do you recollect that beautiful white crape shawl of mamma's which papa gave me two years ago? It has a lovely wreath of embroidery round it; and it came to me the other day that it would make a charming gown, with white surah or something for the under-dress. I should like that better than anything new, because mamma used to wear it, and it would seem as if she were here still, helping me to get ready. Don't you think so?"

"It is a lovely idea," said Clover, the ever-ready tears dimming her happy blue eyes for a moment, "and just like you. Yes, that shall be the dress,—dear mamma's shawl. It will please papa too, I think, to have you choose it."

"I thought perhaps it would," said Katy, soberly. "Then I have a wide white watered sash which Aunt Izzy gave me, and I mean to have that worked into the dress somehow. I should like to wear something of hers too, for she was really good to us when we were little, and all that long time that I was ill; and we were not always good to her, I am afraid. Poor Aunt Izzy! What troublesome little wretches we were,—I most of all!"

"Were you? Somehow I never can recollect the time when you were not a born angel. I am afraid I don't remember Aunt Izzy well. I just have a vague memory of somebody who was pretty strict and cross."

"Ah, you never had a back, and needed to be waited on night and day, or you would recollect a great deal more than that. Cousin Helen helped me to appreciate what Aunt Izzy really was. By the way, one of the two things I have set my heart on is to have Cousin Helen come to my wedding."

"It would be lovely if she could. Do you suppose there is any chance?"

"I wrote her week before last, but she hasn't answered yet. Of course it depends on how she is; but the accounts from her have been pretty good this year."

"What is the other thing you have set your heart on? You said 'two.'"

"The other is that Rose Red shall be here, and little Rose. I wrote to her the other day also, and coaxed hard. Wouldn't it be too enchanting? You know how we have always longed to have her in Burnet; and if she could come now it would make everything twice as pleasant."

"Katy, what an enchanting thought!" cried Clover, who had not seen Rose since they all left Hillsover. "It would be the greatest lark that ever was to have the Roses. When do you suppose we shall hear? I can hardly wait, I am in such a hurry to have her say 'Yes.'"

"But suppose she says 'No'?"

"I won't think of such a possibility. Now go on. I suppose your principles don't preclude a wedding-cake?"

"On the contrary, they include a great deal of wedding-cake. I want to send a box to everybody in Burnet,—all the poor people, I mean, and the old people and the children at the Home and those forlorn creatures at the poor-house and all papa's patients."

"But, Katy, that will cost a lot," objected the thrifty Clover.

"I know it; so we must do it in the cheapest way, and make the cake ourselves. I have Aunt Izzy's recipe, which is a very good one; and if we all take hold, it won't be such an immense piece of work. Debby has quantities of raisins stoned already. She has been doing them in the evenings a few at a time for the last month. Mrs. Ashe knows a factory where you can get the little white boxes for ten dollars a thousand, and I have commissioned her to send for five hundred."

"Five hundred! What an immense quantity!"

"Yes; but there are all the Hillsover girls to be remembered, and all our kith and kin, and everybody at the wedding will want one. I don't think it will be too many. Oh, I have arranged it all in my mind. Johnnie will slice the citron, Elsie will wash the currants, Debby measure and bake, Alexander mix, you and I will attend to the icing, and all of us will cut it up."

"Alexander!"

"Alexander. He is quite pleased with the idea, and has constructed an implement—a sort of spade, cut out of new pine wood—for the purpose. He says it will be a sight easier than digging flower-beds. We will set about it next week; for the cake improves by keeping, and as it is the heaviest job we have to do, it will be well to get it out of the way early."

"Sha'n't you have a floral bell, or a bower to stand in, or something of that kind?" ventured Clover, timidly.

"Indeed I shall not," replied Katy. "I particularly dislike floral bells and bowers. They are next worst to anchors and harps and 'floral pillows' and all the rest of the dreadful things that they have at funerals. No, we will have plenty of fresh flowers, but not in stiff arrangements. I want it all to seem easy and to *be* easy. Don't look so disgusted, Clovy."

"Oh, I'm not disgusted. It's your wedding. I want you to have everything in your own way."

"It's everybody's wedding, I think," said Katy, tenderly. "Everybody is so kind about it. Did you see the thing that Polly sent this morning?"

"No. It must have come after I went out. What was it?"

"Seven yards of beautiful nun's lace which she bought in Florence. She says it is to trim a morning dress; but it's really too pretty. How dear Polly is! She sends me something almost every day. I seem to be in her thoughts all the time. It is because she loves Ned so much, of course; but it is just as kind of her."

"I think she loves you almost as much as Ned," said Clover.

"Oh, she couldn't do that; Ned is her only brother. There is Amy at the gate now."

It was a much taller Amy than had come home from Italy the year before who was walking toward them under the budding locust-boughs. Roman fever had seemed to quicken and stimulate all Amy's powers, and she had grown very fast during the past year. Her face was as frank and childlike as ever, and her eyes as blue; but she was prettier than when she went to Europe, for her cheeks were pink, and the mane of waving hair which framed them in was very becoming. The hair was just long enough now to touch her shoulders; it was turning brown as it lengthened, but the ends of the locks still shone with childish gold, and caught the sun in little shining rings as it filtered down through the tree branches.

She kissed Clover several times, and gave Katy a long, close hug; then she produced a parcel daintily hid in silver paper.

"Tanta," she said,—this was a pet name lately invented for Katy,—"here is something for you from mamma. It's something quite particular, I think, for mamma cried when she was writing the note; not a hard cry, you know, but just two little teeny-weeny tears in her eyes. She kept smiling, though, and she looked happy, so I guess it isn't anything very bad. She said I was to give it to you with her best, *best* love."

Katy opened the parcel, and beheld a square veil of beautiful old blonde. The note said:

This was my wedding-veil, dearest Katy, and my mother wore it before me. It has been laid aside all these years with the idea that perhaps Amy might want it some day; but instead I send it to you, without whom there would be no Amy to wear this or anything else. I think it would please Ned to see it on your head, and I know it would make me very happy; but if you don't feel like using it, don't mind for a moment saying so to

Your loving

Polly.

Katy handed the note silently to Clover, and laid her face for a little while among the soft folds of the lace, about which a faint odor of roses hung like the breath of old-time and unforgotten loves and affections.

"Shall you?" queried Clover, softly.

"Why, of course! Doesn't it seem too sweet? Both our mothers!"

"There!" cried Amy, "you are going to cry too, Tanta! I thought weddings were nice funny things. I never supposed they made people feel badly. I sha'n't ever let Mabel get married, I think. But she'll have to stay a little girl always in that case, for I certainly won't have her an old maid."

"What do you know about old maids, midget?" asked Clover.

"Why, Miss Clover, I have seen lots of them. There was that one at the Pension Suisse; you remember, Tanta? And the two on the steamer when we came home. And there's Miss Fitz who made my blue frock; Ellen said she was a regular old maid. I never mean to let Mabel be like that."

"I don't think there's the least danger," remarked Katy, glancing at the inseparable Mabel, who was perched on Amy's arm, and who did not look a day older than she had done eighteen months previously. "Amy, we're going to make wedding-cake next week,—heaps and heaps of wedding-cake. Don't you want to come and help?"

"Why, of course I do. What fun! Which day may I come?"

The cake-making did really turn out fun. Many hands made light work of what would have been a formidable job for one or two. It was all done gradually. Johnnie cut the golden citron quarters into thin transparent slices in the sitting-room one morning while the others were sewing, and reading Tennyson aloud. Elsie and Amy made a regular frolic of the currant-washing. Katy, with Debby's assistance, weighed and measured; and the mixture was enthusiastically stirred by Alexander, with the "spade" which he had invented, in a large new wash-tub. Then came the baking, which for two days filled the house with spicy, plum-puddingy odors; then the great feat of icing the big square loaves; and then the cutting up, in which all took part. There was much careful measurement that the slices might be an exact fit; and the kitchen rang with bright laughter and chat as Katy and Clover wielded the sharp bread-knives, and the others fitted the portions into their boxes, and tied the ribbons in crisp little bows. Many delicious crumbs and odd corners and fragments fell to the share of the younger workers; and altogether the occasion struck Amy as so enjoyable that she announced—with her mouth full—that she had changed her mind, and that Mabel might get married as often as she pleased, if she would have cake like *that* every time,—a liberality of permission which Mabel listened to with her invariable waxen smile.

When all was over, and the last ribbons tied, the hundreds of little boxes were stacked in careful piles on a shelf of the inner closet of the doctor's office to wait till they were wanted,—an arrangement which naughty Clover pronounced eminently suitable, since there should always be a doctor close at hand where there was so much wedding-cake. But before all this was accomplished, came what Katy, in imitation of one of Miss Edgeworth's heroines, called "The Day of Happy Letters."

CHAPTER II. THE DAY OF HAPPY LETTERS.

The arrival of the morning boat with letters and newspapers from the East was the great event of the day in Burnet. It was due at eleven o'clock; and everybody, consciously or unconsciously, was on the lookout for it. The gentlemen were at the office bright and early, and stood chatting with each other, and fingering the keys of their little drawers till the rattle of the shutter announced that the mail was distributed. Their wives and daughters at home, meanwhile, were equally in a state of expectation, and whatever they might be doing kept ears and eyes on the alert for the step on the gravel and the click of the latch which betokened the arrival of the family news-bringer.

Doctors cannot command their time like other people, and Dr. Carr was often detained by his patients, and made late for the mail, so it was all the pleasanter a surprise when on the great day of the cake-baking he came in earlier than usual, with his hands quite full of letters and parcels. All the girls made a rush for him at once; but he fended them off with an elbow, while with teasing slowness he read the addresses on the envelopes.

"Miss Carr—Miss Carr—Miss Katherine Carr—Miss Carr again; four for you, Katy. Dr. P. Carr,—a bill and a newspaper, I perceive; all that an old country doctor with a daughter about to be married ought to expect, I suppose. Miss Clover E. Carr,—one for the 'Confidante in white linen.' Here, take it, Clovy. Miss Carr again. Katy, you have the lion's share. Miss Joanna Carr,—in the unmistakable handwriting of Miss Inches. Miss Katherine Carr, care Dr. Carr. That looks like a wedding present, Katy. Miss Elsie Carr; Cecy's hand, I should say. Miss Carr once more,—from the conquering hero, judging from the post-mark. Dr. Carr,—another newspaper, and—hollo!—one more for Miss Carr. Well, children, I hope for once you are satisfied with the amount of your correspondence. My arm fairly aches with the weight of it. I hope the letters are not so heavy inside as out."

"I am quite satisfied, Papa, thank you," said Katy, looking up with a happy smile from Ned's letter, which she had torn open first of all. "Are you going, dear?" She laid her packages down to help him on with his coat. Katy never forgot her father.

"Yes, I am going. Time and rheumatism wait for no man. You can tell me your news when I come back."

It is not fair to peep into love letters, so I will only say of Ned's that it was very long, very entertaining,—Katy thought,—and contained the pleasant information that the "Natchitoches" was to sail four days after it was posted, and would reach New York a week sooner than any one had dared to hope. The letter contained several other things as well, which showed Katy how continually she had been in his thoughts,—a painting on rice paper, a dried flower or two, a couple of little pen-and-ink sketches of the harbor of Santa Lucia and the shipping, and a small cravat of an odd convent lace folded very flat and smooth. Altogether it was a delightful letter, and Katy read it, as it were, in leaps, her eyes catching at the salient points, and leaving the details to be dwelt upon when she should be alone.

This done, she thrust the letter into her pocket, and proceeded to examine the others. The first was in Cousin Helen's clear, beautiful handwriting:—

DEAR KATY,—If any one had told us ten years ago that in this particular year of grace you would be getting ready to be married, and I preparing to come to your wedding, I think we should have listened with some incredulity, as to an agreeable fairy tale which could not possibly come true. We didn't look much like it, did we,—you in your big chair and I on my sofa? Yet here we are! When your letter first reached me it seemed a sort of impossible thing that I should accept your invitation; but the more I thought about it the more I felt as if I must, and now things seem to be working round to that end quite marvellously. I have had a good winter, but the doctor wishes me to try the experiment of the water cure again which benefited me so much the summer of your accident. This brings me in your direction; and I don't see why I might not come a little earlier than I otherwise should, and have the great pleasure of seeing you married, and making acquaintance with Lieutenant Worthington. That is, if you are perfectly sure that to have at so busy a time a guest who, like the Queen of Spain, has the disadvantage of being without legs, will not be more care than enjoyment. Think seriously over this point, and don't send for me unless you are certain. Meanwhile, I am making ready. Alex and Emma and little Helen—who is a pretty big Helen now—are to be my escorts as far as Buffalo on their way to Niagara. After that is all plain sailing, and Jane Carter and I can manage very well for ourselves. It seems like a dream to think that I may see you all so soon; but it is such a pleasant one that I would not wake up on any account.

I have a little gift which I shall bring you myself, my Katy; but I have a fancy also that you shall wear some trifling thing on your wedding-day which comes from me, so for fear of being forestalled I will say now, please don't buy any stockings for the occasion, but wear the pair which go with this, for the sake of your loving

Cousin Helen.

"These must be they," cried Elsie, pouncing on one of the little packages. "May I cut the string, Katy?"

Permission was granted; and Elsie cut the string. It was indeed a pair of beautiful white silk stockings embroidered in an open pattern, and far finer than anything which Katy would have thought of choosing for herself.

"Don't they look exactly like Cousin Helen?" she said, fondling them. "Her things always are choicer and prettier than anybody's else, somehow. I can't think how she does it, when she never by any chance goes into a shop. Who can this be from, I wonder?"

"This" was the second little package. It proved to contain a small volume bound in white and gold, entitled, "Advice to Brides." On the fly-leaf appeared this inscription:—

To Katherine Carr, on the occasion of her approaching bridal, from her affectionate teacher,

Marianne Nipson.

1 Timothy, ii. 11.

Clover at once ran to fetch her Testament that she might verify the quotation, and announced with a shriek of laughter that it was: "Let the women learn in silence with all subjection;" while Katy, much diverted, read extracts casually selected from the work, such as: "A wife should receive her husband's decree without cavil or question, remembering that the husband is the head of the wife, and that in all matters of dispute his opinion naturally and scripturally outweighs her own."

Or: "'A soft answer turneth away wrath.' If your husband comes home fretted and impatient, do not answer him sharply, but soothe him with gentle words and caresses. Strict attention to the minor details of domestic management will often avail to secure peace."

And again: "Keep in mind the epitaph raised in honor of an exemplary wife of the last century,—'She never banged the door.' Qualify yourself for a similar testimonial."

"Tanta never does bang doors," remarked Amy, who had come in as this last "elegant extract" was being read.

"No, that's true; she doesn't," said Clover. "Her prevailing vice is to leave them open. I like that truth about a good dinner 'availing' to secure peace, and the advice to 'caress' your bear when he is at his crossest. Ned never does issue 'decrees,' though, I fancy; and on the whole, Katy, I don't believe Mrs. Nipson's present is going to be any particular comfort in your future trials. Do read something else to take the taste out of our mouths. We will listen in 'all subjection.'"

Katy was already deep in a long epistle from Rose.

"This is too delicious," she said; "do listen." And she began again at the beginning:—

My Sweetest of all old Sweets,—Come to your wedding! Of course I shall. It would never seem to me to have any legal sanction whatever if I were not there to add my blessing. Only let me know which day "early in June" it is to be, that I may make ready. Deniston will fetch us on, and by a special piece of good luck, a man in Chicago—whose name I shall always bless if only I can remember what it is—has been instigated by our mutual good angel to want him on business just about that time; so that he would have to go West anyway, and would rather have me along than not, and is perfectly resigned to his fate. I mean to come three days before, and stay three days after the wedding, if I may, and altogether it is going to be a lark of larks. Little Rose can talk quite fluently now, and almost read; that is, she knows six letters of her picture alphabet. She composes poems also. The other day she suddenly announced,—

"Mamma, I have made up a sort of a im. May I say it to you?"

I naturally consented, and this was the

IM.

Jump in the

parlor,

Jump in the hall,

God made us

all!

Now did you ever hear of anything quite so dear as that, for a baby only three years and five months old? I tell you she is a wonder. You will all adore her, Clover particularly. Oh, my dear little C.! To think I am going to see her!

I met both Ellen Gray and Esther Dearborn the other day, and where do you think it was? At Mary Silver's wedding! Yes, she is actually married to the Rev. Charles Playfair Strothers, and settled in a little parsonage somewhere in the Hoosac Tunnel,—or near it,—and already immersed in "duties." I can't think what arguments he used to screw her up to the rash act; but there she is.

It wasn't exactly what one would call a cheerful wedding. All the connection took it very seriously; and Mary's uncle, who married her, preached quite a lengthy funeral discourse to the young couple, and got them nicely ready for death, burial, and the next world, before he would consent to unite them for this. He was a solemn-looking old person, who had been a missionary, and "had laid away three dear wives in foreign lands," as he confided to me afterward over a plate of ice-cream. He seemed to me to be "taking notice," as they say of babies, and it is barely possible that he mistook me for a single woman, for his attentions were rather pronounced till I introduced my husband prominently into conversation; after that he seemed more attracted by Ellen Gray.

Mary cried straight through the ceremony. In fact, I imagine she cried straight through the engagement, for her eyes looked wept out and had scarlet rims, and she was as white as her veil. In fact, whiter, for that was made of beautiful *point de Venise*, and was just a trifle yellowish. Everybody cried. Her mother and sister sobbed aloud, so did several maiden aunts and a grandmother or two and a few cousins. The church resounded with guggles and gasps, like a great deal of bath-water running out of an ill-constructed tub. Mr. Silver also wept, as a business man may, in a series of sniffs interspersed with silk handkerchief; you know the kind. Altogether it was a most cheerless affair. I seemed to be the only person present who was not in tears; but I really didn't see anything to cry about, so far as I was concerned, though I felt very hard-hearted.

I had to go alone, for Deniston was in New York. I got to the church rather early, and my new spring bonnet—which is a superior one—seemed to impress the ushers, so they put me in a very distinguished front pew all by myself. I bore my honors meekly, and found them quite agreeable, in fact,—you know I always did like to be made much of,—so you can imagine my disgust when presently three of the stoutest ladies you ever saw came sailing up the aisle, and prepared to invade *my* pew.

"Please move up, Madam," said the fattest of all, who wore a wonderful yellow hat.

But I was not "raised" at Hillsover for nothing, and remembering the success of our little ruse on the railroad train long ago, I stepped out into the aisle, and with my sweetest smile made room for them to pass.

"Perhaps I would better keep the seat next the door," I murmured to the yellow lady, "in case an attack should come on."

"An attack!" she repeated in an accent of alarm. She whispered to the others. All three eyed me suspiciously, while I stood looking as pensive and suffering as I could. Then after confabulating together for a little, they all swept into the seat behind mine, and I heard them speculating in low tones as to whether it was epilepsy or catalepsy or convulsions that I was subject to. I presume they made signs to all the other people who came in to steer clear of the lady with fits, for nobody invaded my privacy, and I sat in lonely splendor with a pew to myself, and was very comfortable indeed.

Mary's dress was white satin, with a great deal of point lace and pearl passementerie, and she wore a pair of diamond ear-rings which her father gave her, and a bouquet almost but not quite as large, which was the gift of the bridegroom. He has a nice face, and I think Silvery Mary will be happy with him, much happier than with her rather dismal family, though his salary is only fifteen hundred a year, and pearl passementerie, I believe, quite unknown and useless in the Hoosac region. She had loads of the most beautiful presents you ever saw. All the Silvers are rolling in riches, you know. One little thing made me laugh, for it was so like her. When the clergyman said, "Mary, wilt thou take this man to be thy wedded husband?" I distinctly saw her put her fingers over her mouth in the old, frightened way. It was only for a second, and after that I rather think Mr. Strothers held her hand tight for fear she might do it again. She sent her love to you, Katy. What sort of a gown are *you* going to have, by the way?

I have kept my best news to the last, which is that Deniston has at last given way, and we are to move into town in October. We have taken a little house in West Cedar Street. It is quite small and very dingy and I presume inconvenient, but I already love it to distraction, and feel as if I should sit up all night for the first month to enjoy the sensation of being no longer that horrid thing, a resident of the suburbs. I hunt the paper shops and collect samples of odd and occult pattern, and compare them with carpets, and am altogether in my element, only longing for the time to come when I may put together my pots and pans and betake me across the mill-dam. Meantime, Roslein is living in a state of quarantine. She is not permitted to speak with any other children, or even to look out of window at one, for fear she may contract some sort of contagious disease, and spoil our beautiful visit to Burnet. She sends you a kiss, and so do I; and mother and Sylvia and Deniston and grandmamma, particularly, desire their love.

Your loving

Rose Red.

"Oh," cried Clover, catching Katy round the waist, and waltzing wildly about the room, "what a delicious letter! What fun we are going to have! It seems too good to be true. Tum-ti-ti, tum-ti-ti. Keep step, Katy. I forgive you for the first time for getting married. I never did before, really and truly. Tum-ti-ti; I am so happy that I must dance!"

"There go my letters," said Katy, as with the last rapid twirl, Rose's many-sheeted epistle and the "Advice to Brides" flew to right and left. "There go two of your hair-pins, Clover. Oh, do stop; we shall all be in pieces."

Clover brought her gyrations to a close by landing her unwilling partner suddenly on the sofa. Then with a last squeeze and a rapid kiss she began to pick up the scattered letters.

"Now read the rest," she commanded, "though anything else will sound flat after Rose's."

"Hear this first," said Elsie, who had taken advantage of the pause to open her own letter. "It is from Cecy, and she says she is coming to spend a month with her mother on purpose to be here for Katy's wedding. She sends heaps of love to you, Katy, and says she only hopes that Mr. Worthington will prove as perfectly satisfactory in all respects as her own dear Sylvester."

"My gracious, I should hope he would," put in Clover, who was still in the wildest spirits. "What a dear old goose Cecy is! I never hankered in the least for Sylvester Slack, did you, Katy?"

"Certainly not. It would be a most improper proceeding if I had," replied Katy, with a laugh. "Whom do you think this letter is from, girls? Do listen to it. It's written by that nice old Mr. Allen Beach, whom we met in London. Don't you recollect my telling you about him?"

My dear Miss Carr,—Our friends in Harley Street have told me a piece of news concerning you which came to them lately in a letter from Mrs. Ashe, and I hope you will permit me to offer you my most sincere congratulations and good wishes. I recollect meeting Lieutenant Worthington when he was here two years ago, and liking him very much. One is always glad in a foreign land to be able to show so good a specimen of one's young countrymen as he affords,—not that England need be counted as a foreign country by any American, and least of all by myself, who have found it a true home for so many years.

As a little souvenir of our week of sight-seeing together, of which I retain most agreeable remembrances, I have sent you by my friends the Sawyers, who sail for America shortly, a copy of Hare's "Walks in London," which a young *protégée* of mine has for the past year been illustrating with photographs of the many curious old buildings described. You took so much interest in them while here that I hope you may like to see them again. Will you please accept with it my most cordial wishes for your future, and believe me

Very faithfully your friend,
Allen Beach.

"What a nice letter!" said Clover.

"Isn't it?" replied Katy, with shining eyes, "what a thing it is to be a gentleman, and to know how to say and do things in the right way! I am so surprised and pleased that Mr. Beach should remember me. I never supposed he would, he sees so many people in London all the time, and it is quite a long time since we were there, nearly two years. Was your letter from Miss Inches, John?"

"Yes, and Mamma Marian sends you her love; and there's a present coming by express for you,—some sort of a book with a hard name. I can scarcely make it out, the Ru—ru—something of Omar Kay—y— Well, anyway it's a book, and she hopes you will read Emerson's 'Essay on Friendship' over before you are married, because it's a helpful utterance, and adjusts the mind to mutual conditions."

"Worse than 1 Timothy, ii. 11," muttered Clover. "Well, Katy dear, what next? What *are* you laughing at?"

"You will never guess, I am sure. This is a letter from Miss Jane! And she has made me this pincushion!"

The pincushion was of a familiar type, two circles of pasteboard covered with gray silk, neatly over-handed together, and stuck with a row of closely fitting pins. Miss Jane's note ran as follows:—

Hillsover, April 21.

Dear Katy,—I hear from Mrs. Nipson that you are to be married shortly, and I want to say that you have my best wishes for your future. I think a man ought to be happy who has you for a wife. I only hope the one you have chosen is worthy of you. Probably he isn't, but perhaps you won't find it out. Life is a knotty problem for most of us. May you solve it satisfactorily to yourself and others! I have nothing to send but my good wishes and a few pins. They are not an unlucky present, I believe, as scissors are said to be.

Remember me to your sister, and believe me to be with true regard,
Yours,   Jane A. Bangs.

"Dear me, is that her name?" cried Clover. "I always supposed she was baptized 'Miss Jane.' It never occurred to me that she had any other title. What appropriate initials! How she used to J.A.B. with us!"

"Now, Clovy, that's not kind. It's a very nice note indeed, and I am touched by it. It's a beautiful compliment to say that the man ought to be happy who has got me, I think. I never supposed that Miss Jane could pay a compliment."

"Or make a joke! That touch about the scissors is really jocose,—for Miss Jane. Rose Red will shriek over the letter and that particularly rigid pincushion. They are both of them so exactly like her. Dear me! only one letter left. Who is that from, Katy? How fast one does eat up one's pleasures!"

"But you had a letter yourself. Surely papa said so. What was that? You haven't read it to us."

"No, for it contains a secret which you are not to hear just yet," replied Clover. "Brides mustn't ask questions. Go on with yours."

"Mine is from Louisa Agnew,—quite a long one, too. It's an age since we heard from her, you know."

Ashburn, April 24.

Dear Katy,—Your delightful letter and invitation came day before yesterday, and thank you for both. There is nothing in the world that would please me better than to come to your wedding if it were possible, but it simply isn't. If you lived in New Haven now, or even Boston,—but Burnet is so dreadfully far off, it seems as inaccessible as

Kamchatka to a person who, like myself, has a house to keep and two babies to take care of.

Don't look so alarmed. The house is the same house you saw when you were here, and so is one of the babies; the other is a new acquisition just two years old, and as great a darling as Daisy was at the same age. My mother has been really better in health since he came, but just now she is at a sort of Rest Cure in Kentucky; and I have my hands full with papa and the children, as you can imagine, so I can't go off two days' journey to a wedding,—not even to yours, my dearest old Katy. I shall think about you all day long on *the* day, when I know which it is, and try to imagine just how everything looks; and yet I don't find that quite easy, for somehow I fancy that your wedding will be a little different from the common run. You always were different from other people to me, you know,—you and Clover,—and I love you so much, and I always shall.

Papa has taken a kit-kat portrait of me in oils,—and a blue dress,—which he thinks is like, and which I am going to send you as soon as it comes home from the framers. I hope you will like it a little for my sake. Dear Katy, I send so much love with it.

I have only seen the Pages in the street since they came home from Europe; but the last piece of news here is Lilly's engagement to Comte Ernest de Conflans. He has something to do with the French legation in Washington, I believe; and they crossed in the same steamer. I saw him driving with her the other day,—a little man, not handsome, and very dark. I do not know when they are to be married. Your Cousin Clarence is in Colorado.

With two kisses apiece and a great hug for you, Katy, I am always

Your affectionate friend,

Louisa.

"Dear me!" said the insatiable Clover, "is that the very last? I wish we had another mail, and twelve more letters coming in at once. What a blessed institution the post-office is!"

CHAPTER III. THE FIRST WEDDING IN THE FAMILY.

The great job of the cake-making over, a sense of leisure settled on the house. There seemed nothing left to be done which need put any one out of his or her way particularly. Katy had among her other qualities a great deal of what is called "forehandedness." To leave things to be attended to at the last moment in a flurry and a hurry would have been intolerable to her. She firmly believed in the doctrine of a certain wise man of our own day who says that to push your work before you is easy enough, but to pull it after you is very hard indeed.

All that winter, without saying much about it,—for Katy did not "do her thinking outside her head,"—she had been gradually making ready for the great event of the spring. Little by little, a touch here and a touch there, matters had been put in train, and the result now appeared in a surprising ease of mind and absence of confusion. The house had received its spring cleaning a fortnight earlier than usual, and was in fair, nice order, with freshly-beaten carpets and newly-washed curtains. Katy's dresses were ordered betimes, and had come home, been tried on, and folded away ten days before the wedding. They were not many in number, but all were pretty and in good taste, for the frigate was to be in Bar Harbor and Newport for a part of the summer, and Katy wanted to do Ned credit, and look well in his eyes and those of his friends.

All the arrangements, kept studiously simple, were beautifully systematized; and their very simplicity made them easy to carry out. The guest chambers were completely ready, one or two extra helpers were engaged that the servants might not be overworked, the order of every meal for the three busiest days was settled and written down. Each of the younger sisters had some special charge committed to her. Elsie was to wait on Cousin Helen, and see that she and her nurse had everything they wanted. Clover was to care for the two Roses; Johnnie to oversee the table arrangements, and make sure that all was right in that direction. Dear little Amy was indefatigable as a doer of errands, and her quick feet were at everybody's service to "save steps." Cecy arrived, and haunted the house all day long, anxious to be of use to somebody; Mrs. Ashe put her time at their disposal; there was such a superabundance of helpers, in fact, that no one could feel over taxed. And Katy, while still serving as main spring to the whole, had plenty of time to write her notes, open her wedding presents, and enjoy her friends in a leisurely, unfatigued fashion which was a standing wonderment to Cecy, whose own wedding had been of the onerous sort, and had worn her to skin and bone.

"I am only just beginning to recover from it now," she remarked plaintively, "and there you sit, Katy, looking as fresh as a rose; not tired a bit, and never seeming to have anything on your mind. I can't think how you do it. I never was at a wedding before where everybody was not perfectly worn out."

"You never were at such a simple wedding before," explained Katy. "I'm not ambitious, you see. I want to keep things pretty much as they are every day, only with a little more of everything because of there being more people to provide for. If I were attempting to make it a beautiful, picturesque wedding, we should get as tired as anybody, I have no doubt."

Katy's gifts were numerous enough to satisfy even Clover, and comprised all manner of things, from a silver tray which came, with a rather stiff note, from Mrs. Page and Lilly, to Mary's new flour-scoop, Debby's sifter, and a bottle of home-made hair tonic from an old woman in the "County Home." Each of the brothers and sisters had made her something, Katy having expressed a preference for presents of home manufacture. Mrs. Ashe gave her a beautiful sapphire ring, and Cecy Hall—as they still called her inadvertently half the time—an elaborate sofa-pillow embroidered by herself. Katy liked all her gifts, both large and small, both for what they were and for what they meant, and took a good healthy, hearty satisfaction in the fact that so many people cared for her, and had worked to give her a pleasure.

Cousin Helen was the first guest to arrive, five days before the wedding. When Dr. Carr, who had gone to Buffalo to meet and escort her down, lifted her from the carriage and carried her indoors, all of them could easily have fancied that it was the first visit happening over again, for she looked exactly as she did then, and scarcely a day older. She happened to have on a soft gray travelling dress too, much like that which she wore on the previous occasion, which made the illusion more complete.

But there was no illusion to Cousin Helen herself. Everything to her seemed changed and quite different. The ten years which had passed so lightly over her head had made a vast alteration in the cousins whom she remembered as children. The older ones were grown up, the younger ones in a fair way to be so; even Phil, who had been in white frocks with curls falling over his shoulders at the time of her former visit to Burnet, was now fifteen and as tall as his father. He was very slight in build, and looked delicate, she thought; but Katy assured her that he was perfectly well, and thin only because he had outgrown his strength.

It was one of the delightful results of Katy's "forehandedness" that she could command time during those next two days to thoroughly enjoy Cousin Helen. She sat beside her sofa for hours at a time, holding her hand and talking with a freedom of confidence such as she could have shown to no one else, except perhaps to Clover. She had the feeling that in so doing she was rendering account to a sort of visible conscience of all the events, the mistakes, the successes, the glad and the sorry of the long interval that had passed since they met. It was a pleasure and relief to her; and to Cousin Helen the recital was of equal interest, for though she knew the main facts by letter, there was a satisfaction in collecting the little details which seldom get fully put into letters.

One subject only Katy touched rather guardedly; and that was Ned. She was so desirous that her cousin should approve of him, and so anxious not to raise her expectations and have her disappointed, that she would not half say how very nice she herself thought him to be. But Cousin Helen could "read between the lines," and out of Katy's very reserve she constructed an idea of Ned which satisfied her pretty well.

So the two happy days passed, and on the third arrived the other anxiously expected guests, Rose Red and little Rose.

They came early in the morning, when no one was particularly looking for them, which made it all the pleasanter. Clover was on the porch twisting the honeysuckle tendrils upon the trellis when the carriage drove up to the gate, and Rose's sunny face popped out of the window. Clover recognized her at once, and with a shriek which brought all the others downstairs, flew down the path, and had little Rose in her arms before any one else could get there.

"You see before you a deserted wife," was Rose's first salutation. "Deniston has just dumped us on the wharf, and gone on to Chicago in that abominable boat, leaving me to your tender mercies. O Business, Business! what crimes are committed in thy name, as Madame Roland would say!"

"Never mind Deniston," cried Clover, with a rapturous squeeze. "Let us play that he doesn't exist, for a little while. We have got you now, and we mean to keep you."

"How pleasant you look!" said Rose, glancing up the locust walk toward the house, which wore a most inviting and hospitable air, with doors and windows wide open, and the soft wind fluttering the vines and the white curtains. "Ah, there comes Katy now." She ran forward to meet her while Clover followed with little Rose.

"Let me det down, pease," said that young lady,—the first remark she had made. "I tan walk all by myself. I am not a baby any more."

"*Will* you hear her talk?" cried Katy, catching her up. "Isn't it wonderful? Rosebud, who am I, do you think?"

"My Aunt Taty, I dess, betause you is so big. Is you mawwied yet?"

"No, indeed. Did you think I would get 'mawwied' without you? I have been waiting for you and mamma to come and help me."

"Well, we is here," in a tone of immense satisfaction. "Now you tan."

The larger Rose meanwhile was making acquaintance with the others. She needed no introductions, but seemed to know by instinct which was each boy and each girl, and to fit the right names to them all. In five minutes she seemed as much at home as though she had spent her life in Burnet. They bore her into the house in a sort of triumph, and upstairs to the blue bedroom, which Katy and Clover had vacated for her; and such a hubbub of talk and laughter presently issued therefrom that Cousin Helen, on the other side the entry, asked Jane to set her door open that she might enjoy the sounds,—they were so merry.

Rose's bright, rather high-pitched voice was easily distinguishable above the rest. She was evidently relating some experience of her journey, with an occasional splash by way of accompaniment, which suggested that she might be washing her hands.

"Yes, she really has grown awfully pretty; and she had on the loveliest dark-brown suit you ever saw, with a fawn-colored hat, and was altogether dazzling; and, do you know, I was really quite glad to see her. I can't imagine why, but I was! I didn't stay glad long, however."

"Why not? What did she do?" This in Clover's voice.

"Well, she didn't do anything, but she was distant and disagreeable. I scarcely observed it at first, I was so pleased to see one of the old Hillsover girls; and I went on being very cordial. Then Lilly tried to put me down by running over a list of her fine acquaintances, Lady this, and the Marquis of that,—people whom she and her mother had known abroad. It made me think of my old autograph book with Antonio de Vallombrosa, and the rest. Do you remember?"

"Of course we do. Well, go on."

"At last she said something about Comte Ernest de Conflans,—I had heard of him, perhaps? He crossed in the steamer with 'Mamma and me,' it seems; and we have seen a great deal of him. This appeared a good opportunity to show that I too have relations with the nobility, so I said yes, I had met him in Boston, and my sister had seen a good deal of him in Washington last winter.

"'And what did she think of him?' demanded Lilly.

"'Well,' said I, 'she didn't seem to think a great deal about him. She says all the young men at the French legation seem more than usually foolish, but Comte Ernest is the worst of the lot. He really *does* look like an absolute fool, you know,' I added pleasantly. Now, girls, what was there in that to make her angry? Can you tell? She grew scarlet, and glared as if she wanted to bite my head off; and then she turned her back and would scarcely speak to me again. Does she always behave that way when the aristocracy is lightly spoken of?"

"Oh, Rose,—oh, Rose," cried Clover, in fits of laughter, "did you really tell her that?"

"I really did. Why shouldn't I? Is there any reason in particular?"

"Only that she is engaged to him," replied Katy, in an extinguished voice.

"Good gracious! No wonder she scowled! This is really dreadful. But then why did she look so black when she asked where we were going, and I said to your wedding? That didn't seem to please her any more than my little remarks about the nobility."

"I don't pretend to understand Lilly," said Katy, temperately; "she is an odd girl."

"I suppose an odd girl can't be expected to have an even temper," remarked Rose, apparently speaking with a hairpin in her mouth. "Well, I've done for myself, that is evident. I need never expect any notice in future from the Comtesse de Conflans."

Cousin Helen heard no more, but presently steps sounded outside her door, and Katy looked in to ask if she were dressed, and if she might bring Rose in, a request which was gladly granted. It was a pretty sight to see Rose with Cousin Helen. She knew all about her already from Clover and Katy, and fell at once under the gentle spell which seemed always to surround that invalid sofa, begged leave to say "Cousin Helen" as the others did, and was altogether at her best and sweetest when with her, full of merriment, but full too of a deference and sympathy which made her particularly charming.

"I never did see anything so lovely in all my life before," she told Clover in confidence. "To watch her lying there looking so radiant and so peaceful and so interested in Katy's affairs, and never once seeming to remember that except for that accident she too would have been a bride and had a wedding! It's perfectly wonderful! Do you suppose she is never sorry for herself? She seems the merriest of us all."

"I don't think she remembers herself often enough to be sorry. She is always thinking of some one else, it seems to me."

"Well, I am glad to have seen her," added Rose, in a more serious tone than was usual to her. "She and grandmamma are of a different order of beings from the rest of the world. I don't wonder you and Katy always were so good; you ought to be with such a Cousin Helen."

"I don't think we were as good as you make us out, but Cousin Helen has really been one of the strong influences of our lives. She was the making of Katy, when she had that long illness; and Katy has made the rest of us."

Little Rose from the first moment became the delight of the household, and especially of Amy Ashe, who could not do enough for her, and took her off her mother's hands so entirely that Rose complained that she seemed to have lost her child as well as her husband. She was a sedate little maiden, and wonderfully wise for her years. Already, in some ways she seemed older than her erratic little mother, of whom, in a droll fashion, she assumed a sort of charge. She was a born housewife.

"Mamma, you have fordotten your wings," Clover would hear her saying. "Mamma, you has a wip in your seeve, you must mend it," or "Mamma, don't fordet dat your teys is in the top dwawer,"—all these reminders and advices being made particularly comical by the baby pronunciation. Rose's theory was that little Rose was a messenger from heaven sent to buffet her and correct her mistakes.

"The bane and the antidote," she would say. "Think of my having a child with powers of ratiocination!"

Rose came down the night of her arrival after a long, freshening nap, looking rested and bonny in a pretty blue dress, and saying that as little Rose too had taken a good sleep, she might sit up to tea if the family liked. The family were only too pleased to have her do so. After tea Rose carried her off, ostensibly to go to bed, but Clover heard a great deal of confabulating and giggling in the hall and on the stairs, and soon after, Rose returned, the door-bell rang loudly, and there entered an astonishing vision,—little Rose, costumed as a Cupid or a carrier-pigeon, no one knew exactly which, with a pair of large white wings fastened on her shoulders, and dragging behind her by a loop of ribbon a sizeable basket quite full of parcels.

Straight toward Katy she went, and with her small hands behind her back and her blue eyes fixed full on Katy's face, repeated with the utmost solemnity the following "poem:"

"I'm a messender, you see,
Fwom Hymen's Expwess Tumpany.
All these little bundles are
For my Aunty Taty Tarr;
If she knows wot's dood for her
She will tiss the messender."

"You sweet thing!" cried Katy, "tissing the messender" with all her heart. "I never heard such a dear little poem. Did you write it yourself, Roslein?"

"No. Mamma wote it, but she teached it to me so I tould say it."

The bundles of course contained wedding gifts. Rose seemed to have brought her trunk full of them. There were a pretty pair of salt-cellars from Mrs. Redding, a charming paper-knife of silver, with an antique coin set in the handle, from Sylvia, a hand-mirror mounted in brass from Esther Dearborn, a long towel with fringed and embroidered ends from Ellen Gray, and from dear old Mrs. Redding a beautiful lace-pin set with a moonstone. Next came a little *repoussé* pitcher marked, "With love from Mary Silver," then a parcel tied with pink ribbons, containing a card-case of Japanese leather, which was little Rose's gift, and last of all Rose's own present, a delightful case full of ivory brushes and combs. Altogether never was such a satisfactory "fardel" brought by Hymen's or any other express company before; and in opening the packages, reading the notes that came with them and exclaiming and admiring, time flew so fast that Rose quite forgot the hour, till little Rose, growing sleepy, reminded her of it by saying,—

"Mamma, I dess I'd better do to bed now, betause if I don't I shall be too seepy to turn to Aunt Taty's wedding to-mowwow."

"Dear me!" cried Rose, catching the child up. "This is simply dreadful! what a mother I am! Things *are* come to a pass indeed, if babes and sucklings have to ask to be put to bed. Baby, you ought to have been christened Nathan the Wise."

She disappeared with Roslein's drowsy eyes looking over her shoulder.

Next afternoon came Ned, and with him, to Katy's surprise and pleasure, appeared the good old commodore who had played such a kind part in their affairs in Italy the year before. It was a great compliment that he should think it worth while to come so far to see one of his junior officers married; and it showed so much real regard for Ned that everybody was delighted. These guests were quartered with Mrs. Ashe, but they took most of their meals with the Carrs; and it was arranged that they, with Polly and Amy, should come to an early breakfast on the marriage morning.

After Ned's arrival things did seem to grow a little fuller and busier, for he naturally wanted Katy to himself, and she was too preoccupied to keep her calm grasp on events; still all went smoothly, and Rose declared that there never was such a wedding since the world was made,—no tears, no worries, nobody looking tired, nothing disagreeable!

Clover's one great subject of concern was the fear that it might rain. There was a little haze about the sunset the night before, and she expressed her intention to Cousin Helen of lying awake all night to see how things looked.

"I really feel as if I could not bear it if it should storm," she said, "after all this fine weather too; and I know I shall not sleep a wink, anyway."

"I think we can trust God to take care of the weather even on Katy's wedding-day," replied Cousin Helen, gently.

And after all it was she who lay awake. Pain had made her a restless sleeper, and as her bed commanded the great arch of western sky, she saw the moon, a sharp-curved silver shape, descend and disappear a little before midnight. She roused again when all was still, solemn darkness except for a spangle of stars, and later, opened her eyes in time to catch the faint rose flush of dawn reflected from the east. She raised herself on her elbow to watch the light grow.

"It is a fair day for the child," she whispered to herself. "How good God is!" Then she slept again for a long, restful space, and woke refreshed, so that Katy's secret fear that Cousin Helen might be ill from excitement, and not able to come to her wedding, was not realized.

Clover, meantime, had slept soundly all night. She and Katy shared the same room, and waked almost at the same moment. It was early still; but the sisters felt bright and rested and ready for work, so they rose at once.

They dressed in silence, after a little whispered rejoicing over the beautiful morning, and in silence took their Bibles and sat down side by side to read the daily portion which was their habit. Then hand in hand they stole downstairs, disturbing nobody, softly opened doors and windows, carried bowls and jars out on the porch, and proceeded to arrange a great basket full of roses which had been brought the night before, and set in the dew-cool shade of the willows to keep fresh.

Before breakfast all the house had put on festal airs. Summer had come early to Burnet that year; every garden was in bud and blossom, and every one who had flowers had sent their best to grace Katy's wedding. The whole world seemed full of delicious smells. Each table and chimney-piece bore a fragrant load; a great bowl of Jacqueminots stood in the middle of the breakfast-table, and two large jars of the same on the porch, where Clover had arranged various seats and cushions that it might serve as a sort of outdoor parlor.

Nobody who came to that early breakfast ever forgot its peace and pleasantness and the sweet atmosphere of affection which seemed to pervade everything about it. After breakfast came family prayers as usual, Dr. Carr reading the chapter, and the dear old commodore joining with a hearty nautical voice in,—

"Awake my soul! and with the sun,"

which was a favorite hymn with all of them. Ned shared Katy's book, and his face and hers alone would have been breakfast enough for the company if everything else had failed, as Rose remarked to Clover in a whisper, though nobody found any fault with the more substantial fare which Debby had sent in previously. Somehow this little mutual service of prayer and praise seemed to fit in with the spirit of the day, and give it its keynote.

"It's just the sweetest wedding," Mrs. Ashe told her brother. "And the wonderful thing is that everything comes so naturally. Katy is precisely her usual self,—only a little more so."

"I'm under great obligations to Amy for having that fever," was Ned's somewhat indirect answer; but his sister understood what he meant.

Breakfast over, the guests discreetly removed themselves; and the whole family joined in resetting the table for the luncheon, which was to be at two, Katy and Ned departing in the boat at four. It was a simple but abundant repast, with plenty of delicious home-cooked food,— oysters and salads and cold chicken; fresh salmon from Lake Superior; a big Virginia ham baked to perfection, red and translucent to its savory centre; hot coffee, and quantities of Debby's perfect rolls. There were strawberries, also, and ice-cream, and the best of home-made cake and jellies, and everywhere vases of fresh roses to perfume the feast. When all was arranged, there was still time for Katy to make Cousin Helen a visit, and then go to her room for a quiet rest before dressing; and still that same unhurried air pervaded the house.

There had been a little discussion the night before as to just how the bride should make her appearance at the decisive moment; but Katy had settled it by saying simply that she should come downstairs, and Ned could meet her at the foot of the staircase.

"It is the simplest way," she said; "and you know I don't want any fuss. I will just come down."

"I dare say she's right," remarked Rose; "but it seems to me to require a great deal of courage."

And after all, it didn't. The simple and natural way of doing a thing generally turns out the easiest. Clover helped Katy to put on the wedding-gown of soft crape and creamy white silk. It was trimmed with old lace and knots of ribbon, and Katy wore with it two or three white roses which Ned had brought her, and a pearl pendant which was his gift. Then Clover had to go downstairs to receive the guests, and see that Cousin Helen's sofa was put in the right place; and Rose, who remained behind, had the pleasure of arranging Katy's veil. The yellow-white of the old blonde was very becoming, and altogether, the effect, though not "stylish," was very sweet. Katy was a little pale, but otherwise exactly like her usual self, with no tremors or self-consciousness.

Presently little Rose came up with a message.

"Aunty Tover says dat Dr. Tone has tum, and everything is weddy, and you'd better tum down," she announced.

Katy gave Rose a last kiss, and went down the hall. But little Rose was so fascinated by the appearance of the white dress and veil that she kept fast hold of Katy's hand, disregarding her mother's suggestion that she should slip down the back staircase, as she herself proposed to do.

"No, I want to do with my Aunt Taty," she persisted.

So it chanced that Katy came downstairs with pretty little Rose clinging to her like a sort of impromptu bridesmaid; and meeting Ned's eyes as he stood at the foot waiting for her, she forgot herself, lost the little sense of shyness which was creeping over her, and responded to his look with a tender, brilliant smile. The light from the hall-door caught her face and figure just then, the color flashed into her cheeks; and she looked like a beautiful, happy picture of a bride, and all by accident,—which was the best thing about it; for pre-arranged effects are not always effective, and are apt to betray their pre-arrangement.

Then Katy took Ned's arm, little Rose let go her hand, and they went into the parlor and were married.

Dr. Stone had an old-fashioned and very solemn wedding service which he was accustomed to use on such occasions. He generally spoke of the bride as "Thy handmaiden," which was a form that Clover particularly deprecated. He had also been known to advert to the world where there is neither marrying nor giving in marriage as a great improvement on this, which seemed, to say the least, an unfortunate allusion under the circumstances. But upon this occasion his feelings were warmed and touched, and he called Katy "My dear child," which was much better than "Thy handmaiden."

When the ceremony was over, Ned kissed Katy, and her father kissed her, and the girls and Dorry and Phil; and then, without waiting for any one else, she left her place and went straight to where Cousin Helen lay on her sofa, watching the scene with those clear, tender eyes in which no shadow of past regrets could be detected. Katy knelt down beside her, and they exchanged a long, silent embrace. There was no need for words between hearts which knew each other so well.

After that for a little while all was congratulations and good wishes. I think no bride ever carried more hearty good-will into her new life than did my Katy. All sorts of people took Ned off into corners to tell him privately what a fortunate person he was in winning such a wife. Each fresh confidence of this sort was a fresh delight to him, he so thoroughly agreed with it.

"She's a prize, sir!—she's a prize!" old Mr. Worrett kept repeating, shaking Ned's hand with each repetition. Mrs. Worrett had not been able to come. She never left home now on account of the prevailing weakness of carryalls; but she sent Katy her best love and a gorgeous broom made of the tails of her own peacocks.

"Aren't you sorry you are not going to stay and have a nice time with us all, and help eat up the rest of the cake?" demanded Clover, as she put her head into the carriage for a last kiss, two hours later.

"Very!" said Katy; but she didn't look sorry at all.

"There's one comfort," Clover remarked valiantly, as she walked back to the house with her arm round Rose's waist. "She's coming back in December, when the ship sails, and as likely as not she will stay a year, or perhaps two. That's what I like about the navy. You can eat your cake, and have it too. Husbands go off for good long times, and leave their wives behind them. I think it's delightful!"

"I wonder if Katy will think it quite so delightful," remarked Rose. "Girls are not always so anxious to ship their husbands off for what you call 'good long times.'"

"I think she ought. It seems to me perfectly unnatural that any one should want to leave her own family and go away for always. I like Ned dearly, but except for this blessed arrangement about going to sea, I don't see how Katy could."

"Clover, you are a goose. You'll be wiser one of these days, see if you aren't," was Rose's only reply.

CHAPTER IV. TWO LONG YEARS IN ONE SHORT CHAPTER.

Katy's absence left a sad blank in the household. Every one missed her, but nobody so much as Clover, who all her life long had been her room-mate, confidante, and intimate friend.

It was a great help that Rose was there for the first three lonely days. Dulness and sadness were impossible with that vivacious little person at hand; and so long as she stayed, Clover had small leisure to be mournful. Rose was so bright and merry and affectionate that Elsie and John were almost as much in love with her as Clover herself, and sat and sunned themselves in her warmth, so to speak, all day long, while Phil and Dorry fairly quarrelled as to which should have the pleasure of doing little services for her and Baby Rose.

If she could have remained the summer through, all would have seemed easy; but that of course was impossible. Mr. Browne appeared with a provoking punctuality on the morning of the fourth day, prepared to carry his family away with him. He spent one night at Dr. Carr's, and they all liked him very much. No one could help it, he was so cordial and friendly and pleasant. Still, for all her liking, Clover could have found it in her heart to quite detest him as the final moment drew near.

"Let him go home without you," she urged coaxingly. "Stay with us all summer,—you and little Rose! He can come back in September to fetch you, and it would be so delightful to us."

"My dear, I couldn't live without Deniston till September," said the disappointing Rose. "It may not show itself to a casual observer, but I am really quite foolish about Deniston. I shouldn't be happy away from him at all. He's the only husband I've got,—a 'poor thing, but mine own,' as the 'immortal William' puts it."

"Oh, dear," groaned Clover. "That is the way that Katy is going to talk about Ned, I suppose. Matrimony is the most aggravating condition of things for outsiders that was ever invented. I wish nobody *had* invented it. Here it would be so nice for us to have you stay, and the moment that provoking husband of yours appears, you can't think of any one else."

"Too true—much too true. Now, Clovy, don't embitter our last moments with reproaches. It's hard enough to leave you as it is, when I've just found you again after all these years. I've had the most beautiful visit that ever was, and you've all been awfully dear and nice. 'Kiss me quick and let me go,' as the song says. I only wish Burnet was next door to West Cedar Street!"

Next day Mr. Browne sailed away with his "handful of Roses," as Elsie sentimentally termed them (and indeed, Rose by herself would have been a handful for almost any man); and Clover, like Lord Ullin, was "left lamenting." Cousin Helen remained, however; and it was not till she too departed, a week later, that Clover fully recognized what it meant to have Katy married. Then indeed she could have found it in her heart to emulate Eugénie de la Ferronayes, and shed tears over all the little inanimate objects which her sister had left behind,—the worn-out gloves, the old dressing slippers in the shoe-bag. But dear me, we get used to everything, and it is fortunate that we do! Life is too full, and hearts too flexible, and really sad things too sad, for the survival of sentimental regrets over changes which do not involve real loss and the wide separation of death. In time, Clover learned to live without Katy, and to be cheerful still.

Her cheerfulness was greatly helped by the letters which came regularly, and showed how contented Katy herself was. She and Ned were having a beautiful time, first in New York, and making visits near it, then in Portsmouth and Portland, when the frigate moved on to these harbors, and in Newport, which was full and gay and amusing to the last degree. Later, in August, the letters came from Bar Harbor, where Katy had followed, in company with the commodore's wife, who seemed as nice as her husband; and Clover heard of all manner of delightful doings,—sails, excursions, receptions on board ship, and long moonlight paddles with Ned, who was an expert canoeist. Everybody was so wonderfully kind, Katy said; but Ned wrote to his sister that Katy was a great favorite; every one liked her, and his particular friends were all raging wildly round in quest of girls just like her to marry. "But it's no use; for, as I tell them," he added, "that sort isn't made in batches. There is only one Katy; and happily she belongs to me, and the other fellows must get along as they can."

This was all satisfactory and comforting; and Clover could endure a little loneliness herself so long as her beloved Katy seemed so happy. She was very busy besides, and there *were* compensations, as she admitted to herself. She liked the consequence of being at the head of domestic affairs, and succeeding to Katy's position as papa's special daughter,—the person to whom he came for all he wanted, and to whom he told his little secrets. She and Elsie became more intimate than they had ever been before; and Elsie in her turn enjoyed being Clover's lieutenant as Clover had been Katy's. So the summer did not seem long to any of them; and when September was once past, and they could begin to say, "month after next," the time sped much faster.

"Mrs. Hall asked me this morning when the Worthingtons were coming," said Johnnie, one day. "It seems so funny to have Katy spoken of as 'the Worthingtons.'"

"I only wish the Worthingtons would write and say when," remarked Clover. "It is more than a week since we heard from them."

The next day brought the wished-for letter, and the good news that Ned had a fortnight's leave, and meant to bring Katy home the middle of November, and stay for Thanksgiving. After that the "Natchitoches" was to sail for an eighteen months' cruise to China and Japan; and then Ned would probably have two years ashore at the Torpedo Station or Naval Academy or somewhere, and they would start a little home for themselves.

"Meantime," wrote Katy, "I am coming to spend a year and a half with you, if urged. Don't all speak at once, and don't mind saying so, if you don't want me."

The bitter drop in this pleasant intelligence—there generally is one, you know—was that the fortnight of Ned's stay was to be spent at Mrs. Ashe's. "It's her only chance to see Ned," said Katy; "so I know you won't mind, for afterward you will have me for such a long visit."

But they *did* mind very much!

"I don't think it's fair," cried Johnnie, hotly, while Clover and Elsie exchanged disgusted looks; "Katy belongs to us."

"Katy belongs to her husband, on the contrary," said Dr. Carr, overhearing her; "you must learn that lesson once for all, children. There's no escape from the melancholy fact; and it's quite right and natural that Ned should wish to go to his sister, and she should want to have him."

"Ned! yes. But Katy—"

"My dear, Katy *is* Ned," answered Dr. Carr, with a twinkle. Then noticing the extremely unconvinced expression of Johnnie's face, he added more seriously, "Don't be cross, children, and spoil all Katy's pleasure in coming home, with your foolish jealousies. Clover, I trust to you to take these young mutineers in hand and make them listen to reason."

Thus appealed to, Clover rallied her powers, and while laboring to bring Elsie and John to a proper frame of mind, schooled herself as well, so as to be able to treat Mrs. Ashe amiably when they met. Dear, unconscious Polly meanwhile was devising all sorts of pleasant and hospitable plans designed to make Ned's stay a sort of continuous fête to everybody. She put on no airs over the preference shown her, and was altogether so kind and friendly and sweet that no one could quarrel with her even in thought, and Johnnie herself had to forgive her, and be contented with a little whispered grumble to Dorry now and then over the inconvenience of possessing "people-in-law."

And then Katy came, the same Katy, only, as Clover thought, nicer, brighter, dearer, and certainly better-looking than ever. Sea air had tanned her a little, but the brown was becoming; and she had gained an ease and polish of manner which her sisters admired very much. And after all, it seemed to make little difference at which house they stayed, for they were in and out of both all day long; and Mrs. Ashe threw her doors open to the Carrs and wanted some or all of them for every meal, so that except for the name of the thing, it was almost as satisfactory to have Katy over the way as occupying her old quarters.

The fortnight sped only too rapidly. Ned departed, and Katy settled herself in the familiar corner to wait till he should come back again. Navy wives have to learn the hard lesson of patience in the long separations entailed by their husbands' profession. Katy missed Ned sorely, but she was too unselfish to mope, or to let the others know how hard to bear his loss seemed to her. She never told any one how she lay awake in stormy nights, or when the wind blew,—and it seemed to blow oftener than usual that winter,—imagining the frigate in a gale, and whispering little prayers for Ned's safety. Then her good sense would come back, and remind her that wind in Burnet did not necessarily mean wind in Shanghai or Yokohama or wherever the "Natchitoches" might be; and she would put herself to sleep with the repetition of that lovely verse of Keble's "Evening Hymn," left out in most of the collections, but which was particularly dear to her:—

"Thou Ruler of the light and dark,
Guide through the tempest Thine own Ark;
Amid the howling, wintry sea,
We are in port if we have Thee."

So the winter passed, and the spring; and another summer came and went, with little change to the quiet Burnet household, and Katy's brief life with her husband began to seem dreamy and unreal, it lay so far behind. And then, with the beginning of the second winter came a new anxiety.

Phil, as we said in the last chapter, had grown too fast to be very strong, and was the most delicate of the family in looks and health, though full of spirit and fun. Going out to skate with some other boys the week before Christmas, on a pond which was not so securely frozen as it looked, the ice gave way; and though no one was drowned, the whole party had a drenching, and were thoroughly chilled. None of the others minded it much, but the exposure had a serious effect on Phil. He caught a bad cold which rapidly increased into pneumonia; and Christmas Day, usually such a bright one in the Carr household, was overshadowed by anxious forebodings, for Phil was seriously ill, and the doctor felt by no means sure how things would turn with him. The sisters nursed him devotedly, and by March he was out again; but he did not get *well* or lose the persistent little cough, which kept him thin and weak. Dr. Carr tried this remedy and that, but nothing seemed to do much good; and Katy thought that her father looked graver and more anxious every time that he tested Phil's temperature or listened at his chest.

"It's not serious yet," he told her in private; "but I don't like the look of things. The boy is just at a turning-point. Any little thing might set him one way or the other. I wish I could send him away from this damp lake climate."

But sending a half-sick boy away is not such an easy thing, nor was it quite clear where he ought to go. So matters drifted along for another month, and then Phil settled the question for himself by having a slight hemorrhage. It was evident that something must be done, and speedily—but what? Dr. Carr wrote to various medical acquaintances, and in reply pamphlets and letters poured in, each designed to prove that the particular part of the country to which the pamphlet or the letter referred was the only one to which it was at all worth while to consign an invalid with delicate lungs. One recommended Florida, another Georgia, a third South Carolina; a fourth and fifth recommended cold instead of heat, and an open air life with the mercury at zero. It was hard to decide what was best.

"He ought not to go off alone either," said the puzzled father. "He is neither old enough nor wise enough to manage by himself, but who to send with him is the puzzle. It doubles the expense, too."

"Perhaps I—" began Katy, but her father cut her short with a gesture.

"No, Katy, I couldn't permit that. Your husband is due in a few weeks now. You must be free to go to him wherever he is, not hampered with the care of a sick brother. Besides, whoever takes charge of Phil must be prepared for a long absence,—at least a year. It must be either Clover or myself; and as it seems out of the question that I shall drop my practice for a year, Clover is the person."

"Phil is seventeen now," suggested Katy. "That is not so very young."

"No, not if he were in full health. Plenty of boys no older than he have gone out West by themselves, and fared perfectly well. But in Phil's condition that would never answer. He has a tendency to be low-spirited about himself too, and he needs incessant care and watchfulness."

"Out West," repeated Katy. "Have you decided, then?"

"Yes. The letter I had yesterday from Hope, makes me pretty sure that St. Helen's is the best place we have heard of."

"St. Helen's! Where is that?"

"It is one of the new health-resorts in Colorado which has lately come into notice for consumptives. It's very high up; nearly or quite six thousand feet, and the air is said to be something remarkable."

"Clover will manage beautifully, I think; she is such a sensible little thing," said Katy.

"She seems to me, and he too, about as fit to go off two thousand miles by themselves as the Babes in the Wood," remarked Dr. Carr, who, like many other fathers, found it hard to realize that his children had outgrown their childhood. "However, there's no help for it. If I don't stay and grind away at the mill, there is no one to pay for this long journey. Clover will have to do her best."

"And a very good best it will be you'll see," said Katy, consolingly. "Does Dr. Hope tell you anything about the place?" she added, turning over the letter which her father had handed her.

"Oh, he says the scenery is fine, and the mean rain-fall is this, and the mean precipitation that, and that boarding-places can be had. That is pretty much all. So far as climate goes, it is the right place, but I presume the accommodations are poor enough. The children must go prepared to rough it. The town was only settled ten or eleven years ago; there hasn't been time to make things comfortable," remarked Dr. Carr, with a truly Eastern ignorance of the rapid way in which things march in the far West.

Clover's feelings when the decision was announced to her it would be hard to explain in full. She was both confused and exhilarated by the sudden weight of responsibility laid upon her. To leave everybody and everything she had always been used to, and go away to such a distance alone with Phil, made her gasp with a sense of dismay, while at the same time the idea that for the first time in her life she was trusted with something really important, roused her energies, and made her feel braced and valiant, like a soldier to whom some difficult enterprise is intrusted on the day of battle.

Many consultations followed as to what the travellers should carry with them, by what route they would best go, and how prepare for the journey. A great deal of contradictory advice was offered, as is usually the case when people are starting on a voyage or a long railway ride. One friend wrote to recommend that they should provide themselves with a week's provisions in advance, and enclosed a list of crackers, jam, potted meats, tea, fruit, and hardware, which would have made a heavy load for a donkey or mule to carry. How were poor Clover and Phil to transport such a weight of things? Another advised against umbrellas and water-proof cloaks,—what was the use of such things where it never rained?—while a second letter, received the same day, assured them that thunder and hail storms were things for which travellers in Colorado must live in a state of continual preparation. "Who shall decide when doctors disagree?" In the end Clover concluded that it was best to follow the leadings of commonsense and rational precaution, do about a quarter of what people advised, and leave the rest undone; and she found that this worked very well.

As they knew so little of the resources of St. Helen's, and there was such a strong impression prevailing in the family as to its being a rough sort of newly-settled place, Clover and Katy judged it wise to pack a large box of stores to go out by freight: oatmeal and arrowroot and beef-extract and Albert biscuits,—things which Philly ought to have, and which in a wild region might be hard to come by. Debby filled all the corners with home-made dainties of various sorts; and Clover, besides a spirit-lamp and a tea-pot, put into her trunks various small decorations,—Japanese fans and pictures, photographs, a vase or two, books and a sofa-pillow,—things which took little room, and which she thought would make their quarters look more comfortable in case they were very bare and unfurnished. People felt sorry for the probable hardships the brother and sister were to undergo; and they had as many little gifts and notes of sympathy and counsel as Katy herself when she was starting for Europe.

But I am anticipating. Before the trunks were packed, Dr. Carr's anxieties about his "Babes in the Wood" were greatly allayed by a visit from Mrs. Hall. She came to tell him that she had heard of a possible "matron" for Clover.

"I am not acquainted with the lady myself," she said; "but my cousin, who writes about her, knows her quite well, and says she is a highly respectable person, and belongs to nice people. Her sister, or some one, married a Phillips of Boston, and I've always heard that that family was one of the best there. She's had some malarial trouble, and is at the West now on account of it, staying with a friend in Omaha; but she wants to spend the summer at St. Helen's. And as I know you have worried a good deal over having Clover and Phil go off by themselves, I thought it might be a comfort to you to hear of this Mrs. Watson."

"You are very good. If she proves to be the right sort of person, it *will* be an immense comfort. Do you know when she wants to start?"

"About the end of May,—just the right time, you see. She could join Clover and Philip as they go through, which will work nicely for them all."

"So it will. Well, this is quite a relief. Please write to your cousin, Mrs. Hall, and make the arrangement. I don't want Mrs. Watson to be burdened with any real care of the children, of course; but if she can arrange to go along with them, and give Clover a word of advice now and then, should she need it, I shall be easier in my mind about them."

Clover was only doubtfully grateful when she heard of this arrangement.

"Papa always will persist in thinking that I am a baby still," she said to Katy, drawing her little figure up to look as tall as possible. "I am twenty-two, I would have him remember. How do we know what this Mrs. Watson is like? She may be the most disagreeable person in the world for all papa can tell."

"I really can't find it in my heart to be sorry that it has happened, papa looks so much relieved by it," Katy rejoined.

But all dissatisfactions and worries and misgivings took wings and flew away when, just ten days before the travellers were to start, a new and delightful change was made in the programme. Ned telegraphed that the ship, instead of coming to New York, was ordered to San Francisco to refit, and he wanted Katy to join him there early in June, prepared to spend the summer; while almost simultaneously came a letter from Mrs. Ashe, who with Amy had been staying a couple of months in New York, to say that hearing of Ned's plan had decided her also to take a trip to California with some friends who had previously asked her to join them. These friends were, it seemed, the Daytons of Albany. Mr. Dayton was a railroad magnate, and had the control of a private car in which the party were to travel; and Mrs. Ashe was authorized to invite Katy, and Clover and Phil also, to go along with them,—the former all the way to California, and the others as far as Denver, where the roads separated.

This was truly delightful. Such an offer was surely worth a few days' delay. The plan seemed to settle itself all in one minute. Mrs. Watson, whom every one now regretted as a complication, was the only difficulty; but a couple of telegrams settled that perplexity, and it was arranged that she should join them on the same train, though in a different car. To have Katy as a fellow-traveller, and Mrs. Ashe and Amy, made a different thing of the long journey, and Clover proceeded with her preparations in jubilant spirits.

CHAPTER V. CAR FORTY-SEVEN.

It is they who stay behind who suffer most from leave-takings. Those who go have the continual change of scenes and impressions to help them to forget; those who remain must bear as best they may the dull heavy sense of loss and separation.

The parting at Burnet was not a cheerful one. Clover was oppressed with the nearness of untried responsibilities; and though she kept up a brave face, she was inwardly homesick. Phil slept badly the night before the start, and looked so wan and thin as he stood on the steamer's deck beside his sisters, waving good-by to the party on the wharf, that a new and sharp thrill of anxiety shot through his father's heart. The boy looked so young and helpless to be sent away ill among strangers, and round-faced little Clover seemed such a fragile support! There was no help for it. The thing was decided on, decided for the best, as they all hoped; but Dr. Carr was not at all happy in his mind as he watched the steamer become a gradually lessening speck in the distance, and he sighed heavily when at last he turned away.

Elsie echoed the sigh. She, too, had noticed Phil's looks and papa's gravity, and her heart felt heavy within her. The house, when they reached it, seemed lonely and empty. Papa went at once to his office, and they heard him lock the door. This was such an unusual proceeding in the middle of the morning that she and Johnnie opened wide eyes of dismay at each other.

"Is papa crying, do you suppose?" whispered John.

"No, I don't think it can be *that*. Papa never does cry; but I'm afraid he's feeling badly," responded Elsie, in the same hushed tone. "Oh, dear, how horrid it is not even to have Clover at home! What *are* we going to do without her and Katy?"

"I don't know I'm sure. You can't think how queer I feel, Elsie,—just as if my heart had slipped out of its place, and was going down, down into my boots. I think it must be the way people feel when they are homesick. I had it once before when I was at Inches Mills, but never since then. How I wish Philly had never gone to skate on that nasty pond!" and John burst into a passion of tears.

"Oh, don't, don't!" cried poor Elsie, for Johnnie's sobs were infectious, and she felt an ominous lump coming into her own throat, "don't behave so, Johnnie. Think if papa came out, and found us crying! Clover particularly said that we must make the house bright for him. I'm going to sow the mignonette seed [desperately]; come and help me. The trowel is on the back porch, and you might get Dorry's jack-knife and cut some little sticks to mark the places."

This expedient was successful. Johnnie, who loved to "whittle" above all things, dried her tears, and ran for her shade hat; and by the time the tiny brown seeds were sprinkled into the brown earth of the borders, both the girls were themselves again. Dr. Carr appeared from his retirement half an hour later. A note had come for him meanwhile, but somehow no one had quite liked to knock at the door and deliver it.

Elsie handed it to him now, with a timid, anxious look, whose import seemed to strike him, for he laughed a little, and pinched her cheek as he read.

"I've been writing to Dr. Hope about the children," he said; "that's all. Don't wait dinner for me, chicks. I'm off for the Corners to see a boy who's had a fall, and I'll get a bite there. Order something good for tea, Elsie; and afterward we'll have a game of cribbage if I'm not called out. We must be as jolly as we can, or Clover will scold us when she comes back."

Meanwhile the three travellers were faring through the first stage of their journey very comfortably. The fresh air and change brightened Phil; he ate a good dinner, and afterward took quite a long nap on a sofa, Clover sitting by to keep him covered and see that he did not get cold. Late in the evening they changed to the express train, and there again, Phil, after being tucked up behind the curtains of his section, went to sleep and passed a satisfactory night, so that he reached Chicago looking so much better than when they left Burnet that his father's heart would have been lightened could he have seen him.

Mrs. Ashe came down to the station to meet them, together with Mr. Dayton,—a kind, friendly man with a tired but particularly pleasant face. All the necessary transfer of baggage, etc., was made easy, and they were carried off at once to the hotel where rooms had been secured. There they were rapturously received by Amy, and introduced to Mrs. Dayton, a sweet, spirited little matron, with a face as kindly as her husband's, but not so worn. Mr. Dayton looked as if for years he had been bearing the whole weight of a railroad on his shoulders, as in one sense it may be said that he had.

"We have been here almost a whole day," said Amy, who had taken possession, as a matter of course, of her old perch on Katy's knee. "Chicago is the biggest place you ever saw, Tanta; but it isn't so pretty as Burnet. And oh! don't you think Car Forty-seven is nice,—the one we are going out West in, you know? And this morning Mr. Dayton took us to see it. It's the cunningest place that ever was. There's one dear little drawer in the wall that Mrs. Dayton says I may have to keep Mabel's things in. I never saw a drawer in a car before. There's a lovely little bedroom too, and such a nice washing-basin, and a kitchen, and all sorts of things. I can hardly wait till I show them to you. Don't you think that travelling is the most delightful thing in the world, Miss Clover?"

"Yes—if only—people—don't get too tired," said Clover, with an anxious glance at Phil, as he lay back in an easy-chair. She did not dare say, "if Phil doesn't get too tired," for she had already discovered that nothing annoyed him so much as being talked about as an invalid, and that he was very apt to revenge himself by doing something imprudent immediately afterward, to disguise from an observant world the fact that he couldn't do it without running a risk. Like most boys, he resented being "fussed over,"—a fact which made the care of him more difficult than it would otherwise have been.

The room which had been taken for Clover and Katy looked out on the lake, which was not far away; and the reach of blue water would have made a pretty view if trains of cars had not continually steamed between it and the hotel, staining the sky and blurring the prospect with their smokes. Katy wondered how it happened that the early settlers who laid out Chicago had not bethought themselves to secure this fine water frontage as an ornament to the future city; but Mr. Dayton explained that in the rapid growth of Western towns, things arranged themselves rather than were arranged for, and that the first pioneers had other things to think about than what a New Englander would call "sightliness,"—and Katy could easily believe this to be true.

Car Forty-seven was on the track when they drove to the station at noon next day. It was the end car of a long express train, which, Mr. Dayton told them, is considered the place of honor, and generally assigned to private cars. It was of an old-fashioned pattern, and did not compare, as they were informed, with the palaces on wheels built nowadays for the use of railroad presidents and directors. But though Katy heard of cars with French beds, plunge baths, open fireplaces, and other incredible luxuries, Car Forty-seven still seemed to her inexperienced eyes and Clover's a marvel of comfort and convenience.

A small kitchen, a store closet, and a sort of baggage-room, fitted with berths for two servants, occupied the end of the car nearest the engine. Then came a dressing-closet, with ample marble basins where hot water as well as cold was always on tap; then a wide state-room, with a bed on either side, and then a large compartment occupying the middle of the car, where by day four nice little dining-tables could be set, with a seat on either side, and by night six sleeping sections made up. The rest of the car was arranged as a sitting-room, glassed all around, and furnished with comfortable seats of various kinds, a writing-desk, two or three tables of different sizes, and various small lockers and receptacles, fitted into the partitions to serve as catch-alls for loose articles of all sorts.

Bunches of lovely roses and baskets of strawberries stood on the tables; and quite a number of the Daytons' friends had come down to see them off, each bringing some sort of good-by gift for the travellers,—flowers, hothouse grapes, early cherries, or home-made cake. They were all so cordial and pleasant and so interested in Phil, that Katy and Clover lost their hearts to each in turn, and forever afterward were ready to stand up for Chicago as the kindest place that ever was seen.

Then amid farewells and good wishes the train moved slowly out of the station, and the inmates of Car Forty-seven proceeded to "go to housekeeping," as Mrs. Dayton expressed it, and to settle themselves and their belongings in these new quarters. Mrs. Ashe and Amy, it was decided, should occupy the state-room, and the other ladies were to dress there when it was convenient. Sections were assigned to everybody,—Clover's opposite Phil's so that she might hear him if he needed anything in the night; and Mr. Dayton called for all the bonnets and hats, and amid much laughter proceeded to pin up each in thick folds of newspaper, and fasten it on a hook not to be taken down till the end of the journey. Mabel's feathered turban took its turn with the rest, at Amy's particular request. Dust was the main thing to be guarded against, and Katy, having been duly forewarned, had gone out in the morning, and bought for herself and Clover soft hats of whity-gray felt and veils of the same color, like those which Mrs. Dayton and Polly had provided for the journey, and which had the advantage of being light as well as unspoilable.

But there was no dust that first morning, as the train ran smoothly across the fertile prairies of Illinois first, and then of Iowa, between fields dazzling with the fresh green of wheat and rye, and waysides studded with such wild-flowers as none of them had ever seen or dreamed of before. Pink spikes and white and vivid blue spikes; masses of brown and orange cups, like low-growing tulips; ranks of beautiful vetches and purple lupines; escholtzias, like immense sweeps of golden sunlight; wild sweet peas; trumpet-shaped blossoms whose name no one knew,—all flung broadcast over the face of the land, and in such stintless quantities that it dazzled the mind to think of as it did the eyes to behold them. The low-lying horizons looked infinitely far off; the sense of space was confusing. Here and there appeared a home-stead, backed with a "break-wind" of thickly-planted trees; but the general impression was of vast, still distance, endless reaches of sky, and uncounted flowers growing for their own pleasure and with no regard for human observation.

In studying Car Forty-seven, Katy was much impressed by the thoroughness of Mrs. Dayton's preparations for the comfort of her party. Everything that could possibly be needed seemed to have been thought of,—pins, cologne, sewing materials, all sorts of softening washes for the skin, to be used on the alkaline plains, sponges to wet and fasten into the crown of hats, other sponges to breathe through, medicines of various kinds, sticking-plaster, witch-hazel and arnica, whisk brooms, piles of magazines and novels, telegraph blanks, stationery. Nothing seemed forgotten. Clover said that it reminded her of the mother of the Swiss Family Robinson and that wonderful bag out of which everything was produced that could be thought of, from a grand piano to a bottle of pickles; and after that "Mrs. Robinson" became Mrs. Dayton's pet name among her fellow-travellers. She adopted it cheerfully; and her "wonderful bag" proving quite as unfailing and trustworthy as that of her prototype, the title seemed justified.

Pretty soon after starting came their first dinner on the car. Such a nice one!—soup, roast chicken and lamb, green peas, new potatoes, stewed tomato; all as hot and as perfectly served as if they had been "on dry land," as Amy phrased it. There was fresh curly lettuce too, with mayonnaise dressing, and a dessert of strawberries and ice-cream,—the latter made and frozen on the car, whose resources seemed inexhaustible. The cook had been attached to Car Forty-seven for some years, and had a celebrity on his own road for the preparation of certain dishes, which no one else could do as well, however many markets and refrigerators and kitchen ranges might be at command. One of these dishes was a peculiar form of cracked wheat, made crisp and savory after some mysterious fashion, and eaten with thick cream. Like most *chefs*, the cook liked to do the things in which he excelled, and finding that it was admired, he gave the party this delicious wheat every morning.

"The car seems paved with bottles of Apollinaris and with lemons," wrote Katy to her father. "There seems no limit to the supply. Just as surely as it grows warm and dusty, and we begin to remember that we are thirsty, a tinkle is heard, and Bayard appears with a tray,—iced lemonade, if you please, made with Apollinaris water with strawberries floating on top! What do you think of that at thirty miles an hour? Bayard is the colored butler. The cook is named Roland. We have a fine flavor of peers and paladins among us, you perceive.

"The first day out was cool and delicious, and we had no dust. At six o'clock we stopped at a junction, and our car was detached and run off on a siding. This was because Mr. Dayton had business in the place, and we were to wait and be taken on by the next express train soon after midnight. At first they ran us down to a pretty place by the side of the river, where it was cool, and we could look out on the water and a green bank opposite, and we thought we were going to have such a nice night; but the authorities changed their minds, and presently to our deep disgust a locomotive came puffing down the road, clawed us up, ran us back, and finally left us in the middle of innumerable tracks and switches just where all the freight trains came in and met. All night long they were arriving and going out. Cars loaded with cattle, cars loaded with sheep, with pigs! Such bleatings and mooings and gruntings, I never heard in all my life before. I could think of nothing but that verse in the Psalms, 'Strong bulls of Bashan have beset me round,' and could only hope that the poor animals did not feel half as badly as they sounded.

"Then long before light, as we lay listening to these lamentable roarings and grunts, and quite unable to sleep for heat and noise, came the blessed express, and presently we were away out of all the din, with the fresh air of the prairie blowing in; and in no time at all we were so sound asleep that it seemed but a minute before morning. Phil's slumbers lasted so long that we had to breakfast without him, for Mrs. Dayton would not let us wake him up. You can't think how kind she is, and Mr. Dayton too; and this way of travelling is so easy and delightful that it scarcely seems to tire one at all. Phil has borne the journey wonderfully well so far."

At Omaha, on the evening of the second day, Clover's future "matron" and adviser, Mrs. Watson, was to join them. She had been telegraphed to from Chicago, and had replied, so that they knew she was expecting them. Clover's thoughts were so occupied with curiosity as to what she would turn out to be, that she scarcely realized that she was crossing the Mississippi for the first time, and she gave scant attention to the low bluffs which bound the river, and on which the Indians used to hold their councils in those dim days when there was still an "undiscovered West" set down in geographies and atlases.

As soon as they reached the Omaha side of the river, she and Katy jumped down from the car, and immediately found themselves face to face with an anxious-looking little old lady, with white hair frizzled and banged over a puckered forehead, and a pair of watery blue eyes peering from beneath, evidently in search of somebody. Her hands were quite full of bags and parcels, and a little heap of similar articles lay on the platform near her, of which she seemed afraid to lose sight for a moment.

"Oh, is it Miss Carr?" was her first salutation. "I'm Mrs. Watson. I thought it might be you, from the fact that you got out of that car, and it seems rather different—I am quite relieved to see you. I didn't know but something—My daughter she said to me as I was coming away, 'Now, Mother, don't lose yourself, whatever you do. It seems quite wild to think of you in Canyon this and Canyon that, and the Garden of the Gods! Do get some one to keep an eye on you, or we shall never hear of you again. You'll—' It's quite a comfort that you have got here. I supposed you would, but the uncertainty—Oh, dear! that man is carrying off my trunks. Please run after him and tell him to bring them back!"

"It's all right; he's the porter," explained Mr. Dayton. "Did you get your checks for Denver or St. Helen's?"

"Oh, I haven't any checks yet. I didn't know which it ought to be, so I waited till—Miss Carr and her brother would see to it for me I knew, and I wrote my daughter—My friend, Mrs. Peters,—I've been staying with her, you know,—was sick in bed, and I wouldn't let—Dear me! what has that gentleman gone off for in such a hurry?"

"He has gone to get your checks," said Clover, divided between diversion and dismay at this specimen of her future "matron." "We only stay here a few minutes, I believe. Do you know exactly when the train starts, Mrs. Watson?"

"No, dear, I don't. I never know anything about trains and things like that. Somebody always has to tell me, and put me on the cars. I shall trust to you and your brother to do that now. It's a great comfort to have a gentleman to see to things for you."

A gentleman! Poor Philly!

Mr. Dayton now came back to them. It was lucky that he knew the station and was used to the ways of railroads, for it appeared that Mrs. Watson had made no arrangements whatever for her journey, but had blindly devolved the care of herself and her belongings on her "young friends," as she called Clover and Phil. She had no sleeping section secured and no tickets, and they had to be procured at the last moment and in such a scramble that the last of her parcels was handed on to the platform by a porter, at full run, after the train was in motion. She was not at all flurried by the commotion, though others were, and blandly repeated that she knew from the beginning that all would be right as soon as Miss Carr and her brother arrived.

Mrs. Dayton had sent a courteous invitation to the old lady to come to Car Forty-seven for tea, but Mrs. Watson did not at all like being left alone meantime, and held fast to Clover when the others moved to go.

"I'm used to being a good deal looked after," she explained. "All the family know my ways, and they never do let me be alone much. I'm taken faint sometimes; and the doctor says it's my heart or something that's the cause of it, so my daughter she—You ain't going, my dear, are you?"

"I must look after my brother," said poor Clover; "he's been ill, you know, and this is the time for his medicine."

"Dear me! is he ill?" said Mrs. Watson, in an aggrieved tone. "I wasn't prepared for that. You'll have your hands pretty full with him and me both, won't you?—for though I'm well enough just now, there's no knowing what a day may bring forth, and you're all I have to depend upon. You're sure you must go? It seems as if your sister—Mrs. Worthing, is that the name?—might see to the medicine, and give you a little freedom. Don't let your brother be too exacting, dear. It is the worst thing for a young man. I'll sit here a little while, and then I'll—The conductor will help me, I suppose, or perhaps that gentleman might—I hate to be left by myself."

These were the last words which Clover heard as she escaped. She entered Car Forty-seven with such a rueful and disgusted countenance that everybody burst out laughing.

"What is the matter, Miss Clover?" asked Mr. Dayton. "Has your old lady left something after all?"

"Don't call her *my* old lady! I'm supposed to be her young lady, under her charge," said Clover, trying to smile. But the moment she got Katy to herself, she burst out with,—

"My dear, what *am* I going to do? It's really too dreadful. Instead of some one to help me, which is what papa meant, Mrs. Watson seems to depend on me to take all the care of her; and she says she has fainting fits and disease of the heart! How can I take care of her? Phil needs me all the time, and a great deal more than she does; I don't see how I can."

"You can't, of course. You are here to take care of Phil; and it is out of the question that you should have another person to look after. But I think you must mistake Mrs. Watson, Clovy. I know that Mrs. Hall wrote plainly about Phil's illness, for she showed me the letter."

"Just wait till you hear her talk," cried the exasperated Clover. "You will find that I didn't mistake her at all. Oh, why did Mrs. Hall interfere? It would all seem so easy in comparison—so perfectly easy—if only Philly and I were alone together."

Katy thought that Clover was fretted and disposed to exaggerate; but after Mrs. Watson joined them a little later, she changed her opinion. The old lady was an inveterate talker, and her habit of only half finishing her sentences made it difficult to follow the meanderings of her rambling discourse. It turned largely on her daughter, Mrs. Phillips, her husband, children, house, furniture, habits, tastes, and the Phillips connection generally.

"She's the only one I've got," she informed Mrs. Dayton; "so of course she's all-important to me. Jane Phillips—that's Henry's youngest sister—often says that really of all the women she ever knew Ellen is the most—And there's plenty to do always, of course, with three children and such a large elegant house and company coming all the—It's lucky that there's plenty to do with. Henry's very liberal. He likes to have things nice, so Ellen she—Why, when I was packing up to come away he brought me that *repoussé* fruit-knife there in my bag—Oh, it's in my other bag! Never mind; I'll show it to you some other time—solid silver, you know. Bigelow and Kennard—their things always good, though expensive; and my son-in-law he said, 'You're going to a fruit country, and—' Mrs. Peters doesn't think there is so much fruit, though. All sent on from California, as I wrote,—and I guess Ellen and Henry were surprised to hear it."

Katy held serious counsel with herself that night as to what she should do about this extraordinary "guide, philosopher, and friend" whom the Fates had provided for Clover. She saw that her father, from very over-anxiety, had made a mistake, and complicated Clover's inevitable cares with a most undesirable companion, who would add to rather than relieve them. She could not decide what was best to do; and in fact the time was short for doing anything, for the next evening would bring them to Denver, and poor Clover must be left to face the situation by herself as best she might.

Katy finally concluded to write her father plainly how things stood, and beg him to set Clover's mind quite at rest as to any responsibility for Mrs. Watson, and also to have a talk with that lady herself, and explain matters as clearly as she could. It seemed all that was in her power.

Next day the party woke to a wonderful sense of lightness and exhilaration which no one could account for till the conductor told them that the apparently level plain over which they were speeding was more than four thousand feet above the sea. It seemed impossible to believe it. Hour by hour they climbed; but the climb was imperceptible. Now four thousand six hundred feet of elevation was reported, now four thousand eight hundred, at last above five thousand; and still there seemed about them nothing but a vast expanse of flat levels,—the table-lands of Nebraska. There was little that was beautiful in the landscape, which was principally made up of wide reaches of sand, dotted with cactus and grease-wood and with the droll cone-shaped burrows of the prairie-dogs, who could be seen gravely sitting on the roofs of their houses, or turning sudden somersaults in at the holes on top as the train whizzed by. They passed and repassed long links of a broad shallow river which the maps showed to be the Platte, and which seemed to be made of two-thirds sand to one-third water. Now and again mounted horsemen appeared in the distance whom Mr. Dayton said were "cow-boys;" but no cows were visible, and the rapidly moving figures were neither as picturesque nor as formidable as they had expected them to be.

Flowers were still abundant, and their splendid masses gave the charm of color to the rather arid landscape. Soon after noon dim blue outlines came into view, which grew rapidly bolder and more distinct, and revealed themselves as the Rocky Mountains,—the "backbone of the American Continent," of which we have all heard so much in geographies and the newspapers. It was delightful, in spite of dust and glare, to sit with that sweep of magnificent air rushing into their lungs, and watch the great ranges grow and grow and deepen in hue, till they seemed close at hand. To Katy they were like enchanted land. Somewhere on the other side of them, on the dim Pacific coast, her husband was waiting for her to come, and the wheels seemed to revolve with a regular rhythmic beat to the cadence of the old Scotch song,—

"And will I see his face again;
And will I hear him speak?"

But to Clover the wheels sang something less jubilant, and she studied the mountains on her little travelling-map, and measured their distance from Burnet with a sigh. They were the walls of what seemed to her a sort of prison, as she realized that presently she should be left alone among them, Katy and Polly gone, and these new friends whom she had learned to like so much,—left alone with Phil and, what was worse, with Mrs. Watson! There was a comic side to the latter situation, undoubtedly, but at the moment she could not enjoy it.

Katy carried out her intention. She made a long call on Mrs. Watson in her section, and listened patiently to her bemoanings over the noise of the car which had kept her from sleeping; the "lady in gray over there" who had taken such a long time to dress in the morning that she—Mrs. Watson—could not get into the toilet-room at the precise moment that she wished; the newspaper boy who would not let her "just glance over" the Denver "Republican" unless she bought and paid for it ("and I only wanted to see the Washington news, my dear, and something about a tin wedding in East Dedham. My mother came from there, and I recognized one of the names and—But he took it away quite rudely; and when I complained, the conductor wouldn't attend to what I—"); and the bad piece of beefsteak which had been brought for her breakfast at the eating-station. Katy soothed and comforted to the best of her ability, and then plunged into her subject, explaining Phil's very delicate condition and the necessity for constant watchfulness on the part of Clover, and saying most distinctly and in the plainest of English that Mrs. Watson must not expect Clover to take care of her too. The old lady was not in the least offended; but her replies were so incoherent that Katy was not sure that she understood the matter any better for the explanation.

"Certainly, my dear, certainly. Your brother doesn't appear so very sick; but he must be looked after, of course. Boys always ought to be. I'll remind your sister if she seems to be forgetting anything. I hope I shall keep well myself, so as not to be a worry to her. And we can take little excursions together, I dare say—Girls always like to go, and of course an older person—Oh, no, your brother won't need her so much as you think. He seems pretty strong to me, and—You mustn't worry about them, Mrs. Worthing—We shall all get on very well, I'm sure, provided I don't break down, and I guess I sha'n't, though they say almost every one does in this air. Why, we shall be as high up as the top of Mount Washington."

Katy went back to Forty-seven in despair, to comfort herself with a long confidential chat with Clover in which she exhorted her not to let herself be imposed upon.

"Be good to her, and make her as happy as you can, but don't feel bound to wait on her, and run her errands. I am sure papa would not wish it; and it will half kill you if you attempt it. Phil, till he gets stronger, is all you can manage. You not only have to nurse him, you know, but to keep him happy. It's so bad for him to mope. You want all your time to read with him, and take walks and drives; that is, if there are any carriages at St. Helen's. Don't let Mrs. Watson seize upon you, Clover. I'm awfully afraid that she means to, and I can see that she is a real old woman of the sea. Once she gets on your back you will never be able to throw her off."

"She shall not get on my back," said Clover, straightening her small figure; "but doesn't it seem *unnecessary* that I should have an old woman of the sea to grapple with as well as Phil?"

"Provoking things are apt to seem unnecessary, I fancy. You mustn't let yourself get worried, dear Clovy. The old lady means kindly enough, I think, only she's naturally tiresome, and has become helpless from habit. Be nice to her, but hold your own. Self-preservation is the first law of Nature."

Just at dusk the train reached Denver, and the dreaded moment of parting came. There were kisses and tearful good-byes, but not much time was allowed for either. The last glimpse that Clover had of Katy was as the train moved away, when she put her head far out of the window of Car Forty-seven to kiss her hand once more, and call back, in a tone oracular and solemn enough to suit King Charles the First, his own admonitory word, "Remember!"

CHAPTER VI. ST. HELEN'S.

Never in her life had Clover felt so small and incompetent and so very, very young as when the train with Car Forty-seven attached vanished from sight, and left her on the platform of the Denver station with her two companions. There they stood, Phil on one side tired and drooping, Mrs. Watson on the other blinking anxiously about, both evidently depending on her for guidance and direction. For one moment a sort of pale consternation swept over her. Then the sense of the inevitable and the nobler sense of responsibility came to her aid. She rallied herself; the color returned to her cheeks, and she said bravely to Mrs. Watson,—

"Now, if you and Phil will just sit down on that settee over there and make yourselves comfortable, I will find out about the trains for St. Helen's, and where we had better go for the night."

Mrs. Watson and Phil seated themselves accordingly, and Clover stood for a moment considering what she should do. Outside was a wilderness of tracks up and down which trains were puffing, in obedience, doubtless, to some law understood by themselves, but which looked to the uninitiated like the direst confusion. Inside the station the scene was equally confused. Travellers just arrived and just going away were rushing in and out; porters and baggage-agents with their hands full hurried to and fro. No one seemed at leisure to answer a question or even to listen to one.

Just then she caught sight of a shrewd, yet good-natured face looking at her from the window of the ticket-office; and without hesitation she went up to the enclosure. It was the ticket-agent whose eye she had caught. He was at liberty at the moment, and his answers to her inquiries, though brief, were polite and kind. People generally did soften to Clover. There was such an odd and pretty contrast between her girlish appealing look and her dignified little manner, like a child trying to be stately but only succeeding in being primly sweet.

The next train for St. Helen's left at nine in the morning, it seemed, and the ticket-agent recommended the Sherman House as a hotel where they would be very comfortable for the night.

"The omnibus is just outside," he said encouragingly. "You'll find it a first-class house,—best there is west of Chicago. From the East? Just so. You've not seen our opera-house yet, I suppose. Denver folks are rather proud of it. Biggest in the country except the new one in New York. Hope you'll find time to visit it."

"I should like to," said Clover; "but we are here for only one night. My brother's been ill, and we are going directly on to St. Helen's. I'm very much obliged to you."

Her look of pretty honest gratitude seemed to touch the heart of the ticket-man. He opened the door of his fastness, and came out—actually came out!—and with a long shrill whistle summoned a porter whom he addressed as, "Here, you Pat," and bade, "Take this lady's things, and put them into the 'bus for the Sherman; look sharp now, and see that she's all right." Then to Clover,—

"You'll find it very comfortable at the Sherman, Miss, and I hope you'll have a good night. If you'll come to me in the morning, I'll explain about the baggage transfer."

Clover thanked this obliging being again, and rejoined her party, who were patiently sitting where she had left them.

"Dear me!" said Mrs. Watson as the omnibus rolled off, "I had no idea that Denver was such a large place. Street cars too! Well, I declare!"

"And what nice shops!" said Clover, equally surprised.

Her ideas had been rather vague as to what was to be expected in the close neighborhood of the Rocky Mountains; but she knew that Denver had only existed a few years, and was prepared to find everything looking rough and unfinished.

"Why, they have restaurants here and jewellers' shops!" she cried. "Look, Phil, what a nice grocery! We needn't have packed all those oatmeal biscuits if only we had known. And electric lights! How wonderful! But of course St. Helen's is quite different."

Their amazement increased when they reached the hotel, and were taken in a large dining-room to order dinner from a bill of fare which seemed to include every known luxury, from Oregon salmon and Lake Superior white-fish to frozen sherbets and California peaches and apricots. But wonderment yielded to fatigue, and again as Clover fell asleep she was conscious of a deep depression. What had she undertaken to do? How could she do it?

But a night of sound sleep followed by such a morning of unclouded brilliance as is seldom seen east of Colorado banished these misgivings. Courage rose under the stimulus of such air and sunshine.

"I must just live for each day as it comes," said little Clover to herself, "do my best as things turn up, keep Phil happy, and satisfy Mrs. Watson,—if I can,—and not worry about to-morrows or yesterdays. That is the only safe way, and I won't forget if I can help it."

With these wise resolves she ran down stairs, looking so blithe and bright that Phil cheered at the sight of her, and lost the long morning face he had got up with, while even Mrs. Watson caught the contagion, and became fairly hopeful and content. A little leaven of good-will and good heart in one often avails to lighten the heaviness of many.

The distance between Denver and St. Helen's is less than a hundred miles, but as the railroad has to climb and cross a range of hills between two and three thousand feet high, the journey occupies several hours. As the train gradually rose higher and higher, the travellers began to get wide views, first of the magnificent panorama of mountains which lies to the northwest of Denver, sixty miles away, with Long's Peak in the middle, and after crossing the crest of the "Divide," where a blue little lake rimmed with wild-flowers sparkled in the sun, of the more southern ranges. After a while they found themselves running parallel to a mountain chain of strange and beautiful forms, green almost to the top, and intersected with deep ravines and cliffs which the conductor informed them were "canyons." They seemed quite near at hand, for their bases sank into low rounded hills covered with woods, these melted into undulating table-lands, and those again into a narrow strip of park-like plain across which ran the track. Flowers innumerable grew on this plain, mixed with grass of a tawny brown-green. There were cactuses, red and yellow, scarlet and white gillias, tall spikes of yucca in full bloom, and masses of a superb white poppy with an orange-brown centre, whose blue-green foliage was prickly like that of the thistle. Here and there on the higher uplands appeared strange rock shapes of red and pink and pale yellow, which looked like castles with towers and pinnacles, or like primitive fortifications. Clover thought it all strangely beautiful, but Mrs. Watson found fault with it as "queer."

"It looks unnatural, somehow," she objected; "not a bit like the East. Red never was a favorite color of mine. Ellen had a magenta bonnet once, and it always worried—But Henry liked it, so of course—People can't see things the same way. Now the green hat she had winter before last was—Don't you think those mountains are dreadfully bright and distinct? I don't like such high-colored rocks. Even the green looks red, somehow. I like soft, hazy mountains like Blue Hill and Wachusett. Ellen spent a summer up at Princeton once. It was when little Cynthia had diphtheria—she's named after me, you know, and Henry he thought—But I don't like the staring kind like these; and somehow those buildings, which the conductor says are not buildings but rocks, make my flesh creep."

"They'd be scrumptious places to repel attacks of Indians from," observed Phil; "two or three scouts with breech-loaders up on that scarlet wall there could keep off a hundred Piutes."

"I don't feel that way a bit," Clover was saying to Mrs. Watson. "I like the color, it's so rich; and I think the mountains are perfectly beautiful. If St. Helen's is like this I am going to like it, I know."

St. Helen's, when they reached it, proved to be very much "like this," only more so, as Phil remarked. The little settlement was built on a low plateau facing the mountains, and here the plain narrowed, and the beautiful range, seen through the clear atmosphere, seemed only a mile or two away, though in reality it was eight or ten. To the east the plain widened again into great upland sweeps like the Kentish Downs, with here and there a belt of black woodland, and here and there a line of low bluffs. Viewed from a height, with the cloud-shadows sweeping across it, it had the extent and splendor of the sea, and looked very much like it.

The town, seen from below, seemed a larger place than Clover had expected, and again she felt the creeping, nervous feeling come over her. But before the train had fairly stopped, a brisk, active little man jumped on board, and walking into the car, began to look about him with keen, observant eyes. After one sweeping glance, he came straight to where Clover was collecting her bags and parcels, held out his hand, and said in a pleasant voice, "I think this must be Miss Carr."

"I am Dr. Hope," he went on; "your father telegraphed when you were to leave Chicago, and I have come down to two or three trains in the hope of meeting you."

"Have you, indeed?" said Clover, with a rush of relief. "How very kind of you! And so papa telegraphed! I never thought of that. Phil, here is Dr. Hope, papa's friend; Dr. Hope, Mrs. Watson."

"This is really a very agreeable attention,—your coming to meet us," said Mrs. Watson; "a very agreeable attention indeed. Well, I shall write Ellen—that's my daughter, Mrs. Phillips, you know—that before we had got out of the cars, a gentleman—And though I've always been in the habit of going about a good deal, it's always been in the East, of course, and things are—What are we going to do first, Dr. Hope? Miss Carr has a great deal of energy for a girl, but naturally—I suppose there's an hotel at St. Helen's. Ellen is rather particular where I stay. 'At your age, Mother, you must be made comfortable, whatever it costs,' she says; and so I—An only daughter, you know—but you'll attend to all those things for us now, Doctor."

"There's quite a good hotel," said Dr. Hope, his eyes twinkling a little; "I'll show it to you as we drive up. You'll find it very comfortable if you prefer to go there. But for these young people I've taken rooms at a boarding-house, a quieter and less expensive place. I thought it was what your father would prefer," he added in a lower tone to Clover.

"I am sure he would," she replied; but Mrs. Watson broke in,—

"Oh, I shall go wherever Miss Carr goes. She's under my care, you know—Though at the same time I must say that in the long run I have generally found that the most expensive places turn out the cheapest.

As Ellen often says, get the best and—What do they charge at this hotel that you speak of, Dr. Hope?"

"The Shoshone House? About twenty-five dollars a week, I think, if you make a permanent arrangement."

"That *is* a good deal," remarked Mrs. Watson, meditatively, while Clover hastened to say,—

"It is a great deal more than Phil and I can spend, Dr. Hope; I am glad you have chosen the other place for us."

"I suppose it *is* better," admitted Mm Watson; but when they gained the top of the hill, and a picturesque, many-gabled, many-balconied structure was pointed out as the Shoshone, her regrets returned, and she began again to murmur that very often the most expensive places turned out the cheapest in the end, and that it stood to reason that they must be the best. Dr. Hope rather encouraged this view, and proposed that she should stop and look at some rooms; but no, she could not desert her young charges and would go on, though at the same time she must say that her opinion as an older person who had seen more of the world was—She was used to being consulted. Why, Addy Phillips wouldn't order that crushed strawberry bengaline of hers till Mrs. Watson saw the sample, and—But girls had their own ideas, and were bound to carry them out, Ellen always said so, and for her part she knew her duty and meant to do it!

Dr. Hope flashed one rapid, comical look at Clover. Western life sharpens the wits, if it does nothing else, and Westerners as a general thing become pretty good judges of character. It had not taken ten minutes for the keen-witted little doctor to fathom the peculiarities of Clover's "chaperone," and he would most willingly have planted her in the congenial soil of the Shoshone House, which would have provided a wider field for her restlessness and self-occupation, and many more people to listen to her narratives and sympathize with her complaints. But it was no use. She was resolved to abide by the fortunes of her "young friends."

While this discussion was proceeding, the carriage had been rolling down a wide street running along the edge of the plateau, opposite the mountain range. Pretty houses stood on either side in green, shaded door-yards, with roses and vine-hung piazzas and nicely-cut grass.

"Why, it looks like a New England town," said Clover, amazed; "I thought there were no trees here."

"Yes, I know," said Dr. Hope smiling. "You came, like most Eastern people, prepared to find us sitting in the middle of a sandy waste, on cactus pincushions, picking our teeth with bowie-knives, and with no neighbors but Indians and grizzly bears. Well; sixteen years ago we could have filled the bill pretty well. Then there was not a single house in St. Helen's,—not even a tent, and not one of the trees that you see here had been planted. Now we have three railroads meeting at our depot, a population of nearly seven thousand, electric lights, telephones, a good opera-house, a system of works which brings first-rate spring water into the town from six miles away,—in short, pretty much all the modern conveniences."

"But what *has* made the place grow so fast?" asked Clover.

"If I may be allowed a professional pun, it is built up on coughings. It is a town for invalids. Half the people here came out for the benefit of their lungs."

"Isn't that rather depressing?"

"It would be more so if most of them did not look so well that no one would suspect them of being ill. Here we are."

Clover looked out eagerly. There was nothing picturesque about the house at whose gate the carriage had stopped. It was a large shabby structure, with a piazza above as well as below, and on these piazzas various people were sitting who looked unmistakably ill. The front of the house, however, commanded the fine mountain view.

"You see," explained Dr. Hope, drawing Clover aside, "boarding-places that are both comfortable and reasonable are rather scarce at St. Helen's. I know all about the table here and the drainage; and the view is desirable, and Mrs. Marsh, who keeps the house, is one of the best women we have. She's from down your way too,—Barnstable, Mass., I think."

Clover privately wondered how Barnstable, Mass., could be classed as "down" the same way with Burnet, not having learned as yet that to the soaring Western mind that insignificant fraction of the whole country known as "the East," means anywhere from Maine to Michigan, and that such trivial geographical differences as exist between the different sections seem scarcely worth consideration when compared with the vast spaces which lie beyond toward the setting sun. But perhaps Dr. Hope was only trying to tease her, for he twinkled amusedly at her puzzled face as he went on,—

"I think you can make yourselves comfortable here. It was the best I could do. But your old lady would be much better suited at the Shoshone, and I wish she'd go there."

Clover could not help laughing. "I wish that people wouldn't persist in calling Mrs. Watson my old lady," she thought.

Mrs. Marsh, a pleasant-looking person, came to meet them as they entered. She showed Clover and Phil their rooms, which had been secured for them, and then carried Mrs. Watson off to look at another which she could have if she liked.

The rooms were on the third floor. A big front one for Phil, with a sunny south window and two others looking towards the west and the mountains, and, opening from it, a smaller room for Clover.

"Your brother ought to live in fresh air both in doors and out," said Dr. Hope; "and I thought this large room would answer as a sort of sitting place for both of you."

"It's ever so nice; and we are both more obliged to you than we can say," replied Clover, holding out her hand as the doctor rose to go. He gave a pleased little laugh as he shook it.

"That's all right," he said. "I owe your father's children any good turn in my power, for he was a good friend to me when I was a poor boy just beginning, and needed friends. That's my house with the red roof, Miss Clover. You see how near it is; and please remember that besides the care of this boy here, I'm in charge of you too, and have the inside track of the rest of the friends you are going to make in Colorado. I expect to be called on whenever you want anything, or feel lonesome, or are at a loss in any way. My wife is coming to see you as soon as you have had your dinner and got settled a little. She sent those to you," indicating a vase on the table, filled with flowers. They were of a sort which Clover had never seen before,—deep cup-shaped blossoms of beautiful pale purple and white.

"Oh, what are they?" she called after the doctor.

"Anemones," he answered, and was gone.

"What a dear, nice, kind man!" cried Clover. "Isn't it delightful to have a friend right off who knows papa, and does things for us because we are papa's children? You like him, don't you, Phil; and don't you like your room?"

"Yes; only it doesn't seem fair that I should have the largest."

"Oh, yes; it is perfectly fair. I never shall want to be in mine except when I am dressing or asleep. I shall sit here with you all the time; and isn't it lovely that we have those enchanting mountains just before our eyes? I never saw anything in my life that I liked so much as I do that one."

It was Cheyenne Mountain at which she pointed, the last of the chain, and set a little apart, as it were, from the others. There is as much difference between mountains as between people, as mountain-lovers know, and like people they present characters and individualities of their own. The noble lines of Mount Cheyenne are full of a strange dignity; but it is dignity mixed with an indefinable charm. The canyons nestle about its base, as children at a parent's knee; its cedar forests clothe it like drapery; it lifts its head to the dawn and the sunset; and the sun seems to love it best of all, and lies longer on it than on the other peaks.

Clover did not analyze her impressions, but she fell in love with it at first sight, and loved it better and better all the time that she stayed at St. Helen's. "Dr. Hope and Mount Cheyenne were our first friends in the place," she used to say in after-days.

"How nice it is to be by ourselves!" said Phil, as he lay comfortably on the sofa watching Clover unpack. "I get so tired of being all the time with people. Dear me! the room looks quite homelike already."

Clover had spread a pretty towel over the bare table, laid some books and her writing-case upon it, and was now pinning up a photograph over the mantel-piece.

"We'll make it nice by-and-by," she said cheerfully; "and now that I've tidied up a little, I think I'll go and see what has become of Mrs. Watson. She'll think I have quite forgotten her. You'll lie quiet and rest till dinner, won't you?"

"Yes," said Phil, who looked very sleepy; "I'm all right for an hour to come. Don't hurry back if the ancient female wants you."

Clover spread a shawl over him before she went and shut one of the windows.
"We won't have you catching cold the very first morning," she said. "That would be a bad story to send back to papa."

She found Mrs. Watson in very low spirits about her room.

"It's not that it's small," she said. "I don't need a very big room; but I don't like being poked away at the back so. I've always had a front room all my life. And at Ellen's in the summer, I have a corner chamber, and see the sea and everything—It's an elegant room, solid black walnut with marble tops, and—Lighthouses too; I have three of them in view, and they are really company for me on dark nights. I don't want to be fussy, but really to look out on nothing but a side yard with some trees—and they aren't elms or anything that I'm used to, but a new kind. There's a thing out there, too, that I never saw before, which looks like one of the giant ants' nests of Africa in 'Morse's Geography' that I used to read about when I was—It makes me really nervous."

Clover went to the window to look at the mysterious object. It was a cone-shaped thing of white unburned clay, whose use she could not guess. She found later that it was a receptacle for ashes.

"I suppose *your* rooms are front ones?" went on Mrs. Watson, querulously.

"Mine isn't. It's quite a little one at the side. I think it must be just under this. Phil's is in front, and is a nice large one with a view of the mountains. I wish there were one just like it for you. The doctor says that it's very important for him to have a great deal of air in his room."

"Doctors always say that; and of course Dr. Hope, being a friend of yours and all—It's quite natural he should give you the preference. Though the Phillips's are accustomed—but there, it's no use; only, as I tell Ellen, Boston is the place for me, where my family is known, and people realize what I'm used to."

"I'm so sorry," Clover said again. "Perhaps somebody will go away, and Mrs. Marsh have a front room for you before long."

"She did say that she might. I suppose she thinks some of her boarders will be dying off. In fact, there is one—that tall man in gray in the reclining-chair—who didn't seem to me likely to last long. Well, we will hope for the best. I'm not one who likes to make difficulties."

This prospect, together with dinner, which was presently announced, raised Mrs. Watson's spirits a little, and Clover left her in the parlor, exchanging experiences and discussing symptoms with some ladies who had sat opposite them at table. Mrs. Hope came for a call; a pretty little woman, as friendly and kind as her husband. Then Clover and Phil went out for a stroll about the town. Their wonder increased at every turn; that a place so well equipped and complete in its appointments could have been created out of nothing in fifteen years was a marvel!

After two or three turns they found themselves among shops, whose plate-glass windows revealed all manner of wares,—confectionery, new books, pretty glass and china, bonnets of the latest fashion. One or two large pharmacies glittered with jars—purple and otherwise—enough to tempt any number of Rosamonds. Handsome carriages drawn by fine horses rolled past them, with well-dressed people inside. In short, St. Helen's was exactly like a thriving Eastern town of double its size, with the difference that here a great many more people seemed to ride than to drive. Some one cantered past every moment,—a lady alone, two or three girls together, or a party of rough-looking men in long boots, or a single ranchman sitting loose in his stirrups, and swinging a stock whip.

Clover and Phil were standing on a corner, looking at some "Rocky Mountain Curiosities" displayed for sale,—minerals, Pueblo pottery, stuffed animals, and Indian blankets; and Phil had just commented on the beauty of a black horse which was tied to a post close by, when its rider emerged from a shop, and prepared to mount.

He was a rather good-looking young fellow, sunburnt and not very tall, but with a lithe active figure, red-brown eyes and a long mustache of tawny chestnut. He wore spurs and a broad-brimmed sombrero, and carried in his hand a whip which seemed two-thirds lash. As he put his foot into the stirrup, he turned for another look at Clover, whom he had rather stared at while passing, and then changing his intention, took it out again, and came toward them.

"I beg your pardon," he said; "but aren't you—isn't it—Clover Carr?"

"Yes," said Clover, wondering, but still without the least notion as to whom the stranger might be.

"You've forgotten me?" went on the young man, with a smile which made his face very bright. "That's rather hard too; for I knew you at once. I suppose I'm a good deal changed, though, and perhaps I shouldn't have made you out except for your eyes; they're just the same. Why, Clover, I'm your cousin, Clarence Page!"

"Clarence Page!" cried Clover, joyfully; "not really! Why, Clarence, I never should have known you in the world, and I can't think how you came to know me. I was only fourteen when I saw you last, and you were quite a little boy. What good luck that we should meet, and on our first day too! Some one wrote that you were in Colorado, but I had no idea that you lived at St. Helen's."

"I don't; not much. I'm living on a ranch out that way," jerking his elbow toward the northwest, "but I ride in often to get the mail. Have you just come? You said the first day."

"Yes; we only got here this morning. And this is my brother Phil. Don't you recollect how I used to tell you about him at Ashburn?"

"I should think you did," shaking hands cordially; "she used to talk about you all the time, so that I felt intimately acquainted with all the family. Well, I call this first rate luck. It's two years since I saw any one from home."

"Home?"

"Well; the East, you know. It all seems like home when you're out here. And I mean any one that I know, of course. People from the East come out all the while. They are as thick as bumblebees at St. Helen's, but they don't amount to much unless you know them. Have you seen anything of mother and Lilly since they got back from Europe, Clover?"

"No, indeed. I haven't seen them since we left Hillsover. Katy has, though. She met them in Nice when she was there, and they sent her a wedding present. You knew that she was married, didn't you?"

"Yes, I got her cards. Pa sent them. He writes oftener than the others do; and he came out once and stayed a month on the ranch with me. That was while mother was in Europe. Where are you stopping? The Shoshone, I suppose."

"No, at a quieter place,—Mrs. Marsh's, on the same street."

"Oh, I know Mother Marsh. I went there when I first came out, and had caught the mountain fever, and she was ever so kind to me. I'm glad you are there. She's a nice woman."

"How far away is your ranch?"

"About sixteen miles. Oh, I say, Clover, you and Phil must come out and stay with us sometime this summer. We'll have a round-up for you if you will."

"What is a 'round-up' and who is 'us'?" said Clover, smiling.

"Well, a round-up is a kind of general muster of the stock. All the animals are driven in and counted, and the young ones branded. It's pretty exciting sometimes, I can tell you, for the cattle get wild, and it's all we can do to manage them. You should see some of our boys ride; it's splendid, and there's one half-breed that's the best hand with the lasso I ever saw. Phil will like it, I know. And 'us' is me and my partner."

"Have you a partner?"

"Yes, two, in fact; but one of them lives in New Mexico just now, so he does not count. That's Bert Talcott. He's a New York fellow. The other's English, a Devonshire man. Geoff Templestowe is his name."

"Is he nice?"

"You can just bet your pile that he is," said Clarence, who seemed to have assimilated Western slang with the rest of the West. "Wait till I bring him to see you. We'll come in on purpose some day soon. Well, I must be going. Good-by, Clover; good-by, Phil. It's awfully jolly to have you here."

"I never should have guessed who it was," remarked Clover, as they watched the active figure canter down the street and turn for a last flourish of the hat. "He was the roughest, scrubbiest boy when we last met. What a fine-looking fellow he has grown to be, and how well he rides!"

"No wonder; a fellow who can have a horse whenever he has a mind to," said Phil, enviously. "Life on a ranch must be great fun, I think."

"Yes; in one way, but pretty rough and lonely too, sometimes. It will be nice to go out and see Clarence's, if we can get some lady to go with us, won't it?"

"Well, just don't let it be Mrs. Watson, whoever else it is. She would spoil it all if she went."

"Now, Philly, don't. We're supposed to be leaning on her for support."

"Oh, come now, lean on that old thing! Why she couldn't support a postage stamp standing edgewise, as the man says in the play. Do you suppose I don't know how you have to look out for her and do everything? She's not a bit of use."

"Yes; but you and I have got to be polite to her, Philly. We mustn't forget that."

"Oh, I'll be polite enough, if she will just leave us alone," retorted Phil.

Promising!

CHAPTER VII. MAKING ACQUAINTANCE.

Phil was better than his word. He was never uncivil to Mrs. Watson, and his distant manners, which really signified distaste, were set down by that lady to boyish shyness.

"They often are like that when they are young," she told Clover; "but they get bravely over it after a while. He'll outgrow it, dear, and you mustn't let it worry you a bit."

Meanwhile, Mrs. Watson's own flow of conversation was so ample that there was never any danger of awkward silences when she was present, which was a comfort. She had taken Clover into high favor now, and Clover deserved it,—for though she protected herself against encroachments, and resolutely kept the greater part of her time free for Phil, she was always considerate, and sweet in manner to the older lady, and she found spare half-hours every day in which to sit and go out with her, so that she should not feel neglected. Mrs. Watson grew quite fond of her "young friend," though she stood a little in awe of her too, and was disposed to be jealous if any one showed more attention to Clover than to herself.

An early outburst of this feeling came on the third day after their arrival, when Mrs. Hope asked Phil and Clover to dinner, and did *not* ask Mrs. Watson. She had discussed the point with her husband, but the doctor "jumped on" the idea forcibly, and protested that if that old thing was to come too, he would "have a consultation in Pueblo, and be off in the five thirty train, sure as fate."

"It's not that I care," Mrs. Watson assured Clover plaintively. "I've had so much done for me all my life that of course—But I *do* like to be properly treated. It isn't as if I were just anybody. I don't suppose Mrs. Hope knows much about Boston society anyway, but still—And I should think a girl from South Framingham (didn't you say she was from South Framingham?) would at least know who the Abraham Peabodys are, and they're Henry's—But I don't imagine she was much of anybody before she was married; and out here it's all hail fellow and well met, they say, though in that case I don't see—Well, well, it's no matter, only it seems queer to me; and I think you'd better drop a hint about it when you're there, and just explain that my daughter lives next door to the Lieutenant-Governor when she is in the country, and opposite the Assistant-Bishop in town, and has one of the Harvard Overseers for a near neighbor, and is distantly related to the Reveres! You'd think even a South Framingham girl must know about the lantern and the Old South, and how much they've always been respected at home."

Clover pacified her as well as she could, by assurances that it was not a dinner-party, and they were only asked to meet one girl whom Mrs. Hope wanted her to know.

"If it were a large affair, I am sure you would have been asked too," she said, and so left her "old woman of the sea" partly consoled.

It was the most lovely evening possible, as Clover and Phil walked down the street toward Dr. Hope's. Soft shadows lay over the lower spurs of the ranges. The canyons looked black and deep, but the peaks still glittered in rosy light. The mesa was in shadow, but the nearer plain lay in full sunshine, hot and yellow, and the west wind was full of mountain fragrance.

Phil gave little skips as he went along. Already he seemed like a different boy. All the droop and languor had gone, and given place to an exhilaration which half frightened Clover, who had constant trouble in keeping him from doing things which she knew to be imprudent. Dr. Hope had warned her that invalids often harmed themselves by over-exertion under the first stimulus of the high air.

"Why, how queer!" she exclaimed, stopping suddenly before one of the pretty places just above Mrs. Marsh's boarding-house.

"What?"

"Don't you see? That yard! When we came by here yesterday it was all green grass and rose-bushes, and girls were playing croquet; and now, look, it's a pond!"

Sure enough! There were the rose-bushes still, and the croquet arches; but they were standing, so to speak, up to their knees in pools of water, which seemed several inches deep, and covered the whole place, with the exception of the flagged walks which ran from the gates to the front and side doors of the house. Clover noticed now, for the first time, that these walks were several inches higher than the grass-beds on either side. She wondered if they were made so on purpose, and resolved to notice if the next place had the same arrangement.

But as they reached the next place and the next, lo! the phenomenon was repeated and Dr. Hope's lawn too was in the same condition,— everything was overlaid with water. They began to suspect what it must mean, and Mrs. Hope confirmed the suspicion. It was irrigation day in Mountain Avenue, it seemed. Every street in the town had its appointed period when the invaluable water, brought from a long distance for the purpose, was "laid on" and kept at a certain depth for a prescribed number of hours.

"We owe our grass and shrubs and flower-beds entirely to this arrangement," Mrs. Hope told them. "Nothing could live through our dry summers if we did not have the irrigating system."

"Are the summers so dry?" asked Clover. "It seems to me that we have had a thunder-storm almost every day since we came."

"We do have a good many thunderstorms," Mrs. Hope admitted; "but we can't depend on them for the gardens."

"And did you ever hear such magnificent thunder?" asked Dr. Hope. "Colorado thunder beats the world."

"Wait till you see our magnificent Colorado hail," put in Mrs. Hope, wickedly. "That beats the world, too. It cuts our flowers to pieces, and sometimes kills the sheep on the plains. We are very proud of it. The doctor thinks everything in Colorado perfection."

"I have always pitied places which had to be irrigated," remarked Clover, with her eyes fixed on the little twin-lakes which yesterday were lawns. "But I begin to think I was mistaken. It's very superior, of course, to have rains; but then at the East we sometimes don't have rain when we want it, and the grass gets dreadfully yellow. Don't you remember, Phil, how hard Katy and I worked last summer to keep the geraniums and fuschias alive in that long drought? Now, if we had had water like this to come once a week, and make a nice deep pond for us, how different it would have been!"

"Oh, you must come out West for real comfort," said Dr. Hope. "The East is a dreadfully one-horse little place, anyhow."

"But you don't mean New York and Boston when you say 'one-horse little place,' surely?"

"Don't I?" said the undaunted doctor. "Wait till you see more of us out here."

"Here's Poppy, at last," cried Mrs. Hope, as a girl came hurriedly up the walk. "You're late, dear."

"Poppy," whose real name was Marian Chase, was the girl who had been asked to meet them. She was a tall, rosy creature, to whom Clover took an instant fancy, and seemed in perfect health; yet she told them that when she came out to Colorado three years before, she had travelled on a mattress, with a doctor and a trained nurse in attendance.

"Your brother will be as strong, or stronger than I at the end of a year," she said; "or if he doesn't get well as fast as he ought, you must take him up to the Ute Valley. That's where I made my first gain."

"Where is the valley?"

"Thirty miles away to the northwest,—up there among the mountains. It is a great deal higher than this, and such a lovely peaceful place. I hope you'll go there."

"We shall, of course, if Phil needs it; but I like St. Helen's so much that I would rather stay here if we can."

Dinner was now announced, and Mrs. Hope led the way into a pretty room hung with engravings and old plates after the modern fashion, where a white-spread table stood decorated with wild-flowers, candle-sticks with little red-shaded tapers, and a pyramid of plums and apricots. There was the usual succession of soup and fish and roast and salad which one looks for at a dinner on the sea-level, winding up with ice-cream of a highly civilized description, but Clover could scarcely eat for wondering how all these things had come there so soon, so very soon. It seemed like magic,—one minute the solemn peaks and passes, the prairie-dogs and the thorny plain, the next all these portières and rugs and etchings and down pillows and pretty devices in glass and china, as if some enchanter's wand had tapped the wilderness, and hey, presto! modern civilization had sprung up like Jonah's gourd all in a minute, or like the palace which Aladdin summoned into being in a single night for the occupation of the Princess of China, by the rubbing of his wonderful lamp. And then, just as the fruit-plates were put on the table, came a call, and the doctor was out in the hall, "holloing" and conducting with some distant patient one of those mysterious telephonic conversations which to those who overhear seem all replies and no questions. It was most remarkable, and quite unlike her preconceived ideas of what was likely to take place at the base of the Rocky Mountains.

A pleasant evening followed. "Poppy" played delightfully on the piano; later came a rubber of whist. It was like home.

"Before these children go, let us settle about the drive," said Dr. Hope to his wife.

"Oh, yes! Miss Carr—"

"Oh, please, won't you call me Clover?"

"Indeed I will,—Clover, then,—we want to take you for a good long drive to-morrow, and show you something; but the trouble is, the doctor and I are at variance as to what the something shall be. I want you to see Odin's Garden; and the doctor insists that you ought to go to the Cheyenne canyons first, because those are his favorites. Now, which shall it be? We will leave it to you."

"But how can I choose? I don't know either of them. What a queer name,—Odin's Garden!"

"I'll tell you how to settle it," cried Marian Chase, whose nickname it seemed had been given her because when she first came to St. Helen's she wore a bunch of poppies in her hat. "Take them to Cheyenne to-morrow; and the next day—or Thursday—let me get up a picnic for Odin's Garden; just a few of our special cronies,—the Allans and the Blanchards and Mary Pelham and Will Amory. Will you, dear Mrs. Hope, and be our matron? That would be lovely."

Mrs. Hope consented, and Clover walked home as if treading on air. Was this the St. Helen's to which she had looked forward with so much dread,—this gay, delightful place, where such pleasant things happened, and people were so kind? How she wished that she could get at Katy and papa for five minutes—on a wishing carpet or something—to tell them how different everything was from what she had expected.

One thing only marred her anticipations for the morrow, which was the fear that Mrs. Watson might be hurt, and make a scene. Happily, Mrs. Hope's thoughts took the same direction; and by some occult process of influence, the use of which good wives understand, she prevailed on her refractory doctor to allow the old lady to be asked to join the party.

So early next morning came a very polite note; and it was proposed that Phil should ride the doctor's horse, and act as escort to Miss Chase, who was to go on horseback likewise. No proposal could have been more agreeable to Phil, who adored horses, and seldom had the chance to mount one; so every one was pleased, and Mrs. Watson preened her ancestral feathers with great satisfaction.

"You see, dear, how well it was to give that little hint about the Reveres and the Abraham Peabodys," she said. Clover felt dreadfully dishonest; but she dared not confess that she had forgotten all about the hint, still less that she had never meant to give one. "The better part of valor is discretion," she remembered; so she held her peace, though her cheeks glowed guiltily.

At three o'clock they set forth in a light roomy carriage,—not exactly a carryall, but of the carryall family,—with a pair of fast horses, Miss Chase and Phil cantering happily alongside, or before or behind, just as it happened. The sun was very hot; but there was a delicious breeze, and the dryness and elasticity of the air made the heat easy to bear.

The way lay across and down the southern slope of the plateau on which the town was built. Then they came to splendid fields of grain and "afalfa,"—a cereal quite new to them, with broad, very green leaves. The roadside was gay with flowers,—gillias and mountain balm; high pink and purple spikes, like foxgloves, which they were told were pentstemons; painters' brush, whose green tips seemed dipped in liquid vermilion, and masses of the splendid wild poppies. They crossed a foaming little river; and a sharp turn brought them into a narrower and wilder road, which ran straight toward the mountain side. This was overhung by trees, whose shade was grateful after the hot sun.

Narrower and narrower grew the road, more and more sharp the turns. They were at the entrance of a deep defile, up which the road wound and wound, following the links of the river, which they crossed and recrossed repeatedly. Such a wonderful and perfect little river, with water clear as air and cold as ice, flowing over a bed of smooth granite, here slipping noiselessly down long slopes of rock like thin films of glass, there deepening into pools of translucent blue-green like aquamarine or beryl, again plunging down in mimic waterfalls, a sheet of iridescent foam. The sound of its rush and its ripple was like a laugh. Never was such happy water, Clover thought, as it curved and bent and swayed this way and that on its downward course as if moved by some merry, capricious instinct, like a child dancing as it goes. Regiments or great ferns grew along its banks, and immense thickets of wild roses of all shades, from deep Jacqueminot red to pale blush-white. Here and there rose a lonely spike of yucca, and in the little ravines to right and left grew in the crevices of the rocks clumps of superb straw-colored columbines four feet high.

Looking up, Clover saw above the tree-tops strange pinnacles and spires and obelisks which seemed air-hung, of purple-red and orange-tawny and pale pinkish gray and terra cotta, in which the sunshine and the cloud-shadows broke in a multiplicity of wonderful half-tints. Above them was the dazzling blue of the Colorado sky. She drew a long, long breath.

"So this is a canyon," she said. "How glad I am that I have lived to see one."

"Yes, this is a canyon," Dr. Hope replied. "Some of us think it *the* canyon; but there are dozens of others, and no two of them are alike. I'm glad you are pleased with this, for it's my favorite. I wish your father could see it."

Clover hardly understood what he said she was so fascinated and absorbed. She looked up at the bright pinnacles, down at the flowers and the sheen of the river-pools and the mad rush of its cascades, and felt as though she were in a dream. Through the dream she caught half-comprehended fragments of conversation from the seat behind. Mrs. Watson was giving her impressions of the scenery.

"It's pretty, I suppose," she remarked; "but it's so very queer, and I'm not used to queer things. And this road is frightfully narrow. If a load of hay or a big Concord coach should come along, I can't think what we should do. I see that Dr. Hope drives carefully, but yet—You don't think we shall meet anything of the kind to-day, do you, Doctor?"

"Not a Concord coach, and certainly not a hay-wagon, for they don't make hay up here in the mountains."

"Well, that is a relief. I didn't know. Ellen she always says, 'Mother, you're a real fidget;' but when one grows old, and has valves in the heart as I have, you never—We might meet one of those big pedler's wagons, though, and they frighten horses worse than anything. Oh, what's that coming now? Let us get out, Dr. Hope; pray, let us all get out."

"Sit still, ma'am," said the doctor, sternly, for Mrs. Watson was wildly fumbling at the fastening of the door. "Mary, put your arm round Mrs. Watson, and hold her tight. There'll be a real accident, sure as fate, if you don't." Then in a gentler tone, "It's only a buggy, ma'am; there's plenty of room. There's no possible risk of a pedler's wagon. What on earth should a pedler be doing up here on the side of Cheyenne! Prairie-dogs don't use pomatum or tin-ware."

"Oh, I didn't know," repeated poor Mrs. Watson, nervously. She watched the buggy timorously till it was safely past; then her spirits revived.

"Well," she cried, "we're safe this time; but I call it tempting Providence to drive so fast on such a rough road. If all canyons are as wild as this, I sha'n't ever venture to go into another."

"Bless me! this is one of our mildest specimens," said Dr. Hope, who seemed to have a perverse desire to give Mrs. Watson a distaste for canyons. "This is a smooth one; but some canyons are really rough. Do you remember, Mary, the day we got stuck up at the top of the Westmoreland, and had to unhitch the horses, and how I stood in the middle of the creek and yanked the carriage round while you held them? That was the day we heard the mountain lion, and there were fresh bear-tracks all over the mud, you remember."

"Good gracious!" cried Mrs. Watson, quite pale; "what an awful place! Bears and lions! What on earth did you go there for?"

"Oh, purely for pleasure," replied the doctor, lightly. "We don't mind such little matters out West. We try to accustom ourselves to wild beasts, and make friends of them."

"John, don't talk such nonsense," cried his wife, quite angrily. "Mrs. Watson, you mustn't believe a word the doctor says. I've lived in Colorado nine years; and I've never once seen a mountain lion, or a bear either, except the stuffed ones in the shops. Don't let the doctor frighten you."

But Dr. Hope's wicked work was done. Mrs. Watson, quite unconvinced by these well-meant assurances, sat pale and awe-struck, repeating under her breath,—

"Dreadful! What *will* Ellen say? Bears and lions! Oh, dear me!"

"Look, look!" cried Clover, who had not listened to a word of this conversation; "did you ever see anything so lovely?" She referred to what she was looking at,—a small point of pale straw-colored rock some hundreds of feet in height, which a turn in the road had just revealed, soaring above the tops of the trees.

"I don't see that it's lovely at all," said Mrs. Watson, testily. "It's unnatural, if that's what you mean. Rocks ought not to be that color.

They never are at the East. It looks to me exactly like an enormous unripe banana standing on end."

This simile nearly "finished" the party. "It's big enough to disagree with all the Sunday-schools in creation at once," remarked the doctor, between his shouts, while even Clover shook with laughter. Mrs. Watson felt that she had made a hit, and grew complacent again.

"See what your brother picked for me," cried Poppy, riding alongside, and exhibiting a great sheaf of columbine tied to the pommel of her saddle. "And how do you like North Cheyenne? Isn't it an exquisite place?"

"Perfectly lovely; I feel as if I must come here every day."

"Yes, I know; but there are so many other places out here about which you have that feeling."

"Now we will show you the other Cheyenne Canyon,—the twin of this," said Dr. Hope; "but you must prepare your mind to find it entirely different."

After rather a rough mile or two through woods, they came to a wooden shed, or shanty, at the mouth of a gorge, and here Dr. Hope drew up his horses, and helped them all out.

"Is it much of a walk?" asked Mrs. Watson.

"It is rather long and rather steep," said Mrs. Hope; "but it is lovely if you only go a little way in, and you and I will sit down the moment you feel tired, and let the others go forward."

South Cheyenne Canyon was indeed "entirely different." Instead of a green-floored, vine-hung ravine, it is a wild mountain gorge, walled with precipitous cliffs of great height; and its river—every canyon has a river—comes from a source at the top of the gorge in a series of mad leaps, forming seven waterfalls, which plunge into circular basins of rock, worn smooth by the action of the stream. These pools are curiously various in shape, and the color of the water, as it pauses a moment to rest in each before taking its next plunge, is beautiful. Little plank walks are laid along the river-side, and rude staircases for the steepest pitches. Up these the party went, leaving Mrs. Watson and Mrs. Hope far behind,—Poppy with her habit over her arm, Clover stopping every other moment to pick some new flower, Phil shying stones into the rapids as he passed,—till the top of the topmost cascade was reached, and looking back they could see the whole wonderful way by which they had climbed, and down which the river made its turbulent rush. Clover gathered a great mat of green scarlet-berried vine like glorified cranberry, which Dr. Hope told her was the famous kinnikinnick, and was just remarking on the cool water-sounds which filled the place, when all of a sudden these sounds seemed to grow angry, the defile of precipices turned a frowning blue, and looking up they saw a great thunder-cloud gathering overhead.

"We must run," cried Dr. Hope, and down they flew, racing at full speed along the long flights of steps and the plank walks, which echoed to the sound of their flying feet. Far below they could see two fast-moving specks which they guessed to be Mrs. Hope and Mrs. Watson, hurrying to a place of shelter. Nearer and nearer came the storm, louder the growl of the thunder, and great hail-stones pattered on their heads before they gained the cabin; none too soon, for in another moment the cloud broke, and the air was full of a dizzy whirl of sleet and rain.

Others besides themselves had been surprised in the ravine, and every few minutes another and another wet figure would come flying down the path, so that the little refuge was soon full. The storm lasted half an hour, then it scattered as rapidly as it had come, the sun broke out brilliantly, and the drive home would have been delightful if it had not been for the sad fact that Mrs. Watson had left her parasol in the carriage, and it had been wet, and somewhat stained by the india-rubber blanket which had been thrown over it for protection. Her lamentations were pathetic.

"Jane Phillips gave it to me,—she was a Sampson, you know,—and I thought ever so much of it. It was at Hovey's—We were there together, and I admired it; and she said, 'Mrs. Watson, you must let me—' Six dollars was the price of it. That's a good deal for a parasol, you know, unless it's really a nice one; but Hovey's things are always—I had the handle shortened a little just before I came away, too, so that it would go into my trunk; it had to be mended anyhow, so that it seemed a good—Dear, dear! and now it's spoiled! What a pity I left it in the carriage! I shall know better another time, but this climate is so different. It never rains in this way at home. It takes a little while about it, and gives notice; and we say that there's going to be a northeaster, or that it looks like a thunder-storm, and we put on our second-best clothes or we stay at home. It's a great deal nicer, I think."

"I am so sorry," said kind little Mrs. Hope. "Our storms out here do come up very suddenly. I wish I had noticed that you had left your parasol. Well, Clover, you've had a chance now to see the doctor's beautiful Colorado hail and thunder to perfection. How do you like them?"

"I like everything in Colorado, I believe," replied Clover, laughing. "I won't even except the hail."

"She's the girl for this part of the world," cried Dr. Hope, approvingly. "She'd make a first-rate pioneer. We'll keep her out here, Mary, and never let her go home. She was born to live at the West."

"Was I? It seems queer then that I should have been born to live in Burnet."

"Oh, we'll change all that."

"I'm sure I don't see how."

"There are ways and means," oracularly.

Mrs. Watson was so cast down by the misadventure to her parasol that she expressed no regret at not being asked to join in the picnic next day, especially as she understood that it consisted of young people. Mrs. Hope very rightly decided that a whole day out of doors, in a rough place, would give pain rather than pleasure to a person who was both so feeble and so fussy, and did not suggest her going. Clover and Phil waked up quite fresh and untired after a sound night's sleep. There seemed no limit to what might be done and enjoyed in that inexhaustibly renovating air.

Odin's Garden proved to be a wonderful assemblage of rocky shapes rising from the grass and flowers of a lonely little plain on the far side of the mesa, four or five miles from St. Helen's. The name of the place came probably from something suggestive in the forms of the rocks, which reminded Clover of pictures she had seen of Assyrian and Egyptian rock carvings. There were lion shapes and bull shapes like the rudely chiselled gods of some heathen worship; there were slender, points and obelisks three hundred feet high; and something suggesting a cat-faced deity, and queer similitudes of crocodiles and apes,—all in the strange orange and red and pale yellow formations of the region. It was a wonderful rather than a beautiful place; but the day was spent very happily under those mysterious stones, which, as the long afternoon shadows gathered over the plain, and the sky glowed with sunset crimson which seemed like a reflection from the rocks themselves, became more mysterious still. Of the merry young party which made up the picnic, seven out of nine had come to Colorado for health; but no one would have guessed it, they seemed so well and so full of the enjoyment of life. Altogether, it was a day to be marked; not with a white stone,—that would not have seemed appropriate to Colorado,—but with a red one. Clover, writing about it afterward to Elsie, felt that her descriptions to sober stay-at-homes might easily sound overdrawn and exaggerated, and wound up her letter thus:—

"Perhaps you think that I am romancing; but I am not a bit. Every word I say is perfectly true, only I have not made the colors half bright or the things half beautiful enough. Colorado is the most beautiful place in the world. [N.B.—Clover had seen but a limited portion of the world so far.] I only wish you could all come out to observe for yourselves that I am not fibbing, though it sounds like it!"

CHAPTER VIII. HIGH VALLEY.

Clover was putting Phil's chamber to rights, and turning it into a sitting-room for the day, which was always her first task in the morning. They had been at St. Helen's nearly three weeks now, and the place had taken on a very homelike appearance. All the books and the photographs were unpacked, the washstand had vanished behind a screen made of a three-leaved clothes-frame draped with chintz, while a ruffled cover of the same gay chintz, on which bunches of crimson and pink geraniums straggled over a cream-colored ground, gave to the narrow bed the air of a respectable wide sofa.

"There! those look very nice, I think," she said, giving the last touch to a bowl full of beautiful garden roses. "How sweet they are!"

"Your young man seems rather clever about roses," remarked Phil, who, boy-like, dearly loved to tease his sister.

"My young man, as you call him, has a father with a gardener," replied Clover, calmly; "no very brilliant cleverness is required for that."

In a cordial, kindly place, like St. Helen's, people soon make acquaintances, and Clover and Phil felt as if they already knew half the people in the town. Every one had come to see them and deluged them with flowers, and invitations to dine, to drive, to take tea. Among the rest came Mr. Thurber Wade, whom Phil was pleased to call Clover's young man,—the son of a rich New York banker, whose ill-health had brought him to live in St. Helen's, and who had built a handsome house on the principal street. This gilded youth had several times sent roses to Clover,—a fact which Phil had noticed, and upon which he was fond of commenting.

"Speaking of young men," went on Clover, "what do you suppose has become of Clarence Page? He said he should come in to see us soon; but that was ever so long ago."

"He's a fraud, I suspect," replied Phil, lazily, from his seat in the window. He had a geometry on his knees, and was supposed to be going on with his education, but in reality he was looking at the mountains. "I suppose people are pretty busy on ranches, though," he added. "Perhaps they're sheep-shearing."

"Oh, it isn't a sheep ranch. Don't you remember his saying that the cattle got very wild, and they had to ride after them? They wouldn't ride after sheep. I hope he hasn't forgotten about us. I was so glad to see him."

While this talk went on, Clarence was cantering down the lower end of the Ute Pass on his way to St. Helen's. Three hours later his name was brought up to them.

"How nice!" cried Clover. "I think as he's a relative we might let him come here, Phil. It's so much pleasanter than the parlor."

Clarence, who had passed the interval of waiting in noting the different varieties of cough among the sick people in the parlor, was quite of her opinion.

"How jolly you look!" was almost his first remark. "I'm glad you've got a little place of your own, and don't have to sit with those poor creatures downstairs all the time."

"It is much nicer. Some of them are getting better, though."

"Some of them aren't. There's one poor fellow in a reclining-chair who looks badly."

"That's the one whose room Mrs. Watson has marked for her own. She asks him three times a day how he feels, with all the solicitude of a mother," said Phil.

"Who's Mrs. Watson?"

"Well, she's an old lady who is somehow fastened to us, and who considers herself our chaperone," replied Clover, with a little laugh. "I must introduce you by-and-by, but first we want a good talk all by ourselves. Now tell us why you haven't come to see us before. We have been hoping for you every day."

"Well, I've wanted to come badly enough, but there has been a combination of hindrances. Two of our men got sick, so there was more to do than usual; then Geoff had to be away four days, and almost as soon as he got back he had bad news from home, and I hated to leave him alone."

"What sort of bad news?"

"His sister's dead."

"Poor fellow! In England too! You said he was English, didn't you?"

"Yes. She was married. Her husband was a clergyman down in Cornwall somewhere. She was older than Geoff a good deal; but he was very fond of her, and the news cut him up dreadfully."

"No wonder. It is horrible to hear such a thing when one is far from home," observed Clover. She tried to realize how she should feel if word came to St. Helen's of Katy's death, or Elsie's, or Johnnie's; but her mind refused to accept the question. The very idea made her shiver.

"Poor fellow!" she said again; "what could you do for him, Clarence?"

"Not much. I'm a poor hand at comforting any one,—men generally are, I guess. Geoff knows I'm sorry for him; but it takes a woman to say the right thing at such times. We sit and smoke when the work's done, and I know what he's thinking about; but we don't say anything to each other. Now let's speak of something else. I want to settle about your coming to High Valley."

"High Valley? Is that the name of your place?"

"Yes. I want you to see it. It's an awfully pretty place to my thinking,—not so very much higher than this, but you have to climb a good deal to get there. Can't you come? This is just the time,—raspberries ripe, and lots of flowers wherever the beasts don't get at them. Phil can have all the riding he wants, and it'll do poor Geoff lots of good to see some one."

"It would be very nice indeed," doubtfully; "but who could we get to go with us?"

"I thought of that. We don't take much stock in Mrs. Grundy out here; but I supposed you'd want another lady. How would it be if I asked Mrs. Hope? The doctor's got to come out anyway to see one of our herders who's put his shoulder out in a fall. If he would drive you out, and Mrs. Hope would stay on, would you come for a week? I guess you'll like it."

"I 'guess' we should," exclaimed Clover, her face lighting up. "Clarence, how delightful it sounds! It will be lovely to come if Mrs. Hope says yes."

"Then that's all right," replied Clarence, looking extremely pleased. "I'll ride up to the doctor's as soon as dinner's over."

"You'll dine with us, of course?"

"Oh, I always come to Mother Marsh for a bite whenever I stay over the day. She likes to have me. We've been great chums ever since I had fever here, and she took care of me."

Clover was amused at dinner to watch the cool deliberation with which Clarence studied Mrs. Watson and her tortuous conversation, and, as he would have expressed it, "took stock of her." The result was not favorable, apparently.

"What on earth did they send that old thing with you for?" he asked as soon as they went upstairs. "She's as much out of her element here as a canary-bird would be in a cyclone. She can't be any use to you, Clover."

"Well, no; I don't think she is. It was a sort of mistake; I'll tell you about it sometime. But she likes to imagine that she's taking care of me; and as it does no harm, I let her."

"Taking care of you! Great thunder! I wouldn't trust her to take care of a blue-eyed kitten," observed the irreverent Clarence. "Well, I'll ride up and settle with the Hopes, and stop and let you know as I come back."

Mrs. Hope and the doctor were not hard to persuade. In Colorado, people keep their lamps of enjoyment filled and trimmed, so to speak, and their travelling energies ready girt about them, and easily adopt any plan which promises pleasure. The following day was fixed for the start, and Clover packed her valise and Phil's bag, with a sense of exhilaration and escape. She was, in truth, getting very tired of the exactions of Mrs. Watson. Mrs. Watson, on her part, did not at all approve of the excursion.

"I think," she said, swelling with offended dignity, "that your cousin didn't know much about politeness when he left me out of his invitation and asked Mrs. Hope instead. Yes, I know; the doctor had to go up anyway. That may be true, and it may not; but it doesn't alter the case. What am I to do, I should like to know, if the valves of my heart don't open, or don't shut—whichever it is—while I'm left all alone here among strangers?"

"Send for Dr. Hope," suggested Phil. "He'll only be gone one night. Clover doesn't know anything about valves."

"My cousin lives in a rather rough way, I imagine," interposed Clover, with a reproving look at Phil. "He would hardly like to ask a stranger and an invalid to his house, when he might not be able to make her comfortable. Mrs. Hope has been there before, and she's an old friend."

"Oh, I dare say! There are always reasons. I don't say that I should have felt like going, but he ought to have asked me. Ellen will be surprised, and so will—He's from Ashburn too, and he must know the Parmenters, and Mrs. Parmenter's brother's son is partner to Henry's brother-in-law. It's of no consequence, of course,—still, respect—older people—Boston—not used to—Phillips—" Mrs. Watson's voice died away into fragmentary and inaudible lamentings.

Clover attempted no further excuse. Her good sense told her that she had a perfect right to accept this little pleasure; that Mrs. Watson's plans for Western travel had been formed quite independently of their own, and that papa would not wish her to sacrifice herself and Phil to such unreasonable humors. Still, it was not pleasant; and I am sorry to say that from this time dated a change of feeling on Mrs. Watson's part toward her "young friends." She took up a chronic position of grievance toward them, confided her wrongs to all new-comers, and met Clover with an offended air which, though Clover ignored it, did not add to the happiness of her life at Mrs. Marsh's.

It was early in the afternoon when they started, and the sun was just dipping behind the mountain wall when they drove into the High Valley. It was one of those natural parks, four miles long, which lie like heaven-planted gardens among the Colorado ranges. The richest of grass clothed it; fine trees grew in clumps and clusters here and there; and the spaces about the house where fences of barbed wire defended the grass from the cattle, seemed a carpet of wild-flowers.

Clover exclaimed with delight at the view. The ranges which lapped and held the high, sheltered upland in embrace opened toward the south, and revealed a splendid lonely peak, on whose summit a drift of freshly-fallen snow was lying. The contrast with the verdure and bloom below was charming.

The cabin—it was little more—stood facing this view, and was backed by a group of noble red cedars. It was built of logs, long and low, with a rude porch in front supported on unbarked tree trunks. Two fine collies rushed to meet them, barking vociferously; and at the sound Clarence hurried to the door. He met them with great enthusiasm, lifted out Mrs. Hope, then Clover, and then began shouting for his chum, who was inside.

"Hollo, Geoff! where are you? Hurry up; they've come." Then, as he appeared, "Ladies and gentleman, my partner!"

Geoffrey Templestowe was a tall, sinewy young Englishman, with ruddy hair and beard, grave blue eyes, and an unmistakable air of good breeding. He wore a blue flannel shirt and high boots like Clarence's, yet somehow he made Clarence look a little rough and undistinguished. He was quiet in speech, reserved in manner, and seemed depressed and under a cloud; but Clover liked his face at once. He looked both strong and kind, she thought.

The house consisted of one large square room in the middle, which served as parlor and dining-room both, and on either side two bedrooms. The kitchen was in a separate building. There was no lack of comfort, though things were rather rude, and the place had a bare, masculine look. The floor was strewn with coyote and fox skins. Two or three easy-chairs stood around the fireplace, in which, July as it was, a big log was blazing. Their covers were shabby and worn; but they looked comfortable, and were evidently in constant use. There was not the least attempt at prettiness anywhere. Pipes and books and old newspapers littered the chairs and tables; when an extra seat was needed Clarence simply tipped a great pile of these on to the floor. A gun-rack hung upon the wall, together with sundry long stock-whips and two or three pairs of spurs, and a smell of tobacco pervaded the place.

Clover's eyes wandered to a corner where stood a small parlor organ, and over it a shelf of books. She rose to examine them. To her surprise they were all hymnals and Church of England prayer-books. There were no others. She wondered what it meant.

Clarence had given up his own bedroom to Phil, and was to chum with his friend. Some little attempt had been made to adorn the rooms which were meant for the ladies. Clean towels had been spread over the pine shelves which did duty for dressing-tables, and on each stood a tumbler stuffed as full as it could hold with purple pentstemons. Clover could not help laughing, yet there was something pathetic to her in the clumsy, man-like arrangement. She relieved the tumbler by putting a few of the flowers in her dress, and went out again to the parlor, where Mrs. Hope sat by the fire, quizzing the two partners, who were hard at work setting their tea-table.

It was rather a droll spectacle,—the two muscular young fellows creaking to and fro in their heavy boots, and taking such an infinitude of pains with their operations. One would set a plate on the table, and the other would forthwith alter its position slightly, or lift and scrutinize a tumbler and dust it sedulously with a glass-towel. Each spoon was polished with the greatest particularity before it was laid on the tray; each knife passed under inspection. Visitors were not an every-day luxury in the High Valley, and too much care could not be taken for their entertainment, it seemed.

Supper was brought in by a Chinese cook in a pigtail, wooden shoes, and a blue Mother Hubbard, Choo Loo by name. He was evidently a good cook, for the corn-bread and fresh mountain trout and the ham and eggs were savory to the last degree, and the flapjacks, with which the meal concluded, and which were eaten with a sauce of melted raspberry jelly, deserved even higher encomium.

"We are willing to be treated as company this first night," observed Mrs. Hope; "but if you are going to keep us a week, you must let us make ourselves useful, and set the table and arrange the rooms for you."

"We will begin to-morrow morning," added Clover. "May we, Clarence? May we play that it is our house, and do what we like, and change about and arrange things? It will be such fun."

"Fire away!" said her cousin, calmly. "The more you change the more we shall like it. Geoff and I aren't set in our ways, and are glad enough to be let off duty for a week. The hut is yours just as long as you will stay; do just what you like with it. Though we're pretty good housekeepers too, considering; don't you think so?"

"Do you believe he meant it?" asked Clover, confidentially afterward of Mrs. Hope. "Do you think they really wouldn't mind being tidied up a little? I should so like to give that room a good dusting, if it wouldn't vex them."

"My dear, they will probably never know the difference except by a vague sense of improved comfort. Men are dreadfully untidy, as a general thing, when left to themselves; but they like very well to have other people make things neat."

"Mr. Templestowe told Phil that they go off early in the morning and don't come back till breakfast at half-past seven; so if I wake early enough I shall try to do a little setting to rights before they come in."

"And I'll come and help if I don't over-sleep," declared Mrs. Hope; "but this air makes me feel dreadfully as if I should."

"I sha'n't call you," said Clover; "but it will be nice to have you, if you come."

She stood at her window after Mrs. Hope had gone, for a last look at the peak which glittered sharply in the light of the moon. The air was like scented wine. She drew a long breath.

"How lovely it is!" she said to herself, and kissed her hand to the mountain. "Good-night, you beautiful thing."

She woke with the first beam of yellow sun, after eight hours of dreamless sleep, with a keen sense of renovation and refreshment. A great splashing was going on in the opposite wing, and manly voices hushed to suppressed tones were audible. Then came a sound of boots on the porch; and peeping from behind her curtain, she saw Clarence and his friend striding across the grass in the direction of the stock-huts. She glanced at her watch. It was a quarter past five.

"Now is my chance," she thought; and dressing rapidly, she put on a little cambric jacket, knotted her hair up, tied a handkerchief over it, and hurried into the sitting-room. Her first act was to throw open all the windows to let out the smell of stale tobacco, her next to hunt for a broom. She found one at last, hanging on the door of a sort of store-closet, and moving the furniture as noiselessly as she could, she gave the room a rapid but effectual sweeping.

While the dust settled, she stole out to a place on the hillside where the night before she had noticed some mariposa lilies growing, and gathered a large bunch. Then she proceeded to dust and straighten, sorted out the newspapers, wiped the woodwork with a damp cloth, arranged the disorderly books, and set the breakfast-table. When all this was done, there was still time to finish her toilet and put her pretty hair in its accustomed coils and waves; so that Clarence and Mr. Templestowe came in to find the fire blazing, the room bright and neat, Mrs. Hope sitting at the table in a pretty violet gingham ready to pour the coffee which Choo Loo had brought in, and Clover, the good fairy of this transformation scene, in a fresh blue muslin, with a ribbon to match in her hair, just setting the mariposas in the middle of the table. Their lilac-streaked bells nodded from a tall vase of ground glass.

"Oh, I say," cried Clarence, "this *is* something like! Isn't it scrumptious, Geoff? The hut never looked like this before. It's wonderful what a woman—no, two women," with a bow to Mrs. Hope—"can do toward making things pleasant. Where did that vase come from, Clover? We never owned anything so fine as that, I'm sure."

"It came from my bag; and it's a present for you and Mr. Templestowe. I saw it in a shop-window yesterday; and it occurred to me that it might be just the thing for High Valley, and fill a gap. And Mrs. Hope has brought you each a pretty coffee-cup."

It was a merry meal. The pleasant look of the room, the little surprises, and the refreshment of seeing new and kindly faces, raised Mr. Templestowe's spirits, and warmed him out of his reserve. He grew cheerful and friendly. Clarence was in uproarious spirits, and Phil even worse. It seemed as if the air of the High Valley had got into his head.

Dr. Hope left at noon, after making a second visit to the lame herder, and Mrs. Hope and Clover settled themselves for a week of enjoyment. They were alone for hours every day, while their young hosts were off on the ranch, and they devoted part of this time to various useful and decorative arts. They took all manner of liberties, poked about and rummaged, mended, sponged, assorted, and felt themselves completely mistresses of the situation. A note to Marian Chase brought up a big parcel by stage to the Ute Valley, four miles away, from which it was fetched over by a cow-boy on horseback; and Clover worked away busily at scrim curtains for the windows, while Mrs. Hope shaped a slip cover of gay chintz for the shabbiest of the armchairs, hemmed a great square of gold-colored canton flannel for the bare, unsightly table, and made a bright red pincushion apiece for the bachelor quarters. The sitting-room took on quite a new aspect, and every added touch gave immense satisfaction to "the boys," as Mrs. Hope called them, who thoroughly enjoyed the effect of these ministrations, though they had not the least idea how to produce it themselves.

Creature comforts were not forgotten. The two ladies amused themselves with experiments in cookery. The herders brought a basket of wild raspberries, and Clover turned them into jam for winter use. Clarence gloated over the little white pots, and was never tired of counting them. They looked so like New England, he declared, that he felt as if he must get a girl at once, and go and walk in the graveyard,— a pastime which he remembered as universal in his native town. Various cakes and puddings appeared to attest the industry of the housekeepers; and on the only wet evening, when a wild thunder-gust was sweeping down the valley, they had a wonderful candy-pull, and made enough to give all the cow-boys a treat.

It must not be supposed that all their time went in these domestic pursuits. No, indeed. Mrs. Hope had brought her own side-saddle, and had borrowed one for Clover; the place was full of horses, and not a day passed without a long ride up or down the valley, and into the charming little side canyons which opened from it. A spirited broncho, named Sorrel, had been made over to Phil's use for the time of his stay, and he was never out of the saddle when he could help it, except to eat and sleep. He shared in the herders' wild gallops after stock, and though Clover felt nervous about the risks he ran, whenever she took time to think them over, he was so very happy that she had not the heart to interfere or check his pleasure.

She and Mrs. Hope rode out with the gentlemen on the great day of the round-up, and, stationed at a safe point a little way up the hillside, watched the spectacle,—the plunging, excited herd, the cow-boys madly galloping, swinging their long whips and lassos, darting to and fro to head off refractory beasts or check the tendency to stampede. Both Clarence and Geoffrey Templestowe were bold and expert riders; but the Mexican and Texan herders in their employ far surpassed them. The ladies had never seen anything like it. Phil and his broncho were in the midst of things, of course, and had one or two tumbles, but nothing to hurt them; only Clover was very thankful when it was all safely over.

In their rides and scrambling walks it generally happened that Clarence took possession of Clover, and left Geoff in charge of Mrs. Hope. Cousinship and old friendship gave him a right, he considered, and he certainly took full advantage of it. Clover liked Clarence; but there were moments when she felt that she would rather enjoy the chance to talk more with Mr. Templestowe, and there was a look in his eyes now and then which seemed to say that he might enjoy it too. But Clarence did not observe this look, and he had no idea of sharing his favorite cousin with any one, if he could help it.

Sunday brought the explanation of the shelf full of prayer-books which had puzzled them on their first arrival. There was no church within reach; and it was Geoff's regular custom, it seemed, to hold a little service for the men in the valley. Almost all of them came, except the few Mexicans, who were Roman Catholics, and the room was quite full. Geoff read the service well and reverently, gave out the hymns, and played the accompaniments for them, closing with a brief bit of a sermon by the elder Arnold. It was all done simply and as a matter of course, and Clarence seemed to join in it with much good-will; but Clover privately wondered whether the idea of doing such a thing would have entered into his head had he been left alone, or, if so, whether he would have cared enough about it to carry it out regularly. She doubted. Whatever the shortcomings of the Church of England may be, she certainly trains her children into a devout observance of Sunday.

The next day, Monday, was to be their last,—a fact lamented by every one, particularly Phil, who regarded the High Valley as a paradise, and would gladly have remained there for the rest of his natural life. Clover hated to take him away; but Dr. Hope had warned her privately that a week would be enough of it, and that with Phil's tendency to overdo, too long a stay would be undesirable. So she stood firm, though Clarence urged a delay, and Phil seconded the proposal with all his might.

The very pleasantest moment of the visit perhaps came on that last afternoon, when Geoff got her to himself for once, and took her up a trail where she had not yet been, in search of scarlet pentstemons to carry back to St. Helen's. They found great sheaves of the slender stems threaded, as it were, with jewel-like blossoms; but what was better still, they had a talk, and Clover felt that she had now a new friend. Geoff told her of his people at home, and a little about the sister who had lately died; only a little,—he could not yet trust himself to talk long about her. Clover listened with frank and gentle interest. She liked to hear about the old grange at the head of a chine above Clovelley, where Geoff was born, and which had once been full of boys and girls, now scattered in the English fashion to all parts of the world. There was Ralph with his regiment in India,—he was the heir, it seemed,—and Jim and Jack in Australia, and Oliver with his wife and children in New Zealand, and Allen at Harrow, and another boy fitting for the civil service. There was a married sister in Scotland, and another in London; and Isabel, the youngest of all, still at home,—the light of the house, and the special pet of the old squire and of Geoff's mother, who, he told Clover, had been a great beauty in her youth, and though nearly seventy, was in his eyes beautiful still.

"It's pretty quiet there for Isabel," he said; "but she has my sister Helen's two children to care for, and that will keep her busy. I used to think she'd come out to me one of these years for a twelvemonth; but there's little chance of her being spared now."

Clover's sympathy did not take the form of words. It looked out of her eyes, and spoke in the hushed tones of her soft voice. Geoff felt that it was there, and it comforted him. The poor fellow was very lonely in those days, and inclined to be homesick, as even a manly man sometimes is.

"What an awful time Adam must have had of it before Eve came!" growled Clarence, that evening, as they sat around the fire.

"He had a pretty bad time after she came, if I remember," said Clover, laughing.

"Ah, but he had *her*!"

"Stuff and nonsense! He was a long shot happier without her and her old apple, I think," put in Phil. "You fellows don't know when you're well off."

Everybody laughed.

"Phil's notion of Paradise is the High Valley and Sorrel, and no girls about to bother and tell him not to get too tired," remarked Clover. "It's a fair vision; but like all fair visions it must end."

And end it did next day, when Dr. Hope appeared with the carriage, and the bags and saddles were put in, and the great bundle of wild-flowers, with their stems tied in wet moss; and Phil, torn from his beloved broncho, on whose back he had passed so many happy hours, was forced to accompany the others back to civilization.

"I shall see you very soon," said Clarence, tucking the lap-robe round Clover. "There's the mail to fetch, and other things. I shall be riding in every day or two."

"I shall see you very soon," said Geoff, on the other side. "Clarence is not coming without me, I can assure you."

Then the carriage drove away; and the two partners went back into the house, which looked suddenly empty and deserted.

"I'll tell you what!" began Clarence.

"And I'll tell *you* what!" rejoined Geoff.

"A house isn't worth a red cent which hasn't a woman in it."

"You might ride down and ask Miss Perkins to step up and adorn our lives," said his friend, grimly. Miss Perkins was a particularly rigid spinster who taught a school six miles distant, and for whom Clarence entertained a particular distaste.

"You be hanged! I don't mean that kind. I mean—"

"The nice kind, like Mrs. Hope and your cousin. Well, I'm agreed."

"I shall go down after the mail to-morrow," remarked Clarence, between the puffs of his pipe.

"So shall I."

"All right; come along!" But though the words sounded hearty, the tone rather belied them. Clarence was a little puzzled by and did not quite like this newborn enthusiasm on the part of his comrade.

CHAPTER IX. OVER A PASS.

True to their resolve, the young heads of the High Valley Ranch rode together to St. Helen's next day,—ostensibly to get their letters; in reality to call on their late departed guests. They talked amicably as they went; but unconsciously each was watching the other's mood and speech. To like the same girl makes young men curiously observant of each other.

A disappointment was in store for them. They had taken it for granted that Clover would be as disengaged and as much at their service as she had been in the valley; and lo! she sat on the piazza with a knot of girls about her, and a young man in an extremely "fetching" costume of snow-white duck, with a flower in his button-hole, was bending over her chair, and talking in a low voice of something which seemed of interest. He looked provokingly cool and comfortable to the dusty horsemen, and very much at home. Phil, who lounged against the piazza-rail opposite, dispensed an enormous and meaning wink at his two friends as they came up the steps.

Clover jumped up from her chair, and gave them a most cordial reception.

"How delightful to see you again so soon!" she said. Then she introduced them to a girl in pink and a girl in blue as Miss Perham and Miss Blanchard, and they shook hands with Marian Chase, whom they already knew, and lastly were presented to Mr. Wade, the youth in white. The three young men eyed one another with a not very friendly scrutiny, just veiled by the necessary outward politeness.

"Then you will be all ready for Thursday,—and your brother too, of course,—and my mother will stop for you at half-past ten on her way down," they heard him say. "Miss Chase will go with the Hopes. Oh, yes; there will be plenty of room. No danger about that. We're almost sure to have good weather too. Good-morning. I'm so glad you enjoyed the roses."

There was a splendid cluster of Jacqueminot buds in Clover's dress, at which Clarence glared wrathfully as he caught these words. The only consolation was that the creature in duck was going. He was making his last bows; and one of the girls went with him, which still farther reduced the number of what in his heart Clarence stigmatized as "a crowd."

"I must go too," said the girl in blue. "Good-by, Clover. I shall run in a minute to-morrow to talk over the last arrangements for Thursday."

"What's going to happen on Thursday?" growled Clarence as soon as she had departed.

"Oh, such a delightful thing," cried Clover, sparkling and dimpling. "Old Mr. Wade, the father of young Mr. Wade, whom you saw just now, is a director on the railroad, you know; and they have given him the director's car to take a party over the Marshall Pass, and he has asked Phil and me to go. It is *such* a surprise. Ever since we came to St. Helen's, people have been telling us what a beautiful journey it is; but I never supposed we should have the chance to take it. Mrs. Hope is going too, and the doctor, and Miss Chase and Miss Perham,—all the people we know best, in fact. Isn't it nice?"

"Oh, certainly; very nice," replied Clarence, in a tone of deep offence. He was most unreasonably in the sulks. Clover glanced at him with surprise, and then at Geoff, who was talking to Marian. He looked a little serious, and not so bright as in the valley; but he was making himself very pleasant, notwithstanding. Surely he had the same causes for annoyance as Clarence; but his breeding forbade him to show whatever inward vexation he may have felt,—certainly not to allow it to influence his manners. Clover drew a mental contrast between the two which was not to Clarence's advantage.

"Who's that fellow anyway?" demanded Clarence. "How long have you known him? What business has he to be bringing you roses, and making up parties to take you off on private cars?"

Something in Clover's usually soft eyes made him stop suddenly.

"I beg your pardon," he said in an altered tone.

"I really think you should," replied Clover, with pretty dignity.

Then she moved away, and began to talk to Geoff, whose grave courtesy at once warmed into cheer and sun.

Clarence, thus left a prey to remorse, was wretched. He tried to catch Clover's eye, but she wouldn't look at him. He leaned against the balustrade moody and miserable. Phil, who had watched these various interludes with interest, indicated his condition to Clover with another telegraphic wink. She glanced across, relented, and made Clarence a little signal to come and sit by her.

After that all went happily. Clover was honestly delighted to see her two friends again. And now that Clarence had recovered from his ill-temper, there was nothing to mar their enjoyment. Geoff's horse had cast a shoe on the way down, it seemed, and must be taken to the blacksmith's, so they did not stay very long; but it was arranged that they should come back to dinner at Mrs. Marsh's.

"What a raving belle you are!" remarked Marian Chase, as the young men rode away. "Three is a good many at a time, though, isn't it?"

"Three what?"

"Three—hem! leaves—to one Clover!"

"It's the usual allowance, I believe. If there were four, now—"

"Oh, I dare say there will be. They seem to collect round you like wasps round honey. It's some natural law, I presume,—gravitation or levitation, which is it?"

"I'm sure I don't know, and don't try to tease me, Poppy. People out here are so kind that it's enough to spoil anybody."

"Kind, forsooth! Do you consider it all pure kindness? Really, for such a belle, you're very innocent."

"I wish you wouldn't," protested Clover, laughing and coloring. "I never was a belle in my life, and that's the second time you've called me that. Nobody ever said such things to me in Burnet."

"Ah, you had to come to Colorado to find out how attractive you could be. Burnet must be a very quiet place. Never mind; you sha'n't be teased, Clover dear. Only don't let this trefoil of yours get to fighting with one another. That good-looking cousin of yours was casting quite murderous glances at poor Thurber Wade just now."

"Clarence is a dear boy; but he's rather spoiled and not quite grown up yet, I think."

"When are you coming back from the Marshall Pass?" inquired Geoff, after dinner, when Clarence had gone for the horses.

"On Saturday. We shall only be gone two days."

"Then I will ride in on Thursday morning, if you will permit, with my field-glass. It is a particularly good one, and you may find it useful for the distant views."

"When are you coming back?" demanded Clarence, a little later. "Saturday? Then I sha'n't be in again before Monday."

"Won't you want your letters?"

"Oh, I guess there won't be any worth coming for till then."

"Not a letter from your mother?"

"She only writes once in a while. Most of what I get comes from pa."

"Cousin Olivia never did seem to care much for Clarence," remarked Clover, after they were gone. "He would have been a great deal nicer if he had had a pleasanter time at home. It makes such a difference with boys. Now Mr. Templestowe has a lovely mother, I'm sure."

"Oh!" was all the reply that Phil would vouchsafe.

"How queer people are!" thought little Clover to herself afterward. "Neither of those boys quite liked our going on this expedition, I think,—though I'm sure I can't imagine why; but they behaved so differently. Mr. Templestowe thought of us and something which might give us pleasure; and Clarence only thought about himself. Poor Clarence! he never had half a chance till he came here. It isn't all his fault."

The party in the director's car proved a merry one. Mrs. Wade, a jolly, motherly woman, fond of the good things of life, and delighting in making people comfortable, had spared no pains of preparation. There were quantities of easy-chairs and fans and eau-de-cologne; the larder was stocked with all imaginable dainties,—iced tea, lemonade, and champagne cup flowed on the least provocation for all the hot moments, and each table was a bank of flowers. Each lady had a superb bouquet; and on the second day a great tin box of freshly-cut roses met them at Pueblo, so that they came back as gayly furnished forth as they went. Having the privilege of the road, the car was attached or detached to suit their convenience, and this enabled them to command daylight for all the finest points of the excursion.

First of these was the Royal Gorge, where the Arkansas River pours through a magnificent canyon, between precipices so steep and with curves so sharp that only engineering genius of the most daring order could, it would seem, have devised a way through. Then, after a pause at the pretty town of Salida, with the magnificent range of the Sangre de Cristo Mountains in full sight, they began to mount the pass over long loops of rail, which doubled and re-doubled on themselves again and again on their way to the summit. The train had been divided; and the first half with its two engines was seen at times puffing and snorting directly overhead of the second half on the lower curve.

With each hundred feet of elevation, the view changed and widened. Now it was of over-lapping hills set with little mésas, like folds of green velvet flung over the rocks; now of dim-seen valley depths with winding links of silver rivers; and again of countless mountain peaks sharp-cut against the sunset sky,—some rosy pink, some shining with snow.

The flowers were a continual marvel. At the top of the pass, eleven thousand feet and more above the sea, their colors and their abundance were more profuse and splendid than on the lower levels. There were whole fields of pentstemons, pink, blue, royal purple, or the rare scarlet variety, like stems of asparagus strung with rubies. There were masses of gillias, and of wonderful coreopsis, enormous cream-colored stars with deep-orange centres, and deep yellow ones with scarlet centres; thickets of snowy-cupped mentzelia and of wild rose; while here and there a tall red lily burned like a little lonely flame in the green, or regiments of convolvuli waved their stately heads.

From below came now and again the tinkle of distant cow-bells. These, and the plaintive coo of mourning-doves in the branches, and the rush of the wind, which was like cool flower-scented wine, was all that broke the stillness of the high places.

"To think I'm so much nearer heaven
Than when I was a boy,"

misquoted Clover, as she sat on the rear platform of the car, with Poppy, and Thurber Wade.

"Are you sure your head doesn't ache? This elevation plays the mischief with some people. My mother has taken to her berth with ice on her temples."

"Headache! No, indeed. This air is too delicious. I feel as though I could dance all the way from here to the Black Canyon."

"You don't look as if your head ached, or anything," said Mr. Wade, staring at Clover admiringly. Her cheeks were pink with excitement, her eyes full of light and exhilaration.

"Oh dear! we are beginning to go down," she cried, watching one of the beautiful peaks of the Sangre de Cristos as it dipped out of sight. "I think I could find it in my heart to cry, if it were not that to-morrow we are coming up again."

So down, down, down they went. Dusk slowly gathered about them; and the white-gloved butler set the little tables, and brought in broiled chicken and grilled salmon and salad and hot rolls and peaches, and they were all very hungry. And Clover did not cry, but fell to work on her supper with an excellent appetite, quite unconscious that they were speeding through another wonderful gorge without seeing one of its beauties. Then the car was detached from the train; and when she awoke next morning they were at the little station called Cimmaro, at the head of the famous Black Canyon, with three hours to spare before the train from Utah should arrive to take them back to St. Helen's.

Early as it was, the small settlement was awake. Lights glanced from the eating-house, where cooks were preparing breakfast for the "through" passengers, and smokes curled from the chimneys. Close to the car was a large brick structure which seemed to be a sort of hotel for locomotives. A number of the enormous creatures had evidently passed the night there, and just waked up. Clover now watched their antics with great amusement from her window as their engineers ran them in and out, rubbed them down like horses, and fed them with oil and coal, while they snorted and backed and sidled a good deal as real horses do. Clover could not at all understand what all these manœuvres were for,—they seemed only designed to show the paces of the iron steeds, and what they were good for.

"Miss Clover," whispered a voice outside her curtains, "I've got hold of a hand-car and a couple of men; and don't you want to take a spin down the canyon and see the view with no smoke to spoil it? Just you and me and Miss Chase. She says she'll go if you will. Hurry, and don't make a noise. We won't wake the others."

Of course Clover wanted to. She finished her dressing at top-speed, hurried on her hat and jacket, stole softly out to where the others awaited her, and in five minutes they were smoothly running down the gorge, over high trestle-work bridges and round sharp curves which made her draw her breath a little faster. There was no danger, the men who managed the hand-car assured them; it was a couple of hours yet before the next train came in; there was plenty of time to go three or four miles down and return.

Anything more delicious than the early morning air in the Black Canyon it would be difficult to imagine. Cool, odorous with pines and with the breath of the mountains, it was like a zestful draught of iced summer. Close beside the track ran a wondrous river which seemed made of melted jewels, so curiously brilliant were its waters and mixed of so many hues. Its course among the rocks was a flash of foaming rapids, broken here and there by pools of exquisite blue-green, deepening into inky-violet under the shadow of the cliffs. And such cliffs!—one, two, three thousand feet high; not deep-colored like those about St. Helen's, but of steadfast mountain hues and of magnificent forms,—buttresses and spires; crags whose bases were lost in untrodden forests; needle-sharp pinnacles like the Swiss Aiguilles. The morning was just making its way into the canyon; and the loftier tops flashed with yellow sun, while the rest were still in cold shadow.

Breakfast was just ready when the hand-car arrived again at the upper end of the gorge, and loud were the reproaches which met the happy three as they alighted from it. Phil was particularly afflicted.

"I call it mean not to wake a fellow," he said.

"But a fellow was *so* sound asleep," said Clover, "I really hadn't the heart. I did peep in at your curtain, and if you had moved so much as a finger, *perhaps* I should have called you; but you didn't."

The return journey was equally fortunate, and the party reached St. Helen's late in the evening of the second day, in what Mr. Wade called "excellent form." Monday brought the young men from the ranch in again; and another fortnight passed happily, Clover's three "leaves" being most faithfully attentive to their central point of attraction. "Three is a good many," as Marian Chase had said, but all girls like to be liked, and Clover did not find this, her first little experience of the kind, at all disagreeable.

The excursion to the Marshall Pass, however, had an after effect which was not so pleasant. Either the high elevation had disagreed with Phil, or he had taken a little cold; at all events, he was distinctly less well. With the lowering of his physical forces came a corresponding depression of spirits. Mrs. Watson worried him, the sick people troubled him, the sound of coughing depressed him, his appetite nagged, and his sleep was broken. Clover felt that he must have a change, and consulted Dr. Hope, who advised their going to the Ute Valley for a month.

This involved giving up their rooms at Mrs. Marsh's, which was a pity, as it was by no means certain that they would be able to get them again later. Clover regretted this; but Fate, as Fate often does, brought a compensation. Mrs. Watson had no mind whatever for the Ute Valley.

"It's a dull place, they tell me, and there's nothing to do there but ride on horseback, and as I don't ride on horseback, I really don't see what use there would be in my going," she said to Clover. "If I were young, and there were young men ready to ride with me all the time, it would be different; though Ellen never did care to, except with Henry of course, after they—And I really can't see that your brother's much different from what he was, though if Dr. Hope says so, naturally you—He's a queer kind of doctor, it seems to me, to send lung patients up higher than this,—which is high already, gracious knows. No; if you decide to go, I shall just move over to the Shoshone for the rest of the time that I'm here. I'm sure that Dr. Carr couldn't expect me to stay on here alone, just for the chance that you may want to come back, when as like as not, Mrs. Marsh won't be able to take you again."

"Oh, no; I'm quite sure he wouldn't. Only I thought," doubtfully, "that as you've always admired Phil's room so much, you might like to secure it now that we have to go."

"Well, yes. If you were to be here, I might. If that man who's so sick had got better, or gone away, or something, I dare say I should have settled down in his room and been comfortable enough. But he seems just about as he was when we came, so there's no use waiting; and I'd rather go to the Shoshone anyway. I always said it was a mistake that we didn't go there in the first place. It was Dr. Hope's doing, and I have not the least confidence in him. He hasn't osculated me once since I came."

"Hasn't he?" said Clover, feeling her voice tremble, and perfectly aware of the shaking of Phil's shoulders behind her.

"No; and I don't call just putting his ear to my chest, listening. Dr. Bangs, at home, would be ashamed to come to the house without his stethoscope. I mean to move this afternoon. I've given Mrs. Marsh notice."

So Mrs. Watson and her belongings went to the Shoshone, and Clover packed the trunks with a lighter heart for her departure.

The last day of July found Clover and Phil settled in the Ute Park. It was a wild and beautiful valley, some hundreds of feet higher than St. Helen's, and seemed the very home of peace. A Sunday-like quiet pervaded the place, whose stillness was never broken except by bird-songs and the rustle of the pine branches.

The sides of the valley near its opening were dotted here and there with huts and cabins belonging to parties who had fled from the heat of the plains for the summer. At the upper end stood the ranch house,—a large, rather rudely built structure,—and about it were a number of cabins and cottages, in which two, four, or six people could be accommodated. Clover and Phil were lodged in one of these. The tiny structure contained only a sitting and two sleeping rooms, and was very plain and bare. But there was a fireplace; wood was abundant, so that a cheerful blaze could be had for cool evenings; and the little piazza faced the south, and made a sheltered sitting place on windy days.

One pleasant feature of the spot was its nearness to the High Valley. Clarence and Geoff Templestowe thought nothing of riding four miles; and scarcely a day passed when one or both did not come over. They brought wild-flowers, or cream, or freshly-churned butter, as offerings from the ranch; and, what Clover valued as a greater kindness yet, they brought Phil's beloved broncho, Sorrel, and arranged with the owner of the Ute ranch that it should remain as long as Phil was there. This gave Phil hours of delightful exercise every day; and though sometimes he set out early in the morning for the High Valley, and stayed later in the afternoon than his sister thought prudent, she had not the heart to chide, so long as he was visibly getting better hour by hour.

Sundays the friends spent together, as a matter of course. Geoff waited till his little home service for the ranchmen was over, and then would gallop across with Clarence to pass the rest of the day. There was no lack of kind people at the main house and in the cottages to take an interest in the delicate boy and his sweet, motherly sister; so Clover had an abundance of volunteer matrons, and plenty of pleasant ways in which to spend those occasional days on which the High Valley attaches failed to appear.

It was a simple, healthful life, the happiest on the whole which they had led since leaving home. Once or twice Mr. Thurber Wade made his appearance, gallantly mounted, and freighted with flowers and kind messages from his mother to Miss Carr; but Clover was never sorry when he rode away again. Somehow he did not seem to belong to the Happy Valley, as in her heart she denominated the place.

There was a remarkable deal of full moon that month, as it seemed; at least, the fact served as an excuse for a good many late transits between the valley and the park. Now and then either Clarence or Geoff would lead over a saddle-horse and give Clover a good gallop up or down the valley, which she always enjoyed. The habit which she had extemporized for her visit to the High Valley answered very well, and Mrs. Hope had lent her a hat.

On one of these occasions she and Clarence had ridden farther than usual, quite down to the end of the pass, where the road dipped, and descended to the little watering-place of Canyon Creek,—a Swiss-like village of hotels and lodging-houses and shops for the sale of minerals and mineral waters, set along the steep sides of a narrow green valley. They were chatting gayly, and had just agreed that it was time to turn their horses' heads homeward, when a sudden darkening made them aware that one of the unexpected thunder-gusts peculiar to the region was upon them.

They were still a mile above the village; but as no nearer place of shelter presented itself, they decided to proceed. But the storm moved more rapidly than they; and long before the first houses came in sight the heavy drops began to pelt down. A brown young fellow, lying flat on his back under a thick bush, with his horse standing over him, shouted to them to "try the cave," waving his hand in its direction; and hurrying on, they saw in another moment a shelving brow of rock in the cliff, under which was a deep recess.

To this Clarence directed the horses. He lifted Clover down. She half sat, half leaned on the slope of the rock, well under cover, while he stretched himself at full length on a higher ledge, and held the bridles fast. The horses' heads and the saddles were fairly well protected, but the hindquarters of the animals were presently streaming with water.

"This isn't half-bad, is it?" Clarence said. His mouth was so close to Clover's ear that she could catch his words in spite of the noisy thunder and the roar of the descending rain.

"No; I call it fun."

"You look awfully pretty, do you know?" was the next and very unexpected remark.

"Nonsense."

"Not nonsense at all."

At that moment a carriage dashed rapidly by, the driver guiding the horses as well as he could between the points of an umbrella, which constantly menaced his eyes. Other travellers in the pass had evidently been surprised by the storm besides themselves. The lady who held the umbrella looked out, and caught the picture of the group under the cliff. It was a suggestive one. Clover's hat was a little pushed forward by the rock against which she leaned, which in its turn pushed forward the waving rings of hair which shaded her forehead, but did not hide her laughing eyes, or the dimples in her pink cheeks. The fair, slender girl, the dark, stalwart young fellow so close to her, the rain, the half-sheltered horses,—it was easy enough to construct a little romance.

The lady evidently did so. It was what photographers call an "instantaneous effect," caught in three seconds, as the carriage whirled past; but in that fraction of a minute the lady had nodded and flashed a brilliant, sympathetic smile in their direction, and Clover had nodded in return, and laughed back.

"A good many people seem to have been caught as we have," she said, as another streaming vehicle dashed by.

"I wish it would rain for a week," observed Clarence.

"My gracious, what a wish! What would become of us if it did?"

"We should stay here just where we are, and I should have you all to myself for once, and nobody could come in to interfere with me."

"Thank you extremely! How hungry we should be! How can you be so absurd, Clarence?"

"I'm not absurd at all. I'm perfectly in earnest."

"Do you mean that you really want to stay a week under this rock with nothing to eat?"

"Well, no; not exactly that perhaps,—though if you could, I would. But I mean that I would like to get you for a whole solid week to myself. There is such a gang of people about always, and they all want you. Clover," he went on, for, puzzled at his tone, she made no answer, "couldn't you like me a little?"

"I like you a great deal. You come next to Phil and Dorry with me."

"Hang Phil and Dorry! Who wants to come next to them? I want you to like me a great deal more than that. I want you to love me. Couldn't you, Clover?"

"How strangely you talk! I do love you, of course. You're my cousin."

"I don't care to be loved 'of course.' I want to be loved for myself. Clover, you know what I mean; you must know. I can afford to marry now; won't you stay in Colorado and be my wife?"

"I don't think you know what you are saying, Clarence. I'm older than you are. I thought you looked upon me as a sort of mother or older sister."

"Only fifteen months older," retorted Clarence. "I never heard of any one's being a mother at that age. I'm a man now, I would have you remember, though I am a little younger than you, and know my own mind as well as if I were fifty. Dear Clovy," coaxingly, "couldn't you? You liked the High Valley, didn't you? I'd do anything possible to make it nice and pleasant for you."

"I do like the High Valley very much," said Clover, still with the feeling that Clarence must be half in joke, or she half in dream. "But, my dear boy, it isn't my home. I couldn't leave papa and the children, and stay out here, even with you. It would seem so strange and far away."

"You could if you cared for me," replied Clarence, dejectedly; Clover's kind, argumentative, elder-sisterly tone was precisely that which is most discouraging to a lover.

"Oh, dear," cried poor Clover, not far from tears herself; "this is dreadful!"

"What?" moodily. "Having an offer? You must have had lots of them before now."

"Indeed I never did. People don't do such things in Burnet. Please don't say any more, Clarence. I'm very fond of you, just as I am of the boys; but—"

"But what? Go on."

"How can I?" Clover was fairly crying.

"You mean that you can't love me in the other way."

"Yes." The word came out half as a sob, but the sincerity of the accent was unmistakable.

"Well," said poor Clarence, after a long bitter pause; "it isn't your fault, I suppose. I'm not good enough for you. Still, I'd have done my best, if you would have taken me, Clover."

"I am sure you would," eagerly. "You've always been my favorite cousin, you know. People can't *make* themselves care for each other; it has to come in spite of them or not at all,—at least, that is what the novels say. But you're not angry with me, are you, dear? We will be good friends always, sha'n't we?" persuasively.

"I wonder if we can," said Clarence, in a hopeless tone. "It doesn't seem likely; but I don't know any more about it than you do. It's my first offer as well as yours." Then, after a silence and a struggle, he added in a more manful tone, "We'll try for it, at least. I can't afford to give you up. You're the sweetest girl in the world. I always said so, and I say so still. It will be hard at first, but perhaps it may grow easier with time."

"Oh, it will," cried Clover, hopefully. "It's only because you're so lonely out here, and see so few people, that makes you suppose I am better than the rest. One of these days you'll find a girl who is a great deal nicer than I am, and then you'll be glad that I didn't say yes. There! the rain is just stopping."

"It's easy enough to talk," remarked Clarence, gloomily, as he gathered up the bridles of the horses; "but I shall do nothing of the kind. I declare I won't!"

CHAPTER X. NO. 13 PIUTE STREET.

Clover did not see Clarence again for several days after this conversation, the remembrance of which was uncomfortable to her. She feared he was feeling hurt or "huffy," and would show it in his manner; and she disliked very much the idea that Phil might suspect the reason, or, worse still, Mr. Templestowe.

But when he finally appeared he seemed much the same as usual. After all, she reflected, it has only been a boyish impulse; he has already got over it, or not meant all he said.

In this she did Clarence an injustice. He had been very much in earnest when he spoke; and it showed the good stuff which was in him and his real regard for Clover that he should be making so manly a struggle with his disappointment and pain. His life had been a lonely one in Colorado; he could not afford to quarrel with his favorite cousin, and with him, as with other lovers, there may have been, besides, some lurking hope that she might yet change her mind. But perhaps Clover in a measure was right in her conviction that Clarence was still too young and undeveloped to have things go very deep with him. He seemed to her in many ways as boyish and as undisciplined as Phil.

With early September the summering of the Ute Park came to a close. The cold begins early at that elevation, and light frosts and red leaves warned the dwellers in tents and cabins to flee.

Clover made her preparations for departure with real reluctance. She had grown very fond of the place; but Phil was perfectly himself again, and there seemed no reason for their staying longer.

So back to St. Helen's they went and to Mrs. Marsh, who, in reply to Clover's letter, had written that she must make room for them somehow, though for the life of her she couldn't say how. It proved to be in two small back rooms. An irruption of Eastern invalids had filled the house to overflowing, and new faces met them at every turn. Two or three of the last summer's inmates had died during their stay,—one of them the very sick man whose room Mrs. Watson had coveted. His death took place "as if on purpose," she told Clover, the very week after her removal to the Shoshone.

Mrs. Watson herself was preparing for return to the East. "I've seen the West now," she said,—"all I want to see; and I'm quite ready to go back to my own part of the country. Ellen writes that she thinks I'd better start for home so as to get settled before the cold—And it's so cold here that I can't realize that they're still in the middle of peaches at home. Ellen always spices a great—They're better than preserves; and as for the canned ones, why, peaches and water is what I call them. Well—my dear—" (Distance lends enchantment, and Clover had become "My dear" again.) "I'm glad I could come out and help you along; and now that you know so many people here, you won't need me so much as you did at first. I shall tell Mrs. Perkins to write to Mrs. Hall to tell your father how well your brother is looking, and I know he'll be—And here's a little handkerchief for a keepsake."

It was a pretty handkerchief, of pale yellow silk with embroidered corners, and Clover kissed the old lady as she thanked her, and they parted good friends. But their intercourse had led her to make certain firm resolutions.

"I will try to keep my mind clear and my talk clear; to learn what I want and what I have a right to want and what I mean to say, so as not to puzzle and worry people when I grow old, by being vague and helpless and fussy," she reflected. "I suppose if I don't form the habit now, I sha'n't be able to then, and it would be dreadful to end by being like poor Mrs. Watson."

Altogether, Mrs. Marsh's house had lost its homelike character; and it was not strange that under the circumstances Phil should flag a little. He was not ill, but he was out of sorts and dismal, and disposed to consider the presence of so many strangers as a personal wrong. Clover felt that it was not a good atmosphere for him, and anxiously revolved in her mind what was best to do. The Shoshone was much too expensive; good boarding-houses in St. Helen's were few and far between, and all of them shared in a still greater degree the disadvantages which had made themselves felt at Mrs. Marsh's.

The solution to her puzzle came—as solutions often do—unexpectedly. She was walking down Piute Street on her way to call on Alice Blanchard, when her attention was attracted to a small, shut-up house, on which was a sign: "No. 13. To Let, Furnished." The sign was not printed, but written on a half-sheet of foolscap, which was what led Clover to notice it.

She studied the house a while, then opened the gate, and went in. Two or three steps led to a little piazza. She seated herself on the top step, and tried to peep in at the closed blinds of the nearest window.

While she was doing so, a woman with a shawl over her head came hastily down a narrow side street or alley, and approached her.

"Oh, did you want the key?" she said.

"The key?" replied Clover, surprised; "of this house, do you mean?"

"Yes. Mis Starkey left it with me when she went away, because, she said, it was handy, and I could give it to anybody who wished to look at the place. You're the first that has come; so when I see you setting here, I just ran over. Did Mr. Beloit send you?"

"No; nobody sent me. Is it Mr. Beloit who has the letting of the house?"

"Yes; but I can let folks in. I told Mis Starkey I'd air and dust a little now and then, if it wasn't took. Poor soul! she was anxious enough about it; and it all had to be done on a sudden, and she in such a heap of trouble that she didn't know which way to turn. It was just lock-up and go!"

"Tell me about her," said Clover, making room on the step for the woman to sit down.

"Well, she come out last year with her man, who had lung trouble, and he wasn't no better at first, and then he seemed to pick up for a while; and they took this house and fixed themselves to stay for a year, at least. They made it real nice, too, and slicked up considerable. Mis Starkey said, said she, 'I don't want to spend no more money on it than I can help, but Mr. Starkey must be made comfortable,' says she, them was her very words. He used to set out on this stoop all day long in the summer, and she alongside him, except when she had to be indoors doing the work. She didn't keep no regular help. I did the washing for her, and come in now and then for a day to clean; so she managed very well.

"Then,—Wednesday before last, it was,—he had a bleeding, and sank away like all in a minute, and was gone before the doctor could be had. Mis Starkey was all stunned like with the shock of it; and before she had got her mind cleared up so's to order about anything, come a telegraph to say her son was down with diphtheria, and his wife with a young baby, and both was very low. And between one and the other she was pretty near out of her wits. We packed her up as quick as we could, and he was sent off by express; and she says to me, 'Mis Kenny, you see how 't is. I've got this house on my hands till May. There's no time to see to anything, and I've got no heart to care; but if any one'll take it for the winter, well and good; and I'll leave the sheets and table-cloths and everything in it, because it may make a difference, and I don't mind about them nohow. And if no one does take it, I'll just have to bear the loss,' says she. Poor soul! she was in a world of trouble, surely."

"Do you know what rent she asks for the house?" said Clover, in whose mind a vague plan was beginning to take shape.

"Twenty-five a month was what she paid; and she said she'd throw the furniture in for the rest of the time, just to get rid of the rent."

Clover reflected. Twenty-five dollars a week was what they were paying at Mrs. Marsh's. Could they take this house and live on the same sum, after deducting the rent, and perhaps get this good-natured-looking woman to come in for a certain number of hours and help do the work? She almost fancied that they could if they kept no regular servant.

"I think I *would* like to see the house," she said at last, after a silent calculation and a scrutinizing look at Mrs. Kenny, who was a faded, wiry, but withal kindly-looking person, shrewd and clean,—a North of Ireland Protestant, as she afterward told Clover. In fact, her accent was rather Scotch than Irish.

They went in. The front door opened into a minute hall, from which another door led into a back hall with a staircase. There was a tiny sitting-room, an equally tiny dining-room, a small kitchen, and above, two bedrooms and a sort of unplastered space, which would answer to put trunks in. That was all, save a little woodshed. Everything was bare and scanty and rather particularly ugly. The sitting-room had a frightful paper of mingled mustard and molasses tint, and a matted floor; but there was a good-sized open fireplace for the burning of wood, in which two bricks did duty for andirons, three or four splint and cane bottomed chairs, a lounge, and a table, while the pipe of the large "Morning-glory" stove in the dining-room expanded into a sort of drum in the chamber above. This secured a warm sleeping place for Phil. Clover began to think that they could make it do.

Mrs. Kenny, who evidently considered the house as a wonder of luxury and convenience, opened various cupboards, and pointed admiringly to the glass and china, the kitchen tins and utensils, and the cotton sheets and pillow-cases which they respectively held.

"There's water laid on," she said; "you don't have to pump any. Here's the washtubs in the shed. That's a real nice tin boiler for the clothes,—I never see a nicer. Mis Starkey had that heater in the dining-room set the very week before she went away. 'Winter's coming on,' she says, 'and I must see about keeping my husband warm;' never thinking, poor thing, how 't was to be."

"Does this chimney draw?" asked the practical Clover; "and does the kitchen stove bake well?"

"First-rate. I've seen Mis Starkey take her biscuits out many a time,— as nice a brown as ever you'd want; and the chimney don't smoke a mite. They kep' a wood fire here in May most all the time, so I know."

Clover thought the matter over for a day or two, consulted with Dr. Hope, and finally decided to try the experiment. No. 13 was taken, and Mrs. Kenny engaged for two days' work each week, with such other occasional assistance as Clover might require. She was a widow, it seemed, with one son, who, being employed on the railroad, only came home for the nights. She was glad of a regular engagement, and proved an excellent stand-by and a great help to Clover, to whom she had taken a fancy from the start; and many were the good turns which she did for love rather than hire for "my little Miss," as she called her.

To Phil the plan seemed altogether delightful. This was natural, as all the fun fell to his share and none of the trouble; a fact of which Mrs. Hope occasionally reminded him. Clover persisted, however, that it was all fair, and that she got lots of fun out of it too, and didn't mind the trouble. The house was so absurdly small that it seemed to strike every one as a good joke; and Clover's friends set themselves to help in the preparations, as if the establishment in Piute Street were a kind of baby-house about which they could amuse themselves at will.

It is a temptation always to make a house pretty, but Clover felt herself on honor to spend no more than was necessary. Papa had trusted her, and she was resolved to justify his trust. So she bravely withstood her desire for several things which would have been great improvements so far as looks went, and confined her purchases to articles of clear necessity,—extra blankets, a bedside carpet for Phil's room, and a chafing-dish over which she could prepare little impromptu dishes, and so save fuel and fatigue. She allowed herself some cheap Madras curtains for the parlor, and a few yards of deep-red flannel to cover sundry shelves and corner brackets which Geoffrey Templestowe, who had a turn for carpentry, put up for her. Various loans and gifts, too, appeared from friendly attics and store-rooms to help out. Mrs. Hope hunted up some old iron firedogs and a pair of bellows, Poppy contributed a pair of brass-knobbed tongs, and Mrs. Marsh lent her a lamp. No. 13 began to look attractive.

They were nearly ready, but not yet moved in, when one day as Clover stood in the queer little parlor, contemplating the effect of Geoff's last effort,—an extra pine shelf above the narrow mantel-shelf,—a pair of arms stole round her waist, and a cheek which had a sweet familiarity about it was pressed against hers. She turned, and gave a great shriek of amazement and joy, for it was her sister Katy's arms that held her. Beyond, in the doorway, were Mrs. Ashe and Amy, with Phil between them.

"Is it you; is it really you?" cried Clover, laughing and sobbing all at once in her happy excitement. "How did it happen? I never knew that you were coming."

"Neither did we; it all happened suddenly," explained Katy. "The ship was ordered to New York on three days' notice, and as soon as Ned sailed, Polly and I made haste to follow. There would have been just time to get a letter here if we had written at once, but I had the fancy to give you a surprise."

"Oh, it is *such* a nice surprise! But when did you come, and where are you?"

"At the Shoshone House,—at least our bags are there; but we only stayed a minute, we were in such a hurry to get to you. We went to

Mrs. Marsh's and found Phil, who brought us here. Have you really taken this funny little house, as Phil tells us?"

"We really have. Oh, what a comfort it will be to tell you all about it, and have you say if I have done right! Dear, dear Katy, I feel as if home had just arrived by train. And Polly, too! You all look so well, and as if California had agreed with you. Amy has grown so that I should scarcely have known her."

Four delightful days followed. Katy flung herself into all Clover's plans with the full warmth of sisterly interest; and though the Hopes and other kind friends made many hospitable overtures, and would gladly have turned her short visit into a continuous *fête*, she persisted in keeping the main part of her time free. She must see a little of St. Helen's, she declared, so as to be able to tell her father about it, and she must help Clover to get to housekeeping,—these were the important things, and nothing else must interfere with them.

Most effectual assistance did she render in the way of unpacking and arranging. More than that, one day, when Clover, rather to her own disgust, had been made to go with Polly and Amy to Denver while Katy stayed behind, lo! on her return, a transformation had taken place, and the ugly paper in the parlor of No. 13 was found replaced with one of warm, sunny gold-brown.

"Oh, why did you?" cried Clover. "It's only for a few months, and the other would have answered perfectly well. Why did you, Katy?"

"I suppose it *was* foolish," Katy admitted; "but somehow I couldn't bear to have you sitting opposite that deplorable mustard-colored thing all winter long. And really and truly it hardly cost anything. It was a remnant reduced to ten cents a roll,—the whole thing was less than four dollars. You can call it your Christmas present from me, if you like, and I shall 'play' besides that the other paper had arsenic in it; I'm sure it looked as if it had, and corrosive sublimate, too."

Clover laughed outright. It was so funny to hear Katy's fertility of excuse.

"You dear, ridiculous darling!" she said, giving her sister a good hug; "it was just like you, and though I scold I am perfectly delighted. I did hate that paper with all my heart, and this is lovely. It makes the room look like a different thing."

Other benefactions followed. Polly, it appeared, had bought more Indian curiosities in Denver than she knew what to do with, and begged permission to leave a big bear-skin and two wolf-skins with Clover for the winter, and a splendid striped Navajo blanket as a portière to keep off draughts from the entry. Katy had set herself up in California blankets while they were in San Francisco, and she now insisted on leaving a pair behind, and loaning Clover besides one of two beautiful

Japanese silk pictures which Ned had given her, and which made a fine spot of color on the pretty new wall. There were presents in her trunks for all at home, and Ned had sent Clover a beautiful lacquered box.

Somehow Clover seemed like a new and doubly-interesting Clover to Katy. She was struck by the self-reliance which had grown upon her, by her bright ways and the capacity and judgment which all her arrangements exhibited; and she listened with delight to Mrs. Hope's praises of her sister.

"She really is a wonderful little creature; so wise and judgmatical, and yet so pretty and full of fun. People are quite cracked about her out here. I don't think you'll ever get her back at the East again, Mrs. Worthington. There seems a strong determination on the part of several persons to keep her here."

"What do you mean?"

But Mrs. Hope, who believed in the old proverb about not addling eggs by meddling with them prematurely, refused to say another word. Clover, when questioned, "could not imagine what Mrs. Hope meant;" and Katy had to go away with her curiosity unsatisfied. Clarence came in once while she was there, but she did not see Mr. Templestowe.

Katy's last gift to Clover was a pretty tea-pot of Japanese ware. "I meant it for Cecy," she explained. "But as you have none I'll give it to you instead, and take her the fan I meant for you. It seems more appropriate."

Phil and Clover moved into No. 13 the day before the Eastern party left, so as to be able to celebrate the occasion by having them all to an impromptu house-warming. There was not much to eat, and things were still a little unsettled; but Clover scrambled some eggs on her little blazer for them, the newly-lit fire burned cheerfully, and a good deal of quiet fun went on about it. Amy was so charmed with the minute establishment that she declared she meant to have one exactly like it for Mabel whenever she got married.

"And a spirit-lamp, too, just like Clover's, and a cunning, teeny-weeny kitchen and a stove to boil things on. Mamma, when shall I be old enough to have a house all of my own?"

"Not till you are tired of playing with dolls, I am afraid."

"Well, that will be never. If I thought I ever could be tired of Mabel, I should be so ashamed of myself that I should not know what to do. You oughtn't to say such things, Mamma; she might hear you, too, and have her feelings hurt. And please don't call her *that*," said Amy, who had as strong an objection to the word "doll" as mice are said to have to the word "cat."

Next morning the dear home people proceeded on their way, and Clover fell to work resolutely on her housekeeping, glad to keep busy, for she had a little fear of being homesick for Katy. Every small odd and end that she had brought with her from Burnet came into play now. The photographs were pinned on the wall, the few books and ornaments took their places on the extemporized shelves and on the table, which, thanks to Mrs. Hope, was no longer bare, but hidden by a big square of red canton flannel. There was almost always a little bunch of flowers from the Wade greenhouses, which were supposed to come from Mrs. Wade; and altogether the effect was cosey, and the little interior looked absolutely pretty, though the result was attained by such very simple means.

Phil thought it heavenly to be by themselves and out of the reach of strangers. Everything tasted delicious; all the arrangements pleased him; never was boy so easily suited as he for those first few weeks at No. 13.

"You're awfully good to me, Clover," he said one night rather suddenly, from the depths of his rocking-chair.

The remark was so little in Phil's line that it quite made her jump.

"Why, Phil, what made you say that?" she asked.

"Oh, I don't know. I was thinking about it. We used to call Katy the nicest, but you're just as good as she is. [This Clover justly considered a tremendous compliment.] You always make a fellow feel like home, as Geoff Templestowe says."

"Did Geoff say that?" with a warm sense of gladness at her heart. "How nice of him! What made him say it?"

"Oh, I don't know; it was up in the canyon one day when we got to talking," replied Phil. "There are no flies on you, he considers. I asked him once if he didn't think Miss Chase pretty, and he said not half so pretty as you were."

"Really! You seem to have been very confidential. And what is that about flies? Phil, Phil, you really mustn't use such slang."

"I suppose it is slang; but it's an awfully nice expression anyway."

"But what *does* it mean?"

"Oh, you must see just by the sound of it what it means,—that there's no nonsense sticking out all over you like some of the girls. It's a great compliment!"

"Is it? Well, I'm glad to know. But Mr. Templestowe never used such a phrase, I'm sure."

"No, he didn't," admitted Phil; "but that's what he meant."

So the winter drew on,—the strange, beautiful Colorado winter,—with weeks of golden sunshine broken by occasional storms of wind and sand, or by skurries of snow which made the plains white for a few hours and then vanished, leaving them dry and firm as before. The nights were often cold,—so cold that comfortables and blankets seemed all too few, and Clover roused with a shiver to think that presently it would be her duty to get up and start the fires so that Phil might find a warm house when he came downstairs. Then, before she knew it, fires would seem oppressive; first one window and then another would be thrown up, and Phil would be sitting on the piazza in the balmy sunshine as comfortable as on a June morning at home. It was a wonderful climate; and as Clover wrote her father, the winter was better even than the summer, and was certainly doing Phil more good. He was able to spend hours every day in the open air, walking, or riding Dr. Hope's horse, and improved steadily. Clover felt very happy about him.

This early rising and fire-making were the hardest things she had to encounter, though all the housekeeping proved more onerous than, in her inexperience, she had expected it to be. After the first week or two, however, she managed very well, and gradually learned the little labor-saving ways which can only be learned by actual experiment. Getting breakfast and tea she enjoyed, for they could be chiefly managed by the use of the chafing-dish. Dinners were more difficult, till she hit on the happy idea of having Mrs. Kenny roast a big piece of beef or mutton, or a pair of fowls every Monday. These *pièces de résistance* in their different stages of hot, cold, and warmed over, carried them well along through the week, and, supplemented with an occasional chop or steak, served very well. Fairly good soups could be bought in tins, which needed only to be seasoned and heated for use on table. Oysters were easily procurable there, as everywhere in the West; good brown-bread and rolls came from the bakery; and Clover developed a hitherto dormant talent for cookery and the making of Graham gems, corn-dodgers, hoe-cakes baked on a barrel head before the parlor fire, and wonderful little flaky biscuits raised all in a minute with Royal Baking Powder.

She also became expert in that other fine art of condensing work, and making it move in easy grooves. Her tea things she washed with her breakfast things, just setting the cups and plates in the sink for the night, pouring a dipper full of boiling water over them. There was no silver to care for, no delicate glass or valuable china; the very simplicity of apparatus made the house an easy one to keep. Clover was kept busy, for simplify as you will, providing for the daily needs of two persons does take time; but she liked her cares and rarely felt tired. The elastic and vigorous air seemed to build up her forces from moment to moment, and each day's fatigues were more than repaired by each night's rest, which is the balance of true health in living.

Little pleasures came from time to time. Christmas Day they spent with the Hopes, who from first to last proved the kindest and most helpful of friends to them. The young men from the High Valley were there also, and the day was brightly kept,—from the home letters by the early mail to the grand merry-making and dance with which it wound up. Everybody had some little present for everybody else. Mrs. Wade sent Clover a tall india-rubber plant in a china pot, which made a spire of green in the south window for the rest of the winter; and Clover had spent many odd moments and stitches in the fabrication of a gorgeous Mexican-worked sideboard cloth for the Hopes.

But of all Clover's offerings the one which pleased her most, as showing a close observation of her needs, came from Geoff Templestowe. It was a prosaic gift, being a wagon-load of piñon wood for the fire; but the gnarled, oddly twisted sticks were heaped high with pine boughs and long trails of red-fruited kinnikinnick to serve as a Christmas dressing, and somehow the gift gave Clover a peculiar pleasure.

"How dear of him!" she thought, lifting one of the big piñon logs with a gentle touch; "and how like him to think of it! I wonder what makes him so different from other people. He never says fine flourishing things like Thurber Wade, or abrupt, rather rude things like Clarence, or inconsiderate things like Phil, or satirical, funny things like the doctor; but he's always doing something kind. He's a little bit like papa, I think; and yet I don't know. I wish Katy could have seen him."

Life at St. Helen's in the winter season is never dull; but the gayest fortnight of all was when, late in January, the High Valley partners deserted their duties and came in for a visit to the Hopes. All sorts of small festivities had been saved for this special fortnight, and among the rest, Clover and Phil gave a party.

"If you can squeeze into the dining-room, and if you can do with just cream-toast for tea," she explained, "it would be such fun to have you come. I can't give you anything to eat to speak of, because I haven't any cook, you know; but you can all eat a great deal of dinner, and then you won't starve."

Thurber Wade, the Hopes, Clarence, Geoff, Marian, and Alice made a party of nine, and it was hard work indeed to squeeze so many into the tiny dining-room of No. 13. The very difficulties, however, made it all the jollier. Clover's cream-toast,—which she prepared before their eyes on the blazer,—her little tarts made of crackers split, buttered, and toasted brown with a spoonful of raspberry jam in each, and the big loaf of hot ginger-bread to be eaten with thick cream from the High Valley, were pronounced each in its way to be absolute perfection. Clarence and Phil kindly volunteered to "shunt the dishes" into the kitchen after the repast was concluded; and they gathered round the fire to play "twenty questions" and "stage-coach," and all manner of what Clover called "lead-pencil games,"—"crambo" and "criticism" and "anagrams" and "consequences." There was immense laughter over some of these, as, for instance, when Dr. Hope was reported as having met Mrs. Watson in the North Cheyenne Canyon, and he said that knowledge is power; and she, that when larks flew round ready roasted poor folks could stick a fork in; and the consequence was that they eloped together to a Cannibal Island where each suffered a process of disillusionation, and the world said it was the natural result of osculation. This last sentence was Phil's, and I fear he had peeped a little, or his context would not have been so apropos; but altogether the "cream-toast swarry," as he called it, was a pronounced success.

It was not long after this that a mysterious little cloud of difference seemed to fall on Thurber Wade. He ceased to call at No. 13, or to bring flowers from his mother; and by-and-by it was learned that he had started for a visit to the East. No one knew what had caused these phenomena, though some people may have suspected. Later it was announced that he was in Chicago and very attentive to a pretty Miss Somebody whose father had made a great deal of money in Standard oil. Poppy arched her brows and made great amused eyes at Clover, trying to entangle her into admissions as to this or that, and Clarence experimented in the same direction; but Clover was innocently impervious to these efforts, and no one ever knew what had happened between her and Thurber,—if, indeed, anything had happened.

So May came to St. Helen's in due course, of time. The sand-storms and the snow-storms were things of the past, the tawny yellow of the plains began to flush with green, and every day the sun grew more warm and beautiful. Phil seemed perfectly well and sound now; their occupancy of No. 13 was drawing to a close; and Clover, as she reflected that Colorado would soon be a thing of the past, and must be left behind, was sensible of a little sinking of the heart even though she and Phil were going home.

CHAPTER XI. THE LAST OF THE CLOVER-LEAVES.

Last days are very apt to be hard days. As the time drew near for quitting No. 13, Clover was conscious of a growing reluctance.

"I wonder why it is that I mind it so much?" she asked herself. "Phil has got well here, to be sure; that would be enough of itself to make me fond of the place, and we have had a happy winter in this little house. But still, papa, Elsie, John,—it seems very queer that I am not gladder to go back to them. I can't account for it. It isn't natural, and it seems wrong in me."

It was a rainy afternoon in which Clover made these reflections. Phil, weary of being shut indoors, had donned ulster and overshoes, and gone up to make a call on Mrs. Hope. Clover was quite alone in the house, as she sat with her mending-basket beside the fireplace, in which was burning the last but three of the piñon logs,—Geoff Templestowe's Christmas present.

"They will just last us out," reflected Clover; "what a comfort they have been! I would like to carry the very last of them home with me, and keep it to look at; but I suppose it would be silly."

She looked about the little room. Nothing as yet had been moved or disturbed, though the next week would bring their term of occupancy to a close.

"This is a good evening to begin to take things down and pack them," she thought. "No one is likely to come in, and Phil is away."

She rose from her chair, moved restlessly to and fro, and at last leaned forward and unpinned a corner of one of the photographs on the wall. She stood for a moment irresolutely with the pin in her fingers, then she jammed it determinedly back into the photograph again, and returned to her sewing. I almost think there were tears in her eyes.

"No," she said half aloud, "I won't spoil it yet. We'll have one more pleasant night with everything just as it is, and then I'll go to work and pull all to pieces at once. It's the easiest way."

Just then a foot sounded on the steps, and a knock was heard. Clover opened the door, and gave an exclamation of pleasure. It was Geoffrey Templestowe, splashed and wet from a muddy ride down the pass, but wearing a very bright face.

"How nice and unexpected this is!" was Clover's greeting. "It is such a bad day that I didn't suppose you or Clarence could possibly get in. Come to the fire and warm yourself. Is he here too?"

"No; he is out at the ranch. I came in to meet a man on business; but it seems there's a wash-out somewhere between here and Santa Fé, and my man telegraphs that he can't get through till to-morrow noon."

"So you will spend the night in town."

"Yes. I took Marigold to the stable, and spoke to Mrs. Marsh about a room, and then I walked up to see you and Phil. How is he, by the way?"

"Quite well. I never saw him so strong or so jolly. Papa will hardly believe his eyes when we get back. He has gone up to the Hopes, but will be in presently. You'll stay and take tea with us, of course."

"Thanks, if you will have me; I was hoping to be asked."

"Oh, we're only too glad to have you. Our time here is getting so short that we want to make the very most of all our friends; and by good luck there is a can of oysters in the house, so I can give you something hot."

"Do you really go so soon?"

"Our lease is out next week, you know."

"Really; so soon as that?"

"It isn't soon. We have lived here nearly eight months."

"What a good time we have all had in this little house!" cried Geoff, regretfully. "It has been a sort of warm little centre to us homeless people all winter."

"You don't count yourself among the homeless ones, I hope, with such a pleasant place as the High Valley to live in."

"Oh, the hut is all very well in its way, of course; but I don't look at it as a home exactly. It answers to eat and sleep in, and for a shelter when it rains; but you can't make much more of it than that. The only time it ever seemed home-like in the least was when you and Mrs. Hope were there. That week spoiled it for me for all time."

"That's a pity, if it's true, but I hope it isn't. It was a delightful week, though; and I think you do the valley an injustice. It's a beautiful place. Now, if you will excuse me, I am going to get supper."

"Let me help you."

"Oh, there is almost nothing to do. I'd much rather you would sit still and rest. You are tired from your ride, I'm sure; and if you don't mind, I'll bring my blazer and cook the oysters here by the fire. I always did like to 'kitch in the dining-room,' as Mrs. Whitney calls it."

Clover had set the tea-table before she sat down to sew, so there really was almost nothing to do. Geoff lay back in his chair and looked on with a sort of dreamy pleasure as she went lightly to and fro, making her arrangements, which, simple as they were, had a certain dainty quality about them which seemed peculiar to all that Clover did,—twisted a trail of kinnikinnick about the butter-plate, laid a garnish of fresh parsley on the slices of cold beef, and set a glass full of wild crocuses in the middle of the table. Then she returned to the parlor, put the kettle, which had already begun to sing, on the fire, and began to stir and season her oysters, which presently sent out a savory smell.

"I have learned six ways of cooking oysters this winter," she announced gleefully. "This is a dry-pan-roast. I wonder if you'll approve of it. And I wonder why Phil doesn't come. I wish he would make haste, for these are nearly done."

"There he is now," remarked Geoff.

But instead it was Dr. Hope's office-boy with a note.

DEAR C.,—Mrs. Hope wants me for a fourth hand at whist, so I'm staying, if you don't mind. She says if it didn't pour so she'd ask you to come too. P.

"Well, I'm glad," said Clover. "It's been a dull day for him, and now he'll have a pleasant evening, only he'll miss you."

"I call it very inconsiderate of the little scamp," observed Geoff. "He doesn't know but that he's leaving you to spend the evening quite alone."

"Oh, boys don't think of things like that."

"Boys ought to, then. However, I can stand his absence, if you can!"

It was a very merry little meal to which they presently sat down, full of the charm which the unexpected brings with it. Clover had grown to regard Geoff as one of her very best friends, and was perfectly at her ease with him, while to him, poor lonely fellow, such a glimpse of cosey home-life was like a peep at Paradise. He prolonged the pleasure as much as possible, ate each oyster slowly, descanting on its flavor, and drank more cups of tea than were at all good for him, for the pleasure of having Clover pour them out. He made no further offers of help when supper was ended, but looked on with fascinated eyes as she cleared away and made things tidy.

At last she finished and came back to the fire. There was a silence. Geoff was first to break it. "It would seem like a prison to you, I am afraid," he said abruptly.

"What would?"

"I was thinking of what you said about the High Valley."

"Oh!"

"You've only seen it in summer, you know. It's quite a different place in the winter. I don't believe a—person—could live on the year round and be contented."

"It would depend upon the person, of course."

"If it were a lady,—yourself, for instance,—could it be made anyway tolerable, do you think? Of course, one might get away now and then—"

"I don't know. It's not easy to tell beforehand how people are going to feel; but I can't imagine the High Valley ever seeming like a prison," replied Clover, vexed to find herself blushing, and yet unable to help it, Geoff's manner had such an odd intensity in it.

"If I were sure that you could realize what it would be—" he began impetuously; then quieting himself, "but you don't. How could you? Ranch life is well enough in summer for a short time by way of a frolic; but in winter and spring with the Upper Canyon full of snow, and the road down muddy and slippery, and the storms and short days, and the sense of being shut in and lonely, it would be a dismal place for a lady. Nobody has a right to expect a woman to undergo such a life."

Clover absorbed herself in her sewing, she did not speak; but still that deep uncomfortable blush burned on her cheeks.

"What do you think?" persisted Geoff. "Wouldn't it be inexcusable selfishness in a man to ask such a thing?"

"I think;" said Clover, shyly and softly, "that a man has a right to ask for whatever he wants, and—" she paused.

"And—what?" urged Geoff, bending forward.

"Well, a woman has always the right to say no, if she doesn't want to say yes."

"You tempt me awfully," cried Geoff, starting up. "When I think what this place is going to seem like after you've gone, and what the ranch will be with all the heart taken from it, and the loneliness made twice as lonely by comparison, I grow desperate, and feel as if I could not let you go without at least risking the question. But Clover,—let me call you so this once,—no woman could consent to such a life unless she cared very much for a man. Could you ever love me well enough for that, do you think?"

"It seems to me a very unfair sort of question to put," said Clover, with a mischievous glint in her usually soft eyes. "Suppose I said I could, and then you turned round and remarked that you were ever so sorry that you couldn't reciprocate my feelings—"

"Clover," catching her hand, "how can you torment me so? Is it necessary that I should tell you that I love you with every bit of heart that is in me, and need you and want you and long for you, but have never dared to hope that you could want me? Loveliest, sweetest, I do, and I always shall, whether it is yes or no."

"Then, Geoff—if you feel like that—if you're quite sure you feel like that, I think—"

"What do you think, dearest?"

"I think—that I could be very happy even in winter—in the High Valley."

And papa and the children, and the lonely and far-away feelings? There was never a mention of them in this frank acceptance. Oh, Clover, Clover, circumstances *do* alter cases!

Mrs. Hope's rubber of whist seemed a long one, for Phil did not get home till a quarter before eleven, by which time the two by the fire had settled the whole progress of their future lives, while the last logs of the piñon wood crackled, smouldered, and at length broke apart into flaming brands. In imagination the little ranch house had thrown out as many wings and as easily as a newly-hatched dragon-fly, had been beautified and made convenient in all sorts of ways,—a flower-garden had sprouted round its base, plenty of room had been made for papa and the children and Katy and Ned, who were to come out continually for visits in the long lovely summers; they themselves also were to go to and fro,—to Burnet, and still farther afield, over seas to the old Devonshire grange which Geoff remembered so fondly.

"How my mother and Isabel will delight in you," he said; "and the squire! You are precisely the girl to take his fancy. We'll go over and see them as soon as we can, won't we, Clover?"

Clover listened delightedly to all these schemes, but through them all, like that young Irish lady who went over the marriage service with her lover adding at the end of every clause, "Provided my father gives his consent," she interposed a little running thread of protest,—"If papa is willing. You know, Geoff, I can't really promise anything till I've talked with papa."

It was settled that until Dr. Carr had been consulted, the affair was not to be called an engagement, or spoken of to any one; only Clover asked Geoff to tell Clarence all about it at once.

The thought of Clarence was, in truth, the one cloud in her happiness just then. It was impossible to calculate how he would take the news. If it made him angry or very unhappy, if it broke up his friendship with Geoff, and perhaps interfered with their partnership so that one or other of them must leave the High Valley, Clover felt that it would grievously mar her contentment. There was no use in planning anything till they knew how he would feel and act. In any case, she realized that they were bound to consider him before themselves, and make it as easy and as little painful as possible. If he were vexatious, they must be patient; if sulky, they must be forbearing.

Phil opened his eyes very wide at the pair sitting so cosely over the fire when at last he came in.

"I say, have *you* been here all the evening?" he cried. "Well, that's a sell! I wouldn't have gone out if I'd known."

"We've missed you very much," quoth Geoff; and then he laughed as at some extremely good joke, and Clover laughed too.

"You seem to have kept up your spirits pretty well, considering," remarked Phil, dryly. Boys of eighteen are not apt to enjoy jokes which do not originate with themselves; they are suspicious of them.

"I suppose I must go now," said Geoff, looking at his watch; "but I shall see you again before I leave. I'll come in to-morrow after I've met my man."

"All right," said Phil; "I won't go out till you come."

"Oh, pray don't feel obliged to stay in. I can't at all tell when I shall be able to get through with the fellow."

"Come to dinner if you can," suggested Clover. "Phil is sure to be at home then."

Lovers are like ostriches. Geoff went away just shaking hands casually, and was very particular to say "Miss Carr;" and he and Clover felt that they had managed so skilfully and concealed their secret so well; yet the first remark made by Phil as the door shut was, "Geoff seems queer to-night, somehow, and so do you. What have you been talking about all the evening?"

An observant younger brother is a difficult factor in a love affair.

Two days passed. Clover looked in vain for a note from the High Valley to say how Clarence had borne the revelation; and she grew more nervous with every hour. It was absolutely necessary now to dismantle the house, and she found a certain relief in keeping exceedingly busy. Somehow the break-up had lost its inexplicable pain, and a glad little voice sang all the time at her heart, "I shall come back; I shall certainly come back. Papa will let me, I am sure, when he knows Geoff, and how nice he is."

She was at the dining-table wrapping a row of books in paper ready for packing, when a step sounded, and glancing round she saw Clarence himself standing in the doorway. He did not look angry, as she had feared he might, or moody; and though he avoided her eye at first, his face was resolute and kind.

"Geoff has told me," were his first words. "I know from what he said that you, and he too, are afraid that I shall make myself disagreeable; so I've come in to say that I shall do nothing of the kind."

"Dear Clarence, that wasn't what Geoff meant, or I either," said Clover, with a rush of relief, and holding out both her hands to him; "what we were afraid of was that you might be unhappy."

"Well," in a husky tone, and holding the little hands very tight, "it isn't easy, of course, to give up a hope. I've held on to mine all this time, though I've told myself a hundred times that I was a fool for doing so, and though I knew in my heart it was no use. Now I've had two days to think it over and get past the first shock, and, Clover, I've decided. You and Geoff are the best friends I've got in the world. I never seemed to make friends, somehow. Till you came to Hillsover that time nobody liked me much; I don't know why. I can't get along without you two; so I give you up without any hard feeling, and I mean to be as jolly as I can about it. After all, to have you at the High Valley will be a sort of happiness, even if you don't come for my sake exactly," with an attempt at a laugh.

"Clarence, you really are a dear boy! I can't tell you how I thank you, and how I admire you for being so nice about this."

"Then that's worth something, too. I'd do a good deal to win your approval, Clover. So it's all settled. Don't worry about me, or be afraid that I shall spoil your comfort with sour looks. If I find I can't stand it, I'll go away for a while; but I don't think it'll come to that. You'll make a real home out of the ranch house, and you'll let me have my share of your life, and be a brother to you and Geoff; and I'll try to be a good one."

Clover was touched to the heart by these manful words so gently spoken.

"You shall be our dear special brother always," she said. "Only this was needed to make me quite happy. I am so glad you don't want to go away and leave us, or to have us leave you. We'll make the ranch over into the dearest little home in the world, and be so cosey there all together, and papa and the others shall come out for visits; and you'll like them so much, I know, Elsie especially."

"Does she look like you?"

"Not a bit; she's ever so much prettier."

"I don't believe a word of that"

Clover's heart being thus lightened of its only burden by this treaty of mutual amity, she proceeded joyously with her packing. Mrs. Hope said she was not half sorry enough to go away, and Poppy upbraided her as a gay deceiver without any conscience or affections. She laughed and protested and denied, but looked so radiantly satisfied the while as to give a fair color for her friends' accusations, especially as she could not explain the reasons of her contentment or hint at her hopes of return. Mrs. Hope probably had her suspicions, for she was rather urgent with Clover to leave this thing and that for safe keeping "in case you ever come back;" but Clover declined these offers, and resolutely packed up everything with a foolish little superstition that it was "better luck" to do so, and that papa would like it better.

Quite a little group of friends assembled at the railway station to see her and Phil set off. They were laden with flowers and fruit and "natural soda-water" with which to beguile the long journey, and with many good wishes and affectionate hopes that they might return some day.

"Something tells me that you will," Mrs. Hope declared. "I feel it in my bones, and they hardly ever deceive me. My mother had the same kind; it's in the family."

"Something tells me that you must," cried Poppy, embracing Clover; "but I'm afraid it isn't bones or anything prophetic, but only the fact that I want you to so very much."

From the midst of these farewells Clover's eyes crossed the valley and sought out Mount Cheyenne.

"How differently I should be feeling," she thought, "if this were going away with no real hope of coming back! I could hardly have borne to look at you had that been the case, you dear beautiful thing; but I *am* coming back to live close beside you always, and oh, how glad I am!"

"Is that good-by to Cheyenne?" asked Marian, catching the little wave of a hand.

"Yes, it *is* good-by; but I have promised him that it shall soon be how-do-you-do again. Mount Cheyenne and I understand each other."

"I know; you have always had a sentimental attachment to that mountain. Now Pike's Peak is *my* affinity. We get on beautifully together."

"Pike's Peak indeed! I am ashamed of you."

Then the train moved away amid a flutter of handkerchiefs, but still Clover and Phil were not left to themselves; for Dr. Hope, who had a consultation in Denver, was to see them safely off in the night express, and Geoff had some real or invented business which made it necessary for him to go also.

Clover carried with her through all the three days' ride the lingering pressure of Geoff's hand, and his whispered promise to "come on soon." It made the long way seem short. But when they arrived, amid all the kisses and rejoicings, the exclamations over Phil's look of health and vigor, the girls' intense interest in all that she had seen and done, papa's warm approval of her management, her secret began to burn guiltily within her. What *would* they all say when they knew?

And what did they say? I think few of you will be at a loss to guess. Life—real life as well as life in story-books—is full of such shocks and surprises. They are half happy, half unhappy; but they have to be borne. Younger sisters, till their own turns come, are apt to take a severe view of marriage plans, and to feel that they cruelly interrupt a past order of things which, so far as they are concerned, need no improvement. And parents, who say less and understand better, suffer, perhaps, more. "To bear, to rear, to lose," is the order of family history, generally unexpected, always recurring.

But true love is not selfish. In time it accustoms itself to anything which secures happiness for its object. Dr. Carr did confide to Katy in a moment of private explosion that he wished the Great West had never been invented, and that such a prohibitory tax could be laid upon young

Englishmen as to make it impossible that another one should ever be landed on our shores; but he had never in his life refused Clover anything upon which she had set her heart, and he saw in her eyes that her heart was very much set on this. John and Elsie scolded and cried, and then in time began to talk of their future visits to High Valley till they grew to anticipate them, and be rather in a hurry for them to begin. Geoff's arrival completed their conversion.

"Nicer than Ned," Johnnie pronounced him; and even Dr. Carr was forced to confess that the sons-in-law with which Fate had provided him were of a superior sort; only he wished that they didn't want to marry *his* girls!

Phil, from first to last, was in favor of the plan, and a firm ally to the lovers. He had grown extremely Western in his ideas, and was persuaded in his mind that "this old East," as he termed it, with its puny possibilities, did not amount to much, and that as soon as he was old enough to shape his own destinies, he should return to the only section of the country worthy the attention of a young man of parts. Meanwhile, he was perfectly well again, and willing to comply with his father's desire that before he made any positive arrangements for his future, he should get a sound and thorough education.

"So you are actually going out to the wild and barbarous West, to live on a ranch, milk cows, chase the wild buffalo to its lair, and hold the tiger-cat by its favorite forelock," wrote Rose Red. "What was that you were saying only the other day about nice convenient husbands, who cruise off for 'good long times,' and leave their wives comfortably at home with their own families? And here you are planning to marry a man who, whenever he isn't galloping after cattle, will be in your pocket at home! Oh, Clover, Clover, how inconsistent a thing is woman,—not to say girl,—and what havoc that queer deity named Cupid does make with preconceived opinions! I did think I could rely on you; but you are just as bad as the rest of us, and when a lad whistles, go off after him wherever he happens to lead, and think it the best thing possible to do so. It's a mad world, my masters; and I'm thankful that Roslein is only four and a half years old."

And Clover's answer was one line on a postal card,—

"Guilty, but recommended to mercy!"

In the High Valley

CHAPTER I. ALONG THE NORTH DEVON COAST.

IT was a morning of late May, and the sunshine, though rather watery, after the fashion of South-of-England suns, was real sunshine still, and glinted and glittered bravely on the dew-soaked fields about Copplestone Grange.
This was an ancient house of red brick, dating back to the last half of the sixteenth century, and still bearing testimony in its sturdy bulk to the honest and durable work put upon it by its builders. Not a joist had bent, not a girder started in the long course of its two hundred and odd years of life. The brick-work of its twisted chimney-stacks was intact, and the stone carving over its doorways and window frames; only the immense growth of the ivy on its side walls attested to its age. It takes longer to build ivy five feet thick than many castles, and though new masonry by trick and artifice may be made to look like old, there is no secret known to man by which a plant or tree can be induced to simulate an antiquity which does not rightfully belong to it. Innumerable sparrows and tomtits had built in the thick mats of the old ivy, and their cries and twitters blended in shrill and happy chorus as they flew in and out of their nests.

The Grange had been a place of importance, in Queen Elizabeth's time, as the home of an old Devon family which was finally run out and extinguished. It was now little more than a superior sort of farm-house. The broad acres of meadow and pleasaunce and woodland which had given it consequence in former days had been gradually parted with, as misfortunes and losses came to its original owners. The woods had been felled, the pleasure grounds now made part of other people's farms, and the once wide domain had contracted, until the ancient house stood with only a few acres about it, and wore something the air of an old-time belle who has been forcibly divested of her ample farthingale and hooped-petticoat, and made to wear the scant kirtle of a village maid.

Orchards of pear and apple flanked the building to east and west. Behind was a field or two crowning a little upland where sedate cows fed demurely; and in front, toward the south, which was the side of entrance, lay a narrow walled garden, with box-bordered beds full of early flowers, mimulus, sweet-peas, mignonette, stock gillies, and blush and damask roses, carefully tended and making a blaze of color on the face of the bright morning. The whole front of the house was draped with a luxuriant vine of Gloire de Dijon, whose long, pink-yellow buds and cream-flushed cups sent wafts of delicate sweetness with every puff of wind.

Seventy years before the May morning of which we write, Copplestone Grange had fallen at public sale to Edward Young, a well-to-do banker of Bideford. He was a descendant in direct line of that valiant Young who, together with his fellow-seaman Prowse, undertook the dangerous task of steering down and igniting the seven fire-ships which sent the Spanish armada "lumbering off" to sea, and saved England for Queen Elizabeth and the Protestant succession.

Edward Young lived twenty years in peace and honor to enjoy his purchase, and his oldest son James now reigned in his stead, having reared within the old walls a numerous brood of sons and daughters, now scattered over the surface of the world in general, after the sturdy British fashion, till only three or four remained at home, waiting their turn to fly.

One of these now stood at the gate. It was Imogen Young, oldest but one of the four daughters. She was evidently waiting for some one, and waiting rather impatiently.

"We shall certainly be late," she said aloud, "and it's quite too bad of Lion." Then, glancing at the little silver watch in her belt, she began to call, "Lion! Lionel! Oh, Lion! do make haste! It's gone twenty past, and we shall never be there in time."

"Coming," shouted a voice from an upper window; "I'm just washing my hands. Coming in a jiffy, Moggy."

"Jiffy!" murmured Imogen. "How very American Lion has got to be. He's always 'guessing' and 'calculating' and 'reckoning.' It seems as if he did it on purpose to startle and annoy me. I suppose one has got to get used to it if you're over there, but really it's beastly bad form, and I shall keep on telling Lion so."

She was not a pretty girl, but neither was she an ill-looking one. Neither tall nor very slender, her vigorous little figure had still a certain charm of trim erectness and youthful grace, though Imogen was twenty-four, and considered herself very staid and grown-up. A fresh, rosy skin, beautiful hair of a warm, chestnut color, with a natural wave in it, and clear, honest, blue eyes, went far to atone for a thick nose, a wide mouth, and front teeth which projected slightly and seemed a size too large for the face to which they belonged. Her dress did nothing to assist her looks. It was woollen, of an unbecoming shade of yellowish gray; it fitted badly, and the complicated loops and hitches of the skirt bespoke a fashion some time since passed by among those who were particular as to such matters. The effect was not assisted by a pork-pie hat of black straw trimmed with green feathers, a pink ribbon from which depended a silver locket, a belt of deep magenta-red, yellow gloves, and an umbrella bright navy-blue in tint. She had over her arm a purplish water-proof, and her thick, solid boots could defy the mud of her native shire.

"Lion! Lion!" she called again; and this time a tall young fellow responded, running rapidly down the path to join her. He was two years her junior, vigorous, alert, and boyish, with a fresh skin, and tawny, waving hair like her own.

"How long you have been!" she cried reproachfully.

"Grieved to have kept you, Miss," was the reply. "You see, things went contrairy-like. The grease got all over me when I was cleaning the guns, and cold water wouldn't take it off, and that old Saunders took his time about bringing the can of hot, till at last I rushed down and fetched it up myself from the copper. You should have seen cook's face! 'Fancy, Master Lionel,' says she, 'coming yourself for 'ot water!' I tell you, Moggy, Saunders is past his usefulness. He's a regular duffer—a gump."

"There's another American expression. Saunders is a most respectable man, I'm sure, and has been in the family thirty-one years. Of course he has a good deal to do just now, with the packing and all. Now, Lion, we shall have to walk smartly if we're to get there at half-after."

"All right. Here goes for a spin, then."

The brother and sister walked rapidly on down the winding road, in the half-shadow of the bordering hedges. Real Devonshire hedge-rows they were, than which are none lovelier in England, rising eight and ten feet overhead on either side, and topped with delicate, flickering birch and ash boughs blowing in the fresh wind. Below were thick growths of hawthorn, white and pink, and wild white roses in full flower interspersed with maple tips as red as blood, the whole interlaced and held together with thick withes and tangles of ivy, briony, and travellers' joy. Beneath them the ground was strewn with flowers,—

violets, and king-cups, poppies, red campions, and blue iris,—while tall spikes of rose-colored foxgloves rose from among ranks of massed ferns, brake, hart's-tongue, and maiden's-hair, with here and there a splendid growth of Osmund Royal. To sight and smell, the hedge-rows were equally delightful.

Copplestone Grange stood three miles west of Bideford, and the house to which the Youngs were going was close above Clovelly, so that a distance of some seven miles separated them. To walk this twice for the sake of lunching with a friend would seem to most young Americans too formidable a task to be at all worth while, but to our sturdy English pair it presented no difficulties. On they went, lightly and steadily, Imogen's elastic steps keeping pace easily with her brother's longer tread. There was a good deal of up and down hill to get over with, and whenever they topped a rise, green downs ending in wooded cliffs could be seen to the left, and beyond and below an expanse of white-flecked shimmering sea. A salt wind from the channel blew in their faces, full of coolness and refreshment, and there was no dust.

"I suppose we shall never see the ocean from where we are to live," said Imogen, with a sigh.

"Well, hardly, considering it's about fifteen-hundred miles away."

"Fifteen hundred! oh, Lion, you are surely exaggerating. Why, the whole of England is not so large as that, from Land's End to John O'Groat's House."

"I should say not, nothing like it. Why Moggy, you've no idea how small our 'right little, tight little island' really is. You could set it down plump in some of the States, New York, for instance, and there would be quite a tidy fringe of territory left all round it. Of course, morally, we are the standard of size for all the world, but geographically, phew!—our size is little, though our hearts are great."

"I think it's vulgar to be so big,—not that I believe half you say, Lion. You've been over in America so long, and grown such a Yankee, that you swallow everything they choose to tell you. I've always heard about American brag—"

"My dear, there's no need to brag when the facts are there, staring you in the face. It's just a matter of feet and inches,—any one can do the measurement who has a tape-line. Wait till you see it. And as for its being vulgar to be big, why is the 'right little, tight little' always stretching out her long arms to rope in new territory, in that case, I should like to know? It would be much eleganter to keep herself to home—"

"Oh, don't talk that sort of rot; I hate to hear you."

"I must when you talk that kind of—well, let us say 'rubbish.' 'Rot' is one of our choice terms which hasn't got over to the States yet. You're as opiniated and 'narrer' as the little island itself. What do you know about America, any way? Did you ever see an American in your life, child?"

"Yes, several. I saw Buffalo Bill last year, and lots of Indians and cow-boys whom he had fetched over. And I saw Professor—Professor—what was his name? I forget, but he lectured on phrenology; and then there was Mrs. Geoff Templestowe."

"Oh Mrs. Geoff—she's a different sort. Buffalo Bill and his show can hardly be treated as specimens of American society, and neither can your bump-man. But she's a fair sample of the nice kind; and you liked her, now didn't you? you know you did."

"Well, yes, I did," admitted Imogen, rather grudgingly. "She was really quite nice, and good-form, and all that, and Isabel said she was far and away the best sister-in-law yet, and the Squire took such a fancy to her that it was quite remarkable. But she cannot be used as an argument, for she's not the least like the American girls in the books. She must have had unusual advantages. And after all,—nice as she was, she wasn't English. There was a difference somehow,—you felt it though you couldn't say exactly what it was."

"No, thank goodness—she isn't; that's just the beauty of it. Why should all the world be just alike? And what books do you mean, and what girls? There are all kinds on the other side, I can tell you. Wait till you get over to the High Valley and you'll see."

This sort of discussion had become habitual of late between the brother and sister. Three years before, Lionel had gone out to Colorado, to "look about and see how ranching suited him," as he phrased it, and had decided that it suited him exactly. He had served a sort of apprenticeship to Geoffrey Templestowe, the son of an old Devonshire neighbor, who had settled in a place called High Valley, and, together with two partners, had built up a flourishing and lucrative cattle business, owning a large tract of grazing territory and great herds. One of the partners was now transferred to New Mexico, where the firm owned land also, and Mr. Young had advanced money to buy Lionel, who was now competent to begin for himself, a share in the business. He was now going out to remain permanently, and Imogen was going also, to keep his house and make a home for him till he should be ready to marry and settle down.

All over the world there are good English sisters doing this sort of thing. In Australia and New Zealand they are to be found, in Canada, and India, and the Transvaal,—wherever English boys are sent to advance their fortunes. Had her destination been Canada or Australia, Imogen would have found no difficulty in adjusting her ideas to it, but the United States were a terra incognita. Knowing absolutely nothing about them, she had constructed out of a fertile fancy and a few facts an altogether imaginary America, not at all like the real one; peopled by strange folk quite un-English in their ideas and ways, and very hard to understand and live with. In vain did Lionel protest and explain; his remonstrances were treated as proofs of the degeneracy and blindness induced by life in "The States," and to all his appeals she opposed that calm, obstinate disbelief which is the weapon of a limited intellect and experience, and is harder to deal with than the most passionate convictions.

Unknown to herself a little sting of underlying jealousy tinctured these opinions. For many years Isabel Templestowe had been her favorite friend, the person she most admired and looked up to. They had been at school together,—Isabel always taking the lead in everything, Imogen following and imitating. The Templestowes were better born than the Youngs, they took a higher place in the county; it was a distinction as well as a tender pleasure to be intimate in the house. Once or twice Isabel had gone to her married sister in London for a taste of the "season." No such chance had ever fallen to Imogen's lot, but it was next best to get letters, and hear from Isabel of all that she had seen and done; thus sharing the joys at second-hand, as it were.

Isabel had other intimates, some of whom were more to her than Imogen could be, but they lived at a distance and Imogen close at hand. Propinquity plays a large part in friendship as well as love. Imogen had no other intimate, but she knew too little of Isabel's other interests to be made uncomfortable about them, and was quite happy in her position as nearest and closest confidante until, four years before, Geoffrey

Templestowe came home for a visit, bringing with him his American wife, whose name before her marriage had been Clover Carr, and whom some of you who read this will recognize as an old friend.

Young, sweet, pretty, very happy, and "horribly well-dressed," as poor Imogen in her secret soul admitted, Clover easily and quickly won the liking of her "people-in-law." All the outlying sons and daughters who were within reach came home to make her acquaintance, and all were charmed with her. The Squire petted and made much of his new daughter and could not say enough in her praise. Mrs. Templestowe averred that she was as good as she was pretty, and as "sensible" as if she had been born and brought up in England; and, worst of all, Isabel, for the time of their stay, was perfectly absorbed in Geoff and Clover, and though kind and affectionate when they met, had little or no time to spend on Imogen. She and Clover were of nearly the same age, each had a thousand interesting things to tell the other, both were devoted to Geoffrey,—it was natural, inevitable, that they should draw together. Imogen confessed to herself that it was only right that they should do so, but it hurt all the same, and it was still a sore spot in her heart that Isabel should love Clover so much, and that they should write such long letters to each other. She was a conscientious girl, and she fought against the feeling and tried hard to forget it, but there it was all the same.

But while I have been explaining, the rapid feet of the two walkers had taken them past the Hoops Inn, and to the opening of a rough shady lane which made a short cut to the grounds of Stowe Manor, as the Templestowes' place was called.

They entered by a private gate, opened by Imogen with a key which she carried, and found themselves on the slope of a hill overhung with magnificent old beeches. Farther down, the slope became steeper and narrowed to form the sharp "chine" which cut the cliff seaward to the water's edge. The Manor-house stood on a natural plateau at the head of the ravine, whose steep green sides made a frame for the beautiful picture it commanded of Lundy Island, rising in bold outlines over seventeen miles of blue, tossing sea.

The brother and sister paused a moment to look for the hundredth time at this exquisite glimpse. Then they ran lightly down over the grass to where an intersecting gravel-path led to the door. It stood hospitably open, affording a view of the entrance hall.

Such a beautiful old hall! built in the time of the Tudors, with a great carven fireplace, mullioned windows in deep square bays, and a ceiling carved with fans, shields, and roses. "Bow-pots" stood on the sills, full of rose-leaves and spices, huge antlers and trophies of weapons adorned the walls, and the polished floor, almost black with age, shone like a looking-glass.

Beyond opened a drawing-room, low-ceiled and equally quaint in build. The furniture seemed as old as the house. There was nothing with a modern air about it, except some Indian curiosities, a water-color or two, the photographs of the family, and the fresh flowers in the vases. But the sun shone in, there was a great sense of peace and stillness, and beside a little wood-fire, which burned gently and did not hiss or crackle as it might have done elsewhere, sat a lovely old lady, whose fresh and peaceful and kindly face seemed the centre from which all the home look and comfort streamed. She was knitting a long silk stocking, a volume of Mudie's lay on her knee, and a skye terrier, blue, fuzzy, and sleepy, had curled himself luxuriously in the folds of her dress.

This was Mrs. Templestowe, Geoff's mother and Clover's mother-in-law. She jumped up almost as lightly as a girl to welcome the visitors.

"Take your hat off, my dear," she said to Imogen, "or would you rather run up to Isabel's room? She was here just now, but her father called her off to consult about something in the hot-house. He won't keep her long— Ah, there she is now," as a figure flashed by the window; "I knew she would be here directly."

Another second and Isabel hurried in, a tall, slender girl with thick, fair hair, blue eyes with dark lashes, and a look of breeding and distinction. Her dress, very simple in cut, suited her, and had that undefinable air of being just right which a good London tailor knows how to give. She wore no ornaments, but Imogen, who had felt rather well-dressed when she left home, suddenly hated her gown and hat, realized that her belt and ribbon did not agree, and wished for the dozenth time that she had the knack at getting the right thing which Isabel possessed.

"Her clothes grow prettier all the time, and mine get uglier," she reflected. "The Squire says she got points from Mrs. Geoff, and that the Americans know how to dress if they don't know anything else; but that's nonsense, of course,—Isabel always did know how; she didn't need any one to teach her."

Pretty soon they were all seated at luncheon, a hearty and substantial meal, as befitted the needs of people who had just taken a seven-mile walk. A great round of cold beef stood at one end of the table, a chicken-pie at the other, and there were early peas and potatoes, a huge cherry-tart, a "junket" equally large, strawberries, and various cakes and pastries, meant to be eaten with a smother of that delicacy peculiar to Devonshire, clotted cream. Every body was very hungry, and not much was said till the first rage of appetite was satisfied.

"Ah!" said the Squire, as he filled his glass with amber-hued cider,— "you don't get anything so good as this to drink over in America, Lionel."

"Indeed we do, sir. Wait till you taste our lemonade made with natural soda-water."

"Lemonade? phoo! Poor stuff I call it, cold and thin. I hope Geoff has some better tipple than that to cheer him in the High Valley."

"Iced water," suggested Lionel, mischievously.

"Don't talk to me about iced water. It's worse than lemonade. It's the perpetual use of ice which makes the Americans so nervous, I am convinced."

"But, papa, are they so nervous? Clover certainly isn't."

"Ah! my little Clover,—no, she wasn't nervous. She was nothing that she ought not to be. I call her as sweet a lass as any country need want to see. But Clover's no example; there aren't many like her, I fancy,— eh, Lion?"

"Well, Squire, she's not the only one of the sort over there. Her sister, who married Mr. Page, our other partner, you know, is quite as pretty as she is, and as nice, too, though in a different way. And there's the oldest one—the wife of the naval officer, I'm not sure but you would like her the best of the three. She's a ripper in looks,—tall, you know, with lots of go and energy, and yet as sweet and womanly as can be; you'd like her very much, you'd like all of them."

"How is the unmarried one?—Joan, I think they call her," asked Mrs. Templestowe.

"Oh!" said Lionel, rather confused, "I don't know so much about her. She's only once been out to the valley since I was there. She seems a nice girl, and certainly she's mighty pretty."

"Lion's blushing," remarked Imogen. "He always does blush when he speaks of that Miss Carr."

"Rot!" muttered Lionel, with a wrathful look at his sister. "I do nothing of the kind. But, Squire, when are you coming over to see for yourself how we look and behave? I think you and the Madam would enjoy a summer in the High Valley very much, and it would be no end of larks to have you. Isabel would like it of all things."

"Oh, I know I should. I would start to-morrow, if I could. I'm coming across to make Clover and Imogen a long visit the first moment that papa and mamma can spare me."

"That will be a long time to wait, I fear," said her mother, sadly. "Since Mr. Matthewson married and carried off poor Helen's children, the house has seemed so silent that except for you it would hardly be worth while to get up in the morning. We can't spare you at present, dear child."

"I know, mamma, and I shall never go till you can. The perfect thing would be that we should all go together."

"Yes, if it were not for that dreadful voyage."

"Oh, the voyage is nothing," broke in the irrepressible Lionel, "you just take some little pills; I forget the name of them, but they make you safe not to be sick, and then you're across before you know it. The ships are very comfortable,—electric bells, Welsh rabbits at bed-time, and all that, you know."

"Fancy mamma with a Welsh rabbit at bed-time!—mamma, who cannot even row down to Gallantry on the smoothest day without being upset! You must bait your hook with something else, Lionel, if you hope to catch her."

"How would a trefoil of clover-leaves answer?" with a smile,—"she, Geoff, and the boy."

"Ah, that dear baby. I wish I could see the little fellow. He is so pretty in his picture," sighed Mrs. Templestowe. "That bait would land me if anything could, Lion. By the way, there are some little parcels for them, which I thought perhaps you would make room for, Imogen."

"Yes, indeed, I'll carry anything with pleasure. Now I'm afraid we must be going. Mother wants me to step down to Clovelly with a message for the landlady of the New Inn, and I've set my heart upon walking once more to Gallantry Bower. Can't you come with us, Isabel? It would be so nice if you could, and it's my last chance."

"Of course I will. I'll be ready in five minutes, if you really can't stay any longer."

The three friends were soon on their way, under a low-hung sky, which looked near and threatening. The beautiful morning was fled.

"We had better cut down into the Hobby grounds and get under the trees, for I think it's going to be wet," said Imogen.

The suggestion proved a wise one, for before they emerged from the shelter of the woods it was raining smartly, and the girls were glad of their water-proofs and umbrellas. Lionel, with hands in pockets, strode on, disdaining what he was pleased to call "a little local shower."

"You should see how it pours in Colorado," he remarked. "That's worth calling rain! Immense! Noah would feel perfectly at home in it!"

The tax of threepence each person, by which strangers are ingeniously made to contribute to the "local charities," was not exacted of them at the New Road Gate, on the strength of their being residents, and personal friends of the owners of Clovelly Court. A few steps farther brought them to the top of a zig-zag path, sloping sharply downward at an angle of some sixty-five degrees, paved with broad stones, and flanked on either side by houses, no two of which occupied the same level, and which seemed to realize their precarious footing, and hug the rift in which they were planted as limpets hug a rock.

This was the so-called "Clovelly Street," and surely a more extraordinary thing in the way of a street does not exist in the known world. The little village is built on the sides of a crack in a tremendous cliff; the "street" is merely the bottom of the crack, into which the ingenuity of man has fitted a few stones, set slant-wise, with intersecting ridges on which the foot can catch as it goes slipping hopelessly down. Even to practised walkers the descent is difficult, especially when the stones are wet. The party from Stowe were familiar with the path, and had trodden it many times, but even they picked their steps, and went "delicately" like King Agag, holding up umbrellas in one hand, and with the other catching at garden palings and the edges of door-steps to save themselves from pitching headlong, while beside them little boys and girls with the agility of long practice, went down merrily almost at a run, their heavy, flat-bottomed shoes making a clap-clap-clapping noise as they descended, like the strokes of a mallet on wood.

Looking up and above the quaint tenements that bordered the "street," other houses equally quaint could be seen on either side rising above each other to the top of the cliff, in whose midst the crack which held the village is set. How it ever entered into the mind of man to utilize such a place for such a purpose it was hard to conceive. The eccentricity of level was endless, gardens topped roofs, gooseberry-bushes and plum-trees seemed growing out of chimneys, tall trees rose apparently from ridge-poles, and here and there against the sky appeared extraordinary wooden figures of colossal size, Mermaids and Britannias and Belle Savages, figure-heads of forgotten ships which old sea-captains out of commission had set up in their gardens to remind them of perils past. The weather-beaten little houses looked centuries old, and all had such an air of having been washed accidentally into their places by a great tidal wave that the vines and flowers which overhung them affected the new-comer with a sense of surprise.

Down went the three, slipping and sliding, catching on and recovering themselves, till they came to a small, low-browed building dating back for a couple of centuries or so, which was the "New Inn." "Old" and "new" have a local meaning of their own in Clovelly which does not exactly apply anywhere else.

Up two little steps they passed into a narrow entry, with a parlor on one side and on the other a comfortable sort of housekeeper's room, where a fire was blazing in a grate with wide hobs. Both rooms as well as the entry were hung with plates, dishes, platters, and bowls, set thickly on the walls in groups of tens and scores and double-scores, as suited their shape and color. The same ceramic decoration ran upstairs and pervaded the rooms above more or less; a more modern brick-building on the opposite side of the street which was the "annex" of the Inn, was equally full; hundreds and hundreds of plates and saucers and cups,

English and Delft ware chiefly, and blue and white in color. It had been the landlady's hobby for years past to form this collection of china, and it was now for sale to any one who might care to buy.

Isabel and Lionel ran to and fro examining "the great wall of China," as he termed it, while Imogen did her mother's errand to the landlady. Then they started again to mount the hill, which was an easier task than going down, passing on the way two or three parties of tourists holding on to each other, and shrieking and exclaiming; and being passed by a minute donkey with two sole-leather trunks slung on one side of him, and on the other a mountainous heap of hand-bags and valises. This is the only creature with four legs, bigger than a dog, that ever gets down the Clovelly street; and why he does not lose his balance, topple backward, and go rolling continuously down till he falls into the sea below, nobody can imagine. But the valiant little animal kept steadily on, assisted by his owner, who followed and assiduously whacked him with a stout stick, and he reached the top much sooner than any of his biped following. One cannot have too many legs in Clovelly,—a centipede would find himself at an uncommon advantage.

At the top of the street is the "Yellery Gate" through which our party passed into lovely park grounds topping a line of fine cliffs which lead to "Gallantry Bower." This is the name given to an enormous headland which falls into the sea with a sheer descent of nearly four hundred feet, and forms the western boundary of the Clovelly roadstead.

The path was charmingly laid out with belts of woodland and clumps of flowering shrubs. Here and there was a seat or a rustic summer-house, commanding views of the sea, now a deep intense blue, for the rain had ceased as suddenly as it came, and broad yellow rays were streaming over the wet grass and trees, whose green was dazzling in its freshness. Imogen drew in a long breath of the salt wind, and looked wistfully about her at the vivid turf, the delicate shimmer of blowing leaves, and the tossing ocean, as if trying to photograph each detail in her memory.

"I shall see nothing so beautiful over there," she said. "Dear old Devonshire, there's nothing like it."

"Colorado is even better than 'dear old Devonshire,'" declared her brother; "wait till you see Pike's Peak. Wait till I drive you through the North Cheyenne Canyon."

But Imogen shook her head incredulously.

"Pike's Peak!" she answered, with an air of scorn. "The name is enough; I never want to see it."

"Well, you girls are good walkers, it must be confessed;" said Lionel, as they emerged on the crossing of the Bideford road where they must separate. "Isabel looks as fresh as paint, and Moggy hasn't turned a hair. I don't think Mrs. Geoff could stand such a walk, or any of her family."

"Oh, no, indeed; Clover would feel half-killed if she were asked to undertake a sixteen-mile walk. I remember, when she was here, we just went down to the pier at Clovelly for a row on the Bay and back through the Hobby, six miles in all, perhaps, and she was quite done up, poor dear, and had to go on to the sofa. I can't think why American girls are not better walkers,—though there was that Miss Appleton we met at Zermatt, who went up the Matterhorn and didn't make much of it. Good-by, Imogen; I shall come over before you start and fetch mamma's parcels."

CHAPTER II. MISS OPDYKE FROM NEW YORK.

THE next week was a busy one. Packing had begun; and what with Mrs. Young's motherly desire to provide her children with every possible convenience for their new home, and Imogen's rooted conviction that nothing could be found in Colorado worth buying, and that it was essential to carry out all the tapes and sewing-silk and buttons and shoe-thread and shoes and stationery and court-plaster and cotton cloth and medicines that she and Lionel could possibly require during the next five years,—it promised to be a long job.

In vain did Lionel remonstrate, and assure his sister that every one of these things could be had equally well at St. Helen's, where some of them went almost every day, and that extra baggage cost so much on the Pacific railways that the price of such commodities would be nearly doubled before she got them safely to the High Valley.

"Now what can be the use of taking two pounds of pins, for example?" he protested. "Pins are as plenty as blackberries in America. And all those spools of thread too!"

"Reels of cotton, do you mean? I wish you would speak English, at least while we are in England. I shouldn't dare go without plenty of such things. American cotton isn't as good as ours; I've always been told that."

"Well, it's good enough, as you'll find. And do make a place for something pretty; a few nice tea-cups for instance, and some things to hold flowers, and some curtain stuffs for the windows, and photographs. Geoff and Mrs. Geoff have made their house awfully nice, I can tell you. Americans think a deal of that sort of thing. All this haberdashery and hardware is ridiculous, and you'll be sorry enough that you didn't listen to me before you are through with it."

"Mother has packed some cups already, I believe, and I'll take that white Minton jar if you like, but really I shouldn't think delicate things like that would be at all suitable in a new place like Colorado, where people must rough it as we are going to do. You are so infatuated about America, Lion, that I can't trust your opinion at all."

"I've been there, and you haven't," was all that Lionel urged in answer. It seemed an incontrovertible argument, but Imogen made no attempt to overthrow it. She only packed on according to her own ideas, quite unconvinced.

It lacked only five days of their setting out when she and her brother walked into Bideford one afternoon for some last errands. It was June now, and the south of England was at its freshest and fairest. The meadows along the margin of the Torridge wore their richest green, the hill slopes above them were a bloom of soft color. Each court yard and garden shimmered with the gold of laburnums or the purple and white of clustering clematis; and the scent of flowers came with every puff of air.

As they passed up the side street, a carriage with three strange ladies in it drove by them. It stopped at the door of the New Inn,—as quaint in build and even older than the New Inn of Clovelly. The ladies got out, and one of them, to Imogen's great surprise, came forward and extended her hand to Lionel.

"Mr. Young,—it is Mr. Young, isn't it? You've quite forgotten me, I fear,—Mrs. Page. We met at St. Helen's two years ago when I stopped to see my son. Let me introduce you to my daughter, the Comtesse de Conflans, and Miss Opdyke, of New York."

Lionel could do no less than stop, shake hands, and present his sister, whereupon Mrs. Page urged them both to come in for a few minutes and have a cup of tea.

"We are here only till the evening-train," she explained,—"just to see Westward Ho and get a glimpse of the Amyas Leigh country. And I want to ask any quantity of questions about Clarence and his wife. What! you are going out to the High Valley next week, and your sister too? Oh, that makes it absolutely impossible for me to let you off. You really must come in. There are so many messages I should like to send, and a cup of tea will be a nice rest for Miss Young after her long walk."

"It isn't long at all," protested Imogen; but Mrs. Page could not be gainsaid, and led the way upstairs to a sitting-room with a bay window overlooking the windings of the Torridge, which was crammed with quaint carved furniture of all sorts. There were buffets, cabinets, secretaries, delightful old claw-footed tables and sofas, and chairs whose backs and arms were a mass of griffins and heraldic emblems. Old oak was the specialty of the landlady of this New Inn, it seemed, as blue china was of the other. For years she had attended sales and poked about in farmhouses and attics, till little by little she had accumulated an astonishing collection. Many of the pieces were genuine antiques, but some had been constructed under her own eye from wood equally venerable,—pew-ends and fragments of rood-screens purchased from a dismantled and ruined church. The effect was both picturesque and unusual.

Mrs. Page seated her guests in two wide, high-backed chairs, rang for tea, and began to question Lionel about affairs in the High Valley, while Imogen, still under the influence of surprise at finding herself calling on these strangers, glanced curiously at the younger ladies of the party. The Comtesse de Conflans was still young, and evidently had been very pretty, but she had a worn, dissatisfied air, and did not look happy. Imogen learned afterward that her marriage, which was considered a triumph and a grand affair when it took place, had not turned out very well. Count Ernest de Conflans was rather a black sheep in some respects, had a strong taste for baccarat and rouge et noir, and spent so much of his bride's money at these amusements during the first year of their life together, that her friends became alarmed, and their interference had brought about a sort of amicable separation. Count Ernest lived in Washington, receiving a specified sum out of his wife's income, and she was travelling indefinitely in Europe with her mother. It was no wonder that she did not look satisfied and content.

"Miss Opdyke, of New York" was quite different and more attractive, Imogen thought. She had never seen any one in the least like her. Rather tall, with a long slender throat, a waist of fabulous smallness, and hands which, in their gants de Suède, did not seem more than two inches wide, she gave the impression of being as fragile in make and as delicately fibred as an exotic flower. She had pretty, arch, gray eyes, a skin as white as a magnolia blossom, and a fluff of wonderful pale hair—artlessly looped and pinned to look as if it had blown by accident into its place—which yet exactly suited the face it framed. She was restlessly vivacious, her mobile mouth twitched with a hidden amusement every other moment; when she smiled she revealed pearly teeth and a dimple; and she smiled often. Her dress, apparently simple, was a wonder of fit and cut,—a skirt of dark fawn-brown, a blouse of ivory-white silk, elaborately tucked and shirred, a cape of glossy brown fur whose high collar set off her pale vivid face, and a "picture hat" with a wreath of plumes. Imogen, whose preconceived notion of an American girl included diamond ear-rings sported morning, noon, and night, observed with surprise that she wore no ornaments except one slender bangle. She had in her hand a great bunch of yellow roses, which exactly toned in with the ivory and brown of her dress, and she played with these and smelled them, as she sat on a high black-oak settle, and, consciously or unconsciously, made a picture of herself.

She seemed as much surprised and entertained at Imogen as Imogen could possibly be at her.

"I suppose you run up to London often," was her first remark.

"N-o, not often." In fact, Imogen had been in London only once in the whole course of her life.

"Dear me!—don't you? Why, how can you exist without it? I shouldn't think there would be anything to do here that was in the least amusing,—not a thing. How do you spend your time?"

"I?—I don't know, I'm sure. There's always plenty to do."

"To do, yes; but in the way of amusement, I mean. Do you have many balls? Is there any gayety going on? Where do you find your men?"

"No, we don't have balls often, but we have lawn parties, and tennis, and once a year there's a school feast."

"Oh, yes, I know,—children in gingham frocks and pinafores, eating buns and drinking milk-and-hot-water out of mugs. Rapturous fun it must be,—but I think one might get tired of it in time. As for lawn parties, I tried one in Fulham the other day, and I don't want to go to any more in England, thank you. They never introduced a soul to us, the band played out of tune, it was as dull as ditch-water,—just dreary, ill-dressed people wandering in and out, and trying to look as if five sour strawberries on a plate, and a thimbleful of ice cream were bliss and high life and all the rest of it. The only thing really nice was the roses; those were delicious. Lady Mary Ponsonby gave me three,—to make up for not presenting any one to me, I suppose."

"Do you still keep up the old fashion of introductions in America?" said Imogen with calm superiority. "It's quite gone out with us. We take it for granted that well-bred people will talk to their neighbors at parties, and enjoy themselves well enough for the moment, and then they needn't be hampered with knowing them afterward. It saves a lot of complications not having to remember names, or bow to people."

"Yes, I know that's the theory, but I call it a custom introduced for the suppression of strangers. Of course, if you know all the people present, or who they are, it doesn't matter in the least; but if you don't, it makes it a ghastly mockery to try to enjoy yourself at a party. But do tell me some more about Bideford. I'm so curious about English country life. I've seen only London so far. Is it ever warm over here?"

"Warm?" vaguely, "what do you mean?"

"I mean warm. Perhaps the word is not known over here, or doesn't mean the same thing. England seems to me just one degree better than Nova Zembla. The sun is a mere imitation sun. He looks yellow, like a real one, when you see him,—which isn't often,—but he doesn't burn a bit. I've had the shivers steadily ever since we landed." She pulled her fur cape closer about her ears as she spoke.

"Why, what can you want different from this?" asked Imogen, surprised. "It's a lovely day. We haven't had a drop of rain since last night."

"That is quite true, and remarkable as true; but somehow I don't feel any warmer than I did when it rained. Ah, here comes the tea. Let me pour it, Mrs. Page. I make awfully good tea. Such nice, thick cream! but, oh, dear!—here is more of that awful bread."

It was a stout household loaf, of the sort invariable in south-county England, substantial, crusty, and tough, with a "nubbin" on top, and in consistency something between pine wood and sole leather. Miss Opdyke, after filling her cups, proceeded to cut the loaf in slices, protesting as she did so that it "creaked in the chewing," and that

"The muscular strength that it gave to her jaw
Would last her the rest of her life."
"Why, what sort of bread do you have in America?" demanded Imogen, astonished and offended by the frankness of these strictures. "This is the sort every one eats here. I'm sure it's excellent. What is there about it that you don't like?"

"Oh, everything. Wait till you taste our American bread, and you'll understand,—or rather, our breads, for we have dozens of kinds, each more delicious than the last. Wait till you eat corn-bread and waffles."

"I've always been told that the American food was dreadfully messy," observed Imogen, nettled into reprisals; "pepper on eggs, and all that sort of thing,—very messy and nasty, indeed."

"Well, we have deviated from the English method as to the eating of eggs, I admit. I know it's correct to chip the shell, and eat all the white at one end by itself, with a little salt, and then all the yellow in the middle, and last of all the white at the other end by itself; but there are bold spirits among us who venture to stir and mix. Fools rush in, you know; they will do it, even where Britons fear to tread."

"We stopped at Northam to see Sir Amyas Leigh's house," Mrs. Page was saying to Lionel. "It's really very interesting to visit the spots where celebrated people have lived. There is a sad lack of such places in America. We are such a new country. Lilly and Miss Opdyke walked up to the hill where Mrs. Leigh stood to see the Spanish ship come in,—quite fascinating, they said it was."

"You must be sure to stay long enough in Boston to see the house where Silas Lapham lived," put in the wicked Miss Opdyke. "One cannot see too much of places associated with famous people."

"I don't remember any such name in American history," said honest Imogen,—"'Silas Lapham,' who was he?"

"A man in a novel, and Amyas Leigh is a man in another novel," whispered Miss Opdyke. "Mrs. Page isn't quite sure about him, but she doesn't like to confess as frankly as you do. She has forgotten, and fancies that he really lived in Queen Elizabeth's time; and the coachman was so solemnly sure that he did that it's not much wonder. I bought an old silver patch-box in a jeweller's shop on the High Street, and I'm going to tell my sister that it belonged to Ayacanora."

"What an odd idea."

"We are full of odd ideas over in America, you know."

"Tell me something about the States," said Imogen. "My brother is quite mad over Colorado, but he doesn't know much about the rest of it. I suppose the country about New York isn't very wild, is it?"

"Not very," returned Miss Opdyke, with a twinkle. "The buffalo are rarely seen now, and only two men were scalped by the Indians outside the walls of the city last year."

"Fancy! And how do you pass your time? Is it a gay place?"

"Very. We pass our time doing all sorts of things. There's the Corn Dance and the Green Currant Dance and the Water Melon pow wow, of course, and beside these, which date back to the early days of the colony, we have the more modern amusements, German opera and Italian opera and the theatre and subscription concerts. Then we have balls nearly every night in the season and dinner-parties and luncheons and lectures and musical parties, and we study a good deal and 'slum' a little. Last winter I belonged to a Greek class and a fencing class, and a quartette club, and two private dancing classes, and a girls' working club, and an amateur theatrical society. We gave two private concerts for charities, you know, and acted the Antigone for the benefit of the Influenza Hospital. Oh, there is a plenty to pass one's time in New York, I can assure you. And when other amusements fail, we can go outside the walls, with a guard of trappers, of course, and try our hand at converting the natives."

"What tribe of Indians is it that you have near you?"

"The Tammanies,—a very trying tribe, I assure you. It seems impossible to make any impression on them or teach them anything."

"Fancy! Did you ever have any adventures yourself with these Indians?" asked Imogen, deeply excited over this veracious resumé of life in modern New York.

"Oh, dear, yes—frequently."

"Do tell me some of yours. This is so very interesting. Lionel never has said a word about the—Tallamies, did you call them?"

"Tammanies. Perhaps not; Colorado is so far off, you know. They have Piutes there,—a different tribe entirely, and much less deleterious to civilization."

"How sad. But about the adventures?"

"Oh, yes—well, I'll tell you of one; in fact it is the only really exciting experience I ever had with the New York Indians. It was two years ago; I had just come out, and it was my birthday, and papa said I might ride his new mustang, by way of a celebration. So we started, my brother and I, for a long country gallop.

"We were just on the other side of Central Park, barely out of the city, you see, when a sudden blood-curdling yell filled the air. We were horror-struck, for we knew at once what it must be,—the war-cry of the savages. We turned of course and galloped for our lives, but the Indians were between us and the gates. We could see their terrible faces streaked with war-paint, and the tomahawks at their girdles, and we felt that all hope was over. I caught hold of papa's lasso, which was looped round the saddle, and cocked my revolving rifle—all the New York girls wear revolving rifles strapped round their waists," continued Miss Opdyke, coolly, interrogating Imogen with her eyes as she spoke for signs of disbelief, but finding none—"and I resolved to sell my life and scalp as dearly as possible. Just then, when all seemed lost, we heard a shout which sounded like music to our ears. A company of mounted Rangers were galloping out from the city. They had seen our peril from one of the watch-towers, and had hurried to our rescue."

"How fortunate!" said Imogen, drawing a long breath. "Well, go on—do go on."

"There is little more to tell," said Miss Opdyke, controlling with difficulty her inclination to laugh. "The Head Ranger attacked the Tammany chief, whose name was Day Vidbehill,—a queer name, isn't it?—and slew him after a bloody conflict. He gave me his brush, I mean his scalp-lock, afterward, and it now adorns—" Here her amusement became ungovernable, and she went into fits of laughter, which Imogen's astonished look only served to increase.

"Oh!" she cried, between her paroxysms, "you believed it all! it is too absurd, but you really believed it! I thought till just now that you were only pretending, to amuse me."

"Wasn't it true, then?" said Imogen, her tardy wits waking slowly up to the conclusion.

"True! why, my dear child, New York is the third city of the world in size,—not quite so large as London, but approaching it. It is a great, brilliant, gay place, where everything under the sun can be bought and seen and done. Did you really think we had Indians and buffaloes close by us?"

"And haven't you?"

"Dear me, no. There never was a buffalo within a thousand miles of us, and not an Indian has come within shooting distance for half a century, unless he came by train to take part in a show. You mustn't be so easily taken in. People will impose upon you no end over in America, unless you are on your guard. What has your brother been about, not to explain things better?"

"Well, he has tried," said Imogen, candidly, "but I didn't half believe what he said, because it was so different from the things in the books. And then he is so in love with America that it seemed as if he must be exaggerating. He did say that the cities were just like our cities, only more so, and that though the West wasn't like England at all, it was very interesting to live in; but I didn't half listen to him, it sounded so impossible."

"Live and learn. You'll have a great many surprises when you get across, but some of them will be pleasant ones, and I think you'll like it. Good-by," as Imogen rose to go; "I hope we shall meet again some time, and then you will tell me how you like Colorado, and the Piutes, and—waffles. I hope to live yet to see you stirring an egg in a glass with pepper and a 'messy' lump of butter in true Western fashion. It's awfully good, I've always been told. Do forgive me for hoaxing you. I never thought you could believe me, and when I found that you did, it was irresistible to go on."

"I can't make out at all about Americans," said Imogen, plaintively, as after an effusive farewell from Mrs. Page and a languid bow from Madame de Conflans they were at last suffered to escape into the street. "There seem to be so many different kinds. Mrs. Page and her daughter are not a bit like each other, and Miss Opdyke is quite different from either of them, and none of the three resembles Mrs. Geoffrey Templestowe in the least."

"And neither does Buffalo Bill and your phrenological lecturer. Courage, Moggy. I told you America was a sizable place. You'll begin to take in and understand the meaning of the variety show after you once get over there."

"It was queer, but do you know I couldn't help rather liking that girl;" confessed Imogen later to Isabel Templestowe. "She was odd, of course, and not a bit English, but you couldn't say she was bad form, and she was so remarkably quick and bright. It seemed as if she had seen all sorts of things and tried her hand on almost everything, and wasn't a bit afraid to say what she thought, or to praise and find fault. I told you what she said about English bread, and she was just as rude about our vegetables; she said they were only flavored with hot water. What do you suppose she meant?"

"I believe they cook them quite differently in America. Geoff likes their way, and found a great deal of fault when he was at home with the cauliflower and the Brussels sprouts. He declared that they had no taste, and that mint in green-peas killed the flavor. Clover was too polite to say anything, but I could see that she thought the same. Mamma was quite put about with Geoff's new notions."

"I must say that it seems rather impertinent and forth-putting for a new nation like that to be setting up opinions of its own, and finding fault with the good old English customs," said Imogen, petulantly.

"Well, I don't know," replied Isabel; "we have made some changes ourselves. John of Gaunt or Harry Hotspur might find fault with us for the same reason, giving up the 'good old customs' of rushes on the floor, for instance, and flagons of ale for breakfast. There were the stocks and the pillory too, and hanging for theft, and the torture of prisoners. Those were all in use more or less when the Pilgrims went to America, and I'm sure we're all glad that they were given up. The world must move, and I suppose it's but natural that the new nations should give it its impulse."

"England is good enough for me," replied the practical Imogen. "I don't want to be instructed by new countries. It's like a child in a pinafore trying to teach its grandmother how to do things. Now, dear Isabel, let me hear about your mother's parcels."

Mrs. Templestowe had wisely put her gifts into small compass. There were two dainty little frocks for her grandson, and a jacket of her own knitting, two pairs of knickerbocker stockings for Geoff, and for Clover a bit of old silver which had belonged to a Templestowe in the time of the Tudors,—a double-handled porringer with a coat of arms engraved on its somewhat dented sides. Clover, like most Americans, had a passion for the antique; so this present was sure to please.

"And you are really off to-morrow," said Isabel at the gate. "How I wish I were going too."

"And how I wish I were not going at all, but staying on with you," responded Imogen. "Mother says if Lionel isn't married by the end of three years she'll send Beatrice out to take my place. She'll be turned twenty then, and would like to come. Isabel, you'll be married before I get back, I know you will."

"It's most improbable. Girls don't marry in England half so easily as in America. It will be you who will marry, and settle over there permanently."

"Never!" cried Imogen.

Then the two friends exchanged a last kiss and parted.

"My love to Clover," Isabel called back.

"Always Clover," thought Imogen; but she smiled, and answered, "Yes."

CHAPTER III. THE LAST OF DEVON AND THE FIRST OF AMERICA.

WITH the morrow came the parting from home. "Farewell" is never an easy word to say when seas are to separate those who love each other, but the Young family uttered it bravely and resolutely. Lionel, who was impatient to get to work and to his beloved High Valley, was more than ready to go. His face, among the sober ones, looked aggressively cheerful.

"Cheer up, mother," he said, consolingly. "You'll be coming over in a year or two with the Pater, and Moggy and I will give you such a good time as you never had in your lives. We'll all go up to Estes Park and camp out for a month. I can see you now coming down the trail on a burro,—what fun it will be."

"Who knows?" said Mrs. Young, with a smile that was half a sigh. She and her husband had sent a good many sons and daughters out into the world to seek their fortunes, and so far not one of them had come back. To be sure, all were doing well in their several ways,—Cyril in India, where he had an excellent appointment, and the second boy in the army; two were in the navy, and Tom and Giles in Van Diemen's Land, where they were making a very good thing out of a sheep ranch. There was no reason why Lionel should not be equally lucky with his cattle in Colorado; there were younger children to be considered; it was "all in the day's work," the natural thing. Large families must separate, parents could not expect to keep their grown boys and girls with them always. So they dismissed the two who were now going forth cheerfully, uncomplainingly, and with their blessing, but all the same it was not pleasant; and Mrs. Young shed some quiet tears in the privacy of her own room, and her husband looked very serious as he strode down the Southampton docks after saying good-by to his children on board the steamer.

Imogen had never been on a great sea-going vessel before, and it struck her as being very crowded and confused as well as bewilderingly big. She stood clutching her bags and bundles nervously and feeling homesick and astray while farewells and greetings went on about her, and the people who were going and those who were to stay behind seemed mixed in an inextricable tangle on the decks. Then a bell rang, and gradually the groups separated; those who were not going formed themselves into a black mass on the pier; there was a great fluttering of handkerchiefs, a plunge of the screw, and the steamer was off.

Lionel, who had been seeing to the baggage, now appeared, and took Imogen down to her stateroom, advising her to get out all her warm things and make ready for a rough night.

"There's quite a sea on outside," he remarked. "We're in for a rolling if not for a pitching."

"Lion!" cried Imogen, indignantly. "Do you mean to say that you suppose I'm going to be sick,—I, a Devonshire girl born and bred, who have lived by the sea all my life? Never!"

"Time will show," was the oracular response. "Get the rugs out, any way, and your brushes and combs and things, and advise Miss What-d'-you-call-her to do the same."

"Miss What-d'-you-call-her" was Imogen's room-mate, a perfectly unknown girl, who had been to her imagination one of the chief bugbears of the voyage. She was curled up on the sofa in a tumbled little heap when they entered the stateroom, had evidently been crying, and did not look at all formidable, being no older than Imogen, very small and shy, a soft, dark-eyed appealing creature, half English, half Belgic by extraction, and going out, it appeared, to join a lover who for three years had been in California making ready for her. He was to meet her in New York, with a clergyman in his pocket, so to speak, and as soon as the marriage ceremony was performed, they were to set out for their ranch in the San Gabriel Valley, to raise grapes, dry raisins, and "live happily all the days of their lives afterward," like the prince and princess of a fairy tale.

These confidences were not made immediately or all at once, but gradually, as the two girls became acquainted, and mutual suffering endeared them to each other. For, in spite of Imogen's Devonshire bringing up, the English Channel proved too much for her, and she had to endure two pretty bad days before, promoted from gruel to dry toast, and from dry toast to beef-tea, she was able to be helped on deck, and seated, well wrapped up, in a reclining chair to inhale the cold, salty wind which was the best and only medicine for her particular kind of ailment.

The chair next hers was occupied by a pretty, dark-eyed, and very lady-like woman, with whom Lionel had apparently made an acquaintance; for he said, as he tucked Imogen's rugs about her, "Here's my sister at last, you see;" which off-hand introduction the lady acknowledged with a pleasant smile, saying she was glad to see Miss Young able to be up. Her manner was so unaffected and cordial that Imogen's stiffness melted under its influence, and before she knew it they were talking quite like old acquaintances.

Imogen was struck by the sweet voice of the stranger, with its well-bred modulations, and also by the good taste and perfection of all her little appointments, from the down pillow at top of her chair to the fur-trimmed shoes on a pair of particularly pretty feet at the other end. She set her down in her own mind as a London dame of fashion,—perhaps a countess, or a Lady Something-or-other, who was going out to see America.

"Your brother tells me this is your first voyage," said the lady.

"Yes. He has been out before, but none of us were with him. It's all perfectly strange to me"—with a sigh.

"Why do you sigh? Don't you expect to like it?"

"Why no, not like it exactly. Of course I'm glad to be with Lionel and of use to him, but I didn't come away from home for pleasure."

"Pleasure must come to you, then," said the lady, with a smile. "And really I don't see why it shouldn't. In the first place you are acting the part of a good sister; and you know the adage about duty performed making rainbows in the soul. And then Colorado is a beautiful State, with the finest of mountain views, a wonderful climate, and such wild flowers as grow nowhere else. I have some friends living there who are quite infatuated about it. They say there is no place so delightful in the world."

"That is just the way with my brother. It's really absurd the way he talks about it. You would think it was better than England!"

"It is sure to be very different; but all the same, you will like it, I think."

"I hope so"—doubtfully.

Just then came an interruption in the shape of a tall girl of fifteen or sixteen, with a sweet, childish face who came running down the deck accompanied by a maid, and seized the strange lady's hand.

"Mamma," she began, "the first officer says that if you are willing he will take me across to the bows to see the rainbows on the foam. May I go? He says Anne can go too."

"Yes, certainly, if Mr. Graves will take charge of you. But first speak to this young lady, who is the sister of Mr. Young, who was so kind about playing ship-coil with you yesterday, and tell her you are glad she is able to be on deck. Then you can go, Amy."

Amy turned a pair of beautiful, long-lashed, gray eyes on Imogen.

"I'm glad you're better, Miss Young. Mamma and I were sorry you were so sick," she said, with a frank politeness that was charming. "It must be very disagreeable."

"Haven't you been sick, then?" said Imogen, holding fast the little hand that was put in hers.

"No, I'm never sick now. I was, though, the first time we came over, and I behaved awfully. Do you recollect, mamma?"

"Only too well," said her mother, laughing. "You were like a caged bird, beating yourself against the bars in desperation."

Amy lingered a moment, while a dimple played in her pink cheek as if she were moved by some amusing remembrance.

"Ah, there's Mr. Graves," she said. "I must go. I'll come back presently and tell you about the rainbows, mamma."

"I suppose most of these people on board are Americans," said Imogen after a little pause. "It's always easy to tell them, don't you think?"

"Not always. Yes, I suppose a good many of them are—or call themselves so."

"What do you mean by 'call themselves so'? That girl is one, I am sure," indicating a pretty, stylish young person, who was talking rather too loudly for good taste with the ship's doctor.

"Yes, I imagine she is."

"And those people over there," pointing to a large, red-bearded man who lay back in a sea-chair reading a novel, by the side of a fat wife who read another, while their little boy raced up and down the deck quite unheeded, and amused himself by pulling the rugs off the knees of the sicker passengers. "They are Americans, I know! Did you ever see such creatures? The idea of letting that child make a nuisance of himself like that! No one but an American would allow it. I've always heard that children in the States do exactly as they please, and the grown people never interfere with them in the least."

"General rules are dangerous things," said her neighbor, with an odd little smile. "Now, as it happens, I know all about those people. They call themselves Americans because they have lived in Buffalo for ten years and are naturalized; but he was born in Scotland and she in Wales, and the child doesn't belong exactly to any country, for he happened to be born at sea. You see you can't always tell."

"Do you mean, then, that they are English, after all?" cried Imogen, disconcerted and surprised.

"Oh, no. Every body is an American who has taken the oath of allegiance. Those Polish Jews over there are Americans, and that Italian couple also, and the big party of Germans who are sitting between the boats. The Germans have a large shop in New York, and go out every year to buy goods and tell their relations how superior the United States are to Breslau. They are all Americans, though you would scarcely suppose it to look at them. America is like a pudding,— plums from one part of the world, and spice from another, and flour and sugar and flavoring from somewhere else, but all known by the name of pudding."

"How very, very odd. Somehow I never thought of it before in that light. Are there no real Americans, then? Are they all foreigners who have been naturalized?"

"Oh, no. It is not so bad as that. There are a great many 'real Americans.' I am one, for example."

"You!" There was such a world of unfeigned surprise in Imogen's tone that it was impossible for her new friend not to laugh.

"I. Did you not know it? What did you take me for?"

"Why, English of course, like myself. You are exactly like an English person."

"I suppose you mean it for a compliment; thank you, therefore. I like England very much, so I don't mind being taken for an English woman."

"Of course you don't," said Imogen, staring. "It's the height of an American's ambition, I've always heard, to be thought English."

"There you are mistaken. There are a few foolish people who feel so no doubt, and all of us would be glad to copy what is best and nicest in English ways and manners, but a really good American likes his own country best of all, and would rather seem to belong to it than any other."

"And I was thinking how different your daughter is from the American girls!" said Imogen, continuing her own train of thought; "and how her manners were so pretty, and did such credit to us, and would surprise people over there! How very odd. I shall never get to understand the Americans. They're so different from each other as well as from us. There were some ladies from New York at Bideford the other day,—a Mrs. Page and a Comtesse de Something-or-other, her daughter, and a Miss Opdyke from New York. She was very pretty and really quite nice, though rather queer, but all three were as unlike each other as they could be. Do you know them in America?"

"Not Miss Opdyke; but I have met Mrs. Page once in Europe a good while since. It was before her daughter was married. She is a relative of my sister-in-law, Mrs. Worthington."

"Do you mean the Mrs. Worthington whose husband is in the navy? Why, that's Mrs. Geoffrey Templestowe's sister!"

"Do you know Clover Templestowe, then?" said the lady, surprised in her turn. "That is really curious. Was it in England that you met?"

"Yes, and we are on our way to her neighborhood now. My brother has bought a share in Geoff's business, and we are going to live near them at High Valley."

"I do call this an extraordinary coincidence. Amy, come here and listen.

This young lady is on her way to Colorado, to live close to Aunt Clover; what do you think of that for a surprise? I don't wonder that you open your eyes so wide. Isn't it just like a story-book that she should have come and sat down in the next chair to ours?"

"It's so funny that I can't believe it, till I take time to think," said Amy, perching herself on the arm of her mother's seat. "Just think, you'll see Elsie and her baby, and Aunt Clover's baby, and Uncle Geoff and Phil, and all of them. It's the beautifulest place out there that you ever saw. There are whole droves of horses, and you ride all the while, and when you're not riding you can pick flowers and play with the babies. Oh, I wish I were going with you; it would be such fun!"

"But aren't you coming?" said Imogen, much taken by the frankness of the little American maid. "Coax mamma to fetch you out this summer, and come and make me a visit. We're going to have a little cabin of our own, and I'd be delighted to have you. Is it far from where you live?"

"Well, it's what you would call 'a goodish bit' in England," replied Mrs. Ashe,—"two thousand miles or so, nearly three days' journey. Amy would be charmed to come, I am sure, but I am afraid the distance will stand in her way. One doesn't 'step out' to Colorado every summer, but perhaps we may be there some day, and then we shall certainly hope to see you."

This encounter with Mrs. Ashe, who was, in a way, part of the family with whom Imogen expected to be most intimately associated in America, made the remainder of the voyage very pleasant. They sat together for hours every day, talking, and reading, and gradually Imogen waked up to the fact that American life and society was a much more complex and less easily understood affair than she had imagined.

The weather was favorable when the first rough days were past, and after they rounded the curve of the wide sea hemisphere and began to near the American coast it became beautiful, with high-arching skies and very bright sunsets. Accustomed to the low-hung grays and struggling sunbeams of southern England, Imogen could not get used to these novelties. Her surprise over the dazzle of the day and the clear, vivid blue of the heavens was a continual amusement and joy to Mrs. Ashe, who took a patriotic pride in her own climate, and, as it were, made herself responsible for it.

Then came the eventful morning, when, rousing to the first glow of dawn, they found the screw motionless, and the steamer lying off a green island, with a big barrack-building on it, over which waved the American flag. The health officer made his visit, and before long they were steaming up the wide bay of New York, between green, flowery shores, under the colossal Liberty, whose outstretched arm seemed to point to the dim rich mass of roofs and towers and spires of the city which lay beyond. Then they neared the landing-stage, where a black mass of people stood waiting them, and Amy gave a cry of delight as she saw a gold-banded cap among them, and recognized her Uncle Ned.

The little Anglo-Belgian had been more or less ill all the way over, and looked pale and wan, though still very pretty, as she stood with the rest, gazing at the crowd of faces, all of whose eyes were turned toward the steamer. Imogen, who had helped her to dress, remained protectingly by her side.

"What shall you do if he doesn't happen to be there?" she asked, smitten with a sudden fear. "Something might detain him, you know."

"I—I—am not sure," turning pale. "Oh, yes, I am," rallying. "He have aunt in Howbokken. I go there and wait. But he not fail; he will be here." Then her eyes suddenly lit up, and she exclaimed with a little shriek of joy, "He are here! That is he standing by the big timber. My Karl! my Karl! He are here!"

There indeed he was, foremost in the throng, a tall, brown, handsome fellow, with a nice, strong face, and such a look of love and expectation in his eyes that prosaic Imogen suddenly felt that it might be worth while, after all, to cross half the world to meet a look and a husband like that,—a fact which she had disbelieved till now, demurring also in her private mind as to the propriety of such a thing. It was pretty to see the tender happiness in the girl's face, and the answering expression of her lover's. It seemed to put poetry and pathos into an otherwise commonplace scene. The gang-plank was lowered, a crowd of people surged ashore, to be met by a corresponding surge from the on-lookers, and in the midst of it Lieutenant Worthington leaped aboard and hastened to where his sister stood waiting him.

"You're coming up to Newport with me at five-thirty," were his first words. "Katy's all ready, and means to sit up till the boat gets in at two-thirty, keeping a little supper hot and hot for you. The Torpedo Station is in its glory just now, and there's going to be a great explosion on

Thursday, which Amy will enjoy."

"How lovely!" cried Amy, clinging to her uncle's arm. "I love explosions. Why didn't Tanta come too?—I'm in such a hurry to see her."

Then Mr. Worthington asked to be introduced to Imogen and Lionel, and explained that acting on a request from Geoffrey Templestowe, he had taken rooms for them at a hotel, and secured their tickets and sleeping sections in the "limited" train for the next day.

"And I told them to save two seats for Rip Van Winkle to-night till you got there," he added. "If you're not too tired I advise you to go. Jefferson is an experience which you ought not to miss, and you may never have another chance."

"How awfully kind your brother is," said the surprised Imogen to Mrs. Ashe; "all this trouble, and he never saw either of us before! It's very good of him."

"Oh, that's nothing. That's the way American men do. They are perfect dears, there's no doubt as to that, and they don't consider anything a trouble which helps along a friend or a friend's friend. It's a matter of course over here."

"Well, I don't consider it a matter of course at all. I think it extraordinary, and it was so very nice in Geoff to send word to Lion."

Then they parted. Meanwhile the little room-mate had been having a private conference with her "young man." She now joined Imogen.

"Karl says we shall be married directly, in a church, in half an hour," she told her. "And oh, won't you and Mr. Young come to be with us? It is so sad not to have one friend when one is married."

It was impossible to refuse this request; so it happened that the very first thing Imogen did in America was to attend a wedding. It took place in an old church, pretty far down town; and she always afterward carried in her mind the picture of it, dim and sombre in coloring, with the afternoon sun pouring in through a rich rose window and throwing blue and red reflections on the little group of five at the altar, while from outside came the din of wheels and the unceasing tread of busy feet. The service was soon over, the signatures were made, and the little bride went down the chancel on her husband's arm, with her face appropriately turned to the west, and with such a look of secure and unfearing happiness upon it as was good to see. It was an unusual and typical scene with which to begin life in a new country, and Imogen liked to think afterward that she had been there.

Then followed a long drive up town over rough ill-laid pavements, through dirty streets, varied by dirtier streets, and farther up, by those that were less dirty. Imogen had never seen anything so shabby as the poorest of the buildings that they passed, and certainly never anything quite so fine as the best of them. Squalor and splendor jostled each other side by side; everywhere there was the same endless throng of hurrying people, and everywhere the same abundance of flowers for sale, in pots, in baskets, in bunches, making the whole air of the streets sweet. Then they came to the hotel, and were shown to their rooms,— high up, airy, and nicely furnished, though Imogen was at first disposed to cavil at the absence of bed-curtains.

"It looks so bare," she complained. "At home such a thing would be considered very odd, very odd indeed. Fancy a bed without curtains!"

"After you've spent one hot night in America you'll be glad enough to fancy it," replied her brother. "Stuffy old things. It's only in cold weather that one could endure them over here."

The first few hours on shore after a voyage have a delightfulness all their own. It is so pleasant to bathe and dress without having to hold on and guard against lurches and tips. Imogen went about her toilet well-pleased; and her pleasure was presently increased when she found on her dressing-table a beautiful bunch of summer roses, with "Mrs. Geoffrey Templestowe's love and welcome" on a card lying beside it. Thoughtful Clover had written to Ned Worthington to see to this little attention, and the pleasure it gave went even farther than she had hoped.

"I declare," said Imogen, sitting down with the flowers before her, "I never knew anybody so kind as they all are. I don't feel half so home-sick as I expected. I must write mamma about these roses. Of course Mrs. Geoff does it for Isabel's sake; but all the same it is awfully nice of her, and I shall try not to forget it."

Then, when, after finishing her dressing, she drew the blinds up and looked from the windows, she gave a cry of sheer pleasure, for there beneath was spread out a beautiful wide distance of Park with feathery trees and belts of shrubs, behind which the sun was making ready to set in a crimson sky. There was a balcony outside the windows, and Imogen pulled a chair out on it to enjoy the view. Carriages were rolling in at the Park gates, looking exactly like the equipages one sees in London, with fat coachmen, glossy horses, and jingling silvered harness. Girls and young men were cantering along the bridle-paths, and throngs of well-dressed people filled the walks. Beyond was a fairy lake, where gondolas shot to and fro; a band was playing; from still farther away came a peal of chimes from a church tower.

"And this is New York!" thought Imogen. Then her thoughts reverted to Miss Opdyke and her tale of the Tammany Indians, and she flushed with sudden vexation.

"What an idiot she must have considered me!" she reflected.

But her insular prejudices revived in full force as a knock was heard, and a colored boy, entering with a tinkling pitcher, inquired, "Did you ring for ice-water, lady?"

"No!" said Imogen sharply; "I never drink iced water. I rang for hot water, but I got it more than an hour ago."

"Beg pardon, lady."

"Why on earth does he call me 'lady'?" she murmured—"so tiresome and vulgar!"

Then Lionel came for her, and they went down to dinner,—a wonderful repast, with soups and fishes and vegetables quite unknown to her; a bewildering succession of meats and entrées, strawberries such as she had supposed did not grow outside of England, raspberries and currants such as England never knew, and wonderful blackberries, of great size and sweetness, bursting with purple juice. There were ices too, served in the shapes of apples, pears, and stalks of asparagus, which dazzled her country eyes not a little, while the whole was a terror and astonishment to her thrifty English mind.

"Lionel, don't keep on ordering things so," she protested. "We are eating our heads off as it is, I am sure."

"My dear young friend, you are come to the Land of Fat Things," he replied. "Dinner costs just the same, once you sit down to it, whether you have a biscuit and a glass of water, or all these things."

"I call it a sinful waste, then," she retorted. "But all the same, since it is so, I'll take another ice."

"'First endure, then pity, then embrace,'" quoted her brother. "That's right, Moggy; pitch in, spoil the Egyptians. It doesn't hurt them, and it will do you lots of good."

From the dinner-table they went straight to the theatre, having decided to follow Lieut. Worthington's advice and see "Rip Van Winkle." And then they straightway fell under the spell of a magician who has enchanted many thousands before them, and for the space of two hours forgot themselves, their hopes and fears and expectations, while they followed the fortunes of the idle, lovable, unpractical Rip, up the mountain to his sleep of years, and down again, white-haired and tottering, to find himself forgotten by his kin and a stranger in his own home. People about them were weeping on relays of pocket-handkerchiefs, hanging them up one by one as they became soaked, and beginning on others. Imogen had but one handkerchief, but she cried with that till she had to borrow Lionel's; and he, though he professed to be very stoical, could not quite command his voice as he tried to chaff her in a whisper on her emotions, and begged her to "dry up" and remember that it was only a play after all, and that presently Jefferson would discard his white hair and wrinkles, go home to a good supper, and make a jolly end to the evening.

It was almost too exciting for a first night on shore, and if Imogen had not been so tired, and if her uncurtained bed had not proved so deliciously comfortable, she would scarcely have slept as she did till half-past seven the next morning, so that they had to scramble through breakfast not to lose their train. Once started in the "Limited," with a library and a lady's-maid, a bath and a bed at her disposal, and just beyond a daintily appointed dinner-table adorned with fresh flowers,— all at forty miles an hour,—she had leisure to review her situation and be astonished. Bustling cities shot past them,—or seemed to shoot,— beautifully kept country-seats, shabby suburbs where goats and pigs mounted guard over shanties and cabbage-beds, great tracts of wild forest, factory towns black with smoke, rivers winding between blue hill ridges, prairie-like expanses so overgrown with wild-flowers that they looked all pink or all blue,—everything by turns and nothing long. It seemed the sequence of the unexpected, a succession of rapidly changing surprises, for which it was impossible to prepare beforehand.

"I shall never learn to understand it," thought poor perplexed Imogen.

CHAPTER IV. IN THE HIGH VALLEY.

MEANWHILE, as the "Limited" bore the young English travellers on their western way, a good deal of preparation was going on for their benefit in that special nook of the Rocky mountains toward which their course was directed. It was one of those clear-cut, jewel-like mornings which seem peculiar to Colorado, with dazzling gold sunshine, a cloudless sky of deep sapphire blue, and air which had touched the mountain snows somewhere in its nightly blowing, and still carried on its wings the cool pure zest of the contact.

Hours were generally early in the High Valley, but to-day they were a little earlier than usual, for every one had a sense of much to be done. Clover Templestowe did not always get up to administer to her husband and brother-in-law their "stirrup-cup" of coffee; but this morning she was prompt at her post, and after watching them ride up the valley, and standing for a moment at the open door for a breath of the scented wind, she seated herself at her sewing-machine. A steady whirring hum presently filled the room, rising to the floor above and quickening the movements there. Elsie, running rapidly downstairs half an hour later, found her sister with quite a pile of little cheese-cloth squares and oblongs folded on the table near her.

"Dear me! are those the Youngs' curtains you are doing?" she asked. "I fully meant to get down early and finish my half. That wretched little Phillida elected to wake up and demand 'tories' from one o'clock till a quarter past two. 'Hence these tears.' I overslept myself without knowing it."

Phillida was Elsie's little girl, two years and a half old now, and Dr. Carr's namesake.

"How bad of her!" said Clover, smiling. "I wish children could be born with a sense of the fitness of times and seasons. Jeffy is pretty good as to sleeping, but he is dreadful about eating. Half the time he doesn't want anything at dinner; and then at half-past three, or a quarter to eight, or ten minutes after twelve, or some such uncanonical hour, he is so ragingly hungry that he can scarcely wait till I fetch him something. He is so tiresome about his bath too. Fancy a young semi-Britain objecting to 'tub.' I've circumvented him to-day, however, for Geoff has promised to wash him while you and I go up to set the new house in order. Baby is always good with Geoff."

"So he is," remarked Elsie as she moved about giving little tidying touches here and there to books and furniture. "I never knew a father and child who suited each other so perfectly. Phil flirts with Clarence and he is very proud of her notice, but I think they are mutually rather shy; and he always touches her as though she were a bit of eggshell china, that he was afraid of breaking."

The room in which the sisters were talking bore little resemblance to the bare ranch-parlor of old days. It had been enlarged by a semi-circular bay window toward the mountain view, which made it half as long again as it then was; and its ceiling had been raised two feet on the occasion of Clarence's marriage, when great improvements had been undertaken to fit the "hut" for the occupation of two families. The solid redwood beams which supported the floor above had been left bare, and lightly oiled to bring out the pale russet-orange color of the wood. The spaces between the beams were rough-plastered; and on the decoration of this plaster, while in a soft state, a good deal of time had been expended by Geoffrey Templestowe, who had developed a turn for household art, and seemed to enjoy lying for hours on his back on a staging, clad in pajamas and indenting the plaster with rosettes and sunken half-rounds, using a croquet ball and a butter stamp alternately, the whole being subsequently finished by a coat of dull gold paint. He and Clover had themselves hung the walls with its pale orange-brown paper; a herder with a turn for carpentry had laid the new floor of narrow redwood boards. Clover had stained the striped pattern along its edges. In that remote spot, where trained and regular assistance could be had only at great trouble and expense, it was desirable that every one should utilize whatever faculty or accomplishment he or she possessed, and the result was certainly good. The big, homelike room, with its well-chosen colors and look of taste and individuality, left nothing to be desired in the way of comfort, and was far prettier and more original than if ordered cut-and-dried from some artist in effects, to whom its doing would have been simply a job and not an enjoyment.

Clover's wedding presents had furnished part of the rugs and etchings and bits of china which ornamented the room, but Elsie's, who had married into a "present-giving connection," as her sister Johnnie called it, did even more. Each sister was supposed to own a private sitting-room, made out of the little sleeping-chambers of what Clarence Page stigmatized as the "beggarly bachelor days," which were thrown together two in one on either side the common room. Clover and Elsie had taken pains and pleasure in making these pretty and different from each other, but as a matter of fact the "private" parlors were not private at all; for the two families were such very good friends that they generally preferred to be together. And the rooms were chiefly of use when the house was full of guests, as in the summer it sometimes was, when Johnnie had a girl or two staying with her, or a young man with a tendency toward corners, or when Dr. Carr wanted to escape from his young people and analyze flowers at leisure or read his newspaper in peace and quiet.

The big room in the middle was used by both families as a dining and sitting place. Behind it another had been added, which served as a sort of mixed library, office, dispensary, and storage-room, and over the four, extending to the very edge of the wide verandas which flanked the house on three sides, were six large bedrooms. Of these each family owned three, and they had an equal right as well to the spare rooms in the building which had once been the kitchen. One of these, called "Phil's room," was kept as a matter of course for the use of that young gentleman, who, while nominally studying law in an office at St. Helen's, contrived to get out to the Valley very frequently. The interests of the party were so identical that the matter of ownership seldom came up, and signified little. The sisters divided the house-keeping between them amicably, one supplementing the other; the improvements were paid for out of a common purse; their guests, being equally near and dear, belonged equally to all. It was an ideal arrangement, which one quick tongue or jealous or hasty temper would have brought to speedy conclusion, but which had now lasted to the satisfaction of all parties concerned for nearly four years.

That Clarence and Elsie should fancy each other had been a secret though unconfessed dream of Clover's ever since her own engagement, when Clarence had endeared himself by his manly behavior and real unselfishness under trying circumstances. But these dreams are rarely gratified, and she was not at all prepared to have hers come true with such unexpected ease and rapidity. It happened on this wise. Six months after her marriage, when she and Geoff and Clarence, working together, had just got the "hut" into a state to receive visitors, Mr. and Mrs. Dayton, who had never forgotten or lost their interest in their pretty fellow-traveller of two years before, hearing from Mrs. Ashe how desirous Clover was of a visit from her father and sisters, wrote and asked the Carrs to go out with them in car 47 as far as Denver, and be picked up and brought back two months later when the Daytons returned from Alaska. The girls were wild to go, it seemed an opportunity too good to be lost; so the invitation was accepted, and, as sometimes happens, the kindness shown had an unlooked-for return.

Mr. Dayton was seized with a sudden ill turn on the journey, of a sort to which he was subject, and Dr. Carr was able not only to help him at the moment, but to suggest a regimen and treatment which was of permanent benefit to him. Doctor and patient grew very fond of each other, and every year since, when car 47 started on its western course, urgent invitations came for any or all of them to take advantage of it and go out to see Clover; whereby that hospitable housekeeper gained many visits which otherwise she would never have had, Colorado journeys being expensive luxuries.

But this is anticipating. No visit, they all agreed, ever compared with that first one, when they were so charmed to meet, and everything was new and surprising and delightful. The girls were enchanted with the Valley, the climate, the wild fresh life, the riding, the flowers, with Clover's little home made pretty and convenient by such simple means, while Dr. Carr revelled in the splendid air, which seemed to lift the burden of years from his shoulders.

And presently began the excitement of watching Clarence Page's rapid and successful wooing of Elsie. No grass grew under his feet this time, you may be sure. He fell in love the very first evening, deeply and heartily, and he lost no opportunity of letting Elsie know his sentiments. There was no rival in his way at the High Valley or elsewhere, and the result seemed to follow as a matter of course. They were engaged when the party went back to Burnet, and married the following spring, Mr. Dayton fitting up 47 with all manner of sentimental and delightful appointments, and sending the bride and bridegroom out in it,—as a wedding present, he said, but in truth the car was a repository of wedding presents, for all the rugs and portières and silken curtains and brass plaques and pretty pottery with which it was adorned, and the flower-stands and Japanese kakemonos, were to disembark at St. Helen's and help to decorate Elsie's new home. All went as was planned, and Clarence's life from that day to this had been, as Clover mischievously told him, one pæan of thanksgiving to her for refusing him and opening the way to real happiness. Elsie suited him to perfection. Everything she said and did and suggested was exactly to his mind, and as for looks, Clover was dear and nice as could be, of course, and pretty,—well, yes, people would undoubtedly consider her a pretty little woman; but as for any comparison between the two sisters, it was quite out of the question! Elsie had so decidedly the advantage in every point, including that most important point of all, that she preferred him to Geoff Templestowe and loved him as heartily as he loved her. Happiness and satisfied affection had a wonderfully softening influence on Clarence, but it was equally droll and delightful to Clover to see how absolutely Elsie ruled, how the least indication of her least finger availed to mould Clarence to her will,—Clarence, who had never yielded easily to any one else in the whole course of his life!

So the double life flowed smoothly on in the High Valley, but not quite so happily at Burnet, where Dr. Carr, bereft of four out of his six children, was left to the companionship of the steady Dorry, and what he was pleased to call "a highly precarious tenure of Miss Joanna." Miss Joanna was a good deal more attractive than her father desired her to be. He took gloomy views of the situation, was disposed to snub any young man who seemed to be casting glances toward his last remaining treasure, and finally announced that when Fate dealt her last and final blow and carried off Johnnie, he should give up the practice of medicine in Burnet, and retire to the High Valley to live as physician in ordinary to the community for the rest of his days. This prospect was so alluring to the married daughters that they turned at once into the veriest match-makers and were disposed to many Johnnie off immediately,—it didn't much matter to whom, so long as they could get possession of their father. Johnnie resented these manœuvres highly, and obstinately refused to "remove the impediment," declaring that self-sacrifice was all very well, but she couldn't and wouldn't see that it was her duty to go off and be content with a dull anybody, merely for the sake of giving papa up to that greedy Clover and Elsie, who had everything in the world already and yet were not content. She liked to be at the head of the Burnet house and rule with a rod of iron, and make Dorry mind his p's and q's; it was much better fun than marrying any one, and there she was determined to stay, whatever they might say or do. So matters stood at the present time, and though Clover and Elsie still cherished little private plans of their own, nothing, so far, seemed likely to come of them.

Elsie had time to set the room in beautiful order, and Clover had nearly finished her hemming, before the sound of hoofs announced the return of the two husbands from their early ride. They came cantering down the side pass, with appetites sharpened by exercise, and quite ready for the breakfast which Choo Loo presently brought in from the new cooking-cabin, set a little one side out of sight, in the shelter of the grove. Choo Loo was still a fixture in the valley. He and his methods were a puzzle and somewhat of a distress to the order-loving Clover, who distrusted not a little the ways and means of his mysteriously conducted kitchen; but servants were so hard to come by at the High Valley, and Choo Loo was so steady and faithful and his viands on the whole so good, that she judged it wise to ask no questions and not look too closely into affairs but just take the goods the gods provided, and be thankful that she had any cook at all. Choo Loo was an amiable heathen also, and very pleased to serve ladies, who appreciated his attempts at decoration, for he had an eye for effect and loved to make things pretty. Clover understood this and never forgot to notice and praise, which gratified Choo Loo, who had found his bachelor employers in the old days somewhat dull and unobservant in this respect.

"Missie like?" he asked this morning, indicating the wreath of wild cranberry vine round the dish of chicken. Then he set a mound of white raspberries in the middle of the table, starred with gold-hearted brown coreopsis, and asked again, "Missie like dat?" pleased at Clover's answering nod and smile. Noiselessly he came and went in his white-shod feet, fetching in one dish after another, and when all was done, making a sort of dual salaam to the two ladies, and remarking "Allee yeady now," after which he departed, his pigtail swinging from side to side and his blue cotton garments flapping in the wind as he walked across to the cook-house.

Delicious breaths of roses and mignonette floated in as the party gathered about the breakfast table. They came from the flower-beds just outside, which Clover sedulously tended, watered, and defended from the roving cattle, which showed a provoking preference for heliotropes over penstamens whenever they had a chance to get at them. Cows were a great trial, she considered; and yet after all they were the object of their lives in the Valley, their raison d'être, and must be put up with accordingly.

"Do you suppose the Youngs have landed yet?" asked Elsie as she qualified her husband's coffee with a dash of thick cream.

"They should have got in last night if the steamer made her usual time. I dare say we shall find a telegram at St. Helen's to-morrow if we go in," answered her brother-in-law.

"Yes, or possibly Phil will ride out and fetch it. He is always glad of an excuse to come. I wonder what sort of girl Miss Young is. You and Clover never have said much about her."

"There isn't much to say. She's just an ordinary sort of girl,—nice enough and all that, not pretty."

"Oh, Geoff, that's not quite fair. She's rather pretty, that is, she would be if she were not stiff and shy and so very badly dressed. I didn't get on very much with her at Clovelly, but I dare say we shall like her here; and when she limbers out and becomes used to our ways, she'll make a nice neighbor."

"Dear me, I hope so," remarked Elsie. "It's really quite important what sort of a girl Miss Young turns out to be. A stiff person whom you had to see every day would be horrid and spoil everything. The only thing we need, the only possible improvement to the High Valley, would be a few more nice people, just two or three, with pretty little houses, you know, dotted here and there in the side canyons, whom we could ride up to visit, and who would come down to see us, and dine and play whist and dance Virginia reels and 'Sally Waters' on Christmas Eve. That would be quite perfect. But I suppose it won't happen till nobody knows how long."

"I suppose so, too," said Geoff in a tone of well-simulated sympathy. "Poor Elsie, spoiling for people! Don't set your heart on them. High Valley isn't at all a likely spot to make a neighborhood of."

"A neighborhood! I should think not! A neighborhood would be horrid. But if two or three people wanted to come,—really nice ones, you know, perfect charmers,—surely you and Clare wouldn't have the heart to refuse to sell them building lots?"

"We are exactly a whist quartet now," said Clarence, patting his wife's shoulder. "Cheer up, dear. You shall have your perfect charmers when they apply; but meantime changes are risky, and I am quite content with things as they are, and am ready to dance Sally Waters with you at any time with pleasure. Might I have the honor now, for instance?"

"Indeed, no! Clover and I have to work like beavers on the Youngs' house. And, Clare, we are quite a complete party in ourselves, as you say; but there are the children to be considered. Geoffy and Phillida will want to play whist one of these days, and where is their quartet to come from?"

"Down they came, hand in hand, chattering as they went."—Page 111
"Down they came, hand in hand, chattering as they went."—Page 111
"We shall have to consider that point when they are a little nearer the whist age. Here they come now. I hear the nursery door slam. They

don't look particularly dejected about their future prospects, I must say."

Four pairs of eyes turned expectantly toward the staircase, down which there presently came the dearest little pair of children that can be imagined. Clover's boy of three was as big as most people's boys of five, a splendid sturdy little Englishman in build, but with his mother's lovely eyes and skin. Phillida, whose real name was Philippa, was of a more delicate and slender make, with dark brown eyes and a mane of ruddy gold which repeated something of the tawny tints of her father's hair and beard. Down they came hand in hand, little Phil holding tightly to the polished baluster, chattering as they went, like two wood-thrushes. Neither of them had ever known any other child playmates, and they were devoted to each other and quite happy together. Little Geoff from the first had adopted a protecting attitude toward his smaller cousin, and had borne himself like a gallant little knight in the one adventure of their lives, when a stray coyote, wandering near the house, showed his teeth to the two babies, whose nurse had left them alone for a moment, and Geoff, only two then, had caught up a bit of a stick and thrown himself in front of Phillida with such a rush and shout that the beast turned and fled, before Roxy and the collies could come to the rescue. The dogs chased the coyote up the ravine down which he had come, and he showed himself no more; but Clover was so proud of her boy's prowess that she never forgot the exploit, and it passed into the family annals for all time.

One wonderful stroke of good-luck had befallen the young mothers in their mountain solitude, and that was the possession of Roxy and her mother Euphane. They were sister and niece to good old Debby, who for so many years had presided over Dr. Carr's kitchen; and when they arrived one day in Burnet fresh from the Isle of Man, and announced that they had come out for good to better their fortunes, Debby had at once devoted them to the service of Clover and Elsie. They proved the greatest possible comfort and help to the High Valley household. The place did not seem lonely to them, used as they were to a still lonelier cabin at the top of a steep moor up which few people ever came. The Colorado wages seemed riches, the liberal comfortable living luxury to them, and they rooted and established themselves, just as Debby had done, into a position of trusted and affectionate helpfulness, which seemed likely to endure. Euphane was housemaid, Roxy nurse; it already seemed as though life could never have gone on without them, and Clover was disposed to emulate Dr. Carr in objecting to "followers," and in resenting any admiring looks cast by herders at

Roxy's rosy English cheeks and pretty blue eyes.

Little Geoff ran to his father's knee, as a matter of course, on arriving at the bottom of the stairs, while Phillida climbed her mother's, equally as a matter of course. Safely established there, she began at once to flirt with Clarence, making wide coquettish eyes at him, smiling, and hiding her face to peep out and smile again. He seized one of her dimpled hands and kissed it. She instantly pulled it away, and hid her face again.

"Fair Phillida flouts me," he said. "Doesn't baby like papa a bit? Ah, well, he is going to cry, then."

He buried his face in his napkin and sobbed ostentatiously. Phillida, not at all impressed, tugged bravely at the corner of the handkerchief; but when the sobs continued and grew louder, she began to look troubled, and leaning forward suddenly, threw her arms round her father's neck and laid her rose-leaf lips on his forehead. He caught her up rapturously and tossed her high in air, kissing her every time she came down.

"You angel! you little angel! you little dear!" he cried, with a positive dew of pleasure in his eyes. "Elsie, what have we ever done to deserve such a darling?"

"I really don't know what you have done," remarked Elsie, coolly; "but I have done a good deal. I always was meritorious in my way, and deserve the best that is going, even Phillida. She is none too good for me. Come back, baby, to your exemplary parent."

She rose to recapture the child; but Clarence threw a strong arm about her, still holding Phillida on his shoulder, and the three went waltzing merrily down the room, the little one from her perch accenting the dance time with a series of small shouts. Little Geoff looked up soberly, with his mouth full of raspberries, and remarked, "Aunty, I didn't ever know that people danced at breakfast."

"No more did I," said Elsie, trying in vain to get away from her pirouetting husband.

"No more does any one outside this extraordinary valley of ours," laughed Geoff. "Now, partner, if you have finished your fandango, allow me to remind you that there are a hundred and forty head of cattle waiting to be branded in the upper valley, and that Manuel is to meet us there at ten o'clock."

"And we have the breakfast things to wash, and a whole world to do at the Youngs'," declared Elsie, releasing herself with a final twirl. "Now, Clare dear, order Marigold and Summer-Savory, please, to be brought down in half an hour, and tell old José that we want him to help and scrub. No, young man, not another turn. These sports are unseemly on such a busy day as this. 'Dost thou not suspect my place? dost thou not suspect my years?' as the immortal W. would say. I am twenty-five,—nearly twenty-six,—and am not to be whisked about thus."

Everybody went everywhere on horseback in the High Valley, and the gingham riding-skirts and wide-brimmed hats hung always on the antlers, ready to hand, beside water-proofs and top-coats. Before long the sisters were on their way, their saddle-pockets full of little stores, baskets strapped behind them, and the newly made curtains piled on their laps. The distance was about a mile to the house which Lionel Young and his sister were to inhabit.

It stood in a charming situation on the slope of one of the side canyons, facing the high range and backed by a hillside clothed with pines. In build it was very much such a cabin as the original hut had been,—six rooms, all on one floor, the sixth being a kitchen. It was newly completed, and sawdust and fresh shavings were littered freely about the place. Clover's first act was to light a fire in the wide chimney for burning these up.

"It looks bare enough," she remarked, sweeping away industriously. "But it will be quite easy to make it pleasant if Imogen Young has any faculty at that sort of thing. I'm sure it's a great deal more promising than the Hut was before Clarence and Geoff and I took hold of it. See, Elsie,—this room is done. I think Miss Young will choose it for her bedroom, as it is rather the largest; so you might tack up the dotted curtains here while I sweep the other rooms. And that convolvulus chintz is to cover her dress-pegs."

"What fun a house is!" observed Elsie a moment or two later, between her hammer strokes. "People who can get a carpenter or upholsterer to help them at any minute really lose a great deal of pleasure. I always adored baby-houses when I was little, and this is the same thing grown up."

"I don't know," replied Clover, abstractedly, as she threw a last dustpanful of chips into the fire. "It is good fun, certainly; but out here one has so much of it that sometimes it comes under the suspicion of being hard work. Now, when José has the kitchen windows washed it will all be pretty decent. We can't undertake much beyond making the first day or two more comfortable. Miss Young will prefer to make her own plans and arrangements; and I don't fancy she's the sort of girl who will enjoy being too much helped."

"Somehow I don't get quite an agreeable idea of Miss Young from what you and Geoffrey say of her. I do hope she isn't going to make herself disagreeable."

"Oh, I'm sure she won't do that; but there is a wide distance between not being disagreeable and being agreeable. I didn't mean to give you an unpleasant impression of her. In fact, my recollections about her are rather indistinct. We didn't see a great deal of her when we were at Clovelly, or perhaps it was that Isabel and I were out so much and there was so much coming and going."

"But are not she and Isabel very intimate?"

"I think so; but they are not a bit alike. Isabel is delightful. I wish it were she who was coming out. You would love her. Now, my child, we must begin on the kitchen tins."

It was an all-day piece of work which they had undertaken, and they had ordered dinner late accordingly, and provided themselves with a basket of sandwiches. By half-past five all was fairly in order,—the windows washed, the curtains up, kitchen utensils and china unpacked and arranged, and the somewhat scanty supply of furniture placed to the best advantage.

"There! Robinson Crusoe would consider himself in clover; and even Miss Young can exist for a couple of days, I should think," said Elsie, standing back to note the effect of the last curtain. "Lionel will have to go in to St. Helen's and get a lot of things out before it will be really comfortable, though. There come the boys now to ride home with us. No, there is only one horse. Why, it is Phil!"

Phil indeed it was, but such a different Phil from the delicate boy whom Clover had taken out to Colorado six years before. He was now a broad-shouldered, muscular, athletic young fellow, full of life and energy, and showing no trace of the illness which at that time seemed so menacing. He gave a shout when he caught sight of his sisters, and pushed his broncho to a gallop, waving a handful of envelopes high in air.

"This despatch came last night for Geoff," he explained, dismounting, "and there were a lot of letters besides, so I thought I'd better bring them out. I left the newspapers and the rest at the house, and fetched your share on. Euphane told me where you two were. So this is where the young Youngs are going to live, is it?"

He stepped in at the door and took a critical survey of the interior, while Clover and Elsie examined their letters.

"This telegram is for Geoff," explained Clover. "The Youngs are here," and she read:—

Safely landed. We reach Denver Thursday morning, six-thirty.

Lionel Young.
"So they will get here on Thursday afternoon. It's lucky we came up to-day. My letters are from Johnnie and Cecy Slack. Johnnie says—"

She was interrupted by a joyful shriek from Clover, who had torn open her letter and was eagerly reading it.

"Oh, Elsie, Elsie, what do you think is going to happen? The most enchanting thing! Rose Red is coming out here in August! She and Mr. Browne and Röslein! Was there ever anything so nice in this world! Just hear what she says:"—

Boston, June 30.
My Ducky-Daddles and my dear Elsie girl,—I have something so wonderful to tell that I can scarcely find words in which to tell it. A kind Providence and the A. T. and S. F. R. R. have just decided that Deniston must go to New Mexico early in August. This would not have been at all delightful under ordinary circumstances, for it would only have meant perspiration on his part and widowhood on mine, but most fortunately, some angels with a private car of their own have turned up, and have asked all three of us to go out with them as far as Santa Fé. What do you think of that? It is not the Daytons, who seem only to exist to carry you to and fro from Burnet to Colorado free of expense, this time, but another batch of angels who have to do with the road,— name of Hopkinson. I never set eyes on them, but they appear to my

imagination equipped with the largest kind of wings, and nimbuses round their heads as big as shade-hats.

I have always longed to get out somehow to your Enchanted Valley, and see all your mysterious husbands and babies, and find out for myself what the charm is that makes you so wonderfully contented there, so far from West Cedar Street and the other centres of light and culture, but I never supposed I could come unless I walked. But now I am coming! I do hope none of you have the small-pox, or pleuro-pneumonia, or the "foot-and-mouth disease" (whatever that is), or any other of the ills to which men and cattle are subject, and which will stand in the way of the visit. Deniston, of course, will be forced to go right through to Santa Fé, but Röslein and I are at your service if you like to have us. We don't care for scenery, we don't want to see Mexico or the Pacific coast, or the buried cities of Central America, or the Zuñi corn dance,—if there is such a thing,—or any alkaline plains, or pueblos, or buttes, or buffalo wallows; we only want to see you, individually and collectively, and the High Valley. May we come and stay a fortnight? Deniston thinks he shall be gone at least as long as that. We expect to leave Boston on the 31st of July. You will know what time we ought to get to St. Helen's,—I don't, and I don't care, so only we get there and find you at the station. Oh, my dear Clovy, isn't it fun?

I have seen several of our old school-set lately, Esther Dearborn for one. She is Mrs. Joseph P. Allen now, as you know, and has come to live at Chestnut Hill, quite close by. I had never seen her since her marriage, nearly five years since, till the other day, when she asked me out to lunch, and introduced me to Mr. Joseph P., who seems a very nice man, and also—now don't faint utterly, but you will! to their seven children! He had two of his own when they married, and they have had two pairs of twins since, and "a singleton," as they say in whist. Such a houseful you never did see; but the twins are lovely, and Esther looks very fat and happy and well-to-do, and says she doesn't mind it a bit, and sees more clearly every day that the thing she was born for was to take the charge of a large family. Her Joseph P. is very well off, too. I should judge that they "could have cranberry sauce every day and never feel the difference," which an old cousin of my mother's, whom I dimly remember as a part of my childhood, used to regard as representing the high-water mark of wealth.

Mary Strothers has been in town lately, too. She has only one child, a little girl, which seems miserably few compared with Esther, but on the other hand she has never been without neuralgia in the face for one moment since she went to live in the Hoosac Tunnel, she told me, so there are compensations. She seems happy for all that, poor dear Mary. Ellen Gray never has married at all, you know. She goes into good works instead, girls' Friendlies and all sorts of usefulnesses. I do admire her so much, she is a standing reproach and example to me. "Wish I were a better boy," as your brother Dorry said in his journal.

Mother is well and my father, but the house seems empty and lonely now. We can never get used to dear grandmamma's loss, and Sylvia is gone too. She and Tom sailed for Europe in April, and it makes a great difference having them away, even for a summer. My brother-in-law is such a nice fellow, I hope you will know him some day.

And all this time I have forgotten to tell you the chief news of all, which is that I have seen Katy. Deniston and I spent Sunday before last with her at the Torpedo station. She has a cosey, funny little house, one of a row of five or six, built on the spine, so to speak, of a narrow, steep island, with a beautiful view of Newport just across the water. It was a superb day, all shimmery blue and gold, and we spent most of our time sitting in a shady corner of the piazza, and talking of the old times and of all of you. I didn't know then of this enchanting Western plan, or we should have had a great deal more to talk about. The dear Katy looks very well and handsome, and was perfectly dear, as she always is, and she says the Newport climate suits her to perfection. Your brother-in-law is a stunner! I asked Katy if she wasn't going out to see you soon, and she said not till Ned went to sea next spring, then she should go for a long visit.

Write at once if we may come. I won't begin on the subject of Röslein, whom you will never know, she has grown so. She goes about saying rapturously, "I shall see little Geoff! I shall see Phillida! I shall see Aunt Clovy! Perhaps I shall ride on a horse!" You'll never have the heart to disappoint her. My "milk teeth are chattering with fright" at the idea of so much railroad, as one of her books says, but for all that we are coming, if you let us. Do let us!

Your own Rose Red.
"Let them! I should think so," cried Clover, with a little skip of rapture. "Dear, dear Rose! Elsie, the nicest sort of things do happen out here, don't they?"

CHAPTER V. ARRIVAL.

THE train from Denver was nearing St. Helen's,—and Imogen Young looked eagerly from the window for a first sight of the place. Their journey had been exhaustingly hot during its last stages, the alkaline dust most trying, and they had had a brief experience of a sand-storm on the plains, which gave her a new idea as to what wind and grit can accomplish in the way of discomfort. She was very tired, and quite disposed to be critical and unenthusiastic; still she had been compelled to admit that the run down from Denver lay over an interesting country. The town on its plateau was shining in full sunshine, as it had done when Clover landed there six years before, but its outlines had greatly changed with the increase of buildings. The mountain range opposite was darkly blue from the shadows of a heavy thunder gust which was slowly rolling away southward. The plains between were of tawny yellow, but the belts of mesa above showed the richest green, except where the lines of alfalfa and grain were broken by white patches of mentzelia and poppies. It was wonderfully beautiful, but the town itself looked so much larger than Imogen had expected that she exclaimed with surprise:—

"Why, Lion, it's a city! You said you were bringing me out to live in the wilderness. What made you tell such stories? It looks bigger than Bideford."

"It looks larger than it did when I came away," replied her brother. "Two, three, six,—eight fine new houses on Monument Avenue, by Jove, and any number off there toward the north. You've no idea how these Western places sprout and thrive, Moggy. This isn't twenty years old yet."

"I can't believe it. You are imposing on me. And why on earth did you let me bring out all those pins and things? There seem to be any number of shops."

"I let you! Oh, I say, that is good! Why, Moggy, don't you remember how I remonstrated straight through your packing. Never a bit would you listen to me, and here is the result," pulling out a baggage memorandum as he spoke, and reading aloud in a lugubrious tone, "Extra weight of trunks, thirteen dollars, fifty-two cents."

"Thirteen fifty," cried Imogen with a gasp. "My gracious! why, that's nearly three pounds! Lion! Lion! you ought to have made me listen."

"I'm sure I did all I could in that way. But cheer up! You'll want your pins yet. You mustn't confound this place with High Valley. That's sixteen miles off and hasn't a shop."

The discussion was brought to end by the stopping of the train. In another moment Geoff Templestowe appeared at the door.

"Hallo, Lion! glad to see you. Imogen," shaking hands warmly, "how are you? Welcome to Colorado. I'm afraid you've had a bad journey in this heat."

"It has been beastly. Poor Moggy's dead beat, I'm afraid. Neither of us could sleep a wink last night for the dust and sand. Well, it's all well that ends well. We'll cool her off in the valley. How is everything going on there? Mrs. Templestowe all right, and Mrs. Page, and the children? I declare," stretching himself, "it's a blessing to get a breath of good air again. There's nothing in the world that can compare with Colorado."

A light carryall was waiting near the station, whose top was little more than a fringed awning. Into this Geoffrey helped Imogen, and proceeded to settle her wraps and bags in various seat boxes and pockets with which the carriage was cleverly fitted up. It was truly a carry-all and came and went continually between the valley and St. Helen's.

"Now," he remarked as he stuffed in the last parcel, "we will just stop long enough to get the mail and some iced tea, which I ordered as I came down, and then be off. You'll find a cold chicken in that basket, Lion. Clover was sure you'd need something, and there's no time for a regular meal if we are to get in before dark."

"Iced tea! what a queer idea!" said Imogen.

"I forgot that you were not used to it. We drink it a great deal here in summer. Would you rather have some hot? I didn't fancy that you would care for it, the day is so warm; but we'll wait and have it made, if you prefer."

"Oh, no. I won't delay you," said Imogen, rather grudgingly. She was disposed to resent the iced tea as an American innovation, but when she tried it she found herself, to her own surprise, liking it very much.

"Only, why do they call it tea," she meditated. "It's a great deal more like punch—all lemon and things." But she had to own that it was wonderfully refreshing.

The sun was blazing on the plain; but after they began to wind up the pass a cool, strong wind blew in their faces and the day seemed suddenly delightful. The unfamiliar flowers and shrubs, the strange rock forms and colors, the occasional mountain glimpses, interested Imogen so much that for a time she forgot her fatigue. Then an irresistible drowsiness seized her; the talk going on between Geoffrey Templestowe and her brother, about cows and feed and the prospect of the autumn sales, became an indistinguishable hum, and she went off into a series of sleeps broken by brief wakings, when the carryall bumped, or swayed heavily from side to side on the steep inclines. From one of the soundest of these naps she was roused by her brother shaking her arm and calling,—

"Moggy, wake, wake up! We are here."

With a sharp thump of heart-beat she started into full consciousness to find the horses drawing up before a deep vine-hung porch, on which stood a group of figures which seemed to her confused senses a large party. There was Elsie in a fresh white dress with pale green ribbons, Clarence Page, Phil Carr, little Philippa in her nurse's arms, small Geoff with his two collies at his side, and foremost of all, ready to help her down, hospitable little Clover, in lilac muslin, with a rose in her belt and a face of welcome.

"How the Americans do love dress!" was Imogen's instant thought,— an ungracious one, and quite unwarranted by the circumstances. Clover and Elsie kept themselves neat and pretty from habit and instinct, but the muslin gowns were neither new nor fashionable, they had only the merit of being fresh and becoming to their wearers.

"You poor child, how tired you must be!" cried Clover, as she assisted Imogen out of the carriage. "This is my sister, Mrs. Page. Please take her directly to her room, Elsie, while I order up some hot water. She'll be glad of that first of all. Lion, I won't take time to welcome you now. The boys must care for you while I see after your sister."

A big sponging-bath full of fresh water stood ready in the room to which Imogen was conducted; the white bed was invitingly "turned down;" there were fresh flowers on the dressing-table, and a heap of soft cushions on a roomy divan which filled the deep recess of a range of low windows. The gay-flowered paper on the walls ran up to the peak of the ceiling, giving a tent-like effect. Most of the furnishings were home-made. The divan was nothing more or less than a big packing-box nicely stuffed and upholstered; the dressing-table, a construction of pine boards covered and frilled with cretonne. Clover had plaited the chintz round the looking-glass and on the edges of the book-shelves, while the picture-frames, the corner-brackets, and the impromptu washstand owed their existence to Geoff's cleverness with tools. But the whole effect was pretty and tasteful, and Imogen, as she went on with her dressing, looked about her with a somewhat reluctant admiration, which was slightly tinctured with dismay.

"I suppose they got all these things out from the East," she reflected. "I couldn't undertake them in our little cabin, I'm sure. It's very nice, and really in very good taste, but it must have cost a great deal. The Americans don't think of that, however; and I've always heard they have a great knack at doing up their houses and making a good show."

"Go straight to bed if you feel like it. Don't think of coming down. We will send you up some dinner," Clover had urged; but Imogen, tired as she was, elected to go down.

"I really mustn't give in to a little fatigue," she thought. "I have the honor of England to sustain over here." So she heroically put on her heavy tweed travelling-dress again, and descended the stairs, to find a bright little fire of pine-wood and cones snapping and blazing on the hearth, and the whole party gathered about it, waiting for her and dinner.

"What an extraordinary climate!" she exclaimed in a tone of astonishment. "Melting with heat at three, and here at a quarter past seven you are sitting round a fire! It really feels comfortable, too!"

"The changes are very sharp," said Geoff, rising to give her his chair. "Such a daily drop in temperature would make a sensation in our good old Devonshire, would it not? You see it comes from the high elevation. We are nearly eight thousand feet above the sea-level here; that is about twice as high as the top of the highest mountain in the United Kingdom."

"Fancy! I had no idea of it. Lionel did say something about the elevation, but I didn't clearly attend." She glanced about the room, which was looking its best, with the pink light of the shaded candles falling on the white-spread table, and the flickering fire making golden glows and gleams on the ceiling. "How did you get all these pretty things out here?" she suddenly demanded.

"Some came in wagons, and some just 'growed,'" explained Clover, merrily. "We will let you into our secrets gradually. Ah, here comes dinner at last, and I am sure we shall all be glad of it."

Choo Loo now entered with the soup-tureen, a startling vision to Imogen, who had never seen a Chinaman before in her life.

"How very extraordinary!" she murmured in an aside to Lionel. "He looks like an absolute heathen. Are such things usual here?"

"Very usual, I should say. Lots of them about. That fellow has a Joss in his cabin, and very likely a prayer-wheel; but he's a capital cook. I wish we could have the luck to happen on his brother or nephew for ourselves."

"I don't, then," replied his scandalized sister. "I can't feel that it is right to employ such people in a Christian country. The Americans have such lax notions!"

"Hold up a bit! What do you know about their notions? Nothing at all."

"Come to dinner," said Clover's pleasant voice. "Geoff, Miss Young will sit next to you. Put a cushion behind her back, Clarence."

Dinner over, Imogen concluded that she had upheld the honor of England quite as long as was desirable, or in fact possible, and gladly accepted permission to go at once to bed. She was fairly tired out.

She woke wonderfully restored by nine hours' solid sleep in that elastic and life-giving atmosphere, and went downstairs to find every one scattered to their different tasks and avocations, except Elsie, who was waiting to pour her coffee. Clover and Lionel were gone to the new house, she explained, and they were to follow them as soon as Imogen had breakfasted.

Elsie's manner lacked its usual warmth and ease. She had taken no fancy at all to the stiff, awkward little English woman, in whom her quick wits detected the lurking tendency to cavil and criticise, and was discouraging accordingly. Oddly enough, Imogen liked this offish manner of Elsie's. She set it down to a proper sense of decorum and retenue. "So different from the usual American gush and making believe to be at ease always with everybody," she thought; and she made herself as agreeable as possible to Elsie, whom she considered much prettier than Clover, and in every way more desirable. These impressions were doubtless tinctured by the underlying jealousy from which she had so long suffered, and which still influenced her, though Isabel Templestowe was now far away, and there was no one at hand to be jealous about.

The two rode amicably up the valley together.

"There, that's your new home," said Elsie, when they came in sight of the just finished cabin. "Didn't Lionel choose a pretty site for it? And you have a most beautiful view."

"Well, Moggy," cried her brother, hurrying out to help her dismount, "here you are at last. Mrs. Templestowe and I have made you a fire and done all sorts of things. How do you like the look of it? It's a decent little place, isn't it? We must get Mrs. Templestowe to put us up to some of her nice little dodges about furniture and so on, such as they have at the other house. She and Mrs. Page have made it all tidy for us, and put up lots of nice little curtains and things. They must have worked awfully hard, too. Wasn't it good of them?"

"Very," said Imogen, rather stiffly. "I'm sure we're much obliged to you, Mrs. Templestowe. I fear you have given yourself a great deal of trouble."

The words were polite enough, but the tone was distinctly repellent.

"Oh, no," said Clover, lightly. "It was only fun to come up and arrange a little beforehand. We were very glad to do it. Now, Elsie, you and I will ride down, and leave these new housekeepers to discuss their plans in peace. Dinner at six to-night, Lionel; and please send old José down if you need anything. Don't stay too long or get too tired, Miss Young. We shall have lunch about one; but if you are doing anything and don't want to leave so early, you'll find some sardines and jam and a tin of biscuits in that cupboard by the fire."

She and Elsie rode away accordingly. When they were out of hearing, Clover remarked,—

"I wonder why that girl dislikes me so."

"Dislikes you! Clover, what do you mean? Nobody ever disliked you in your life, or ever could."

"Yes, she does," persisted Clover. "She has got some sort of queer twist in her mind regarding me, and I can't think what it is. It doesn't really matter, and very likely she'll get over it presently; but I'm sorry about it. It would be so pleasant all to be good friends together up here, where there are so few of us."

Her tone was a little pathetic. Clover was used to being liked.

"Little wretch!" cried Elsie, with flashing eyes. "If I really thought that she dared not to like you, I'd—I'd—, well, what would I do?—import a grisly bear to eat her, or some such thing! I suppose an Indian could be found who for a consideration would undertake to scalp Miss Imogen Young, and if she doesn't behave herself he shall be found. But you're all mistaken, Clovy; you must be. She's only stiff and dull and horribly English, and very tired after her journey. She'll be all right in a day or two. If she isn't, I shall 'go for' her without mercy."

"Well, perhaps it is that." It was easier and pleasanter to imagine Imogen tired than to admit that she was absolutely unfriendly.

"After all," she added, "it's for Miss Young's sake that I should regret it if it were so, much more than for my own. I have Geoff and you and Clare,—and papa and Johnnie coming, and dear Rose Red,—all of you are at my back; but she, poor thing, has no one but Lionel to stand up for her. I am on my own ground," drawing up her figure with a pretty movement of pride, "and she is a stranger in a strange land. So we won't mind if she is stiff, Elsie dear, and just be as nice as we can be to her, for it must be horrid to be so far away from home and one's own people. We cannot be too patient and considerate under such circumstances."

Meanwhile the moment they were out of sight Lionel had turned upon his sister sharply, and angrily.

"Moggy, what on earth do you mean by speaking so to Mrs. Templestowe?"

"Speaking how? What did I say?" retorted Imogen.

"You didn't say anything out of the common, but your manner was most disagreeable. If she hadn't been the best-tempered woman in the world she would have resented it on the spot. Here she, and all of them, have been doing all they can to make ready for us, giving us such a warm welcome too, treating us as if we were their own kith and kin, and you return it by putting on airs as if she were intruding and interfering in our affairs. I never was so ashamed of a member of my own family before in my life."

"I can't imagine what you mean," protested Imogen, not quite truthfully. "And you've no call to speak to me so, Lionel, and tell me I am rude, just because I don't gush and go about making cordial speeches like these Americans of yours. I'm sure I said everything that was proper to Mrs. Templestowe."

"Your words were proper enough, but your manner was eminently improper. Now, Moggy," changing his tone, "listen to me. Let us look the thing squarely in the face. You've come out here with me, and it's awfully good of you and I sha'n't ever forget it; but here we are, settled for years to come in this little valley, with the Templestowes and Pages for our only neighbors. They can be excellent friends, as I've found, and they are prepared to be equally friendly to you; but if you're going to start with a little grudge against Mrs. Geoff,—who's the best little woman going, by Jove, and the kindest,—you'll set the whole family against us, and we might as well pack up our traps at once and go back to England. Now I put it to you reasonably; is it worth while to upset all our plans and all my hopes,—and for what? Mrs. Templestowe can't have done anything to set you against her?"

"Lion," cried Imogen, bursting into tears, "don't! I'm sure I didn't mean to be rude. Mrs. Geoff never did anything to displease me, and certainly I haven't a grudge against her. But I'm very tired, so please don't s-c-o-ld me; I've got no one out here but you."

Lionel melted at once. He had never seen his sister cry before, and felt that he must have been harsh and unkind.

"I'm a brute," he exclaimed. "There, Moggy, there, dear—don't cry. Of course you're tired; I ought to have thought of it before."

He petted and consoled her, and Imogen, who was really spent and weary, found the process so agreeable that she prolonged her tears a little. At last she suffered herself to be comforted, dried her eyes, grew cheerful, and the two proceeded to make an investigation of the premises, deciding what should go there and what here, and what it was requisite to get from St. Helen's. Imogen had to own that the ladies of the Valley had been both thoughtful and helpful.

"I'll thank them again this evening and do it better," she said; and Lionel patted her back, and told her she really was quite a little brick when she wasn't a big goose,—a brotherly compliment which was more gratifying than it sounded.

It was decided that he should go into St. Helen's next day to order out stores and what Lionel called "a few sticks" that were essential, and procure a servant.

"Then we can move in the next day," said Imogen. "I feel in such a hurry to begin house-keeping, Lionel, you can't think. One is always a stranger in the land till one has a place of one's own. Geoff and his wife are very kind and polite, but it's much better we should start for ourselves as soon as possible. Besides, there are other people coming to stay; Mrs. Page said so."

"Yes, but not for quite a bit yet, I fancy. All the same, you are right, Moggy; and we'll set up our own shebang as soon as it can be managed. You'll feel twice as much at home when you have a house of your own. I'll get the mattresses and tables and chairs out by Saturday, and fetch the slavey out with me if I can find one."

"No Chinese need apply," said Imogen. "Get me a Christian servant, whatever you do, Lion. I can't bear that creature with the pig-tail."

"I'll do my possible," said her brother, in a doubtful tone; "but you'll come to pig-tails yet and be thankful for them, or I miss my guess."

"Never!"

Imogen remembered her promise. She was studiously polite and grateful that evening, and exerted herself to talk and undo the unpleasant impression of the morning. The little party round the dinner-table waxed merry, especially when Imogen, under the effect of her gracious resolves, attempted to adapt her conversation to her company and gratify her hosts by using American expressions.

"People absquatulate from St. Helen's toward autumn, don't they?" she remarked. Then when some one laughed she added, "You say 'absquatulate' over here, don't you?"

"Well, I don't know. I never did hear any one say it except as a joke," replied Elsie.

And again: "Mother would be astonished, Lion, wouldn't she, if she knew that a Chinese can make English puddings as well as the cooks at home. She'd be all struck of a heap."

And later: "It really was dreadful. The train was broken all to bits, and nearly every one on board was hurt,—catawampously chawed up in fact, as you Americans would say. Why, what are you all laughing at? Don't you say it?"

"Never, except in the comic newspapers and dime novels," said Geoffrey Templestowe when he recovered from his amusement, while Lionel, utterly overcome with his sister's vocabulary, choked and strangled, and finally found voice to say,—

"Go on, Moggy. You're doing beautifully. Nothing like acquiring the native dialect to make a favorable impression in a new country. Oh, wherever did she learn 'catawampus'? I shall die of it."

CHAPTER VI. UNEXPECTED.

IMOGEN'S race-prejudices experienced a weakening after Lionel's return from St. Helen's with the only "slavey" attainable, in the shape of an untidy, middle-aged Irish woman, with red hair, and a hot little spark of temper glowing in either eye. Putting this unpromising female in possession of the fresh, clean kitchen of the cabin was a trial, but it had to be done; and the young mistress, with all the ardor of inexperience, bent herself to the task of reformation and improvement, and teaching Katty Maloney—who was old enough to be her mother—a great many desirable things which she herself did not very well understand. It was thankless work and resulted as such experiments usually do. Katty gave warning at the end of a week, affirming that she wasn't going to be hectored and driven round by a bit of a miss, who didn't well know what she wanted; and that the Valley was that lonesome anyhow that she'd not remain in it; no, not if the Saints themselves came down from glory and kivered up every fut of soil with shining gold, and she a-starving in the mud,—that she wouldn't! Imogen saw her go with small regret. She had no idea how difficult it might be to find a successor, and it was not till three incompetents of the same nationality had been lured out by the promise of high wages, only to decide that the place was too "lonely" for them and incontinently depart, that she realized how hard was the problem of "help" in such a place. It was her first trial at independent housekeeping, and with her English ideas she had counted on neatness, respectfulness of manner, and a certain amount of training as a matter of course in a servant. One has to learn one's way in a new country by the hardest, and perhaps, the least hard part of Imogen's lesson were the intervals when she and Lionel did the work themselves, with only old José to scrub and wash up; then at least they could be quiet and at peace, without daily controversies. Later, relief and comfort came to them in the shape of a gentle Mongolian named Ah Lee, procured through the good offices of Choo Loo, whom Imogen was only too thankful to accept, pig-tail and all, for his gentleness of manner, general neatness and capacity, and the good taste which he gave to his dishes. In fact, she confessed one day to Lionel, privately in a moment of confidence, that rather than lose him, she would herself carve a joss stick and nail it up in the kitchen; which concession proves the liberalizing and widening effect of necessity upon the human mind. But this is anticipating.

The cabin was a pleasant place enough when once fairly set in order.

There was an abundance of sunshine, fire-wood was plenty, and so small a space was easily kept tidy. Imogen, when she reviewed her resources, realized how wise Lionel had been in recommending her to bring more ornamental things and fewer articles of mere use, such as tapes and buttons. Buttons and tapes were easy enough to come by; but things to make the house pretty were difficult to obtain and cost a great deal. She made the most of her few possessions, and supplied what was lacking with wild flowers, which could be had in any quantity for the picking. Lionel had hunted a good deal during his first Colorado years, and possessed quite a good supply of fox, wolf, and bear skins. These did duty for rugs on the floor. Elk and buffalo horns fastened on the walls served as pegs on which to hang whips and hats. Some gay Mexican pots adorned the chimney-piece; it all looked pretty enough and quite comfortable. Imogen would fain have tried her hand at home-made devices of the sort in which the ladies at the lower house excelled, but somehow her attempts turned out failures. She lacked lightness of touch and originality of fancy, and the results were apt to be what Elsie privately stigmatized as "wapses of red flannel and burlaps without form or comeliness," at which Lionel jeered, while visitors discreetly averted their eyes lest they should be forced to express an opinion concerning them.

Imogen's views as to the character and capacities of American women underwent many modifications during that first summer in the Valley. It seemed to her that Mrs. Templestowe and her sister were equal to any emergency however sudden and unexpected. She was filled with daily wonder over their knowledge of practical details, and their extraordinary "handiness." If a herder met with an accident they seemed to know just what to do. If Choo Loo was taken with a cramp or some odd Chinese disease without a name, and laid aside for a day or two, Clover not only nursed him but went into the kitchen as a matter of course, and extemporized a meal which was sufficiently satisfactory for all concerned. If a guest arrived unexpectedly they were not put out; if some article of daily supply failed, they seemed always able to devise a substitute; and through all and every contingency they managed to look pretty and bright and gracious, and make sunshine in the shadiest places.

Slowly, for Imogen's mind was not of the quick working order, she took all this in, and her respect for America and Americans rose accordingly. She was forced to own that whatever the rest of womankind in this extraordinary new country might be, these particular specimens were of a sort which any land, even England, might be justly proud to claim.

"And with all they do, they contrive to look so nice," she said to herself. "I can't understand how they manage it. Their gowns fit so well, and they always seem to have just the right kind of thing to put on. It is really wonderful, and it certainly isn't because they think a great deal about it. Before I came over I always imagined that American women spent their time in reading fashion magazines and talking over their clothes. Mrs. Geoff and Mrs. Page certainly don't do that. I don't often hear them speak about dresses, or see them at work at them; and both of them know a great deal more about a house than I do, or any other English girl I ever saw. Mrs. Geoff, and Mrs. Page too, can make all sorts of things,—cakes and puddings and muffins and even bread; and they read a good deal as well. The Americans are certainly a cleverer people than I supposed."

The mile of distance between what Clarence called "the Hut and the Hutlet" counted for little, and a daily intercourse went on, trending chiefly, it must be owned, from the Hut to the Hutlet. Clover was unwearied in small helps and kindnesses. If Imogen were cookless, old José was sure to appear with a loaf of freshly baked bread, or a basket of graham gems; or Geoff with a creel of trout and an urgent invitation to lunch or dinner or both. New books made their appearance from below, newspapers and magazines; and if ever the day came when Imogen felt hopelessly faint-hearted, lonely, and over-worked, she was sure to see the flutter of skirts, and her pretty, cordial neighbors would come riding up the trail to cheer her, and to propose something pleasant or helpful. Sometimes Elsie would have her baby on her knee, trusting to "Summer Savory's" sure-footed steadiness; sometimes little Geoff would be riding beside his mother on a minute burro. Always it seemed as though they brought the sun with them; and she learned to watch for their coming on dull days, as if they were in the secret of her moods and knew just when they were most wanted. But they came so often that these coincidences were not so wonderful, after all.

Imogen did appreciate all this kindness, and was grateful, and, after her manner, responsive; still the process of what Elsie termed "limbering out Miss Young" went on but slowly. The English stock, firm-set and sturdily rooted, does not "limber" readily, and a bent toward prejudice is never easily shaken. Compelled to admit that Clover was worth liking, compelled to own her good nature and friendliness, Imogen yet could not be cordially at ease with her. Always an inward stiffness made itself apparent when they were together, and always Clover was aware of the fact. It made no difference in her acts of good-will, but it made some difference in the pleasure with which she did them,— though on no account would she have confessed it, especially to Elsie, who was so comically ready to fire up and offer battle if she suspected any one of undervaluing her sister. So the month of July went.

It was on the morning of the last day, when the long summer had reached its height of ripeness and completeness, and all things seemed making themselves ready for Rose Red, who was expected in three days more, that Clover, sitting with her work on the shaded western piazza, saw the unwonted spectacle of a carriage slowly mounting the steep road up the Valley. It was so unusual to see any wheeled vehicle there, except their own carryall, that it caused a universal excitement. Elsie ran to the window overhead with Phillida in her arms; little Geoff stood on the porch staring out of a pair of astonished eyes, and Clover came forward to meet the new arrivals with an unmistakable look of surprise in her face. The gentleman who was driving and the lady beside him were quite unknown to her; but from the back part of the carriage a head extended itself,—an elderly head, with a bang of oddly frizzled gray hair and a pair of watery blue eyes, all surmounted by an eccentric shade hat, and all beaming and twittering with recognition and excitement. It took Clover a moment to disentangle her ideas; then she perceived that it was Mrs. Watson, who, when she and Phil first came out to Colorado, years before, came with them, and for a time had been one of the chief trials and perplexities of their life there.

"Well, my dear, and I don't wonder that you look astonished, for no one would suppose that after all I went through with I should ever again— This is my daughter, and her husband, you know, and of course their coming made it seem quite— We are staying in the Ute Valley; only five miles over, they said it was, but such miles! I'd rather ride ten on a level, any day, as I told Ellen, and—well, they said you were living up here; and though the road was pretty rough, it was possible to— And if ever there was a man who could drive a buggy up to the moon, as Ellen declares, Henry is the—but really I was hardly prepared for—but any way we started, and here we are! What a wild sort of place it is that you are living in, my dear Miss Carr—not that I ought to call you Miss Carr, for— I got your cards, of course, and I was told then that— And your sister marrying the other young man and coming out to live here too! that must be very— Oh, dear me! is that little boy yours? Well, I never!"

"I am very glad to see you, I am sure," said Clover, taking the first opportunity of a break in the torrent of words, "and Mrs. Phillips too,—this is Mrs. Phillips, is it not? Let me help you out, Mrs. Watson, and Geoffy dear, run round to the other door and ask Euphane to send somebody to take the horses."

"Thank you," said Mrs. Phillips. "Let me introduce my husband, Mrs. Templestowe. We are at the hotel in the Ute Valley for three days, and my mother wished so much to drive over and see you that we have brought her. What a beautiful place your valley is!"

Mrs. Phillips, tall, large-featured, dark and rather angular, with a pleasant, resolute face, and clear-cut, rather incisive way of speaking, offered as complete a contrast to her pale, pudgy, incoherent little mother as could well be imagined. Clover's instant thought was, "Now I know what Mr. Watson must have been like." Mr. Phillips was also tall, with a keen, Roman-nosed face, and eye-glasses. Both had the look of people who knew what was what and had seen the world,—just the sort of persons, it would seem, to whom a parent like Mrs. Watson would be a great trial; and it was the more to their credit that they never seemed in the least impatient, and were evidently devoted to her comfort in all ways. If she fretted them, as she undoubtedly must, they gave no sign of it, and were outwardly all affectionate consideration.

"Why, where is your little boy gone? I wanted to see him," said Mrs. Watson, as soon as she was safely out of the carriage. "He was here just this moment, and then—I must say you have got a beautiful situation; and if mountains were all that one needed to satisfy—but I recollect how you used to go on about them at St. Helen's— Take care, Ellen, your skirt is caught! Ah, that's right! Miss Carr is always so—but I mustn't call her that, I know, only I never— And now, my dear, I must have a kiss, after climbing up all this way; and there were gopher holes—at least, a man we met said they were that, and I really thought— Tell me how you are, and all about— That's right, Henry, take out the wraps; you never can tell how— Of course Miss Carr's people are all— I keep calling you Miss Carr; I really can't help it. What a beautiful view!"

Clover now led the way in-doors. The central room, large, cool, and flower-scented, was a surprise to the Eastern guests, who were not prepared to find anything so pretty and tasteful in so remote a spot.

"This is really charming!" said Mr. Phillips, glancing from fireplace to wall, and from wall to window; while his wife exclaimed with delight over the Mariposa lilies which filled a glass bowl on the table, and the tall sheaves of scarlet penstamens on either side the hearth. Mrs. Watson blinked about curiously, actually silent for a moment, before her surprise took the form of words.

"Why, how pretty it looks, doesn't it, Ellen? and so large and spacious, and so many— I'm all the more surprised because when we were together before, you wouldn't go to the Shoshone House, you remember, because it was so expensive, and of course I— Well, circumstances do alter; and it is a world of changes, as Dr. Billings said in one of his sermons last spring. And I'm sure I'm glad, only I wasn't prepared to— Ellen! Ellen! look at that etching! It's exactly the same as yours, which Jane Phillips gave you and Henry for your tin wedding. It was very expensive, I know, for I was with her when she got it, and so—at Doll's it was; and his things naturally—but I really think the frame of this is the handsomest! Now, my dear Miss Carr, where did you get that?"

"It was one of our gifts," said Clover, smiling. "There is a double supply of wedding presents in this house, Mrs. Watson, for my sister's are here as well as our own. So we are rather rich in pretty things, as you see, but not in anything else, except cows; of those we have any number. Now, if you will all excuse me for a moment, I will go up and tell Mrs. Page that you are here."

Up she went, deliberately till she was out of sight, and then at a swift, light run the rest of the way.

"Elsie dear," she cried, bursting into the nursery, "who do you think is here? Mrs. Watson, our old woman of the Sea, you know. She has her son-in-law and daughter with her, and they look like rather nice people, strange to say. They have driven over from the Ute Valley, and of course they must have some lunch; but as it happens it is the worst day of the whole year for them to choose, for I have sent Choo Loo into St. Helen's to look up a Chinese cook for Imogen Young, and I meant to starve you all on poached eggs and raspberries for lunch. I can't leave them of course, but will you just run down, my darling duck, and see what can be done, and tell Euphane? There are cans of soup, of course, and sardines, and all that, but I fear the bread supply is rather short. I'll take Phillida. She's as neat as a new pin, happily. Ah, here's Geoffy. Come and have your hair brushed, boy."

She went down with one child in her arms and the other holding her hand,—a pretty little picture for those below.

"My sister will come presently," she explained. "This is her little girl. And here is my son, Mrs. Watson."

"Dear me,—I had no idea he was such a big child," said that lady. "Five years old, is he, or six?—only three! Oh, yes, what am I thinking about; of course he—Well, my little man, and how do you like living up here in this lonesome place?"

"Very much," replied little Geoff, backing away from the questioner, as she aimlessly reached out after him.

"He has never lived anywhere else," Clover explained; "so he cannot make comparisons. Ignorance is bliss, we are told, Mrs. Watson."

Euphane, staid and respectable in her spotless apron, now entered with the lunch-cloth, and Clover convoyed her guests upstairs to refresh themselves with cold water after the dust of the drive. By the time they returned the table was set, and presently Elsie appeared, cool and fresh in her pretty pink and white gingham with a knot of rose-colored ribbon in her wavy hair, her cheeks deepened to just the becoming tint, the very picture of a dainty, well-cared-for little lady. No one would have suspected that during the last half-hour she had stirred and baked a pan of brown "gems," mixed a cream mayonnaise for the lettuce, set a glass dish of "junket" to form, and skimmed two pans of cream, beside getting out the soup and sweets for Euphane, and trimming the dishes of fruit with kinnikinick and coreopsis. The little feast seemed to have got itself ready in some mysterious manner, without trouble to any one, which is the last added grace of any feast.

"It is perfectly charming here," said Mrs. Phillips, more and more impressed. "I have seen nothing at all like this at the West."

"No one would have suspected that she had skimmed two pans of cream"—Page 166. "No one would have suspected that she had skimmed two pans of cream"—Page 166.
"There isn't any other place exactly like our valley, I really think. Of course there are other natural parks among the ranges of the Rockies, but ours always seems to me quite by itself. You see we lie so as to catch the sun, and it makes a great difference even in the winter. We have done very little to the Valley, beyond just making ourselves

comfortable."

"Very comfortable indeed, I should say."

"And so you married the other young man, my dear?" Mrs. Watson was remarking to Elsie. "I remember he used to come in very often to call on your sister, and it was easy enough to see,—people in boarding-houses will notice such things of course, and we all used to think— But there—of course she knew all the time, and it is easy to make mistakes, and I dare say it's all for the best as it is. You look very young indeed to be married. I wonder that your father could make up his mind to let you."

"I am not young at all, I'm nearly twenty-six," replied Elsie, who always resented remarks about her youth. "There are three younger than I am in the family, and they are all grown up."

"Oh, my dear, but you don't look it! You don't seem a day over twenty. Ellen was nearly as old as you are before she ever met Henry, and they were engaged nearly two— But she never did look as young as most of the girls she used to go with, and I suppose that's the reason that now they are all got on a little, she seems younger than— Well, well! we never thought while I was with your sister at St. Helen's, helping to take care of your poor brother, you know, how it would all turn out. There was a young man who used to bring roses,—I forget his name,— and one day Mrs. Gibson said— Her husband had weak lungs and they came out to Colorado on that account, but I believe he— They were talking of building a house, and I meant to ask— But there, I forgot; one does grow so forgetful if one travels much and sees a good many people; but as I was saying—he got well, I think."

"Who, Mr. Gibson?" asked Elsie, quite bewildered.

"Oh, no! not Mr. Gibson, of course. He died, and Mrs. Gibson married again. Some man she met out at St. Helen's, I believe it was, and I heard that her children didn't like it; but he was rich, I believe and of course— Riches have wings,—you know that proverb of course,—but it makes a good deal of difference whether they fly toward you or away from you."

"Indeed it does," said Elsie, much amused. "But you asked me if somebody got well. Who was it?"

"Why, your brother of course. He didn't die, did he?"

"Oh dear, no! He is living at St. Helen's now, and perfectly well and strong."

"Well, that must be a great comfort to you all. I never did think that he was as ill as your sister fancied he was. Girls will get anxious, and when people haven't had a great deal of experience they— He used to laugh a great deal too, and when people do that it seems to me that their lungs— But of course it was only natural at her age. I used to cheer her up all I could and say— The air is splendid there, of course, and the sun somehow never seems to heat you up as it does at the East, though it is hot, but I think when people have weak chests they'd better— Dr. Hope doesn't think so, I know, but after all there are a great many doctors beside Dr. Hope, and— Ellen quite agrees with me— What was I saying."

Elsie wondered on what fragment of the medley she would fix. She was destined never to know, for just then came the trample of hoofs and the "Boys" rode up to the door.

She went out on the porch to meet them and break the news of the unexpected guests.

"That old thing!" cried Clarence, with unflattering emphasis. "Oh, thunder! I thought we were safe from that sort of bore up here. I shall just cut down to the back and take a bite in the barn."

"Indeed you will do nothing of the sort. Do you suppose I came up to this place, where company only arrives twice a year or so, to be that lonesome thing a cowboy's bride, that you might slip away and take bites in barns? No sir—not at all. You will please go upstairs, make yourself fit to be seen, and come down and be as polite as possible. Do you hear, Clare?"

She hooked one white finger in his buttonhole, and stood looking in his face with a saucy gaze. Clarence yielded at once. His small despot knew very well how to rule him and to put down such short-lived attempts at insubordination as he occasionally indulged in.

"All right, Elsie, I'll go if I must. They're not to stay the night, are they?"

"Heaven forbid! No indeed, they are going back to the Ute Valley."

He vanished, and presently re-appeared to conduct himself with the utmost decorum. He did not even fidget when referred to pointedly as "the other young man," by Mrs. Watson, with an accompaniment of nods and blinks and wreathed smiles which was, to say the least, suggestive. Geoff's manners could be trusted under all circumstances, and the little meal passed off charmingly.

"Good-by," said Mrs. Watson, after she was safely seated in the carriage, as Clover sedulously tucked her wraps about her. "It's really been a treat to see you. We shall talk of it often, and I know Ellen will say— Oh, thank you, Miss Carr, you always were the kindest— Yes, I know it isn't Miss Carr, and I ought to remember, but somehow— Good-by, Mrs. Page. Somehow—it's very pretty up here certainly, and you have every comfort I'm sure, and you seem— But it will be getting dark before long, and I don't like the idea of leaving you young things up here all by yourselves. Don't you ever feel a little afraid in the evenings? I suppose there are not any wild animals—though I remember— But there, I mustn't say anything to discourage you, since you are here, and have got to stay."

"Yes, we have to stay," said Clover, as she shook hands with Mr. Phillips, "and happily it is just what we all like best to do." She watched the carriage for a moment or two as it bumped down the road, its brake grinding sharply against the wheels, then she turned to the others with a look of comically real relief.

"It seems like a bad dream! I had forgotten how Phil and I used to feel when Mrs. Watson went on like that, and she always did go on like that. How did we stand her?"

"Ellen seems nice," remarked Elsie,—"Poor Ellen!"

"Geoff," added Clarence, vindictively, "this must not happen again. You and I must go to work below and shave off the hill and make it twice as steep! It will never do to have the High Valley made easy of access to old ladies from Boston who—"

"Who call you 'the other young man,'" put in naughty Elsie. "Never mind, Clare. I share your feelings, but I don't think there is any risk. There is only one of her, and I am quite certain, from the scared look with which she alluded to our 'wild beasts,' that she never proposes to come again."

CHAPTER VII. THORNS AND ROSES.

GEOFF," said Clover as they sat at dinner two days later, "couldn't we start early when we go in to-morrow to meet Rose, and have the morning at St. Helen's? There are quite a lot of little errands to be done, and it's a long time since we saw Poppy or the Hopes."
"Just as early as you like," replied her husband. "It's a free day, and I am quite at your service."

So they breakfasted at a quarter before six, and by a quarter past were on their way to St. Helen's, passing, as Clover remarked, through three zones of temperature; for it was crisply cold when they set out, temperately cool at the lower end of the Ute Pass, and blazing hot on the sandy plain.

"We certainly do get a lot of climate for our money out here," observed Geoff.

They reached the town a little before ten, and went first of all to see Mrs. Marsh, for whom Clover had brought a basket of fresh eggs. She never entered that house without being sharply carried back to former days, and made to feel that the intervening time was dreamy and unreal, so absolutely unchanged was it. There was the rickety piazza on which she and Phil had so often sat, the bare, unhomelike parlor, the rocking-chairs swinging all at once, timed as it were to an accompaniment of coughs; but the occupants were not the same. Many sets of invalids had succeeded each other at Mrs. Marsh's since those old days; still the general effect was precisely similar.

Mrs. Marsh, who only was unchanged, gave them a warm welcome. Grateful little Clover never had forgotten the many kindnesses shown to her and Phil, and requited them in every way that was in her power. More than once when Mrs. Marsh was poorly or overtired, she had carried her off to the High Valley for a rest; and she never failed to pay her a visit whenever she spent a day at St. Helen's.

Their next call was at the Hopes'. They found Mrs. Hope darning stockings on the back piazza which commanded a view of the mountain range. She always claimed the entire credit of Clover's match, declaring that if she had not matronized her out to the Valley and introduced her and Geoff to each other, they would never have met. Her droll airs of proprietorship over their happiness were infinitely amusing to Clover.

"I think we should have got at each other somehow, even if you had not been in existence," she told her friend; "marriages are made in Heaven, as we all know. Nobody could have prevented ours."

"My dear, that is just where you are mistaken. Nothing is easier than to prevent marriages. A mere straw will do it. Look at the countless old maids all over the world; and probably nearly every one of them came within half an inch of perfect happiness, and just missed it. No, depend upon it, there is nothing like a wise, judicious, discriminating friend at such junctures, to help matters along. You may thank me that Geoff isn't at this moment wedded to some stiff-necked British maiden, and you eating your head off in single-blessedness at Burnet."

"Rubbish!" said Clover. "Neither of us is capable of it;" but Mrs. Hope stuck to her convictions.

She was delighted to see them, as she always was, and no less the bottle of beautiful cream, the basket full of fresh lettuces, and the bunch of Mariposa lilies which they had brought. Clover never went into St. Helen's empty-handed.

Here they took luncheon No. 1,—consisting of sponge-cake and claret-cup, partaken of while gazing across at Cheyenne Mountain, which was at one of its most beautiful moments, all aerial blue streaked with sharp sunshine at the summit. It was the one defect of the High Valley, Clover thought, that it gave no glimpse of Cheyenne.

Luncheon No. 2 came a little later, with Marian Chase, whom every one still called "Poppy" from preference and long habit. She was perfectly well now, but she and her family had grown so fond of St. Helen's that there was no longer any talk of their going back to the East. She had just had some beautiful California plums sent her by an admirer, and insisted on Clover's eating them with an accompaniment of biscuits and "natural soda water."

"I want you and Alice Perham to come out next week for two nights," said Clover, while engaged in this agreeable occupation. "My friend Mrs. Browne arrives to-day, and she is by far the greatest treat we have ever had to offer to any one since we lived in the Valley. You will delight in her, I know. Could you come on Monday in the stage to the Ute Hotel, if we sent the carryall over to meet you?"

"Why, of course. I never have any engagements when a chance comes for going to the dear Valley; and Alice has none, I am pretty sure. It will be perfectly delightful! Clover, you are an angel,—'the Angel of the Penstamen' I mean to call you," glancing at the great sheaf of purple and white flowers which Clover had brought. "It's a very good name. As for Elsie, she is 'Our Lady of Raspberries;' I never saw such beauties as she fetched in week before last."

Some very multifarious shopping for the two households followed, and by that time it was two o'clock and they were quite ready for luncheon No. 3,—soup and sandwiches, procured at a restaurant. They were just coming away when an open carriage passed them, silk-lined, with a crest on the panel, jingling curb-chains, and silver-plated harnesses, all after the latest modern fashion, and drawn by a pair of fine gray horses. Inside was a young man, who returned a stiff bow to Clover's salutation, and a gorgeously gowned young lady with rather a handsome face.

"Mr. and Mrs. Thurber Wade, I declare," observed Geoffrey. "I heard that they were expected."

"Yes, Mrs. Wade is so pleased to have them come for the summer. We must go and call some day, Geoff, when I happen to have on my best bonnet. Do you think we ought to ask them out to the Valley?"

"That's just as you please. I don't mind if he doesn't. What fine horses. Aren't you conscious of a little qualm of regret, Clover?"

"What for? I don't know what you mean. Don't be absurd," was all the reply he received, or in fact deserved.

And now it was time to go to the train. The minutes seemed long while they waited, but presently came the well-known shriek and rumble, and there was Rose herself, dimpled and smiling at the window, looking not a whit older than on the day of Katy's wedding seven years before. There was little Rose too, but she was by no means so unchanged as her mother, and certainly no longer little, surprisingly tall on the contrary, with her golden hair grown brown and braided in a pig-tail, actually a pig-tail. She had the same bloom and serenity, however, and the same sedate, investigating look in her eyes. There was Mr. Browne too, but he was a brief joy, for there was only time to shake hands and exchange dates and promises of return, before the train started and bore him away toward Pueblo.

"Now," said Rose, who seemed quite unquenched by her three days of travel, "don't let's utter one word till we are in the carriage, and then don't let's stop one moment for two weeks."

"In the first place," she began, as the carryall, mounting the hill, turned into Monument Avenue, where numbers of new houses had been built of late years, Queen Anne cottages in brick and stone, timber, and concrete, with here and there a more ambitious "villa" of pink granite, all surrounded with lawns and rosaries and vine-hung verandas and tinkling fountains. "In the first place I wish to learn where all these people and houses come from. I was told that you lived in a lodge in the wilderness, but though I see plenty of lodges the wilderness seems wanting. Is this really an infant settlement?"

"It really is. That is, it hasn't come of age yet, being not quite twenty-one years old. Oh, you've no notion about our Western towns, Rose. They're born and grown up all in a minute, like Hercules strangling the snakes in his cradle. I don't at all wonder that you are surprised."

"'Surprised' doesn't express it. 'Flabbergasted,' though low, comes nearer my meaning. I have been breathless ever since we left Albany. First there was that enormous Chicago which knocked me all of a heap, then Denver, then that enchanting ride over the Divide, and now this! Never did I see such flowers or such colored rocks, and never did any one breathe such air. It sweeps all the dust and fatigue out of one in a minute. Boston seems quite small and dull in comparison, doesn't it, Röslein?"

"It isn't so big, but I love it the most," replied that small person from the front seat, where she sat soberly taking all things in. "Mamma, Uncle Geoff says I may drive when we get to the foot of a long hill we are just coming to. You won't be afraid, will you?"

"N-o; not if Uncle Geoff will keep his eye on the reins and stand ready to seize them if the horses begin to run. Rose just expresses my feelings," she continued; "but this is as beautiful as it is big. What is the name of that enchanting mountain over there,—Cheyenne? Why, yes,—that is the one that you used to write about in your letters when you first came out, I remember. It never made much impression on me,—mountains never seem high in letters, somehow, but now I don't wonder. It's the loveliest thing I ever saw."

Clover was much pleased at Rose's appreciation of her favorite mountain, and also with the intelligent way in which she noted everything they passed. Her eyes were as quick as her tongue; chattering all the time, she yet missed nothing of interest. The poppy-strewn plain, the green levels of the mesa delighted her; so did the wide stretches of blue distance, and she screamed with joy at the orange and red pinnacles in Odin's Garden.

"It is a land of wonders," she declared. "When I think how all my life I have been content to amble across the Common, and down Winter Street to Hovey's, and now and then by way of adventure take the car to the Back Bay, and that I felt all the while as if I were getting the cream and pick of everything, I am astonished at my own stupidity. Rose, are you not glad I did not let you catch whooping cough from Margaret Lyon? you were bent on doing it, you remember. If I had given you your way we should not be here now."

Rose only smiled in reply. She was used to her little mother's vagaries and treated them in general with an indulgent inattention.

The sun was quite gone from the ravines, but still lingered on the snow-powdered peaks above, when the carriage climbed the last steep zigzag and drew up before the "Hut," whose upper windows glinted with the waning light. Rose looked about her and drew a long breath of surprise and pleasure.

"It isn't a bit like what I thought it would be," she said; "but it's heaps and heaps more beautiful. I simply put it at the head of all the places I ever saw." Then Elsie came running on to the porch, and Rose jumped out into her arms.

"I thank the goodness and the grace
That on my birth has smiled,
And brought me to this blessed place
A happy Boston child!"
she cried, hugging Elsie rapturously. "You dear thing! how well you look! and how perfect it all is up here! And this is Mr. Page, whom I have known all about ever since the Hillsover days! and this is dear little Geoff! Clover, his eyes are exactly like yours! And where is your baby, Elsie?"
"Little wretch! she would go to sleep. I told her you were coming, and I did all I could, short of pinching, to keep her awake,—sang, and repeated verses, and danced her up and down, but it was all of no use.

She would put her knuckles in her eyes, and whimper and fret, and at last I had to give in. Babies are perfectly unmanageable when they are sleepy."

"Most of us are. It's just as well. I can't half take it in as it is. It is much better to keep something for to-morrow. The drive was perfect, and the Valley is twice as beautiful as I expected it to be. And now I want to go into the house."

Elsie had devoted her day to setting forth the Hut to advantage. She and Roxy had been to the very top of the East Canyon for flowers, and returned loaded with spoil. Bunches of coreopsis and vermilion-tipped painter's-brush adorned the chimney-piece; tall spikes of yucca rose from an Indian jar in one corner of the room, and a splendid sheaf of yellow columbines from another; fresh kinnikinick was looped and wreathed about the pictures; and on the dining-table stood, most beautiful and fragile of all, a bowlful of Mariposa lilies, their delicate, lilac-streaked bells poised on stems so slender that the fairy shapes seemed to float in air, supported at their own sweet will. There were roses, too, and fragrant little knots of heliotrope and mignonette. With these Rose was familiar; the wild flowers were all new to her.

She ran from vase to vase in a rapture. They could scarcely get her upstairs to take off her things. Such a bright evening followed! Clover declared that she had not laughed so much in all the seven years since they parted. Rose seemed to fit at once and perfectly into the life of the place, while at the same time she brought the breath of her own more varied and different life to freshen and widen it. They all agreed that they had never had a visitor who gave so much and enjoyed so much. She and Geoffrey made friends at once, greatly to Clover's delight, and Clarence took to her in a manner astonishing to his wife, for he was apt to eschew strangers, and escape them when he could.

They all woke in the morning to a sense of holiday.

"Boys," said Elsie at breakfast, "this isn't at all a common, every-day day, and I don't want to do every-day things in it. I want something new and unusual to happen. Can't you abjure those wretched beasts of yours for once, and come with us to that sweet little canyon at the far end of the Ute, where we went the summer after I was married? We want to show it to Rose, and the weather is simply perfect."

"Yes, if you'll give us half an hour or so to ride up and speak to

Manuel."

"All right. It will take at least as long as that to get ready."

So Choo Loo hastily broiled chickens and filled bottles with coffee and cream; and by half-past nine they were off, children and all, some on horseback, and some in the carryall with the baskets, to Elsie's "sweet little canyon," over which Pike's Peak rose in lonely majesty like a sentinel at an outpost, and where flowers grew so thickly that, as Rose wrote her husband, "it was harder to find the in-betweens than the blossoms." They came back, tired, hungry, and happy, just at nightfall; so it was not till the second day that Rose met the Youngs, about whom her curiosity was considerably excited. It seemed so odd, she said, to have "only neighbors," and it made them of so much consequence.

They had been asked to dinner to meet Rose, which was a very formal and festive invitation for the High Valley, though the dinner must perforce be much as usual, and the party was inevitably the same. Imogen felt that it was an occasion, and wishing to do credit to it, she unpacked a gown which had not seen the light before since her arrival, and which had done duty as a dinner dress for two or three years at Bideford. It was of light blue mousselaine-de-laine, made with a "half-high top" and elbow sleeves, and trimmed with cheap lace. A necklace of round coral beads adorned her throat, and a comb of the same material her hair, which was done up in a series of wonderful loops filleted with narrow blue ribbons. She carried a pink fan. Lionel, who liked bright colors, was charmed at the effect; and altogether she set out in good spirits for the walk down the Pass, though she was prepared to be afraid of Rose, of whose brilliancy she had heard a little too much to make the idea of meeting her quite comfortable.

The party had just gathered in the sitting-room as they entered. Clover and Elsie were in pretty cotton dresses, as usual, and Rose, following their lead, had put on what at home she would have considered a morning gown, of linen lawn, white, with tiny bunches of forget-me-nots scattered over it, and a jabot of lace and blue ribbon. These toilettes seemed unduly simple to Imogen, who said within herself, complacently, "There is one thing the Americans don't seem to understand, and that is the difference between common dressing and a regular dinner dress,"—preening herself the while in the sky-blue mousselaine-de-laine, and quite unconscious that Rose was inwardly remarking, "My! where did she get that gown? I never saw anything like it. It must have been made for Mrs. Noah, some years before the ark. And her hair! just the ark style, too, and calculated to frighten the animals into good behavior and obedience during the bad weather. Well, I put it at the head of all the extraordinary things I ever saw."

It is just as well, on the whole, that people are not able to read each other's thoughts in society.

"You've only just come to America, I hear," said Rose, taking a chair near Imogen. "Do you begin to feel at home yet?"

"Oh, pretty well for that. I don't fancy that one ever gets to be quite at home anywhere out of their own country. It's very different over here from England, of course."

"Yes, but some parts of America are more different than some other parts. You haven't seen much of us as yet."

"No, but all the parts I have seen seemed very much alike."

"The High Valley and New York, for example."

"Oh, I wasn't thinking of New York. I mean the plains and mountains and the Western towns. We didn't stop at any of them, of course; but seen from the railway they all look pretty much the same,—wooden houses, you know, and all that."

"What astonished us most was the distance," said Rose. "Of course we all learned from our maps, when we were at school, just how far it is across the continent; but I never realized it in the least till I saw it. It seemed so wonderful to go on day after day and never get to the end!"

"Only about half-way to the end," put in Clover. "That question of distance is a great surprise; and if it perplexes you, Rose, it isn't wonderful that it should perplex foreigners. Do you recollect that Englishman, Geoff, whom we met at the table d'hôte at Llanberis, when we were in Wales, and who accounted for the Charleston earthquake by saying that he supposed it had something to do with those hot springs close by."

"What hot springs did he mean?"

"I am sure you would never guess unless I told you. The hot springs in the Yellowstone Park, to be sure,—simply those, and nothing more! And when I explained that Charleston and the Yellowstone were about as distant from each other as Siberia and the place we were in, he only stared and remarked, 'Oh, I think you must be mistaken.'"

"And are they so far apart, then?" asked Imogen, innocently.

"Oh, Moggy, Moggy! what were your geography teachers thinking about?" cried her brother. "It seems sometimes as if America were entirely left out of the maps used in English schools."

"Lionel," said his sister, "how can you say such things? It isn't so at all; but of course we learned more about the important countries." Imogen spoke quite artlessly; she had no intention of being rude.

"Great Scott!" muttered Clarence under his breath, while Rose flashed a look at Clover.

"Of course," she said, sweetly, "Burmah and Afghanistan and New Zealand and the Congo States would naturally interest you more,— large heathen populations to Christianize and exterminate. There is nothing like fire and sword to establish a bond."

"Oh, I didn't mean that. Of course America is much larger than those countries."

"'Plenty of us such as we are'" quoted the wicked Rose.

"And pretty good what there is of us," added Clover, glad of the appearance of dinner just then to create a diversion.

"That's quite a dreadful little person," remarked Rose, as they stood at the doorway two hours later, watching the guests walk up the trail under the light of a glorious full moon. "Her mind is just one inch across. You keep falling off the edge and hurting yourself. It's sad that she should be your only neighbor. I don't seem to like her a bit, and I predict that you will yet have some dreadful sort of a row with her, Clovy."

"Indeed we shall not; nothing of the kind. She's really a good little thing at bottom; this angularity and stiffness that you object to is chiefly manner. Wait till she has been here long enough to learn the ways and wake up, and you will like her."

"I'll wait," said Rose, dryly. "How much time should you say would be necessary, Clover? A hundred years? I should think it would take at least as long as that."

"Lionel's a dear fellow. We are all very fond of him."

"I can understand your being fond of him easily enough. Imogen! what a name for just that kind of girl. 'Image' it ought to be. What a figure of fun she was in that awful blue gown!"

The two weeks of Rose's visit sped only too rapidly. There was so much that they wanted to show her, and there were so many people whom they wanted her to see, and so many people who, as soon as they saw her, became urgent that she should do this and that with them, that life soon became a tangle of impossibilities. Rose was one of those charmers that cannot be hid. She had been a belle all her days, and she would be so till she died of old age, as Elsie told her. Her friends of the High Valley gloried in her success; but all the time they had a private longing to keep her more to themselves, as one retires with two or three to enjoy a choice dainty of which there is not enough to go round in a larger company. They took her to the Cheyenne Canyons and the top of Pike's Peak; they carried her over the Marshall Pass and to many smaller places less known to fame, but no less charming in their way. Invitations poured in from St. Helen's, to lunch, to dinner, to afternoon teas; but of these Rose would none. She could lunch and dine in Boston, she declared, but she might never come to Colorado again, and what she thirsted for was canyons, and not less than one a day would content her insatiable appetite for them.

But though she would not go to St. Helen's, St. Helen's in a measure came to her. Marian Chase and Alice made their promised visit; Dr. and Mrs. Hope came out more than once, and Phil continually; while smart Bostonians whom Clover had never heard of turned up at Canyon Creek and the Ute Valley and drove over to call, having heard that Mrs. Deniston Browne was staying there. The High Valley became used to the roll of wheels and the tramp of horses' feet, and for the moment seemed a sociable, accessible sort of place to which it was a matter of course that people should repair. It was oddly different from the customary order of things, but the change was enlivening, and everybody enjoyed it with one exception.

This exception was Imogen Young. She was urged to join some of the excursions made by her friends below, but on one excuse or another she refused. She felt shy and left out where all the rest were so well-acquainted and so thoroughly at ease, and preferred to remain at home; but all the same, to have the others so gay and busy gave her a sense of loneliness and separation which was painful to bear. Clover tried more than once to persuade her out of her solitary mood; but she was too much occupied herself and too absorbed to take much time for coaxing a reluctant guest, and the others dispensed with her company quite easily; in fact, they were too busy to notice her absence much or ask questions. So the fortnight, which passed so quickly and brilliantly at the Hut, and was always afterward alluded to as "that delightful time when Rose was here," was anything but delightful at the "Hutlet," where poor Imogen sat homesick and forlorn, feeling left alone on one side of all the pleasant things, scarcely realizing that it was her own choice and doing, and wishing herself back in Devonshire.

"Lion seems quite taken up with these new people and that Mrs. Browne," she reflected. "He's always going off with them to one place or another. I might as well be back in Bideford for all the use I am to him." This was unjust, for Lionel was anxious and worried over his sister's depressed looks and indisposition to share in the pleasures that were going on; but Imogen just then saw things through a gloomy medium, and not quite as they were. She felt dull and heavy-hearted, and did not seem able to rouse herself from her lassitude and weariness.

Out of the whole party no one was so perfectly pleased with her surroundings as the smaller Rose. Everything seemed to suit the little maid exactly. She made a delightful playfellow for the babies, telling them fairy stories by the dozen, and teaching them new games, and washing and dressing Phillida with all the gravity and decorum of an old nurse. They followed her about like two little dogs, and never left her side for a moment if they could possibly help it. All was fish that came to her happy little net, whether it was playing with little Geoff, going on excursions with the elders, scrambling up the steep side-canyons under Phil's escort in search of flowers and curiosities, or riding sober old Marigold to the Upper Valley as she was sometimes allowed to do. The only cloud in her perfect satisfaction was that she must some day go away.

"It won't be very pleasant when I get back to Boston, and don't have anything to do but just walk down Pinckney Street with Mary Anne to school, and slide a little bit on the Common when the snow comes and there aren't any big boys about, will it, mamma?" she said, disconsolately. "I sha'n't feel as if that were a great deal, I think."

"I am afraid the High Valley is a poor preparation for West Cedar Street," laughed Rose. "It will seem a limited career to both of us at first. But cheer up, Poppet; I'm going to put you into a dancing-class this winter, and very likely at Christmas-time papa will treat us both to a Moral Drayma. There are consolations, even in Boston."

"That 'even in Boston' is the greatest compliment the High Valley ever received," said Clover, who happened to be within hearing. "Such a moment will never come to it again."

And now the last day came, as last days will. Mr. Browne returned from Mexico, with forty-eight hours to spare for enjoyment, which interval they employed in showing him the two things that Rose loved most,—namely, the High Valley from top to bottom, and the North Cheyenne Canyon. The last luncheon was taken at Mrs. Hope's, who had collected a few choice spirits in honor of the occasion, and then they all took the Roses to the train, and sent them off loaded with fruit and flowers.

"Miss Young was extraordinarily queer and dismal last night," said Rose to Clover as they stood a little aside from the rest on the platform. "I can't quite see what ails her. She looks thinner than when we came, and doesn't seem to know how to smile; depend upon it she's going to be ill, or something. I wish you had a pleasanter neighbor,—especially as she's likely to be the only one for some time to come."

"Poor thing. I've neglected her of late," replied Clover, penitently. "I must make up for it now that you are going away. Really, I couldn't take my time for her while you were here, Rosy."

"And I certainly couldn't let you. I should have resented it highly if you had. Oh dear,—there's that whistle. We really have got to go. I hoped to the last that something might happen to keep us another day. Oh dear Clover,—I wish we lived nearer each other. This country of ours is a great deal too wide."

"Geoff," said Clover, as they slowly climbed the hill, "I never felt before that the High Valley was too far away from people, but somehow I do to-night. It is quite terrible to have Rose go, and to feel that I may not see her again for years."

"Did you want to go with her?"

"And leave you? No, dearest. But I am quite sure that there are no distances in Heaven, and when we get there we shall find that we all are to live next door to each other. It will be part of the happiness."

"Perhaps so. Meanwhile I am thankful that my happiness lives close to me now. I don't have to wait till Heaven for that, which is the reason perhaps that for some years past Earth has seemed so very satisfactory to me."

"Geoff, what an uncommonly nice way you have of putting things," said Clover, nestling her head comfortably on his arm. "On the whole I don't think the High Valley is so very far away."

CHAPTER VIII. UNCONDITIONAL SURRENDER.

HAVE you seen Imogen Young to-day?" was Clover's first question on getting home.

"No. Lionel was in for a moment at noon, and said she was preserving raspberries; so, as I had a good deal to do, I did not go up. Why?"

"Oh, nothing in particular. I only wanted to know. Well, here we are, left to ourselves with not a Rose to our name. How we shall miss them! There's a letter from Johnnie for you by way of consolation."

But the letter did not prove in the least consoling, for it was to break to them a piece of disappointing news.

"The Daytons have given up their Western trip," wrote Johnnie. "Mrs. Dayton's father is very ill at Elberon; she has gone to him, and there is almost no chance of their getting away at all this summer. It really is a dreadful disappointment, for we had set our hearts on our visit, and papa had made all his arrangements to be absent for six weeks,—which you know is a thing not easily done, or undone. Then Debby and Richard had been promised a holiday, and Dorry was going in a yacht with some friends to the Thousand Islands. It all seemed so nicely settled, and here comes this blow to unsettle it. Well, Dieu dispose,— there is nothing for it but resignation, and unpacking our hopes and ideas and putting them back again in their usual shelves and corners. We must make what we can of the situation, and of course, it isn't anything so very hard to have to pass the summer in Burnet with papa; still I was that wild with disappointment at the first, that I actually went the length of suggesting that we should go all the same, and pay our own travelling expenses! You can judge from this how desperate my state of mind must have been! Papa, as you may naturally suppose, promptly vetoed the proposal as impossible, and no doubt he was right. I am growing gradually resigned to Fate now, but all the same I cannot yet think of the blessed Valley and all of you, and—and the happy time we are not going to have, without feeling quite like 'weeping a little weep.' How I wish that we possessed a superfluous income!"

"Now," said Elsie, and her voice too sounded as if a "little weep" were not far off, "isn't that too bad? No papa this year, and no Johnnie. I suppose we are spoiled, but the fact is, I have grown to count on the Daytons and their car as confidently as though they were the early and the latter rain." Her arch little face looked quite long and disconsolate.

"So have I," said Clover. "It doesn't bear talking about, does it?"

She had been conscious of late of a great longing after her father. She had counted confidently on his visit, and the sense of disappointment was bitter. She put away her bonnet and folded her gloves with a very sober face. A sort of disenchantment seemed to have fallen on the Valley since the coming of this bad news and the departure of Rose.

"This will never do," she told herself at last, after standing some moments at the window looking across at the peak through a blur of tears,—"I must brace up and comfort Elsie." But Elsie was not to be comforted all at once, and the wheels of that evening drave rather heavily.

Next morning, as soon as her usual tasks were despatched, Clover ordered Marigold saddled and started for the Youngs'. Rose's last remarks had made her uneasy about Imogen, and she remembered with compunction how little she had seen of her for a fortnight past.

No one but Sholto, Lionel's great deerhound, came out to meet her as she dismounted at the door. His bark of welcome brought Ah Lee from the back of the house.

"Missee not velly well, me thinkee," he observed.

"Is Missy ill? Where is Mr. Young, then?"

"He go two hours ago to Uppey Valley. Missee not sick then."

"Is she in her room?" asked Clover. "Tie Marigold in the shade, please, and I will go in and see her."

"All litee."

The bed-room door was closed, and Clover tapped twice before she heard a languid "Come in." Imogen was lying on the bed in her morning-dress, with flushed cheeks and tumbled hair. She looked at Clover with a sort of perplexed surprise.

"My poor child, what is the matter? Have you a bad headache?"

"Yes, I think so, rather bad. I kept up till Lion had had his breakfast, and then everything seemed to go round, and I had to come and lie down. So stupid of me!" impatiently; "but I thought perhaps it would pass off after a little."

"And has it?" asked Clover, pulling off her gloves and taking Imogen's hand. It was chilly rather than hot, but the pulse seemed weak and quick. Clover began to feel anxious, but did her best to hide it under a cheerful demeanor lest she should startle Imogen.

"Were you quite well yesterday?" she asked.

"Yes,—that is, I wasn't ill. I had no headache then, but I think I haven't been quite right for some time back, and I tried to do some raspberries and felt very tired. I dare say it's only getting acclimated. I'm really very strong. Nothing ever was the matter with me at home."

"Now," said Clover, brightly, "I'll tell you what you are going to do; and that is to put on your wrapper, make yourself comfortable, and take a long sleep. I have come to spend the day, and I will give Lion his luncheon and see to everything if only you will lie still. A good rest would make you feel better, I am sure."

"Perhaps so," said Imogen, doubtfully. She was too miserable to object, and with a docility foreign to her character submitted to be undressed, to have her hair brushed and knotted up, and a bandage of cold water and eau de cologne laid on her forehead. This passive compliance was so unlike her that Clover felt her anxieties increase. "Matters must be serious," she reflected, "when Imogen Young agrees meekly to any proposal from anybody."

She settled her comfortably, shook up the pillows, darkened the window, threw a light shawl over her, and sat beside the bed fanning gently till Imogen fell into a troubled sleep. Then she stole softly away and busied herself in washing the breakfast things and putting the rooms to rights. The young mistress of the house had evidently felt unequal to her usual tasks, and everything was left standing just as it was.

Clover was recalled by a cry from the bedroom, and hurried back to find Imogen sitting up, looking confused and startled.

"What is it? Is anything the matter?" she demanded. Then, before Clover could reply, she came to herself and understood.

"Oh, it is you," she said. "What a comfort! I thought you were gone away."

"No, indeed, I have no idea of going away. I was just in the other room, straightening things out a little. It was settled that I was to stay to lunch and keep Lionel company, you remember."

"Ah, yes. It is very good of you, but I'm afraid there isn't much for luncheon," sinking back on her pillows again. "Ah Lee will know. I don't seem able to think clearly of anything." She sighed, and presently was asleep again, or seemed to be so, and Clover went back to her work.

So it went all day,—broken slumbers, confused wakings, increasing fever, and occasional moments of bewilderment. Clover was sure that it was a serious illness, and sent Lionel down with a note to say that either Geoff or Clarence must go in at once and bring out Dr. Hope, that she herself was a fixture at the other house for the night at least, and would like a number of things sent up, of which she inclosed a list. This note threw the family into a wild dismay. Life in the High Valley was only meant for well people, as Elsie had once admitted. Illness at once made the disadvantages of so lonely and inaccessible a place apparent,—with the doctor sixteen miles distant, and no medicines or other appliances of a sick-room to be had short of St. Helen's.

Dr. Hope reached them late in the evening. He pronounced that Imogen had an attack of "mountain fever," a milder sort of typhoid not uncommon in the higher elevations of Colorado. He hoped it would be a light case, gave full directions, and promised to send out medicines and to come again in three days. Then he departed, and Clover, as she watched him ride down the trail, felt as a shipwrecked mariner might, left alone on a desert island,—astray and helpless, and quite at a loss as to what first to do.

There were too many things to be done, however, to allow of her long indulging this feeling, and presently her wits cleared and she was able to confront the task before her with accustomed sense and steadiness. Imogen could not be left alone, that was evident; and it was equally evident that she herself was the person who must stay with her. Elsie could not be spared from her baby, and Geoffrey, beside being more especially interested in the Youngs, would be far more amenable and less refractory than Clarence at a curtailment of his domestic privileges.

So, pluckily and reasonably, she "buckled to" the work so plainly set for her, established herself and her belongings in the spare chamber, gathered the reins of the household and the sick-room into her hands, and began upon what she knew might prove to be a long, hard bout of patience and vigilance, resolved to do her best each day as it came and let the next day take care of itself, minding nothing, no fatigue or homesickness or difficulty, if only Imogen could be properly cared for and get well.

After the first day or two matters fell into regular grooves. The attack proved a light one, as the doctor had hoped. Imogen was never actually in danger, but there was a good deal of weakness and depression, occasional wandering of mind, and always the low, underlying fever, not easily detected save by the clinical thermometer. In her semi-delirious moments she would ramble about Bideford and the people there, or hold Clover's hand tight, calling her "Isabel," and imploring her not to like "Mrs. Geoff" better than she liked her. It was the first glimpse that Clover had ever caught of this unhappy tinge of jealousy in Imogen's mind; it grieved her, but it also explained some things that had been perplexing, and she grew very pitiful and tender over the poor girl, away from home among strangers, and so ill and desolate.

The most curious thing about it all was the extraordinary preference which the patient showed for Clover above all her other nurses. If Euphane came to sit beside her, or Elsie, or even Lionel, while Clover took a rest, Imogen was manifestly uneasy and unhappy. She never said that she missed Clover, but lay watching the door with a strained, expectant look, which melted into relief as soon as Clover appeared. Then she would feebly move her fingers to lay hold of Clover's hand, and holding it fast, would fall asleep satisfied and content. It seemed as if the sense of comfort which Clover's appearance that first morning had given continued when she was not quite herself, and influenced her.

"It's queer how much better she likes you than any of the rest of us," Lionel said one day. Clover felt oddly pleased at this remark. It was a new experience to be preferred by Imogen Young, and she could not but be gratified.

"Though very likely," she told herself, "she will stiffen up again when she gets well; so I must be prepared for it, and not mind when it happens."

Meanwhile Imogen could not have been better cared for anywhere than she was in the High Valley. Clover had a natural aptitude for nursing. She knew by instinct what a sick person would like and dislike, what would refresh and what weary, what must be remembered and what avoided. Her inventive faculties also came into full play under the pressure of the little daily emergencies, when exactly the thing wanted was sure not to be at hand. It was quite wonderful how she devised substitutes for all sorts of deficiencies. Elsie, amazed at her cleverness, declared herself sure that if Dr. Hope were to say that a roc's egg was needful for Imogen's recovery, Clover would reply, as a matter of course, "Certainly,—I will send it up directly," and thereupon proceed to concoct one out of materials already in the house, which would answer as well as the original article and do Imogen just as much good. She cooked the nicest little sick-room messes, giving them variety by cunningly devised flavors, and she originated cooling drinks out of sago and arrowroot and tamarinds and fruit juices and ice, which Imogen would take when she refused everything else. Her lightness of touch and bright, equable calmness were unfailing. Dr. Hope said she would make the fortune of any ordinary hospital, and that she was so evidently cut out for a nurse that it seemed a clear subversion of the plans of Providence that she should ever have married,—a speech for which the doctor got little thanks from anybody, for Clover declared that she hated hospitals and sick folks, and never wanted to nurse anybody but the people she loved best, and then only when she couldn't help herself; while Geoffrey treated the facetious physician to the blackest of frowns, and privately confided to Elsie that the doctor, good fellow that he was, deserved a kicking, and he shouldn't mind being the one to administer it.

By the end of a fortnight the fever was conquered, and then began the slow process of building up exhausted strength, and fanning the dim spark of life once again into a generous flame. This is apt to be the most trying part of an illness to those who nurse; the excitement of anxiety and danger being past, the space between convalescence and complete recovery seems very wide, and hard to bridge over. Clover found it so. Imogen's strength came back slowly; all her old vigor and decision seemed lost; she was listless and despondent, and needed to be coaxed and encouraged and cheered as much as does an ailing child.

She did not "stiffen," however, as Clover had feared she might do; on the contrary, her dependence upon her favorite nurse seemed to increase, and on the days when she was most languid and hopeless she clung most to her. There was a wistful look in her eyes as they followed Clover in her comings and goings, and a new, tender tone in her voice when she spoke to her; but she said little, and after she was able to sit up just lay back in her chair and gazed at the mountains in a dreamy fashion for hours together.

"This will never do," Lionel declared. "We must hearten her up somehow," which he proceeded to do, after the blundering fashion of the ordinary man, by a series of thrilling anecdotes about cattle and their vagaries, refractory cows who turned upon their herders and "horned" them, and wild steers who chased mounted men, overtook and gored them; how Felipe was stampeded and Pepe just escaped with his life. The result of this "heartening," process was that Imogen, in her weak state, conceived a horror of ranch work, and passed the hours of his absence in a subdued agony of apprehension concerning him. He was very surprised and contrite when scolded by Clover.

"What shall I talk to her about, then?" he demanded ruefully. "I can't bear to see her sit so dull and silent. Poor Moggy! and cattle are the only subjects of conversation that we have up here."

"Talk about yourself and herself and the funny things that happened when you were little, and pet her all you can; but pray don't allude to horned animals of any kind. She's so quiet only because she is weak. Presently we shall see her brighten."

And so they did. With the first breath of autumn, full of cool sparkle and exhilaration, Imogen began to rally. Color stole back to her lips, vigor to her movements; each day she could do a little and a little more. Her first coming out to dinner was treated as a grand event. She was placed in a cushioned chair and served like a queen. Lionel was in raptures at seeing her in her old place, at the head of the table, "better than new," as he asserted; and certainly Imogen had never in her life been so pretty. They had cut her long hair during the illness because it was falling out so fast; the short rings round her face were very becoming, the sunburn of the summer had worn off and her complexion was delicately fair. Clover had dressed her in a loose jacket of pale-pink flannel which Elsie had fitted and made for her; it was trimmed with soft frills of lace, and knots of ribbon, and Geoff had brought up a half-opened tea rose which exactly matched it.

"I shall carry you home with me when I go," she told Imogen as she helped her undress. "You must come down and make us a good long visit. I can't and won't have you left alone up here, to keep the house and sit for hours every day imagining that Lionel is being gored by wild bulls."

"When you go?" repeated Imogen, in a dismayed tone; "but yes, of course you must go—what was I thinking of?"

"Not while you need me," said Clover, soothingly. "But you are nearly well now, and will soon be able to do everything for yourself."

"I am absolutely silly," said Imogen, with her eyes full of tears. "What extraordinary things fevers are! I declare, I am as bad as any child. It is absurd, but the mere idea of having to give you up makes me quite cold and miserable."

"But you won't have to give me up; we are going to be neighbors still, and see each other every day. And you won't be ill again, you know. You are acclimated now, Dr. Hope says."

"Yes—I hope so; I am sure I hope so. And yet, do you know, I almost think I would go through the fever all over again for the sake of having you take care of me!"

"Why, my dear child, what a thing to say! It's the greatest compliment I ever had in my life, but yet—"

"It's no compliment at all. I should never think of paying you compliments. I couldn't."

"That is sad for me. Compliments are nice things, I think."

Imogen suddenly knelt down and put her arms on Clover's lap as she sat by the window.

"I want to tell you something," she said in a broken voice. "I was so unjust when I came over,—so rude and unkind in my thoughts. You will hardly believe it, but I didn't like you!"

"I can believe it without any particular difficulty. Everybody can't like me, you know."

"Everybody ought to. You are simply the best, dearest, truest person I ever knew. Oh, I can't half say what you are, but I know! You have heaped coals of fire on my head. Perhaps that's the reason my hair has fallen off so," with a mirthless laugh. "I used to feel them burn and burn, on those nights when I lay all scorching up with fever, and you sat beside me so cool and sweet and patient. And there is more still. I was jealous because I fancied that Isabel liked you better than she did me. Did you ever suspect that?"

"Never till you were ill. Some little things that you muttered when you were not quite yourself put the idea into my head."

"I can't think why I was so idiotic about it. Of course she liked you best,—who wouldn't? How horrid it was in me to feel so! I used to try hard not to, but it was of no use; I kept on all the same."

"But you're not jealous now, I hope?"

"No, indeed," shaking her head. "The feeling seems all burnt out of me. If I am ever jealous again it will be just the other way, for fear you will care for her and not at all for me."

"I do believe you are making me a declaration of attachment!" cried Clover, amazed beyond expression at this outburst, but inexpressibly pleased. The stiff, reserved Imogen seemed transformed. Her face glowed with emotion, her words came in a torrent. She was altogether different from her usual self.

"Attachment! If I were not attached to you I should be the most ungrateful wretch going. Here you have stayed away from home all these weeks, and worked like a servant making me all those lovely lemon-squashes and things, and letting your own affairs go to wrack and ruin, and you never seemed to remember that you had any affairs, or that there was such a thing as getting tired,—never seemed to remember anything except to take care of me. You are an angel—there is nobody like you. I don't believe any one else in the world would have done what you did for a stranger who had no claim upon you."

"That is absurd," said Clover, frightened at the probable effect of all this excitement on her patient, and trying to treat the matter lightly. "You exaggerate things dreadfully. We all have a claim on each other, especially here in the Valley where there are so few of us. If I had been ill you would have turned to and helped to nurse me as I did you, I am sure."

"I shouldn't have known how."

"You would have learned how just as I did. Emergencies are wonderful teachers. Now, dear Imogen, you must get to bed. If you excite yourself like this you will have a bad night and be put back."

"Oh, I'll sleep. I promise you that I will sleep if only you will let me say just one more thing. I won't go on any more about the things you have done, though it's all true,—and I don't exaggerate in the least, for all that you say I do; but never mind that, only please tell me that you forgive me. I can't rest till you say that."

"For what,—for not liking me at first; for being jealous of Isabel? Both were natural enough, I think. Isabel was your dearest friend; and I was a new-comer, an interloper. I never meant to come between you, I am sure; but I daresay that I seemed to do so, and I can understand it all easily. There is no question of forgiving between us, dear, only of forgetting. We are friends now, and we will both love Isabel; and I will love you if you will let me, and you shall love me."

"How good you are!" exclaimed Imogen, as Clover bent over for a good-night kiss. She put her arms round Clover's neck and held her tight for a moment.

"Yes, indeed," she sighed. "I don't deserve it after my bad behavior, but I shall be only too glad if I may be your friend. I don't believe any other girl in the world has two so good as you and Isabel."

"Don't lie awake to think over our perfections," said Clover, as she withdrew with the candle. "Go to sleep, and remember that you are coming down to the Hut with me for a visit, whenever I go."

Dr. Hope, however, negatived this suggestion decidedly. He was an autocrat with his sick people, and no one dared dispute his decisions.

"What your young woman needs is to get away from the Valley for a while into lower air; and what you need is to have her go, and forget that you have been nursing her," he told Clover. "There is a look of tension about you both which is not the correct thing. She'll improve much faster at St. Helen's than here, and besides, I want her under my eye for a while. Mary shall send up an invitation to-morrow, and mind that you make her accept it."

So the next day came the most cordial of notes from Mrs. Hope, asking

Imogen to spend a fortnight with her.

"Dr. Hope wishes to consider you his patient a little longer," she wrote, "and says the lower level will do you good; and I want you as much as he does for other reasons. St. Helen's is rather empty just now, in this betwixt-and-between season, and a visitor will be a real God-send to me. I am so afraid that you will be disobliging, and say 'No,' that I have made the doctor put it in the form of a prescription; and please tell Clover that we count upon her to see that you begin to take the remedy without delay."

And sure enough, on the doctor's prescription paper, with the regular appeal to Jupiter which heads all prescriptions, a formula was enclosed setting forth with due professional precision that Miss Imogen Young was to be put in a carryall, "well shaken" on the way down, and taken in fourteen daily doses in the town of St. Helen's. "Immediate."

"How very good of them!" said Imogen. "Everybody is so wonderfully good to me! I think America must be the kindest country in the world!"

She made no difficulty about accepting the invitation, and resigned herself to the will of her friends with a docility that was astonishing to everybody except Clover, who was in the secret of her new-born resolves. They packed her things at once, and Lionel drove her down to St. Helen's the very day after the reception of Mrs. Hope's note. Imogen parted from the sisters with a warm embrace, but she clung longest to Clover.

"You will let me come for a night or two when I return, before I settle again at home, won't you?" she said. "I shall be half-starved to see you, and a mile is a goodish bit to get over when you're not strong."

"Why, of course," said Clover, delighted. "We shall count on it, and Lion has promised to stay with us all the time you are away."

"I do think that girl has experienced a change of heart," remarked Elsie, as they turned to go in-doors. "She seems really fond of you, and almost fond of me. It is no wonder, I am sure, so far as you are concerned, after all you have done for her. I never supposed she could look so pretty or come so near being agreeable as she does now. Evidently mountain-fever is what the English emigrant of the higher classes needs to thaw him out and attune him to American ways. It's a pity they can't all be inoculated with it on landing.

"Now, Clovy,—my dear, sweet old Clovy,—what fun it is to have you at home again!" she went on, giving her sister a rapturous embrace. "I wouldn't mention it so long as you had to be away, but I have missed you horribly. 'There's no luck about the house' when you are not in it. We have all been out of sorts,—Geoff quite down in the mouth, little Geoff not at all contented with me as a mother; even Euphane has worn a long face and exhibited a tendency to revert to the Isle of Man, which she never showed so long as you were to the fore. As for me, I have felt like a person with one lung, or half a head,—all broken up, and unlike myself. Oh, dear! how good it is to get you back, and be able to consult you and look at you! Come upstairs at once, and unpack your things, and we will play that you have never been away, and that the last month is nothing but a disagreeable dream from which we have waked up."

"It is delightful to get back," admitted Clover; "still the month has had its nice side, too. Imogen is so sweet and grateful and demonstrative that it would astonish you. She is like a different girl. I really think she has grown to love me."

"I should say that nothing was more probable. But don't let's talk of Imogen now. I want you all to myself."

The day had an ending as happy as unexpected. This was the letter that Lionel Young brought back that evening from Johnnie at Burnet:—

Dearest Sisters,—What do you think has happened? Something as enchanting as it is surprising! I wrote you about Dorry's having the grippe; but I would not tell you what a serious affair it was, because you were all so anxious and occupied about Miss Young that I did not like to add to your worries more than I could help. He was pretty ill for nearly a week; and though on the mend now, he is much weakened and run down, and papa, I can see, considers him still in a poor way. There is no chance of his being able to go back to the works for a couple of months yet, and we were casting about as to the best way of giving him a change of air, when, last night, came a note from Mr. Dayton to say that he has to take a business run to Salt Lake, with a couple of his directors, and there are two places in car 47 at our service if any of us still care to make the trip to Colorado, late as it is. We had to answer at once, and we took only ten minutes to make up our minds. Dorry and I are to start for Chicago to-morrow, and will be with you on Thursday if all goes well,—and for a good long visit, as the company have given

Dorry a two months' vacation. We shall come back like common folks at our own charges, which is an unusual extravagance for the Carr family; but papa says sickness is a valid reason for spending money, while mere pleasure isn't. He thinks the journey will be the very thing for Dorry. It has all come so suddenly that I am quite bewildered in my mind. I don't at all like going away and leaving papa alone; but he is quite decided about it, and there is just the bare chance that Katy may run out for a week or two, so I am going to put my scruples in my pocket, and take the good the gods provide, prepared to be very happy. How perfectly charming it will be to see you all! Somehow I never pined for you and the valley so much as I have of late. It was really an awful blow when the August plan came to nothing, but Fate is making amends. Thursday! only think of it! You will just have time to put towels in our rooms and fill the pitchers before we are there. I speak for the west corner one in the guest cabin, which I had last year. Our dear love to you all.

Your affectionate Johnnie.
P.S. Please tell Mr. Young how happy we are that his sister is recovering.

"This is too delicious!" said Elsie, when she had finished reading this letter. "Dorry, who never has been here, and John, and for October, when we so rarely have anybody! I think it is a sort of 'reward of merit' for you, Clover, for taking such good care of Imogen Young."

"It's a most delightful one if it is. I half wish now that we hadn't asked Lion to stay while his sister is gone. He's a dear good fellow, but it would be nicer to have the others quite to ourselves, don't you think so?"

"Clover dear," said Elsie, looking very wise and significant, "did it never occur to you that there might be a little something like a sentiment or tenderness between John and Lionel? Are you sure that she would be so thoroughly pleased if we sent him off and kept her to ourselves?"

"Certainly not. I never thought of such a thing."

"You never do think of such things. I am much sharper about them than you are, and I have observed a tendency on the part of Miss John to send messages to that young man in her letters, and always in postscripts. Mark that, postscripts! There is something very suspicious in postscripts, and he invariably blushes immensely when I deliver them."

"You are a great deal too sharp," responded Clover, laughing. "You see through millstones that don't exist. It would be very nice if it were so, but it isn't. I don't believe a word about your postscripts and blushes; you've imagined it all."

"Some people are born stupid in these directions," retorted Elsie. "I'll bet you Phillida's back-hair against the first tooth that Geoffy loses that I am right."

CHAPTER IX. THE ECHOES IN THE EAST CANYON.

LIONEL certainly did redden when Johnnie's message was delivered to him. The quick-eyed Elsie noted it and darted a look at Clover, but Clover only shook her head slightly in return. Each sister adhered to her own opinion.

They were very desirous that the High Valley should make a favorable impression on Dorry, for it was his first visit to them. The others had all been there except Katy, and she had seen Cheyenne and St. Helen's, but to Dorry everything west of the Mississippi was absolutely new. He was a very busy person in these days, and quite the success of the Carr family in a moneyed point of view. The turn for mechanics which he exhibited in boyhood had continued, and determined his career. Electrical science had attracted his attention in its earlier, half-developed stages; he had made a careful study of it, and qualified himself for the important position which he held under the company, which was fast revolutionizing the lighting and street-car system of Burnet, now growing to be a large manufacturing centre. This was doing well for a young fellow not quite twenty-five, and his family were very proud of him. He was too valuable to his employers to be easily spared, and except for the enforced leisure of the grippe it might probably have been years before he felt free to make his sisters in Colorado a visit, in which case nothing would have happened that did happen.

"Dear, steady old Sobersides!" said Elsie, as she spread a fresh cover over the shelf which did duty for a bureau in the Bachelors' Room; "I wonder what he will think of it all. I'm afraid he will be scandalized at our scrambling ways, and our having no regular church, and consider us a set of half-heathen Bohemians."

"I don't believe it. Dorry has too much good sense, and has seen too much of the world among business men to be easily shocked. And our little Sunday service is very nice, I think; Geoff reads so reverently,— and for sermons, we have our pick of the best there are."

"I know, and I like them dearly myself; but I seem to feel that Dorry will miss the pulpit and sitting in a regular pew. He's rather that sort of person, don't you think?"

"You are too much inclined to laugh at Dorry," said Clover, reprovingly, "and he doesn't deserve it of you. He's a thoroughly good, sensible fellow, and has excellent abilities, papa says,—not brilliant, but very sound. I don't like to have you speak so of him."

"Why, Clovy—my little Clovy, I almost believe you are scolding me! Let me look at you,—yes, there's quite a frown on your forehead, and your mouth has the firm look of grandpapa Carr's daguerreotype. I'll be good,—really I will. Don't fire again,—I've 'come down' like the coon in the anecdote. Dorry's a dear, and you are another, and I'm ever so glad he's coming; but really, it's not in human nature not to laugh at the one solemn person in a frivolous family like ours, now is it?"

"See that you behave yourself, then, and I'll not scold you any more," replied Clover, magisterially, and ignoring the last question. She marred the effect of her lecture by kissing Elsie as she spoke; but it was hard to resist the temptation, Elsie was so droll and coaxing, and so very pretty.

They expected to find Dorry still something of an invalid, and made preparations accordingly; but there was no sign of debility in his jump from the carriage or his run up the steps to greet them. He was a little thinner than usual, but otherwise seemed quite himself.

"It's the air," explained Johnnie, "this blessed Western air! He was forlorn when we left Burnet, and so tired when we got to Chicago; but after that he improved with every mile, and when we reached Denver this morning he seemed fresher than when we started. I do think Colorado air the true elixir of life."

"It is quite true, what she says. I feel like a different man already," added Dorry. "Clover, you look a little pulled down yourself. Was it nursing Miss What's-her-name?"

"I'm all right. Another day or two will quite rest me. I came home only day before yesterday, you see. How delicious it is to have you both here! Dorry dear, you must have some beef-tea directly,—Euphane has a little basin of it ready,—and dinner will be in about an hour."

"Beef-tea! What for? I don't need anything of the sort, I assure you. Roast mutton, which I seem to smell in the distance, is much more in my line. I want to look about and see your house. What do you call that snow-peak over there? This is a beautiful place of yours, I declare."

"Papa would open his eyes if he could see him," remarked Johnnie, confidentially, when she got her sisters to herself a little later. "It's like a miracle the way he has come up. He was so dragged and miserable and so very cross only three days ago. Now, you dear things, let me look at you both. Are you quite well? How are the brothers-in-law? Where are the babies, and what have you done with Miss Young?"

"The brothers-in-law are all right. They will be back presently. There is a round-up to-day, which was the reason we sent Isadore in with the carriage; no one else could be spared. The babies are having their supper,—you will see them anon,—and Imogen has gone for a fortnight to St. Helen's."

"Oh!" Johnnie turned aside and began to take down her hair. "Mr. Young is with her, I suppose."

"No, indeed, he is here, and staying with us. You will see him at dinner."

"Oh!" said Johnnie again. There was a difference between these two "ohs," which Elsie's quick ear detected.

"Please unlock that valise," went on Johnnie, "and take out the dress on top. This I have on is too dreadfully dusty to be endured."

Joanna Carr had grown up very pretty; many people considered her the handsomest of the four sisters. Taller than any of them except Katy, and of quite a different build, large, vigorous, and finely formed, she had a very white skin, hair of pale bronze-brown, and beautiful velvety dark eyes with thick curling lashes. She had a turn for dress too, and all colors suited her. The woollen gown of cream-yellow which she now put on seemed exactly what was needed to throw up the tints of her hair and complexion; but she would look equally well on the morrow in blue. With quick accustomed fingers she whisked her pretty locks into a series of artlessly artful loops, with little blowing rings about the forehead, and stuck a bow in here and a pin there, talking all the time, and finally caught little Phillida up in her strong young arms, and ran downstairs just in time to greet the boys as they dismounted at the door, and shake hands demurely with Lionel Young, who came with them. All three had raced down from the very top of the Upper Valley at breakneck speed, to be in time to welcome the travellers.

There is always one moment, big with fate, when processes begin to take place; when the first fine needle of crystallization forms in the transparent fluid; when the impulse of the jellying principle begins to work on the fruit-juice, and the frost principle to inform the water atoms. These fateful moments are not always perceptible to our dull apprehensions, but none the less do they exist; and they are apt to take us by surprise, because we have not detected the fine gradual chain of preparation which has made ready for them.

I think one of these fateful moments occurred that evening, as Lionel Young held Joanna Carr's hand, and his straight-forward English eyes poured an ardent beam of welcome into hers. They had seen a good deal of each other two years before, but neither was prepared to be quite so glad to meet again. They did not pause to analyze or classify their feelings,—people rarely do when they really feel; but from that night their attitude toward each other was changed, and the change became more apparent with every day that followed.

As these days went on, bright, golden days, cloudless, and full of the zest and snap of the nearing cold, Dorry grew stronger and stronger. So well did he feel that after the first week or so he began to allude to himself as quite recovered, and to show an ominous desire to get back to his work; but this suggestion was promptly scouted by everybody, especially by John, who said she had come for six weeks at least, and six weeks at least she should stay,—and as much longer as she could; and that Dorry as her escort must stay too, no matter how well he might feel.

"Besides," she argued, "there's all your life before you in which to dig away at dynamos and things, and you may never be in Colorado again. You wouldn't have the heart to disappoint Clover and Elsie and hurry back, when there's no real necessity. They are so pleased to have a visit from you."

"Oh, I'll stay! I'll certainly stay," said Dorry. "You shall have your visit out, John; only, when a fellow feels as perfectly well as I do, it seems ridiculous for him to be sitting round with his hands folded, taking a mountain cure which he doesn't need."

Autumn is the busiest season for cattlemen everywhere, which made it the more singular that Lionel Young should manage to find so much time for sitting and riding with Johnnie, or taking her to walk up the steepest and loneliest canyons. They were together in one way or another half the day at least; and during the other half Johnnie's face wore always a pre-occupied look, and was dreamily happy and silent.

Even Clover began to perceive that something unusual was in the air, something that seemed a great deal too good to be true. She and Elsie held conferences in private, during which they hugged each other, and whispered that "If! whenever!—if ever!— Papa would surely come out and live in the Valley. He never could resist three of his girls all at once." But they resolved not to say one word to Johnnie, or even look as if they suspected anything, lest it should have a discouraging effect.

"It never does to poke your finger into a bird's nest," observed Elsie, with a sapient shake of the head. "The eggs always addle if you do, or the young birds refuse to hatch out; and of course in the case of turtle-doves it would be all the more so. 'Lay low, Bre'r Fox,' and wait for what happens. It all promises delightfully, only I don't see exactly, supposing this ever comes to anything, how Imogen Young is to be disposed of."

"We won't cross that bridge till we come to it," said Clover; but all the same she did cross it in her thoughts many times. It is not in human nature to keep off these mental bridges.

At the end of the fortnight Imogen returned in very good looks and spirits; and further beautified by a pretty autumn dress of dark blue, which Mrs. Hope had persuaded her to order, and over the making of which she herself had personally presided. It fitted well, and set off to admiration the delicate pink and white of Imogen's skin, while the new warmth of affection which had come into her manner was equally becoming.

"Why didn't you say what a pretty girl Miss Young was?" demanded Dorry the very first evening.

"I don't know, I'm sure. She looks better than she did before she was ill, and she's very nice and all that, but we never thought of her being exactly pretty."

"I can't think why; she is certainly much better-looking than that Miss Chase who was here the other day. I should call her decidedly handsome; and she seems easy to get on with too."

"Isn't it odd?" remarked Elsie, as she retailed this conversation to Clover. "Imogen never seemed to me so very easy to get on with, and Dorry never before seemed to find it particularly easy to get on with any girl. I suppose they happen to suit, but it is very queer that they should. People are always surprising you in that way."

What with John's recently developed tendency to disappear into canyons with Lionel Young, with the boys necessarily so occupied, and their own many little tasks and home duties, there had been moments during the fortnight when Clover and Elsie had found Dorry rather heavy on their hands. He was not much of a reader except in a professional way, and still less of a horseman; so the two principal amusements of the Valley counted for little with him, and they feared he would feel dull, or fancy himself neglected. With the return of Imogen these apprehensions were laid at rest. Dorry, if left alone, promptly took the trail in the direction of the "Hutlet," returning hours afterward looking beaming and contented, to casually mention by way of explanation that he had been reading aloud to Miss Young, or that he and Miss Young had been taking a walk.

"It's remarkably convenient," Elsie remarked one evening; "but it's just as remarkably queer. What can they find to say to each other do you suppose?"

If Dorry had not been Dorry, besides being her brother, she would probably have arrived at a conclusion about the matter much sooner than she did. Quick people are too apt to imagine that slow people have nothing to say, or do not know how to say it when they have; while all the time, for slow and quick alike, there is the old, old story for each to tell in his own way, which makes the most halting lips momentarily eloquent, and which both to speaker and listener seems forever new, fresh, wonderful, and inexhaustibly interesting.

In a retired place like the High Valley intimacies flourish with wonderful facility and quickness. A month in such a place counts for more than half a year amid the confusions and interruptions of the city. Dorry had been struck by Imogen that first evening. He had never got on very well with girls, or known much about them; there was a delightful novelty in his present sensations. There was not a word as to the need of getting back to business after she dawned on his horizon. Quite the contrary. Two weeks, three, four went by; the original limit set for the visit was passed, the end of his holiday drew near, and still he stayed on contentedly, and every day devoted himself more and more to Imogen Young.

She, on her part, was puzzled and fluttered, but not unhappy. She was quite alive to Dorry's merits; he was her first admirer, and it was a new and agreeable feature of life to have one, "like other girls," as she told herself. Lionel was too much absorbed in his own affairs to notice or interfere; so the time went on, and the double entanglement wound itself naturally and happily to its inevitable conclusion.

It was in the beautiful little ravine to the east, which Clover had named "Penstamen Canyon," from the quantity of those flowers which grew there, that Dorry made his final declaration. There were no penstamens in the valley now, no yuccas or columbines, only a few belated autumn crocuses and the scarlet berried mats of kinnikinick remained; but the day was as golden-bright as though it were still September.

"We have known each other only four weeks," said Dorry, going straight to the point in his usual direct fashion; "and if I were going to stay on I should think I had no right, perhaps, to speak so soon,—for your sake, mind, not for my own; I could not be surer about my feelings for you if we had been acquainted for years. But I have to go away before long, back to my home and my work, and I really cannot go without speaking. I must know if there is any chance for me."

"I like you very much," said Imogen, demurely.

"Do you? Then perhaps one day you might get to like me better still. I'd do all that a man could to make you happy if you would, and I think you'd like Burnet to live in. It's a big place, you know, with all the modern improvements,—not like this, which, pretty as it is, would be rather lonely in the winters, I should think. There are lots of nice people in Burnet, and there's Johnnie, whom you already know, and my father,—you'd be sure to like my father."

"Oh, don't go on in this way, as if it were only for the advantages of the change that I should consent. It would be for quite different reasons, if I did." Then, after a short pause, she added, "I wonder what they will say at Bideford."

It was an indirect yes, but Dorry understood that it was yes.

"Then you'll think of it? You don't refuse me? Imogen, you make me very happy."

Dorry did look happy; and as bliss is beautifying, he looked handsome as well. His strong, well-knit figure showed to advantage in the rough climbing-suit which he wore; his eyes sparkled and beamed as he looked at Imogen.

"May I talk with Lionel about it?" he asked, persuasively. "He represents your father over here, you know."

"Yes, I suppose so." She blushed a little, but looked frankly up at Dorry. "Poor Lion! it's hard lines for him, and I feel guilty at the idea of deserting him so soon; but I know your sisters will be good to him, and I can't help being glad that you care for me. Only there's one thing I must say to you, Theodore [no one since he was baptized had ever called Dorry 'Theodore' till now!], for I don't want you to fancy me nicer than I really am. I was horribly stiff and prejudiced when I first came out. I thought everything American was inferior and mistaken, and all the English ways were best; and I was nasty,—yes, really very nasty to your sisters, especially dear Clover. I have learned her worth now, and I love her and America, and I shall love it all the better for your sake; but all the same, I shall probably disappoint you sometimes, and be stiff and impracticable and provoking, and you will need to have patience with me: it's the price you must pay if you marry an English wife,—this particular English wife, at least."

"It's a price that I'll gladly pay," cried Dorry, holding her hand tight. "Not that I believe a word you say; but you are the dearest, truest, honestest girl in the world, and I love you all the better for being so modest about yourself. For me, I'm just a plain, sober sort of fellow. I never was bright like the others, and there's nothing in the least 'subtle' or hard to understand about me; but I don't believe I shall make the worse husband for that. It's only in French novels that dark, inscrutable characters are good for daily use."

"Indeed, I don't want an inscrutable husband. I like you much better as you are." Then, after a happy pause, "Isabel Templestowe—she's Geoff's sister, you know, and my most intimate friend at home—predicted that I should marry over here, but I never supposed I should. It didn't seem likely that any one would want me, for I'm not pretty or interesting, like your sisters, you know."

"Oh, I say!" cried Dorry, "haven't I been telling you that you interest me more than any one in the world ever did before? I never saw a girl whom I considered could hold a candle to you,—certainly not one of my own sisters. You don't think your people at home will make any objections, do you?"

"No, indeed; they'll be very pleased to have me settled, I should think. There are a good many of us at home, you know."

Meanwhile, a little farther up the same canyon, but screened from observation by a projecting shoulder of rock, another equally satisfactory conversation was going on between another pair of lovers. Johnnie and Lionel had strolled up there about an hour before Dorry and Imogen arrived. They had no idea that any one else was in the ravine.

"I think I knew two years ago that I cared more for you than any one else," Lionel was saying.

"Did you? Perhaps the faintest suspicion of such a thing occurred to me too."

"I used to keep thinking about you at odd minutes all day, when I was working over the cattle and everything, and I always thought steadily about you at night when I was falling asleep."

"Very strange, certainly."

"And the moment you came and I saw you again, it flashed upon me what it meant; and I perceived that I had been desperately in love with you all along without knowing it."

"Still stranger."

"Don't tease me, darling Johnnie,—no, Joan; I like that better than Johnnie. It makes me think of Joan d'Arc. I shall call you that, may I?"

"How can I help it? You have a big will of your own, as I always knew. Only don't connect me with the ark unless you spell it, and don't call me Jonah."

"Never! He was the prophet of evil, and you are the good genius of my life."

"I'm not sure whether I am or not. It plunges you into all sorts of embarrassments to think of marrying me. Neither of us has any money. You'll have to work hard for years before you can afford a wife,—and then there's your sister to be considered."

"I know. Poor Moggy! But she came out for my sake. She will probably be only too glad to get home again whenever—other arrangements are possible. Will you wait a while for me, my sweet?"

"I don't mind if I do."

"How long will you wait?"

"Shall we say ten years?"

"Ten years! By Jove, no! We'll say no such thing! But eighteen months,—we'll fix it at eighteen months, or two years at farthest. I can surely fetch it in two years."

"Very well, then; I'll wait two years with pleasure."

"I don't ask you to wait with pleasure! That's carrying it a little too far!"

"I don't seem able to please you, whatever I say," remarked Johnnie, pretending to pout.

"Please me, darling Joan! You please me down to the ground, and you always did! But if you'll wait two years,—not with pleasure, but with patience and resignation,—I'll buckle to with a will and earn my happiness. Your father won't be averse, will he?"

"Poor papa! Yes, he is very averse to having his girls marry, but he's somewhat hardened to it. I'm the last of the four, you know, and I think he would give his blessing to you rather than any one else, because you would bring me out here to live near the others. Perhaps he will come too. It is the dream of Clover's and Elsie's lives that he should."

"That would be quite perfect for us all."

"You say that to please me, I know, but you will say it with all your heart if ever it happens, for my father is the sweetest man in the world, and the wisest and most reasonable. You will love him dearly. He has been father and mother and all to us children. And there's my sister Katy,—you will love her too."

"I have seen her once, you remember."

"Yes; but you can't find Katy out at once,—there is too much of her.

Oh, I've ever so many nice relations to give you. There's Ned Worthington; he's a dear,—and Cousin Helen. Did I ever tell you about her? She's a terrible invalid, you know, almost always confined to her bed or sofa, and yet she has been one of the great influences of our lives,—a sort of guardian angel, always helping and brightening and cheering us all, and starting us in right directions. Oh, you must know her. I can't think how you ever will, for of course she can never come to Colorado; but somehow it shall be managed. Now tell me about your people. How many are there of you?"

"Eleven, and I scarcely remember my oldest brother, he went away from home so long ago. Jim was my chum,—he's no end of a good fellow. He's in New Zealand now. And Beatrice—that's the next girl to Imogen—is awfully nice too, and there are one or two jolly ones among the smaller kids. Oh, you'll like them all, especially my mother. We'll go over some day and make them a visit."

"That will be nice; but we shall have to wait till we grow rich before we can take such a long journey. Lion, do you think by-and-by we could manage to build another house, or move your cabin farther down the Valley? I want to live nearer Clover and Elsie. You'll have to be away a good deal, of course, as the other boys are, and a mile is 'a goodish bit,' as Imogen would say. It would make all the difference in the world if I had the sisters close at hand to 'put my lips to when so dispoged.'"

"Why, of course we will. Geoff built the Hutlet, you know; I didn't put any money into it. I chose the position because—well, the view was good, and I didn't know how Moggy would hit it off with the rest, you understand. I thought she might do better a little farther away; but with you it's quite different of course. I dare say the Hutlet could be moved; I'll talk to Geoff about it."

"I don't care how simple it is, so long as it is near the others," went on Johnnie. "It's easy enough to make a simple house pretty and nice. I am so glad that your house is in this valley, Lion."

A little pause ensued.

"What was that?" asked Johnnie, suddenly.

"What?"

"That sound? It seemed to come from down the canyon. Such a very odd echo, if it was an echo!"

"What kind of a sound? I heard nothing."

"Voices, I should say, if it were not quite impossible that it could be voices,—very low and hushed, as if a ghost were confabulating with another ghost about a quarter of a mile away."

"Oh, that must be just a fancy," protested Lionel. "There isn't a living soul within a mile of us."

And at the same moment Dorry, a couple of hundred feet distant, was remarking to Imogen:—

"These canyons do have the most extraordinary echoes. There's the strangest cooing and sibilating going on above."

"Wood pigeons, most probably; there are heaps of them hereabout."

Presently the pair from above, slowly climbing down the ravine hand-in-hand, came upon the pair below, just rising from their seat to go home. There was a mutual consternation in the four countenances comical to behold.

"You here!" cried Imogen.

"And you here!" retorted Lionel. "Why, we never suspected it. What brought you up?—and Carr, too, I declare!"

"Why—oh—it's a pretty place," stammered Imogen. "Theodore—Mr. Carr, I mean— Now, Lionel, what are you laughing at?"

"Nothing," said her brother, composing his features as best he could; "only it's such a very odd coincidence, you know."

"Very odd indeed," remarked Dorry, gravely. The four looked at one another solemnly and questioningly, and then—it was impossible to help it—all four laughed.

"By Jove!" cried Lionel, between his paroxysms, "I do believe we have all come up here on the same errand!"

"I dare say we have," remarked Dorry; "there were some extremely queer echoes that came down to us from above."

"Not a bit queerer, I assure you, than some which floated up to us from below," retorted Johnnie, recovering her powers of speech.

"We thought it was doves."

"And we were sure it was ghosts,—affectionate ghosts, you know, on excellent terms with each other."

"Young, I want a word with you," said Dorry, drawing Lionel aside.

"And I want a word with you."

"And I want several words with you," cried Johnnie, brightly, putting her arm through Imogen's. She looked searchingly at her.

"I'm going to be your sister," she said; "I've promised Lionel. Are you going to be mine?"

"Yes,—I've promised Theodore—"

"Theodore!" cried Johnnie, with a world of admiration in her voice. "Oh, you mean Dorry. We never call him that, you know."

"Yes, I know, but I prefer Theodore. Dorry seems a childish sort of name for a grown man. Do you mean to say that you are coming out to the Valley to live?"

"Yes, by-and-by, and you will come to Burnet; we shall just change places. Isn't it nice and queer?"

"It is a sort of double-barrelled International Alliance," declared Lionel. "Now let us go down and astonish the others."

The others were astonished indeed. They were prepared for Johnnie's confession, but had so little thought of Dorry's that for some time he and Imogen stood by unheeded, waiting their turn at explanation.

"Why, Dorry," cried Elsie at last, "why are you standing on one side like that with Miss Young? You don't look as surprised as you ought. Did you hear the news before we did? Imogen dear,—it isn't such good news for you as for us."

"Oh, yes, indeed it is. I am quite as happy in it as you can be."

"Ladies and gentlemen," cried Lionel, who was in topping spirits and could not be restrained, "this shrinking pair also have a tale to tell. It is a case of 'change partners all round and down the middle.' Let me introduce to you Mr. and Mrs. Theo—"

"Lion, you wretched boy, stop!" interrupted Johnnie. "That's not at all the right way to do it. Let me introduce them. Friends and countrymen, allow the echoes of the Upper East Canyon to present to your favorable consideration the echoes of the Lower East Canyon. We've all been sitting up there, 'unbeknownst,' within a few feet of each other, and none of us could account for the mysterious noises that we heard, till we all started to come home, and met each other on the way down."

"What kind of noises?" demanded Elsie, in a suffocated voice.

"Oh, cooings and gurglings and soft murmurs of conversation and whisperings. It was very unaccountable indeed, very!"

"Dorry," said Elsie, next day when she chanced to be alone with him, "Would you mind if I asked you rather an impertinent question? You needn't answer if you don't want to; but what was it that first put it into your head to fall in love with Imogen Young? I'm very glad that you did, you understand. She will make you a capital wife, and I'm going to be very fond of her,—but still, I should just like to know."

"I don't know that I could tell you if I tried," replied her brother. "How can a man explain that sort of thing? I fell in love because I was destined to fall in love, I suppose. I liked her at the start, and thought her pretty, and all that; and she seemed kind of lonely and left out among you all. And then she's a quiet sort of girl, you know, not so ready at talk as most, or so quick to pick at a fellow or trip him up. I've always been the slow one in our family, you see, and by way of a change it's rather refreshing to be with a woman who isn't so much brighter than I am. The rest of you jump at an idea and off it again while I'm gathering my wits together to see that there is an idea.

Imogen doesn't do that, and it rather suits me that she shouldn't. You're all delightful, and I'm very fond of you, I'm sure; but for a wife I think I like some one more like myself."

"Of all the droll explanations that I ever heard, that is quite the drollest," said Elsie to her husband afterward. "The idea of a man's falling in love with a woman because she's duller than his own sisters! Nobody but Dorry would ever have thought of it."

CHAPTER X. A DOUBLE KNOT.

THE next few days in the High Valley were too full of excitement and discussions to be quite comfortable for anybody. Imogen was seized with compunctions at leaving Lionel without a housekeeper, and proposed to Dorry that their wedding should be deferred till the others were ready to be married also,—a suggestion to which Dorry would not listen for a moment. There were long business-talks between the ranch partners as to hows and whens, letters to be written, and innumerable confabulations between the three sisters, in which Imogen took part, for she counted as a fourth sister now. Clover and Elsie listened and planned and advised, and found their chief difficulty to consist in hiding and keeping in the background their unfeigned and flattering joy over the whole arrangement. It made matters so delightfully easy all round to have Imogen engaged to Dorry, and it was so much to their own individual advantage to exchange her for Johnnie that they really dared not express their delight too openly.

The great question with all was how papa would take the announcement, and whether he could be induced to carry out his half promise of leaving Burnet and coming to live with them in the Valley. They waited anxiously for his reply to the letters. It came by telegraph two days before they had dared to hope for it, and was as follows:—

God bless you all four! Genesis xliii. 14.

P. Carr.

This Biblical addition nearly broke John's heart. Her sisters had to comfort her with all manner of hopeful auguries and promises.

"He'll be glad enough over it in time," they told her. "Think what it would have been if you had been going to marry a Californian, or a man with an orange plantation in Florida. He'll see that it's all for the best as soon as he gets out here, and he must come. Johnnie, you must never let him off. Don't take 'no' for an answer. It is so important to us all that he should consent."

They primed her with persuasive messages and arguments, and both Clover and Elsie wrote him a long letter on the subject. On the very eve of the departure came a second telegram. Telegrams were not every-day things in the High Valley, the nearest "wire" being at the Ute Hotel five miles away; and the arrival of the messenger on horseback created a momentary panic.

This telegram was also from Dr. Carr. It was addressed to Johnnie,—

Following just received: "Miss Inches died to-day of pneumonia." No particulars.

P. Carr.

It was a great shock to poor Johnnie. She and "Mamma Marian," as she still called her god-mother, had been warm friends always; they corresponded regularly; Johnnie had made her several long visits at Inches Mills, and she had written to her among the first with the news of her engagement.

"She never got it. She never will know about Lionel," she kept repeating mournfully. "And now I can never tell her about any of my plans, and she would have been so pleased and interested. She always cared so much for what I cared about, and I hoped she would come out here for a long visit some day, and see you all. Oh dear, oh dear! what a sad ending to our happy time!"

"Not an ending, only an interruption," put in the comforting Clover. But John for a time could not be consoled, and the party broke up under a cloud, literal as well as metaphorical, for the first snow-storm was drifting over the plain as they drove down the pass, the melting flakes instantly drunk up by the sand; all the soft blue of distance had vanished, and a gray mist wrapped the mountain tops. The High Valley was in temporary eclipse, its brightness and sparkle put by for the moment.

But nothing could long eclipse the sunshine of such youthful hearts and hopes. Before long John's letters grew cheerful again, and presently she wrote to announce a wonderful piece of news.

"Something very strange has happened," she began. "I am an heiress! It is just like the girls in books! Yesterday came a letter from a firm of lawyers in Boston with a long document enclosed. It was an extract from Mamma Marian's will; and only think,—she has left me a legacy of thirty thousand dollars! Dear thing! and she never knew about my engagement either, or how wonderfully it was going to help in our plans. She just did it because she loved me. 'To Joanna Inches Carr, my namesake and child by affection,' the will says; and I think it pleases me as much as having the money. That frightens me a little, it seems so much. At first I did not like to take it, and felt as if I might be robbing some one else; but papa says that she had no very near relations, and that I need not hesitate. Oh, my darling Clover, is it not wonderful? Now Lion and I need not wait two years, unless he prefers it, and can just go on and make our plans happily to suit ourselves and all of you,—and I shall love to think that we owe it all to dear Mamma Marian; only it will be a sore spot always that she never got the letter telling of our engagement. It came just after she died, and they returned it to me.

"Ned has his orders at last. He goes to sea in April, and Katy writes to papa that she will come and spend a year with him if he likes, while Ned is away. But papa won't be here. He has quite decided, I think, to leave Burnet and make his home for the future with us in the High Valley. Three different physicians have already offered to buy out his practice, and it is arranged that Dorry shall rent the old house of him, and the furniture too, except the books and a few special things which papa wishes to keep. He is going to write to you about the building of what he is pleased to call 'a separate shanty;' but please don't let the shanty be really separate; he must be in with all of us somehow, or we shall never be satisfied. Did Lionel decide to move the Hutlet? Of course Katy will spend her year in the Valley instead of Burnet. I am beginning to get my little trousseau together, and have set up a 'wedding bureau' to put the things in; but it is no fun at all without any sisters at home to help and sympathize. I am the only one who has had to get ready to be married all by herself. If Katy were not coming in two months I should be quite desperate. The chief thing on my mind is how to arrange about the two weddings with the family so scattered as it is."

This difficulty was settled by Clover a little later. Both the weddings she proposed should take place in the Valley.

"It is a case of Mahomet and mountain," she wrote. "Look at it dispassionately. You and papa and Katy and Dorry have got to come out here any way,—the rest of us are here; and it is clearly impossible that all of us should go on to Burnet to see you married,—though if you persist some of us will, inconvenient and expensive as it would be. But just consider what a picturesque and romantic place the Valley is for a wedding, with the added advantage that you would be absolutely the first people who were ever married in it since the creation of the world! I won't say what may happen in the remote future, for Rose Red writes that she is going to change its name and call it henceforward 'The Ararat Valley,' not only because it contains 'a few souls, that is eight,' but also because all the creatures who go into it seem to enter pell-mell and come out two by two in pairs. You will inaugurate the long procession at all events! Do please think seriously of this, dear John. 'Consider, cow, consider,—' and write me that you consent.

"We are building papa the most charming little bungalow ever seen,—a big library and two bedrooms, one for himself and one to spare. It is just off the southwest corner, and a little covered way connects it with our piazza; for we are quite decided that he is to take his meals with us and not have the bother of independent housekeeping. Then if you decide to put your bungalow on the other side of his, as we hope you will, we shall all be close together. Lion will do nothing about the building till you come. You are to stay on indefinitely with us, and oversee the whole thing yourself from the driving of the first nail. We will all help, and won't it be fun?

"There is something very stately and comforting in the idea of a 'resident physician.' Elsie declares that now Phillida may have croup or any other infant disease she likes, and I sha'n't lie awake at night to wonder what we should do in case Geoffey was thrown from the burro and broke a bone. I am not sure but we may yet attain to the dignity of a 'resident pastor' as well, for Geoff has decided not to move the Hutlet, but leave it as it is, putting in a little simple furniture, and offer it from time to time to some invalid clergyman who needs Colorado air and would be glad to spend a few months in the Valley. Who knows but it may grow some day into a little church? Then indeed we should have a small world of our own, with the learned professions all represented; for of course Phil by that time will be qualified to do our law for us, in case we quarrel and require writs and replevins or habeas corpuses, or any last wills and testaments drawn up.

"I have begun on new curtains for Katy's room already, and Elsie and I have all manner of beautiful projects for the weddings. Now Johnnie darling, write at once and say that you agree to this plan. It really does seem a perfect one for everybody. The time must of course depend on when Dorry can get his leave, but we will be all ready whenever it comes."

Clover's arguments were unanswerable, and every one gradually gave in to the plan which she had so much at heart. Dorry got a fortnight's holiday, beginning on the 15th of June; so the twentieth was fixed as the day for the double wedding, and the preparations went merrily on. Early in May Katy arrived in Burnet; and after that Johnnie had no need to complain of being unsistered, for Katy was a host in herself, and gave all her time to helping everybody. She sewed and finished, she packed and advised, she assisted to box her father's books, and went with Dorry to choose the new papers and rugs which were to make the old house freshly bright for Imogen; she exclaimed and rejoiced over each wedding present that arrived, and supplied that sweet atmosphere of mutual interest and sympathy which is the vital breath of a family occasion. All was ready in time; the old home was in exact and perfect order for its new mistress, the good-bys were said, and on the morning of the fifteenth the party started for Colorado.

Quite a little group waited for them on the platform of the St. Helen's station three days later. Lionel had of course come in to meet his bride, and Imogen her bridegroom; and Geoff had come, and Clover, to meet her father and Katy, and Phil was also in waiting. It was truly a wonderful moment when the train drew up, and Johnnie, all beautiful in smiles and dimples, encountered Lionel; while Dorry jumped out to greet Imogen, who was in blooming health again, and very pleased to see him.

"We have brought the two carryalls," Clover explained. "Geoff got a new one the other day, that the means of transportation may keep pace with the increase of population, as he says. I think, Geoff, we will put the brides and bridegrooms together in the new one. Then the 'echoes' from the back seat can mix with the 'echoes' from the front seat; and it will be as good as the East Canyon, and they will all feel at home."

So it was arranged, and the party started.

"Katy," cried Clover, looking at her sister with eyes that seemed to drink her in, "I had forgotten quite how dear you are! It seems to me that you have grown handsome, my child; or is it only that you are a little fatter?"

"I am afraid the latter," replied Katy, with a laugh. "No one but Ned was ever so deluded as to call me handsome."

"Where is Ned? It is such a shame that he can't be here,—the only one of the family missing!"

"He is on his way to China," said Katy, with a little suppressed sigh. "Yes, it is too bad; but it can't be helped. Naval orders are like time and tide, and wait for no man, and most of all for no woman." She paused a moment, and changed the subject abruptly. "Did I tell you," she asked, "that after I broke up at Newport I went to Rose for a week?"

"Johnnie wrote that you were to go."

"It was such a bright week! Boston was beautiful, as it always is in spring, with the Public Garden a blaze of flowers, and all the pretty country about so green and sweet! Rose was most delightful; and I saw ever so many of the old Hillsover girls, and even had a glimpse of Mrs. Nipson!"

"That must have been rather a bad joy."

"N—o, not exactly. I was rather glad, on the whole, to meet her again. She isn't as bad as we made her out. School-girls are almost always unjust to their teachers."

"Oh, come, now," said Clover, making a little face. "This is a happy occasion, certainly, and I am in a benignant frame of mind, but really I can't stand having you so horridly charitable. 'There is no virtue, madam, in a mush of concession.' Mrs. Nipson was an unpleasant old thing,—so there! Let us talk of something else. Tell me about your visit to Cousin Helen."

"Oh, that was a sweet visit all through. I stayed ten days, and she was better than usual, it seemed to me. Did I write about little Helen's ball?"

"No."

"She is just nineteen, and it was her first dance. Such a pretty creature, and so pleased and excited about it! and Cousin Helen was equally so. She gave Helen her dress complete, down to the satin shoes, and the fan and the long gloves, and a turquoise necklace, and turquoise pins for her hair. You never saw anything so charming as the way in which she enjoyed it. You would have supposed that Helen was her own child, as she lay on the sofa, with such bright beaming eyes, while the pretty thing turned round and round to exhibit her finery."

"There certainly never was any one like Cousin Helen. She is embodied sympathy," said Clover. "Now, Katy, I want you to look. We are just turning into our own road."

It was a radiant afternoon, with long, soft shadows alternating with golden sunshine, and the High Valley was at its very best as they slowly climbed the zigzag pass. With every turn and winding Katy's pleasure grew; and when they rounded the last curve, and came in sight of the little group of buildings, with their picturesque background of forest and the splendid peak soaring above, she exclaimed with delight:—

"What a perfect situation! Clover, you never said enough about it! Surely the half was not told me, as the Queen of Sheba remarked! Oh, and there is Elsie on the porch, and that thing in white beside her is Phillida! I never dreamed she could be so large! How glad I am that I didn't die of measles when I was little, as dear Rose Red used to say."

Katy's coming was the crowning pleasure of the occasion to all, but most of all to Clover. To have her most intimate sister in her own home, and be able to see her every day and all day long, and consult and advise and lay before her the hopes and intentions and desires of her heart, which she could never so fully share with any one else, except Geoff, was a delight which never lost its zest, and of which Clover never grew weary.

To settle Dr. Carr in his new quarters was another pleasure, in which they all took equal part. When his books and microscopes were unpacked, and the Burnet belongings arranged pretty much in their old order, the rooms looked wonderfully homelike, even to him. The children soon learned to adore him, as children always had done; the only trouble was that they fought for the possession of his knee, and would never willingly have left him a moment for himself. His leisure had to be protected by a series of nursery laws and penances, or he would never have had any; but he said he liked the children better than the leisure. He was born to be a grandfather; nobody told stories like him, or knew so well how to please and pacify and hit the taste of little people.

But all this, of course, came subsequently to the double wedding, which took place two days after the arrival of the home-party. The morning of the twentieth was unusually fine, even for Colorado,—fair, cloudless, and golden bright, as if ordered for the occasion,—without a cloud on the sky from dawn to sunset. The ceremony was performed by a clergyman from Portland, who with his invalid wife were settled in the Hutlet for the summer, very glad of the pleasant little home offered them, and to escape from the crowd and confusion of Mrs. Marsh's boarding-house, where Geoff had found them. Two or three particular friends drove out from St. Helen's; but with that exception the whole wedding was "valley-made," as Elsie declared, including delicious raspberry ice-cream, and an enormous cake, over which she and Clover had expended much time and thought, and which, decorated with emblematical designs in icing and wreathed with yucca-blossoms, stood in the middle of the table.

The ceremony took place at noon precisely, when, as Phil facetiously observed, "the shadows of the high contracting parties could never be less." There was little that was formal about it, but much that was reverent and sweet and full of true feeling. Imogen and Johnnie had both agreed to wear white muslin dresses, very much such dresses as they were all accustomed to wear on afternoons; but Imogen had on her head her mother's wedding-veil, which had been sent out from England, and John wore Katy's, "for luck," as she said. Both carried a big bouquet of Mariposa lilies, and the house was filled with the characteristic wild-flowers of the region most skilfully and effectively grouped and arranged.

A hospitably hearty luncheon followed the ceremony, of which all partook; then Imogen went away to put on her pretty travelling-suit of pale brown, and the carry-all came round to take Mr. and Mrs. Theodore Carr to St. Helen's, which was the first stage on their journey of life.

The whole party stood on the porch to see them go. Imogen's last word and embrace were for Clover.

"We are sisters now," she whispered. "I belong to you just as much as Isabel does, and I am so glad that I do! Dear Clover, you have been more good to me than I can say, and I shall never forget it."

"Nonsense about being good! You are my Dorry's wife now, and our own dear sister. There is no question about goodness,—only to love one another."

She kissed Imogen warmly, and helped her into the carriage. Dorry sprang after her; the wheels revolved; and Phil, seizing a horseshoe which hung ready to hand on the wall of the house, flung it after the departing vehicle.

"It's more appropriate than any other sort of old shoe for this Place of Hoofs," he observed. "Well, the Carr family are certainly pretty well disposed of now. I am 'the last ungathered rose on my ancestral tree.' I wonder who will tear me from my stem!"

"You can afford to hang on a while longer," remarked Elsie. "I don't consider you fairly expanded yet, by any means. You'll be twice as well worth gathering a few years from now."

"Oh, very fine!—years indeed! Why, I shall be a seedy old bachelor! That would never do! And Amy Ashe, whom I have had in my eye ever since she was in pinafores, will be married to some other fellow!"

"Don't set your heart on Amy," said Katy. "She's not seventeen yet; and I don't think her mother has any idea of having her made into Ashes of Roses so early!"

"There's no harm in having a girl in one's eye," retorted Phil, disconsolately. "I declare, you all look so contented and so satisfied with yourselves and one another, that it's enough to madden a fellow, left out, as I am, in the cold! I shall go back to St. Helen's with Dr. and Mrs. Hope."

The others, left to themselves in their happy loneliness, gathered together in the big room after the last guest had gone. Geoff touched a match to the ready-laid fire; Clover wheeled an armchair forward for her father, and sat down beside him with her arm on his knee; John and Lionel took possession of a big sofa.

"Now let us enjoy ourselves," said Clover. "The world is shut out, we are shut in; there are none to molest and make us afraid; and, please Heaven, there is a whole, long, happy year before us! I never did suppose anything so perfectly perfect could happen to us all as this. Now, papa,—dear papa,—just say that you like it as much as we all do."

Elsie perched herself on the arm of her father's chair; Katy stood behind, stroking his hair. Dr. Carr held out his hand to Johnnie, who ran across the room, knelt down, caught it in both hers, and fondly laid her cheek upon it.

"I like it quite as much as you do," he said. "Where my girls are is the place for me; and I am going to be the most contented old gentleman in America for the rest of my days."

Printed in Great Britain
by Amazon